YOUR

FACE

TOMORROW

Also by Javier Marías, Available from New Directions

JAVIER MARÍAS

YOUR

FACE

TOMORROW

Volume Three
Poison, Shadow and Farewell

Translated from the Spanish by Margaret Jull Costa

A NEW DIRECTIONS BOOK

First published in Spain in 2007 as *Tu rostro mañana, 3 Veneno y sombra y adiós* by Alfaguara, Grupo Santillana de Ediciones, S.A.

Published by arrangement with Mercedes Casanovas Agencia Literaria, Barcelona, and in association with Chatto & Windus, The Random House Group UK.

The translator would like to thank Javier Marías, Annella McDermott, Palmira Sullivan, and Ben Sherriff for all their help and advice.

Grateful acknowledgment is made to Random House, Inc., for permission to reprint from *The Selected Poetry of Rainer Maria Rilke* the line from the first "Duino Elegy," copyright © 1989 by Stephen Mitchell. The Eliot lines are quoted from "The Love Song of J. Alfred Prufrock," copyright 1917 by T. S. Eliot.

The publication of this book has been assisted with a translation subvention from the Director of Books, Archives, and Libraries of the Cultural Ministry of Spain.

Manufactured in the United States of America
New Directions Books are printed on acid-free paper.
First published clothbound in 2009 and as a New Directions Paperbook (NDP1206) in 2011.
Design by Semadar Megged

Library of Congress Cataloging-in-Publication Data

Marías, Javier.
[Tu rostro mañana. English]
Your face tomorrow : fever and spear/Javier Marías ; translated from the Spanish by Margaret Jull Costa.   p. cm.
Volume I, Fever and Spear ISBN: 978-0-8112-1612-8
Volume II, Dance and Dream ISBN: 978-0-8112-1656-2
Volume III, Poison, Shadow and Farewell ISBN: 978-0-8112-1812-2
(alk. paper)
I. Costa, Margaret Jull.   II. Title.
PQ6663.A7218T8313 2005
863'.64—dc22
2005000992

1 3 5 7 9 10 8 6 4 2

New Directions Books are published for James Laughlin
by New Directions Publishing Corporation
80 Eighth Avenue, New York 10011

C o n t e n t s

For Carmen López M, who has been kind
enough to hear me out patiently until the end

And for my friend Sir Peter Russell and
my father, Julián Marías,
who generously lent me
a large part of their lives,
in memoriam.

5
Poison

'While it isn't ever something we would wish for, we would all nonetheless always prefer it to be the person beside us who dies, whether on a mission or in battle, in an air squadron or under bombardment or in the trenches when there were trenches, in a mugging or a raid on a shop or when a group of tourists is kidnapped, in an earthquake, an explosion, a terrorist attack, in a fire, it doesn't matter: even if it's our colleague, brother, father or even our child, however young. Or even the person we most love, yes, even them, anyone but us. Whenever someone covers another person with his own body, or places himself in the path of a bullet or a knife, these are all extraordinary exceptions, which is why they stand out, and most are fictitious and only appear in novels and films. The few real-life instances are the result of unthinking reflexes or else dictated by a strong sense of decorum of a sort that is becoming ever rarer, there are some who couldn't bear for a child or a loved one to pass into the next world with, as their final thought, the knowledge that a parent or lover had done nothing to prevent their death, had not sacrificed themselves, had not given their own life to save them, it's as if such people had internalized a hierarchy of the living, which seems so quaint and antiquated now, whereby children have more right to live than women and women more than men and men more than the old, or something of the sort, at least that's how it used to be, and such old-fashioned chivalry still persists in a dwindling band of people, those who still believe in that decorum, which, when you think about it, is quite absurd, after all, what do such final thoughts, such transient feelings of pique or disappointment matter when, a moment later, the person concerned will be dead and incapable of feeling either pique or disappointment, incapable, indeed, of thinking? It's true that there are still a few people who harbor this deep-seated belief and to whom it does matter, and they are, in fact, acting so that the person they are saving can bear witness, so that he or she will think well of them and remember them with eternal admiration and gratitude; what they don't realize at that decisive moment, or at least not fully, is that they will never enjoy that admiration or gratitude because they will be the ones who, a moment later, will be dead.'

And what came into my head while he was talking was an expression that was both difficult to grasp and possibly untranslatable, which is why, at first, I didn't mention it to Tupra, it would have taken me too long to explain. My initial thought was: 'It's what we call "*vergüenza torera*," literally "a bullfighter's sense of shame,"' and then: 'Because bullfighters, of course, have loads of witnesses, a whole arenaful, plus sometimes a TV audience of millions, so it's perfectly understandable that they should think: "I'd rather leave here with a ruptured femoral artery or dead than be thought a coward in the presence of all these people who will go on to talk about it endlessly and forever." Bullfighters fear narrative horror like the plague, that final defining wrong move, they really care about how their lives end, it's the same with Dick Dearlove and almost any other public figure, I suppose, whose story is played out in full view of everyone at every stage or chapter, right up to the dénouement that can mark a whole life and give it an entirely false and unfair meaning.' And then I couldn't help saying it out loud, even though it meant briefly interrupting Tupra. But it did, after all, add to what he was saying and was also a way of pretending that this was a dialogue:

'That's what we call "*vergüenza torera*."' And I said the two words in Spanish, then immediately translated them. 'I'll explain to you exactly what it means another day, since you don't have bullfighters here.' Although at that moment, I wasn't even sure there would be another day, another day at his side, not one.

'OK, but don't forget. And no, you're right, we don't have

bullfighters here.' Tupra was always curious to hear the turns of phrase in my own language about which I occasionally enlightened him, whenever they seemed relevant or were particularly striking. Now, however, he was enlightening me (I knew where he was heading, and both he and the path he was taking aroused my curiosity over and above the foreseeable revulsion I would feel at the end of the journey), and so he continued: 'From there to letting someone die in order to save yourself is only a step, and trying to ensure that someone else dies in your place or even bringing that about (you know the kind of thing, it's him or me) is just one more short step, and both steps are easily taken, especially the first, in fact, in an extreme situation, almost everyone takes that step. How else explain why it is that in a fire at a theater or a disco more people are crushed or trampled to death than burned or asphyxiated, or why when a ship sinks there are people who don't even wait for the lifeboat to be full before lowering it into the water, just so that they can get away quickly and without being burdened by other passengers, or why the expression "Every man for himself" exists, which, after all, means discarding all consideration for others and reverting to the law of the jungle, which we all accept and to which we return without a second's thought, even though we've spent more than half our lives with that law in abeyance or under control. The reality is that we're doing violence to ourselves by not following and obeying it at all times and in all circumstances, but even so we apply that law far more often than we acknowledge, but surreptitiously, under cover of a thin veneer of civility or in the guise of other more respectful laws and regulations, more slowly and with numerous detours and stages along the way, it's all very laborious but, deep down, it's the law of the jungle that rules, that holds sway. It is, think about it. Among individuals and among nations.'

Tupra had used the English equivalent of '*Sálvese quien pueda,*' which means literally 'Save yourself if you can,' whereas 'Every man for himself' denotes perhaps even fewer scruples: let each man save his own skin and worry only about himself, save himself by whatever means are available to him, and let others look after themselves, the weaker, the slower, the more ingenuous and the more stupid (and the more protective, too, like my son Guillermo). At that moment, you can allow yourself to shove and trample and kick others out of the way, or use an oar to smash in the head of anyone trying to hold onto your boat and get into it when it's already sliding down into the water with you and yours inside it, and there's no room for anyone else, or you simply don't want to share it or run the risk of capsizing. The situations may be different, but that commanding voice belongs to the same family or type as three other voices: the voice that issues an instruction to fire at will, to slaughter, to beat a disorderly retreat or to flee en masse; the one that orders to shoot at close range and indiscriminately whoever you happen to see or catch, the voice urging us to bayonet or knife someone, to take no prisoners, to leave not a soul alive ('Give no quarter,' is the command, or worse 'Show no mercy'); and the voice that tells us to fly, to withdraw and break ranks, *pêle-mêle* in French or *pellmell* in its English form; soldiers fleeing en masse when there are not enough escape routes to flee alone, each listening only to his own survival instinct and therefore indifferent to the fate of his companions, who no longer count and who have, in fact, ceased to be companions, even though we're all still in uniform and feel, more or less, the same fear in that shared flight.

I sat looking at Tupra in the light of the lamps and in the light of the fire, the latter making his complexion more coppery than usual, as if he had Native American blood in his veins—it occurred to me then that his lips could perhaps be Sioux—his complexion now not so much the color of beer as of whisky. He had not yet reached his destination, he had only begun his journey and would not be slow about it, and I was sure that sooner or later he would ask me that question again: 'Why can't one do that? Why can't one, according to you, go around beating people up and killing them?' And I still had no answers that would convince him, I had to keep thinking about something we never do think about because we take it as universally agreed, as immutable and normal and right. The answers going round in my head were fine for the majority, so much so that anyone could have given them, but not for Reresby, if he still was Reresby or perhaps he never ceased being him and was always all of them, simultaneously, Ure and Dundas and Reresby and Tupra, and who knows how many other names in the course of his turbulent life in all those different places, although now he did seem to have settled down. Doubtless his names were legion and he wouldn't be able to remember every last one or, indeed, every first one, people who accumulate many experiences tend to forget what they did at a particular time or at various times. There's not a trace in them of who they were then, and it's as if they had never been.

'But in those situations, there are always people willing to lend a hand,' I murmured feebly. 'People willing to help someone else into the boat or risk their own life by rescuing someone from the flames. Not everyone flees in terror or runs for cover. Not everyone simply abandons strangers to their fate.'

And my eyes remained fixed on the flames. When we'd arrived, there had still been the embers of a fire in the grate, and it had taken Tupra little effort to revive it, doubtless because he enjoyed an open fire or else to save on heating, which, I noticed, was turned down low—a lot of English people, even the filthy rich, like to economize on such things. This meant either that he must have servants or else didn't live alone, there in his three-storey house which was, as I'd speculated, in Hampstead, a very plush area, a place for the wealthy, perhaps he earned much more than I imagined (not that I'd given it much thought), he was, after all, only a functionary, however high up he was in the hierarchy, and I didn't think he was particularly high up. So perhaps it wasn't his house, but Beryl's and he was there thanks to their as yet unannulled marriage, or more likely thanks to his first marriage and to an advantageous divorce settlement, Wheeler had told me that Tupra had been married twice and that Beryl was considering trying to win him back because, since their separation, her life had signally failed to improve. Or perhaps Tupra enjoyed other sources of income apart from that of his known profession, or perhaps the extras that this brought him ('the frequent pleasant surprises, paid in kind,' as Peter put it) far exceeded my imaginative capabilities. It seemed to me improbable that he would have inherited such a house from the first British Tupra or, indeed, from the second, one or the other must have been immigrants from some low-ranking country. Although who knows, perhaps his grandfather or father had been quick off the mark and swiftly amassed a fortune, anything's possible, by dirty dealings or through usury or banking, it comes to the same thing, such fortunes appear in a flash, like lightning, but with one difference, they persist and grow, or perhaps those first Tupras had married into money, unlikely, unless they already possessed the gift of making themselves irresistible to women and that gift was the legacy they bequeathed to Tupra, their descendant.

We were in a large sitting room, which was clearly not the

only one in the house (I'd glimpsed another from the corridor, unless it was just a billiards room, for it contained a green baize table), well furnished, well carpeted, with very expensive bookshelves (something I do know about) and on them some very fine and costly books (I can tell that, too, from afar, at a single glance), and I spotted on the walls what was certainly a Stubbs equine portrait and what looked to me like a Jean Béraud, a large-scale work depicting some elegant casino of the time, at Baden-Baden or Monte Carlo, and a possible De Nittis of rather more modest dimensions (I know about paintings as well), society people in a park with thoroughbreds in the background, and none of these pictures, it seemed to me, were copies. Someone in that house knew or had known a thing or two about art, someone keen on horse-racing or on betting in general, and my host, of course, was keen on the former, as he was on soccer or at least on the Chelsea Blues. To acquire such works one doesn't necessarily have to be a pound or euro multimillionaire, but you do need either to have some surplus cash or to be absolutely sure that more money will be forthcoming after each extravagance. The place felt more like the home of a well-to-do diplomat or some eminent professor who doesn't depend on his salary—the kind who works not so much to earn a living as to gain recognition—than the home of an army employee appointed to carry out certain obscure and indefinable civilian tasks, I couldn't forget that the initials MI6 and MI5 meant Military Intelligence; and then it occurred to me that Tupra might be a high-ranking officer, a Colonel, a Major or perhaps the Commander of a frigate, like Ian Fleming and his character James Bond, especially if he was from the Navy, from the former OIC, the Operational Intelligence Centre, which, according to Wheeler, had provided the best men, or from the NID, the Naval Intelligence Division, of which it was part. I was gradually reading and learning about the organization and distribution of these services from the books that Tupra kept in his office and which I sometimes leafed through when I was alone, working late at the building with no name, or arrived early to start or to finish some report, and when I might find the young

Pérez Nuix drying her bare torso with a towel because she'd spent the night there, or so she said.

I fixed my weary eyes on the fire that Reresby had lit and which contributed in no small part to transforming his sitting room into a story-book setting, a place of enchantment, and there came into my mind the image of a more welcoming and, in fact, unusual, but, how I can put it, not entirely non-existent London, the London of Wendy's parents in the Disney version of *Peter Pan*, with its square windowpanes framed by strips of white lacquered wood and its equally white bookshelves, its clusters of chimneys and its peaceful attic rooms, at least that's how I recalled the home I had seen in the dark in my childhood, cartoons so comforting that one wanted to live in them. Yes, Tupra's house was cosy and comfortable, the kind of house that helps you to forget about things and relax, it also had something about it of the house inhabited by Professor Higgins, as played by Rex Harrison in *My Fair Lady*, although his was in Marylebone and Wendy's in Bloomsbury, I think, and Tupra's was there in Hampstead, further to the north. Perhaps he needed these benign, tranquil surroundings in order to cancel out and isolate himself from his many intersecting, murky and even violent activities, perhaps his background as a low-born foreigner or his origins in Bethnal Green or in some other depressing area had made him aspire to a mode of decor so opposed to the sordid that it's almost only ever found in fiction, intended for children if they're by Barrie or for adults if they're by Dickens, he was bound to have seen that film based on the work of the former, the dramatist, when it came out, as did every child in our day in any country in this world of ours, I'd seen it dozens of times in my own childhood world.

He took out one of his Egyptian cigarettes and offered it to me, he was my host now and was mechanically aware of that, he'd also offered me a drink which, for the moment, I'd declined, he'd poured himself a port not from an ordinary bottle, but from one with a little medal about its neck, like those passed swiftly round in a clockwise direction by the guests (there were always several bottles, they never stopped coming) during the dessert course at the high tables to which I was occasionally invited by colleagues in my distant Oxford days, perhaps *his* Oxford colleagues still sent him some of that extraordinary port wine from the college cellars and which one can find nowhere else. I hadn't kept up with how much Tupra had drunk during that long, interminable evening which had still not yet ended, although he had, I imagined, drunk no less than I had, and I didn't want and couldn't hold another drop, he, however, seemed unaffected by the alcohol or else its ravages were not apparent. The quantity of alcohol consumed, however, had had nothing to do with his terrorizing and punishing or beating or thrashing of De la Garza, for he had behaved throughout with precision and calculation. Who knows, though, perhaps it *had* influenced his decision to demonstrate to De la Garza his variant—varying— modes of death and to leave both De la Garza and me alive so that we would always remember them, it's rare for the resolve to do something and the actual execution of that act to coincide, even though the two things may follow on and appear to be simultaneous, perhaps he'd taken that decision when his head was still fuzzy, still hot, and his head had cleared and cooled during the few minutes I'd spent waiting for him in the handicapped toilet along with our trusting victim, for I'd tricked De la Garza into going there with the false promise of a line of cocaine, although I didn't know at the time why I was putting him, the victim, where I'd been asked to put him or that the promise was a mere pretext. I should have imagined it, I should have foreseen it. I should have refused to have anything to do with it. I'd prepared him for Tupra, served him up on a plate, I had, in the end, been a part of it all. I was about to ask him, out of curiosity: 'Was it real cocaine you gave the poor devil?' But, as often happens after long silences, we both spoke at once and he got in just a fraction of a second before me, in order to reply to the last thing I'd said:

'Yes, of course,' murmured Reresby almost lazily. 'You'll always get the kind of person who watches himself acting, who sees himself as if in some continuous performance. Who believes there'll be witnesses to report his generous or contempt-

No, probably not,' he went on, without giving me time to reply, 'which is yet further proof of how inappropriate and gratuitous and exaggerated that "M" was when it came to giving a name to the complex. Anyway, we've called it that for quite some time now, it's become the custom, and it's used almost exclusively in-house. Although, believe it or not,' he said, correcting himself, 'I've known some high officials use it too, having picked it up from us presumably, and the term has even appeared in the odd book.'

'I believe I do remember Jayne Mansfield,' I said, taking advantage of that minimal pause.

'Really?' Tupra seemed surprised. 'Well, you're certainly old enough, but I wasn't sure if such frivolous films would have made it into your country. During the dictatorship, I mean.'

'The only thing we weren't cut off from was the movies. Franco loved films and had his own projection room in the palace of El Pardo. We saw almost everything, apart from a few things that the censor strictly forbade (they weren't forbidden to Franco, of course: he enjoyed being shocked, the way priests do, at the vile deeds committed in the outside world from which he was protecting us). Others were cut or had the dialogue changed in the dubbing process, but most movies got shown. Yes, I think I do remember Jayne Mansfield. I can't quite recollect her face, but I can recall her general appearance. She was a voluptuous platinum blonde, wasn't she, very curvaceous. She made comedies in the fifties and possibly the sixties. And she had fairly big boobs.'

'Fairly big? Good grief, you clearly don't remember her at all, Jack. Wait, I'm going to show you a funny photo, I have it here.' Tupra had little difficulty in finding it. He got up, went over to one of the shelves, wiggled his fingers about as if he were trying the combination of a safe and then took from the shelf what seemed to be a hefty volume but which turned out to be a wooden rather than a metal box, disguised as a book. He took it down, opened it there and then, and rummaged for a couple of minutes among the letters kept inside, heaven knows who they were from, given that he knew exactly where to locate them and kept them so easily to hand. While he was doing this, he tapped the holder of his Rameses II cigarette and nonchalantly tipped ash onto the carpet, as if it didn't matter. He must have had servants. Permanent staff. Finally, he carefully removed a postcard from an envelope, using his index and middle finger as tweezers, then held it out to me. 'Here it is. Take a look. You'll remember her clearly now, as clear as clear. In a sense, she's unforgettable, especially if you discovered her as a boy. You can understand Mulryan's fascination. Our friend must be more lecherous than he seems. Doubtless in private. Or in his day perhaps,' he added.

I took the black-and-white photo from Tupra—like him with index and middle finger—and it immediately made me smile, even while he was commenting on it in words very similar to those going through my own head. Seated at a table, elbow to elbow, in the middle of supper or before or possibly afterwards (there are a few disorienting bowls), are two actresses famous at the time, to the left of the image Sophia Loren and to the right Jayne Mansfield, whose face ceased to be vague the moment I saw it again. The Italian, who was herself far from flat-chested— she had been another dream for many men, a long-lasting one too—is wearing a dress with a very modest neckline and she's giving Mansfield a sideways look, but making no attempt to conceal the fact, her eyes drawn irresistibly, with a mixture of envy, perplexity and fright, or perhaps incredulous alarm, to the far more abundant and far barer breasts of her American colleague, which really are very eye-catching and prominent (they make Loren's bust seem positively paltry in comparison), and even more so in an age when augmentative surgery was unlikely or certainly infrequent. Mansfield's breasts, as far as one can judge, are natural, not stiff and hard, but endowed with a pleasant, mobile softness—or so one would imagine ('If only I'd encountered breasts like that tonight and not Flavia's rock-hard pair,' I thought fleetingly), and must have caused a tremendous stir in that restaurant—whether in Rome or America who knows—the waiter who can be seen in the background, between the two women, maintains a praiseworthy impassivity, although we can only see his body, his face is in shadow, and one does wonder if tage, Reresby and I laughed in unison with the kind of laughter that creates a disinterested bond between people, as had happened once before in his office, when I was telling him about the hypothetical clogs worn by some minor tyrant—albeit elected, voted in—and about the patriotically starry print on the shirt I saw him wearing once on television, and when I said 'liki-liki,' that comical word which it's impossible to hear or read without immediately wanting to repeat it: *liki-liki*, like that. I had asked myself then, apropos of that disarming laughter, his and mine united, whether, in the future, he or I would be the one to be disarmed, or if, perhaps, both of us would.

'He's got some balls,' I thought crudely, in De la Garza style, feeling irritated, 'he's managed to make me laugh out loud. Only a while ago I was furious with him and still am, those feelings won't just go away; a while ago I was witness to his brutality, afraid he was going to kill a poor wretch with methodical coldness, that he was going to cut his throat for no real reason, if there ever can be a reason for doing so; that he was going to strangle De la Garza with his own ridiculous hairnet and drown him in the blue water; and I saw from up close the beating he gave him without ever using his own hands to deal a single blow, despite the threatening gloves he was wearing.' Tupra hadn't forgotten about those gloves: the first thing he'd done after getting the fire going again was to take them out of his overcoat pocket and throw them on the flames along with the pieces of toilet paper he'd wrapped them in. The smell of burning leather and wool was finally fading and what predominated was that of burning wood, the gloves must have dried off considerably since we left the handicapped toilet, 'The smell won't last,' he'd said as he threw them onto the fire with an almost mechanical gesture, like someone putting down his keys or loose change when he arrives home. He had kept them with him until he had the opportunity to destroy them, I noticed, and in his own house too. He was cautious even when he had no need to be. 'And now there he is, perfectly at ease, showing me a funny photo and cheerily commenting on it. (The sword is still in his overcoat, when will he take it out, when will he put it away?) And I'm equally at ease, seeing the funny side of the scene in the photo and laughing with him—oh, he's a pleasant fellow all right, in the first and the next-to-last instance, we can't help it, we get on well, we like each other.' (He wasn't so pleasant in the *last* instance, but that didn't usually occur, although that night it had.) I quickly traced back in my mind (it did little for my recovered anger, but it was better than nothing) why he had shown me the postcard in the first place. For a few moments, I'd forgotten what that photo was doing there, and what he and I were doing there. It was no night for laughter, and yet we'd laughed together only a short time after his transformation into Sir Punishment. Or Sir Revenge perhaps. But if the latter, what had he been avenging? It had been so over-the-top, so excessive, and for what? A trifle, a nothing.

I returned the postcard to him, he was standing next to my armchair, looking over my shoulder at me looking at the two actresses or bygone sex symbols—one far more remote than the other—sharing or rather studying my unexpected amusement.

'Why Jayne Mansfield?' I asked. 'What's she got to do with Kennedy? I presume you mean President Kennedy? Was he her lover too? Isn't it Marilyn Monroe who was supposed to have had an affair with him—didn't she sing him some sexy version of "Happy Birthday" at a party? Mansfield must have been an imitation of her.'

'Oh, well, there were several of them,' said Tupra, while he was returning the photo to its envelope, the envelope to the box and the box to the shelf, all in order. 'We even had one in England, Diana Dors. You probably don't remember her. She was pretty much for national consumption only. She was coarser, not bad-looking or a bad actress, but with a rather stupid face and eyebrows too dark for her platinum blonde locks, I don't know why she didn't have them dyed as well. In fact, I met her when she was in her forties, we went to some of the same places in Soho that were fashionable then, in the late sixties and early seventies, she was already beginning to get a bit matronly, but she'd always been drawn to the bohemian lifestyle, she thought it made her more youthful, more modern. Yes, she was coarser than Mansfield, and somehow darker too, not so jolly,' he added, as if this were something he had pondered for a moment. 'But if *she'd* been sitting at the table in that postcard, I don't know who would have been most startled. In her youth, Diana Dors had a real hourglass figure.' And he made the familiar movement with his hands that many men make to indicate a woman with a lot of curves, I think the Coca-Cola bottle imitated that gesture and not the other way round. I hadn't seen anyone do that for a long time, well, gestures, like words, fall into disuse, because they're nearly always substitutes for words and therefore share the same fate: they're a way of saying something without using words, sometimes very serious things, which, in the past, might have proved the motive for a duel, and even nowadays can provoke violence and death. And so even when nothing is said, one can still speak and signify and tell, what a curse; if I'd patted myself under my chin two or three times with the back of my hand in Manoia's presence, he would have understood me to be making the Italian gesture indicating scornful dismissal of one's companion and would have unsheathed his sword against me, if he, too, had one hidden about his person, who knows, compared with him, Reresby seemed reasonable and mild.

Yes, Tupra was distracting me with his anecdotes, his conversation—or was it merely chatter? I was still furious, even though I sometimes forgot to be, and I wanted to show him that I was, to call him to account for his savage behavior, properly and more thoroughly than I had during our false farewell opposite the door to my house in the square, but he kept leading me from one thing to another, never getting to the point of what he had announced or almost demanded that I should hear, and I doubted if he would ever tell me anything about Constantinople or Tangiers, places he had mentioned while sitting at the wheel of his car, he'd specialized in Medieval History at Oxford, although you'd never know it, and in that field he might well have been an unofficial disciple of Toby Rylands, who, to his regret, had very briefly been Toby Wheeler, in that distant, forgotten New Zealand, just like his brother Peter. Tupra had also promised to show me some videos which he kept at home and not at the office, 'they're not for just anyone's eyes,' he had said, and yet he was going to show them to me, what could they possibly be about and why did I have to see them, I might wish I never had; I could always close my eyes, although whenever you decide to do that, you inevitably close them just a little too late not to catch a glimpse of something and to get a horrible idea of what's going on, too late not to understand. Or else, with your eyes screwed tight shut, once you think that the vision or scene has finished—sound deceives, and silence more so—you open them too soon.

'What happened to Jayne Mansfield, then? What did she have to do with Kennedy?' I asked again. I wasn't going to allow him to continue wandering and digressing, not on a night prolonged at his insistence; nor was I prepared to allow him to drift from an important matter to a secondary one and from there to a parenthesis, and from a parenthesis to some interpolated fact, and, as occasionally happened, never to return from his endless bifurcations, for when he started doing that, there almost always came a point when his detours ran out of road and there was only brush or sand or marsh ahead. Tupra was capable of keeping you distracted indefinitely, of arousing your interest in a subject totally lacking in interest and entirely incidental, for he belonged to that rare class of individuals who seem themselves to be the embodiment of interest or else have the ability to generate it, they somehow carry it around inside them, it resides on their lips. They are the most slippery characters of all and the most persuasive.

He eyed me ironically, and I know he gave in only because he wanted to, he would have been perfectly capable of sustaining a protracted silence, withstanding it long enough for my two questions to dissolve in the air and thus be erased, letting them vanish as if no one had ever asked them and as if I were not there. But I was.

'Nothing. They're just two people marked by the final episode of their life. Exaggeratedly so, to the point that it defines or configures both of them and almost cancels out everything they did before, even if they had done important things, which

Mansfield clearly hadn't. If they'd known what the end had in store for them, those two people would have had good reason to suffer from narrative horror, as you said of Dick Dearlove. Both Jack Kennedy and Jayne Mansfield would have suffered from their own complex, K–M as we call it, if they'd guessed or feared how they would die. There are, naturally, many more such examples, from, say, James Dean to Abraham Lincoln, from Keats to Jesus Christ. The first and almost only thing anyone remembers about them is the way—shocking or unusual, premature or bizarre—their lives ended. Dean dead at twenty-four in a car crash, with an extraordinary career as a movie star still before him and the whole world at his feet; Lincoln assassinated by John Wilkes Booth, highly theatrically, in a box at the theatre, shortly after winning the War of Secession and having been re-elected; Keats dead in Rome from tuberculosis, at twenty-five, such a loss to literature; Christ on the cross at thirty-three, a mature adult in the eyes of the age he lived in, even a little slow off the mark in carrying out his work, but young, if not in years, and gone to an early grave according to our idle, long-lived times. As I said, it was at Mulryan's insistence that we called it the K–M complex, but any of those other names would have done, or many more, quite a few people owe their great celebrity or the fact of not being forgotten to the manner of their death or its timing, when it might be said that they weren't ready or that it was unfair. As if death knew anything about fairness or was concerned with meting it out, or could even understand the concept, quite absurd. At most, death is arbitrary, capricious, by which I mean that it establishes an order it doesn't always follow, one that it chooses either to follow or discard: sometimes it approaches filled with resolve and, as if intent on its business, draws near, flies over us, looks down, and then suddenly decides to leave it for another day. It must have a very good memory to be able to recall every living being and not miss a single one. Death's task is infinite, and yet it's been carrying it out with exemplary thoroughness for centuries. What an efficient slave, one that never stands idle and never wearies. Or forgets.'

His way of referring to death, of personalizing it, again made me think that he must have had more dealings with it than most, that he must have seen it in action many times and had perhaps, on a few occasions, himself taken on the role of death. That very night he had approached De la Garza filled with resolve, he had drawn near, flown over him wielding his Landsknecht sword just like the helicopter with its whirling blades that had so frightened Wheeler and me in his garden by the river: in the end, it had merely ruffled our hair, and Tupra had merely cut off De la Garza's fake ponytail and plunged his head into the water and beaten him, and left him for another day, as if he really were Sir Death on a night when he had decided not to follow his own established order of things. Or perhaps Tupra, as a medievalist, albeit non-practicing, was accustomed to the anthropomorphic vision of past centuries: the decrepit old woman with her scythe or Sir Death in full armor and bearing a sword and a lance; but just whose 'efficient slave' did he think death was: God's, the Devil's, mankind's, or life's, even though life only has this one method of proceeding?

'I know what happened, I mean I know, as does everyone else, how President Kennedy died,' I replied. 'But I don't know what happened to Jayne Mansfield. In fact, I know almost nothing about her and her extraordinary hourglass figure.' And after humorously quoting his own words back at him, I added a Spanish note to what I had said: 'I suppose García Lorca would fit that complex too. We wouldn't evoke him so frequently, he wouldn't be remembered or read in the same way if he hadn't died the way he did, shot and thrown into a common grave by the Francoists, before he was even forty. However good a poet he was, he wouldn't be missed or praised half as much.'

'Exactly, that's another clear example of a death defining a life, of ever-present death enfolding and sweeping someone along,' replied Tupra, not really listening to what I'd said; I wondered how much he knew about the circumstances of Lorca's murder. 'Throughout her brief and brilliant career and her almost equally brief decline, Jayne Mansfield was always ready to turn her hand—and certainly her bust—to doing whatever was necessary to attract the attention of the press and to publicize herself. She always kept her door open to reporters, wherever she was, in motels when she was on the road, in the suites she stayed in and even in hotel bathrooms; she loved them to come and photograph her in her pink Spanish-style mansion on Sunset Boulevard in Beverly Hills, full of dogs and cats, and she would wear provocative outfits and strike suggestive poses, and nothing was ever too ridiculous or too trifling, she would welcome anyone, however stupid or malicious, from even the most mediocre of publications. She posed nude for *Playboy* a couple of times, married a muscle-bound Hungarian, and would happily show off her swimming pool and her bed, both of which were heart-shaped, to the least significant of provincial hacks. She divorced the strong man and the odd subsequent husband, went to Vietnam to cheer up the troops with her saucy remarks and her tight sweaters, and when even Las Vegas would no longer have her, she toured Europe appearing in tacky shows and Italian films about Hercules. She took to drinking, she picked fights and worked very hard at creating scandals, but as her career declined, she found this increasingly difficult because no one took much notice and, besides, she wasn't very talented. It was said that she converted to the Church of Satan, a nonsense invented by one Anton LaVey, its High Priest, a bald fellow sporting a puerile diabolical goatee and fake horns on his bald head, who claimed, falsely, to be of Hungarian or Transylvanian origin, and was just as publicity-hungry as she was, as well as being a compulsive con artist: he claimed to be the author of *The Satanic Bible*, which was blatantly plagiarized from four or five different writers, among them the famous Renaissance alchemist John Dee and the novelist H. G. Wells; he claimed, also, to have had an affair with Marilyn Monroe and, needless to say, with Mansfield too. This was all complete fantasy, of course, but then, as you know, people will believe all manner of vile and despicable things about celebrities. He was mad for her and she would sometimes phone him from Beverly Hills, surrounded by her friends, so that she could laugh at and make fun of his demoniacal ardor, filling his shaven head with titillating thoughts from afar. Later, it was rumoured that a vengeful LaVey put a curse on Mansfield's then lover, a lawyer named Brody, and there begins the legend of her death. In June 1967, she was driving in the early hours from a place called Biloxi in Mississippi, where she'd been standing in at a club for her friend and rival Mamie Van Doren, en route to New Orleans, where she was going to be interviewed the next day on a local TV program, as you see, nothing was ever too much trouble or too trivial. The Buick she was travelling in was crammed with people: the young man who was driving, namely Brody, Mansfield and three of her five children, the ones from her marriage to the muscle-bound Hungarian, plus four chihuahuas; really it's hardly surprising that they had a crash. About twenty miles from their destination, the car slammed into the back of a truck that had braked suddenly when it came upon a slow-moving municipal vehicle spraying a swamp for mosquitoes, Mulryan always emphasized that sordid, boggy, Southern detail. The impact was such that the roof of the Buick was sliced clean off. Mansfield and Brody—her driver and lover—died instantly and their bodies were hurled out onto the road. The three children, asleep in the back, only suffered bruises, and there's no news of the chihuahuas, probably because they were unharmed and perhaps escaped.' Tupra paused, threw something onto the fire, I didn't see what, perhaps a speck of fluff from his jacket or a match I hadn't seen him light and which he had been holding between his fingers. He told the story as if it were a report he had in his head, memorized. It occurred to me that, given his profession, he might have hundreds and thousands of such reports stored away, reports on both real events and possibilities, on proven facts and speculation, written not only by him, but by me and by Pérez Nuix, Mulryan, Rendel and others; and by other people in the past such as Peter Wheeler and, who knows, Peter's wife Valerie and Toby Rylands and even Mrs. Berry. Perhaps Tupra was a walking archive. 'Jayne Mansfield's ostentatious blonde wig fell onto the bumper,' he went on, 'which gave rise to two rumors, both equally unpleasant, which is probably why they became so fixed in people's imaginations: according to one rumor, the actress had been scalped in the accident, her scalp torn off as if by an Indian from the Wild West;

according to the other, she had been decapitated along with the roof of the Buick, and her head had rolled across the asphalt into the swampy mosquito-infested area by the side of the road. Both ideas proved irresistible to popular malice: it wasn't enough that the woman whose opulent curves had for a decade adorned the walls of garages, workshops and dives, as well as trucks and the lockers of students and soldiers, should suffer an extremely violent death at the age of thirty-four, when she was still desirable despite her rapid decline and when she might still have profited from her physical splendors; it was much more satisfying to know that death had also left her bald and ugly, or grotesquely decapitated and with her head in the mud. People like cruel punishments and the sarcastic turns that fortune takes, they like it when someone who had it all is suddenly dispossessed of everything, not to mention the ultimate dispossession of sudden death, especially a bloody death.'

'Why is he talking to me about heads being cut off,' I thought, 'when only a short while ago, he was about to cut one off himself, right before my eyes?' And it seemed to me that Tupra was using this gruesome story in order to drive me to some destination much closer than either New Orleans or Biloxi. However, I didn't interrupt him with questions, I merely quoted back to him the words he'd said to me at our first meeting:

'And besides, everything has its moment to be believed, isn't that what you think?'

'You don't know how true that is, Jack,' he replied, then immediately took up his story again. 'It was then, after her death, that LaVey started to boast in public about his affair with her (as you know, the dead are very quiet and never raise any objections) and to put it about in the press that the spectacular accident had been the result of a curse he'd put on her lover Brody, a curse so powerful that it had blithely carried her off too, since she was seated beside him, in the place of highest risk. And people love conspiracies and settlings of scores, the weird and the wonderful and the dangers that come to pass. Most people deny the existence of chance, they loathe it, but then most people are stupid.' I remembered hearing him say the same thing or something similar to Wheeler, perhaps it was one of the beliefs on which our group had always based itself, as does every government. 'If Jayne Mansfield had been attracted by or flirted with the Church of Satan, no less, it was hardly odd that her pretty face should have ended up like that, in a swamp, being nibbled by animals until it was picked up; or with her celebrated platinum blonde hair snatched from her skull, for it had always been her second most striking feature, the first being the one on such conspicuous display in the postcard I showed you. The rabble demands explanations for everything'—Tupra used that word 'rabble,' which is so frowned upon now—'but it wants explanations that are ridiculous, improbable, complicated and conspiratorial, and the more those explanations are all those things, the more easily it accepts and swallows them, the happier it is. Incomprehensible as it may be, that's the way of the world. And so that bald, horned grotesque LaVey was listened to and believed, so much so that those who still remember Mansfield and worship her (and there are plenty of them, just take a look on the Internet, you'll be surprised), what survives of Jayne Mansfield are not the four or five amusing Hollywood comedies she made, nor her two flamboyant *Playboy* covers, nor the wilful, dissolute scandals she was involved in, nor her crazy pink mansion on Sunset Boulevard, nor even the bold fact that she was the first star of the modern era to show her tits in a conventional American film, but the dismal legend of her death, so humiliating for a sex symbol like her and created perhaps by a satanist, a pervert, a wizard. This, ironically, caused more of a sensation and brought her more publicity than anything she ever did during a lifetime spent pursuing the limelight, daily renouncing all privacy and what the overwhelming mass of people would call dignity. What a shame she couldn't enjoy the thousands of reports about her and the accident, and see whole pages devoted to her horrible death, like something out of a novel. It made no odds that the coffin in which she was buried was pink: her name was forever swathed in black, the blackness of a fatal, diabolical curse and a sinful life crowned by punishment, a dark road surrounded by mud, and a lovely head separated from its voluptuous body until the end of time. If she hadn't died in that way, with the possibly invented details that so fire the rabble's imagination, she would have been almost completely forgotten. Kennedy wouldn't, obviously, if he'd simply suffered a heart attack in Dallas, but you can be quite sure that he would be remembered infinitely less and with only slight emotion if his name were not immediately associated with being gunned down and with various convoluted, unresolved conspiracy theories. That, in essence, is the Kennedy-Mansfield complex, the fear of having one's life forever marked and distorted by the manner of one's death, the fear that one's whole life will come to be viewed as merely an intermediary stage, a pretext, on the way to the lurid end that will eternally identify us. Mind you, we all run the same risk, even if we're not public figures, but obscure, anonymous, secondary individuals. We are all witnesses to our own story, Jack. You to yours and I to mine.'

'But not everyone fears such an ending,' I said. 'There are those who desire and seek out theatrical, spectacular deaths, even if, lacking any other recourse, they can only achieve this with words. You have no idea the care many writers have taken to utter a few memorable last words. Although, of course, it's hard to know which will truly be your last word, and more than one writer has blown the opportunity, by being over-hasty and speaking too soon. Then, at the final moment, nothing suitable has come to mind and they've spouted some utter nonsense instead.'

'Yes, I agree, but it's still a response based on fear. Anyone who yearns to die a memorable death does so because he fears not living up to his reputation or his greatness, whether assigned to him by others or by himself in private—it makes no difference. The person who feels, to use your term, narrative horror, as you believe Dick Dearlove does, is as afraid of someone spoiling his image or the story he's been telling as someone might be who's planning his own brilliant or theatrical and eccentric dénouement, it depends on the character of the individual and on the nature of the blot, which some will confuse with a flourish, but death is always a blot. Killing and being killed and committing suicide are not the same thing. Nor is being an executioner, or being mad with despair, or a victim, or being a heroic victim or a foolish one. Obviously, it's never good to die before one's time—and, still worse, foolishly—but the living Jayne Mansfield wouldn't have disapproved of the legend of her death, although she would might well have wished she hadn't worn a wig on that particular car journey. And I don't think your Lorca or that rebellious, provocative Italian filmmaker, Pasolini, would have been entirely displeased with the kind of blot that fell on them, from an aesthetic or, if you like, narrative point of view. They were both of them somewhat exhibitionist, and their memories have benefitted from their unjust, violent deaths, both of which have shades of martyrdom about them, don't you think? In the minds of yokels, that is. You and I know that neither one nor the other consciously sacrificed himself for anything, they were just unlucky.'

Tupra had used the word 'rabble' twice and now he was using the word 'yokel' (or was it 'fool,' I can't quite remember now). 'He can't think much of people,' I thought, 'to use such words so easily and so casually, and with a kind of natural, unaffected scorn. However, in the latter category he's including both the cultivated and the common, from biographers to journalists and sociologists, from men and women of letters to historians, all those people, in short, who view those two famous murder victims—made even more famous by their murders—as martyrs to a political or even a sexual cause. Reresby clearly doesn't think much of death either, he doesn't see it as anything extraordinary; perhaps that's the reason he asked me why it was that one couldn't go around dealing it out, or maybe he thinks it's just another instance of chance, and he neither denies nor loathes chance, nor does he require explanations for everything, unlike stupid people who need to see signs and connections and links everywhere. It could be that he loathes chance so little that he doesn't mind joining forces with it now and then, and setting himself up as Sir Death with his sword and playing serf to that efficient slave. He must have been a yokel himself once, possibly even for quite a long time.'

'You don't think much of people, do you?' I said. 'You don't think much of death either, of other people's deaths.'

Tupra moistened his lips, not with his tongue but with his lips themselves, as if pressing them together would be enough—they were, after all, very large and fleshy and would always have a little saliva on them. Then he took a sip from his glass, and I had the disquieting sense that he was licking his lips. He again offered me some port, and this time I accepted, my palate felt as if it were covered by a communion wafer or a veil, he poured from the bottle until I raised my hand to say 'Enough.'

'Now you're beginning to get there,' he replied, which again made me think that he was driving or leading me; yes, as long as I was the one demanding an explanation, he was the person doing the leading. A bad defendant and a bad witness. He looked at me smugly from his blue or grey eyes, from his eyelashes shaped like half-moons, which gleamed in the firelight. 'Now you're going to start criticizing me again, asking why I did what I did and all that. You're too much a man of your time, Jack, and that's the worst thing to be, because it's hard if you always feel other people's suffering, there's no room for maneuver when everyone agrees and sees things the same way and gives importance to the same things, and the same things are deemed serious or insignificant. There's no light, no breathing space, no ventilation in unanimity, nor in shared commonplaces. You have to escape from that in order to live better, more comfortably. More honestly too, without feeling trapped in the time in which you were born and in which you'll die, there's nothing more oppressive, nothing so clouds the issue as that particular stamp. Nowadays, enormous importance is given to individual deaths, people make such a drama out of each person who dies, especially if they die a violent death or are murdered; although the subsequent grief or curse doesn't last very long: no one wears mourning any more and there's a reason for that, we're quick to weep but quicker still to forget. I'm talking about our countries, of course, it's not like that in other parts of the world, but what else can they do in a place where death is an everyday occurrence. Here, though, it's a big deal, at least at the moment it happens. So-and-so has died, how dreadful; such-and-such a number of people have been killed in a crash or blown to pieces, how terrible, how vile. The politicians have to rush around attending funerals and burials, taking care not to miss any—intense grief, or is it pride, requires them as ornaments, because they give no consolation nor can they, it's all to do with show, fuss, vanity and rank. The rank of the self-important, super-sensitive living. And yet, when you think about it, what right do we have, what is the point of complaining and making a tragedy out of something that happens to every living creature in order for it to become a dead creature? What is so terrible about something so supremely natural and ordinary? It happens in the best families, as you know, and has for centuries, and in the worst too, of course, at far more frequent intervals. What's more, it happens all the time and we know that perfectly well, even though we pretend to be surprised and frightened: count the dead who are mentioned on any TV news report, read the birth and death announcements in any newspaper, in a single city, Madrid, London, each list is a long one every day of the year; look at the obituaries, and although you'll find far fewer of them, because an infinitesimal minority are deemed to merit one, they're nevertheless there every morning. How many people die every weekend on the roads and how many have died in the innumerable battles that have been waged? The losses haven't always been published throughout history, in fact, almost never. People were more familiar with and more accepting of death, they accepted chance and luck, be it good or bad, they knew they were vulnerable to it at every moment; people came into the world and sometimes disappeared at once, that was normal, the infant mortality rate was extraordinarily high until eighty or even seventy years ago, as was death in childbirth, a woman might bid farewell to her child as soon as she saw its face, always assuming she had the will or the time to do so. Plagues were common and almost any illness could kill, illnesses we know nothing about now and whose names are unfamiliar; there were famines, endless wars, real wars that involved daily fighting, not sporadic engagements like now, and the generals didn't care about the losses, soldiers fell and that was that, they were only individuals to themselves, not even to their families, no family was spared the premature death of at least some of its members, that was the norm; those in power would look grim-faced, then carry out another levy, recruit more troops and send them to the front to continue dying in battle, and almost no one complained. People expected death, Jack, there wasn't so much panic about it, it was neither an insuperable calamity nor a terrible injustice; it was something that could happen and often did. We've become very soft, very thin-skinned, we think we should last forever. We ought to be accustomed to the temporary nature of things, but we're not. We insist on not being temporary, which is why it's so easy to frighten us, as you've seen, all one has to do is unsheathe a sword. And we're bound to be cowed when confronted by those who still see death, their own or other people's, as part and parcel of their job, as all in a day's work. When confronted by terrorists, for example, or by drug barons or multinational mafia men. And so it's true, Iago.' I didn't like it when he called me by the name of that troublemaker; it sounded grubby to me, it wasn't a name I wanted to answer to (I, who answered to so many). 'It's important that some of us don't think much of death. Of other people's deaths, as you said, outraged, oh, I noticed despite your neutral tone, it was a good try, but not enough. It's lucky that some of us can step out of our own era and look at things as they used to in more robust times, past and future (because those times will return, I assure you, although I don't know whether you and I will live to see them), so that we don't collectively suffer the fate described by a French poet: *Par délicatesse j'ai perdu ma vie.*' And he took the trouble to translate these words for me, and in that I saw a remnant of the yokel he had left behind: 'Out of delicacy I lost my life.'

I glanced down at his feet, his shoes, as I had during one of our first meetings, fearing that he might be wearing some abomination, short green boots in alligator skin, like Marshal Bonanza, or even clogs. This wasn't the case, he always wore elegant brown or black lace-ups, they were certainly not the shoes of a yokel; only the waistcoats he was rarely seen without were questionable, although now they looked more old-fashioned and dated than ever, like a leftover from the seventies, at the time when he would have been starting to take life more seriously, I mean, to be fully aware of his responsibilities and the consequences of his actions, or with a proper sense of the options available to him. Nevertheless, there was something about him that did not quite ring true: his work, his gestures, his surroundings, his accent, even that very comfortable English house, so textbook perfect, like something out of an expensive film, or a picture in a storybook. Perhaps it was the abundant curls on his bulging cranium, or the apparently dyed ringlets at his temples, perhaps the soft mouth seemingly lacking consistency, a piece of chewing gum before it goes hard. Many people doubtless found him attractive, despite that slightly repellent element I could never entirely identify or isolate or pin down with any exactitude, perhaps it didn't depend on just one characteristic, but on the whole. Perhaps I was the only person to see it, women clearly didn't pick it up. Not even perceptive women like Pérez Nuix, accustomed to noticing and intuiting everything, and with whom he had probably been to bed. That's something we would have in common, Tupra and I, or should that be I and Reresby. Or Ure or Dundas.

'And because of that you allow yourself to beat up and scare to death a poor inoffensive fool, and with my help too; except, of course, I had no idea what you were planning to do to him. And for no reason, just because, because one shouldn't take death too seriously. Well, I couldn't disagree with you more. By the way, I believe that line is from Rimbaud,' I added to make him feel inadequate, he'd already gained far too much ground. I was taking a risk, though, because I wasn't sure at all.

He paid no attention; I was cultured, I knew other languages, I had taught at Oxford in the past, and so he didn't give me any credit for knowing that. He would expect me to recognize the quotation. He gave a wry laugh, just one, a mere simulacrum of bitterness.

'There are no inoffensive people, Jack. None,' he said. 'And you don't seem to take into account that it was all your fault. Think about it.'

'What do you mean? Because I introduced him to the lady and they hit it off? She was longing to be courted by the first mameluke who appeared, whoever he was. Just think back a bit. You yourself warned me about it.' The word '*mameluco*' had been going round and round in my head ever since Manoia confirmed to me that it was the same word in Italian, and words don't go away until you've spoken them, however many times it takes. Of course, 'mameluke' sounded more recherché in English, and inappropriate too, it doesn't even have the same principal meaning as in Spanish, namely 'numbskull.'

'That wasn't the only reason. I asked you to find them and to bring Flavia back, I told you not to take too long and to remove that De la Garza fellow from the scene. You failed. So I had to go after you and sort things out. And still you complain. By the time I found them, Mrs. Manoia already had a great welt on her face. If I hadn't stepped in, it would have been far worse, you don't know her husband, I do. I couldn't just have that useless Spaniard thrown out.' It occurred to me that he sometimes forgot that I, too, was a Spaniard, and possibly a useless one as well. 'Given that Flavia had a mark, a wound on her face, that wouldn't have been enough for him. He would have gone up to your friend and, if your friend was lucky, torn off his arm, if not his head. You criticize me for some trifling, unimportant thing that I did, but you live in a tiny world that barely exists, sheltered from the violence that has always been the norm and still is in most parts of the world, it's like mistaking the interlude for the whole performance, you haven't a clue, you people who never step outside of your own time or travel beyond countries like ours in which, up until the day before yesterday, violence also ruled. What I did was nothing. The lesser of two evils. And it was your fault.'

The lesser of two evils. So Tupra belonged to that all-too-familiar group of men who have always existed and of whom I've known a few myself, there are always so many of them. The sort who justify themselves by saying: 'I had to do it in order to avoid a greater evil, or so I believed; others would have done the same, only they would have behaved more cruelly and caused more harm. I killed one so that ten would not be killed, and ten so that a hundred would not die, I don't deserve to be punished, I deserve a prize.' Or those who answer: 'I had to do it, I was defending my God, my King, my country, my culture, my race; my flag, my legend, my language, my class, my space; my honour, my family, my strongbox, my purse and my socks. And in short, I was afraid.' Fear, which exonerates as much as love, and of which it's so easy to say and to believe 'It's stronger than I am, it's not in my power to stop it' or that allows one to resort to the words 'But I love you so much,' as an explanation for one's actions, as an alibi or an excuse or as a mitigating factor. Perhaps he even belonged to those who would claim: 'It was the times we lived in, and unless you were there, you couldn't possibly understand. It was the place, it was unhealthy, oppressive; unless you were there, you couldn't possibly imagine our feelings of alienation, the spell we were under.' On the other hand, at least he would not be one of those who dodged the issue altogether, he would never pronounce those other words: 'I didn't intend to do it, I knew nothing about it, it happened against my will, as if befuddled by the tortuous smokescreen of dreams, it was part of my theoretical, parenthetical life, the life that doesn't really count, it only half-happened and without my full consent.' No, Tupra would never stoop to the sort of pathetic excuses even I have used to justify to myself certain episodes in my own life. Just then, however, I prefered not to go into that aspect of things, and so I replied to the last thing he'd said to me:

'I work for you, Bertram, I do my job. Don't ask me to do any more than that. I'm here to interpret and to write reports, not to deal with drunken boors. Nor even to entertain ladies in their declining years, clasping them to me, sternum to breast.'

Tupra couldn't help being amused despite himself. Up until then we hadn't had the chance to talk about my torment, still less to laugh about it, or for him to laugh at me, at my bad luck and my imperfect stoicism.

'Rocky peaks, eh?' And he let out a genuine guffaw. 'There's no way I would have accepted her invitation to dance, not with those bulwarks of hers.' He used the word 'bulwarks,' which might best be rendered in Spanish as 'baluartes.'

He'd done it again. I myself sometimes laugh at things despite myself. I couldn't suppress my own laughter, my anger vanished for a moment, or was postponed because it was no longer relevant. For a few seconds, we both laughed together, simultaneously, with neither of us hanging back or preempting the other, the laughter that creates a kind of disinterested bond between men and that suspends or dissolves their differences. This meant that, for all my irritation and my growing feelings of apprehension—or was it perhaps unease, aversion, repugnance—I hadn't entirely withdrawn my laughter from him. I might have been on the way to rationing it out, but I hadn't removed or denied him my laughter. Not altogether, not yet.

Yes, we would have that in common, our having slept with young Pérez Nuix, I was almost sure of it, although it had never occurred to me to ask him, still less her, even though sharing a bed while awake arbitrarily marks the frontier between discretion and trust, between secrecy and revelation, between deferential silence and questions with their respective answers or, perhaps, evasions, as if briefly entering another's body broke down not only physical barriers but others too: biographical, sentimental, certainly the barriers of pretense, caution or reserve, it's absurd really that two people, having once entwined, feel that they can, with authority and impunity, probe the life and thoughts of whoever was above or below, or standing up facing forwards or backwards if no bed was needed, or else describe both life and thoughts at length, in the most verbose and even abstracted fashion, there are people who only screw someone so that they can then rabbit on at them to their heart's content, as if that intertwining had given them a license to do so. This is something that has often bothered me following one of my occasional flings, one that lasted a night or a morning or an afternoon, and, in the first instance, all such encounters are just that—flings—as long as they're not repeated, and all encounters start out the same with neither party knowing if it will end right there, or, rather, one of the parties knows, knows at once, but politely says nothing and thus gives rise to a misunderstanding (politeness is a poison, our undoing); they pretend that this relationship isn't going to come to an immediate halt, but that something really has opened up and there's no reason why it should ever be closed again; the most terrible mess and confusion ensues. And sometimes you know this before you've even entered that new body, you know you only want to do it that one time, just to find out, or perhaps to brag about it to yourself or to shock yourself, or you might even make a mental note of the occasion so that you can recall or remember it or, even more tenuously, have it on record, so that you'll be able to say to yourself: 'This happened in my life,' especially in old age or in one's maturer years when the past often invades the present and when the present, grown bored or skeptical, rarely looks ahead.

Yes, it's often bothered me that the other person involved has then gone on to describe to me her characteristics, her inner world, painted me a portrait of herself, not, of course, entirely true-to-life, or has tried to make out that with me it's different ('This has never happened to me with any other man'), partly to flatter me and partly to save a reputation upon which no one had cast a doubt. I've found it irritating when she's started moving about my house or apartment—if that's where we were—with excessive familiarity and nonchalance and with an appropriative attitude (asking, for example, 'Where do you keep the coffee?' taking it for granted that I do keep coffee and that she can make some herself; or else announcing 'I'm just nipping to the bathroom,' instead of asking if she can, as she would have done a little while before, when she was still dressed and as yet unskewered; although that verb is too extreme). It has infuriated me when one of them has settled down to spend the whole night in my bed without even consulting me, taking it for granted that she has an open invitation to linger in my sheets just because she's lain on the mattress for a while or rested her hands on it to keep her balance while bending over, her back to me, *more ferarum*, with her skirt hitched up and the heels of her shoes firmly planted on the floor. It has angered me when, a day or so later, that same woman has turned up at my door, to say a fond and spontaneous hello, but really in order deliberately to repeat what happened before and to make herself more at home, on the baseless assumption that I will let her in and devote time to her at any hour or in any circumstances, whether I'm busy or not, whether I have other visitors or not, whether I feel pleased or regretful (though I've more than likely forgotten) that I allowed her to set foot on my territory the day before. When I want to be alone or I'm missing Luisa. And it's really riled me when one such woman has phoned up later saying 'Hi, it's me,' as if yesterday's bit of carnal knowledge had conferred on her exclusivity or uniqueness, or made her instantly identifiable, or guaranteed her a prominent place in my thoughts, or obliged me to recognize a voice that possibly—if I was lucky—uttered only a single groan or a few, purely out of politeness.

However, what has most enraged me has been the feeling that I was somehow in her debt (absurd in this day and age) for allowing me to sleep with her. This is probably a hangover from the era into which I was born, when it was still considered that all the interest and insistence came from the man and that the woman merely gave in or, more than that, conceded or assented, and that she was the one making a valuable gift or granting a large favor. Not always, but all too frequently, I have judged myself to be the architect or the person ultimately responsible for what has happened between us, even if I hadn't sought or anticipated it—although I've seen it coming on most occasions, suspected it—and assumed that they would regret it as soon as it was over and I'd withdrawn or moved away, or while they were getting dressed again or smoothing or adjusting their clothes (there was even a married woman once who asked to borrow my iron: her tight skirt, by then, looked like a concertina, and she was going straight on to a dinner party with some very proper married couples and didn't have time to go home first; I lent her my iron and she left looking very pleased with herself, her skirt silent and showing no trace of its recent ups and downs), or perhaps later on, when they were alone and in pensive or reflective mood, gazing up at the same moon—to which I would be oblivious—through windows that, for them, had suddenly taken on a nuptial feel, as they dozed in the early hours.

And so I have often felt an impulse to repay them at once, by being sensitive, patient or prepared to hear them out; by attending meekly to their woes or engaging with their chatter;

by watching over their unfamiliar sleep or bestowing on them inappropriate caresses that certainly didn't come from the heart, but which I dredged up from somewhere; by thinking up complicated excuses so that I could leave their house before dawn, like a vampire, or leave my own house in the early hours, thus letting it be understood that they couldn't stay overnight and that they had to get dressed and go downstairs with me and pick up their car or get a taxi (with me having paid the driver in advance), instead of admitting to them that I could no longer stand seeing them, listening to them or even lying breathing sleepily by their side. And sometimes my impulse has been to reward them, symbolically and ridiculously, and then I've improvised a gift or prepared them a good breakfast if it was that time of the morning and we were still together, or I've bowed to some wish that it was within my power to grant and which they had expressed not to me but to the air, or agreed to some implicit and unformulated request, made long enough ago for the two things not to be connected or only if there was a stubborn insistence on bringing together word and flesh. Not, on the other hand, if the request was made explicitly and immediately after the event, because then I've never been able to shake off the unpleasant feeling that some sort of transaction or exchange has taken place, which falsifies what has happened and makes it seem somehow sordid or, indeed, glossed over, as if it had never happened.

Perhaps that's why Pérez Nuix asked me for the favor early on, when it still hadn't even occurred to me that by the end of the night we would get so close and even reach the morning without entirely letting go of each other. Well, actually the idea had crossed my mind, not as a possible possibility but as a hypothetical improbability (a strange idea in the back of the mind, acknowledging to yourself that you would accept something that is clearly never going to happen), and the first time had been while she was repeatedly zipping and unzipping her boots and drying herself on my towel and there was a snag in one of her stockings that degenerated into a long, wide run, and she had blithely revealed her thighs to me and thus indicated that she did not exclude me. 'She doesn't rule me out, but that's as far as it goes,' I had thought. 'Nothing more, that's all, I am the one who notices and bears it in mind. In reality, though, it's nothing.' And: 'There's a great gulf between feeling desire and not entirely rejecting someone, between affirmation and the unknown, between willingness and the simple absence of any plan, between a "Yes" and a "Possibly," between a "Fine" and a "We'll see" or even less than that, an "Anyway" or an "Hmm, right" or something which doesn't even formulate itself as a thought, a limbo, a space, a void, it's not something I've ever considered, it hadn't even occurred to me, it hadn't even crossed my mind.' I was still invisible to her when she asked me the favor, and perhaps I remained so throughout the night and even into the morning. Except perhaps for that brief moment when she cupped my face with her open hands as if professing some affection for me, the two of us, by then, lying in my bed ready to go to sleep, her soft hands; when she looked into my eyes and smiled at me and laughed and delicately held my face, just as Luisa sometimes used to do when her bed was still mine and we were not yet sleepy, or not enough to say goodnight and turn our backs on each other until the morning.

But that came later. And as almost always happens when you ask a string of questions one after the other, young Pérez Nuix began by answering the last one. 'You still haven't asked me the favor, what is it exactly, I still don't know. And which private private individuals do you mean?' had been my two questions, repeating the expression she had used 'private private individuals.'

'Strange though it may seem to us today, Jaime, with our nerves constantly on edge and with everyone in a permanent state of panic over terrorism,' she said, 'there was a period of a few years, quite recently in fact, although it seems a long time ago to us now, when MI5 and MI6, shall we say, lacked work. After the fall of the Berlin Wall, their duties diminished as did their concerns, and the budgets they had at their disposal collapsed, which, as we now know, was a great mistake. For example, the budget for MI5 went from £900 million in 1994 to less than £700 million in 1998. Then it gradually started creeping up again, but until the attack on the Twin Towers in 2001, which set all the alarm bells ringing and provoked much breast-beating and many dismissals from the ranks of middle management, there were about seven or eight years when a large part of the world's Intelligence Service, and, of course, our own, felt almost useless and superfluous, how can I put it, unoccupied, unnecessary, idle and, worse, bored. Many of the people who had spent decades studying the Soviet Union found themselves not unemployed exactly, but surplus to requirements, with a sense that they had not only wasted their time, but also a large portion of their lives, which were abruptly coming to an end. A sense that they had become the past. Those who knew German, Bulgarian, Hungarian, Polish and Czech were called on less frequently, and even Russian experts lost prominence and work. Suddenly, there was a kind of unacknowledged superfluity, suddenly, people who had been of fundamental importance were no longer needed, or only for minor matters. The situation was so depressing that even the department heads realized how demoralizing it was, and I can assure you that in any job anywhere, they are always the least likely to notice their subordinates' problems. Anyway, the fact is that they did finally cotton on, incredibly late—and only a few days before September 11th, if I remember rightly, the press, *The Independent*, I believe, reported that MI5, through the then Director General, Sir Stephen Lander, was preparing to offer its espionage services to the major companies of the land, like British Telecom, Allied Domecq, Cadbury Schweppes and others, whom it could provide with very useful information about their foreign competitors. Apparently, it was the agency that approached the companies, and not the other way round, in the course of a seminar held at their headquarters in Mill-bank, the very first time, if I'm not mistaken, that representatives from industry and the financial world, both from the public and the private sectors, had been invited there. The reason given was that it was just as important and as patriotic to help the British economy and make it more competitive in the world, as well as shielding our large companies from the foreign spies who doubt-less exist, as it was to protect the nation from dangers and threats to its security, be they internal or external, political, military or terrorist. The idea was basically to commercialize the activities of the SIS'—I remembered this acronym, I'd heard Tupra and Wheeler use it: the Secret Intelligence Service, she said the acronym in English, *s, i, s,* or to Spanish ears, *es, ai, es,* even though we were speaking Spanish— 'to win lucrative contracts, which was tantamount to a partial privatizion of the agency, to reap immediate large rewards and rescue from boredom a good number of the idle and depressed by sending them to work more or less directly for these companies. And that, of course, brought with it a real risk of dividing their loyalties. Lander roundly denied this through a spokesman, who stated that offering to spy for private companies in exchange for remuneration would go beyond the competence of MI5 and that such a proposal would be illegal. He admitted that MI5 had, for some time, been mounting operations with a view to uncovering foreign spies in British companies, and that they provided free advice mainly to the defense industry and to those developing new technologies when they were preparing to sign large contracts or if there was any suspicion of computer fraud. The spokesman added, however, that Lander's controversial paper at the seminar, whose theme had been 'Secret Work in an Open Society,' had dealt only with the growing threat from hackers, and that he had offered advice, with no mention of money, to public and private companies on the best ways of guarding against hackers and of combating software piracy. Several of the invited guests, however, acknowledged in private that Lander's initiative had been quite different, and that he had promised to aid them in their business dealings with a constant stream of privileged information about companies and individuals, 'if they asked for it.'

Young Pérez Nuix paused and now she did accept my offer of a drink, her mouth must have been getting dry after her long speech, a mouth with attractive firm red lips, like Capitán Trueno's Viking lady love, Sigrid, or some other character out of a children's comic, one always looks at the lips of anyone who talks for any length of time, students look at their teachers' lips, audiences look at actors' lips, spectators at the lips of speakers and politicians (the latter always make a bad impression). I got up, went into the kitchen, and from there (not very far away, my apartment was not that big) I called out to her what I had in the house, only Coca-Cola, beer, wine and water, I was perhaps a less than perfect host because in London I wasn't in the habit of being one, almost everyone who came to see me, and they were very few, came to do just that, to be only briefly occupied with me. I also offered her a black coffee, perhaps a glass of milk, or a white coffee if she preferred something warm and comforting, and she replied that she'd like wine as long as it was white and chilled. I remembered that I had six unopened bottles of Sangre y Trabajadero sent to me by a kind, long-standing friend from Cádiz, but I couldn't be bothered to set about opening a crate at that hour.

'Here you are. It's cold enough for me, but it may not be for you,' I said, placing before her knees, on two coasters (I'm a clean fellow) the bottle of Ruländer that I opened there and then (I don't know much about wine) and a not entirely suitable glass, which she allowed me to fill almost to the brim. 'If she's drinking because she's thirsty, she'll be drunk in no time,' I thought when she didn't raise her hand to stop me. The run in her stockings kept growing each time she made a movement, however slight or delicate, or when she crossed her legs, and she crossed and uncrossed them often, with the consequent upward movement of her skirt, this was only minimal with each crossing and uncrossing, but her skirt was gradually creeping up (until she tugged it down again). She still hadn't noticed the damage being wrought, when perhaps she should have. Given the nature of runs, it didn't look out of place on her leg, although it did seem destined to reduce her tights to tatters if our conversation lasted long enough, and she had, it seemed, completely forgotten that, in her words, 'it'll only take a moment,' and, in part, forgotten about me too. I realized that, after the initial surprise and my sense that the visit would only be a brief one, I was in fact enjoying her prolonged presence there, especially with the dog at her feet, for dogs, when they are still, do make one feel calmer, even comfortable. The creature, which had apparently dried off considerably, was still dozing with one eye open, lying close to his mistress. ('Sleep with one eye open, when you slumber,' I sometimes sing or repeat to myself.) He seemed kindly and ingenuous and honest, the very opposite of a joker or a trickster.

'Aren't you having anything?' Pérez Nuix asked. 'Don't tell me you're not going to join me. It's embarrassing drinking alone.' And she immediately overcame any embarrassment by emptying the glass as if she were Lord Rymer the Flask in one of his greedier moments. She was probably thirsty, which was perfectly normal after that walk in the rain, what was odd was that she hadn't asked me for a drink earlier. I refilled her glass, not quite to the top this time.

'Later, in a few minutes,' I replied. 'Go on.' And so that this did not sound like an order, I leaned down and again stroked the dog's head and back, felt his thin bones. This time he didn't even lift his neck, he must have got used to my presence and simply took no notice of me, he was very dignified that pointer. Everyone thinks it makes you look like a nicer person if you behave affectionately towards animals, and that was the effect I wanted then. (If there's one thing I can't stand it's writers, and there are hundreds of them, who have themselves photographed with their dogs or cats in order to project a more amiable image when, in fact, they just come across as affected and twee.) I took advantage of my friendly bowed position to take a long look at Pérez Nuix's thighs from close up, I will not deny that they continued to attract me. I suppose she pretended not to notice, she certainly didn't cover them up or move them a fraction of an inch. At that point, I did feel as puerile as De la Garza, but then the sexual admiration that precedes sex is always puerile, and there's nothing to be done about it.

'I don't know what happened to those measures, they may have gone ahead, but under cover and with much less fuss than planned,' she went on, having, without a pause, downed half of her second glass of wine: I hoped that her speech wouldn't start to become slurred. 'Because shortly after came September 11th and from that day on no one was entirely superfluous. However, those measures, especially if they were genuine, came too late and were, anyway, hardly original, they simply made official what had been going on for years without the intervention and almost without the knowledge of the high-ranking officers in the service, well, they half-knew about it, but that knowledge was accompanied by a degree of passivity, a lot of turning a blind eye, little curiosity and a desire not to cramp anyone's style. The agents with the least to do, once they'd got over the long period of confusion that followed the fall of the Berlin Wall, had started looking for external clients, both occasional and otherwise, according to their respective fields and possibilities. Some, who felt sidelined, actually resigned, those who could simply left (depending on how much responsibility you've been given, that isn't easy and sometimes impossible). The majority, though, didn't manage to do so or simply didn't want to, and although still employed by the State, started getting other work here and there, which meant they were serving different masters. They offered their skills to the highest bidder or accepted the best-paid commissions. And what kind of people or private institutions were or are interested in employing agents? Well, some were given work more suited to private detectives, confirming an infidelity, investigating cases of embezzlement or misappropriation of funds, collecting money from debtors in arrears; or working as bodyguards to protect show-business types or tycoons at public events, things like that. Others gave a hand or two to those ex-colleagues of theirs who had become mercenaries, of whom there were quite a few, and there's never any shortage of that kind of work in Africa. The range of jobs kept widening, and eventually the lower-ranking field agents began to suggest and supply such work to the middle-ranking officials and I imagine that, by 2001, the latter had convinced the higher-ranking officials of the advantages of not working solely for the State. The fact is that during those seven or eight years, during that long interval without a principal enemy, a parallel network of diverse clients of every kind was created. More than once, members of MI5 and MI6, whether knowingly or not, or preferring not to know but sensing it, would doubtless have worked for criminals or even criminal organizations, and perhaps, at the darker, more remote end of the chain, for foreign governments.

It's possible, no one knows and no one's going to try to find out, for at this point in time nothing's very clear and everything's very muddled. You get used to not asking who is paying the bill, and besides, almost everything is dealt with and discussed by intermediaries and front men. If you first had to carry out an investigation to discover who was behind each commission, you'd never finish and never start, and any deal would be worthless.'

Young Pérez Nuix paused and finished off the second half of her second glass of wine. I hesitated, but, out of courtesy, made a very slight move as if to refill it, without actually touching the bottle. Up until then, I had noticed no hesitancy or difficulty in speaking on her part, but if she carried on at the same rate, this might well happen at any moment, or if not that, incoherence or somnolence, and now I wanted to hear everything she had to say. There were, however, no signs of any such symptoms, she must have been accustomed to drinking wine. Even her vocabulary was select and precise, that of a well-read person, she used unusual words, such as '*arrumbados*' for 'sidelined,' '*encomienda*' for 'commission,' '*rasos*' for 'non-commissioned.' Perhaps, despite her ancestry on her father's side, she was like certain English people who have learned my language more from books than from speaking it, and whose Spanish therefore seems rather bookish. And so I got up and, before she could say 'Yes' or 'No' to my hint of an interrogative gesture, announced:

'I'm going to get a glass for myself, I'm ready for a drink now too.' And I then ventured the following warning or caution: 'Do you think it's wise to drink three glasses one after the other like that? That's drinking English-fashion, not like a Spaniard. Anyway, I'll bring a few snacks just in case.'

When I came back with my glass and a few olives and chips in their respective bowls, I caught her inspecting the run in her tights. In the corridor, before going into the room and almost hidden from view—I stopped and spied on her for a few seconds: one, two, three; and four—I saw her looking at it and carefully running her index finger over it (a finger moistened with saliva perhaps or a drop of nail varnish, which is what women used to apply to a catch in their stockings in order to stop a run, to see if the stocking would stay decent at least until they got home; although it was too late now to stop anything). When I rejoined her, she, with arms and legs crossed now, made no reference to this imperfection in her apparel, which was odd: it would have been the moment to express surprise and regret and, if she so chose, to apologize for the theoretically scruffy appearance the run conferred upon her, although it didn't displease me in the least or trouble me, I found it rather entertaining being able discreetly to observe its progress. I wondered how much longer she would keep up the fiction that she hadn't yet noticed, and why, since it was beyond concealment now. And for the first time that evening—for the first time ever—it occurred to me that not only did she not exclude me, but that, without a word or a touch or a look—although she looked straight at me when she spoke, as if there were nothing more to that look than her explanatory, neutral remarks—she was telling me that what did finally occur could occur, quite a lot later and when I was no longer expecting it, despite our insistent nearness in my bed, which was not that big: the opening of silk or nylon as a simile or promise or sign, its steadily growing length and width, the fact that she did not try to stop or remedy it by going to the bathroom and taking off her tights and even changing them (I know women who always carry a spare pair in their bag, Luisa is one of them), allowing the run to continue to grow and expose an ever larger expanse of thigh and soon, possibly, the front part of the calf, for which I've never known the name, if it has one, perhaps shank or shinbone, but neither word seems quite right; that area, of course, was covered by her boots, although her boots had opened fleetingly too, been unzipped, as soon as their drenched owner had arrived and sat down; yes, the run in her tights was like a zipper without teeth, uncivilized and autonomous and uncontrollable, with the added rogue element of being a thing that can be torn, except that this was a tear in which neither my hand nor anyone else's was intervening, the cloth was coming apart of its own accord, while still clinging to the leg, covering and uncovering at the same time and pointing up the contrast, the unveiled flesh advancing in both directions, down and up, and we men know what lies hidden at the top of a long female thigh. (I would accidentally see it myself—a dark triangle—in the ladies' toilet of a disco, where a woman would say to me with great self-confidence: 'You come and see.')

I felt slightly ashamed, almost embarrassed, when I realized I was having these thoughts, that I was thinking them. They were entirely inappropriate, they had taken me pretty much by surprise, and the worst thing is that once an idea gets into your head, it's impossible not to have had it and very hard to drive it out or erase it, whatever it might be: anyone plotting an act of revenge is very likely to attempt to carry it out, and if he can't, out of cowardice or vassalage, or if he has to wait a long time for the right circumstances, then it's probable that he nevertheless already lives with the act and that it sours his light sleep with its nocturnal beating; if one feels a sudden hostility towards someone, it would be odd if that were not translated into machinations and defamations and acts of bad faith, of the sort that seek to cause harm, or lie there watching, in the rear guard, oozing resentment until the long-awaited morning comes; if the temptation to make some amorous conquest arises, the normal thing would be for the *conquistador* to get straight down to work, with infinite patience and intrigue if necessary, but if he lacks the courage, he will be unable fully to abandon the project until the far-off day when he finally grows bored with so much uncertainty, with such theoretical, future-oriented, and therefore imaginary activities, and only then does the condensation that hangs over his misty wakenings dissipate; if what lies ahead is the possibility of killing someone—or, as is more frequent, of having someone killed—it will be easy enough at least to ascertain the current rates charged by hit men and tell yourself they'll always be there or, if not, their sons will, so that you can approach them once you've overcome your vacillations and your anticipated remorse; and if it's a case of sudden sexual desire, as unexpected as the desire that erupts in our dreams, and as involuntary perhaps, it will be difficult then not to feel it at every moment, for as long as that desire remains unsatisfied and the person inflaming it is still there before us, even though we're not prepared to take a single step towards satisfying it and cannot imagine doing so at any point in what remains of our existence. What remains of the past no longer counts, as regards yearnings or fantasies, or even avarice. Or regret. Although it does as regards speculations.

When I recalled this in Tupra's house, in his comfortable living room that invited a sense of confidence bordering on easeful calm, I wondered if I had spied on Pérez Nuix's run and thighs with the same apprehensive, unguarded look Sophia Loren had turned on the white breasts of Jayne Mansfield floating above the tablecloth in a restaurant, although my gaze would have been filled with admiration and desire rather than envy and suspicion. If I had, she would have noticed and very quickly too (the person being observed can sense such looks). I filled my glass and Pérez Nuix moved hers a little closer, and I couldn't not fill it without appearing paternalistic or stingy when it came to wine, both of which are extremely unattractive qualities; and so she immediately started on her third glass, taking only a small sip, and at least she ate a couple of olives and a potato chip. My thoughts were, I felt, vain and idiotic, but I was nonetheless convinced that they were right, sometimes idiotic things are. 'It could be,' I thought, 'that she's allowing that run to grow so as to show me the way to unexpected lust, to guide me, but be careful: she *is* about to ask me a favor, she hasn't done so yet in any detail, we're still at the stage when she can't afford to annoy me and when offering me something, or who knows, even giving it to me, must seem to her advisable even though I've made no demands or dropped any hints, a stage that will last at least until I answer "Yes" or "No," or "I'll see what I can do, I'll do my best," or "But I'll want this in exchange." And it would be only natural if this stage were to last still longer, for several days, until I had done what I said I would do, with irreversible words or deeds, beyond the promise or announcement or the half-open possibility of a "Let me think about it" or a "We'll see" or a "It all depends." However, she hasn't yet formulated her petition to me, not entirely, and therefore the moment hasn't yet come for me to speak, to concede or deny, to put off, to play hard to get or to be ambivalent.'

'Anyway,' she went on, holding another of my Karelias cigarettes from the Peloponnese, 'once a field has been opened up, it's very hard to set bounds on it again, especially if there's no real will to do so. What do you want me to say?'—Yes, Pérez Nuix spoke both languages very well (the expression 'to set bounds on something' is not that common), but now and then she came out with some strange anglicisms—for example '*¿Cómo me quieres que diga?*'—when she spoke my language, or, rather, ours. 'You open a crack, and if there's a storm blowing outside, there's no way you'll close it. Something growing isn't programmed to shrink but to expand, and almost no one is willing to give up a ready income, still less if he's already started earning it and has grown used to it. The field agents were pioneers in accepting external commissions during the period when there was a gap in activities, let's call it that anyway, although it's not quite accurate, and don't go thinking that even now, when they're working at full capacity again, they earn high salaries, most earn no more than you and I, and that's not much, or so they feel, given the risks they sometimes have to run and the time involved in finding out some trivial piece of information. Many of them have families, many get into debt, they spend long periods traveling and not always at someone else's expense. They're asked to justify their expenses and sometimes that's not possible: you're hardly likely to get a signed receipt from the person you're bribing or paying for a tip-off, or from traitors, informers or moles, or from someone who does the occasional job for you or covers for you or hides you, not to mention the thugs you sometimes have to hire to get out of a tight corner or remove obstacles, or the person you have to pay to spare your life, because the only way to do that is to give him more money than he was given to kill you, a form of auction really. How are people like that going to give you receipts? The financial bureaucracy is irrational, counterproductive, absurd, and deeply unhelpful, a burden really, and discontent is always rife among the agents, they have a sense that they do more than they're given credit for, that they're soiling their hands and having a lousy time in order to protect a society that not only knows nothing about their sacrifices and their acts of bravery and occasional acts of barbarism, but one that also, by definition and on principle, doesn't even know their names. They don't know them even when they die in service, it's forbidden to reveal them, you see, however many decades they've been pushing up daisies. They get depressed and ask themselves every day why they're doing what they're doing. They're not selfless individuals or simple patriots, satisfied to think that they're doing their best for their country without anyone ever knowing, not their friends or their neighbors or, for the most part, their families. That attitude belongs to another era or to the kind of innocent era that soon gets left behind. Some might have been like that to begin with, when they joined, but, I can assure you, any feeling of personal satisfaction doesn't last, there comes a point when everyone wants to do well and get some thanks, a pat on the back, a little flattery, to see their name mentioned and their good works, even if it's only in an internal memo from the firm they work for. And since they're not going to get that, they at least want money, ease, a little luxury, to enjoy themselves when they're not working, to give their children the best, to buy their wives or husbands nice presents, to be able to afford lovers and keep them, and since agents are often absent or unavailable, they have to recompense said children or spouses or lovers, and that costs money, having fun is expensive, pleasing people is expensive, showing off is expensive, making others love you is expensive. They want what everyone else wants in a world in which there's no longer any discipline, and so they don't look too closely at the people who come to them with extra work. And since their bosses don't want to upset the agents on whom they depend, they ignore these other missions when they hear about them and, later, some even go on to travel the same path. Why do you think you and I earn so much, relatively speaking, that is? It's not much for a field agent, who might be away from home for long periods, endure certain hardships or even risk his own life, and who probably, in the most extreme cases, will have to decide whether or not to take another man's life. Nevertheless, it's a lot of money for what we do and for where and how we do it, with fairly relaxed working hours and no danger involved, in considerable comfort, with a glass screen between us and them and without exactly working our asses off.'—Again I thought how rich her vocabulary was compared with the norm in Spain, she was clearly a person well-read in superior literature, not like the low-grade stuff you get now, any ignoramus can publish a novel and be praised to the skies for it: most of my compatriots would barely know how to use words like '*cundir*'—to be rife—'*holgura*'—ease—'*transitar*'—to travel—'*deslomarse*'—to work one's ass off. I had never heard Pérez Nuix talk so much or for so long, it was as if I were meeting her for the first time, and this second impression was as unusual as the first. She stopped for a moment, took another meager sip of wine and concluded: 'How do you think Bertie manages to live so well and to have so much? Of course we all work for private private individuals now and then, knowingly or not, possibly more often than we think, as I've said, it's not our responsibility, we just take orders. And besides, why shouldn't we do that work, why not make use of our abilities? So what if we do, Jaime? It's been going on at all levels for years now and it really doesn't matter very much. You can be quite sure that nothing very essential changes because of it, it doesn't make the lives of citizens more dangerous. On the contrary. Well, perhaps, but the more avenues we explore, the more fingers we'll have in more pies, and the better equipped we'll be to protect them.'

I remained silent for a moment, I couldn't help shooting another surreptitious, Lorenesque glance at the run, which was still following its course. It wouldn't be long before her tights split apart, and then she'd have to take them off, and what would happen then?

'Wasn't James Bond supposed to be a field agent?' I asked unexpectedly, unexpectedly to her at least, because she gave a startled laugh and answered, still laughing:

'Yes, of course. But what's that got to do with anything?

'I don't know, but he spends money like water, and it's never seemed to me that he has any problems with budget restraints.'

Young Pérez Nuix laughed again, and perhaps not only out of politeness, but because my facile joke had genuinely amused her. It may have been the wine or her growing sense of ease and confidence, but her laughter, I noticed, bubbled up unaffectedly and unimpeded, just like Luisa's laughter when she was in a good mood or caught off guard. This wasn't to me an entirely new facet of her personality. I had seen it in the building with no name and on the occasional night out with Tupra and the others, but, at work, people's qualities and characteristics seem muffled: feelings of annoyance are contained and amusement postponed, there's not enough room or time. Her laughter also contributed to the further destruction of her already injured tights.

'Bear in mind,' she replied, 'that real-life agents have never enjoyed Fleming's fortune nor the financial backing of the Broccolis. And without them, everything is harder, meaner and more prosaic.'

She said this as if I should know who the last rather comically-named people were, if, that is, it was a real name ('broccoli' in Italian is the plural of 'broccolo' which has the unfortunate secondary meaning of 'idiot'). And I had no idea who they were.

'I don't know who they are,' I confessed, not bothering to pretend I knew more than I did. They were obviously well-known in England, despite their evident Italian origins, but I'd never heard of them.

'For decades Albert Broccoli was the producer of the Bond films, along with a guy named Saltzman. In the more recent movies, his name has been replaced by those of a Barbara Broccoli and a Tom Pevsner. I suppose she must be the daughter and that her father is now dead, in fact, I seem to recall reading an obituary a few years ago. The family must have made a fortune, because the films, can you believe it, have been going since 1962, and they're still making them I think—anyway, I always go and see a Bond movie when I can.'

'I must ask Peter about it,' I thought, 'before he dies,' and it seemed odd to me that such a fear and such an idea should occur to me: despite his advanced age I never imagined the world without him or him without the world. He wasn't one of those old people who wear their imminent disappearance on their face or in the way they speak or walk. On the contrary. Both the adult and the young man he had been were still so present in him that it seemed impossible that they would cease to exist merely because of something as absurd as accumulated time, it doesn't make any sense at all that it should be time that determines and dictates, that it should prevail over free will. Or perhaps, as his brother, Toby Rylands, had said many, many years before, 'When one is ill, just as when one is old or troubled, things are done half with one's own will and half with someone else's in exactly equal measure. What isn't always clear is who the part of the will that isn't ours belongs to. To the illness, to the doctors, to the medicine, to the sense of unease, to the passing years, to times long dead? To the person we no longer are and who carried off our will when he left?' 'To the face we wore yesterday,' I could have added, 'we'll always have that as long as we're remembered or some curious person pauses to look at old photographs of us, and, on the other hand, there will come a day when all faces will be skulls or ashes, and then it won't matter, we'll all be the same, us and our enemies, the people we loved most and the people we loathed.' Yes, I would have to ask Wheeler about those dedications from the fortunate and ill-fated Ian Fleming, who had known great success but few years in which to enjoy it, how they had met and how well they had known each other, 'who may know better. *Salud!*'—that is what Fleming had written in Wheeler's copy in 1957. Since starting work with Tupra I'd had less time to go and visit Peter in Oxford, or perhaps it was rather that I had too much time and my spirits were heavier, but then again my visits to him always helped fill up the former and somewhat lift the latter. However, we never let more than two weeks go by without talking for a while on the phone. He would ask how I was getting on with my new boss and with my colleagues and in my new and imprecise trade, but without demanding any details or enquiring into the present-day activities of the group, that is into our translations of people or interpretations of lives. Perhaps he knew better than anyone how fundamentally reserved I was, or perhaps he didn't need to ask, perhaps he had a direct line to Tupra and knew all about my main activities, my advances and retreats. Sometimes I thought I sensed in him, however, a desire not to meddle, not to draw me out and even not to hear me if I began telling some story related to my work, as if he didn't want to know, or as if being on the outside made him jealous—that was possible, when someone like me was on the inside, and I was, after all, a foreigner, an upstart—or as if he felt slightly hurt to have lost, in part, my company and to have brought about that loss himself in his role as intermediary, through his intrigues and his influence. I never noticed in him a hint of spite, nor of self-reproach, nor resentment at my absence, but something resembling the mixture of grief and pride, or unspoken regret and suppressed satisfaction, that sometimes assails patrons when their protégés break free, or teachers when they see themselves outstripped by their students in audacity, talent or fame, even though both parties pretend that this hasn't happened and won't happen in their lifetimes.

The person he was most interested in was Pérez Nuix, despite his growing distance from that group to which he had belonged in another age, so remote and so different. I wasn't sure whether this was because he had heard so much from Tupra about her qualities ('That very competent half-Spanish girl of his,' he had said of her when I had still not met her, 'I can never remember her name, but he says that, with time, she'll be the best of the group, if he can hold on to her for long enough.' And he had added as if remembering another such case: 'That's one of the difficulties, most of them get fed up and leave') or because he occasionally thought I might get together with her and thus leave behind me my sentimental daze and my occasional sexual toings and froings, far less frequent than he imagined, the old tend to deem anyone whom they believe to be still virile, and therefore still young, as promiscuous—I mean truly and successfully so. Wheeler could see that the months were passing and that the situation with Luisa had still not been sorted out, as he would have preferred—there wasn't so much as a flicker, not even a tremor, even of the kind that leaves the doors more firmly shut than before; because even if they only open a crack, there is still a slight fluster of agitation—and so from his distance, fumblingly, not to say blindly, with a touch of ingenuousness and respectful paternalism, he would act as a very tentative matchmaker whenever a female name cropped up in our conversations, and that of Patricia Pérez Nuix was, inevitably, the most persistent and enduring.

'Do you get on well with her? Are you, would you say, comrades?' he asked me once. 'Contrary to what is generally believed, the best relationship you can have with the opposite sex is one of comradeship, it's the best way to make conquests and it lasts longer too.' On another occasion, he questioned me about her abilities: 'Do you find her talk interesting, her view of things, the details she picks up on? Is she as good as Tupra says she is? Do you have fun with her?' And on a third occasion, he was even more direct or more curious: 'Is the girl pretty? Apart from her youth, I mean. Do you find her attractive?'

And I had answered every time, without alacrity but with due deference: 'Yes, the beginnings of comradeship, I mean it could happen. But it's early days for that, we haven't found ourselves yet in a situation where we could unequivocally help each other, get each other out of a difficulty or a dilemma, because those are the kinds of things that create comradeship. Or long habit, and the unremarked passage of time.' And then: 'Yes, she is good, she's sharp and perceptive; she's subtle too, but never overembellishes, she doesn't invent or show off; and she's certainly fun, I don't get irritated or bored when I have to interpret alongside her, I'm always glad and willing to listen to her.' And later: 'Yes, she is rather pretty, but not too pretty. And she's funny and physical and she laughs easily, which is so often the most attractive thing about women. I don't know that I find her so attractive that I'd go to the kind of bother I might have once or actually take a step in that direction, but I certainly wouldn't turn up my nose if the opportunity happened to arise.' I remember that I resorted to Spanish for the whole of that last sentence, well, there isn't any real equivalent in other languages for 'no hacer ascos,' although 'to turn up your nose at something' comes close, and I added: 'It's just a hypothesis: it's not something I think about, not something I'm considering doing. Besides, it would be inappropriate, she's much younger than me. In theory, she's not someone I could ever aspire to.'

Wheeler responded with genuine bemusement:

'Really? Since when have you set such limits on yourself? Or put obstacles in your way? I think I'm right in saying that you're younger than Tupra, and as far as I know, he doesn't set limits on himself or put obstacles in his way in that or any other field.'

He could have been speaking in general or making a specific reference to the liaison between Tupra and Pérez Nuix about which I had so many suspicions. This was another piece of information to back up those suspicions.

'We're not all alike, Peter,' I replied. 'And the older men get, the more unlike we become, don't you think? You should know. Tupra and I are very different. We probably always were, right from childhood.'

He paid no attention to this remark, however, or else took it as a joke.

'Oh, come now. You're not going to persuade me that you've suddenly gone all shy, Jacobo. Or that you've developed a complex about your age and with it all kinds of scruples. What do ten or twenty years matter? Once someone becomes an adult, that's it, and things even out very quickly from then on. It's a point from which there's no return, I'm pleased to say, although there are some people who never achieve adulthood, not in how they live their lives or intellectually—in fact, there are more and more such people, they're real pests, I can't abide them, and yet shops, hotels and offices, even hospitals and banks, are full of them. It's a deliberate ploy, fostered by the societies we live in. For reasons I can't understand, they choose to create irresponsible people. It's incomprehensible. It's as if they set out to create people with a handicap. How old is this bright young thing?'

'Twenty-seven at most, I would say. Certainly not much less.'

'She's a grown woman, then, she'll already have crossed Conrad's shadow line, or will be about to do so. It's the age at which life takes charge of you, if you haven't already taken charge of it yourself. The line that separates the closed from the open, the written from the blank page: it's when possibilities begin to run out, because the ones you discard become ever more irrecoverable, and more so with each day you live through. Each date a shadow, or a memory, which comes to the same thing.'

'Yes, that would be so in Conrad's day, Peter. Now, at twenty-seven, most people feel as if they're only just starting, with the doors of life flung open and real life as yet unbegun and eternally waiting. People graduate from the school of irresponsibility at a much later age now. If, as you say, they ever do.'

'Be that as it may, your age will be a matter of indifference to that girl, if you interest her or she takes a liking to you. And if she has such a keen eye as you and Tupra say, she won't have fallen asleep in puberty or childhood, she won't have dug herself in, but will be fully incorporated into the world, she'll have scrambled aboard as quickly as she could, perhaps obliged by circumstance. And if she's as acute as all that, she won't be the kind of girl who likes very young men. They'll seem too transparent, overly decipherable, she'll have read their whole story even with the book closed.' Wheeler paused for a long time, the kind of pause that announced he was weary of talking, he tired very quickly on the phone, in the hand of an old man even a phone weighs heavy, and his arm would find it tiring to hold. Before saying goodbye, he added: 'You and Tupra are not so very different, Jacobo. Well, you *are* different, but not as much as you think, or as you would like. And you ought not to spend so much time alone there in London, I've told you before, even though you have more to do now and are busier. It's not the same thing.'

And there she was before me, that bright and not-too-pretty young woman, in my apartment, at night, on my sofa, with her dog, a run in her tights, and drinking too much wine, all in order to ask me a favor, and outside I could see the steady, comfortable rain, so strong and sustained that it alone seemed to light up the night with its continuous threads like flexible metal bars or endless spears, it was as if it were excluding clear skies for good and discounting the possibility of any other weather ever appearing in the sky—or even the idea of its own absence, just like embraces when they are given willingly and with feeling and just like repugnance when repugnance is the only thing that still exists between those same two people who once embraced; the one before and the other afterwards, things almost always happen in that order and not the other way round. There was young Pérez Nuix, probably the best of us—there was no need to allow any more time to pass before saying so—the one who saw most and the most gifted of our group in the building with no name, the one who took the biggest risks and saw most deeply, more than Tupra and more than me and much more than Mulryan and Rendel, I wondered if she would guess or know what my reactions and my response would be when she finally asked me straight out what she had come to ask me after her long walk, drenched despite her umbrella. And I thought she would doubtless have made her measurements, her calculations and her prognostications, and that she would probably know what I still did not know about myself—perhaps she had her own kind of prescience; I must tread very carefully and sidestep her predictions, or deliberately prove them wrong, but that would be difficult, because she was also capable of foreseeing when and how I would intentionally and far-sightedly sidestep the predictions I had foreseen. We could end up cancelling each other out and our conversation would then lack both truth and meaning, as was the case with everything we did. When two equal forces meet, that is the time to lay down one's weapons: when the spear is thrown to one side and the shield is lowered and laid on the grass, the sword is stuck into the ground and the helmet hung on its hilt. I should just relax and try not to get ahead of myself or act against my own best interests; I should try not to be artificial, but drink a little more of my wine calmly and unconcernedly, knowing that in the end I could answer either 'Yes' or 'No' and still direct the conversation.

'Broccoli, Saltzman, Pevsner, they're all foreign names, I mean non-British. It's striking, isn't it, a little odd, that the producers of Bond should be German or Italian in origin.' That is what I in turn replied, taking a sip of my drink and at the same time giving in to my onomastic-geographical curiosity and not urging her to get to the point. They must have been false Englishmen and women too, the members of those wealthy families. For one reason or another, there really were quite a lot of them. 'Even if they had British nationality or were born here, they still sound false.'

'Well, it seems perfectly normal to me, I don't know what you mean by "false." People have the mistaken idea that there isn't much of a racial mix here or that any foreign presence is very recent, like that Abramovich man who's taken over Chelsea or Al Fayed or other millionaire Arabs. Great Britain has been full of non-English surnames for centuries. Look at Tupra, look at me, look at Rendel, look at you. The only one of us whose name doesn't come from elsewhere is Mulryan, and he, I bet, is really an Irishman.'

'But I'm not English, I don't count,' I said. 'I'm to all intents and purposes a Spaniard, and I'm only here temporarily. At least I think I am, that's my feeling, although, who knows, I might end up staying. And you're only half-British, aren't you? Your father is Spanish. Nuix, I assume, is a Catalan name.' I pronounced it as it should be pronounced, not as a Castilian would, but as if it were written 'Nush.' I had noticed that the English, on the other hand, called her 'Niux,' as if her name were written 'Nukes.'

'He was Spanish, yes, but he isn't any more,' replied young Nukes. 'Anyway, I'm not half anything, I'm English. As English as Michael Portillo, the politician, you know who I mean, at one point it looked as if he might be the next Tory Prime Minister, his father, though, was an exile from the Spanish Civil War. The next leader of the Tories was that fellow Howard, he may have changed his surname, but he's Romanian originally. And many years ago in Ireland, there was that President with the unequivocally Spanish name De Valera, as nationalistic as any O'Reilly, and who, incredibly enough, emerged out of Sinn Fein. Then you have the Korda brothers, who for decades dominated this country's film industry and the painter Freud, and the composer Finzi, and the conductor Sir John Barbirolli, and that director who made *The Full Monty*, Cattaneo or Cataldi, I can't quite remember. There's Cyril Tourneur, a contemporary of Shakespeare, and the poets Dante and Christina Rossetti, and Byron's lugubrious friend, Dr. John Polidori, and Conrad's real name was Korzeniowski. Gielgud is a Lithuanian or Polish name, and yet no one spoke better English on the stage; Bogarde was Dutch, and then there was that old actor Robert Donat, who played Mr. Chips, his name was an abbreviation of Donatello, I believe. There were prestigious publishers like Chatto and Victor Gollancz, and the bookseller Rota. Then you have Lord Mountbatten, who started off as Battenberg, and even the Rothschilds. Not to mention the Hanoverians, who have reigned here for centuries now, however they may conceal the fact by calling their dynasty Windsor, a name-change that only occurred thanks to George V. There have always been loads of such examples, and most are or were as British as Churchill or Blair or Thatcher. Or as Disraeli, for that matter, Prime Minister during Queen Victoria's reign, and there's very little that's English about his name.' She paused for a moment. She was better informed and more cultivated than I had thought, she had probably studied at Oxford, like so many civil servants; or perhaps because she herself had a foreign surname she had learned all these antecedents by heart and identified with them. She felt entirely English, which was interesting, she would never suffer any conflicts of loyalty; it seemed to me that her reaction betrayed even a certain patriotism, which was more worrying, as is anyone's patriotism. She finished off her third glass of wine, lit another of my Peloponnese cigarettes and took two puffs, one after the other, as if she had finally decided to come to grips with her subject and these were her final preparations, the equivalent to the little mental run-up she often took at work before she came over to talk to me, beyond I mean just greeting me or asking me some isolated question; taking a drink and smoking a cigarette marked a new paragraph. All this movement (she had been gesticulating during her proclamation of Britishness and her assurance that she was no compatriot of mine, contrary to my belief or, rather, feeling) had caused the run in her stockings to advance downwards and it was getting close to the top of her boot now; on its upward path it had already reached the edge of her skirt, and so I would not see it grow further in that direction unless her skirt inched up a little or she hitched it up herself, but why would she do that, though it wasn't impossible that she would do so distractedly, or perhaps that was just wishful thinking on my part. The paragraph, however, turned out to be a full stop: 'Oddly enough,' she said in another tone, 'the favor I want to ask you has to do with English people with foreign surnames, and with a daughter and a father, I'm the daughter, and the father is my own, which is why this is such a big favor. We're not as rich as the Broccoli family, of course, and that's part of the problem.' She stopped, as if unsure whether it was appropriate to slip in the odd joke, hesitating between solemnity and frivolity, almost everyone who ends up asking for something opts for the former, fearing that otherwise their plea will lack force. And exaggeration is obligatory, it's up to the person listening to water down the gravity of the request. Lying and fantasy are less obligatory, but it's still as well to assume their presence—absolute credulity when given an account of some drama or danger can prove disastrous to the person hearing it. And so while I did not prepare myself to suspend belief, I did prepare to combat or undermine it because I am, by nature, credulous until, that is, I hear a false note.

'Tell me what it's about. Tell me and I'll see what I can do, if I can do anything. What's happened to Mr. Pérez Nuix, both names are his, are they not?' I couldn't help saying this in the patronizing tone of someone preparing to listen, consider, think it over, be a momentary enigma, keep the other person dangling and then concede or deny or be merely ambiguous. It always makes you feel rather important, knowing that you'll take equal pleasure in saying a 'Yes' and a 'No' and a 'Possibly' ('I'm being so good,' you say to yourself; or 'I'm so hard, so implacable, I wasn't born yesterday and no one's putting anything over on me'; or 'If I don't give a decision right now, I will be the lord of uncertainty'), and so you magnanimously, patiently draw the other person out: 'What is it?' or 'Tell me' or 'Explain what you mean'; or else speak threateningly and urgently: 'Come on, spit it out' or 'You've got two minutes, make the most of them and get straight to the point' (or 'Make it short')—I was giving that young woman all the time in the world that night, the rain outside removed all sense of haste.

'Yes, my mother's maiden name was Waller. He hyphenates his two names,' she said, and she drew the hyphen in the air, 'but I don't. I'm like Conan Doyle.' She smiled, and that, I thought, would be the last smile for quite some time, for as long as it took her to present her case. 'My father's getting on a bit now, he had me quite late, from his second marriage, I've got a half-sister and half-brother somewhere who are much older than me, but I've never had much to do with them. Even though my mother was considerably younger than him, she died six years ago from galloping cancer. He was already retired by then; well, insofar as anyone can retire from doing far too many things, most of them unproductive and vague and never entirely abandoned. He was always a womanizer, and still is within his limitations, but he was quite lost or perhaps disconcerted when my mother died: he even lost interest in other women. Naturally, this didn't last very long, just a few months of playing the part of the suddenly aged widower, but he soon recovered his youth. He'd had a terrible time as a child in Spain, during the War and afterwards, until his father managed to get him out and bring him to England, my grandfather had left in 1939 and couldn't send for him until '45, when the war against Germany ended; my father was fifteen when he arrived and was always torn between the two countries, he'd left some older brothers behind in Barcelona, who, when they had the chance, chose not to change countries. And he didn't have an easy time in London at first either, until he started to make his own way. He married well, both times; not that it was hard for him, he was a charming man and very handsome. It was a great error and injustice, to use his words, that he'd had such a difficult start in life, but he, of course, forgot about the difficulties and soon made up for them. And he'd laugh when he said this. He maintains, and always has, that we come into this world in order to have a good time, and anyone who doesn't see it like that is in the wrong place, that's what he says. He was a very good-humored man, and still is, he's one of those people who avoids sadness and is bored by suffering; even if he has real reason to suffer, he'll shake it off eventually, it just seems to him like a stupid waste of time, like a period of involuntary, enforced tedium that interrupts the party and may even ruin it. He was terribly shaken by my mother's death, I could see that, his grief was very real, some days it bordered on despair, he was almost mad with it, shut up at home, which was unheard of for a man who has spent his entire life going to sociable places in search of diversion. However, he was incapable of remaining anchored in sorrow for more than a few months. He can only cope with pain, his own or other people's, as if it were a brief performance in need of encouragement and compliments, and he would have seen wallowing in grief as not making the most of life, as a waste.'

That was the word both Wheeler and my father had used to refer to a very different thing, to the war dead, especially once the fighting's over and it becomes clear that everything has remained more or less the same, more or less as it probably would have been without all the bloodshed. That, with few exceptions, is how we all feel about wars, when we become distanced from them by passing time, and people don't even know about the crucial battles without which they might not have been born. According to young Pérez Nuix's father, time spent on heartbreak and mourning was also a waste. And it occurred to me that perhaps his idea was not so very different from that of my two old men, simply more categorical: not only were deaths a waste, whether in wartime or peacetime, it was just as much a waste to allow ourselves to be saddened or dragged down by them and not recover or be happy again. Like a knee pressing into our chest, like lead upon our soul.

'What was your father's name, I mean, what *is* his name?' I asked, correcting myself at once. I had been influenced by her temporal oscillations, 'He maintains, and always has,' 'He said, he says,' 'He was, he is,' I imagined that she kept slipping into the wrong tense because her father was old, and she would find it harder and harder to see in him the father of her childhood; it happens to all of us, we take the fathers and mothers of our childhood to be the real, essential and almost only ones, and later, even though we still recognize and respect and support them, we see them slightly as impostors. Perhaps they, in turn, see us like that, in youth and adulthood. (I was absenting myself from my children's childhood, who knows for how much longer; the only advantage, if that banishment were to prove prolonged, would be that, later, we would not see each other as impostors, they would not see me that way, nor I they. More like uncle and nephews, something strange like that.)

'Alberto. Albert. Or Albert.' The second time, she said the name as it would be pronounced in Catalan, with the stress on the second syllable, and the third time as it is in English, with the stress on the first. I deduced from this that she must have ended up pronouncing her father's name in that third way in his adopted country, and that this is what friends and acquaintances would call him, and his second wife when they were at home, and how the child Pérez Nuix would have heard him addressed before she relinquished that pretentious hyphen. 'Why do you ask?'

'Oh, no reason. When someone is talking to me about a person I don't know, I always get a clearer idea of them if I know their first name. Names can be very influential sometimes. For example, it's not insignificant that Tupra is called Bertram.' And with my next words, I took advantage of my temporary position in the control seat, it was an attempt to make her feel insecure, or to instill in her a sense of now unnecessary haste, I was used to the situation now and to her agreeable presence, my living room was infinitely more welcoming with her inside it, and more entertaining. 'I still don't know why you're telling me all this about your father. Not that I don't find it interesting, mind. Plus, of course, I'm interested in you.'

'Don't worry, I haven't really been beating about the bush, or not entirely, I'm getting to the point now,' she replied, slightly embarrassed. My words had had an effect, sometimes it's very easy to make someone feel nervous, even people who are not the nervous type. She was one such person, as were Tupra, Mulryan and Rendel. And presumably I was as well, given that they'd made me a member of the group, although I didn't believe that to be a virtue I possessed, not at least that I was aware of, I often feel like a real bundle of nerves. Of course it might be that we were all pretending or that we simply kept our cool at work, but were less successful at doing so outside. 'Anyway, since my mother died, my father has spent the last six years more out of control than ever, more desperate for activity and company. And after a certain age, however sociable and charming you might be, getting both those things can cost money, and without my mother there to keep a check on him, he's been spending it hand over fist.'

'You mean he let her manage his affairs?'

'Not exactly. It's just that the money was largely hers, she was the one with the income, from her family, and all more or less in order and assured. Not that she was rich, she didn't own a fortune or anything, but she had enough not to suffer any financial difficulties and to spend a life, or even a life and a half, in comfort. His earnings were sporadic. He would plunge optimistically into various risky businesses, film and television production, publishing houses, fashionable bars, would-be auction houses that never got off the ground. One or two went well and brought him large profits for a year or two, but they were never very stable. Others went disastrously wrong, or else he was cheated and lost everything he'd invested. Either way, he never changed his lifestyle, or went without his usual entertainments and celebrations. My mother did try to curb his excesses and ensure that he didn't squander so much money that it constituted a danger to her finances. But that ended six years ago. And about a month ago now, I found out that he's incurred enormous gambling debts. He's always loved the races and betting on his beloved horses; but now he bets on anything, whatever it might be—and he's widened the field to the Internet where the possibilities are endless; he frequents gambling dens and casinos, places where there's never any shortage of overexcited people, which for as long as I can remember is what has always attracted him, and so those places have become his principal way of keeping the party going, given that for him, the world is one long party; and to go to those places, he doesn't have to charm anyone or wait to be invited, which is a great advantage for a man getting on in years. Then he took to disappearing from home for long periods, and I'd hear nothing from him until it occurred to him to call me up one night from Bath or Brighton or Paris or Barcelona or from here in London, where he'd taken it into his head to book into a hotel, in the city where he has his own house, and a very nice house too, simply in order to feel more a part of the hustle and bustle, to wander through the foyer and strike up conversations in the various reception rooms, usually with absurd American tourists, who are always the keenest to chat with the natives. I also learned that, up until only a few months ago and for decades now, he'd been renting a little suite in a family-run hotel, the Basil Street Hotel, which isn't luxurious and a bit old-fashioned, but, still, imagine the expense, and imagine what he must have used it for, and hospitality is the thing that always costs most. At least that debt has been paid, the people at the hotel were very understanding and I came to an agreement with them. That isn't the case with the gambling debts, of course, which have got completely out of hand, as tends to happen to innocent aficionados, especially those who like to ingratiate themselves with their new acquaintances, and my father loves to keep refreshing his circle of friends.' Young Pérez Nuix paused for breath (albeit unostentatiously), she uncrossed and crossed her legs, inverting their position (the one beneath on top, and the one on top beneath, I thought I heard the run advance still further, I was keeping my eye on it), and she pushed her glass towards me an inch, propelling it forward by its base. I would have preferred her not to drink so much, although she seemed to hold her drink well. I pretended not to notice, I would wait until she insisted, or until she pushed it a little closer. 'Fortunately, the debts aren't too widely spread, which is something. So he doesn't entirely lack sense, and he borrowed money from a bank, well, from a banker friend, on a semi-personal basis, the banker was really a friend of my mother's and only my father's friend by proximity and association. However, this gentleman, Mr. Vickers, brought in a front man, in order, I understand, not to involve his bank in any way: he's a man with very varied business dealings, he's into lotteries and betting and a thousand other things, including acting as an occasional moneylender. The sums always came from the banker in this case, but the front man was charged with delivering the money and recovering it, along, shall we say, with the bank's interest. And if he can't recover the money, then he'll have to answer to Vickers and pay him the money out of his own pocket, now are you beginning to get some idea of the mess my father is in?'

'I'm not sure; they'd report him, wouldn't they? Or how does it work? Can't you come to some arrangement with this man Vickers, if he was a friend of your mother's?'

'No, that isn't how it works at all, you don't understand,' said Pérez Nuix, and in those last few words there was, for the first time, a hint of desperation. 'The money is originally his, but to all practical effects it's as if it wasn't. It's as if he had given the order: "Lend this gentleman up to this amount and have him return it to you with this much interest and by this deadline, and if he doesn't return it, bring me the money anyway." Officially, he doesn't even touch it, when it comes to handing it over or to recovering it. It's not up to him to worry about the transactions, these are the responsibility of the front man from start to finish, and the banker exercises no control over them whatsoever; and that is precisely how he wants it; consequently, he refuses to intervene, nor would he wish to. He doesn't even want to know if the money he receives on a certain date comes from the debtor or not; he will receive it from the person who received it from him in the first place, which is how it should be. That's all. The rest is not his responsibility. And so my father doesn't have a problem with Vickers, but with this other man, and he's not the sort to go to the police to make some pointless formal complaint. It isn't like it was in Dickens' day when people went to prison for the most paltry debts. What would he gain by that anyway, putting a seventy-five-year-old man behind bars? Assuming that were a possibility.'

'Wouldn't they first impound your father's goods or something?'

'Forget about all those slow, legal routes, Jaime, this man would never resort to anything like that in order to settle an outstanding bill, and I assume that's why Vickers and other people use him, so that no one has to waste time and so that everything turns out as planned.'

'Couldn't your father sell something, his house or whatever else he has left?' Pérez Nuix's look, a flicker of impatience despite her inferior or disadvantageous position (she had now started asking me the favor), made me realize that such a solution was impossible, either because the house had been sold already or because she wasn't prepared to leave her father without his own home, which is the one thing that consoles and calms the old and the sick when the time comes to rest, however fond they've been of wandering. I didn't insist, I changed tack at once. 'Well, if what you're saying is that you're afraid they'll beat him up or knife him, I don't see what they'd gain from that, the banker or his front man. The corpse of an elderly man turning up in the river.'—'I've seen too many old films,' I thought then. 'I always imagine the Thames giving back swollen, ashen bodies, rocked by the waters.'

'The front man would pay the banker, so the banker's no longer involved, you can forget about him; he merely triggered the whole thing, and although the money comes from him, it doesn't any more.'—'According to that theory,' I thought, 'matters are not triggered by the person doing the asking, but by the person who grants the request; I'd better take note'—'As for the front man, he might suffer a loss on this occasion, but on others, he'll have made a profit and will continue to do so. What he can't allow is for there to be a precedent, for someone not to keep their word and for nothing to happen to him. Nothing bad I mean. Do you understand?' And again there was that note in her voice, perhaps it was more incipient exasperation than anything else. 'Not that they'll necessarily inflict physical harm on my father, although that can't be ruled out at all. One thing is sure, though, they will seriously harm him in some way. Possibly through me, if they can find no better way of teaching him a lesson, or, from their point of view, of applying the rules, penalizing non-payment and seeing justice done. They couldn't let a bold seafarer who has failed to pay the toll go unreprimanded. Besides, that isn't what most worries me, what might happen to me I mean, and it's unlikely they would turn on me, they know that I know some influential people, that on some flanks I'm protected and can look after myself; I'm not protected against a beating or a knife attack, obviously, but they wouldn't take that route with me, they'd try instead to discredit me, to make sure I didn't get to work again in any of the fields that interest me, to ruin my future, and doing that to a young person isn't at all easy, the world keeps turning and sometimes, inevitably, things right themselves again. What I most fear is what they might do to him, physically or morally, or biographically. He walks so proudly through life that he wouldn't understand what was happening to him. That would be the worst thing, his confusion, he would never recover. I don't know, they would spoil what remains of his life, or else shorten it. Always assuming, of course, touch wood, fingers crossed, that they don't decide simply to take his life.' And she touched wood and crossed her fingers. 'It's very easy to ruin an old man, or indeed, heaven forbid, to kill him.' And she again crossed her fingers. 'He'd fall over if you pushed him.'

She fell silent for a moment and sat looking at her empty glass, but this time she preferred not to or didn't even think to push it closer to me. She used the same two fingers to stroke the base of the glass. It was as if she could see her blithe, frivolous, fragile father in that glass, and you would only need to tip it over to shatter it.

'But what can I do about it? Where do I come into all this?'

She glanced up at once and looked at me with her bright, quick eyes, they were brown and young and not yet overburdened with tenacious visions that refuse to go away.

'The man you're due to interpret the day after tomorrow or the next, or at the latest next week,' she replied, barely letting me finish my second question, like someone who has spent a long time in the fog waiting for the lighthouse to appear and who cries out when she does finally spot it. 'Well, he's the front man, our problem, *the* problem. And he's another Englishman with a strange surname. He's called Vanni Incompara.'

Vanni or Vanny Incompara, that, she said, was how he was known, although his official name was John, and he was presumably English, but she wasn't sure whether he was so by birth—she was currently trying to put together facts about his past, but the search kept throwing up unexpected lacunae, and he was turning out to be a most elusive man—or by virtue of a very rapidly acquired citizenship, thanks to influential contacts or to some strange secret subterfuge, and so she didn't know whether he was a first- or second-generation immigrant, like her and Tupra, who had both been born in London, although for all she knew, Bertram might be third- or fourth- or nth-generation, perhaps his family had been settled on the island for centuries. She had never asked him about that, nor about the origin of his strange surname, she didn't know if it was Finnish, Russian, Czech, or Armenian—or Turkish as I guessed and as Wheeler had suggested to me the first time he mentioned the person who would later become my boss, slightly mocking his name before I had even met Tupra—or, as she suddenly suggested, Indian; the fact is she had no idea, perhaps she would ask him one day, he never mentioned his roots, nor any relatives alive or dead or distant or close, that is, blood relatives—she must have been thinking about Beryl when she added this, and I, of course, thought of her too—as if he had sprung into being by spontaneous generation; although there was no reason why he should mention his roots, in England people tended to be reserved if not opaque when it came to personal matters, he sometimes talked about himself and his experiences, but always in vague terms, never giving a place or a date to his exploits, recalling each one with almost no context, isolated from the others, as if he were showing us only tiny fragments of shattered tombstones.

It was possible that this John Incompara had arrived in England not that many years ago, which might explain why he still liked to be called by the diminutive form of his Italian name, Giovanni, she explained, didactic and helpful, just in case I hadn't picked up on that. Anyway, his activities had only come to light fairly recently, and he was clearly an able fellow: he had quickly made himself some money—or perhaps he had brought it with him—and some relatively important friendships, and if, as was likely, he was breaking the law, he was careful to disguise or camouflage any illegalities with other entirely legitimate deals and to leave no proof or evidence of the more drastic, more brutal actions he was suspected of carrying out. She could find nothing incriminating, or, rather, nothing she could use as a negotiating tool to persuade him to write off the paternal debt. The only thing she had now was me. Vanni Incompara was going to be examined, studied and interpreted by the group and I had been assigned to do this work alongside Tupra. As far as she knew, this report had been commissioned by a third party, by some private private individual who was doubtless considering doing business with Incompara and wanted to be extra careful and find out more—to what extent he could be trusted and to what extent he would deceive, to what extent he was constant and to what extent resentful or patient or dangerous or resolute, and so on, the usual thing. In turn, should the opportunity arise during this probable encounter with Tupra, Incompara wanted to try and establish the beginnings of a relationship or even friendship with him, for he knew that Tupra had excellent contacts in almost every sphere and could prove a fruitful introduction to many celebrities and other wealthy people. What Pérez Nuix was asking of me was no big deal really, she said. It would be a huge favor to her but would not require much effort from me, she said again, despite my earlier protests, now that she was explaining what would be required. I merely had to help Incompara—insofar as this was possible and prudent—to emerge from this scrutiny with a Good or a Pass; to give a favorable opinion about his trustworthiness, his attitude towards associates and allies—could he prove dangerous, did he hold a grudge—his ability to resolve problems and overcome difficulties, his personal courage; but neither must I exaggerate or diverge too much from what Tupra saw in him or from what I believed Tupra saw (he didn't tend to give his own opinion in our presence, instead he would ask us and urge us on, and that way we would guess where he was leading us and where he was heading), but introduce shades and nuances—which would be easy enough—so that I would not present our boss with a picture lit by only one light or painted all one color, which he would be inclined to distrust on principle because it was far too simple; I must, in short, in no way prejudice Incompara's chances. And if I happened to notice the slightest hint of affinity or sympathy between the two men, I should foment and encourage this later, although again unemphatically, discreetly, even indifferently; just a quiet echo, a whisper, a murmur. 'The tranquil and patient or reluctant and languid murmur,' I thought, 'of words that slip by gently or indolently, without the obstacle of the alert reader, or of vehemence, and which are then absorbed passively, as if they were a gift, and which resemble something easy and incalculable that brings no advantage. Like the words carried along or left behind by rivers in the middle of a feverish night, when the fever has abated; and that is one of the times when anything can be believed, even the craziest, most unlikely things, even a nonexistent drop of blood, just as one believes in the books that speak to you then, to your weariness and your somnambulism, to your fever, to your dreams, even if you are or believe yourself to be wide awake, and books can persuade us of anything then, even that they're a connecting thread between the living and the dead, that they are in us and we are in them, and that they understand us.' And immediately I remembered more or less what Tupra had said at Sir Peter Wheeler's buffet supper by the River Cherwell in Oxford: 'Sometimes that moment lasts only a matter of days, but sometimes it lasts forever.'

'But if this man won't even write off the debt of a defenseless old man,' I said to Pérez Nuix after we had both fallen silent for a few seconds; I had rested my right cheek on my fist while I listened to her, and I was still in that same position; and I realized that she had done the same while she was talking to me, both of us in that identical posture, like an old married couple who unconsciously imitate each other's gestures, 'and if you believe him capable of brutal acts and if that's what you most fear about him in your father's case; and if he's not the dissembling type, as you said a little while ago ("I know this, I know him," you said), then I don't see how I could possibly persuade Tupra not to see what is glaringly obvious. Maybe you're attributing to me gifts I don't possess, or too much influence, or else you take Bertram for a scatterbrain and a greenhorn, which I find hard to believe. He's far more experienced than I am, not to mention more knowledgeable and more perceptive. Probably even more than you, more experienced, I mean.' I made this unnecessary clarification, thinking of Tupra's own views on her abilities, at least according to Wheeler, and also because I didn't want to downgrade her. She didn't, however, pick up the indirect compliment.

'No, you haven't fully understood me, Jaime,' she replied, again with that instantly suppressed note of desperation or exasperation. 'I didn't explain myself properly when I said that. I've been with Incompara, I've met him a couple of times now, to see what I could get out of him or what could be done for my father, to try and calm him down and gain time, to see what he's interested in and to see if I have some bargaining chip in my hand I wasn't aware of, and it turns out I do have one. If you will help me. It's true, he's not the dissembling type. By which I mean that you can tell at once that he'll have no scruples he can't set aside if he needs to. And that he's probably brutal about it. Not personally perhaps (I can't imagine him beating anyone up himself), but in the orders he might give and the decisions he might take. There's his rigidity about any agreements he makes, the obsessive importance he gives to obligations being met, in a way he's a stickler for the rules, although that might just be an act he's putting on for my benefit to justify his intransigence in my affair. He only cares about other people meeting their obligations, of course, not about meeting his own. A characteristic he shares with far too many people nowadays, never have so many eyes been so contented to wear their beams with pride.' She didn't use the Spanish word '*vigas*' here, but the English 'beams'; this happened very rarely, but it did happen now and then; as she herself said, she was, after all, English. 'But none of these things is necessarily bad or negative or off-putting in a prospective colleague. On the contrary, and that's precisely why he's used by people like Mr. Vickers, an honorable man who simply doesn't want to bother with or know anything about the confusing or unpleasant details. Bertie will, of course, see all of that in Incompara, and you won't say anything to contradict it, because you'll observe that too and there would no point in arguing over something so obvious. No doubt about it, Incompara is a frightening guy (if he wasn't, my situation wouldn't be so serious), and in that respect it's not a matter of him dissembling, that would be extremely hard for him to do. I'm not really asking you to lie about anything very much, Jaime, especially when there would be no point. There's no point to any lie unless it's believable. Well, unless it's believed. Forgive me for insisting so much on this, but while I'm really not asking you for very much, *I* would gain enormously.'

'What would you gain exactly?'

'Vanni Incompara would be willing to write off the entire debt in exchange for this.'

'In exchange for what exactly?' I asked, repeating the word "exactly." 'What would satisfy this man? What would the consequences be? What would your part in all this be? And do you believe him?'

'Yes, I do in this case. He wouldn't hesitate to teach my father a lesson or anyone else who didn't keep his word, but I'm also sure that he would always rather save himself the bother. He won't mind not getting the money back if he's compensated for it with something worthwhile; he's got plenty of money. He knows that someone has asked our group to assess him, I mean, that they've asked Bertie, since he's the one who receives instructions from above as well as most of the private commissions, those of any substance. I don't know who has asked for the report, Incompara hasn't told me, but that doesn't matter to us, does it? We don't usually know anyway. Whoever they are, it's important to him that he wins their approval and that they don't reject him, or that he reaches an agreement with them or strikes a deal or gets to participate in their projects. He'd consider the debt paid off entirely if I made all or any of those things happen—if he's accepted by the people who are submitting him to this examination, that's all he needs. He would, he says, put it down to my intervention, to my collaboration, however partial, as long as it did the trick; he's obviously not a hundred percent sure of himself, he must know what his weak points are and will imagine a trained eye would detect them, well, we all feel that way under scrutiny. It would take a few days to know the result, perhaps a week or more, but meanwhile . . . well, at the worst, we would have bought my father a deferment.' Yes, her Spanish was decidedly bookish: she didn't manage '*vigas*,' but she did use '*escarmentar*'—to teach someone a lesson—'*entablar negocios*'—to strike a deal—and '*enjundia*'—substance. She had made the matter her own, she wanted to leave her father out of it as much as possible, to spare him even the negotiations, she had taken on his debt, which is why she had said 'He'd consider the debt paid off entirely' and 'my situation' and 'my affair.' No 'we' or 'our.'

'Why are you so sure that I'll be the one chosen to interpret this fellow Incompara? It could be you, and then you'd have no problem and wouldn't have to ask anyone for a favor.'

'I've worked with Bertie for several years now,' she replied. 'I usually know who's going to be assigned to whom, when it's not routine work and I'm told about it beforehand. When there's a lot of money involved or if, for whatever reason, special tact is required—for example, if we had to make a study of the Prince's current girlfriend (and it will happen, we'll be asked to do that sooner or later)—he would use me for the task. To help him out, shall we say, for a second opinion, as a contrast, because he wouldn't delegate such a task to just anyone. Otherwise, he follows a complex system of turn-taking, depending on our individual characteristics. He doesn't stick to it rigidly, but according to that system and to my calculations, it's your turn. I'd love it if he chose me to interpret Incompara. If only . . . And if I'm wrong and that's what happens, I can assure you I'll be the first to celebrate, more than you or him, more than anyone. That would make things much easier for me, I'd prefer not to have to depend on you. Not to have to bother you with this or get you mixed up in it all. I gave all this a lot of thought before asking you. I've been thinking about it for the last few days, and just now, during the walk over here, more than once I was on the verge of turning around and going home. What I can't do is offer myself for the job, or show a particular interest in taking it on, because Bertie would immediately wonder why and ask me questions and get suspicious; he never shies away from suspicions or brushes them under the carpet, he never thinks anyone is above suspicion. Not even his own mother, if she's still alive, although, as I said, I've never heard him mention his family. And there's another element too: from what I know, Incompara must have a finger in a lot of pies. Bertie will probably think that, among other factors, you are the least exposed to previous chance contaminations because you haven't been in London all that long.'

I sat looking at her and then poured her the glass of wine I'd denied her before, the fourth. I could see that she was tired, or perhaps beginning to feel the effort of having to persuade and to ask, which takes a lot of energy, and that she was tense too, which is exhausting, and there's always a moment when, however enthusiastically we might have begun an assault, we doubt that we'll get what we want, that we'll succeed. The whole thing suddenly seems pointless, we're convinced people will say 'No' or even take pleasure in saying 'No' and refuse, and that they'll be able to come up with cast-iron reasons for doing so: 'I'm a bit hard up at the moment,' 'I don't want to get involved,' 'Sorry, you're asking too much of me,' 'It won't work, I'm no good at that kind of thing,' 'I have my loyalties,' 'It's too big a risk,' 'If it was up to me, I'd do it, but there are other people involved'; or more clearly, 'What's in it for me?' Perhaps young Pérez Nuix, in a sudden loss of faith, was already asking herself which of these formulae I would opt for. Yes, what *was* in it for me? I could see no benefit at all, and she would know that I couldn't, because there was none. She hadn't even tried that route, at least not yet, and hadn't even attempted to invent some benefit. During those moments when she seemed distracted, almost resigned, I again glanced at the run in her stockings, at her ever more naked leg. I hoped she would do something before her tights exploded (that would be a shock) or went all baggy and loose (that would be repellent) or suddenly dropped to the floor (that would be humiliating), none of these three possibilities appealed to me, but they would break the spell of that torn but still taut fabric. And so I indicated her thighs with a lift of my chin and said (the words just came out, my will did not intervene, or appeared not to):

'I don't know if you've noticed, but you've got an enormous run in your stockings. It must have happened while you were walking. Or perhaps the dog did it.'

'Yes,' she replied easily, unsurprised, 'I noticed it a while ago, but didn't want to interrupt you. I'd better just nip to the bathroom and take them off. How embarrassing.' She stood up (farewell, vision) and picked up her bag, the dog got to his feet as well, ready to follow her, but she stopped him with two words in English (he was, of course, a native English dog), persuaded him to lie down again, and disappeared. 'How embarrassing,' she said again when she was already in the corridor, out of my field of vision. But she didn't seem in the least embarrassed. 'She isn't really that tired or discouraged or depressed,' I thought. 'Interrupt *me*? That can't have been a mistake or a slip. Not even after all the wine she's drunk. She's the one doing the talking, the telling, the one who came here to plead with me, although she hasn't really done that yet, neither by her tone of voice or her choice of vocabulary nor by being tedious or insistent. Yet she is, nevertheless, pleading, only without actually running the risk of provoking a flat refusal, which would be counterproductive. She's asking me something, but without a hint of pathos and without humiliating herself, almost as if she weren't asking for anything, but she isn't doing so out of pride. She's simply setting out the information.' When she returned, she was no longer wearing any stockings, so she wasn't one of those far-sighted women who always carry a spare pair; or perhaps she was, but had decided not to put them on, preferring boots against her bare skin, and it wasn't cold in the apartment. She crossed her legs as if nothing had happened (the vision returned, rather improved in fact), she picked up two olives, nibbled a chip and took a timid sip of her wine, perhaps she was watching what she was drinking more closely than I thought. 'So, Jaime, what do you say? Can I count on your help? It's a big favor I'm asking you.'

I had been sitting down for too long. I got up and went over to the window, I opened it for a few seconds and put my head out and looked up at the sky, at the street, my cheeks and the back of my neck got slightly wet, the rain wouldn't stop for several days and nights, it looked as if it were going to hang over the city for some time, or over the country which for her was '*país*' or perhaps also '*patria*,' the dangerous, empty concept and the dangerous, inflammatory word, which would allow a mother to say in justification of her son's actions: '*La patria es la patria*'— one's country is one's country—and when it comes to defending one's country, lies are no longer lies. Poor trapped mother, the mother of the man who betrayed not his country, but his former friend, it's always safer to betray an individual, however close to them we might be, than some vague, abstract idea that anyone can claim to represent, for then, at every step, we might find ourselves accused by strangers, by standard-bearers we have never seen before, who will feel betrayed by our actions or lack of action; that's the bad thing about ideas, their self-declared representatives keep crawling out of the woodwork, and anyone can take up an idea to suit their needs or interests and proclaim that they'll defend it by whatever means necessary, bayonet or betrayal, persecution or tank, mortar or defamation, brutality or dagger, anything goes. Perhaps it would be easier for me than for Pérez Nuix to try and betray Tupra. For me he was a single individual and nothing more, while for her, he might, in some measure, represent her country or at least embody an idea. The deception would come from her, but via an intermediary, namely me, and such intermediaries help enormously to diffuse blame, it's as if one were less involved or, once the thing is done, almost not involved at all, in the eyes of others, but also in one's own eyes, which is why people so often resort to front men, hired assassins, soldiers, thugs, straw men, paid killers and the police, and even the courts, which often serve as the executive branch of our passions, if we first manage to draw them in and later convince them. It's easier to do away with someone or bring about their ruin if you only give the order or set the appropriate mechanisms going, or pay the money or hatch a plot or approach the appropriate person with a tip-off, or if you merely make a formal complaint and conspire and have other people lead your victim to the cell, not to mention execute him once he has passed through the hands of innumerable intermediaries, all of them legal, who share the blame out among themselves as they follow that long road and return to us only the lukewarm leftovers, a few insubstantial crumbs, and all we receive at the end of the process that we originated are a few terse words, a mere communiqué and sometimes only an enigmatic phrase: 'Sentence has been passed,' or 'It's done,' or 'Problem solved,' or 'No need to worry any more,' or 'The torment's over' or 'You can sleep easy now.' Or even 'I have done the deed' (in the words of that ancient Scotsman). It would be less sinister in my case, merely a matter of phoning Patricia one day or not even that, of whispering to her in the office, when we met or passed: 'He fell for it.' The first traitor's name, Del Real it was, had also used intermediaries against my father: first, he recruited the second traitor, that Professor Santa Olalla who lent his signature to back up a complaint against someone he didn't even know, and then . . . Those two men did not go in person to get Juan Deza on the feast day of San Isidro in 1939, they sent Franco's police to arrest him and put him in prison, and then others intervened, witnesses, a prosecutor, a sham lawyer and judge, almost nothing is ever done directly or face to face, we don't even see the face of the person bringing about our ruin, there is almost always someone in the middle, between you and me, or between me and the dead man, between him and her.

'Why haven't you gone straight to Tupra and asked him? Surely if you explained, as you have to me, about your father he'd understand and grant you this one favor? He'll be sure to make an exception. You know him much better than you know me, you seem quite close, you share a kind of ironic affection, if I can put it like that, as if you had an out-of-office relationship too.' I didn't want to continue along that route, I didn't want to insinuate what I suspected existed between them; although I didn't believe that it still existed, I imagined it to be more a thing of the past, and possibly only a very transient thing, or only half-voluntary. I was speaking to her now from more of a distance, with my back against the open window, I could feel the air through my shirt, fortunately it wasn't raining hard, I would have to shut the window as soon as the smoke cleared. 'In fact, you hardly know me at all. What made you think I would be more accessible than him, readier to agree to what you're asking, more helpful? I'm sure he must owe you some debt of gratitude, even if only for the years of collaboration and the good work you've done. I, on the other hand,' I hesitated for a moment, did a swift recap and found nothing, 'I as yet have no reason to be grateful to you, as far as I know or can recall.'

'You're Spanish,' she said, 'and therefore less rigid when it comes to principles. You're new to the job, you might leave soon and you're on a salary. Not that Bertram has that many principles—in the usual understanding of the term—nor are they of the noblest kind; obviously he's capable of making exceptions, he has no alternative in his job, or indeed in most jobs. But the principles he has, he holds to, and one of them is not to mess around in any way with his work. If a mistake occurs, he'll accept that, but not if it's due to negligence or if it's a deliberate, a false mistake. He only accepts unavoidable errors, when we really are misled or are wrong or we miss something, it happens to us all from time to time, not seeing clearly and getting things totally wrong. No, this is one favor he wouldn't grant. He'd urge me to find other solutions, he'd think that there must be some other way, but I know there isn't, I've gone over and over it in my head. More than that, if he knew about the situation, he'd take it as just another bit of information on Incompara, he'd use it in the report and possibly to Incompara's disadvantage, I would run the risk of everything turning out exactly as I don't want it to, and it would be all my fault. He cares about his own prestige and fancies himself as an expert. He doesn't think he's infallible, but he does believe he renders a real service to the State and to our clients, I mean, the people who come to him aren't just anybody. He also believes he has a very good eye when it comes to choosing the staff he works with. He doesn't take on just anyone, in case you hadn't noticed. You started as an interpreter of languages. The fact that you've gone on to other things is because he saw that you had real ability and because he trusts you. You've risen really fast. The last thing he would expect would be for one of us to deliberately distort an interpretation or ask him to do so. I get the impression with you, though, that none of this really matters. I have the feeling you're just waiting and meantime earning some money, doing something that you find fairly easy, and more fun than working for the radio. Waiting to know what to do, to see what to do, or to be summoned to Madrid, waiting for someone to say "Come back." Don't take this the wrong way, but I don't think your heart is really in this job. That's why I'm asking you and not Bertie. What does it matter to you? And it really is a big favor.'

'Come, come, I was so wrong about you before,' I thought. 'Sit down here beside me, somehow I just couldn't see you clearly before. Come here. Come with me. Come back and stay here forever.' The nights continued to pass and I heard no such words, nothing like them, not even a contradictory murmur or a false echo. Perhaps Pérez Nuix was right, perhaps I was just there waiting, 'waiting without hope,' in the words of an English poet whom so many have copied since. But if the voice never came, over the phone or in some unexpected letter, or in person when I finally went to see my children, there would come a day when I would wake up with the feeling that I was no longer waiting. ('Last night I was still all right, but today? I'm another day older, that's the only difference and yet my existence has changed. I'm no longer waiting.') On that morning, I would discover that I had become used to London, to Tupra and to Pérez Nuix, to Mulryan and to Rendel, to the office with no name and to my day-to-day work and, from time to time, to Wheeler, who had known Luisa and would soon become a link with my forgetting. I would discover that I had got used to everything—I mean to the point of not feeling surprised when I opened my eyes or not even thinking about any of them. These others would become my everyday and my world, the thing that requires no reason to exist, my air, and I would no longer miss Luisa, or my former city and life. Only my children.

I closed the window, I was starting to feel a little chilly and, more to the point, I noticed that she was too: she was no longer wearing stockings, and I saw that she was tempted to pull her skirt down over her thighs, thus depriving me of that pleasant view. However, I stayed where I was, with my back to the street, the sky and the rain. And I thought: 'As she doubtless foresaw, this woman is well on the way to persuading me. But it's still up to me to answer "Yes" or "No" or "Maybe."'

'Before, you said that I wouldn't really have to lie about anything very much,' I said. 'What exactly is that "nothing very much"? What should I tell Tupra that I see or don't see in Incompara and that I probably will or won't see? In any case, won't he also see or not see the same thing?'

Young Pérez Nuix was hardly drinking at all now. Either her furious thirst had passed or she knew exactly how much she could drink and how fast. She was, however, smoking. She lit another Karelias cigarette, she must have liked the slightly spicy taste. With the lighter still in her hand, she uncrossed her legs and left them slightly apart, and from where I was, I thought I could see as far as her crotch, a flash of white panties. I was careful not to let my eyes remain fixed on that point, she would have noticed at once. I merely allowed myself the occasional fleeting glance.

'There are some fundamental things that are not at all easy to pick up on at a meeting, during a conversation or on a video, and I don't know if there is a video of Incompara that Bertie could show you. It's unlikely, but possible—he can get hold of video footage of almost anyone. It isn't easy to see, for example, that a person is a coward, and that in a moment of great danger he'll leave you in the lurch, especially if there's some physical danger or, let's say, a risk of prison. But that's certainly been my impression on the couple of occasions I've met Incompara. I may be wrong, however, and it would be inadvisable for the report to reflect that; it would cause him irreparable harm. The people who have commissioned the report would want nothing to do with Incompara if such a characteristic were attributed to him, that's for sure. Well, it's not a characteristic anyone likes, it makes you feel vulnerable, unsafe. In fact, it's everyone's worst nightmare, thinking that if things were to take an unexpected turn or if a situation got nasty, the person who should be helping would simply take off, duck out and leave us high and dry or, worse, pin the blame on us in order to save himself. If you get that feeling too, you mustn't mention it to Bertie, that's where you would have to lie, or, rather, say nothing. And if Bertie also picks up on it, you'll have to try, very carefully, to persuade him that it isn't so.' She paused very briefly and her gaze grew abstracted, as if she really were thinking or puzzling something out even as she was speaking, and people rarely do that. 'It's one of the hardest things to identify, as is its opposite. It's where we're most likely to slip up, and even when we think we know, there's always a nagging doubt that won't go away until we've had a chance to put it to the test. Not that one has to try very hard to sow that seed of doubt. People's forecasts or declarations on the matter, regarding their valiant or pusillanimous character, are almost no use at all. It's the thing they hide best, although the verb "hide" is inappropriate really: most of the time, they conceal it so well because they themselves have no idea how they'd react, just as a new recruit doesn't know how he'll react to his baptism of fire. People tend to imagine what they would do in accordance with their hopes or fears; but almost none of us knows just how we'd respond if placed in a dangerous situation. At most, we find out when we're put to the test, but that doesn't happen very often in our normal lives and might never happen, we usually get through the day with no major upsets or dangers. Not that

the discovery that we behaved with valor or cowardice in a particular circumstance proves anything anyway, because the next
time we might behave quite differently, possibly in exactly the
opposite way. We can never guarantee either boldness or panic,
and if we ourselves know nothing about this facet of our character, it would take enormous skill on the part of an observer, an
interpreter, to discern it in someone else, that is, to manage to
foresee a response about which even the person in question has
his doubts, and to which he is, indeed, half-blind. That, among
other reasons, is why you're here: you have a good eye for that
characteristic, better even than Rendel, and that's not just my
opinion, I've heard Bertie say so and he's not exactly lavish with
compliments. He clearly trusts you in that field more than anyone, including himself. So it wouldn't be hard for you to make
him waver, anything you said certainly wouldn't go unheeded.
You would have more difficulty when it came to other aspects,
for example, Incompara's relative lack of scruples, his harshness
towards those over whom he has power, the brutality by proxy
that I mentioned before. You wouldn't have to lie about those
things, though, nor even keep quiet about them; as I said, they
wouldn't prevent the people who've asked for this investigation
from taking him on or letting him in or whatever, such qualities would be seen, rather, as advantages and virtues. Cowardice, on the other hand, brings no benefits at all. No one thinks
of it as a desirable quality. I mean other people's cowardice, of
course, not our own. We all have to come to terms with our
own.' She didn't use the normal Spanish expression here either,
but translated it literally as '*llegar a términos*.' Maybe, although it
didn't show, she *was* a bit tired or slightly drunk, which is when
language tends to falter.

It's true, almost no one knows, not even when put to the
test. If that night someone had asked me how I would react
when confronted by a man who suddenly produced a sword in
a public toilet and threatened to cut off another man's head in
my presence, I wouldn't have had the slightest idea or, if I had
ventured an opinion, I would have been quite wrong. It would
have seemed to me so improbable, so anachronistic, so unlikely

that I might perhaps have dared to respond, with the optimism that always accompanies our imaginings of something that isn't going to happen, or which is purely hypothetical and therefore impossible: 'I'd stop him, I'd grab his arm and block the blow, I'd force him to drop the sword, I'd disarm him.' Or else, if the image had seemed real and I had believed it or, for a moment, fully accepted it, I would have been able to reply: 'God, what a nightmare, how dreadful. I'd run away, without a backward glance, take to my heels so that no two-edged sword fell on me, so that I wouldn't be the one for the chop.' The incident in the toilet had happened not long after that night of rain, and I had, so to speak, been caught between those two extremes. I had neither confronted him nor fled. I didn't move and didn't close my eyes as De la Garza had closed his and as I closed mine later on at Tupra's house, where I was not so much in real or physical danger, but perhaps in moral danger, or perhaps my conscience was; I had stood there astonished and terrified and had shouted at him, I had resorted to words, which are sometimes more effective than the hand and quicker and sometimes quite useless and go entirely unheeded, and I had also looked on impotently, or perhaps prudently, more concerned about saving my own as yet unscathed skin than about the already condemned man, who couldn't be rescued from his fate. I don't know if such a reaction is natural or pure cowardice.

Yes, Pérez Nuix was right: you can almost never precisely pin down the nature of such a reaction or what it consists of because it wears an infinite number of masks and disguises, and never appears in its pure state. Most of the time, you don't even recognize it, because there's no way of separating it from everything else that makes up our personality, of splitting it off from the nucleus that is us, nor of isolating or defining it. We don't recognize the reaction in ourselves and yet, oddly enough, we do in others. I wasn't at all convinced by what she and apparently Tupra believed, that I had a particular ability to spot and predict this in a person before it even revealed itself. What I knew for sure was that I couldn't see it in myself, any more than I could see courage, before or after either had shown its face. It's burdensome having to live with such ignorance, knowing, too, that we will never learn, but that is how we live.

'I think you overestimate my influence,' I said, 'the influence I can bring to bear on Tupra and his opinions, in that particularly tricky area or in any other. I don't believe that any view I took of a person would make Tupra abandon or modify his own, I mean assuming he'd already formulated his own, had noticed something, and he always notices lots of things. The very first time I met him, I was struck by his gaze, so warm and all-embracing and appreciative. Those flattering and at the same time fearsome eyes are never indifferent to what is there before them, eyes whose very liveliness gives the immediate impression that they're going to get to the bottom of whatever being or object or gesture or scene they alight upon. As if they absorbed and captured any image set before them. However elusive a quality cowardice may be, it wouldn't escape him. And if I do notice it in your friend, as you suggest, Tupra will notice it too and form his own idea. And I won't be able to shift him from that view, even if I try. Even if I get him drunk.'

Young Pérez Nuix burst out laughing, a pleasant, slightly maternal laugh, with no mockery in it or, if so, only the kind of mockery with which one might greet a child's naïve response or angry retort, and I took advantage of that momentary lowering of her guard to direct my eyes to the place at which I'd been trying not to look, at least not fixedly—she had not yet re-crossed her legs.

'I'm sorry,' she said, 'it just amuses me that even an intelligent man like you should suffer from the same inability. It's astonishing how wrong our perception of ourselves always is, how hopeless we are at gauging and weighing up our strengths and weaknesses. Even people like us—gifted and highly trained in examining and deciphering our fellow man—become one-eyed idiots when we make ourselves the object of our studies. It's probably the lack of perspective and the impossibility of observing yourself without knowing that you're doing so. Whenever we become spectators of ourselves that's when we're most likely to play a role, distort the truth, clean up our act.' She paused and looked at me with a mixture of jovial stupefaction and unwitting pity. She'd described me as 'intelligent' and had done so quite spontaneously; if this was flattery, she had disguised it very well. 'Don't you realize, Jaime, how much Bertie likes you? How stimulating and amusing he finds you? That he's so fond of you that he'll make a genuine effort to accept your view of things, as long, of course, as it's not arrant nonsense, and to believe what you tell him you can see, even if only to confirm to himself that you are his most magnificent acquisition, his most successful hire? Remember, too, that you came to him recommended not only by Wheeler, but by his teacher Rylands, from beyond the grave. Not that this situation will necessarily last; he'll grow tired of it one day, or get used to your presence; he'll even disapprove of you sometimes or scorn you, Bertie is not the most constant of people and he quickly tires of almost everything, or his enthusiasms come and go. Now, though, you're the latest novelty and, besides, you really do seem to have hit it off, in that sober, masculine, unspoken way of yours—or whatever it is—but I know what I'm talking about. At the moment, you have far more influence over him than you think, and yet it seems to me you haven't even noticed. It's a rather temporary state of affairs, and partial too, because Bertie never entirely trusts anyone and he's not a man to be manipulated or led and certainly not deflected. But there are a few areas where he can be made to entertain doubts, and you're in a position to sow a few doubts now. I know because I've been through the same process and can recognize it. I recognize his pleasure and enjoyment, how being with you amuses and stimulates him, just as he used to find my company enlivening too. We really hit it off as well, and that lasted a long time. Not in the same masculine way in which you and he get on. And it's not as if we don't any more, I have no complaints about the high esteem in which he holds me or his professional respect for me. But I no longer represent for him the small daily celebration that I did at first and even later on too, that's what he felt about me for quite a while, and I know I shouldn't say so, but it's true, ask Mulryan or Rendel, or Jane Treves, who, being a woman, naturally suffered more from jealousy, I'm sure you'll meet her one day, she felt positively neglected when she and I were both there with Tupra. You can persuade him, Jaime. Not about just anything, that won't happen either today or indeed ever, but if it's about some area he's unsure of and in which he believes you to be an expert, as with cowardice and bravery; there, as I said, he's convinced of your expertise. I am too, by the way, you're really very good. Anyway, that's what I'm asking you, Jaime. The man will then cancel the debt and my father will be safe. As you see, it's a big favor to ask.'

She had used the word 'favor' several times, it was a way of saying 'please' or '*por favor*' without actually saying it or not in so many words—words that denote pleading or begging, especially when repeated, 'Please, please, please'—'*Por favor, por favor, por favor.*' She crossed her legs, blocking my view, but I could instead direct my gaze anywhere with impunity, I could still see her bare thighs for example. She took a small sip of wine and put another Karelias cigarette to her red lips—again that flashback to childhood cartoons—without lighting it. The dog was fast asleep, as if he had got used to the idea that he might be staying there all night, and lying down like that, he seemed even whiter. I glanced out of the window, then moved away, nothing had changed, the flexible metal bars or endless spears of the ever more dominant rain continued to fall, as if excluding the possibility of clear skies for good. I took a few steps and then sat down where I had been sitting before. I had the feeling that the silence was not a pause this time, but that Pérez Nuix had finished her presentation; that she considered her plea to be over and done with: her few timid attempts at flattery, her various lines of argument and her deployment of prudent powers of persuasion. I felt that I now had to give an answer, that she was not going to add anything more. To answer 'Yes' or 'No' or 'Possibly' or 'We'll see.' To give her a little more hope without actually committing myself to anything: 'I'll see what I can do, I'll do my best.' 'It depends' would not, of course, put an end to the conversation or the visit. And I wasn't sure I wanted either to end, and so I didn't give her an answer, but asked her another question:

'How much is the debt exactly?'

She lit the cigarette and I thought I saw her blush for a moment, or perhaps it was just the glow from the match, or a lurking embarrassment, as when in the office with no name, I would sense in her a brief gathering of energy before she came over to talk to me, that is, beyond greeting me or asking me some isolated question, as if she had to gather momentum or take a run-up, and that was what gave me the idea that she didn't rule me out, although probably without knowing that she didn't, nor having even considered the possibility. I thought: 'She's embarrassed to tell me how much. Either because it's so low, and then I'll know that she can't afford to pay even that, or because it's so high, and then I'll find out what an enormous sum it is, or how crazy her father is, and perhaps how crazy she is as well.'

'Nearly two hundred thousand pounds,' she said after a few seconds, and she raised her eyebrows in a gesture that was not, of course, English, as if she were adding: 'You see the fix I'm in.' Though what she did, in fact, say was not so very different. 'What do you think?'

I made a rapid calculation. It was nearly three hundred thousand euros or fifty million pesetas, I had still not quite reaccustomed myself to the pound and will perhaps never get used to the euro when it comes to the kind of large quantities one does not deal with every day.

'I think that, considering his defects, Incompara is very generous,' I replied. 'Or else that report is worth an awful lot to him.' And then I asked another question, perhaps the one I least expected to ask, although I don't know if she was quite as surprised as I was, that depended on how well she knew me, on how much more she knew of me than I did of myself, on how much and in what depth she had translated or interpreted me—to employ the terminology we sometimes used to describe our indefinable work—during those months of working together. It occurred to me as a joke really and I saw no reason to resist. Besides, it would force her to put something on the table, to put a value on my participation, to consider me and the risk I was taking, to consider the possible damage to me and the unlikely benefits. Asking a favor is easy, even comfortable, the difficult, disquieting thing is hearing the request and then having to decide whether to grant or deny it. A transaction involves more work and more care and calculation for both parties. With a favor, only one of the parties has to decide and calculate, the one who is or isn't going to agree to it, because no one is obliged to return a favor or even be grateful. You ask, wait and receive a 'Yes' or a 'No'; then, in either case, you can calmly leave, having offloaded a problem or created a conflict. No, favors granted are not binding, they carry with them no contract, no debt, or only moral ones, and that's nothing, mere air, nothing practical. So, to my surprise, what I said was: 'And what's in it for me?'

Pérez Nuix, however, had not fallen into my trap, into my improvised and semi-unintentional trap. She didn't immediately go on to offer me something, a reward, a sum of money, a percentage, a gift, not even the promise of her eternal gratitude. She doubtless knew that the latter has no tangible or even symbolic meaning. People say it far too much, 'I'll be eternally grateful' is one of the most vacuous statements ever uttered and yet one hears it often, always with that unvarying epithet, always that same irresponsible 'eternally,' another clue to its absolute lack of reality, or truth or meaning, and sometimes the person saying it will add: 'If there's ever anything I can do for you, now or later on, you only have to ask,' when the fact is that almost no one immediately asks a favor in return, that would seem exploitative—a case of *do ut des*—and if, in the future, one does ask for something, the empty words will have been long forgotten and, besides, no one resorts to that, rarely does anyone remind the other person: 'Some time ago, you said . . .'; and if they do, they're likely to meet with this response: 'Did I say that? How very odd. Did I really? I don't remember that,' or else 'No, ask anything but that, that's the one thing I can't grant you, the very worst thing, please, don't ask me' or else 'I'm so sorry, I'd love to help, but it's simply not in my power, if only you'd come to me a few years ago, but things have changed.' And so the person who was only seeking the return of an old favor ends up asking a new favor, as if nothing had happened before, and is reduced almost to begging ('Please, please, please'). She was intelligent enough not to promise me chimeras or outlandish rewards in kind, nothing graspable or ungraspable, present or future.

'Nothing,' she said. 'For the moment, nothing, Jaime. It's simply a favor I'm asking and you can say "No" if you want to, you're not going to get anything out of it, you'll get nothing in return, although I really don't think it will be all that hard for you or that you'll be running any risk. If things don't work out, if he doesn't take the bait, you can always tell Bertie you made a mistake, it happens to us all, even to him, he knows perfectly well that no one's infallible. His hero Rylands wasn't, nor was Wheeler, something Wheeler, later on, had great cause to regret, apparently. Vivian wasn't either, nor were Cowgill, Sinclair or Menzies, people from another age, some of the best and most renowned, both in our field and beyond.' She knew how to pronounce that last name like a good Englishwoman or like a good spy, she too said 'Mingiss.' 'Nor were the big names of more recent times, Dearlove, Scarlett, Manningham-Buller and Remington, they all blundered at some point, in some way. Even Montagu wasn't infallible, nor were Duff Cooper or Churchill. That's why I said earlier that while this was a big favor for me, it wasn't such a big deal for you. That bothered you at the time, but it's true nonetheless. No, I don't think you'll get anything in return or profit in any way. But you won't suffer any misfortunes or any losses either. Anyway, Jaime, it's entirely up to you whether you say "Yes" or "No." You're under no obligation. And I can't think of any way I could tempt you.'

'"Dearlove" did you say? Who? Richard Dearlove?' I recalled that this was one of the unlikely and to me unfamiliar names I'd stumbled across while rifling through some old restricted files one day at the office. It had struck me as a name more suited to some idol of the masses than to a high-ranking official or civil servant, which is why I used it for the singer-celebrity whom here I call Dick Dearlove to protect his real identity, a vain endeavor. My immediate curiosity proved too much for me and so I put off giving my answer a little longer. And there was something else I was curious about, a curiosity that demanded satisfaction, less immediately perhaps but more insistently.

'Yes,' she said. 'Sir Richard Dearlove. For several years, until not long ago in fact, he was our invisible leader, didn't you know? The head of MI6, "C" or "Mr. C."' She pronounced this initial English-fashion, 'Mr. Si,' we Spaniards would say. 'No one has published a recent photograph of him, it's forbidden, no one has seen him or knows what he looks like; not even now, when he's no longer in that post. And so none of us could identify him; no one would recognize him if he walked by in the street. That's a great advantage, don't you think? I wish I had the same advantage.'

'And have we never done a report on him? I mean a video interview, although I can't imagine he would have been taken up to Tupra's office so that we could spy on him from our hiding-place in the train carriage, from our cabin.' I realized at once that I had said 'we' and 'our' as if I already considered myself part of the group and had since even before my arrival. I was developing a strange and entirely involuntary sense of belonging. But I preferred not to think about that just then.

'I don't know,' she said half-heartedly. 'Ask Bertie. As I said, he has videos of everyone.' I had the feeling she was growing impatient with my delay, or with my waffling around, I still hadn't heard that order, or was it a kind of motto, 'Don't linger or delay,' not that I've ever taken any notice of it, either before or since. She must simply have wanted to know where she stood and then she could leave. Certainly if my final answer was 'No,' she would leave there and then and not waste any more of the night on me, but set off with her gentle dog, doubtless feeling rather ridiculous and perhaps filled as well with a sense of instant rancor or even lasting grievance. If the answer was 'Yes,' on the other hand, perhaps she would stay longer, to celebrate her relief or to issue new instructions, now that what she had come for was in the bag. She must have found it irritating that I should bother her now with questions about Sir Richard Dearlove, the real Dearlove this time, or about any other person or subject. That I should, at this point, open a parenthesis or invent tangents. She would just have to put up with it, I was still the one guiding the conversation and determining its course, and she could not afford to upset me—yet. That, when you think about it, is the only calculation anyone asking a favor must make really, once they've taken the first step and made their request (before that, it's different, they have to be more cautious, estimating whether it's worthwhile or even advisable for them to reveal their deficiencies and inabilities): they have to be pleasant and patient and even unctuous, to keep to the tempo being set for them, to consider their steps and their words and the degree to which they can insist, until they get what they've asked for. Unless, that is, they're someone so important that doing them a favor is in itself an honor for the person granting it, a privilege. This was not the case here, and so she added in another tone of voice: 'No, I don't think so, but anything's possible. I suppose photos of him must exist, nowadays you can track down pictures of anyone; and if only very few have access to his photos, it wouldn't surprise me at all if Bertie was one of them.'

'Why did you say that Wheeler regretted not being infallible? What happened? What happened to him? What did you mean?' That was the deeper, more insistent curiosity demanding satisfaction.

Again I noticed her annoyance, her frayed nerves, her mutable state of exhaustion, which came and went. I was probably annoying her or driving her mad. But she once more suppressed her feelings or pulled herself together, she had still not lost heart.

'I don't know what happened to him, Jaime, it was a long time ago, during or after World War II, and I don't know him personally. People say that he made an interpretative error that cost him dearly. He failed to foresee something and that left him feeling dreadfully guilty, useless, destroyed, I don't know exactly. I've heard it mentioned in passing as an example of great misfortune, but I've never asked or no one's ever given me an answer, most of our work is still secret even after sixty or more years, it may remain so forever, at least officially. Any leaks usually come from outside and are often pure speculation, not to be trusted. Or they come from people with an axe to grind, who either resigned or were sacked, and who distort the facts. It's difficult to know anything very precise about our past, especially about us insiders, who tend to be the most discreet and the least curious, it's as if we had no history. We're the most keenly aware of what should not be told, because we live with that all the time. So, I'm sorry, but I can't help. You'll have to ask Wheeler himself. You know him well, he was your champion, your sponsor, the one who introduced you to the group.'

She, I noticed, used 'we' and 'our' without even thinking, naturally and frequently—she had been part of the group for much longer than me and felt herself to be an heir to the original group, the one that had been created by Menzies or Ve-Ve Vivian or Cowgill or Hollis or even Philby or Churchill himself to fight the Nazis, Wheeler thought Churchill had been the one who sparked the idea, being the brightest and boldest of the lot, and the least afraid of ridicule.

'Who have you heard mention it? Tupra? Can you remember if what happened involved Wheeler's wife? Her name was Valerie. Does that ring any bells?'

'I don't know who I heard it from, Jaime. It could have been Bertie, it probably was, or Rendel, or Mulryan, or perhaps some other person in some other place, I don't recall now. But that's all I know, nothing more—that something bad happened, that he failed in some way, or at least he thought so, and I believe he came close to withdrawing from the group altogether, to giving it up. It was all a very long time ago.'

I didn't know if she was telling me the truth or if she didn't feel authorized to tell me the story or if she simply wanted to get away from my endless questions and not—at this late hour of the night—get into some obscure, possibly long tale about someone else, which she would, at best, know only at second hand and which bore no relation to her current problems, the problems that had brought her to my house after much thought and much trudging through the rain: her father and that man Vanni Incompara and the banker Vickers and that leap-frogging debt of two hundred thousand pounds, I'm amazed at some people's ability to accumulate sums of money they don't have, and in a way I envy them—it's quite a talent, if not a gift; it requires a cheerful mindset—although any envy I might feel is purely theoretical or fictional, literary and cinematographic, Pérez Nuix's vicarious position at that point was not in the least enviable. For the first time, I felt sorry for her (pity always intervenes), perhaps because tiredness made her seem more childlike, or perhaps it was the suppressed anxiety that surfaced now and then in her bright darting eyes and at the corners of her mouth, which kept trying to form brief, fearful smiles, to please me. I decided that it was time to put her out of her misery: she had expended a lot of effort, she had followed me for a long time through that half-deserted city, getting drenched in the process, she had pondered what to do, she had put her case and she had expended on me, first, her indecision and her time and then her resolve and still more time.

'All right, Patricia,' I said, bringing to an end my session of interrogations and postponements. 'I'll try, although I still think Tupra will see whatever there is to see, and more than me. But I'll do what I can, I'll try my best.'

This was the lowest level of commitment I could give. I might fail and make a mistake and not do as well as I had hoped, she herself had said as much and so she wouldn't be able to reproach me with failure. Nor be disappointed, for I had given her due warning. This left me much freer than if my answer had been 'I want this in return,' mainly because now I ran no risk of beginning to desire or to hope for what I had demanded from her, and thus to fear my own defeat. More than that, if you're not afraid, your chances of success will probably increase, and there'll still be time later on to raise your hand and demand a prize and say: 'I want this as a reward.' Naturally, this could be denied to us outright, with no explanation or excuse: there's no moral obligation then, no link, no agreement, nothing explicit, and there may very soon be no trace left of the immense favor we granted, just like the drop of blood or its rim that one looks for after it has disappeared, having been scrubbed and rubbed away, or the infinite crimes and noble acts not known about since their commission or which the slow centuries amuse themselves by very slowly diluting until they're completely erased and then by pretending that they've never been. As if everything always fell like snow on our shoulders, slippery and docile, even things that make a great din and spread fires. (And from our shoulders it vanishes into the air or else melts or falls to the ground. And the snow always stops, eventually.)

Almost no trace remains of what happened next or only the faintest of vestiges in my more languid memory and perhaps in hers too, but we will never find out—I mean she and I, face to face, through an exchange of words. It happened as if in the very moment it was occurring we both wanted to pretend that it wasn't happening, or preferred not to notice, not to register it, to pretend it didn't matter, or to keep it so hushed up that later on we could deny it to each other, or to others if one of us let the cat out of the bag or started boasting about it, even if each of us only did so to ourselves, as if we both knew that something of which there is no record or no explicit recognition and which is never mentioned simply doesn't exist; something which, in a way, is committed secretly or behind the backs of its perpetrators and without their full consent or with only a drowsing awareness: something we do while telling ourselves we're not doing it, something that occurs even as we're persuading ourselves that it isn't happening, something not as strange as it sounds or seems, indeed, it happens all the time and causes us almost no alarm or doubts about our own judgement. We convince ourselves that we never had that unworthy or evil thought, that we never desired that woman or that death—the death of an enemy, husband or friend—that we never felt even momentary scorn or hostility towards the person we most respected or to whom we owed the greatest debt of gratitude, nor envied our irksome children who will go on living when we're no longer here and who will appropriate everything and quickly take our place; that we never intrigued or betrayed or plotted, never sought the ruin of anyone when in fact we diligently sought that of several people, that we were never tempted to do anything we might feel ashamed of; that we never acted in bad faith when we recounted some malicious gossip to someone so that he could defend himself—or so we argued, thus becoming instantly virtuous and charitable—and so that he would stop being so naïve and realize just who he was dealing with; and—even more extraordinary, because it affects actual events and not just the easily-deceived mind—that we didn't flee when in fact we ran away for all we were worth and left all regrets behind us, that we didn't push or shove a child out of the way to make room for ourselves in the lifeboat when the ship was sinking, that we didn't shield ourselves behind someone else when things were at their worst, so that the blows or the knife-thrusts or the bullets hit the person next to us who was, perhaps, expecting our protection: who knows, perhaps the person we loved most in the world, to whom we declared a thousand times that we would unhesitatingly give up our life for him or her, and it turns out that we did hesitate and didn't and haven't given up our life, nor would we if a second opportunity were to arise; that we didn't lay the blame for something we did on someone else nor make a false accusation in order to save ourselves, that we never acted out of the most terrible egotism and fear. We really believe that we weren't born when and where we came into the world, that we're younger than we are and from some nobler, less obscure place, that our parents aren't our parents and bear a much less vulgar surname; that we earned by our own merit what we stole or was given to us, that we fairly inherited some scepter or throne or mere stick or chair without using guile and without usurping them, that we came up with witticisms and ideas written or spoken by other wiser and more thoughtful men, whose dread names we never mention and whom we loathe for having 'got in' before us, although deep down we know, in some small surviving corner of our consciousness, that there was no question of their 'getting in before us' and that if they hadn't 'preceded' us, those ideas so personal to them would be even less our ideas, indeed could never be ours; we believe ourselves to be the person we most admire, and to make this come true, we set out to destroy him, believing we can supplant and obliterate him with our achievements which we owe entirely to him and drive him from the world's fickle memory, reassuring ourselves with the thought that he was only a pioneer whom we have exceeded and absorbed, and thus made highly dispensable; we persuade ourselves that the past does not weigh on us because we have never traversed it ('It wasn't me, it didn't happen to me, I never lived through that, I didn't see anything, I know nothing about it, it's the fruit of someone else's imaginings, someone else's memory that has somehow or other been transplanted into mine or else infected it') and that we never said what we said or stole what we stole, that we never cheered the dictator or betrayed our best friend who was so unbearably much better than us from the first day to the last ('He brought it on himself, I had nothing to do with it, I kept my mouth shut, he was a hothead, he made his own fate, he stood out when he shouldn't have and didn't change sides in time, didn't even want to'); and we don't even call ourselves by our real name, but only by a false one or by whichever of the ever-changing names that keep coming along and being added, be it Rylands or Wheeler, or Ure or Reresby or Tupra or Dundas, or Jacques the Fatalist or Jacobo or Jaime.

People believe what they want to believe, and that's why it's only logical—and so easy—that everything should have its time to be believed. We'll believe anything: even something that's manifestly untrue and contradicts what we can see with our own eyes, yes, even that has its time to be believed, each separate event in its own time and, in the fullness of time, everything. Everyone is prepared to look away and turn a deaf ear, to deny what's there before them and not to hear the shouting, and to maintain that there are no screams only a vast peaceful silence; to modify events and what has happened as much as they need to— the one-legged man still able to feel his leg and the one-armed man his arm and the decapitated man staggering three steps forward as if he hadn't yet lost both will and consciousness—but above all their own thoughts, feelings, memories and their anticipated future, which is sometimes mistaken for prescience. 'It wasn't like that. This isn't going to happen or won't have happened. This isn't happening' is the constant litany that distorts the past, the future and the present, and thus nothing is ever fixed or intact, neither safe nor certain. Everything that exists also doesn't exist or carries within itself its own past and future nonexistence, it doesn't last or endure, and even the gravest of events run that same risk and will end up visiting and traveling through one-eyed oblivion, which is no steadier or more stable or more capable of giving shelter. That's why all things seem to say 'I'm still here, therefore I must have been here before' while they are still alive and well and growing and have not yet ceased. Perhaps that's their way of clinging grimly to the present, a resistance to disappearing put up by the inanimate, by objects too, not only by people, who hang on and grow desperate and almost never give in ('But it's not time yet, not yet,' they mutter in their panic, with their dwindling strength), perhaps it's an attempt to leave their mark on everything, to make it harder for them to be denied or erased or forgotten, their way of saying 'I have been' and to stop other people saying 'No, this was never here, no one saw it or remembers it or ever touched it, it simply never was, it neither strode the world nor trod the earth, it didn't exist and never happened.'

It was nothing very grave, almost insignificant given the times we live in, and pleasurable too, the thing that happened without happening between young Pérez Nuix and me late that night, perhaps at the hour the Romans called the *conticinio* and which doesn't really exist in our cities now, for there is no time when everything is still and silent. She gave a sigh of satisfaction or relief and thanked me for my promise that was not a promise, for my declaration that I would do my best, which is hardly a major commitment. She seemed suddenly very tired, but this lasted only a moment, she immediately sprang to her feet, went over to the window and looked more closely at the tireless rain. She stretched discreetly—just her hands and wrists, not her arms; and her thighs, but without standing on tiptoe or rocking back on her heels—and then she asked me if she could stay. She couldn't face going home at that hour, she said, and I needn't worry, she'd get up very early to take the dog out, she'd leave in time to go back to her place and shower and change ('And put on a new pair of stockings,' I thought at once), and we wouldn't have to go together to the building with no name, like some strange married couple who, when they set off to work, don't go their separate ways. No one there would guess that we had met outside of work to conspire nor that we had said goodbye only a short time before. I agreed, how could I refuse such a minor request after granting the major one (well, at least its attempt), even though they were quite different in nature; it was a filthy night to be heading off out into the street again and who knew how long it would take for a taxi to come, and I'd have to phone for one first, if, that is, anyone answered the phone. Besides, I would prefer, for reasons of dramatic delicacy, that she didn't just leave as soon as she'd got what she wanted (or at least a declaration of intent), which would have made her visit exclusively utilitarian. It was, of course, utilitarian, as we both knew, but it would be best not to draw attention to that, nor was it appropriate given how much remained to be done in the next days, especially by me, for I would have to interpret and perhaps meet Incompara. I offered to sleep on the sofa and let her have the bed; she, however, wouldn't allow this; she, after all, was the intruder, the unexpected guest, she couldn't possibly deprive me of my mattress and my sheets.

'No, I'll take the sofa,' she said. But when she looked at it properly and saw how uncomfortable it was, and possibly still wet from her and the rain she'd brought in, she made the only suggestion someone of her age and self-assurance could make: 'I don't see what's wrong with us sharing the bed, as long as you don't mind, that is. I don't. Is it fairly wide?'

Of course I didn't mind, I had been young during an age when you were happy to sleep in any bed and alongside new acquaintances wherever you happened to find yourself after a night of wild excess or induced ecstasy or supposed spirituality or partying—the seventies, so effortfully spontaneous and so unhygienic, not to say downright grubby at times, and part of the eighties, which continued in the same vein. And of course I did mind, I no longer was that young man nor was I accustomed to sleeping anywhere but in my own bed, and I had spent too many years getting used to sleeping only beside Luisa, not even by the side of that stupid short-lived lover who ruined much of what I had, or what I treasured, even though Luisa never knew for certain about her existence; and later, in London, only beside a few sporadic women—three, to be exact—with whom the unhygienic or, if you like, grubby part had happened earlier and with whom, therefore, there was no danger that I'd want to grope them for the first time in dreams or while half-asleep, nor that I'd try to brush up against them, holding my breath and pretending to have done so purely by chance, nor that I'd want to observe them in the dark with my five senses alert and my eyes wide open, and with pointless intensity.

So it was that I found myself in bed with young Pérez Nuix, so aware of her warmth and her presence that I couldn't really get to sleep, and what made it even more difficult was the question that kept going round and round in my head as to whether the same thing was happening to her, if she was waiting or fearing that I would move closer, a slow, stealthy approach, so gradual at first that she would doubt it was happening, just like those men who used to feel women up on buses or trams or on the underground, using as their excuse the crush of people and the swaying motion, and who would rub and even press themselves against the uncomplaining bosom of the chosen woman, but never using their hands—so 'feeling up' is perhaps not quite the right phrase—and always with the excuse that any contact was entirely involuntary and attributable to the overwhelming pressure of the crowd and the bends in the road and the jolting. I speak of this in the past, because it's been ages since I saw this embarrassing spectacle on any form of public transportation and I don't know if it still happens in this day and age, which is more respectful at least in that one area; I often saw it during my childhood and adolescence, and I can't rule out having timidly done the same myself when I was thirteen or fourteen, when, in the minds of we fledgling men, everything is imaginary or frustrated sex. And I suppose it's because I associate such scenes with the remote past that I mention trams, which have been ghosts for decades now, as are those nice Madrid doubledeckers that they withdrew only a short while ago, and which were identical to the London ones, except that they were blue not red, and had the same doorless entrance, just an open platform at the rear with a vertical bar to grab hold of and haul yourself aboard—on the right rather than the left, in keeping with the side of the road we drive on in my country. Genitalia, women's that is, are also like entrances with no doors, I mean that if they're unobstructed by clothes there's no need to open them in order to enter. I let her get into bed first, alone, I waited in the living room for a while so that she could get ready and get undressed as she wished, and so when I eventually went into the bedroom, after those few minutes, young Pérez Nuix was already in bed and I had no way of knowing which clothes or how many she had removed before lying down. I had lent her a clean T-shirt, short-sleeved, because that's what I wear when it looks like it might be cold, I don't own any proper pajamas. 'That'll do fine, thank you,' she had said, which meant that this was probably all she was wearing and that her legs were bare, although I was almost sure she would have kept her panties on out of modesty, or out of consideration, or out of cleanliness, so as not to stain someone else's sheets, just as I kept on my boxer shorts and also donned a T-shirt, less because it was cold that night than to avoid any chance contact with her, skin on skin, flesh on flesh, such contact would happen only with our legs, my hairy ones against her smooth ones, for she was one hundred per cent Spanish as regards waxing her legs. However, before turning out the light—the bedside lamp—which she had left on so that I wouldn't have to enter the room in the dark, I pretended I was making sure my clothes weren't mixed up with hers, for we had both placed them on the same armchair, and then I could see and count the items of clothing she had taken off, and I counted not only her bra, as I had imagined, but also her other underwear, as I hadn't imagined at all, for there, neatly folded, were her white panties, they were tiny, which is to say normal, and I thought at once: 'I'm taller than she is, so the T-shirt will probably be long enough for her to feel covered.' This thought, though, was of no use to me, and from the moment the room was in darkness and I had slipped in between the sheets, I realized that I would spend the whole night unable to forget that strange and unexpected fact and that it would be almost impossible for me to go to sleep, as I lay agonizing over it and looking for some meaning: what did she mean by taking off her panties and leaving her genitalia—how can I put it—exposed, so close to me and to mine, we were separated by only a few inches and two bits of flimsy cloth or not even that, by the cloth of my boxer shorts with their ready-made opening and that of her borrowed T-shirt, if, of course, it hadn't ridden up when she was getting into bed and she hadn't bothered to pull it down, for then it was possible that her bottom—she had lain down on the other side of the bed and so had her back to me—was bare and very close to my irremediably aroused member, it was hopeless, I wouldn't get a wink of sleep in that state of physical alertness and repetitive mental activity, thinking and thinking about the singular fact, about my member, about her buttocks and below, about the nearness of everything and the absence of doors and of any barrier, even a barrier of cloth, wondering whether to approach surreptitiously and alight tentatively, making it look as if it were unconscious, something done in dreams, something merely instinctive, involuntary, animal almost, all the time waiting tensely, wide awake, to see if she would escape at once, if she would shy away at the first contact or accept it and stay where she was and not flee, neither surrender nor let me fall into the air, into the void, into emptiness; I didn't dare expect any pressure or stimulus from her, all of this was going on in my mind, which, in such circumstances, immediately becomes obsessed, it's the kind of doubt or idea which, once started, won't dissolve or withdraw, still less if the blood has gathered and impedes all abatement and all breathing, all appeasement or distraction or truce, and the temptation then becomes fixed. After a while spent listening to her breathing—it didn't sound to me like that of someone sleeping—and holding in, almost stopping my own, it occurred to me that I should get up and go and sleep on the sofa, with a blanket, but the truth was I didn't want to leave the bed or lose the unlikely proximity thus far achieved, it was a kind of promise that was its own satisfaction and which allowed me to remain in that state of mortifying, hopeful ignorance, to fantasize about what might happen at any moment if we did touch and neither of us avoided it or started away, we were only a little way apart and it's all a question of time and space and of coinciding in those two dimensions, we had the time and, very nearly, the space as well, all that was needed was a slight slippage, a minimal shift, for things to be completely in our favor, it was so easy that it seemed impossible it would not occur, one first tentative caress perhaps and my member would slip inside her and then both would be in the same place, one inside the other almost without our realizing, we could even pretend not to know and to be asleep even though we were both fully awake, I knew I was and thought the same was true of her; I was pretty convinced but not certain, of course, and that was what held me back or one of the things.

This situation of sexual imminence was not new to me, that is, it was new with young Pérez Nuix, but not in my previous existence, it had happened more than once with Luisa, silently and peacefully at first, after the initial tentative caress and the minimal shift that had caused us to coincide in both space and time, that's what matters, that's what determines important events, which is why it's so vital sometimes not to linger or delay, although it can also be what saves us, we never know what would be for the best and what is the right thing to do; if bullet and head or knife and chest or sword-blade and neck do not coincide in the same place and moment, no one dies, and that's why De la Garza was still alive, because his neck and Reresby's Landsknecht sword, or his *Katsbalger*, had not coincided exactly, despite having been on the point of doing so several times. However, with Luisa, her acquiescence was almost certain, and from her I could expect both pressure and stimulus, after all, we got into the same bed each night, she earlier and I later, as if I were coming to visit her in her dreams and I were her ghost, and the rest formed part of the foreseeable and the probable, or at least the possible. And if one of us said 'No,' either her or even me, it was a chance rejection, reasoned and momentary ('I'm exhausted,' or 'I'm too preoccupied today, my mind's on other things' or even more trivial 'I have to get up really early tomorrow'), not essential either to the totality or to the act itself, as young Pérez Nuix's refusal might be, expressed in unequivocal and crushing terms:

'What the hell are you are up to? Who do you think you are?' or perhaps gentler and more diplomatic, 'I wouldn't continue down that road if I were you, you won't get anywhere,' or more humiliating: 'Huh, I thought you'd have more self-control, more maturity, I didn't have you down as your average Spanish sex maniac, or an old-fashioned Spanish macho-man.'

None of these wounding words were spoken, indeed no words of any sort were uttered when I finally dared to make that tentative approach and lightly rested my member against her buttocks and was immediately aware that I was touching not T-shirt but firm, warm flesh, she was probably one of those women who are really sensitive to the cold, but who give off the heat they themselves don't feel, they're like a warm oven to the person who touches them, even though they themselves may be shivering, like someone with a fever. Nothing was said, there was no reaction, no movement either towards me or away, no discouragement and no encouragement, it really was as if she were deep asleep, I wondered if she really could be sleeping so profoundly that she wouldn't notice the touch of skin on skin with nothing in between, I thought not and that she must be pretending, but when it comes to other people, and possibly even when it comes to yourself, you can never be absolutely sure about anything, or almost anything. I got a little closer, pressed a little harder, but so very little that I wasn't even sure of having done so, sometimes you think you've moved or shifted, or pushed or caressed, but your approach is so timid and terrified that you can sometimes deceive yourself, and your advance or even your touch may prove imperceptible to the other person. And that was where I was, caught between a yes and a no, between irresistible desire and fearful or perhaps civilized restraint, applying such minute pressure that it might not have been pressure at all, when a thought suddenly, ridiculously, occurred to me: 'A condom,' I thought. 'I can't do anything without a condom on, and for that I need a minimum of consent, permission, agreement. If I get up now and fetch one and then come back to bed with it, I'll have lost my position, lost this closeness, I'd have to start all over again, she might move away or perhaps prove less accessible. And with a condom on I would no longer have an alibi, I would no longer be able to say to her, if she told me off or pulled me up short: "Oh, sorry, I didn't mean to, I was fast asleep and didn't realize I was touching you. It wasn't intentional, I'm sorry, I'll keep to my side of the bed," because the ridiculous sheath would be irrefutable proof that it *was* intentional and premeditated as well.'

This thought immediately made me draw back a little, enough to lose contact, and that reaffirmed me in my uncertain belief that there had been contact and that the ghostly pressure had been neither avoided nor rejected; and after a few seconds, I abandoned my position ('Goddamn condoms,' I thought, 'in my youth, we despised them, it never even occurred to me to buy them, now, though, we always have to use them') and no longer lay behind her, in that privileged place, but on my back, wondering what to do or how to do it or whether I should give up despite my growing hopes and try to go to sleep and do nothing. I put my arm under the pillow the better to rest my head, an involuntary gesture of deliberation, and in doing so I uncovered my chest, almost as far as my waist, and uncovered her shoulders. And that was enough—or a pretext—for young Pérez Nuix to wake up or pretend she did. And for the first and only time in the whole of that night we spent together I was not invisible to her, despite our being in darkness: she turned over and placed the open palms of her hands on my cheeks as if to show her fondness for me, they were very soft palms; she looked into my eyes for a few seconds (one, two, three, four; and five; or six, seven, eight; and nine; or ten, eleven, twelve; and thirteen) and smiled at me or laughed as she delicately cupped or held my face, as Luisa sometimes used to do when her bed was still mine and we weren't yet sleepy or not sleepy enough to say goodnight and turn our backs on each other until the next day, or when I came to her late like a ghost she'd arranged to meet and for whom she was waiting, and welcomed me. Only then was I not invisible to Pérez Nuix, when there was no light. My eyes were accustomed to seeing in the half-dark of my room without blinds or shutters, like almost all bedrooms on that large island whose inhabitants sleep with one eye open; but not her eyes, which were unfamiliar with the space. Nevertheless, she looked at me and smiled and laughed, it was very brief. Then she turned over again and offered me her back, adopting the same position as before, as if that gazing at each other in the dark hadn't taken place and she were ready to continue sleeping. But it had taken place, and that for me was the necessary sign of consent, permission, agreement I needed, it made me get out of bed for a moment and rapidly search out a condom, put it on and return with much more confidence and aplomb to my previous position, and to the rubbing and touching and gentle pushing, not against her buttocks now but slightly lower down, towards the dampness and the passage, the passageway, *more ferarum*, in the manner of the beasts, that's the Latin tag for it. She didn't move, at least not as I began to slide in, easily now ('I'm screwing her,' I thought as I entered her, I couldn't help it), she just let me, she didn't participate if one can say that or if that's possible, at any rate, we didn't speak, there was no indication on either side that what was happening was happening, how can I put it, we pretended to pretend to be asleep, to be unaware, to recognize nothing of what was going on as if it were taking place in our absence or without our knowledge, although occasionally she did utter a few sounds and perhaps I did too when I came, I conscientiously repressed them though, telling myself I had merely breathed more deeply, at most sighed, but who knows, one hears oneself so little, and anyway sounds and even groans are permissible during sleep, some people even deliver whole speeches while asleep, but they're never accused of being awake. Almost nothing was heard or seen, I could see only the back of her neck in the darkness and from far too close, and that's doubtless why I kept picturing things, the same things I had just spent a long time contemplating in the living room ('It'll only take a moment,' she had announced from the street, I wondered if she knew just how wrong she would be), the zippers on her boots going up and down, the run in her stockings advancing in all directions along her thigh, but especially upwards, as if pointing the way, and another older vision, that of her naked breast, a tight skirt, and in her hand a towel and a raised arm that added an additional nakedness to the image by unembarrassedly revealing her clean, smooth, newly washed and, needless to say, shaven armpit, early one morning in the building with no name, that time when she did not blush, making me think that young Pérez Nuix did not rule me out, or did not entirely exclude me, although she didn't necessarily feel attracted to me either, having been seen by me and having decided not to cover herself up, or perhaps no decision was involved. It was all very silent and timid, ghostly really, and it remained so, except that, after a while, I noticed that she was pushing too, it wasn't just me now and neither of us was pretending not to push or else pushing only gently, it was as if we were locked in a tight embrace, but without making use of our arms, she was pressed against me and I against her, but with just one part of our body, the same part, as if we were only those parts or as if we consisted solely of that, it was as if we had been forbidden to entwine in any other way, with our arms or our legs or round the waist or by way of kisses. I don't think we even held hands.

Yes, we almost certainly shared that in common, Tupra and I, or Ure or Reresby or Dundas, or who knows how many other names he would have used in other countries and which he perhaps now never used in this more sedentary stage of his life, safe and settled in London, where it was possible that he felt slightly bored, although he did go off now and then on short trips, or perhaps not, maybe he had already grown weary of all that gadding about, and of spreading outbreaks of cholera and malaria and plague and of igniting fires in far-off countries. His house was not that of a man who felt either temporary or in a hurry, that of someone who goes out and comes in, takes a quick look around, then leaves and returns and smokes a cigarette and never lingers anywhere. Perhaps the thing we shared in common was, nonetheless, very limited: I had slept with Pérez Nuix in a manner that was utterly tacit and clandestine, not only as regards other people, but as regards ourselves as well. On the other hand (and this was only a suspicion, but a strong one), he would have known her intimately over perhaps a long or at least a not insignificant period of time, perhaps when she was still a novelty and the person who most stimulated and amused him and was an important element in creating for him that sense of a small, or large, daily celebration. They would, at any rate, have seen each other's faces when they slept together, they would have talked afterwards, they would have told each other something of their lives and their opinions (although Tupra would have done so only in his usual fragmentary way, that is, very little), and when they were together in a room, they would have known for certain that what was happening was really happening, unlike me, for I felt certain of nothing—even less certain, given that what happened immediately became the past—when I withdrew from that passage, the end of which one never reaches, and emerged from it as carefully and tentatively as I had approached and entered; when I moved away and turned over onto my side and for the first time presented my back to that young woman just as she had presented hers to me for almost the whole time—except when she looked at me and cupped my face in her hands—and I slipped one arm under the pillow, not this time in order to think or to curse, but in order to summon sleep.

Perhaps the only thing Tupra and I would have in common was a pale, vague relationship of which most men know nothing and which languages fail to include, although they recognize the sentiment and, on occasion, the feelings of jealousy or even of camaraderie; apart, that is, from the Anglo-Saxon language as I read once in a book, not by an Englishman, but by a compatriot of mine, and not in an essay or a book on linguistics, but in a fiction, a novel, whose narrator recalled the existence of a word in that ancient language which described the relationship or kinship acquired by two or more men who had lain or slept with the same woman, even if this had happened at different times and with the different faces worn by that woman in her lifetime, her face of yesterday or today or tomorrow. That curious notion remained fixed in my mind, although the narrator wasn't sure if it was a verb, whose nonexistent modern equivalent would be 'co-fornicate' (or 'co-fuck' in coarse, contemporary parlance), or a noun, which would denote the 'co-fornicators' (or 'co-fuckers') or the action itself (let's call it 'co-fornication'). One of the possible forms of the words, I don't know which, was *ge-brȳd-guma*, I had remembered it without trying to and without effort, and sometimes it was there on the tip of my tongue, or the tip of my thoughts: 'Good God, that's what I am, I've become this man's *ge-brȳd-guma*, how degrading, how horrible, how cheap, how dreadful,' whenever I saw or heard that an old lover or girlfriend of mine was pairing up or spending too much time with some despicable, odious man, with an imbecile or an *untermensch*; it happens all too often or so it seems, and besides we're constantly exposed to it and can do nothing about it. (I had decided that the word was pronounced 'gebrithgoomer,' although, naturally, I had no idea.)

When I first met Tupra, I had thought or feared that I might acquire that relationship with him through Luisa, in some bizarre, unreal way—or, rather, I had been glad that she was in Madrid and that they would never meet and that this would never happen—when I saw that almost no woman could resist him and that I wouldn't stand a chance against him if I ever had to compete with him in that field, regardless of whether I got there first, or second, or at the same time. And now it seemed that I had probably acquired such a relationship through another unexpected and more frivolous activity, one that made me the person who came *afterwards* not the person who was or had been there *before*: the former is in a slightly more advantageous position, because he can hear and find out things from the latter, but he is also the one most at risk of contagion if there's any disease involved, and that—a disease if there is one—is the only tangible manifestation of that strange, weak link to which no one gives a thought any more, even though it exists without being named and hovers unnoticed above the relations between men and between women, and between men and women. No one speaks that medieval language any more and hardly anyone knows it. And when you think about it, there is, in some cases, something else that is transmitted by the person in the middle, from the one who was with her *before* to the one who was with her *afterwards*, but which is neither tangible nor visible: influence. Throughout my conversation that night with young Pérez Nuix, I had now and then had the feeling that Tupra was speaking through her, but this could also have been because they had worked and been in continual contact for several years, not necessarily because they were ex-lovers. The truth is that we never know from whom we originally get the ideas and beliefs that shape us, those that make a deep impression on us and which we adopt as a guide, those we retain without intending to and make our own.

From a great-grandparent, a grandparent, a parent, not necessarily ours? From a distant teacher we never knew and who taught the one we did know? From a mother, from a nursemaid who looked after her as a child? From the ex-husband of our beloved, from a *ġe-brȳd-guma* we never met? From a few books we never read and from an age through which we never lived? Yes, it's incredible how much people say, how much they discuss and recount and write down, this is a wearisome world of ceaseless transmission, and thus we are born with the work already far advanced but condemned to the knowledge that nothing is ever entirely finished, and thus we carry—like a faint booming in our heads—the exhausting accumulated voices of the countless centuries, believing naïvely that some of those thoughts and stories are new, never before heard or read, but how could that be, when ever since they acquired the gift of speech people have never stopped endlessly telling stories and, sooner or later, everything is told, the interesting and the trivial, the private and the public, the intimate and the superfluous, what should remain hidden and what will one day inevitably be broadcast, sorrows and joys and resentments, certainties and conjectures, the imagined and the factual, persuasions and suspicions, grievances and flattery and plans for revenge, great feats and humiliations, what fills us with pride and what shames us utterly, what appeared to be a secret and what begged to remain so, the normal and the unconfessable and the horrific and the obvious, the substantial—falling in love—and the insignificant—falling in love. Without even giving it a second thought, we go and we tell.

'Believe me, I wouldn't have either, if I'd had the choice,' I said to Tupra when we'd finished our shared, disinterested laughter, with me laughing despite myself, about the 'bulwarks' onto which he had thrown me. 'But you made me do it, just as you've made me do everything else tonight, including still being here at this unearthly hour,' I said in my sometimes rather bookish English, literally *'a una hora no terrenal'* in Spanish. 'I don't know if you realize, but you've done nothing all day but give me orders, most of them after hours. It's time I left. I need to sleep, I'm tired.' And so I shifted again from brief treacherous laughter to a more enduring seriousness, if not annoyance. And I made a movement as if to suggest that I was thinking about getting up, but no more than that, because he wouldn't let me leave just yet: he wanted to talk to me about Constantinople and Tangiers in centuries past, there are always more exhausting voices and stories that we have not yet heard. However, he didn't start again and probably wasn't going to, there are some things that are mentioned but never returned to, that are sown and then abandoned, like verbal decoys; and he was supposed to be showing me his private tapes, or perhaps DVDs. That didn't happen either. 'If you don't tell me about Tangiers and Constantinople right now, Bertram, I'm leaving. I've had enough. I'm dog tired and I'm in no mood to go on chatting.'

Tupra emitted a kind of dull roar, halfway between a brief guffaw and a stifled snort of scorn. He stood up and said:

'Don't be impatient, Jack, this is no time to be in a hurry. I'm going to show you the videos I told you about, you'll learn a lot from them and it will be useful for you to see them. Not immediately useful, they're not at all pleasant and they may well drive away any current desire for sleep that you feel, at least for the next few hours, but I've already given you permission not to come to work tomorrow, or rather today, so let's waste no more time.' He glanced rapidly at his watch; so did I: it was an unearthly hour for London, but not for Madrid. The children would be asleep, but I had no idea what Luisa would be up to, she might still be awake, with someone else or with no one. 'But it'll be useful to you later on to have seen them. In a matter of days really, and they'll always come in handy. It may be that you are already someone who gives no importance to the unimportant, because that's the first thing everyone should be taught and yet everyone behaves as if exactly the opposite were true: people are brought up nowadays to think that any idiot can make a great drama out of any kind of nonsense. People are brought up to suffer for no reason, and you get nowhere suffering over everything or tormenting yourself. It paralyzes, overwhelms, stops growth and movement. As you see, though, people nowadays beat their breast over harming a plant, and if it's an animal, what a crime, what a scandal! They live in an unreal, delicate, soft, twee world.'—'*Cursi*,' I thought, 'English doesn't have that useful, wide-ranging word'—'Their minds are permanently wrapped in cotton wool.' And he briefly made that strange roaring noise again; it sounded this time like a short sarcastic cough. 'In *our* countries, that is. And when something happens here that's perfectly normal in other places, common currency, we find ourselves vulnerable, at a loss what to do, helpless, easy prey, and it takes us a while to react, and we do so disproportionately and blindly, missing the target. And with too much retrospective fear as well, as happened with the attacks here and in your own city of Madrid, not to mention the attacks on New York and Washington.'

'Nothing much has changed in Madrid,' I said. 'It's almost as if it had never happened.'

But he wasn't listening, he had his own agenda. His deep voice had grown mournful. It always did sound slightly mournful, like the sound made by a bow moving over the strings of a cello. Sometimes, though, that tonality was more marked and it produced in the person hearing it a gentle, almost pleasant feeling that eased all affliction; at least in me it did.

'I'm not saying there's nothing to be afraid of, you understand. It's just that we should have been frightened before and to have taken fear as much for granted as the air we breathe, and to have instilled fear too. Instilling and feeling fear, all the time, that's the unchanging way of the world, which we've forgotten. It's normal in other countries that are more alert to these things. But no one here realizes it and we fall asleep without keeping one eye open, we get caught unawares and then we can't believe it's happened. Retrospective fear is useless, even more so than anticipatory fear. That's not much good either, but at least it puts one, if not on one's guard, at least in a state of expectancy. It's always best to be in a position to instil fear in others. Anyway, let me show you these scenes, they're not long. Some I'll fast-forward for you.'

He poured me some port without first consulting me, thinking perhaps that I would need it in order to face these unpleasant but instructive scenes, then he picked up his own glass and, at his urging, I picked up mine; he beckoned to me with a motion of his head and one finger and led me to a smaller room which he unlocked with a key from his key-ring. Given that Tupra clearly didn't want anyone to enter that room without his permission or alone, I wondered who else lived in the house, or perhaps it was just the domestic staff who were barred. He turned on a couple of lights. It was a kind of study which immediately reminded me of his office in the building with no name, it was full of books as costly as those in the living room or possibly more so—perhaps they were his bibliophile's jewels; on the other hand, there were no paintings, only the framed drawing of a soldier, just head and shoulders, with a slightly curled mustache, perhaps some idol of his from MI6 or whatever it used to be called; it appeared at first sight to date from the First World War or, at the latest, from the 1920s, I didn't think it was an ancestor, a Tupra, for he was wearing the uniform of a British officer, though what rank I couldn't say. There was a desk with a computer on it; a chair on casters behind the desk, which must be where Reresby worked when he was at home; and two ottomans. He maneuvered these with his foot so that they were in front of a low cabinet whose wooden doors he opened to reveal a television inside, an absurd piece of camouflage, like the minibars you get in certain posh hotels, ashamed of having them in their rooms. He indicated that I should sit down on one of the ottomans and I did so. He went over to the desk, walked round it and removed a DVD from a drawer, which, again, he opened with a key, he obviously kept a few DVDs in there, well, more than one and probably more than two. He turned on the television, the DVD player was underneath and he put the disk in. He sat down on the other ottoman, to my left, almost next to me and a little behind, both of us were very close to the now blue screen, but I was closest, he picked up the remote control, I had to look at him out of the corner of my eye and turn my neck if I wanted to see the expression on his face. We were each holding a glass, he did everything with one hand or else, as I said, with his foot.

'So what are we going to watch, what are you going to show

me?' I asked with a mixture of impatience and self-assurance. 'It's not a film, is it? It's hardly the right time for that.'

I still felt no fear, I was prevented from doing so by irritation and tiredness, it seemed unlikely to me that anything could wake me up. Besides, I'd seen quite enough unpleasant and painfully instructive things for one night, and not on a video but in palpable, breathable reality, right next to me, I could still feel in my body, albeit less keenly, the shock of that sword being brought down on the numbskull's neck, and in my head was the echo of the useless thoughts that had assailed me then: 'He's going to kill him, no, he can't, he won't, yes, he is, he's going to decapitate him right here, separate his head from his trunk, this man full of rage, and I can do nothing about it because the blade is going to come down and it's a two-edged sword, it's like thunderless lightning that strikes in silence, and he's going to cut right through him.' I didn't believe there could be anything worse, and whatever Tupra showed me would, moreover, belong to the past, it would be something that had already happened, that was over and had been filmed, and in which I would not be expected to intervene. There would be nothing to be done about it; with every viewing, the same thing would be repeated identically. But I must have felt it, the dread, the apprehension, the cringing, the shrinking back in fear, from the moment when Tupra's voice had suddenly grown more mournful than usual and awoken in me a suggestion of motiveless, meaningless anguish, the way mournful music does, for no reason—yes just a few notes on a cello or violin or viola da gamba, or on a piano—as if he knew all there was to know about those retrospective disasters which could, nevertheless, be reproduced and made present again an infinite number of times, because they had been recorded or registered, the kind of disaster of which I had no knowledge or even the tiniest suspicion.

'What you're going to see is secret. Never talk about it or mention it, not even to me after tonight, because tomorrow I will never have shown it to you. These are recordings we keep just in case we need them one day.'—'Just in case,' I thought, 'that, it seems, is our motto.'—'They contain shameful or embarrassing things, as well as crimes that have never been reported or pursued, committed by individuals of some consequence but against whom no steps have been taken or charges made because it wasn't or isn't worth it or because it's still not the moment or because little would be gained. It makes much more sense to hang on to them, to keep them, in case there's ever a use for them in the future, with some of them we could obtain a great deal in exchange. In exchange for them staying buried here, never seen by anyone, you understand, only us. With others we've already obtained a lot, made good use of them and, besides, their possible benefits are never exhausted, because we never destroy anything or hand it over, we just show them occasionally to the people who appear in them, to the interested parties, if they don't trust us or don't believe that such recordings exist and want to see them to make quite sure. Don't worry, they don't come here (very few people ever have), well, it's so easy now to make copies and you can even show them on your mobile phone or send them. So these videos are a real treasure: they can persuade, dissuade, bring in large sums of money, force some insalubrious candidate to stand down, they can seal lips, obtain concessions and agreements, foil maneuvers and conspiracies, put off or mitigate conflicts, provoke fires, save lives. You're not going to like the content, but don't scorn or condemn them. Bear in mind their value and the uses they can be put to. And the service they render, the good they sometimes do for our country.'—He had used a similar expression the first time we met at Wheeler's buffet supper in Oxford, when I had asked him what he did and he had been evasive in his reply: 'My real talent has always been for negotiating, in different fields and circumstances. Even serving my country, one should if one can, don't you think, even if the service one does is indirect and done mainly to benefit oneself.' He had repeated the word 'country' which can be translated as *'patria'* in my language, a word which, given our history and our past, has become a disagreeable and dangerous term that reveals a great deal, all of it negative, about those who use it; its imperfect English equivalent lacks that emotive, pompous quality. 'Our country,' he had said.

How odd. Tupra had again forgotten that his country and mine were not the same, that I wasn't an Englishman but a Spaniard, probably, like De la Garza, a useless Spaniard. That was the moment when I came closest to believing that I had gained his trust without his noticing, that is, without his having decided to give it to me: when, late that night, in his house that almost no one ever visited, before the as yet blank screen, when he was about to show me those confidential images, he lost sight of the fact that as long as I was working for him, I was serving him, for a salary, and not working for his country. Nor, of course, mine. As for him, it was impossible to guess what services, indirect or otherwise, he rendered to his country, or if he always acted mainly to benefit himself. Perhaps, in his mind, the two things were now indistinguishable. He added: 'Prepare yourself. We're going to start. And not a word to anyone, is that clear?'

And he pressed Play.

What I saw thereafter should not be told, and I should do so only in short bursts. Partly because some scenes were shown in fast-forward mode, as Tupra had promised, and so fortunately I just caught glimpses of them, but always enough and more than I would have wanted; partly because for a few seconds—one, two, three, four; and five—I turned away or closed my eyes, and on a couple of occasions I held my hand like a visor at eyebrow height, with my fingers ready, so that I could choose to see or not see what I was seeing. But I saw or half-saw enough of each film or episode, because Reresby urged me to keep looking ('Don't turn away, resist the desire not to look, I'm not showing you this so that you can cover your eyes, don't hide,' he ordered me when, in one way or another, I tried to avoid the screen, 'and tell me now if what you witnessed earlier was so very terrible, tell me now that I went too far, tell me now that it was of any importance at all'; and by 'earlier' he was referring to what had happened or to what he had made happen in the handicapped toilet, in my presence and in the face of my impotence, my passivity and fear, my cowardice pure and simple). And partly, last of all, because I dare not describe it or I'm not capable of doing so, not fully.

As I looked and half-looked and saw, a poison was entering

me, and when I use that word 'poison,' I'm not doing so lightly or purely metaphorically, but because something entered my consciousness that had not been there before and provoked in me an immediate feeling of creeping sickness, of something alien to my body and to my sight and to my mind, like an inoculation, and that last term is spot on etymologically, for it contains at its root the Latin 'oculus,' from which it comes, and it was through my eyes that this new and unexpected illness entered, through my eyes which were absorbing images and registering them and retaining them, and which could no longer erase them as one might erase a bloodstain on the floor, still less not have seen them. (Perhaps only when my eyes had recovered could I begin to doubt those images: when the time that levels and dissolves and mingles had passed.) And thus they entered, as if through a slow needle, things that were quite external to me and of which I was entirely ignorant, things I had never foreseen or conceived or even dreamed of, things so beyond my experience that it was of no use to me having read about similar cases in the press, for there they always seem remote and exaggerated, or in novels, or indeed in films, which we never quite believe because, deep down, we know it's all fake, however much we care about the characters or identify with them. Nevertheless, the first scenes Tupra showed me on the screen contained, relatively speaking, a deceptively comic element, which is why I could still make jokes and ask him about it (had he begun with what followed, I would probably have been struck dumb from the start):

'What's this? Porn?'

And this was tantamount to giving Reresby permission to enlighten me as much as he wanted—never very much, always concisely—about that initial recording and about others or most of them, although about two or three he kept a strange and total—or perhaps significant—silence, as if there were no need to say anything.

'That was neither the intention nor the result,' he replied very coldly, my comment had clearly not amused him. 'That woman is a very influential figure in the Conservative Party, one of the old school, and currently has high hopes of being promoted, as a reassuring counterweight for the more hard-line Tory voters; and since she usually gives fiery speeches about the decline in society's morals and habits, and about unbridled sex and all that, it's interesting to see what she gets up to in this video, and one day it might be useful to show it to her. Her husband, of course, is not present.'

There were no preliminaries, by which I mean that it had probably been cut to show only the basics, or the nitty-gritty, which I rather regretted because I would have liked to know where they had come from, or what they had proposed to her, or how they had reached that situation, the two guys who—the scene began, as I say, *in medias res*—were already enjoying a sex sandwich, the three of them writhing about on a rather faded green carpet, or perhaps it was the film quality, which was only fair, but clear enough for me to recognize the woman, that is, I remembered having seen her before on television, in Parliament or on the news. I even remembered her rather gruff voice, a voice like a hairdryer, she was one of those people who, even if they try, cannot or don't know how to speak softly or even to pause for a moment, which must be a torment for her nearest and dearest. Fortunately, there was no sound, if there had been, judging by the look of double ecstasy on her face at being impaled simultaneously by the two men, one from in front, one from behind—or intermittently, they were not very well synchronised or not always a very good fit, they came apart—her howls would have sounded to us like a gale or else a handsaw. As far as one could tell from their scant clothing, the two men might have been civil servants and neither was very young or very svelte, and one of them—with only his fly open, a sign of laziness rather than urgency—was wearing a pair of very bracing braces over his bare torso, which gave him an incongrous air, as if he were an impossible blend of office worker and butcher. As for the woman, she was about forty years old and, in turn, had not bothered to remove her skirt, which was transformed now into a crumpled belt, nor was she particularly attractive despite her bare and ample bosom, clearly unaugmented by surgery. They could have been in a hotel room or in an office, the narrow field of vision did little to clarify this, the camera being focused only on the fornicators, the two jerks in question were both fully paid-up ğe-brȳd-guma, indeed, they were being so there and then. It really did look like a low-budget or amateur porn movie made with understudies. Just who had filmed the scene and how was, needless to say, a mystery, but nowadays anyone would be able to do it, by using their mobile phone or even from a distance, without being present at all, and so no one is safe from being caught on camera in the most intimate or the most outrageous situations.

After about a minute or less, Tupra pressed the fast-forward button, for which I was grateful, there was no point in watching all that effort in order to reach an ending that would be of no surprise to anyone. I got as far as glimpsing a look on the Conservative lady's face at the conclusion of her double-decker experience, a look of pleased surprise, as if she were saying: 'How amazing. How could I have done such a thing? I'll have to try it again just to see if it really was as good as I think it was.' Perhaps it was her first act of daring duplicity. My boss returned the tape to its normal speed then, and we moved on at once to the second episode, with sound this time, which showed two famous actors and a third individual, unknown to me, spouting nonsense and falling about laughing while snorting cocaine in a living room, on a sofa, with the large, not to say enormous lines of cocaine set out on the coffee table, which they were gradually snuffling up like someone taking sips from a glass.

'I don't know who he is,' I said, pointing to the man on the right and making it clear to Tupra that I had recognized the two juvenile leads.

'He's a member of the royal family. A long way down the line of succession, very secondary. It would have been suited us perfectly if it had been someone more prominent, someone closer to the throne.' And he again pressed the fast-forward button, it was very dull footage, nothing but moronic laughter and that banquet of cocaine.

His remark momentarily gave me food for thought, I wondered why it would have suited them perfectly (I took 'us' to mean MI6, or the Secret Services as a whole, rather than our group) for anyone to take drugs, commit adultery, engage in corruption or break the law. They should have been glad that the Queen's closest relatives were not, like that trio, up to their eyeballs in cocaine.

'I don't understand,' I said, bewildered. 'Why would that have suited you?' And I made a point of not including myself.

Tupra froze the image in order to answer me.

'That's a very naïve question, Jack, you disappoint me sometimes. Anything like that suits us, with anyone of any importance, weight, decision-making ability, fame or influence. The more blots and the higher up the person, the better it suits us. Just as it suits everyone everywhere with those close to them. It's in your interests that your neighbor should be in your debt or that you should have caught him out in some way and be in a position to hurt him by reporting him or doing him the favor of keeping quiet about it. If people didn't infringe the law or try to get round the rules or if they never made mistakes or committed base acts, we would never get anything, it would be very hard for us to have any bargaining power and almost impossible to bend their wills or oblige them to. We'd have to resort to force and physical threats, and we tend not to use that much any more, we've been trying to give it up for some time now, because you never know if you'll emerge from that kind of thing unscathed or if they'll end up taking you to court and ruining you. Truly powerful people can do that, they can make your life very difficult and have you dismissed, they can pull strings and make you the scapegoat. We still use force on insignificant people like your friend Garza. There's no more effective method, I can assure you. With people who won't utter so much as a murmur of complaint. But with other people, it's always a risk. You can't influence them with money either, because they have so much. On the other hand, almost all are capable of weighing things up and making a judgment, of listening to reason, of seeing what's in their best interests. Everyone has something to hide, as you know; I've never known anyone who wasn't prepared to give in, either a little or a lot, in order to keep something quiet, so that it didn't get around or, at least, didn't reach the ears of one particular person. How could it possibly not suit us that people should be weak or base or greedy or cowardly, that they should fall into temptation and drop the occasional very large gaffe, or even be party to or commit misdemeanors? That's the basis of our work, the very substance. More than that, it's the bedrock of the State. The State needs treachery, venality, deceit, crime, illegal acts, conspiracy, dirty tricks (on the other hand, it needs very few acts of heroism, or only now and then, to provide a contrast). If those things didn't exist, or not enough, the State would have to invent them. It already does. Why do you think new offenses are constantly being created? What wasn't an offense becomes one, so that no one is ever entirely clean. Why do you think we intervene in and regulate everything, even where it's unnecessary or where it doesn't concern us? We need laws to be violated and broken. What would be the point of having laws if everyone obeyed them? We'd never get anywhere. We couldn't exist. The State needs infractions, even children know that, although they don't know that they know. They're the first to commit them. We're brought up to join in the game and to collaborate right from the start, and we keep playing the game until the very last, even when we're dead. The debt is never settled.'

I kept occasionally turning my head a little to look at him out of the corner of my eye, but Tupra, who was behind me in relation to my position on the ottoman, was mainly addressing my back. His voice sounded very close and very gentle, almost a whisper, he had no reason to speak more loudly, there was nothing but silence all around. That last 'us' ('where it doesn't concern us') had been even more comprehensive than the previous one, he felt himself to be part of the State, its representative, possibly its guardian, possibly a servant of the nation, despite his tendency to consider his own benefit before all else. I imagined that he, too, would be capable of treachery, even if only to keep the country's supplies topped up, to satisfy its needs.

'The State *needs* treachery?' I asked, somewhat puzzled (although only slightly, for I was beginning to see what he meant). 'Of course, Jack. Especially in time of siege or invasion or war. That is what we most commemorate, what most unites people, what nations most remember over the centuries. Where would we be without it?'

It occurred to me that when I betrayed him with my interpretation of Incompara, I had perhaps been inadvertently useful to him in his role as man of the State, but this in no way helped me to feel that my debt had been paid off. This was doubtless partly why I put up with him—I could always leave—why I showed him such consideration, such leniency, or so I believed, because of that enduring sense of unease and because of that deliberate mistake of mine, I was still not sure if he had realized just how deliberate it had been. It was also because we liked each other, much to my regret sometimes and perhaps to his as well, young Pérez Nuix was far too optimistic in that regard. That night Tupra had put my liking for him to the test, and was still doing so with this film-show.

He stopped talking and immediately pressed the play button again. The previous scene ended abruptly and a new one appeared on the screen, and that was when the poison began to enter me. Two men in T-shirts and camouflage trousers and short boots, soldiers presumably, were standing over a third man, who was wearing a hood and sitting on a stool, his hands and feet shackled. There was sound this time, but all I could hear was a desperate panting coming from the prisoner, as if he had just run five hundred yards or were having a panic or anxiety attack. It was distressing, that loud, fast, somehow unquenchable breathing, it was quite possible that it was brought on by fear, being tied up and unable to see must make you dread every next second, and the seconds pass relentlessly. The room was lit from above, although the source of that light was offscreen, probably a lamp with a shade hanging from the ceiling, which revealed all three men or, rather, lit the two in camouflage trousers only intermittently because they kept prowling round the hooded man and, as they did so, were plunged every now and then into shadow. Beyond the circle of light, at the back, there were two or three other people, sitting in a row against the wall, arms folded, but in the darkness I couldn't make out their faces and only barely their shapes. The soldiers stopped their pacing and roughly hauled the prisoner to his feet and made him stand on the stool, helping him up. I saw them grab a rope, and although the hooded man's head was out of the frame now—the shot was fixed, the camera static—everything led me to believe that they had put the rope around his neck and that the rope was tied to a beam or some other high, horizontal bar, because one of the T-shirted men suddenly kicked away the stool and the victim was left dangling, unable to touch the floor, even though it was very near; this was a hanging.

I started, perhaps gasped or panted unexpectedly, I turned to Tupra and said in alarm:

'What's this?'

As he fell, the prisoner must have struck or perhaps brushed against the invisible lamp, because for a few seconds the light swayed gently back and forth.

'Don't turn away, keep looking, it isn't finished yet,' Tupra said imperiously. And he tapped my elbow with his stiff fingers, as if I were a disobedient child.

When I again fixed my eyes on the screen, I saw the feet of the hanged man still flailing around for support, while his panting gave way to a kind of guttural groan, a choking sound that never became more than that—it couldn't. The feet, however, suddenly found some support: one of the men in camouflage trousers grabbed the man's two legs and lifted them up as high as he could while the other man retrieved the stool and placed it once again beneath the hanged man's feet. Once he was firmly installed, they removed the rope and lowered him to ground level. Then they gave him a shove and he sat down again on the stool, and the two soldiers recommenced their prowling round the prisoner, who was now coughing, his lungs must have been bursting. The short boots made more noise this time, as if their owners were marching in unison and deliberately bringing their feet down hard in order to make that threatening noise, evocative of a roll on the drums at the circus announcing some still more dangerous feat or in public squares just before a much-anticipated execution. And after about thirty seconds—or perhaps ninety—they repeated the whole operation, that is, they made the hooded man stand on the stool and again pretended to hang him, or, to be more exact, they started to hang him—the stool kicked away as before—and then, soon afterwards, stopped. On that occasion, the prisoner lost a shoe during his desperate kicking, perhaps this time the hanging went on slightly longer than before. He was wearing very ordinary shoes, old lace-ups without the laces. He wasn't wearing socks. 'This is just like Tupra in the handicapped toilet,' I managed to think confusedly, 'when he raised and lowered the sword and then raised and lowered it again. Each time I thought he was going to cut the moron's head off, and now, although what he's showing me is over and done with and although he can freeze the action on the video, or even leave it for another day as if it really didn't matter (the scene will still be there unchanged), right now, I've no idea if those guys will end up hanging the poor devil on one of these dummy runs or not, and I want to know, even though the man's a stranger and I can't even see his face. He wouldn't have known how it would end either, when it was still not yet the past. He can't be a young man, not with those old battered brown shoes.' Before sitting the man down again, they put his shoe back on, as if driven by some mysterious impulse to maintain tidiness and good order. One of the soldiers started waving his hand about in front of his nose, as if some terrible smell were suddenly emanating from the man. They still said nothing, no one spoke, not even the obscure spectators, and that's bound to fill anyone unable to see or move with even more fear, more than surly voices or insults, unless they're asked something in an unfamiliar language, and that's the most frightening thing, I think, not understanding what is being said to you in a life-or-death situation.

They went on to repeat the whole operation a third time,

exactly the same, with the prisoner's head at first out of the frame only to reappear later along with the already taut rope, the body dropping straight down, albeit only a short way, so that nothing irreparable happened during the fall, the light swaying briefly either because he had brushed against it or perhaps from the sudden jolting, the second or third time they may have left him hanging there for fewer seconds, although, in my distress, it seemed much longer. The victim would be getting weaker with each cruel attempt, he had probably dislocated something and his heart would be racing. Obviously his neck hadn't been broken, that would have been the end, the men in the camouflage trousers didn't leave him long enough for that to happen, they were well trained, they must have known at what point it would be too late, not, I imagined, that it would matter very much if they got it wrong and the man snuffed it, perhaps no one in the world knew of his fate, nor even where he was. Everyone seemed relatively relaxed, both executioners and witnesses, diligent or alert but without malice, as if they were carrying out or watching some unpleasant procedure, but which was nothing more than that, a procedure.

Tupra froze the image when the prisoner had again been taken down and was coughing, his legs very weak and uncooperative, and on that occasion they did not sit him down. He still had on the black hood, with a single opening for mouth and nose (with adhesive tape covering the mouth), but none for the eyes. They seemed about to take him away, perhaps back to a cell, perhaps to the infirmary. His breathing was once more gradually slowing to a pant.

'Did you see?' Tupra asked. And in his voice I heard a note of almost amused excitement, to me inexplicable, for I was already aware of the poison entering me.

'What are you doing?' I replied. 'I want to know how it ends, to know if they finish off the poor guy.'

'That's where it ends, there isn't any more, it moves on to something else. But did you see him?' he said, referring clearly now to a man, not to an object or a particular detail or to the episode itself, in that case, he would have said 'it' not 'him.'

'Whom?' I asked, falling perhaps into hypercorrection, another example of that mysterious impulse to impose excessive good order and tidiness in the midst of the shock I was feeling.

Tupra tut-tutted in spontaneous scorn.

'You're being very slow on the uptake, Jack. Come on, what are your eyes for? The eye is quick and catches everything. You've done better than this in the past, you're losing your powers, or perhaps you're just tired.' Then he rewound the images with the remote control, found a particular point in the recording and froze it again, he did this quickly and skilfully, he was obviously very practiced. It was one of the moments in which the prisoner was falling, the rope tightening, the stool kicked away, and the light swaying very briefly and gently, hardly at all and less and less with each movement, and covering a shorter distance. Two, at most three movements back and forth, but in that moment, just for a fraction of a second, the three men in the background were suddenly lit up by the shifting light. I looked at them, I couldn't quite make them out, but there was something familiar about them. 'What do you see now?'

'Wait,' I said, still uncertain, screwing up my eyes to see more clearly. 'Wait.'

Tupra did not wait, he activated the zoom and framed their faces in enlarged form, he had a DVD player with far more features than I had on mine in Madrid, I still hadn't bought one for myself in London. And then I clearly saw the familiar square, lined face, known to half of humanity, the half that watches television and reads the newspapers, with his unmistakable glasses and his look of some German doctor or chemist, or rather some Nazi doctor or chemist or scientist, whenever I'd seen him on screen or in a photo, I'd had no difficulty at all in imagining him wearing a white coat over his tie, more than that, his face almost cried out for, no, demanded that white coat, it seemed strange that he didn't wear one. He, like all democratic world leaders and politicians, had repeatedly and publicly denied having anything to do with such things, or having given orders, approved or consented or even known about such practices, even ones that were less brutal and merely humiliating. No one in the outside world knew what I knew now: that, far from not knowing, he had been present, at least once, at the triple half-hanging of a man chained hand and foot, and that he had literally sat idly by, arms folded, impassive, the highest authority there, as he would have been almost anywhere. As Tupra had said, those videos could not be seen by just anyone (a journalist would have been jumping up and down). And the reason they were treasured as if they were gold dust was because each of them contained the fixed image—indefinitely repeatable—of someone famous or powerful or wealthy or someone with prestige and influence. After a while, I had forgotten all about that and focused only on the main action, how could I not? Perhaps for Tupra, on the other hand, the only thing that counted was the dark backdrop, or that one illuminated moment. Obviously, he had seen it before, it didn't take him by surprise. His attitude confirmed to me, at any rate, that he gave little importance to someone's possible death, but that neither was he a sadist. At least he took no pleasure in the suffering of another, those dummy hangings were not an object of fascination, they were merely the necessary framework for what really interested him.

'Yes, I can see him now,' I said. 'But why do you keep this? He's an American, an ally, one of yours.' And I realized at once that I hadn't said 'one of ours,' as would perhaps have seemed logical to Tupra and as would have been logical at that point; it seemed to me that, without even realizing it, I had entered some very murky territory. Yes, I was inside and I knew it, I really did belong to one particular side, despite feeling that I belonged to none. And what was even more unexpected and would have seemed unthinkable a year or even six months ago: I had seen something that was forbidden to almost all other eyes in the world, or, rather, had seen only the half of it.

'So what if he is? You never know.' He took a sip of port, I no longer felt much like drinking mine. He took out and lit a Rameses II. He only offered me one afterwards, when his cigarette was already smoking, and that I did accept. 'We don't even know who is "one of ours," or if they'll still be one of ours

135

tomorrow, it's best not to worry too much about that aspect of things. That's something I can't know about you or you about me. Anyway, let's continue.'

And he resumed the session, the injection of poison, and, at my side and slightly behind me, occasionally spoke to make some brief point or comment, almost as used to happen at slide-shows, with a projector and a screen, given after a journey considered unusual for the times—in my childhood, for example—with the travelers, the ones showing the slides to relatives or friends, placing each one in its context and giving an explanation: 'Here we are on top of the Empire State Building, the tallest skyscraper in the world,' when it still was, 'it's enough to give you vertigo, isn't it?' And vertigo, yes, vertigo was exactly what I felt with each new scene. Some were innocuous, people caught performing perfectly normal sexual acts, but which if made public or seen by others become strangely anomalous, especially if performed by famous people or very serious people or people of a certain age or respectable people, there's always something laborious and ridiculous about objectified sex, and it's hard to understand why, today, there are so many people who film themselves for pleasure, to bask later on in the semi-embarrassment of it all. There were also individuals offering and accepting bribes, some in cash, some whose faces I knew, the occasional Spaniard or, rather, one particular Spanish woman, the blonde hypocrite, but Tupra fast-forwarded over all of these and only returned to normal speed when the scene involved violence or something bizarre. Bizarre to me, that is; not to him, of course; who knows, perhaps they would have seemed so to Pérez Nuix and Mulryan and Rendel, they might never have seen such images either or perhaps they were fully aware of them and knew every detail; perhaps, who knows, such images would have struck Wheeler as bizarre too, or maybe he would have seen more than enough of such things during his youth, and not on screen. But I had not, I had never seen an execution before, except in films, or more recently on television, where the news they show always seems as unreal as the cinema; three men and a woman standing quite still on the seashore, waiting, their hands untied, they're helpless, so why tie them up, a dawn light, it reminded me at once of that painting in the Prado, by Gisbert, at least that's the name that came to me, the shooting of Torrijos and his liberal companions in Málaga, you can see the sand and the waves, perhaps a little of the countryside behind and, in the center, a large group of condemned men, and when I looked it up on the Internet later that morning, I counted sixteen if you include the wife and child to whom one of them is clinging, but doubtless wife and child were merely saying goodbye to their soon-to-be-dead husband and father and would not meet the same fate, so there were fourteen and four more already fallen, with their eyes blindfolded, and nearby, on the ground, there's a top hat that one of the corpses must have tenaciously kept on his head until the moment he became a corpse, they would have killed them in batches to make things manageable, fifty or so men fell there in 1831 ('Late at night they killed him, along with all his company,' I recalled Lorca's great ballad on the subject and quoted it to myself), the six most smartly dressed are grouped on the right, the troops are bunched together on the left and the man in the Phrygian hat looks disdainful and proud (social class matters even in a shared death), more so than the bespectacled fellow who forms part of the gentlemen's group, Torrijos must be the one with fairish hair ('the noble general, with the clear brow'), or perhaps not, he must be the one wearing boots and holding the hands of two of his comrades ('A gentleman among the dukes, a heart of finest silver'), betrayed on his return to the country by the Governor of Málaga ('they drew him there with deceitful words, which he, alas, believed'), he, too, had sought refuge in England for several years, it's always dangerous returning to Spain, where faces change so much between today and tomorrow, even if you were a hero of the Peninsular War or the War of Independence ('The Vizconde de La Barthe, who commanded the militias, should have cut off his own hand rather than commit such villainy'), and there were the friars who are always present at our most somber events (and if not them, priests and if not priests, then nuns), one reading or praying and two applying blindfolds, all three are ominous figures, and behind stand the blurred and waiting

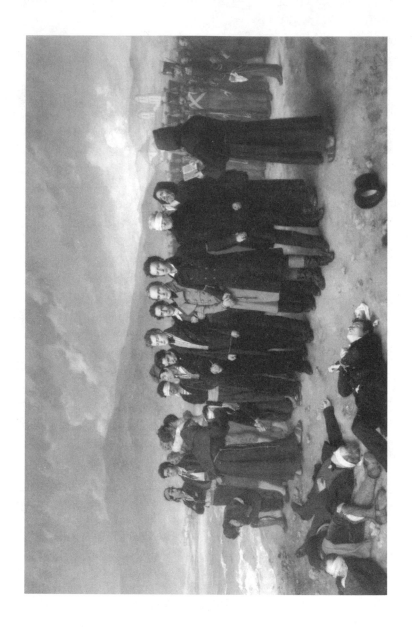

shapes of the firing squad ('Great clouds are building above the Mijas mountains'), it's possible that the man commanding them let fall the white handkerchief he's holding in his left hand, or attached it perhaps to the point of his saber, at the same time shouting 'Fire!' ('Amongst the sound of the waves the rifle shots rang out, and he lay dead upon the sand, bleeding from three wounds . . . Death, being death, did not wither his smile'); and I remembered, too, those who were executed without trial or given, at most, a sham version of justice, on those same Málaga beaches by the man who took the city more than a century later with his Francoist and Moorish hordes and with the Blackshirts of Roatta or 'Mancini': the Duque de Sevilla was his untimely title, the man who strewed with corpses the shore and the water and the barracks and the prisons and the hotels and the walls, about four thousand, it was claimed, and so what if it was fewer; and in front of the condemned men and woman stood two men with machine-guns or something similar, I don't know much about these things, two men wearing ties and with their hair neatly combed, I bet they always carried a comb in their pocket as I do, as do most southerners, and when one of them said '*Dai*,' they both unleashed interminable bursts of gunfire, they fired and fired, squandering bullets as if they had to get rid of them all, while the bodies were falling and once they had fallen too, the woman and one man face upwards and the other two on their sides, the gunmen moved closer, still firing, holding their weapons almost vertically now, the sand jumped and it seemed as if the flesh and the modest clothes of the already very dead dead, bleeding from twenty wounds, also jumped at every gratuitous shot. 'This is a settling of accounts on some secluded beach on the Golfo de Taranto, probably not far from Crotone in Calabria, a few years ago now,' murmured Reresby, correctly stressing the first syllable of Taranto, and he spoke so very softly now, it was as if his voice were emerging from inside a helmet. 'It's interesting. One of the executioners has since carved out a career for himself, first in the construction industry, then in politics, and he now has an excellent post in the current government. The other man, however is dead, he was bumped off straight away, in reprisal for this. It's useful for us to have this video, don't you think?' And I sensed in that question a kind of collector's pride, and maybe he was right to feel proud.

Nor had I ever seen, or even conceived of, an arranged bestial rape, with spectators as if they were at a tryout for young fighting bulls, a small arena, or perhaps the central courtyard of a group of houses, well-dressed men sitting beneath white, red and green awnings, a vicious sun, thick mustaches and Texan hats and not a few Havana cigars clenched between teeth, there was the festive sound of a brass band in the background, encouraging shouts in Spanish and in English, and in the arena, a woman, a horse, a few *mamporreros*—men employed to help stallions mate with mares—and something tearing, I couldn't bear it, I closed my eyes, 'Don't close your eyes!' and so I looked away, 'Don't look away!' But I did, except for the odd moment, this I really couldn't stand because I couldn't believe it, I'd never imagined such a thing were possible in the world, purely as a form of entertainment, and it really was a mortal poison, the images—what I glimpsed of them, for my eyelids and my turned-away face were quick to save me—entered my mind as if they were an ugly reptile or a kind of serpent, or perhaps an eel, or leeches under the skin, how can I put it, internal leeches, the images slipped inside me like a foreign body that caused me immediate pain and a sense of oppression and suffocation and the urgent need for someone to remove it ('Let me sit heavy on thy soul'), but you cannot root out what enters through the eyes, nor what enters through the ears, it installs itself inside you and there's nothing to be done about it, or else you have to wait some time in order to be able to persuade yourself that you did not see or hear what you did see or hear—there's always a doubt or the trace of a doubt—that it was imagination or a misunderstanding or a mirage or a hallucination or a malicious misinterpretation, we are none of us immune from them when our thoughts and our perceptions become twisted and we judge everything in the same slanted sinister light. 'This is Ciudad Juárez, in the state of Chihuahua, in Mexico,' murmured Tupra in his ever more sunken voice and in a tone that wasn't in the least indifferent, but almost sorrowful, grave, and it didn't sound to me as if he were putting it on, 'and there you have one of the thousand women who have disappeared and about whom so much has been written in the press. That, however, is not what matters to us, important though it is, but, rather, that man there, to the right in the second row, the one all in white and wearing a red tie.' This forced me to look for a moment, reluctantly and out of the corner of my eye—how hard it is to resist curiosity when someone points a finger at something—I saw a man in the audience, a fat, smiling, middle-aged man with shiny skin and thick hair, though I couldn't help but see, as well, the terrible irrationality and more tearing and some blood now—like a sword or a spear—and I turned away again, towards where Reresby was sitting, his eyes fixed on the screen, but screwed up now, as if he needed glasses or were preparing to close them at any moment, perhaps that episode, even though he had seen it before and knew how it would end, really set his teeth on edge or provoked anguish or even repugnance ('Bloody and guilty, guiltily awake'), no one can bear everything and, as I said, he was not a sadist. 'At the time, and this is a few years ago now, he was a very rich businessman, not yet a tycoon. Now he is, though, and he's standing for the post of mayor in an important town, in another region, in another state on the border with the United States, Coahuila. And he'll get it too. It will be useful for us to have this film of him enjoying the show.' He mispronounced Coahuila, saying it as if it were an English word—it's less well known than Chihuahua—something like 'koh-hoo-why-lah.' The worst thing was that the event seemed not to be a single episode, I certainly didn't get the impression that everything had been arranged for this one occasion, the band, the awnings, the horse and its experienced handlers, the invitation, doubtless made over the Internet and in code, or through messages left on cell phones, doubtless in a whisper. What I glimpsed had probably happened before, perhaps with minor variations, with a different animal perhaps, but I didn't want to go down that road and I tore out all further imaginings by the roots.

'It's pronounced koh-ah-wee-lah,' I said, unable to resist the desire to correct him, a further example of that mysterious impulse to impose good order and unnecessary precision at all costs. I said this while looking at him. But he wasn't looking at me, he still kept his eyes glued to the screen for a few more seconds, almost half-closed now, his expression one of scorn and disgust for what he was seeing, his wasn't the face of a man unmoved by cruelty and by the suffering of others, he was judging them severely; then he fast-forwarded again and, after a while, froze the image.

'It's all right, you can look now. I've stopped at another scene, the next one. But Jack,' he added with barely suppressed irritation, yet almost kindly, 'I'm not showing you all this in order for you not to look at it, quite the opposite. Otherwise, what's the point?'

'I don't want to see any more, Bertie,' I said. 'If it's all like that, I don't want to see anything. I think I understand where you're going with this, and I don't need to know any more; besides, why don't you use these images to do something about it? You could use them to find out, through that fat man you appear to know so well and who's been so very successful, just what's going on in that place and to stop it. I don't understand your passivity, the organization's passivity.'

'Do you really think that the Mexicans and the Americans don't already have a copy of this tape? If *they* don't intervene in the matter, there's not much we can do at our end; and it's not always easy to take action; in some countries, such a video would be unacceptable as proof, the way it was obtained would invalidate it. And what would we accuse our fat friend of? Attending an illegal event? Doing nothing? Refusing to help? Bah. I can understand why they might simply keep it filed away for a better occasion, just in case. I can't criticize them for that, we do the same with most of the footage that concerns us and our territories. You might save more lives by forcing one individual to do something later on than by immediately coming down hard on the less important people. And we're always interested in saving lives. We're always making calculations, weighing up whether it's worth letting one person die now if that will mean many others will live. Our priority, understandably enough, is saving British lives. As it would be in time of war. We have to get the most benefit out of everything, even if that means waiting a few years. It's the same with the day-to-day work in the office, sometimes you have to wait until someone is in a position to carry out what we have predicted that he or she is capable of doing. Including the things you predict, Jack, the things you tell us about. Everything you tell me counts, nothing is wasted. And it's the same with this.' He did finally look at me as he spoke these last few sentences, his eyes—grey in the gloom—no longer half-closed, his now wide-open, absorbent eyes that made anyone they alighted on feel worthy of attention and of interpretation; and it seemed to me that his words had been intended to increase that feeling in me. I had still not yet turned back to the screen again, despite his reassuring words. 'Go on, look. You must see at least one more recording. I'll fast-forward more quickly, I'll jump over a few, since you find them so upsetting.' Here he did not spare me his sarcasm.

I didn't care. I held up my hand to indicate that it was not yet the moment, that there was something I wanted to clear up first. Perhaps I needed a minute to recover from what I had seen and another to get myself used to the idea that there were doubtless still more unpleasant things to see, more poison. However, I disguised this by asking, as if my curiosity needed to be urgently assuaged:

'Where do you get them from? How do you find them? The things you've shown me up until now, I mean. None of them is a situation where cameras would be permitted.'

'From anywhere, from all kinds of places and in all kinds of ways, the opportunities are endless nowadays. On the one hand, we have our own traditional means: our installers and our infiltrators and other people we bribe to do the filming. But people sell images too, there's a whole floating market out there and we just buy whatever might be of interest to us, we get them cheap when the seller doesn't know the identity of the people who appear in them. We usually *do* know or we can find out, whether they're mere minions or obscure hired assassins or people of a certain importance. It's the same as in the art market: if the buyer knows the true value and the seller doesn't, then the result is a bargain. Now every fool owns and carries a mini-camera in his pocket or has one on his cell phone, and if a tourist chances to capture some serious incident, even a crime, he's more likely to try and make some money out of it than take it to the police. The police don't pay, but we do, as do others, through inter-mediaries. It's the same if they catch some celebrity naked or screwing someone, they'll put it up for sale to the sensationalist magazines and TV shows, it's good to have someone keeping an eye on such things. At other times, our colleagues in other countries send us videos, and we reciprocate with anything that might be of use to them, satellites pick up a lot too. Nowadays, it's the easiest thing in the world, there are recordings of every-thing. People no longer have any idea where cameras might be hidden or still don't believe that there are quite that many, the most sensible thing is to assume that they're everywhere all the time, even in hotel rooms and in brothels and in saunas and in public toilets (not in the handicapped toilets, though, they don't tend to put them there), and even in private houses. No one is safe any more from being filmed doing anything and in any circumstances, whether committing a crime or indulging in depraved sexual acts, always good possibilities. We aren't al-ways so lucky, of course, and what we get hold of and watch is a tiny fraction of what's available. We can make immediate use, I mean legal use, of very little. But our archive is pretty good for future or hypothetical use, with a view to reaching private agreements. People really care about their image and can always be persuaded to withdraw or to make some kind of pact. You'd be surprised how much they care, even the non-famous, even businessmen who are unknown to most people, I mean, to those who watch television and read newspapers, because they know they would immediately cease to be unknown. It's very wide-spread that panic of yours, that narrative panic or horror, as you called it, everyone is convinced that they could have a story or could provide the material for a story, they just need someone to tell it, to decide to tell it. And there's nothing easier than rescuing someone from anonymity. Many people struggle and do their utmost to drag themselves out of anonymity, you know the kind of thing, they offer up their daily life on the Internet, twenty-four hours a day, they plan scandals or notorious frauds, they try to launch themselves into celebrity even of the ugliest kind, they invent some ridiculous piece of tittle-tattle in order to be invited to talk about it on the most obscure and paltry of programs in the small hours, they seek out the indirect contagion of someone else's fame, however vile, or they pick a fight in the TV studio and trade insults, and try to have stupid, inane photos taken of themselves with an actor, a soccer star, a singer, a millionaire, a politician, a member of the royal family, a model. They'll even murder an acquaintance or a stranger in the most gruesome, complicated way, in a particularly cruel or striking or spine-chilling fashion, a child killing a much younger child, an adolescent killing his parents, a young woman killing a weaker colleague, an adult staging a massacre in a public place or secretly doing in seven people, one after the other, hoping to be discovered at last and to amaze the world. Because anyone—even the most stupid person—can kill someone. And they don't know that all they have to do is carry on with their lives until someone finds them interesting and adopts the appropriate point of view and decides to tell their story, or at least takes an interest and pays them some attention. As long as there is in that life some shameful, untold episode, a stain or an anomaly. And that's not so very difficult, Jack, because we all have something of the sort in our past, possibly without even knowing that we do or without being able to put our finger on it. It depends on who's looking at us. And the worst that can happen to anyone is for no one to look at them. People can't bear it and go into a decline. Some people die of it or kill.'

And he paused long enough for me to think: 'Tupra has adopted my theory, or snippets of it. He has the delicacy not to use my exact words or, when he does, to acknowledge that he has done so, "as you called it" or "to use your term," he says when he's quoting me verbatim. He has the good taste not to appropriate, at least not in my presence, the idea that people hate being left out or passed over and prefer always to be seen and judged, for good or ill or even for worse, and even need this and yearn for it; the idea that they still cannot do without the supposed eye of God that observed and watched us for centuries, without that companionable belief that some being is aware of us at all times and knows everything about us and follows every detail of our trajectory like someone following a story of which we are the protagonist; what they can't bear and won't allow is to remain unobserved by anyone, to be neither approved nor disapproved of, neither rewarded nor punished nor threatened, to be unable to count on any spectator or witness regardless of whether they are for us or against us; and they seek out or invent substitutes for that eye, which is now closed or wounded, or weary or inert, or bored or blind, or which has simply looked away from what I am doing; perhaps that's why people today care so little about being spied on and filmed, and often even provoke it, through exhibitionism, although that can prove detrimental and draw down upon them precisely the thing they most dread, the conversion of their story into a disaster. It's a contradictory double need: I want it to be known that I exist and have existed, and I want my deeds to be known, but that frightens me too, because it might ruin forever the picture I'm painting of myself. And so when I'm not there, Tupra will probably have no qualms about appropriating wholesale everything I said to him when I talked about Dick Dearlove or indeed on other occasions, and he'll think he thought of it himself (in that regard he'll be like any other boss). Perhaps Pérez Nuix was right and I do have more influence over him than I think, perhaps I do stimulate and amuse him. Maybe that's why he has a soft spot for me and invites or drags me to his house and shows me this collection of horrible videos, and is so patient with me, and lets me get away with so many things, even letting me cover my eyes and not look at what he's generous enough to show me, in an act of great trust, or to watch it with only one eye open.'

And I immediately went on to think: "But everything has its end, and banks will only honor your checks while there's still cash in your account, so I mustn't take anything for granted.' And then I said:

'All right, show me what you've got to show me and let's get it over with. It's very late and I want to go home.'

'Ah, of course,' he replied ironically. 'Those lights. Do you think she'll still be waiting for you? If so, it won't be easy for you to get away afterwards, she'll be very insistent.' He glanced at his watch and added: 'You've certainly kept her hanging around. Do give her my deepest apologies.'

He was the kind of man who feels excited by the mere thought of women, by the idea of them, whoever they may be, and still more by the thought of his friends' wives or girlfriends and of sending messages to those female strangers through their husbands or boyfriends. That way, he thinks, they'll find out about him, they'll at least know of his existence and perhaps feel curious and imagine what he might be like, and thus indulge in a form of aimless, imaginary flirtation.

'I've told you already, Bertram, no one is waiting for me and no one has my keys.' I downed my drink in one, as if to show that at least something had been concluded. 'Come on, get on with it, what else do you want me to see?' And I indicated the TV with a lift of my chin.

He pressed Play again and then the fast-forward button, although he put it on at its second fastest speed, not at maximum, so that I could still see the images fairly clearly, albeit without sound, and they were all of them unpleasant to a greater or lesser degree, the worst kept feeding the poison into me, while others were, at best, boring or sordid, two guys with grey hair and reddish skin lying on a bed in their underpants, sniffing cocaine (drugs really provide a lot of material, perhaps that's why no government wants to legalize them, it would mean reducing the number of possible offenses), people who were of no interest to me and made no impression whatsoever, so I abstained from asking who they were, they were probably well-known or important folk, perhaps British or Canadian or Australian, perhaps police officers, one of them had on an incongruous navy-blue peaked cap worn at a jaunty angle; I very nearly went back on my resolve and came close to giving in to jocular curiosity when there appeared on the screen a Spanish politician, a nationalist, whom we're all heartily sick of seeing (he, of course, would have objected to being described as Spanish), standing before a full-length mirror in the process of meticulously disguising himself as a lady or, rather, as an old-fashioned whore, it took him ages to get his stockings on straight, every time they became twisted or wrinkled he had to take them off and start again, he tore two pairs in the process and glumly flung them down, he was also wrestling with a kind of girdle, it was a half-comic, half-pathetic sight, for which someone in my country would have paid good money; anyway, as I say, I was tempted, but I stopped myself in time and succeeded in not asking Tupra to play it at its proper speed, I wanted to finish as quickly as possible; in a billiard hall, four sinister-looking men were beating up some poor man of advancing years and distinguished appearance, they flung him face down on the green baize and beat him with billiard cues, holding the thin ends and thrashing him with the thick ends, then they rolled him over and immediately set to smashing his glasses and continued hitting him in the face—with glass flying everywhere and doubtless embedding itself in his skin with each new blow—and then they beat him all over his body, his ribs and his hips and his legs and his testicles, yes, they even beat him there, with the cues held upright, they must have broken his kneecaps and his tibia, the man didn't know how best to protect himself, they must have broken his hands too as he tried in vain to cover himself, four billiard cues are a lot when they're raised and lowered and raised and lowered, again and again, like swords. Here, I couldn't help commenting:

'You're not going to tell me that one of these savages is now a prominent figure in some lofty position. I can hardly believe it of thugs like them.'

Tupra stopped the film for a moment, he wasn't going to let me miss any of those barbaric acts, even in fast-forward. The image remained frozen on the poor man, his castigators already withdrawn, lying motionless on the table, bleeding from his nose and eyebrows, possibly from his cheekbones and from other cuts, a swollen, wounded heap.

'That wouldn't be impossible, not at all. But no,' he replied from behind me, this time I hadn't turned round to look at him, just as well, I thought afterwards. 'The important figure here is the old man, who would feel deeply ashamed of this scene. Bear in mind that some people want to hide the fact that they have been the victim as much as or more than if they'd been the executioner. There are people who would do almost anything to keep people from knowing what happened to them, what barbarous, humiliating things have been done to them, and who would go to still greater lengths to prevent that being seen. So that their loved ones, for example, never see or know about it, because they would suffer and be heartbroken and be unable to ever forget it, I mean, imagine if this man were your father. But he's important in a different way from the others you've seen, he's another type altogether. He has little power or influence, at least not directly. Don't you know who he is? Really?' And without even giving me time to answer 'No,' he told me. 'It's Mr. Pérez Nuix, our Patricia's father.' And he pronounced that double-barreled surname English-style, so that it sounded as if he'd said something like 'Pears-Nukes.'

It was then that I thought how glad I was he couldn't see my face. I felt a sudden wave of heat spreading over both face and neck and then throughout my body, just like when I'd been caught red-handed at school, with no possibility of arguing or lying my way out of the situation. 'I obviously didn't deceive him,' I thought at once, 'and he doubtless knows that I tried to do so deliberately. That I lied to him about Incompara, perhaps he realized this at once and so it was all pointless, useless, because he didn't take the bait, and Incompara didn't get what he wanted, and so the debt wasn't cancelled, or the man paid off his debt with this brutal beating, but filmed by whom, they must have arranged to meet the father at that billiard hall to sort things out, they set a trap, and probably Reresby knew about it beforehand, knew what was really awaiting the old man, ordered a hidden camera to be installed there or else paid the manager or a fifth thug who doesn't appear in the frame because he wasn't taking part in the thrashing and was only directing it or witnessing it so that he could report back afterwards that the deed was done, meanwhile filming it on his cell phone or on his miniature camera. Thoughts crowded into my mind and also a feeling of intense shame that took various forms, or perhaps they were all different, simultaneous shames. But I couldn't give myself away so easily, silence was hardly the normal response after such a revelation, that would have been tantamount to acknowledging that I knew everything or at least a part of it.

'But why?' I asked nervously. Such a question wasn't suspicious, any nervousness on my part could be attributed to the vicious attack I had just witnessed, fortunately with the sound off. 'Why? Why him? What did he do to those guys?'

'He had a lot of gambling debts, and you know what happens with things like that. It depends who you owe the money to, but they never let you off.'

'He's pretending,' I thought, 'he's telling me this as if I didn't already know, when he must be aware that I know a lot. He's testing me. He wants to see if I'll cave in and confess or if I'll play the innocent until the end, without giving anything away. He wants to see how I handle being found out.'

'When does this video date from, when did it happen?'

'Relatively recently,' he replied. 'A couple of months ago or less.'

'Does Patricia know? I mean, has she seen this?'

She had said nothing to me, perhaps because my favor or my pretense had failed so completely: why give me the bad news which, after all, did not concern me, why make me feel responsible, why get me any more involved than I already was? She hadn't told me the opposite either, that everything had turned out well and the debt had been settled, thanks, in part, to my good offices. Then again, it had never occurred to me that she would and I hadn't asked her about it, she had only asked me that one favor, after all, and that ought to be respected; contrary to popular belief, the first occasion doesn't necessarily give rise to a second, whatever it might be.

Tupra gave that same laugh, like a short cough, which indicated sarcasm or incredulity at what he was hearing.

'No, of course she hasn't seen it. What do you take me for? It was bad enough for her seeing him in the hospital. Her father spent a long time there, in fact he may only have been sent home a short time ago, I'm not sure, and it's still unclear whether he'll recover, and well, he's getting on a bit now, he'll never completely get over something like that, they gave the poor devil a real going-over.'

Yes, there was young Pérez Nuix's poor father, whom she loved so much, frozen before my eyes at his saddest moment, his eyes were half-closed, and what little expression could be read in them bespoke disappointment, as if he had never expected the world to inflict such cruelty or that he would experience it in his own flesh, that frivolous man who found suffering tedious; I felt guilty for what they had done to him and that was one of the various shames I felt, perhaps I hadn't been convincing enough when I gave my views on Incompara, it's hard to lie when one doesn't oneself believe the lie, I should have tried harder, have been more insistent and underwritten my words with my thoughts thus making them true, or perhaps it wasn't a failure on my part at all and Tupra had merely seen what he had seen, which was, moreover, as clear as day: that Vanni Incompara was not to be trusted in any way and that he was also utterly ruthless, Pérez Nuix would have picked that up, but would have had to deceive herself, which is what we all do, even those who

have the gift, even the most gifted, when what we see affects us
and proves unbearable. Perhaps it had been an impossible under-
taking, that of persuading my boss that things were otherwise,
the same boss who was now showing me this video for who
knows what reason, or was it pure coincidence and he had no
ulterior motive, after all, I could have said nothing, and then he
wouldn't have paused the tape, but let it run without making any
further reference to it and without telling me who the victim
was. 'And yet he seems to be saying to me: "Take a good look,
you didn't deceive me, just see where your attempt at deceit has
led, Iago, your cunning plan didn't work, and I paid no attention
to your treachery, I wasn't taken in by your recommendations
and so I rejected him, and then, of course, he flew into a rage because of the false expectations you had aroused in him; it would
have been so much better if you hadn't bothered, he might have
been more magnanimous with that cheerful and distinguished
old man, your compatriot, and sent him only one thug instead
of four, armed perhaps with a blackjack, not a long hard billiard
cue, or else he would have found another way to settle the matter, without anger or violence. You really made a blunder there
and underestimated me too, thinking you could pull the wool
over my eyes, but you've a long way to go before you'll manage that. A whole lifetime." It could also be that he's not saying
anything to me.'

'But why didn't you stop it, when you knew he was Patricia's
father?' I continued to act dumb; once you set off along a path
you have to follow it until it's cut off by the sea, a precipice, a
wall, the desert, or the jungle. 'You're not telling me you knew
nothing about this, or that the camera filming it was there by
chance, that you had nothing to do with it and bought the video
on the market. That would be a coincidence, don't you think,
the father of a colleague being beaten up?'

Tupra remained impassive, or so I imagined. I still had my
back to him, preferring not to see his expression and for him not
to see mine. His voice sounded calm:

'Of course it wasn't a coincidence. It was precisely because it
involved a colleague that they brought it to us, offered it to us.

They thought it might be of interest, either by revealing where her weaknesses might lie, or to help us carry out reprisals against the aggressors. You know, in our group, we don't talk much about our personal problems—Pat says almost nothing. If it hadn't been for this tape, I would hardly have known a thing. All she told me was that her father had had an accident and was in the hospital. We don't tend to mix socially, as you know.'

'And didn't you take reprisals? Not even in a case like this? Then why keep the tape?'

'As I told you, nothing here gets thrown away or given away or destroyed, and this beating is perfectly safe here, it's not going to be shown to anyone. Although, who knows, it might be necessary to show it to Pat one day, to convince her of something, perhaps to stay, not to leave us, you never can tell. For the moment, though, there's no point in taking reprisals, those four men are rank nobodies, they do things like that—a hundred similar things for a hundred different masters—and they're sure to get caught now and then with no need for us to go after them, they're used to prison. As for the men behind it, as I've explained, it's best to wait, as we so often do, to make some better future use of it.'

'Is that what you wanted me to see?' I knew it wasn't, if it had been, he wouldn't have been fast-forwarding over it, risking me not saying anything and depriving him of the opportunity to enlighten me. He had still more poison with which to inoculate me, or more torment to put me through.

'No, that's not it. Let's get on.'

And more scenes, albeit fewer, sped silently by, I could still see most of them, I saw a man screaming at another man who was sitting in a car in an underground parking lot, I mean a private not a public one, he was leaning against the car and screaming at him, resting one elbow on the open window so that the other man couldn't wind it up, their two faces so close that he must have been spraying him with spit, I saw how with a rapid movement he took a pistol from his jacket pocket and placed the barrel beneath the ear lobe of his adversary or victim, I saw how he took not even three seconds to squeeze the trigger and shoot him right there, beneath the ear lobe, at point-blank range. I put my hand to my eyes, so that I could see only through the chinks between my fingers, ridiculous I know, I saw blood spurt out and tiny bits of bone, but that way you somehow feel that you're seeing less or could at least stop seeing it at any moment, although that moment never arrives because you never draw your fingers together. The blood spattered the murderer too, not that this appeared to bother him, there must be a shower nearby or else he has a fresh shirt in his car, another suit, or perhaps this was the underground parking lot for his own apartment building, he turned and disappeared, returning the pistol to his pocket, it was a very brief sequence, but judging by the cut of his trousers—rather short and narrow and made of shiny grey fabric—I would have said he was American, and the fact that Tupra kept the video must mean that the man belonged to the CIA or something similar, the Army perhaps, I refrained from asking questions, perhaps he was now one of its highest-ranking officers, who knows, well, Reresby would.

Immediately after this, I saw someone being beaten to death with a hammer, at least I assume he was killed, a woman of about thirty was wielding the weapon, she was wearing a skirt and high heels and a pearl necklace over her tight V-necked sweater—the clothing and shoes in the same matching green, she looked like someone out of the 1950s or the early sixties, a secretary or an executive or a bank clerk, certainly an office worker—she felled a man considerably taller than herself with a savage hammer blow to the forehead, he was my age or Tupra's, but heavier and broader than either of us, this was probably taking place in a hotel room, the burly man fell backwards and she sat astride him hitting him with the hammer, smashing his skull, which is why I assume that he died, she must have feared or hated him intensely, her necklace jiggled up and down, her skirt was all rucked up; strangely enough, despite her autumnal outfit, she wasn't wearing stockings, perhaps she'd taken them off before and perhaps her panties too, in order to have sex fully clothed, or perhaps she didn't have to take off her panties, or he took them off so as to rape her and would have liked to have her like that, on top of him, or underneath with her legs spread, what would that have made her then, what was she now and who was the victim, I still said nothing, the recording ended abruptly, the woman poised with her hammer in the air, like Tupra with his sword, she had not yet finished delivering her blows, I couldn't help remembering that rather odd actress Constance Towers in that old movie, *The Naked Kiss*, in Spain it was called *Una luz en el hampa*—*A Light in the Underworld*—a slightly ridiculous title—in which she did something similar in the first scene, not with a hammer but with the sharp heel of her shoe, or was it a telephone, and while she was committing this crime her hair fell off, it turned out she was wearing a blonde wig and was revealed to the viewers as completely bald, and maybe that's what was most shocking, like those false stories about Jayne Mansfield; and the image of Luisa also crossed my mind, the dread image I had fantasized about in my darkest or maddest moments, attacked by the man who would replace me, a devious sort who wouldn't give her so much as a moment's breathing space and would isolate her totally, and who, one rainy night, when they were stuck at home, would close his large hands around her throat while the children—my children—watched from a corner, pressing themselves into the wall as if wishing the wall would give way and disappear and, with it, that awful sight, and the choked-back tears that longed to burst forth, but could not, the bad dream, and the strange, long-drawn-out noise their mother made as she died, I just hoped she had a hammer at hand so that she wouldn't be the one to die, but the devious man, the despotic possessive man who wasn't like that in the early stages, on their first dates, but deferential, respectful, even cautious, who, like me, didn't stay the night, even if begged to do so, but put all his clothes back on despite the lateness of the hour, the exhaustion and the cold, and when he went out into the street once again put his gloves on, that man so similar to Tupra.

It's also possible that I was too tired to say a word, as scene succeeded scene, I felt more and more shrivelled, diminished, atrophied ('Dream on, dream on, of bloody deeds and death'), as if that one facet of the world I was being shown were driving out all the other more usual ones, not just the happy smiling ones, but also the anodyne and the neutral, the indifferent, the routine, which—especially the latter—are our salvation and essence. That is what poison does, it infiltrates and contaminates everything. The tiredness, however, must have been cumulative because, at the same time, I realized that, despite all I had seen, nothing being paraded before me made such a painful impact on me as the incident I had witnessed with my own eyes, unmediated by a screen, in the handicapped toilet. Violence that happens right next to you and that breathes and stains is not the same as violence projected onto a screen, even if you know it's real and not fictitious, television doesn't spatter us, it only frightens us. And now and then, Tupra's question would resurface in my mind, the question he had asked me in the car before setting off and that had made him decide to drive us both to his house, 'Why can't one go around beating up people and killing them? That's what you said.' What nonsense, everyone knows why, anyone could have given him the answer. But in the light of what he was showing me ('Let these visions sit heavy on thy soul; and lay down thy edgeless sword and let thy shield roll away; take off thy helmet and let fall thy lance'), I could still find only idiotic puerile answers, inherited but never thought through, the usual trite and vacuous ones that everyone has learned by rote and is ready to trot out without ever having given them a thought, however paltry or vague, without ever having questioned them: why is it wrong, because it's immoral, because it's against the law, because you can get sent to prison or to the gallows in some countries, because you shouldn't do unto others what you wouldn't want done unto you, because it's a crime, because there is such a thing as pity, because it's a sin, because it's bad, because life is sacred, because once it's done it's done and cannot be undone. Tupra was clearly asking me something that went beyond all that.

I saw more flurries of activity, perhaps I shouldn't describe them, I saw worse things, more confused, almost run together. Reresby had increased the speed, he needed to sleep too, yes, maybe he was growing sleepy, although he sounded wide awake, perhaps he was at last in sympathy with my desire to get it over with as quickly as possible, I wanted an end to the fever, my pain, the word, the dance, the image, the poison, the dream, at least for that day and for that very long night, the things that compromise or accuse are not very varied—weird sex, violent sex, adulterous or merely laughable sex, beatings, drug consumption, a bit of torture, cruelty and sadism, corruption, bribes, con tricks and betrayals and debts, failed conspiracies and treacheries exposed, improvised homicides and planned murders, and not much else really, almost everything can be reduced to that, but then there are the massacres, I saw another machine-gunning, on a larger scale this time, of civilians in some African country, twenty or so women and men and children and old people, they fell in quick succession, like dominoes, and thus it seemed less grave or even less true, executed by black soldiers or marksmen under orders from a white officer in uniform, whether regulation or half-invented I don't know, perhaps he was a mercenary who later rejoined his army, there are Englishmen and South Africans and Belgians who have made that return journey, and Frenchmen too, I believe. If that were the case, Tupra had that European soldier exactly where he wanted him, he would have allowed him to rise, make a career for himself, he certainly wouldn't have warned him of the existence of that film nor would he have denounced him, he would be waiting until he reached some lofty position, in his own country, in NATO, so that he could then ask him an enormous favor, or, rather, in the light of that video, force him to grant the favor.

And finally he stopped, I mean that he resumed normal speed for one particular sequence and with it restored the sound, he had to rewind a little to catch the beginning.

'Here it is,' he said. 'This is what I want you to see before you go home. Take a good look, and when you're lying in bed think about me and think about this.'

It was, like all the others, a short scene, he hadn't lied about that, even though I seemed to have been there forever, almost all the episodes had been edited together onto that one DVD with barely any preamble, what mattered was the brutality, the crime or the farce, not what came before or afterwards, but what could be used to blackmail the subject of the film. Three men were in a kind of hut, in the background I could make out the tail of an animal whisking back and forth, probably a cow or an ox, there was straw scattered about the floor, I could imagine how it must have smelled in there. Two of the men were standing and they had tied up the third man, who was sitting on a wicker chair, his hands behind his back and each foot tied to a chair leg, to the front legs, of course. There was a cassette or a radio playing, I could hear a tune that I half-recognized, with my reliable memory for music: Comendador had taken a liking to the local songs during his prison stay in Palermo after being arrested by customs because of a drop of blood that trickled from his nose at an inopportune or perhaps opportune moment and aroused the suspicions of a border guard with a very sharp or deductive eye, and who literally set the drug-sniffing dogs on him. He had sent me a couple of CDs as a present, one by Modugno and the other by someone called Zappulla, and I was almost sure that it was the latter's voice I could hear at full volume in the cowshed, singing a song that appeared on my CD, I could remember some of the titles: 'I puvireddi,' 'Suspirannu,' 'Luntanu,' 'Bidduzza,' or 'Moro pe ttia,' pretty, pleasant songs, slightly tacky in their melancholy, and I had enjoyed listening to them, over and over, during a melancholy and rather tacky period of my own life, that cowshed must then be in Sicily, an idea confirmed by the presence of the weapon one of the men standing guard wore slung over his shoulder on a chain, a *lupara*, the sawn-off shotgun once used there for hunting and for settling scores, and perhaps still used for both, the other man had a large pistol in a holster under his arm, his jacket draped elegantly over his shoulders, the sleeves hanging empty, and his shirtsleeves rolled up, a large square watch on his wrist, his hand resting on the back of the chair in which sat the prisoner, stouter and older than the two younger and thinner men, and all three were mouthing the words of the song, they all knew it by heart and were singing along with Zappulla, and although each was doing this of his own accord, so to speak, absorbed and isolated, as if to himself and not in unison, there was nonetheless something very odd about them all momentarily sharing that melody, as if they weren't two guards and their captive or two executioners and their victim, and as if nothing bad awaited the latter, and the tails of the animals in the background seemed to move to the same rhythm, all the living beings in that out-of-the-way place were strangely and incongruously in tune, the man carrying the *lupara* was even swaying slightly, not lifting his feet, but just moving his legs and his torso and the twin-barreled shotgun, dancing to the lilting melody of '*I puvireddi*' or '*Moro pe ttia*,' which mean, in dialect, 'The poor devils' or 'I'm dying for you.'

This lasted only a few seconds, then the door was flung open—a glimpse of grass, a pleasant field—and three other men came in, closing the door behind them, and the first man, the man in charge, was Arturo Manoia. There he was with his glasses—the glasses of a rapist or of a civil servant—which he kept pushing up with his thumb even when they had not slipped down, I noticed that he was doing the same thing there, while standing up and active and occupied, and his gaze, almost invisible due to the reflected light and to his incessantly shifting, lusterless eyes (the color of milky coffee), as if he found it hard to keep them still for more than a few seconds, or else could not stand for people to be able to examine them. I recognized him at once, I had just spent a whole unforgettable evening with him and he didn't look very much younger, so it must have been a recent video or else he was one of those men who don't age and who, unlike his wife, don't change either, there he was with his invasive, too-long chin, perhaps not long enough to be termed prognathous, but still meriting the word *bazzone*. And there he was, with his evident readiness to take revenge. The moment I met him, I thought he would be likely to lash out without the slightest provocation or on the slightest pretext or even with no need for either, that he was an irascible man, although he would doubtless be considered, instead, as measured, because he would almost never give vent to that anger. But I had also thought that on the few occasions when his rage did surface, it would doubtless be terrifying and best not witnessed. And now, having said goodbye to him and seen the last of him in person, there, unexpectedly, at the end of the night, I was about to witness one of his attacks of rage on screen. It was almost, it seemed to me, a curse and I knew this as soon as I saw him, in suit and tie, come in through the door of the cowshed. I prepared myself, I told myself that, whatever happened, I would not look away or cover my eyes. I wanted to show Tupra that I had toughened up during our late-night session or had created inside myself an antidote to his poison, or at least some resistance.

The music didn't stop when the three newcomers arrived, they didn't even turn down the volume, and so I heard little of what Manoia was saying to the bound man and understood still less, he seemed to me to be speaking with an exaggerated southern accent or else mixing dialect and Italian. I could tell, though, that he was speaking to him proudly, indignantly, scornfully—his wounding voice raised in anger now—waving his hands around and giving the man the occasional smack across the face as if this were simply another gesture made in passing, a way of underlining each reproof, almost involuntary or as if he were barely aware of what he was doing, which is a sure sign that the person being slapped is now worthless and has become a mere thing. The other man answered as best he could, and *he* was definitely speaking in dialect, because I couldn't understand a word, he managed only truncated sentences, constantly interrupted by the swift ceaseless flow of words from Manoia, I tried not to look too much at the prisoner, the less I perceived him as an individual, the less it would matter to me what happened to him in the end, because something horrible was about to happen, that much was certain, the situation demanded it and, besides, the scene was part of that specially chosen and edited DVD of embarrassing or downright vile episodes, but I did look at him despite myself, out of habit, he was a plump man, with a small mouth and a large head, short, curly, straw-colored hair, bulging eyes, and the weather-beaten skin of a small landowner who still walks his own fields, well-dressed in a country way, and about forty or so years old. Finally, Manoia's cascade of words ceased—but not his rage—or else he made a brief pause, and then I did understand what he said: '*Tappategli la bocca*,' he ordered his henchmen, although it sounded more like '*Dabbadegli la bogga*,' with unvoiced consonants converted into voiced, or perhaps I understood this *a posteriori* from the images, when I saw how the man with the pistol and the man with the shotgun stuffed two wads of cloth into the man's mouth, one after the other, I don't know how there was room, and on top of that placed a large strip of adhesive tape, from ear to ear, so that he couldn't cough freely as he needed to, his face grew red and inflamed, his eyes seemed, for a moment, about to pop out of their sockets, his cheeks puffed up like boils, the henchmen used red-and-white checked cloths, perhaps napkins from a *trattoria*, and the ends stuck out above and below the tape, what could he have done that was so very terrible or so grave, had he been an informer like Del Real, had he betrayed someone, lost his nerve, failed, fled, fallen asleep, he did not seem like a mere enemy, although he could well have been, perhaps someone had died because of him, some agent from the Sismi who wasn't due to die, always assuming Manoia belonged to the Sismi. Manoia then took an object out of his jacket pocket, I couldn't see what it was, something short, a small penknife, a teaspoon, a sharp metal file, a pencil. '*Adesso vedrai*,' he said, 'Now you'll see,' and those words I did hear clearly despite the music. The seated man's head was at the same height as Manoia's chest and arms. Manoia moved closer, only a couple of steps, and with whatever he was holding in his hand he made two rapid movements over the man's face, the gesture of an old-fashioned dentist preparing to pull out a tooth by main force, first one, then the other, and he did pull them out, he really did, by the roots, but not the man's teeth, he sliced them out the way someone uses a dessert knife to cut out the stone from a peach half, or the seeds from a watermelon, or walnuts from their shells after the initial struggle to open them, and then I had to close mine, despite my earlier resolution, what else could I do, but I tried not to cover them with my hand so that Tupra might think that I had kept them open, while Zappulla kept singing and I caught only the occasional word, '*sfortunate*,' '*mangiare*,' '*cerco*,' '*soffro*,' '*senza capire*,' '*malate*,' 'unhappy,' 'eat,' 'I seek,' 'I suffer,' 'without understanding,' 'sick,' not enough to make any sense of them, although one can always give meaning to anything, unhappy the empty sockets of my eyes, they force me to eat napkins or cloths, I seek to save myself and I suffer mutilations, without understanding the cruelty of these sick beasts . . . '*E quando son le feste di Natale,*' that didn't help in the least even though it was the longest phrase my ears had caught, because I could still hear the inhuman snorts of incredulity and despair and pain, but no screams, there could be no shouts with those checked cloths stuffed in his mouth, but at least I couldn't see, which was something, even though I was trying to make Reresby believe the opposite and possibly succeeding.

And in short, I was afraid ('O that I could forget what I have been or not remember what I must be now'). Afraid of Manoia and afraid of Tupra and also vaguely afraid of myself, because I was mixed up with them ('Yes, O that I could not remember what I must be now'). Tupra used the remote control to freeze the image, he had inoculated me with the last drop of his poison and through the eyes too, as indicated by its etymology. I knew he had stopped the film because I could no longer hear the sound. I opened my eyes, I dared to look, fortunately the film was frozen at a moment when Manoia's back was covering the face of the now blind man.

'You've seen enough,' said Tupra, 'although the scene isn't over yet: our friend heaps further insults on his victim and then slits his throat, but I'll spare you that—there's a lot of blood—just as he could have spared that man, I mean, why make someone suffer like that when you're going to kill him anyway, and only a few seconds later?' He said this in a tone of genuine perplexity and horror, and as if he had given much thought to that 'why' but never managed to get beyond it. 'I don't understand it, do you, Jack? Do you understand it, Jack?'

I had fallen silent, I preferred not to say a word for a few moments because I was afraid that if I spoke, I would crumble and my voice would shake, and I might even cry, and I couldn't let that happen under any circumstances, I wouldn't allow myself to do so in that place and at that time. I clenched my jaw and kept it clenched, and finally I felt sufficiently composed to respond with what I intended to be an imitation of sarcasm:

'You should have asked him. You missed an opportunity there. You had all night to find out.' This seemed to disconcert him slightly, he obviously hadn't been expecting such a response. I went on: 'Perhaps when he did that first thing he didn't know he was going to kill him. Maybe he hadn't yet decided. Sometimes a first punishment isn't enough to satisfy one's fury and you have to go still further. Perhaps he had no option but to kill him. For some people even that isn't enough, and they try to kill the person twice, to vainly try and kill the already dead. They mutilate the corpse or profane the tomb— they even regret having killed him because they can't now kill him again. It happened a lot during our Civil War. It happens now with ETA, for whom once isn't enough.' Then I went back to my first question: 'But why ask me, he's your friend, you should have asked him.'

Tupra lit another cigarette, I heard the sound of the lighter, I had still not turned around to face him. He stopped the DVD, got up, removed the disk, stood in front of me, holding it delicately between his fingers, and said:

'Certainly not, Manoia doesn't even know I have this video, he hasn't a clue. Well, he'll assume I have something on him, but he won't know what. And it would never occur to him that it would be this. Anyway, as you can see, I very likely saved that imbecile Garza's life. Instead of getting angry with me, you should be grateful that I took charge of his punishment, to use your word. He would never have gotten away scot-free, that's for sure.'

I had known for some time now where he was heading. 'I had to do it in order to avoid a greater evil, or so I believed; I killed one so that ten would not be killed, ten so that a hundred would not fall, a hundred in order to save a thousand,' and so on, ad infinitum, the old excuse that so many would spend centuries preparing and elaborating in their Christian and non-Christian tombs, waiting for the Judgment that never comes, and many still believe in that Judgment at the hour of their departing, certainly almost all murderers and instigators of murder throughout history. However, I wasn't concerned so much with heaping more blame on him as with holding myself together, which I was managing only with difficulty, how I would love to have appeared completely indifferent. And so I asked him a genuine question, that is, one I would have wanted to ask him anyway, when I was more myself.

'If he assumes you have something on him and you've got something like that, how come you were pussyfooting around him all evening? It looked like you were trying to placate him, not making any demands. According to what you've just told me, these videos are used above all to make it easier to wheedle concessions out of people, to blackmail them, but my impression was that you were having a hard time persuading him to do whatever it was you were trying to persuade him to do, or getting out of him what you wanted.'

Tupra looked at me in a slightly amused, slightly irritated way. I had still not moved from the ottoman, and so he was looking down on me.

'How do you know he doesn't have some footage of *us*? We could lose our advantage or it could be cancelled out.' He said 'of us,' not 'of me,' I thought that it could be footage of Rendel or Mulryan, although the latter seemed a very cautious type, and I couldn't imagine Pérez Nuix behaving like Manoia in that cowshed. Or it could be Tupra, of course, or someone above him or, rather, above us, for I, too, was 'us.' Or a compromising video of another sort, not equivalent, not comparable, not as vile, or so at least I hoped. What I had seen in that film from Sicily was utterly repellent, as were the scenes shot in Ciudad Juárez and other places, I would never be able to forget them or, better still, erase them: as if they had never existed or trod the earth or strode the world, or passed before my eyes.

'That was in Sicily, wasn't it?' I asked then, adopting a technical tone of voice, which is the most helpful when one is on the verge of collapse.

'Very good, Jack, you get better and better,' he replied and made as if to applaud me, although he couldn't do so while holding the disk in one hand and his cigarette in the other. 'How did you glean that, from the song, the language or both things?'

'Three things—there was the guy with the *lupara* as well. It wasn't that hard.' I assumed he would know that word, even if he didn't know Italian. I was wrong, and this surprised me.

'The what?'

'The *lupara*.' And I spelled it out for him. 'That's what they call that kind of double-barreled shotgun in Sicily.'

'Well, you do know a lot.' Perhaps he was bothered because I was managing to put on a semblance of composure; after spending so much time covering my eyes, he must have felt sure that I would completely fall apart when I saw the man with whom I had shared both supper and drinks, whose hand I had shaken, with whose wife I had danced, gouging out a person's eyes. And of course I had fallen apart, I was trembling inside and I wanted to get out of that room as quickly as possible, but I wasn't going to let Tupra see that, he had tormented me quite enough for one night and I wasn't prepared to give him still more pleasure. Flavia would have no inkling of her husband's sadistic side, it's astonishing how little we know the faces of those we love, today or yesterday, let alone tomorrow.

'What I'd like to know is how come there was a camera in what I assume to be a remote cowshed somewhere in the back of beyond? Isn't that rather strange?' I tried to maintain that technical tone of voice, and I was doing quite well with my efforts to pull myself together.

Tupra again looked down at me from above, more amused now than irritated.

'Yes, it would have been very strange, Jack, if the fellow with the *lupara*, you see what a quick learner I am'—he pronounced the word as if it were English, 'looparrah,' he didn't have a very good ear—'hadn't hidden it there beforehand. If they'd discovered it, he might have ended up just like the man in the chair.'

I didn't really want an answer to my next question, but I asked it purely in order to shore myself up, until the moment when I could leave, and I asked it in that same technical tone:

'You're not telling me that guy's English, are you, looking like that? You're not telling me he's our agent?' I almost said 'your,' but I corrected myself or changed my mind in time, possibly ironically, possibly because in some way it suited me.

The answer was obvious, 'What else do you think we spend our money on?' or 'Why else do we have contacts?' or 'Why else do we resort to blackmail?' but Tupra, at that late hour, wanted to draw the attention back to himself. The fact is he had been doing this intermittently all night.

'That's a big question, Jack.' He moved away from me, went to the desk from which he had taken the disk, carefully put the disk back inside, and locked the drawer with the key, the key to his treasures. Then he turned to ask me the question again, from the other side of the desk, in the near-darkness. He said it with his large mouth—with his overly soft and fleshy mouth, as lacking in consistency as it was over-endowed in breadth—at the same time blowing out smoke: 'You've had plenty of time to think about it, so answer the question I asked you in the car. Now that you've seen things you'd never seen before and, I hope, never will again. Tell me now, why, according to you, one can't go around beating people up and killing them? You've seen how much of it goes on, everywhere, and sometimes with an utter lack of concern. So explain to me why one can't.'

None of the classic responses would work with him, I had known that from the start. I hadn't expected Reresby to come back to it, although I don't know why, given that like me and like Wheeler, he never lost the thread or forgot any unresolved matter or let go of his prey if he didn't want to. I looked stupidly around me, as if I might find an answer on the walls; the room lay in semi-darkness, the lights down low. For a moment, my eyes rested on the one image, perhaps as a respite from all the others, from those I had seen on that wretched television screen and from Tupra's living image: the portrait of a British officer wearing a tie and curled mustache and a Military Cross, his hair grown into a widow's peak, his eyebrows thick and an elegiac look no doubt like mine in his eyes, and in that mournful look I saw a reflection of my own exhaustion, a look that might give me away to Tupra, despite my artificial tone of voice. I could just make out the signature on the drawing, 'E. Ken-

nington. 17,' a name I had heard in Wheeler's mouth when he spoke to me about the Careless Talk Campaign of 1917, during World War One, the war that both he and my father had experienced as children, it seemed incredible that the two of them had still not been erased from the world, that they were not safe more or less in one-eyed, uncertain oblivion as the officer in the portrait would certainly be, unless Tupra knew his identity, the killing in that conflict had been worse than in any other, I mean people were killed in the very worst of ways, with new techniques but also in hand-to-hand combat and with bayonets, and those who had fallen at the front were uncountable, or no one had dared to count them. I tried a slight diversionary tactic, playing for time:

'Who's that military gentleman?' And I pointed to the drawing.

Reresby's answer was contradictory, as if he simply wanted to get rid of the question:

'I don't know. My grandfather. I like his face.' Then he immediately returned to the matter at hand. 'Tell me why one can't.'

I didn't know what to reply, I was still very shaken, still dismayed and upset. I nevertheless said something, almost without intending to and certainly without thinking, purely in order not to remain silent:

'Because then it would be impossible for anyone to live.'

I couldn't judge the effect of these words or indeed if they had one, I never found out if he would have laughed or not, if he would have mocked them, if he would have refuted them or scornfully allowed them to fall without even bothering to pick them up, because just then, the moment after I had spoken them, I heard a woman's voice behind me:

'Who are you with, Bertie, and what are you doing? You're keeping me awake, do you know what time it is, aren't you coming to bed?'

This was said in a domestic tone of voice. I turned round. The woman had switched on the light in the corridor and her shadowy figure on the threshold was silhouetted against the brightness, she had opened the door but her face was invisible. She was wearing a transparent, ankle-length dressing gown, made of gauze or something similar, tied with a belt or else in another way caught in around the waist and the rest was loose and flimsy, at least that was my impression, her apparently naked figure could be clearly seen through the gauze, although it was unlikely she would be naked, if she had heard my voice, or our voices; she had on slippers with high slender heels, as if she were an old-fashioned model of lingerie or negligees or nightdresses, a pin-up girl from the 1950s or the early '60s, a woman from my childhood. She looked like a calendar girl. She smelled good too, a sexual smell that wafted into the room from the doorway, creating the illusion of dissipating its horrors. She didn't have an hourglass figure nor that of a Coca-Cola bottle, but very nearly, it was outlined perfectly and very attractively against the bright light behind her; she was tall and had long legs, a toboggan down which to slide, so she could have been his ex-wife Beryl, who had so inflamed and aroused De la Garza. I suddenly thought of him perhaps still lying on the floor of the handicapped toilet—less clean now—badly injured and unable to move. I felt a twinge of conscience, but I would not be the one, that night, to go and find him and see how he was, I felt shattered, drained. I'd phone the Embassy another day, someone, sooner or later, was bound to pick him up and call an ambulance. The Manoias, on the other hand, would have long since been sleeping in their beds in the Ritz, placid and reconciled, and Flavia would be satisfied and content to have enjoyed a nocturnal triumph and to have provoked an incident, although she would also have asked herself as she closed her eyes: 'Tonight, I was all right, but will I be all right tomorrow? I'll be another day older.' Whoever the woman on the threshold was, her appearance there obliged me to leave, or finally allowed me to—it didn't seem to me that Tupra was about to introduce me to her.

'Just working late with a colleague. I'll be right with you, my dear,' he said from behind the desk, and he used that rather old-fashioned term 'my dear.'

'So there was someone waiting for him, and he doesn't live alone, or at least on some nights he doesn't lack for loving company,' I thought, standing up. 'So he does have a weak point, someone at his side. And he likes the old ways, which isn't quite the same as what he calls the way of the world. Perhaps the way of the world was there in what I had seen on the screen, and in the handicapped toilet, and that's what he's just poisoned me with.'

6
Shadow

I didn't hurry, I lingered and delayed, and allowed a few months to pass before that 'other day' came when I finally decided to go in person to the Embassy to see how De la Garza was. Not that I wasn't concerned about his fate, I often pondered it with unease and sorrow, and in the days that followed that long unpleasant night, I kept an attentive eye on the London papers to see if they carried any report of the incident, but none of them picked it up, probably because Rafita hadn't reported the assault to the police. Tupra's intimidation, or mine when I translated Tupra's words giving those very precise instructions, had clearly had its effect. I also bought *El País* and *Abc* each day (the latter because it took more interest than most in the vicissitudes of diplomats, as well as those of bishops), but during the first few days nothing appeared in those either. Only after about ten days, in an article on the comparative dangers of European capitals, did *El País's* London correspondent mention in passing: 'There was some alarm among the Spanish colony in London a week or so ago when an Embassy employee was admitted to a hospital after being beaten up one night by complete strangers, for no apparent reason and in the middle of the street, according to his initial version of events. Later, he admitted that the brutal attack (which left him with many bruises and several broken ribs) had taken place in a fashionable disco and had been the result of a fight. This somewhat reassured people, since it was clearly a chance, isolated event that he possibly brought on himself and that was, at least, directed at him personally.'

It would have been impossible for De la Garza to conceal his state from superiors and colleagues, and so in order to justify being away on sick leave, he would have told that story, saying, perhaps, that some brutish louts had provoked him, or that he had acted in defense of a lady (offenders of ladies like to pass themselves off as the exact opposite: I could still remember his words 'Women are all sluts, but for looks you can't beat the Spanish'), or that someone had insulted Spain and he'd had no alternative but to get rough and come to blows, I was curious to know what fantasy he would have invented in order to emerge from the episode relatively unscathed (well, unscathed from his point of view and according to his account of things, because whoever it was had clearly thrashed him): 'Oh, they gave me a thorough pummelling, true enough, but I gave as good as I got and beat the shit out of them,' he would have crowed, still mingling coarseness with pedantry, like so many Spanish writers past and present, a veritable plague. Only the antipathy felt for him among his own circle could explain the words: 'that he possibly brought on himself,' it was a little uncalled-for, and the correspondent would doubtless have received a reprimand for his lack of objectivity. It amused me to imagine myself as a hard Mafia type, and at least I learned that Tupra had been spot on, he had diagnosed it right there, in the toilet, two broken ribs, maybe three, at most four, perhaps he was one of those men who could estimate the effect of each blow and each cut, depending on the part of the body and the force with which the blow was dealt, like surgeons or hitmen, perhaps he was experienced in this and had learned to gauge the intensity and depth and never went too far, but knew exactly how much damage he was inflicting and tried not to get carried away, unless, of course, he intended to. It would clearly be best not to get into a fight with him, a physical fight I mean.

And so I let time pass, telling myself that it would be better to phone De la Garza or to go and see him when he was more recovered and the anger and shock had subsided a little; and the fear, of course, which would be the feeling that had gone deepest. As far as I knew, he had obeyed us, Tupra and me, he had done as we said; he hadn't even gone telling tales to

Wheeler or to his father, Don Pablo, with his now waning influence. I hadn't visited Wheeler for some time, but I still spoke to him on the phone every week or every two weeks, and while these were, as almost always, delightful stimulating conversations, they were, nonetheless, fairly routine. One day, I casually mentioned Rafita and he interrupted me at once: 'Oh, haven't you heard? It was terrible, he got beaten up good and proper and is still in the hospital, I believe. I haven't heard anything from him directly, he's not yet in a state to speak to anyone, only from people at the Embassy and from his father, who flew over to London to be with him and look after him during the first few days, and since he didn't leave Rafa's bedside for a moment, he had no time to come up to Oxford, and since I never go anywhere now, we didn't see each other.' 'Good heavens, what happened?' I asked hypocritically. 'I don't know exactly,' he said. 'He must have been drunk and he has, apparently, changed his story several times, contradicting himself, he probably doesn't know what happened either or doesn't remember because he was too far gone, you've seen how fond he is of the bottle, do you remember when he was here, how he immediately bonded with Lord Rymer? He went too far with his impertinence, I imagine, with that crude and to me incomprehensible lexicon he occasionally adopts, apparently it was some compatriots of his, of yours, that is, who beat the living daylights out of him in a toilet in a disco, as if they'd been waiting there to pounce on him, it sounds like something schoolboys would do, which fits of course. But the fact is they beat him to a pulp, and there's nothing schoolboyish about that, they broke several major bones. And in a handicapped toilet of all places; that doesn't bode very well, does it?' Wheeler couldn't help seeing the comical side of almost everything and he added slightly mischievously (I could imagine the twinkle in his eyes): 'Apparently he's completely encased in plaster. When the other patients catch a glimpse of him from the corridor, they mistake him for The Mummy.' And he immediately moved on to another subject, to do with the peculiar Spanish expression he had used—*zurrarle la badana a alguien*—to beat the living daylights out of someone: 'Do you still say that in Spanish or is it very old hat now? By the way, I've never known what "*badana*" means, do you?' I realized that I hadn't the faintest idea and felt the same embarrassment I used to feel years ago when my Oxford students would confront me with their malicious questions, and I would find myself having to lie to them in class and to improvise ridiculous, false etymologies which they diligently noted down. 'It's quite common in Spanish not to know the actual meaning of what you're saying, far more so than in English or in other languages,' Sir Peter went on, 'and yet you Spaniards come out with those phrases with such pride and aplomb: for example, what the devil does "*joder la marrana*" mean? Literally. Or "*a pie juntillas*" (I've noticed that some ignorant authors write "*a pies juntillas*," and I don't know about now, but that used to be considered unacceptable)? Or "*a pie enjuto*" or "*a dos velas*" or "*caérsele los anillos*"? Why have an idiom about rings falling off when rings, if they do anything, tend, on the contrary, to get stuck. And why do you call street blocks "*manzanas*"? Apparently no one knows, I've even asked members of the Real Academia Española, but they just shrug unconcernedly and with not a flicker of embarrassment. I mean, why "apples"? It's absurd. Street blocks don't look anything like apples, even from above. And why do you make that odd gesture signifying "*a dos velas*" where you place the index and middle fingers of your right hand on either side of your nose and draw them down towards your upper lip, it's very strange, I can't see any connection at all with being down to your last two candles, which is presumably what it means. You use gestures a lot when you talk, but most of them make no sense at all, they're virtually opaque and often seem to have nothing to do with their meaning—like that one where you rest the fingers of one hand on the upright palm of the other, do you know the one I mean, I'd demonstrate it for you if you could see me, but I never see you, you hardly ever come now, is Tupra exploiting you or have you got a girlfriend? Anyway, I think it's used to indicate "Stop, don't go on" or perhaps "Let's go."'

Wheeler was tireless when it came to discussing linguistic matters and idioms, he paused and lingered over them and momentarily forgot about everything else, and, as I knew, from the days when I first taught translation and Spanish at Oxford, I was profoundly ignorant of my own language, not that it mattered much, for it's an ignorance I share with almost all my compatriots and they couldn't care less. I was beginning to think that sometimes his mind wavered slightly, rather as he occasionally lost the ability to speak. Not in the same way, he didn't go blank, not at all, and he didn't talk nonsense or get confused, but he strayed from the subject more than usual and didn't listen with his usual alacrity and attention, as if he were less interested in the external, and as if the internal were gaining ground—his disquisitions, his deliberations, his insistent thoughts—and, as is often the case with the old, perhaps his memories too, although he didn't care to tell or share these, but maybe he did go over them in his mind, put them in order, unfold them to himself, and explain and weigh them up, or perhaps it was simply a matter of putting them straight and contemplating them, like someone taking a few steps back and surveying his library or his paintings or his rows of tin soldiers if he collects them, everything he has accumulated and arranged over a lifetime, probably with no other objective—this does happen—than that of stepping back and looking at them.

This form of loquacious introspection, which I noticed when we spoke on the phone, occasionally made me fear that I didn't have much time left in which to ask him all the things I'd always wanted to ask him and which I kept postponing for reasons of discretion, respect and a dislike of worming things out of people and stealing from them what they are keeping in reserve or storing away, or of seeming overly curious or even impertinent, together with a natural tendency to wait for people to tell me only what they really want to and not what they are tempted to tell me because of a particular conversational thread or the direction a conversation is taking or because they feel flattered or moved—the temptation to tell is as strong as it is transient, and it soon vanishes if you resist it or, indeed, give in to it, except that in the latter case, there's no remedy but regret or, as the Italians put it, *rimpianto*, a kind of sorrowful regret to be ruminated upon in private. And the truth is that I wanted to ask him those things before it became problematic or impossible, I wanted to know, however briefly and anecdotally, about his involvement in the Spanish Civil War—a war that had so marked my parents—and about which I had known nothing until recently; about his adventures with MI6, his special missions in the Caribbean, West Africa, and South East Asia between 1942 and 1946, according to *Who's Who*, in Havana and in Kingston and in other unknown places, although he was still not allowed to talk about them even after sixty years nor, doubtless, after however many years of life remained to him; he would take his story to the grave if I didn't get it out of him, that Acting Lieutenant-Colonel Peter Wheeler, born in the antipodes as Rylands; about his unspoken relationship with his brother Toby, whom I had known first and admired and mourned, with no idea that they were related; as well as about his activities with the group that had no name when it was created and still has none now, nor any 'interpreters of people,' 'translators of lives' or 'anticipators of stories,' indeed, he had criticized Tupra for employing such terms in private: 'Names, nicknames, sobriquets, aliases, euphemisms are quickly taken up and, before you know it, they've stuck,' he had said, 'you find yourself always referring to things or people in the same way, and that soon becomes the name they're known by. And then there's no getting rid of it, or forgetting it'; and it was true, I couldn't forget those terms now, because I was part of that group and those were the terms I'd learned from Wheeler's diminished contemporary heirs; and I wanted to know, too, about the death of his young wife Val or Valerie, although he always preferred to leave that for another day and, besides, he believed, deep down, that one should never tell anything.

It even seemed to me—I had no proof of this, it was only a suspicion—that Wheeler might be loosening the grip of that hand that never let go of its prey, as was not yet the case with Tupra or with me or, probably, with young Pérez Nuix, all three of us were still at the restless or at least vigilant age, how long do those energetic years last, the years of anxiety and quickened pulses, the years of movement, unexpected reversals, and vertigo, the years when all of that and so much more occurs, so many doubts and torments, in which we struggle and plot and fight and try to inflict scratches on others and avoid getting scratched ourselves and to turn things to our own advantage, and when all of those activities are sometimes so very skilfully disguised as noble causes that even we, the creators of those disguises, are fooled. I mean that Wheeler was distancing himself from his machinations and his plans, at least that was the impression he gave me, as if his will and determination were finally on the wane or as if he suddenly scorned them and saw them as pointless and futile, after decades of building and cultivating and feeding them and, of course, of applying them. He was focused entirely on himself, and little else interested him. But then he was over ninety, and so this was hardly surprising or deserving of reproach, it was high time really.

And despite these warnings and my growing fear that I didn't have, as I'd always felt I had, unlimited time with him, I continued putting off my visits and my questions and still did not go and see him. I would also have liked him to tell me more about Tupra, about his antecedents, his history, his potential dangerousness, his character, the 'probabilities that ran in his veins'—he would know more about those, he had known him for longer—especially after that night of the sword and the videos, the memory of which had been bothering me for weeks and would do so indefinitely; but given that I'd decided not to leave or decamp, not yet to abandon my post and with it my work, salary and general state of confusion, perhaps I was avoiding the possibility of really finding out and—if Wheeler did as I asked him and deciphered Tupra fully—of having to stop what I had, for the moment, not without some violence to myself, determined to continue. I realized that I had reached a point when each passing day made it harder and harder for me to go back, let alone just to pack it all in and return to Madrid—doing what exactly, living how, just to be closer to Luisa as she moved further away from me?—a place which, nevertheless, I had still not entirely left. My mind was largely there, but not my body, and the latter was growing accustomed to strolling about London and breathing in its smells on waking and on going to sleep (always with one eye open, because of the lack of shutters, and like just one more inhabitant of that large island), to spending part of the day in the company of Tupra and Pérez Nuix and Mulryan and Rendel and, on occasions, Jane Treves or Branshaw, to the initially saving grace of certain routines in which, unexpectedly, you suddenly find yourself caught as in a spider's web, unable to imagine any other way of life, even if it isn't any great shakes and happened purely by chance and without your asking. No, it was no longer easy for me to think of myself taking another less comfortable and less well-paid job, less attractive and less varied, after all, each morning I was confronted by new faces or else went deeper into familiar ones, and it was a real challenge to decipher them. To guess at their probabilities, to predict their future behavior, it was almost like writing novels, or at least biographical sketches. And sometimes there were outings, on-the-spot translations and the occasional trip out of London.

And so I also kept delaying my return to Madrid, I mean, to see my children and my father and my siblings and my friends, too many months had passed without my setting foot in my own city and, therefore, without seeing or hearing Luisa, which was what most attracted and frightened me. I had told her, two days after that night when I'd phoned to consult her about botox and the blood stains left by women, that I would not be back for a while. 'The kids have been asking when you'll be coming to see them,' she had said, taking great care not to include herself and making it plain that she wasn't the one doing the asking. 'Not in the immediate future I shouldn't think,' I had replied and mentioned that I had a trip with my boss coming up, I didn't know exactly when yet, but it could be any time, so I was busy until then. And it was true, Tupra had told me this, although, in the end, he dragged me off, instead, on several different trips during that month, short hops lasting only a couple of days, three within the large island itself and one to Berlin, to the Continent. We went to Bath with Mulryan, to Edinburgh on our own and to York with Jane Treves, who, it seems, was from Yorkshire and knew the terrain, although it didn't seem to me that you needed to be an expert to find your way around those very human-sized cities. He didn't take Pérez Nuix with him, perhaps to punish her for trying to deceive him in the matter of Incompara and her poor beaten father, in which he must have considered me to be merely a naïve and secondary accomplice, or perhaps, it occurred to me, so that she and I did not end up in the same hotel: sometimes I had the feeling that there was nothing he didn't know about, and that he was therefore sure to know what had happened in my apartment, in my bed, in silence and as if it hadn't happened, on that night of constant rain.

In each of those cities we only ever had one meeting at which I could prove useful as an interpreter, of languages or people, and if Tupra saw more people, as I imagined he did, he did so on his own and never invited me to join him. In Bath, he stayed at a very fine hotel, the Royal Crescent if I remember rightly (Mulryan and I stayed in another which was pleasant rather than fine—we, after all, occupied a different place in the hierarchy), in which there lived 'on an almost permanent basis,' according to my boss, a Mexican millionaire, 'officially retired but still very active from a distance and from the shadows,' with whom he wished to come to some agreement. This elderly man—with white hair and mustache, the vestiges of what was, by then, a very precarious elegance and a resemblance to the old actor César Romero, and whose two surnames were Esperón Quigley—spoke impeccable English with a thick Spanish accent (it happens to many Latins on both sides of the Atlantic), and my help was only necessary on a few occasions, when the gentleman's diction proved so opaque to the purely English ear of Tupra and to the half-Irish ear of Mulryan that perfectly correct words became completely unrecognizable in Esperón Quigley's eccentric pronunciation. As usual, I paid no attention to what they were discussing, it was no business of mine, I was bored by it a priori and preferred not to know. The rest of the time I was free, and I spent it walking, looking at the River Avon, visiting the Roman baths and a few antique shops, and rereading Jane Austen in a place where she had spent a few years of scant literary productivity, as well as the odd page by William Beckford, who'd shut himself away there for a long time and where he reluctantly lived and died, far from his beloved Fonthill Abbey, which had led him to his ruin. On one of my strolls about the city, I was amazed to come across a shop, a rather average jeweler's, which, implausibly, bore the name of Tupra. It wasn't far from another shop with larger pretensions and which, if memory serves me right, declared itself in its window to be a supplier to the Admiralty (I imagine this referred only to watches, and not to precious stones and glass beads for the navy). When I mentioned this coincidence to Tupra, he replied tartly:

'Oh, yes, I know. Nothing to do with my family though. No relation at all. None.' This might have been true or totally false, and the watchmaker might have been his father. However, I didn't dare press the matter further.

Even so, I couldn't resist making a private joke:

'Nevertheless, it would be more appropriate for Tupra's jeweler's shop to be made supplier to the Admiralty rather than that other shop nearby which, I noticed, lays claim to just that. Even if only because of your connections, or, rather, our connections with the former OIC, don't you think?' I remembered what Wheeler had said that Sunday before lunch, in Oxford, when he spoke to me about the difficulties they'd had recruiting the first members of the group, just after it had been formed: 'It was necessary to comb the country for recruits as quickly as possible. Most came from the Secret Services, from the Army, a few from the former OIC, which you've probably never heard of, the Navy's Operational Intelligence Centre, there weren't many of them, but they were very good, possibly the best; and, of course, from our Universities.' And I saw a look of surprise and slight suspicion appear on Tupra's face (as if hearing that old acronym in my mouth—an odd thing for a twenty-first- or even late-twentieth-century Spaniard to know—made him wonder what else I knew and if he had underestimated how much I had learned).

He also allowed me some free time during the two days we spent in Edinburgh, and there, too, I walked and reread the work of two of that city's finest sons, Conan Doyle and Stevenson, just a few of their stories, and climbed up Calton Hill to see the view which so enthused the latter, and which is still astonishing even after all the time that has passed. I also took away with me a few poems by Stevenson and a little book about the city, subtitled *Picturesque Notes* and published in 1879 no less. In it he talks about Greyfriars, telling of how, close to this verdant cemetery, from the window of a house since demolished, but whose site was pointed out to him by a grave-digger, the body-snatcher Burke used to keep watch, for he and his mate Hare would disinter the still-fresh bodies from their graves in order to sell them to scientists and anatomists, and had eventually taken to murdering people so as to speed up the process and to prevent business from falling off: 'Burke, the resurrection man,' as Stevenson noted with irony, 'infamous for so many murders at five shillings a head, used to sit thereat, with pipe and nightcap, to watch burials going forward on the green.' Now there, I thought, was a man who lacked the patience to wait for tomorrow's faces to be revealed to him, no, he preferred to sit, smoking, and watch them file past, as they had been yesterday and would be always.

And on the train journey up to Edinburgh, the two of us alone, I read out to Tupra some lines that Stevenson had written towards the end of his life in the South Seas, in Apemama, lines filled by a strange and yet very real nostalgia for 'our scowling town': 'The belching winter wind, the missile rain, the rare and welcome silence of the snows, the laggard morn, the haggard day, the night, the grimy spell of the nocturnal town, do you remember? Ah, could one forget!' he wrote, genuinely nostalgic for that desolate scene. And further on, he added: 'When the lamp from my expiring eyes shall dwindle and recede, the voice of love fall insignificant on my closing ears, what sound shall come but the old cry of the wind in our inclement city? What return but the image of the emptiness of youth, filled with the sound of footsteps and that voice of discontent and rapture and despair?' Another poem is infused with the same spirit, scorning the warm distant seas he had so diligently sought out and yearning terribly for the 'inclement city' of Edinburgh: 'A sea uncharted, on a lampless isle, environs and confines their wandering child in vain. The voice of generations dead summons me, sitting distant, to arise, my numerous footsteps nimbly to retrace, and all mutation over, stretch me down in that denoted city of the dead.' And so I read him those lines, in his language of course, in the language of Tupra and of the lines themselves: 'The belching winter wind, the missile rain, the rare and welcome silence of the snows, the laggard morn, the haggard day, the night . . .'

'Do you think that always happens, Bertram?' I asked; he was sitting opposite me, with him facing the engine and me with my back to it. 'You know a lot about deaths,' I added somewhat cruelly, 'do you think that, in the end, we all turn to that first place, however humble or depressing or gloomy it was, however much our life has changed and our affections have been transformed, however many unimaginable fortunes and achievements we have amassed along the way? Do you think that we always look back at our earlier poverty, at the impoverished quarter we grew up in, at the small provincial town or dying village from which we peered out at the rest of the world, and which for so many years it seemed impossible to leave, and that we miss it? They say that the very old remember their childhood most clearly of all and almost shut themselves away in it, mentally I mean, and that they have a sense that everything that happened between that distant time and their present decline, their greeds and their passions, their battles and their setbacks, was all false, an accumulation of distractions and mistakes and of tremendous efforts to achieve things that really weren't important; and they wonder then if everything hasn't been an interminable detour, a pointless voyage, all merely to return to the essence, to the origin, to the only thing that truly counts at the end of the day.'—And I thought then: 'Why all that conflict and struggle, why did they fight instead of just looking and staying still, why were they unable to meet or to go on seeing each other, and why so much sleep, so many dreams, and why that scratch, my pain, my word, your fever, and all those doubts, all that torment?'—'You must know a lot about that, you must have seen many people die. And you can see how it was with Stevenson: he traveled halfway around the world and yet in the end, in Polynesia, there he was thinking only of the city where he was born. Look how this one begins: 'The tropics vanish, and meseems that I, from Halkerside, from topmost Allermuir, or steep Caerketton, dreaming gaze again . . .'

'Those are hills close to Edinburgh,' Tupra said, interrupting me as if he were a footnote, and then fell silent again. I waited for him to reply to my questions and for him to add something more. I hadn't read those lines to him purely for pleasure or to pass the time. I had mentioned impoverished quarters and provincial towns trusting that he might take the hint and think of Bethnal Green, if that's where he came from, or of the watchmaker of Bath, if he had spent part of his childhood with him, for example, and that he might tell me a little about them. Tupra, however, as I should have known, only answered the questions he wanted to answer. 'As I remember,' he said after a few seconds, 'Stevenson went to Samoa chiefly for his health's sake, not in search of adventures. Besides, he wasn't old. He died when he was forty-four.'

'That doesn't matter,' I said. 'When he wrote those poems, he must have known that the end was not far off, and all he could think about, with enormous nostalgia, was the inhospitable city of his childhood. Listen to what he says: "When . . . the voice of love fall insignificant on my closing ears . . ." You see, not even having his wife near will count for much, or so he imagines, in his final consciousness of the world, in his final seconds, only those momentary pictures from the past that "gleam and fade and perish." He set this out clearly in the closing lines: "These shall I remember, and then all forget," that's what he says.'

Tupra remained thoughtful for a while. I know from experience that no one can resist analyzing texts.

'How can that be? Read me the bit about insignificant love again.'

And I did:

'When . . . the voice of love fall insignificant on my closing ears . . .'

'Nonsense,' said Tupra, again cutting me off. 'Nonsense. That's not Stevenson at his best. Poetry wasn't his forte really.' He fell silent again, as if to underline his verdict, and then, to my surprise, added: 'Read me a bit more, go on.'

Almost everyone likes being read to. And so I did:

'Far set in fields and woods, the town I see spring gallant from the shallows of her smoke, cragg'd, spired, and turreted, her virgin fort beflagg'd.' And as I read I stole occasional glances at Tupra and saw that he was enjoying it, even though he didn't like Stevenson's poetry. 'There, on the sunny frontage of a hill, hard by the house of kings, repose the dead, my dead, the ready and the strong of word. Their works, the salt-encrusted, still survive; the sea bombards their founded towers; the night thrills pierced with their strong lamps. The artificers, one after one, here in this grated cell, where the rain erases and the rust consumes, fell upon lasting silence.'

Who knows, perhaps no one had read to him since he was a child.

There in Edinburgh, by the Firth of Forth, to the south of Fife, Tupra only required my services on one night, for another supper -*cum*-celebrities or -*cum*-buffoons, which was also a supper-*cum*-Dick Dearlove, that is, the global singer to whom I've chosen to give that name. Fortunately, Tupra did not also oblige me to go to the concert Dearlove was giving at the Festival beforehand, although he did force me to pretend that I'd watched the concert from the first chord to the last with indescribable enthusiasm: 'Remember to mention his fantastic renditions of "Peanuts from Heaven" and the miraculous "Bouncing Bowels," he always comes up with strange new versions, and they sound different every time, even though they're two of his all-time classics,' he warned me, just in case anyone or even Dearlove himself should ask, for Tupra had engineered things so that I would be sitting near the singer. 'On the pretext of entertaining those two compatriots of yours who are often in his entourage now, try to get him talking, even at the risk of appearing nosy and boring, the worst that can happen is that he'll ignore you or change places to avoid you. Talk to him about the tremendous success he enjoys in Spain, but, whatever you do, don't say "especially in the Basque Country": even though that's true, it might offend him, as being too local, too limited. Get his attention, charm him, encourage him to confide in you, draw him out as much as you can on his supposed role as a universal sex symbol wherever he goes, or so he believes. Make him feel flattered and in the mood to boast, invent Spanish people you know who've got the hots for him, who would love to get their hands on his basket, acquaintances of yours, real people, anything to inflame his imagination, any young things you happen to know, your own children perhaps, how old *are* they, oh no, they're far too young, well, then, your nephews and nieces, whoever, but probe him to see what you can get out of him, he's always exhausted after a performance, but euphoric too, his guard's down, and he's eager to talk, what with all the excitement and the acclaim plus whatever he took before the concert to cope with the whole insane affair, I'm surprised he's lasted this long really, after all these years of supercharged love-fests. He knows me too well, but with a stranger he'll never see again (I don't think he remembers you from last time), with someone like you, he might reveal much more than he would to me or to some other Englishman, he'll feel less vulnerable, besides, stars love to show off to newcomers, they're always in need of a fresh influx of the easily impressed. With luck he'll describe an affair he's had, some striking sexual triumph, some exploit, anyway, that's the route you need to pursue, even if it seems impertinent—as I say, the worst that can happen is that he'll turn his back on you and refuse to take the bait. Let's see if we can get some confirmation, a clearer idea, of just how capable he is or would be of endangering the way people see him and his life, to what extent he would risk exposing himself to that narrative horror of yours and end up swelling the ranks of the Kennedy-Mansfield fraternity, from which there is no possible escape.' That's how Tupra often spoke, especially when he was giving us instructions or asking us to do something, with that mixture of colloquialisms and old-fashioned turns of phrase, some peculiar to him alone, as if he brought together in his speech his probable origins in some slum and his undoubted Oxford education as a medievalist under the tutelage of Toby Rylands, of which I frequently had to remind myself, or was it just that the figure of Toby was gradually fading from my mind, absorbed by that of his brother Peter, sometimes the living do incorporate or embrace or superimpose themselves on the dead to whom they were close, and even cancel them out.

I felt that what Tupra was asking was an impossible enterprise: to get Dick Dearlove to talk to me in those terms, and about such things, much less with other people around, at a supper for twenty or more guests, all gazing at him reverently. Nevertheless, I had a go; Tupra was determined that I should get results. He placed me almost opposite the idol, and while the people on either side tried to capture his attention through flattery, I managed to slip in a few remarks that aroused his curiosity, more because of their peculiarly Spanish nature than because of me.

'Why are the Spanish so sexually permissive?' he asked after a brief exchange of comments on customs and laws. 'For a long time we always had exactly the opposite impression.'

'And your impression was correct,' I replied, and in order to see if I could get anything more out of him, I refrained from saying that his current impression was also correct, and said instead: 'Why do *you* think we're so permissive now, Mr. Dearlove?'

'Oh, please, call me Dick,' he said at once. 'Everyone does, and with good reason too.' And he gave a rather weary laugh, which his neighbors echoed. I assumed this was a joke he had made thousands of times during a lifetime of being lauded and idolized (but there's always someone who hasn't heard it, and he was aware of this, that nothing has ever been entirely wrung dry, however hard you squeeze it), punning crudely on one of the meanings of the word 'dick,' which is, of course, '*polla*.' He was, after all, famous for his hypersexuality or pansexuality or heptasexuality or whatever it was, although he never acknowledged this in public, that is, in the press. 'Well, I don't know what kind of life you lead in your country,' he said paternalistically, 'but you're obviously missing out. Whenever I've been on tour there, I haven't had the energy or the time to meet the enormous demand. Everyone seems to be up for a roll in the hay, women, men, even children it seems.' And he gave a slightly less time-worn guffaw. 'With the exception of the Basque Country, where they don't seem to know about sex or else restrict themselves to performing only a pale imitation of it because they've heard about it in other places, but in the rest of Spain, I've had to hold auditions to choose who to invite into my bed, or my bathroom if it's just for a quickie, because there's so much on offer after each concert, and beforehand too: lines have formed in hotel lobbies for a chance to come up to my room for a while, and I've nearly always found it worth interrupting my well-earned rest. They're much more ardent than they are here, and much easier too; incredible though it may seem, people are more chaste in Great Britain, though the Irish are as prim as the Basques.' Suddenly, it bothered me that he should speak of my compatriots in these terms, in that offhand manner, like sex-mad hordes. It bothered me to think that this famous fool should take young women and young men to his bed—through no merit of his own and with no effort—in Barcelona, Gijón, Madrid or Seville or wherever, each time he set foot in Spain, and he'd given quite a few concerts there over the years. I was even glad to hear that he'd had a harder time of it in San Sebastián and Bilbao, that was some consolation; and when I noticed this puerile idiotic reaction of mine, I realized that we never entirely free ourselves from patriotism, it all depends on the circumstances and where we're from and who's speaking to us, for some vestige, some remnant, to burst to the surface. I can think and say dreadful things about my country, which, personally, I consider now completely debased and coarsened in far too many respects, but if I hear those criticisms in the mouth of a despicable fatuous foreigner, I feel a strange, almost inexplicable pang, something similar to what that primitive creature De la Garza must have felt when he saw that I was not prepared to defend him from the sword-wielding Englishman who was about to decapitate him, and he perhaps considered squealing on me to the Judge later on 'when all those legs and arms and heads, chopped off in battle, shall join together at the latter day, and cry all, "We died at such a place,"' at the end of the uncountable centuries: 'This man killed me with a sword and cut me in two, and this other man was there, he saw it all and didn't lift a finger; and the man who watched and did nothing spoke my language and we were both from the same land, further south, not so very far away, albeit separated by the sea; he just stood there like a statue, his face frozen in horror, a guy from Madrid, can you believe it, a fellow Spaniard, one of us, and he didn't even try to grab the other guy's arm.' It does make it worse being from the same country, and that's how I always felt when my father told me terrible tales from our own War: they were both from the same country, the militiawoman and the child whose head she smashed against the wall of a fourth-floor apartment on the corner of Alcalá and Velázquez, so were Emilio Marés and the men who baited him like a bull in Ronda, and even more so the man from Málaga in the red beret who killed him, gave him the coup de grâce, and then couldn't resist castrating him too. Del Real the traitor and my father were, as was Santa Olalla, the professor who contributed his weightier and more authoritative signature to the formal complaint, and even that novelist who enjoyed a certain degree of tawdry commercial success, Darío Flórez, who appeared as witness for the prosecution and delivered that sinister warning to the betrayed man via my mother, when she wasn't yet my or anyone else's mother: 'If Deza forgets that he ever had a career, he'll live; otherwise, we'll destroy him.' For me they had always been the names of treachery, which should never be protected, and they were traitors because they all came from the same country, my father and them and, in two of the cases, because they had been friends before and he had never given them any reason to withdraw or cancel their friendship, on the contrary.

I brushed aside my absurd feelings of bruised patriotism. I had to—not only to carry out my assignment from Tupra (broaching the subject had been much easier than expected; and I could see my boss's grey eyes in the distance, near the head of the table, observing me, intrigued, wondering how I was getting on), but also because there was no sense in clinging on to bruises. Dearlove's comments could have been made by a compatriot of mine, De la Garza to look no further, had he been a pop idol and able to choose on tour from among dozens of girls to sleep with, and I would have been equally put out by such arrogant and disrespectful comments. And yet, and yet . . . there was an added bitterness, I could not deny it, something irrational, disquieting, disagreeable, atavistic. Perhaps Tupra felt the same when, in his presence, people spoke scornfully of Great Britain or of the British, especially when those people were from the Continent or from across the Atlantic or from the green isle of Erin, where such talk is almost the norm. And perhaps for that reason, which would be logical, he had no hesitation in doing what he did, possibly with more dedication and diligence than I thought, and perhaps it was true what he had said to me shortly after we met, albeit tempered with a touch of cynicism: 'Even serving my country, one should if one can, don't you think, even if the service one does is indirect . . .' I understood then, rather late, that he probably served his country ceaselessly as long as it was in his own best interests, and that in time of need, in time of war, or when the moment came, I would be no more to him than another useless Spaniard whom he wouldn't hesitate to have shot, just as, during my burst of patriotic feeling, Dearlove had been for me merely a conceited English bastard I'd happily have slapped.

One of the other guests nearby, a designer of extravagant clothes who was getting on in years (she herself was wearing an incomprehensible jumble of petticoats, feathers and rags) unwittingly gave me a helping hand in keeping that conversation going along the path that most suited me:

'Really?' she said. 'And there I was thinking that it was only in Britain that everyone found you irresistible, Dickie, but it turns out that it's Spain where you've got both bed and bathroom jam-packed.' She used that expression 'jam-packed'—'*de bote en bote*' or '*a reventar*' in Spanish.

It was clear that they were friends and knew each other well, or perhaps Dick Dearlove (as also seemed to be the case) spoke openly to almost anyone about even the most intimate things, to me for example; this often happens with the very famous and the constantly praised, they end up thinking that anything they say or do will be well received because it's all part of their ongoing performance, and there comes a point when they can no longer distinguish between public and private (unless there's a photographer or a journalist around, and then they're either more discreet or more exhibitionist depending on the circumstances): if they're so warmly applauded in the first sphere, and so spoiled, why shouldn't they be equally so in the second, given that in both spheres they are the undisputed protagonists every day of their life until the end?

'As you know better than I do, Viva, even though you're a woman,' replied Dick Dearlove, in a tone that was half-ironic and half-regretful, 'at our age, however famous we might be, and I'm much more famous than you are, there are occasions when we have no option but to pay, cash or in kind. There's a certain kind of particularly tasty morsel that I almost always have to pay for here in Britain, I hardly ever get it for free now, although just a few years ago I still did, half the nation has turned into a load of tight-asses; whereas in Spain, you see, I've never had to spend a euro, it's as if the young people in Spain aren't really so interested in the act itself—at my age I'm hardly going to boast about my performance, I mean, my body can no longer keep up with my imagination—that's indefatigable, in fact I rather wish my mind would slow down a bit, oh, if only the two things were more compatible, it's all very badly thought out, at least in my view—no, people are more interested in being able to tell their friends afterwards, or spill the beans on some TV program. It's extraordinary how much people there experience things not because they really want to, it seems, but simply in order to talk about it afterwards, it's a country that really revels in gossip and boasting, isn't it, a country very given to tattle-tales—and ab-solutely shameless about it.'—These rhetorical questions were directed at me, as someone who knew the territory.—'Everyone tells everything and asks everything, it cracks me up at press con-ferences and interviews, dodging questions, they're so coarse and brazen and have no sense of shame at all, which is unheard of in a European country. I've fucked a few Spaniards who I could see were simply desperate to get it over with, not because they weren't having a reasonably good time—I haven't entirely lost my touch, you know—but because they couldn't wait to leave and spread the news, I can imagine them striding proudly into their local bar or into school the next day: "I bet you can't guess who's just had me good and hard and every which way too."' He paused for a moment and smiled rather dreamily, as if he had found the situation so amusing that he was able to retrieve it intact years later, in the middle of a post-concert supper in Edinburgh. But also as if he were recalling something from the past, something lost that might never return. 'I don't know if their friends will believe them, they might not prove that easy to convince, and that could become a problem, because some of them come along now armed with their digital camera or their cell phone, I'm sure they want photographic evidence, although they all say it's because they don't go anywhere without them, so they have to be frisked before I let them in, it would be no joke being photographed in the act. Anyway, now I routinely check them out, I've got one of those gadgets they have at airports, you know a sort of wand-like thing—I touch them up with it in the process, which they love and which makes them laugh like crazy, and you get an idea of what to expect too, although they're all usually pretty well-endowed. And they let you do this, meek as lambs, just to get into your bedroom. In Britain, though, they're much less compliant and less fun too, they don't try to sneak in cameras or anything, but that's the downside: it's not that big a deal, going and telling someone else and boasting about it, though maybe people here have just grown tired of me. That's partly why I have to pay probably, you know how word gets around, and they know I'm a soft touch and that they'll be able to get some money out of me. But sometimes you don't get much even when you pay, we're easy prey—eh, Viva?—in our beloved England, Scotland and Wales. Now don't go depressing me by telling me that you're doing just fine.'

I was the one who was getting depressed. Dick Dearlove was over fifty now, and although he was still extremely famous, he wasn't as famous as he had been at the peak of his career. His concerts were still packed and wildly successful, but perhaps more because of his name and his history than because of his present-day powers, the common fate of most of the enduring British singers from the 1970s and 1980s who continue to per-form, from Elton John to Rod Stewart and the Rolling Stones. Dearlove wore his hair pathetically long for a man his age, very blonde and curly, he looked like a former member of Led Zep-pelin or King Crimson or Emerson, Lake & Palmer who, thirty years on, was trying to preserve, unchanged, his perennially youthful appearance. From behind, with that almost frizzy mop of hair, he could easily be mistaken for Olivia Newton-John at the end of *Grease*, except that if he turned around or offered his profile, his features were the very opposite of that sweet young Australian or New Zealander or whatever she was: his nose, while still aquiline, had become sharper and more prominent rather than more hooked, growing along the horizontal plane only; his eyes, which had always been small, seemed much bigger, but in a rather strange and creepy way, as if he had managed to emphasize them by resorting to the drastic method of shaving off his eyelashes or having his eyelids surgically reduced or some such barbarity; and his evident efforts not to put on weight had had the unfortunate consequence of leaving him with a scraggy neck and deep lines on cheeks, chin and forehead (perhaps his most recent dose of botox had worn off), and yet these efforts had not, on the other hand, prevented a slight paunch developing in the middle of an otherwise thin and toned body. None of this was apparent from a distance, when he was writhing around on stage, but it became so as soon as he stepped off the stage or in the close-ups on the giant screens, of which there were not that many. He had moved his chair away from the table and was now sitting sideways on so as to be face to face with the designer Genevieve Seabrook and had crossed his extremely long legs, so that I could see with surprise and dismay that he had, at some point, beslippered himself, that is, on the way to the restaurant, he had discarded his trademark musketeer boots—he wore them at every performance and had done so for three decades or more, even in hot weather—and had put on a pair of ridiculous gold and black slippers with a curved pointed toe (his bare heels, I observed queasily, were tattooed), which lent him a domestic or almost summery air that only added to my depression. He seemed as much of a buffoon as the first time I met him and even more repellent, but I also felt very slightly sorry for him because of the candor with which he acknowledged his current amatorial difficulties, having no option now but to chip in some money, at least when it came to his British encounters with those 'tasty morsels.' I hoped not to find out just how tasty they could be during what remained of that aberrant conversation, I certainly didn't intend to investigate further despite being charged by Tupra with that depressing mission. Indeed, I decided not to ask or enquire anything further of Dearlove (after all, I had little opportunity with so many other guests around, admiring, sycophantic and even extremely famous in their own right), what I had heard would be quite enough for me to write a brief report, and I could always invent the rest if Ure insisted or demanded more of me (it occurred to me that Tupra would tend to call himself Ure in Scotland, or perhaps he would prefer to be known as Dundas in Edinburgh).

'No, I won't do that, dear Dickie,' replied Viva Seabrook with a smile that was as affectionate as it was mischievous, at least insofar as I could ascertain, the layers of lurid makeup she applied must have been as thick as an Egyptian, by which I mean a Pharaoh's, death mask. 'You must bear in mind that very young boys will do almost anything as long as they get to dip their wick in some woman. So I'm lucky that way, although they do sometimes cover my face with the sheet or even with my own skirt and that does make me feel pretty bad. Well, not so much now, but the first time one of them stuck a pillow over my face, I hit the roof, and the boy fled, terrified by my insults and cursing. I consider myself rather attractive, but naturally they might associate me with their mothers or their aunts, and that could be a bit of a turn-off and, generally speaking, they're so primitive, so utterly heartless and brutal . . . Well, you know what I mean.'

I found it odd that she, too, should speak so bluntly in front of a complete stranger like me. Perhaps the milieu and their vanity spurred them on; perhaps they didn't notice the people around them, as if only the very famous really connected with each other, and the rest of the world was just a mist that didn't matter or counted only as an audience or a claque who might cheer and applaud, or, in the worst case, maintain a respectful or constrained silence and, as if sitting in the dark of a theater, merely listen to this celebrity dialogue. In a sense, it was as if they were there all alone, just the two of them. And what Dearlove said in reply, having first rested his curls for a few moments on

Seabrook's vast decolletage, as if seeking consolation or refuge in the bosom of an old friend, confirmed me in that impression:

'Oh, Viva, how much longer have we got, how much longer have I got? A day will come when I'll be nothing but a memory for the elderly, and that memory will gradually fade as those who keep it alive all die, one after the other—with the number of those who remember me steadily decreasing, with no chance of it ever increasing—after it had been constantly growing for years and years, that's what I can't bear. It's not just that I will grow old and disappear, it's that everyone who might talk about me will gradually disappear too, those who have seen me and heard me and those who have slept with me, however youthful they were at the time, they'll become old and fat and will die too, as if they're all under some kind of curse. It's unlikely that my songs will survive and that future generations will continue to hear them—what will become of my songs when I'm no longer here to defend and repeat them, when I'm no longer up to performing concerts like tonight's? They'll never be played again. I've hardly written a thing in the last fifteen years, great tunes that others might rediscover and sing tomorrow, even if they're in ghastly new versions; I no longer have the energy to sit down and write new ones. Besides, I doubt I could come up with anything very memorable.' And he added disconcertingly. 'I mean if not even Lennon and McCartney have managed to write anything for ages and ages now, how could I? I'll be entirely forgotten, Viva. Not a trace of me will be left.'

There was something rather theatrical about his tone of voice and about the gestures that accompanied these laments, but it was clear that they contained some truth as well. He again stretched his legs, and I leaned forward a little to get a better look at those hideous ink-daubed heels of his, I felt curious to know what design or motto he'd had tattooed on his skin.

'But John Lennon has been dead for thirty years,' I couldn't help saying. 'How the hell *could* he compose anything?'

'That doesn't matter,' Dearlove responded sharply. 'He wasn't much good anyway. If someone hadn't shot him, his songs would probably make people nowadays throw up.'—'Another candidate for the Kennedy-Mansfield brotherhood,' I thought.—'Such a wet, pretentious git, and he couldn't sing either.'—And he shot me a fulminating glance with his once small and now unnaturally large eyes with their cropped lids, as if I were a staunch defender of Lennon, which I never have been and never will be. I rather agreed with former dentist Dearlove's diagnosis, but telling him so would have seemed like the lowest form of sycophancy.

At least my imprudent intervention had the virtue of briefly angering him, that is, of enlivening and rescuing him from the melancholy state into which he had subsided, and during the rest of supper he was once again a jolly man making rather inopportune jokes that verged on the tedious. I spent most of the time in silence, now and then attempting to lean over discreetly and crane my neck so as to read his heels, but without success.

Later on, thoroughly fed up, I gave Ure or Dundas the shortest possible report:

'I can confirm everything I told you before, but with this one amendment: he is so concerned about his posterity that, who knows, he might one day commit some atrocity in order to be remembered just for that. He doesn't believe that his music will last any longer than he will. So, in a moment of desperation, far from avoiding such a blot at all costs, he might very well blot his own life and thus deliberately enter the ranks of the Kennedy-Mansfield clan, as you call them. However, this would have to be while he was in the grip of a deep depression or else confused, or in a few years' time when he's retired and no longer gives concerts or enjoys the protective adoration of the crowd. He's so focused on himself that he sees it as some kind of unfair curse that those who admire him and have met him should die, as if this were something that didn't touch and wasn't shared by all those who have trod the earth or strode the world.' And I added at once: 'Listen, you know him better than I do, what is it he has tattooed on the heels of his feet?' I thought it best to formulate the question in this rather absurd way, because, in English, 'heel' can also mean the heel of a shoe.

Tupra, however, ignored me. He wasn't satisfied and I had to recount every last sentence exchanged over supper, by Dearlove, by Viva Seabrook, by my show-business compatriot who had been sitting near us and by anyone else who had made a contribution, however minimal, to the conversation. I loathed having scrupulously to reproduce these dialogues and being forced to relive them. I felt like those vacuous diary writers recording their mean little lives in great detail and then publishing them, to the tedium of unwary readers or perhaps readers who are equally mean and vacuous.

Why he took me with him to York, I don't know. We walked a long way around the very long wall surrounding the city, as if we were two sentinels or two princes. He wanted us to drive out to the neighboring village of Coxwold, where, two and half centuries before, the writer Laurence Sterne had his home in Shandy Hall, named in honor of his most important novel, *Tristram Shandy*. I attributed Tupra's interest to the influence of Toby Rylands, who, when I knew him, had already spent years working on 'the best book ever written,' as Rylands told me once—not so much immodestly as with conviction—about Sterne's other major work, *A Sentimental Journey*; as if Tupra wanted in this way to pay homage to his former teacher at Oxford or at MI6 or both, and I had nothing against the idea, on the contrary, and besides who was I to object? Nevertheless, as soon as we arrived, he sought out the man in charge of that house-*cum*-museum, a man younger than either of us, and whom he introduced to me with the unlikely name of Mr. Wildgust before shutting himself up with him in his office, having first urged me to have a look around the house and garden on my own. In each room of that pleasant, peaceful, two-storey mansion was an elderly man or woman—volunteers, doubtless retired people—who, whether you wanted them to or not, provided you, the visitor, with extensive information about the life and habits of its eighteenth-century owner and about the renovation work carried out on the mansion, both in the days of a certain Mr. Monkman, revered founder of the Laurence Sterne Trust (I gladly made a small contribution to the cause) and now. In the spacious garden I did something that is probably punishable by law: I uprooted a tiny plant, which I concealed and kept moist for the rest of the trip, and later, in London, with barely any care or effort on my part, it grew into a plant of extraordinary lushness and vigor, although I never discovered its name, in English or in Spanish (I was thrilled to have carried off and preserved some living thing from the garden of the Shandy family). Tupra didn't bother to visit the house, he had done so before, he said, and this was doubtless true. After an hour, he reappeared with Wildgust, a semi-youth of an affable, innocent, jolly appearance, with glasses and rather long fair hair, and we returned to York, where Tupra may have met up with someone else, but I did not. He didn't ask me to provide him with an interpretation of anyone or an opinion on anything, not even on Sterne or York's endless city wall or Shandy Hall.

It was hard to believe that such a practical man as Tupra would have anything but a professional relationship with Coxwold or with Mr. Wildgust, and it was equally hard to imagine why he would go and see the latter in person or of what possible use he could be to him, a mere employee leading an apparently contemplative life—he obviously didn't have much to do: when we arrived, he was immersed in reading a novel at the stall selling souvenirs and postcards, with not a customer in sight—stranded in a Yorkshire village where, in his day, the worldly, irreverent and not very vocational Reverend Sterne had been appointed curate. Nor was it easy to comprehend what business he might have with the Berlin shoemaker whom we visited in a tiny elegant shop called Von T (bespoke shoes for gentlemen), on the one occasion when we traveled to the Continent, shortly after these other trips on the large island. To be sure, Reresby did try on and buy some shoes, and it was at Tupra's urging that Herr Von Truschinsky of Bleibtreustrasse, using beautiful hand-crafted wooden tools the like of which I had never seen before, took the exact and complete measurements of my two feet—length and width, height, instep and tattooable heel—in the confident belief, he said with modesty and tact and in excellent English, that I would be pleased and inspired enough to follow my boss's example and order more pairs in future, from England or from

Spain, and the truth is that, despite the high prices, I bought two pairs, with excellent results and a consequent improvement to my appearance at ground level. (And to think that I had once feared that Tupra might wear boots or clogs or worse, if there is anything worse.) The odd thing is that the shoes bought by Reresby and myself were both English brands I had never heard of before—perhaps because they were so exquisite—Edward Green of Northampton, established 1890, and Grenson, from I don't know where, established 1866. It seemed somewhat extravagant to travel to Berlin in order to get them—Tupra chose two models, one called Hythe and the other Elmsley, the first in 'Chestnut Antique' and the second in 'Burnt Pine Antique,' and I chose Windermere in 'Black' and Berkeley in 'Tobacco Suede'—instead of buying them in our own country, that is in Tupra's country in which I was living at the time. After the measuring ceremony, carried out with extreme delicacy and care by the owner and sole employee, Tupra went into the back of the shop with Von Truschinsky and they conversed behind the curtain for about fifteen minutes, while I amused myself looking through catalogues of fine shoes, which is why I know so much about the actual names of the colors and why some of the shoes I wear now were created by the superlative John Hlustik, which did not mean much to me at the time, but sounded important and Czech. The murmur that reached me was not English, but neither did I have the impression that it was German.

As in York, Tupra didn't require me to interpret anyone in Berlin or to meet anyone else. He left me free to do as I pleased and did not invite me to a supper he attended with people from the city. On the flight back, I thought he would at least ask me for my necessarily superficial opinion of the shoemaker and, perhaps belatedly, of Mr. Wildgust, even though I hadn't been present for a substantial part of either conversation. But since, after an hour of discomfort in the air, Tupra was still talking to me only about horse-racing and soccer (he was infuriated by the unnatural Russian wealth and Lusitanian antipathy of the soccer team he had supported all his life, Chelsea), I couldn't resist asking him:

'Just out of curiosity, what language were you and Mr. Von Truschinsky speaking when you and he were alone?'

He looked at me with such an accomplished show of surprise that I even thought it might be real.

'What language would we be speaking? English, of course. The same language in which I was speaking to you. Why would I change? Besides, I hardly know any German.'

It wasn't true that they had been speaking in English, but I didn't want to argue. So I changed the subject, or perhaps not that much:

'Listen, Bertram, I can understand why you asked me to accompany you to Bath and Edinburgh, and I hope I proved useful to you there. But I can't understand why you wanted me to go with you to York nor why I came to Berlin. You didn't set me any task, and I can't see what use I was. And don't tell me that it was to keep you company, that you don't like traveling alone. In York, you had the company of Jane, although in the end we hardly made use of her at all.' Jane Treves hadn't been part of the excursion to Coxwold nor had she walked for a long time around the medieval city wall. We had merely had supper with her. It could be, why not, that he had made use of her and that she had slept in his room.

'She was very busy seeing relatives. I included her in the trip more than anything so that she would have the chance to see them. She hasn't visited them for ages. I'm very pleased with her work. She's hardly stopped lately.'

'And yet, on the other hand, with all these short trips, you're forcing me to postpone my journey to Madrid. You may not realize it, but it's been ages since I saw my kids; I'll hardly recognize them. Or my father. My father's very old, you know, he's only a year younger than Peter. Sometimes I'm afraid I won't see him again.' And here I did insist. 'Why did you ask me to come with you to Berlin? To buy shoes? To renew my footwear?'

Tupra smiled with his thick lips that hardly grew any thinner when stretched.

'I wanted to introduce you to Clemens von T, he's an old friend of mine now and provides a magnificent service, you can trust him absolutely. I'm sure that, from now on, you'll be much better shod. And you'll be able to deal with him direct. Anyway, I have no trips planned for next month, so if you want to spend a few weeks in Madrid—two or three if you like—that will be fine.'

Such a generous amount of leave. I was taken aback. I thanked him. But there was no way he was going to reply to a question to which he was determined not to reply, I knew that all too well, nor would he explain something he either shouldn't or couldn't explain. I gave up. I assumed that when he mentioned my being able to deal direct with Clemens von T, he was not refering to shoes, and that in future he would ask me to consult him about something other than footwear. Nevertheless, the truth is that even now, when that time of fever and dream has long passed, I continue to order my handsome long-lasting pairs of shoes from that tiny shop in Berlin.

Tupra meant what he said on the plane, and so I arranged my trip to Madrid for the following month, a stay of two weeks, I realized this would be quite long enough, possibly even too long, I mean, once I had seen everyone, I wouldn't know what to do with my time.

Nostalgia, or missing some place or person, regardless of whether for reasons of absence or abandonment or death, is a very strange and contradictory business. At first, you think you can't live without someone or far from someone, the initial grief is so intense and so constant that you experience it as a kind of endless sinking or an interminably advancing spear, because each moment of privation counts and weighs, you feel it and it chokes you, and all you want is for the hours of the day to pass, knowing that their passing will lead to nothing new, only to more waiting for more waiting. Each morning you open your eyes—if you've had the benefit of sleep which, while it doesn't allow you to forget everything, does at least numb and confuse—thinking the same thought that oppressed you just before you closed them, for example, 'She's not here and she won't be coming back' (whether that means her coming back to you or back from death), and you prepare yourself not to trudge through the day, because you're not even capable of looking that far ahead or of differentiating one day from another, but through the next five minutes and then the next, and so you'll continue from five minutes to five minutes, if not from minute to minute, becoming entangled in them all and, at most, trying to distract yourself for just two or three minutes from your consciousness, or from your ponderous paralysis. If that happens, it has nothing to do with your will, but with some form of blessed chance: a curious item on the television news, the time it takes to complete or begin a crossword, an irritating or solicitous phone call from someone you can't stand, the bottle that falls to the floor and obliges you to gather up the fragments so that you don't cut yourself when out of laziness you wander about barefoot, or the dire TV series that nonetheless amuses you—or that you simply took to straight away—and to which you surrender yourself with inexplicable relief until the final credits roll, wishing another episode would start immediately and allow you to keep clinging on to that stupid thread of continuity. These are the found routines that sustain us, what remains of life, the foolish and the innocuous, that neither enthuses nor demands participation or effort, the padding that we despise when everything is fine and we're busy and have no time to miss anyone, not even the dead (in fact, we use those busy times to shrug them off, although this only works for a short while, because the dead insist on staying dead and always come back later on, the pin prick pressing into our chest and the lead upon our souls).

Time passes, and at some ill-defined point, we go back to being able to sleep without suddenly starting awake and without remembering what has happened in our dreams, and to shaving not at chance moments or at odd times, but each morning; no bottles are broken and we remain unirritated by any phone call, we can make do without the TV soap opera, the crossword, the random soothing routines that we look at oddly as we bid farewell to them because now we can scarcely understand why we ever needed them, and we can even make do without the patient people who entertained us and listened to us during our monotonous, obsessive period of mourning. We raise our head and once more look around us, and although we see nothing particularly promising or attractive, nothing that can replace the person we long for and have lost, we begin to find it hard to sustain that longing and wonder if it was really such a loss. We're filled by a kind of retrospective laziness regarding the time when we loved or were devoted or got over-excited or anxious, and feel incapable of ever giving so much attention to anyone again, of trying to please them, of watching over their sleep and concealing from them what can be concealed or what might hurt them, and one finds enormous relief in that deep-rooted absence of alertness. 'I was abandoned,' we think, 'by my lover, by my friend, by my dead, so what, they all left, and the result was the same, I just had to get on with my own life. They'll regret it in the end, because it's nice to know that one is loved and sad to know one's been forgotten, and now I'm forgetting them, and anyone who dies knows more or less what fate awaits him or her. I did what I could, I held firm, and still they drifted away.' Then you quote these words to yourself: 'Memory is a tremulous finger.' And add in your own words: 'And it doesn't always succeed when it tries to point at us.' We discover that our finger can no longer be trusted, or less and less often, and that those who absorbed our thoughts night and day and day and night, and were fixed there like a nail hammered firmly in, gradually work loose and become of no importance to us; they grow blurred and, yes, tremulous, and one can even begin to doubt their existence as if they were a bloodstain rubbed and scrubbed and cleaned, or of which only the rim remains, which is the part that takes longest to remove, and then that rim, too, finally submits.

More time passes, and there comes a day, just before the last trace vanishes, when the mere idea of seeing the lost person suddenly seems burdensome to us. Even though we may not be happy and may still miss them, even though their remoteness and loss still occasionally wounds us—one night, lying in bed, we look at our shoes alone by the leg of a chair, and we're filled with grief when we remember that her high heels once stood right next to them, year after year, telling us that we were two even in sleep, even in absence—it turns out that the people we most loved, and still love, have become people from another era, or have been lost along the way—along our way, for we each have our own—have become almost preterite beings to whom we do not want to return because we know them too well and the thread of continuity has been broken. We always view the past with a feeling of proud superiority, both it and its contents, even if our present is worse or less fortunate or sick and the future promises no improvement of any kind. However brilliant and happy our past was, to us it seems contaminated with ingenuousness, ignorance and, in part, silliness: in the past we never knew what would come after and now we do, and in that sense the past is inferior, in objective, practical terms; that's why it always carries within it an element of hopeless foolishness and makes us feel ashamed that we lived for so long in a fantasy world, believing what we now know to be false, or perhaps it wasn't false then, but which has, anyway, ceased to be true by not resisting or persevering. The love that seemed rock solid, the friendship we never doubted, the living person whom we always relied upon to live forever because without him the world was inconceivable or it was inconceivable that the world would still be the world and not some other place. We cannot help looking down slightly at our most beloved dead, the more so as more time passes and in passing wastes them, not just with sadness but with pity too, knowing, as we do, that they know nothing—how naïve they were—of what happened after their departure, whereas we do. We went to the funeral and listened to what was said there, as well as to what people muttered under their breath, as if afraid the departed might still be able to hear them, and we saw those who had harmed him boasting that they had been his closest friends and pretending to mourn him. He neither saw nor heard anything. He died deceived, like everyone else, without ever knowing enough, and that's precisely what makes us pity them and consider them all to be poor men and poor women, poor grown-up children, poor devils.

Those whom we left behind or who left our side know nothing about us either, as far as we're concerned they've become as fixed and immovable as the dead, and the mere prospect of meeting again and having to talk to them and hear them seems to us like hard work, partly because we feel that neither they nor we would want to talk about or hear anything. 'I can't be bothered,' we think, 'it's been far too long since she was a witness to my days. She used to know almost everything about me, or at least the most important things, and now a gap has opened up that could never be filled, even if I were to tell her in great detail all that has happened, everything of which she did not have immediate knowledge. I can't be bothered with having to get to know each other again and explain ourselves, how upsetting to recognize at once the old reactions and the old vices and the old anxieties and the old tones of voice in which I addressed her and she me; and even the same suppressed jealousies and the same passions, albeit unspoken now. I'll never be able to see her as someone new, nor as part of my daily existence, she'll seem simultaneously stale and alien. I'll go home to see Luisa and the children, and once I've spent a good long time with them and they're starting to get used to me, I'll sit down beside her for a rather shorter time, perhaps before going out to supper at a restaurant, while we wait for the babysitter who's late arriving, on the sofa we shared for so many years, but where I sit now like a visiting stranger, dependable or otherwise, and we won't know how to behave. There'll be pauses and clearings of the throat and, given that we're face to face, extraordinarily inane remarks such as 'So, how are things with you?' or 'You're looking really good.' And then we'll realize that we can't be together without really being together, and that we don't want that. We will be neither completely natural nor completely artificial, it's not possible to be superficial with someone we've known deeply and since forever, nor deep with someone who has lost all track of us and covered her own tracks completely, for both of us there is so much that is now unknown. And after half an hour, perhaps one, two at the most, over dessert, we'll consider that there's nothing more to be said and, even stranger, that once is quite enough, and then I'll have thirteen days' holiday left to kill. And even if the unthinkable happened and we fell into each other's arms and she said the words I've been wanting to hear for so long now: "Come, come, I was so wrong about you before. Sit down here beside me again. I haven't yet shooed away your ghost, this pillow is still yours, I just couldn't see you clearly before. Come and embrace me. Come to me. Come back. And stay here for ever"; even if that happened and I gave up my London apartment and said farewell to Tupra and Pérez Nuix, to Mulryan and Rendel and even to Wheeler, and began the swift task of transforming them into a long parenthesis—even seemingly interminable parentheses close eventually and then they can be jumped over—and returned to Madrid to be with her—and I'm not saying that I wouldn't, given the opportunity, if that happened—I would do so knowing that what has been interrupted cannot be resumed, that the gap would remain there always, hidden perhaps but constant, and knowing that a before and an after can never be knit together.'

And so, despite my genuine desire to return to my city and to see my family again, even the one person who no longer considered herself mine, to see yesterday's faces, having absented myself from today and from their today, and to find myself, without preparation or warning, confronted by tomorrow's faces, I not only planned a stay of two weeks rather than the three my boss had offered me, I also postponed my departure for a little longer on our return from Berlin, in order to find out first what had happened to De la Garza.

I thought of simply phoning him out of the blue and enquiring after his health, but it occurred to me that if I gave my name, he might not even want to speak to me, and that if I gave a false name or invented an excuse or some fabricated query, it would be difficult then to move the conversation on and ask about his physical state, suddenly and for no reason, given that I was supposedly a stranger. So I decided instead to pay him a surprise visit, that is, without making a prior appointment. However, since nowadays no official organization will allow in anyone unless they have first specified the purpose of their visit or proved that they have some legitimate business there, I phoned an ex-colleague at the BBC with whom I had worked on various tedious programs about terrorism and tourism at the start of my life in London—before I was recruited by Tupra or, rather, by Wheeler—and who, like me, had managed to escape his boring post and had doubtless improved his lot by taking on a vague although not entirely insignificant job with the Spanish Embassy at the Court of my patron saint St. James, or San Jacobo.

The name of this unctuous, treacherous individual, part-despot, part-serf (despite the apparent contradiction, the two often go together), was Garralde and when it came to ensuring his own well-being he lacked all scruples; he was always ready to be servile, not just with the powerful and the famous, but also with those he reckoned would one day enjoy a little power and fame, however minimal, enough, at any rate, to do him some future favor or for him to feel able to ask for one; in just the same way, he was scornful of those who, in his view, would never be of any use to him, although he had no qualms about suddenly and cynically turning on the charm if he discovered later on that he had been wrong. He had a broad face, like an almost full moon, small eyes, very porous skin, like pulp, and rather widely spaced teeth, the latter giving him a highly salacious appearance which, as far as I know, accorded only with his greedy mentality—he looked as if he were constantly secreting juices—but not with his activities: he was the kind of man who laughingly pays everyone amorous compliments—probably both women and men, although he would do so only implicitly and, how can I put it, interrogatively with the latter, by taking a great interest in them—but on the rare occasions when one of his flatterees responded in kind, he would, equally laughingly, make his escape, fearful that he would not be able to oblige. He had the strangest hair too, it looked just like Davy Crockett's hat (without the beaver or racoon tail or whatever it was, there were quite enough dangly bits in that Embassy with De la Garza; although the latter didn't wear his hairnet to work), and I always wondered if that hairstyle-*cum*-cap wasn't in fact a wig, so thick and flamboyant that no one dared suspect it was false. Whenever I saw him, I felt like giving it a good tug, under the guise of masculine affection or in manly, boorish jest, just to see if it came off in my hand and, in passing, to find out what it felt like (it bore a creepy resemblance to velvet).

He had never paid me much attention—poor radio hack that I was—when we first knew each other—he always thought he was better than that, even though he was a hack too at the time—but now he had me down as someone with influence and a touch of mystery. He didn't know exactly what I did or who I worked for, but he knew something about my occasional appearances at chic discos, expensive restaurants, racecourses, celebrity suppers, Stamford Bridge, as well as ghastly dives no Spaniard would ever venture into (Tupra's sociable spells sometimes went on for weeks), and all of this in the company of the natives, which is rare in England for almost any foreigner, even diplomats. (On this occasion, moreover, he would have noticed me wearing those extraordinary shoes made by Hlustik and Von Truschinsky, and Garralde had a keen eye for such things and an infuriating tendency to copy them.) He felt what it best behooves acquaintances to feel about oneself: confusion and curiosity. This led him to imagine that I had all kinds of contacts and powers, which meant that he would do anything I asked. And so, offering no explanation, I asked if I could come and see him at the Embassy and, once I was there at his desk, immediately clarified the situation (in a prudently low voice, for Garralde shared a room with three other functionaries; if he was thinking of staying there, he still had quite some way to go before he made it to the top).

'I haven't actually come to see you, Garralde. I made the appointment so that I wouldn't have any problems getting in. I'll just spend a couple of minutes with you, if that's all right. We can have a proper chat over lunch another day, I've just discovered this fantastic new place, you'll love it, you see lots of people there, fresh out of bed. They skip breakfast, you see.'—For him 'people' meant 'important people,' the only kind he was interested in. He spattered his Spanish with really ghastly foreign expressions like 'the cream of society' or even worse '*la crème de la crème*,' 'the *haut monde*' and 'the jet set'; he talked about 'big names' and people being 'top-notch,' and said that at weekends he was 'unplugged.' He might climb quite high with his blend of groveling and abuse, but he would never be anything more than a social yokel. He would also exclaim '*Oro!*' whenever he thought something particularly wonderful or remarkable, having heard an Italian friend use the expression and finding it highly original. 'As soon as we finish here (it will only take two minutes), I want you to tell me where I can find the office of a colleague of yours, Rafael de la Garza. He's the person I really want to see, but I don't want him to know I'm coming.'

'But why didn't you ask him for an appointment?' asked the vile Garralde, more out of nosiness than to make any difficulties. 'I'm sure he'd have said "Yes."'

'I don't think so. He's upset with me over some nonsense or other. I want to make up with him, it was all a misunderstanding. But he mustn't know that I'm here. Just show me where his office is and I'll turn up there on my own.'

'But wouldn't it be best if I told him you were here? He's a higher rank than me.'

It was as if he hadn't heard what I'd said. He may have been clever when it came to manipulating friends and acquaintances, but he was basically an oaf. He irritated me, and I was on the point of hurling myself on his abundant hair, its similarity to the legendary hat of Davy Crockett, king of the wild frontier, was really quite incredible (although it looked more matted than on other occasions, perhaps it was beginning to bear more of a resemblance to a Russian fur hat). I once again restrained myself, after all, he *was* about to do me a small favor that he would soon ask me to pay back, he was not the sort to wait.

'What did I just say, Garralde? If you announce me, he'll refuse to see me, and besides, it might get you into trouble.'

Since he was a base creature, this last argument sharpened his wits a little. He would never want to make an enemy of a superior, or to annoy him, even if that person wasn't his direct superior. For a moment, I felt sorry for him: how could he possibly consider Rafita de la Garza his superior? Our world is very badly ordered and unfair and corrupt if it allows other people to be at the orders of that prize dickhead. It was just pathetic. Of course, it was equally shocking to think that someone might have Garralde as their superior and have to obey him.

'Fine, if that's what you want,' he said. 'Let me just check if he's on his own. It wouldn't do you much good to burst in on him if he's in a meeting. You wouldn't be able to undo the misunderstanding with witnesses present, now would you?'

'I'll go with you. You can show me the way and the right

door. Don't worry, I'll wait outside and before I go in, I'll give you plenty of time to clear off. He'll never know you had anything to do with my visit.'

'And what about lunch?' he asked before we even set off. He had to make sure he got his reward, at least the minimum and immediate one. He would try to get something better out of me later, that was his way of charging interest. But I didn't care a fig about that or indeed about our lunch date, which I probably wouldn't keep. He'd be momentarily angry, but it would only increase his respect for me and his curiosity when he saw how little care I took over my social commitments. 'I'd love to go to that restaurant you mentioned.'

'What about Saturday? I have to fly over to Madrid for a few days after that. I'll phone you tomorrow and we'll arrange a time. I'll reserve a table.'

'*Oro!*'

I couldn't bear him saying that. Well, I couldn't bear anything about him. I decided there and then that I would not damn well reserve a table nor would I damn well phone him, I'd invent some convincing excuse later on.

He led me down carpeted and slightly labyrinthine corridors, we changed direction at least six times. Finally, he stopped at a prudent distance from a door that stood ajar or almost open, we could hear declamatory voices, or rather one voice, barely audible, which sounded as if it were reciting poetry in a strange, insistent rhythm, or perhaps it was a litany.

'Is he alone?' I whispered.

'I'm not sure. He might be, although, of course, he is speaking. No, wait, now I remember: Professor Rico is here today. He's giving a lecture this evening at the Cervantes Institute. They're probably rehearsing.' And then he felt it necessary to enlighten me: 'Yes, Professor Francisco Rico, no less. You may not know it, but he's a great expert, really top-notch, and very stern. Apparently he treats anyone he deems stupid or importunate like dirt. He's much feared, very disrespectful and has a caustic wit. There's absolutely no way we can interrupt them, Deza. He's a member of the Spanish Academy.'

'It would be best if the Professor didn't see you, then. I'll wait here until they've finished. You'd better go, you don't want to get a dressing down. Thanks for everything and, don't worry, I'll be all right.'

Garralde hesitated for a moment. He didn't trust me. Quite right too. However, he must have thought that whatever happened next and whatever I did, it would be best if he wasn't there. He set off back down those corridors, turning round every now and then and repeating noiselessly to me until he had disappeared from view (it was easy enough to read his lips):

'Don't go in. Don't even think of interrupting them. He's a member of the Academy.'

I had learned from Tupra and Rendel how to move almost silently, and to silently open closed doors, if there were no complications, and how to jam them shut, as with the door of the handicapped toilet. And so I made my way over to De la Garza's office, keeping close to the farther side of the corridor. From there I could see practically the whole room, I could certainly see both men, the numbskull and Rico, whose face I was familiar with from television and the newspapers and which was, besides, pretty much unmistakable, he was a bald man who, curiously and audaciously, did not behave like a bald man, he had a disdainful or sometimes even weary look in his eye, he must get very tired of the ignorance surrounding him, he must constantly curse having been born into an illiterate age for which he would feel nothing but scorn; in his statements to the press and in his writings (I had read the occasional article) he gave the impression that he was addressing himself not to a few cultivated people in the future, in whose existence he doubtless did not trust, but to readers from the past, all good and dead, as if he believed that in books—on both sides of the divide: for books speak in the middle of the night just as the river speaks, quietly and reluctantly, and their murmur, too, is tranquil or patient or languid—being alive or dead was merely a secondary matter, a matter of chance. He perhaps thought, like his compatriot and mine, that 'time is the only dimension in which the living and the dead can talk to each other and communicate, the only dimension they have

215

in common and that binds them together,' and that all time is therefore inevitably indifferent and shared (we all existed and will exist in time), and the fact that we coincide in it physically is purely incidental, like arriving late or early for an appointment. I saw his characteristically large mouth, well-formed and rather soft, slightly reminiscent of Tupra's mouth, but less moist, less cruel. His mouth was closed, his lips almost pressed together, so the primitive rhythms I could hear were emanating not from there, but from Rafita, who, it seems, not only considered himself to be a black rapper by night, in chic and idiotic clubs, but a white hip-hopper in the broad light of day and in his office at the Embassy, although he was dressed perfectly conventionally now and wasn't wearing a stiff, over-large jacket, or a gipsy earring in one ear, or some faux matador's hairnet or a hat or a bandana or a Phrygian cap, or anything else on his empty head. His recitation droned to a halt, and he said with satisfaction to Francisco Rico, that man of great learning:

'So what did you think, Professor?'

The Professor was wearing a pair of large spectacles with thick frames and lenses possibly made of anti-glare glass, but even so I could see his icy gaze, his look of sad stupefaction, as if he were not so much angry as unable to believe De la Garza's pretentiousness or presumptuousness.

'It doesn't thrill me. *Ps. Tah.* Not in the least.'—That's what he said, '*Ps.*' Not even the more traditional '*Pse,*' which means 'So-so' or 'No great shakes' (or '*Ni fu ni fa,*' which Spaniards use all the time, even though no one really knows what it means). '*Ps,*' especially when followed by '*Tah,*' was far more discouraging, in fact it was deeply disheartening.

'Let me lay another one on you, Professor. This one's more elaborate, has more ass to it, it's more, like, kickin."

There he was again with his semi-crude, semi-youth slang; no one could dishearten or discourage Rafita. I felt relieved to see that he was little changed since the last time I had seen him, beaten and lying on the floor, literally with the fear of death in his shaking, silently supplicant body, his eyes dull and his gaze averted, not even daring to look at us, at his punisher and at me, his punisher's companion by association. I saw that he had recovered, his injuries couldn't have been so very grave if he were still prepared to importune anyone anywhere with his nonsense. He must be the kind of man who never learned, a hopeless case. It was, of course, unlikely that Professor Rico would draw a sword or a dagger on him, or grab him by the neck and bang his head on the table several times. At most, he would give a loud, dismissive snort, or bluntly tell him what he thought of him, because, as the vile Garralde had said, he did have a reputation for being caustic and wounding and for not keeping to himself his harsh opinions or his insults when he considered them to be justified. He was seated indolently in an armchair, his head thrown back like a disinterested, skeptical judge, his legs elegantly crossed, his right forearm resting on the back of the chair and in his hand a cigarette whose ash he was allowing to fall onto the floor, helped by an occasional light tap on the filter with his thumbnail. It was clear that unless someone placed an ashtray immediately underneath his cigarette, he was not going to bother looking for one. He sometimes blew the smoke out through his nose, a somewhat old-fashioned thing to do nowadays, and for that reason still stylish. He probably couldn't care less about the ban on smoking in offices. He was well dressed and well shod, his shirt and suit looked to me as if they were by Zegna or Corneliani or someone similar, but his shoes were definitely not by Hlustik, that much was sure, they, too, must have come from the South. Rafita was standing in front of him, clearly rather worked up, as if he genuinely wanted to know Rico's opinion, to which, however, he paid no attention because that opinion was not, for the moment, benevolent. There are more and more such people in the world, who only hear what pleases and flatters them, as if anything else simply passes them by. It started off as a phenomenon among politicians and mediocre artists hungry for success, but now it has infected whole populations. I was watching the two of them as if from the fifth row in a theater, and if I centered myself opposite the half-open door, both appeared in my field of vision uncut.

'Look here, young De la Garza,' Rico said in an offensively

paternalistic tone, 'it's as plain as day that God has not called you to follow the path of foolish nonsensical verse. You're light years away from *Struwwelpeter,* and Edward Lear could run rings around you.' The Professor was being deliberately pedantic, that is, he was having fun at Rafita's expense, because he probably knew that Rafita wouldn't have heard of either name, I knew of Edward Lear purely by chance, from my pedantic years in Oxford, the other name meant nothing to me, although I've found out more since. 'And I feel you should not oppose His wishes, *derr,* and that way you won't waste any more time. He obviously hasn't called you to the higher path either, why, you wouldn't even be capable of writing something like '*Una alta ricca rocca,*' even though you have six long centuries of progress on your side.' He spoke this line in an immaculate Italian accent, and so I assumed it was not Spanish but Italian, despite the similarity of vocabulary; perhaps it was from Petrarch, on whom he was an expert, as he was on so many other world authors and doubtless on *Struwwelpeter,* too, his knowledge was immeasurable. 'There are some things, *ets,* that simply cannot be. So give up now, *pf.*' I was struck by the fact that, despite his role as member of the Spanish Academy, he used so much onomatopoeia that was strange to our language and initially indecipherable, although, at the same time, I found it all perfectly comprehensible and clear, perhaps he had a special gift for it and was a master of onomatopoeia, an inventor, a creator even. '*Derr*' obviously indicated some sort of prohibition. '*Ets*' sounded to me like a very serious warning. '*Pf*' seemed to me to indicate a lost cause.

But Rafita was very much a man of his age and preferred not to hear or perhaps did not hear, and maybe the plethora of other people like him nowadays are just the same. And so he continued unabashed:

'No, you'll really like this one, Professor, it'll blow your mind. Here goes.' Then I saw him doing ridiculous things with his hands and arms just like a rapper (I'm applying the word 'ridiculous' not to him, although he was ridiculous, but to all those who devote themselves to gesticulating and mumbling that witless, worthless drivel, as if the religious doggerel we had to chorus when we were kids, God help us, was making a comeback after all these years), he flailed about, making undulating movements in an attempt to emulate the angry gestures of some low-life black man, although every now and then his Spanish roots would reveal themselves and he'd end up striking poses more like those of a flamenco dancer in full flow. It was truly pathetic, as were his awful so-called verses, a ghastly dirge accompanied by a constant bending of the knees in time to the supposed rhythm of some thin, imaginary tune: 'I'm gonna turn you baby into my ukelele,' was how it began, with that so-called rhyme, 'I'm food for the snakes, like a fine beefsteak, I'll fill you up with venom just for wearin' denim, don't go stepping on my toes if you want to keep your nose, hoo-yoo, yoo-hoo.'—And then, without even pausing to take a breath, he attacked another strophe or section or whatever it was: 'My bullets want some fun, no point in trying to run, and they're looking for your brain and are out to cause you pain, to burn up your grey matter, send it pouring down the gutter, flushing down the can, you'll be shit down the pan, hoo-yoo, yoo-hoo.'

'Enough!'—The very eminent Professor Rico had looked him straight in the eye ('*de hito en hito*,' another phrase that everyone understands without knowing quite what it means); and I suppose he had listened to him '*de hito en hito*' as well, if that's possible, which I doubt, although I really don't know. He had, at any rate, turned pale on hearing those defiling dactyls, as must I, I imagine, although there were no mirrors to confirm this. Immediately afterwards, however, I felt a wave of heat to my face and I must have blushed, out of a mixture of fury and embarrassment (not for myself but for De la Garza): how did that great nincompoop dare to waste the admirable Francisco Rico's time and bother him with such out-and-out bunkum and baloney? How could he possibly think that his crude ditty had any poetic value whatsoever, not even as a kind of pseudo-limerick, and how could he expect to receive the approval of one of Spain's leading literary authorities, a great expert, on a visit to London, perhaps still tired from his journey, perhaps needing time to put the finishing touches to his magisterial lecture that evening? I felt as indignant as when I saw De la Garza on the fast dance floor at the disco, flailing the imprudent Flavia's face with his ludicrous hairnet. My one brief, simple thought then had been: 'I'd like to smash his face in,' and at the time I knew nothing of the imminent traumatic consequences of that incident. I had remembered that thought much later, with sadness, with a kind of vicarious regret (on my own behalf, but also, vaguely, on behalf of Tupra, who seemed to regret nothing, as was only natural in someone so single-minded and conscientious; he had no regrets, at least about work-related matters), both during and after the thrashing—and, of course, before—each time that Reresby's Landsknecht sword rose and fell. How could De la Garza not have learned his lesson, how could he not have grown more discreet? How could he have composed anything, however incoherent and grotesque, that contained elements of violence, when he himself, courtesy of us, had such painful first-hand experience of it? How could he even mention the words 'pan' and 'can,' when he had nearly been drowned in the blue water of a toilet? 'Perhaps that's why,' I thought to myself as I stood in the corridor, still unnoticed, invisible, a voyeur and an eavesdropper. 'Perhaps he's obsessed with what happened to him, and this is his one (idiotic) way of coming to terms with it or overcoming it, by believing (in his clumsy, puerile way) that he could be Reresby and fill someone with bullets or at least with fear, or poison them, or blow their brains out, or do all those things to Tupra himself, of whom he must be scared witless and whom he doubtless prayed each day never to meet again—in this city that they shared. Fantasizing is free, we know this from childhood on; we continue to know it as we grow older, but we learn to fantasize very little, and less and less as the years pass, when we realize that there's no point.' I immediately felt rather sorry for him and that feeling tempered my indignation, although this was not the case with the illustrious Professor, of course, who shared neither my thoughts nor my outstanding debts: 'Enough!' he cried, without actually raising his voice, but the way he projected his voice it sounded like a shout, rather in the way that waiters in Madrid bars can bawl out orders to the people in the kitchen or at the bar, above or below the hubbub from the customers. 'Are you out of your tiny mind, De la Garza? Just what *has* got into you? Do you really think I could possibly be interested in hearing that string of inanities,' he paused, 'that tom-tom-like tosh you were spouting? What filth! *Regh*. What dross!'—Many of the expressions he used were old-fashioned or perhaps it was simply that the lexicon used by Spaniards nowadays has become so reduced that almost all expressions seem old-fashioned, things like '*¿qué ventolera te ha dado?*—'what *has* got into you?' or '*sarta de necedades*'—'string of inanities' or '*tabarra*'—'dross,' as well as '*no estar en sus cabales*'—'to be out of your mind,' and I was pleased to see that I was not the only one to use them; for a second, I identified with Rico, a self-identification I found flattering, unexpectedly or perhaps not (he *is* a very eminent man). His latest onomatopoeia, '*Regh*,' seemed to me as transparent and eloquent as the previous ones, conveying disgust, both moral and aesthetic.

The Professor did not move, did not get up, he was clearly capable of controlling his body, it was enough for him occasionally to unleash his tongue, however briefly. He merely deposited his cigarette end in a handy pencil-holder and touched the bridge of his glasses, first with his index finger and then with his middle finger, twice, as if he wanted to make sure they hadn't flown off his nose when he erupted. De la Garza stood paralyzed, knees momentarily bent, not the most graceful of poses, as if he were about to crouch down. Then he straightened up. And since he'd had nothing to drink, he might well have felt alarmed.

'Oh, forgive me, Professor, I'm so sorry, I don't understand, I'd read somewhere that you were interested in hip-hop, that you saw a connection with certain archaic forms of poetry, with doggerel, you know, chapbooks, songbooks, ballads, and all that . . .'

'You're confusing me with Villena,' Rico cut in, referring to a very well-known Spanish poet with a sharp eye (a sharp eye for all the latest trends). He didn't say this in an offended tone, but in a purely professorial and explanatory one.

'. . . that you'd said you found it very medieval . . .'

And then it happened. He stopped speaking because that was

when it happened. As he was shaking his head to express his incomprehension and his contrition, shocked by Rico's blunt or rough reaction (which he'd brought on himself), he saw me and immediately recognized me, as if he had been fearing just such an encounter for some time or had often dreamed of me or as if, in his nightmares, I was a crushing weight on his chest. When he glanced to the right, he saw me there, straight ahead of him, standing on the other side of the corridor like a specter at the feast, and instantly recognized me. And I saw the effect of that surprise and that recognition. De la Garza shrank back, every bit of him, the way an insect sensing danger contracts, curls up, rolls into a ball, tries to disappear and erase itself so that death will not touch it, so as not to be picked out or seen, to cease to exist and thus deny its own existence ('No, really, I'm not what you see, I'm not here'), because the only sure way of avoiding death is no longer to be, or perhaps even better, never to have been at all. He clamped his arms to his sides, not like a boxer about to defend or cover himself, but as if he'd suddenly been seized with cold and were shivering. He drew in his head too, much as he had done in the handicapped toilet, when he turned his head and for the first time spotted the blurred gleam of metal overhead and saw, at the very periphery of his vision, the double-edged sword about to swoop down on him: he instinctively hunched up his shoulders as if in a spasm of pain, the deliberate or unwitting gesture made by all the victims of the guillotine over two hundred years or of the axe over hundreds of centuries, even chickens and turkeys must have made that gesture from the moment it occurred to the first bored or hungry man to decapitate one. As happened then, too, his top lip lifted, almost folded back on itself in a rictus, re- vealing dry gums on which the inner part of his lip got stuck for lack of saliva. And in his eyes I saw an irrational, overwhelming, all-excluding fear, as if my mere presence had plucked him from reality and as if, in a matter of seconds, he had forgotten where he was, in the Spanish Embassy in the Court of St. James or San Jacobo or San Jaime, where he worked or spent time every day surrounded by guards and colleagues who would protect him, they were only a step away; he had forgotten that before him sat the prestigious and very irritated Professor Rico and that, given the situation, I could do nothing to him. What I found most disquieting, what left me troubled and transfixed, was that I didn't want to do anything to him, quite the contrary, I wanted to ask if he'd recovered, inquire after his health, make sure that nothing irreparable had happened, and, if the opportunity arose, and even though I couldn't stand the man, to say how sorry I was. How sorry I was that I hadn't done more, that I hadn't stopped it, that I hadn't helped him to flee, that I hadn't defended him or made Tupra see reason (although with Tupra everything was always calculated and he never rushed into anything or lost his reason). And I would even have liked to convince the dickhead that, all in all, he'd been lucky and got off lightly, and that my colleague Reresby, despite his brutality and incredible though it might seem, had done him an enormous favor by stepping in and thus preventing the bloodthirsty Manoia (whom I had seen and not seen in action on that video, now *he* really was Sir Cruelty, I'd closed my eyes, I hadn't wanted to cover them, but that scene really cried out for a blindfold) from taking charge of the punishment himself. But I neither could nor should tell him any of that, still less in front of Rico, who, on seeing Rafita's transformation, glanced with disdainful curiosity in my direction (he must have despised everything about De la Garza and considered him a peabrain and a madman).

It was a very disagreeable feeling, more than that, it was incomprehensible, to discover that I could provoke such fear in someone. It was doubtless by association, by assimilation, after all, I hadn't even touched him, perhaps De la Garza assumed that we always went around together and was afraid that Tupra might suddenly hove into view behind me. I was, however, alone and had gone there without the knowledge of my boss, who would not have been in the least amused by my visit. 'Tell him not to phone you to demand an explanation, but to leave you alone, to forget he ever knew you,' Tupra had told me to tell him, to translate those words to the fallen man, before he abandoned De la Garza, brushing his face with the tail of his armed coat as he left. 'Tell him to accept that there's no reason to demand an explanation, that there are no grounds for complaints or protest. Tell him not to talk to anyone, to keep quiet, not even to recount it later as some kind of adventure. But tell him always to remember.' And Rafita had followed those instructions to the letter, he had invented some tall story to explain his battered state to friends and colleagues. And, of course, he would have remembered, indeed, he would have done little else since then, a bundle of nerves day and night, awake and asleep, night and day, even though he later had the cheek to sing a rap song to Rico and commit other unimaginable acts of nincompoopery. When he saw me there, so close, in the corridor, perhaps, from his point of view, stalking him, he might have been panicked into thinking that I was the one who would never leave him in peace or forget him. 'He could have been left with no head, he came very close,' Reresby had added. 'But since he didn't lose it, tell him there's still time, another day, any day, we know where to find him. Tell him never to forget that, tell him the sword will always be there.' I had omitted those last few words, I hadn't translated them, I had refused to endorse them, but I had translated the rest. Everything would have remained engraved on De la Garza's memory, despite his diminished consciousness after the shock of the sharp steel and being hurled against the blunt cylindrical bars: 'We know where to find you.' Nothing could be truer, and now I had found him and I was his terror, his threat.

'He's absolutely terrified of me,' I thought fleetingly. 'But how can that be, I can't recall having terrified anyone very much before, and yet here's this man, frozen to the spot and consumed with the horror he feels on seeing me, even though he's here in his inviolable office, in the Embassy, along with a member of the Spanish Academy, objectively speaking safe and sound, why, all he'd have to do is shout and fellow diplomats and the odd vigilante or guard would be here in a trice. However, his feeling is that they would arrive too late if I had a gun or a sword or a knife and used them on him right away, with no thought for my own fate and without saying a word, that is what he knows intuitively, or perhaps the memory is still all too vivid of that moment when he first glimpsed the double-edged sword and knew there was nothing he could do to save himself: death comes in a second, one moment you're alive and the next, without realizing it, you're dead, that's how it is sometimes and, of course, all the time during wars and bombardments from on high, that widespread practice, which, however customary and accepted it may have become, is always illegitimate and always dishonorable, far more so than the crossbow in the days of Richard Yea and Nay, that changeable *Coeur de Lion* who was slain by an arrow from a dishonorable crossbow at the end of the twelfth century: you hear the bang and see and hear nothing more, and it won't be you, but possibly someone else who's still alive, who will hear the whistle of the bullet that embeds itself in your forehead. Yes, right now, this man would do anything I ordered him to do, his dread of me—or rather of Tupra, whose representative or henchman or symbol I am—is something he not only experienced in reality for a few minutes that would have seemed to him, as they had to me, an eternity, he would also often have anticipated it, asleep and awake: perhaps he saw us striding towards him like two hired assassins come to slice him up, perhaps we had appeared in his nightmares of being chased and caught, then chased and caught again, and perhaps we have sat heavy on his soul since then.' Because 'even dreams know that your pursuer usually catches up with you, and they've known it since the *Iliad*,' as Tupra had said to me that night, somewhat later, the two of us sitting in his car outside the door to my apartment, where he believed someone was waiting for me, but where there was no one, only the lights still on and possibly the dancer opposite.

Then I strode quickly into the room and spoke. I walked into the office and said confidently, almost jovially:

'So, how are you doing, Rafita? I can see you've made an excellent recovery.' And I added at once, so that he would see I was keen to keep up appearances and that my intentions were not violent or aggressive. 'Forgive me bursting in like this. Won't you introduce me?' And I went straight over to Professor Rico, who made not the slightest effort to get up, but merely held out one hand to me, the way grand ladies used to do, reaching out as far as he could without actually moving, he had a most distinguished hand and a most elegant shirt-cuff, by Cuprì or Sensatini at the very least, excellent brands, I shook it warmly (his hand that is). And since De la Garza still did not respond or utter a word (he just stared at me, terrified, so afraid that he didn't even stop me approaching Rico, in fact, he wouldn't have stopped me doing anything, I could, I realized, do what I liked), I introduced myself: 'Jacques Deza, Jacobo Deza. You're Don Francisco Rico, aren't you? The celebrated scholar.'

It pleased him to be recognized and he deigned to answer, doubtless for that reason alone, for his general attitude revealed no actual interest (whoever I might be, I was, after all, already stigmatized as someone he associated with that rapper-attaché).

'Deza, Deza . . . Aren't you a friend or acquaintance or student . . . or, er, whatever . . . of Sir Peter Wheeler? Your name rings a bell.' Both men were great scholarly figures, and I was aware that they knew and admired each other.

'Yes, I'm a very good friend of his, Professor.'

'I knew the name rang a bell. I recognized it. He must have mentioned you to me once, although I've no idea why. But it definitely rang a bell,' he said, pleased with his own retentive memory.

De la Garza wasn't listening to this superficial exchange. He had moved away from me and was now standing behind his desk as if his desk would protect him and so that he could run away if necessary.

'What the fuck do you want?' he asked suddenly, but despite the expletive, his tone was neither hostile nor ill-tempered, but imploring, as if all he wanted was for me to magically disappear (for the terrible vision, the bad dream to go away) and wishing with all his might that I would reply: 'I'm off now. I don't want anything. I was never here.'

'Nothing, Rafita, I just wanted to reassure myself that you'd recovered from your accident, that there weren't any aftereffects. I happened to be passing and it occurred to me to pop in and ask you, I've been worried. It's a purely friendly visit, I won't stay long, so don't get uptight about it. So, are you all right? Completely better? I'm really sorry about what happened, I mean it.'

'What happened? What accident?' asked Rico skeptically.

'Having seen what I've seen and heard what I've heard, no accident could possibly be serious enough,' he added under his breath, but perfectly audibly.

Rafita, however, paid no attention to this harsh comment, he had relegated the Professor and his annoyance to the background, he was too preoccupied with me, alert and tense, as if he feared that at any moment, I would leap at his throat like a tiger. This was an odd sensation for me, almost amusing at first, because I knew myself to be incapable of harming him and had no wish to do so. *I* knew that, but he did not and contrary to what teachers believe, knowledge is not transmissible; one can only persuade. I found the gulf between his perception and my knowledge almost funny, and yet, at the same time, it was distressing to have someone see me that way, as a danger, as someone threatening and violent. De la Garza was almost beside himself, on tenterhooks.

'Believe me, I just wanted to find out how you are,' I said, trying to calm him, convince him. 'I know you made a real nuisance of yourself and really put your foot in it, but I certainly didn't expect my boss to react like that, and I'm sorry. It took me completely by surprise and was totally disproportionate. I had no idea what he was planning and could do nothing to avoid it.'

'What boss? Sir Peter, you mean? I'm completely lost, what *are* you talking about, *élgar*. If he did turn nasty, I'm not surprised, Sir Peter's far too old for such imbecilities.' Rico returned to the charge, not so much because the matter interested him, but because he was bored. He appeared to be the sort of man who cannot bear his brain to be inactive for a moment, because if you don't understand something immediately, you soon will if you wait, but such waiting is unbearable for people who are constantly thinking. That '*élgar*' denoted a need to know.

'Look, go away, just go away,' said the nincompoop childishly. He took no notice of what I was saying, he wouldn't listen to reason, he probably hadn't even heard me. He'd lost his nerve completely and so very quickly that it reaffirmed me in my view that Tupra and I must often have strolled through his nightmares, in which we were probably inseparable. 'Please leave, I beg you,

leave me alone, shit, what more do you want, I haven't said anything, I haven't told anyone the truth, surely that's enough.'

Rico lit another cigarette, having realized that this obscure
conflict was a matter exclusively and perhaps pathologically
between De la Garza and me, and that he was not going to
glean anything more. He made a dismissive gesture, indicating
that he was happy to abandon any further attempts at clarification, and he gave vent to one more of his varied repertoire of
onomatopoeia.

'*Esh*,' he said. It sounded to me exactly like: 'To hell with
these two idiots, I'm going to think my own thoughts and not
waste any more time on them.'

I saw how shaken Rafita was—his clenched fists still held
close to his body (not as a weapon, but as a shield), his eyes
wild, his breathing agitated—gripped by a panic that he was
now reliving and which he had perhaps been dreading for
months, he had also developed an intermittent cough, which,
when the fit took him, proved uncontrollable. That cloud
of perpetual fear would last for some time yet, it wouldn't
be quick to clear. He must have suffered greatly that night,
because one is always instantly aware when there is any real
danger of death, even if, in the end, it turns out to be something that merely frightened one half to death. It was pointless trying to talk to him. I wondered what state he would
have been in if it had been Reresby and not me who had
appeared unexpectedly at the door of his office. He would
have fainted, had a seizure, a heart attack. I had gone there
out of consideration for him (insofar as that was possible),
and there was no sense in making him suffer further with my
continued presence. On the other hand, I could leave with
a clear conscience. He looked fine physically. He might still
suffer some pain or other damage, but he had, on the whole,
fully recovered. His present and future feelings of insecurity
were, however, quite another thing, and they would stay with
him for a long time. He would feel uncomfortable in the
world, with the added inconvenience of fear and a permanent
sense of unease. Not that this would prevent him spouting

nonsense, but it would have dealt a fatal blow to his sense of pride at its deepest level.

'Anyway, I'll go now, so don't upset yourself. I can see that you're fine, although not perhaps at this precise moment. It's my fault, I suppose. You seemed in pretty good form while you were singing your rhyming couplets. I'll come and see you again some other time.' I realized that these last innocent words had terrified him still more. From his point of view it was the equivalent of a threat. I let it go, however, I didn't try to put him right, he wouldn't have listened, and I didn't really care. In a moment of weakness and guilt I had chosen to visit him and had paid the price for both weakness and guilt. 'Goodbye, Professor. It's been an honor to meet you. I'm only sorry it was so brief and so . . . odd.'

'Everything about young De la Garza is odd,' he said scornfully, playing down the importance of the episode, he had probably seen worse; and he stood up, not in order to shake my hand, but to leave. His anger had passed, the situation had nothing to do with him, and his mind was already wandering pastures new. 'Wait, I'm leaving too. I'll see you this evening, Rafita. I doubt I'll have the good fortune of you missing my lecture.'

And there we left De la Garza, still barricaded behind his desk, not daring even to sit down. He didn't say goodbye, he obviously still wasn't capable of articulating any civilized words. And while we, the Professor and I, walked back along those slightly labyrinthine corridors towards the exit, I couldn't help at least attempting an apology:

'You see we had a bit of a falling-out and he still hasn't got over it.'

'No,' he said. 'You should feel very pleased with yourself: you had him scared shitless. You're lucky you can keep him at arm's length like that. He's terribly clinging. I'm vaguely friendly with his father, which is why I put up with the son. Only from time to time, fortunately, and only when I come to London for one of these dull official dos.'

Once we were out in the street and we went our separate ways, I noticed (strangely enough, I hadn't noticed before) that

Rafita's fear had cast me in a rather flattering light. Imposing re-spect, instilling fear, seeing oneself as a danger had its pleasurable side. It made one feel more confident, more optimistic, stronger. It made one feel important and—how can I put it—masterful. But before I hailed a taxi, there was time for me to find this un-expected vanity repugnant too. Not that the latter feeling drove out conceit, they lived alongside each other. The two things were mingled, until they dissipated and were forgotten.

When you haven't been back for some time to a place you know well, even if it's the city you were born in, the city to which you're most accustomed, where you've lived for the longest time and which is still home to your children and your father and your siblings and home even to the love that stood firm for many years (even if that place is as familiar to you as the air you breathe), there comes a moment when it begins to fade and your recollection of it dims, as if your memory were suddenly afflicted by myopia and—how can I put it—by cinematography: the different eras become juxtaposed and you start to feel unsure as to which of those cities you left or departed from when you last set off, the city of your childhood or your youth or the city of your manhood or maturity, when where you live dwindles in importance, and, hard though it is to admit, the truth is you'd be happy enough with your own little corner almost anywhere in the world.

That's how I'd come to see Madrid during my now prolonged absence: faded and dim, accumulative, oscillating, a stage-set that concerned me very little despite having invested so much in it—so much of my past and so much of my present, albeit at a distance—and, more to the point, one that could get along without me quite happily (it had, after all, dismissed me, expelled me from its modest production). Of course any city can do without anyone, we're not essential anywhere, not even to the few people who say they miss our presence or claim they couldn't live without us, because everyone seeks substitutes and, sooner or later, finds them, or else ends up resigned to our absence and feels so comfortable in that mood of resignation that they no longer wish to introduce any changes, not even to allow the lost or much-mourned person to return, not even to take us in again . . . Who knows who will replace us, we know only that we will be replaced, on all occasions and in all circumstances and in every role, and the void or gap we believed we left or really did leave is of no importance, regardless of how we disappeared or died, whether far too young or after a long life, whether violently or peacefully: it's the same with love and friendship, with work and influence, with machinations and with fear, with domination and even longing itself, with hatred, which also wearies of us in the end, and with the desire for vengeance, which darkens and changes its objective when it lingers and delays, as Tupra had urged me not to do; with the houses we inhabit, with the rooms we grew up in and the cities that accept us, with the corridors we raced madly along as children and the windows we gazed dreamily out of as adolescents, with the telephones that persuade and patiently listen to us and laugh in our ear or murmur agreement, at work and at play, in shops and in offices, at our counters and our desks, playing card games or chess, with the childhood landscape we thought was ours alone and with the streets that grow exhausted from seeing so many fade away, generation after generation, all meeting the same sad end; with restaurants and walks and pleasant parks and fields, on balconies and belvederes from which we watched the passing of so many moons they grew bored with looking at us, and with our armchairs and chairs and sheets, until not a trace, not a vestige of our smell remains and they're torn up to make rags or cloths, and even our kisses are replaced and the person left behind closes her eyes when she kisses the easier to forget us (if the pillow is still the same, or so that we don't reappear in some sudden, treacherous, irrepressible mental vision); with memories and thoughts and daydreams and with everything, and so we are all of us like snow on shoulders, slippery and docile, and the snow always stops . . .

It had been some time since I visited Madrid, from which I, too, had evaporated or faded, leaving not a trace behind or so it seemed, or perhaps all that remained of me was the rim, (which is the part that takes longest to remove), and also my own first name, which I had not yet left behind me, not having yet reached that state of strangeness. I hadn't ceased to exist, of course, in my father's house, not there, but I wasn't referring to his home, but to the home that was once mine. And now I would perhaps find out who had replaced me, even if he was only temporary and had no intention of staying, the permanent replacement takes his time or patiently awaits his turn, the one who will truly replace us always hangs back and lets others go ahead to be burned on the pyre that Luisa one day lit for us and which continues to burn, consuming all who come near, and which does not automatically extinguish itself once we've been burned to a cinder. I wouldn't need to worry that much about whoever happened to be by her side now, or only a little, just a touch, because of the mere fact that he *was* by her side and by the side of my children too.

I had decided not to give them prior warning from London, but to wait until I arrived, so that my phone call could be followed immediately by a semi-surprise visit. I wanted to make sure they were home—I knew the hours they kept, but there are always exceptions and emergencies—and then turn up a few minutes later, full of smiles and laden with presents. To see the children's excitement and, out of the corner of my eye, Luisa's amused, perhaps briefly nostalgic expression, that would allow me a simulacrum of triumph and a flicker of illusory hope, enough perhaps to sustain me during that artificial two-week sojourn, which seemed to me far too long the moment the plane touched down.

I stayed at a hotel and not at my father's house, for I had learned from my brothers and my sister—rather than from him, for he never spoke about his problems—that his health had deteriorated badly over the last two months, after the doctors discovered that he'd had three mini-strokes—as they called them—of which he had been entirely unaware, not even knowing when they'd occurred; and although my brothers, my sister, some of his grand-daughters and my sisters-in-law often dropped in to see him, there had, in the end, been no alternative but to provide him with a live-in caregiver, a rather nice Colombian lady, who slept in the bedroom I would have occupied, and who relieved his maid, who was getting on in years now, of some of her tasks. I didn't want to upset the new order with my presence. With my current salary, I could easily afford the Palace Hotel, and so I booked a suite there. It was easier for me to stay at a hotel than in someone else's house, even that of my father or of my best friends, male and female, the women being rather more hospitable: with them I would not only have felt like an intruder but also an exile from my own home, whereas in a hotel, I could pretend I was a visiting foreigner, although not a tourist, and feel less acutely that unpleasant sense of having been repudiated and then offered shelter.

I spoke to my father on the phone, as usual a brief conversation, although now he didn't have the excuse that I was calling him from England, which he assumed must be a very expensive thing to do (he belonged to a thrifty generation who only used the phone to give or receive messages, although Wheeler wasn't like that, so perhaps it was a generation that existed only in Spain), and I arranged to see him the next day. His voice sounded normal, just as it had on the last few occasions when I had called from London, I phoned him every week or even more frequently sometimes; he sounded slightly tired, but no more than that, and disliked having to hold the phone to his ear for too long. The strange thing was, though, that he made no fuss about the prospect of seeing me and expressed no excitement, as if we had seen each other only a couple of days before, if not yesterday. It was as if he suddenly had little sense of time or its passing, and kept those people closest to him, those he knew best, always in his thoughts, either so as not to miss them quite so much, their palpable presence I mean, or so as not really to notice their absence. I was simply me, one of his children, and therefore unchanging and sufficently established in his mind for him not to feel my physical absence or my distance or the unusually long gaps between visits or, rather, the non-existence of those visits. He hardly went out now. 'I've flown over from

London, Papa,' I said, 'I'll be here for a couple of weeks.' 'Good. And how are things?' he asked, showing no particular surprise. 'Oh, not too bad. But we'll have a proper talk tomorrow when I come and see you. Today, I want to go and see the kids. I probably won't even recognize them.' 'They were here a few days ago with their mother. She doesn't visit that often, but she comes when she can. And she phones me.' Luisa was not as fixed and stable as I was, which is why he could remember when she came to see him and when she didn't—she was, up to a point, still new to him. 'She must be incredibly busy,' I said as if she were still part of my life and I had to apologize for her. I knew there was no need, she was very fond of my father, and, besides, her own father had died a few years before, and she had, insofar as such a thing is possible, replaced that lost figure with *my* father. If she didn't go and see him more often, it must be because she really couldn't find the time. 'Was she looking pretty?' I asked stupidly. 'Luisa is always pretty. Why do you ask? You must see her more than I do.' He knew about our separation, I hadn't hidden it from him, as one does occasionally hide potentially upsetting news from the elderly. 'I'm living in England now, Papa,' I reminded him, 'and I haven't seen her for a while.' He said nothing for a moment, then: 'I know you're living in England. Well, if that's what you want. I hope your stay in Oxford is proving fruitful.' It wasn't that he didn't know I was living in London, but now and then he got the different times confused, which isn't that surprising really, since time is a continuum in which we are all caught up until we apparently cease to be.

I had to phone Luisa before going to her house, not only to make sure the children would be there, but out of respect for her. I still had the keys to the apartment and she wouldn't necessarily have changed the locks; I could probably just walk in, without warning, causing first shock and then surprise; but that seemed an abuse to me, she wouldn't like it at all, and besides I risked bumping into my temporary replacement, whoever he was, assuming she had granted him habitual access. It was unlikely, but when in doubt, it's best to do nothing: it would have been embarrassing and I would have liked it even less than she. It turned my stomach, the mere idea of finding a complete stranger sitting in my place on the sofa or preparing a quick supper in the kitchen or watching television with the children in order to appear all fatherly and friendly, or making out he was Guillermo's buddy. I was prepared to be told this as a fact, but not actually to see it and then, unable to forget it, have that picture in my mind once I was back in London.

I dialed her number, it was mid-afternoon, the children would be back from school. She picked up the phone, and when I told her I was in Madrid, she was really shocked and took a while to respond, as if she were rapidly taking stock of the situation in the light of this unforeseen event, and then: why didn't you warn me, how could you, it's not fair; I wanted to give you all a surprise, well, the kids mostly, and I'd still like it to be a surprise, so don't tell them I'm here, just let me walk through the door without them knowing a thing, they're not going out this evening, I assume, can I come over now?

'They're not going out, but I am,' she replied hastily and somewhat flustered, so much so that I even wondered—I couldn't help it—if it was true or if she had just made a last-minute decision to leave the house, I mean, to skedaddle, so as not to be there when I arrived, so that she wouldn't have to see me or meet me.

'You've got to go out now?' I had counted on her presence, on her benevolent gaze when the four of us met once more, it wouldn't be the same without her as witness.

'Yes, any moment actually, I'm just waiting for the babysitter,' she said. 'In fact, let me phone her right now, before she sets off, to warn her that you're coming. She doesn't know you, and she might not want to let you in unless she's forewarned, I've told her not to open the door to strangers under any circumstances, and you, I'm afraid, would be a stranger to her. Hang up now so that I can call her, and I'll call you right back. Where are you?'

I gave her the numbers of the hotel and my room. It was as if she were in the most terrific hurry, besides, nowadays you can track down a babysitter anywhere and at any time even if they're not at home, they all have cell phones. It occurred to me that she had not in fact yet spoken to the babysitter and was phoning her now so that the babysitter could race over to deal with this unexpected situation—hence the urgency—and have time to arrive, and give Luisa time to leave, before I appeared. Even if this was a genuine spur-of-the-moment decision to go out, she would never just assume that my key would still work and thus leave the children alone, not even for a minute, to wait for me there unaware they were waiting. I had the awful feeling she was trying to avoid me. But I couldn't be sure, perhaps I'd grown too used to interpreting people, those I came across at work and outside as well, to analyzing every inflection of voice and every gesture and to seeing something hidden behind any show of haste or delay. This was no way to go about the world, all it did was feed my imaginings.

She took what seemed an age to call back, long enough for me to grow impatient, to rekindle my suspicions, and to hope she would dispel them by telling me she'd cancelled her date. And to think, too, that she was playing for time, I mean, allowing time for the babysitter to get there and so delay me setting off in the same direction, towards our apartment which was no longer mine. I sat motionless on the bed, which is what you do when you're expecting something to happen from one moment to the next, a wretched expression that makes every second seem an eternity and leaves us dangling. More than a quarter of an hour had passed when the phone finally rang.

'Hi, it's me,' said Luisa, as young Pérez Nuix had done when she rang my doorbell on that night of heavy, sustained rain, but with much more justification, after all, as far as I was concerned she had been an unequivocal 'me' for many years—that's usually taken for granted in marriages, that there is only one 'me'— and, by then, I had been waiting for her call for some time. She was also within her rights to assume that I would recognize her without any need for further identification—who else would it be, who else but me, but her—from the first word and the first instant, and she could be almost sure of occupying most or many of my thoughts, although that wouldn't be high on her agenda just then, her mind was elsewhere, or she was trying to combine that elsewhere with my unwanted presence, for I couldn't shake off the feeling that I was just that, a nuisance. 'Sorry, the babysitter's phone was busy, and I've only just managed to get through to her. Anyway, she knows you'll be coming and that she's not to spoil your surprise, so she won't say anything to the children. How long will it take you to get here?'

'I don't know, about twenty minutes I should think, I'll take a cab.'

'Then would you mind not leaving for another fifteen or twenty minutes, that will give her time to settle in and sort the kids out. And please try not to keep them up too long past their bedtime, otherwise they'll be worn out tomorrow and they've got school in the morning. If possible, make sure they're in bed by eleven at the latest, which is already much later than usual. You'll have other opportunities to see them. How long are you staying?'

'Two weeks,' I said, and again it seemed to me that this created another unforeseen problem for her, that it was even an annoyance, a bother, something she would have to wrestle with.

'That long?' She couldn't suppress her feelings, she sounded more alarmed than glad. 'How come?'

'As I think I told you, I had to accompany my boss on a trip. In the end, it turned out to be four trips, one after the other. Anyway, he's rewarded me, I suppose, with a longer trip just for me.' And I added: 'So I won't see you tonight, then?'

'No, I don't think so, by the time I get back the children will be in bed. The babysitter will stay as long as she needs to, so don't worry about that; as soon as they're in bed, you can leave, don't wait up for me. If you'd warned me you were coming, I'd have arranged things differently. We'll talk later, when we've got more time.'

The same city, which, just the day before, was faded and dim, becomes suddenly crystal-clear as soon as you set foot in it again; time condenses, yesterday disappears—or becomes just an interval—and it's as if you had never left. You suddenly know once more which streets to take, and in which order, to get from one place to another, wherever they may be, and how much time to allow. I had reckoned on twenty minutes by taxi to my apartment through the abominable traffic, and I was almost exactly right. And instead of thinking excitedly about my children, whom I would be seeing at last after a long absence, I couldn't help worrying about Luisa instead during the whole disenchanted journey. It wasn't that I had expected her to give me a wonderful reception, but I'd thought at least she'd show a little curiosity and sympathy, as she had on the phone whenever I'd spoken to her from London, what had changed, why had she turned against me, was it because I was now breathing the same air as her? Perhaps she had only felt that sympathy and that vague curiosity about me from a distance, as long as I was far away, as long as I was just a voice in her ear, a voice with no face, no body, no eyes, no arms; then she could allow herself those feelings, but not here, not where we had lived happily together and where, later on, we had wounded each other. This was where she had survived without me, become unaccustomed to me, and so she didn't quite know what to do with me any more: I hadn't been around for quite some time. She said not a word about her date, which had arisen, or so it seemed to me, as soon as she learned that I was there in the flesh. She was under no obligation to tell me, of course, and I hadn't asked, nor had I suggested that she cancel, which is easy enough and perfectly free and something that people do on the slightest pretext, simply because they feel like it ('Oh, please, please, today's a really special day, I would so love to see all of you together, surely you can change it, go on, why don't you try?'); and people usually do give explanations even if they're not asked, and provide needless excuses, and tell you about their inane life and speak at length and babble on, out of the sheer pleasure of using language, or so as to provide superfluous information or to avoid silences, or to provoke jealousy or envy or so as not to arouse suspicions by being enigmatic. 'The fatal word,' Wheeler had called it. 'The curse of the word. Talking and talking, without stopping, that is the one thing for which no one ever lacks ammunition. That is the wheel that moves the world, Jacobo, more than anything else; that is the engine of life, the one that never becomes exhausted and never stops, that is its life's breath.' Luisa had held in that breath and said only: 'They're not going out, but I am,' without even adding the minimal excuses usual in such cases, 'It's an appointment I can't break, I made it weeks ago,' or 'It's too late to cancel,' or 'I can't postpone it because the people I'm meeting are visiting Madrid and they're leaving tomorrow.' Nor had she expressed polite regret at the clash, even if that regret was false (it still gives some small consolation to the jilted person and makes him feel better): 'Oh, how annoying, what bad luck, what a shame, I would love to have seen the children's reaction when they saw it was you. If only I'd known about it beforehand. Are you sure you can't wait until tomorrow? It's been such a long time.' She had kept her mouth shut, just as if she didn't know who her date was or where she was going, more as if she had just made it up than as if she wanted to keep it secret. That was my suspicion, an occupational hazard perhaps, acquired in England. She must have somewhere to go, somewhere to spend a few hours, the hours I would spend in her apartment. She was sure by now to have a boyfriend, a lover, however transient. It would just be a matter of finding him, or probably not even that if he'd already given her the keys to his place. 'It's as if she doesn't want to see me,' I thought in the taxi. 'But she's going to, that's for sure. I didn't come here to spend yet another day without seeing her, without once more seeing her face.'

The children were hugely surprised. At first, Marina gave me a hard, distrustful stare, then she got used to me, but more in the way that small children get used to strangers—it takes only a matter of minutes if the adult in question has a way with kids—than as if she really remembered me clearly and in detail. It also helped that her brother filled her in right from the start ('It's Papa, silly, don't you see?'). The presents helped to ease matters too, and the babysitter's approving, almost beatific smile, she was a very able young woman who came to open the door to me: I didn't dare try my key in the lock, in case it had been changed, I rang the bell like any other visitor. Marina asked me absurd questions ('Where do you live?' 'Have you got a dog?' 'Does it always rain there?' 'Are there any bears?'), while Guillermo was in charge of asking questions of a more reproachful kind ('Why don't we ever see you?' 'Do you like it better there than here?' 'Have you met any English children?') as well as of the bookish-adventure film variety, he read quite a lot and watched films all the time ('Have you visited Harry Potter's school?' 'And what about Sherlock Holmes' house?' 'Aren't you afraid to go out at night with all that fog and with Jack the Rippers about, or aren't there any Jack the Rippers in London now?' 'Is it true that if the real person stands next to his wax figure at Madame Tussaud's, you can't tell which is which?') I hadn't visited Harry Potter's school, but I had been to 221B Baker Street, because I lived nearby and often popped in; and in York, I had discovered the dark, neglected grave of Dick Turpin, the highwayman in the red jacket, mask, three-cornered hat and thigh-high boots, and next to him was buried his faithful horse, or rather mare, *Black Bess*, and I had seen the place where, still elegantly dressed, he had been hanged at the Tyburn, just outside York. One night, a white dog had followed me, tis tis tis, through the streets and squares and parks to my house, he was all alone in the heavy rain, for children it would be much more mysterious if I didn't mention his mistress; I let him dry himself and sleep in my apartment, and yes, I would have kept him, but he left the following morning when I took him out for a walk, and I've never seen him since, perhaps he didn't like my human food, well, I didn't have any dog food. On another night, I saw a man take out a sword in a disco, a two-edged sword, he produced it from inside his coat and threatened people, who drew back in terror; he sliced through several things with great skill and mastery, a table, a couple of chairs, some curtains, he shattered a few bottles and ripped the skirts of two women without causing them the slightest harm, he judged things perfectly, he was a real artist; then he put the sword back in the sheath inside his long coat, put the coat on—this made him walk very stiffly, like a ghost—and he left just like that, and no one dared to stop him; I didn't either, what do you mean, are you mad, he would have made mincemeat of me in seconds, he was so fast with that sword (like thunderless lightning that kills silently). I was about to tell them that I had spent a third night at the house of Wendy, Peter Pan's girlfriend, but I held back: Marina was young enough to believe it, but not Guillermo, and I didn't want to recall the videos I had been shown there, in fact, I didn't want ever to remember them and yet I thought of them constantly ('The wind moves the sea and the boats withdraw, with hurrying oars and full sails. Amongst the sound of the waves the rifle shots rang out . . . Cursèd be the noble heart that puts its trust in evil men! . . . Aboard the boats, all the sailors were crying, and the most beautiful women, all in black and distraught, walk, crying, through the lemon groves.' That poem about Torrijos would always be associated in my mind with that string of evil scenes). And I realized—I had forgotten, it was such a long time since I'd spoken to Guillermo and Marina—that almost everything that happens to one, can, with very few changes, easily be converted into a story for children. Intriguing or sinister tales, the kind that protect and prepare them and make them resourceful.

Once they had gone to bed, I was sure for the first time in many months that they were safe and sound; time again condensed or concertinaed, and for a few seconds I felt as if I had never left their side and never known Tupra or Pérez Nuix, Mulryan or Rendel; when, shortly afterwards, I tiptoed into their respective rooms, to turn out the lights and to check if they were all right, the Tintin book the boy must have been reading just before he fell asleep had slipped to the floor without waking him, and the girl was embracing a little bear destined once more to be smothered by the diminutive arm of her simple dreams. Almost nothing had changed in my absence. Only Luisa, who wasn't there, and although I was, I still hadn't seen her. In her place was a discreet babysitter, and she had kept out of the way, hadn't interfered in the reunion at all, she had merely helped with the children when it was time for supper and bed. She said her name was Mercedes, even though she was Polish: perhaps it was an adopted name, to hispanicize herself more quickly. She spoke good Spanish, she had learned it during the three years she had been there, before that, she hadn't known a word, she said, but her boyfriend was from Madrid, and she was thinking of getting married and settling there (I noticed she wore a little crucifix around her neck), she told me all this while I was playing for time. 'Don't wait up for me,' Luisa had warned, well, it had sounded to me rather like a warning. She was perfectly within her rights not to want me there while she was not, I might have started snooping, looking for anything that might have changed and poking around in her mail, opening her wardrobes and sniffing her clothes, going into her bathroom and smelling her shampoo and her cologne, checking to see if she still kept a photo of me in her bedroom (unlikely), although in the living room there were still a few family snapshots in which I appeared, the four of us together, she wouldn't want the children to forget me completely, at least not my face.

'Do you often come here?' I asked Mercedes. 'The children seem to know you well and they do as they're told.' This wasn't an entirely innocent question.

'Yes, sometimes, but not that often. Luisa doesn't go out much at night. Although she has gone out more lately, usually in the evening.' And then she betrayed Luisa, although she certainly didn't intend to, but she did, without lingering or delaying— people just have to start speaking in order to tell too much, even when they don't seem to be telling anything; they supply the listener with information as soon as they open their mouth, without being asked and without realizing that it *is* information, and so they give someone away without intending to, or they betray themselves, and no sooner are the words out than it's too late: 'Oh, I didn't realize, how stupid of me, I didn't mean to'—'She was lucky to find me in. She doesn't normally leave it so late to call me, she always phones at least the day before. I might have been booked somewhere else, because I babysit for four different families. Four, excluding Luisa.'

'She was lucky then. How much notice did she give you?'

'None. Just enough time for me to get here. I normally have to catch a bus and a metro, but tonight she said she'd pay for my taxi. The thing is, there aren't that many taxis where I live, which is why it took me so long. "Come as soon as you can," she said, "something urgent's cropped up." She told me about your visit and that I should let you in. But I would have looked through the peephole and let you in anyway, because I know you from the photographs.' And she gestured shyly towards them, as if she were embarrassed to have noticed.

So my suspicions had been right, perhaps all that practice in the office with no name had not been in vain. Luisa hadn't intended to go out, she'd done so in order not to see me. She hadn't dared make me postpone my meeting with the kids, she would have found it far harder to come up with a credible excuse ('That long,' she had said, aware that it really was a long time). Where would she have gone, it isn't easy to spend hours away from home if you've nothing planned, when evening starts to come on, at twilight. She could have gone to the movies, any film would do, or gone shopping downtown, although she really hated that; she could have sought refuge with her lover, or gone to see a friend or her sister. She would have to kill an awful lot of time until I left, until she reckoned that I would have left the apartment and the coast would be clear, and she would know, too, how hard I'd find it to drag myself away, I felt very comfortable there, almost nothing had changed.

It was past eleven o'clock, which was the very latest the children were allowed to stay up on special occasions, we'd had a very entertaining few hours, but I could see they were tired too, it hadn't been particularly hard to persuade them that it was high time they went to bed, and Mercedes was in equal parts persuasive and firm. It wouldn't be long before Luisa was back. If I hung on for another half an hour, we'd almost certainly meet. I could at least say hello, give her a kiss on the cheek, perhaps a hug if that seemed appropriate, hear her voice, no longer disembodied, see how she had changed, whether she had grown slightly faded or was perhaps more beautiful now that I was far away and she had someone more flattering closer to hand; I could at least see her face. I wanted no more than that, so very little, but I was filled with impatience, an unbearable impatience. Added to that were feelings of insecurity, intrigue, possibly rancor, or perhaps wounded pride: she didn't even share my elementary curiosities, but how could that be after we had been each other's main motive for so many years, it seemed positively insulting that nothing should remain, that she was quite happy to wait another whole day and not even necessarily see me tomorrow—there was no guarantee that, on various pretexts, she wouldn't also avoid me tomorrow and the day after and the day after that, and so on, during the whole of my stay; she might even suggest I pick up the kids downstairs at the entry door on my next visit and take them out somewhere or arrange it so that when I arrived, she'd always be out, or else she might drop them off at my father's apartment so that I could spend time with them there and they'd get to see their grandfather as well. Yes, it was rude of her to be in so little hurry to recognize me in the changed man, the absent man, the solitary man, the foreigner returned; not to immediately want to find out what I was like without her, or who I had become. ('What a disgrace it is to me to remember thy name, or to know thy face tomorrow,' I thought.)

'Do you mind if I stay a bit, until Luisa comes?' I asked the false Mercedes. 'I'd like to see her, just for a moment. She won't be much longer, I shouldn't think.'—'What a painful irony,' I thought, 'here I am asking the permission of a young Polish baby-sitter whom I've never seen in my life to stay a little longer in my own apartment or what was my apartment, and which I chose and set up and furnished and decorated along with Luisa, in which we lived together for a long time, and which I still pay for, indirectly. Once you abandon a place you can never go back, not in the same way, any gap you leave is instantly filled or else your things are thrown away or dumped, and if you do reappear it's only as an incorporeal ghost, with no rights, no key, no claims and no future. With nothing but a past, which is why we can be shooed away.'

'Luisa said I should stay until she got back,' she said. 'She's going to pay for my taxi home as well, if she's very late. So that I don't have to wait to catch a *buho*, there aren't many during the week.'—The word *buho* rang a bell in that context, they were, I seemed to recall, the late-night buses or metros, I'd forgotten all about them.—'There's really no point in waiting,' she added. 'She's likely to be some time yet. I'll be here if the children should wake up, if they need anything.'

She was very discreet, but her words sounded discouraging, almost like orders. As if Luisa had briefed her when she phoned and what she was really saying to me was: 'No, the best thing would be if you left, because Luisa doesn't want to see you. And she doesn't want you hanging around when she's not here, unchecked and unwatched—my presence isn't enough; I don't have any authority—she doesn't trust you any more, she stopped trusting you some time ago.' Or else: 'She's erased you, all these months she's been scrubbing away at the stain you left and now she's struggling to remove the rim, the final remnant. She doesn't want you to leave any more stains and to see all her hard work ruined. So please be so kind as to go, if not, you'll be considered an intruder.' And these last two interpretations of her words were what made me decide once and for all to stay.

'No, I think I'll wait for her anyway,' I said and sat down on the sofa, after first having taken a book from the shelves. The books hadn't changed, they were in the same arrangement and order in which I had left them, there was my entire library, I mean, our library, we hadn't divided the books up, and I had nowhere to put mine, everything in England was provisional and, besides, I had no space, and I wasn't going to start moving things if I didn't know where I was going to live, either in the short term or the long. Mercedes wouldn't dare oppose me, she wouldn't dare throw me out if I sat down and read and said nothing, if I asked her no more questions and didn't bother her or try to worm things out of her. She hadn't realized that was what I was doing, or perhaps only when it was too late. 'I'm in no hurry,' I added, 'I've just arrived from London. This way I'll be able to say hello to her—in Madrid and in person.'

I waited and waited, reading in silence, listening to the small noises that seemed either eerily familiar or instantly recognizable: the fridge with its changing moods, occasional distant footfalls in the apartment above and a sound like drawers being opened and closed—the upstairs neighbors obviously hadn't moved and kept up their nocturnal customs; there were also the faint notes of a cello coming from the boy who lived with his widowed mother across the landing and who always practiced before he went to bed, he might well be almost an adolescent by now, his playing had improved a lot, he got stuck or stopped less often from what I could hear, which wasn't much, the boy always tried not to play too loudly, he was well-brought-up and used to say 'Good afternoon' to us even when he was only small, but in a friendly not a cloying way, I tried to work out if he was playing something by Purcell or by Dowland, but I couldn't, the chords were very tenuous and my musical memory was out of training, in London I listened to music at home and rarely went to concerts, not that I spent much time at home, where I couldn't rely on the consoling daze that sustained me daily and liberated me from the curse of having to make plans. The only thing I knew for sure was that the music being played wasn't Bach.

The Polish babysitter got out her cell phone and made a call, retreating into the kitchen so that she could talk to her boyfriend where I wouldn't hear her, perhaps out of modesty, perhaps in order not to bother me with a schmaltzy or perhaps obscene conversation (however Catholic she was, you never can tell). It occurred to me that if I hadn't been there, she would have used

Luisa's landline, on which she could talk at greater length because she would be saving herself the expense, for that reason alone it must have really irritated her that I hadn't left when I should have. I had taken *Henry V* down from the shelves, because Wheeler had quoted from it and referred to it in his house by the River Cherwell, and since then I had kept it handy and dipped into it or leafed through it now and then, even though I had long since found the fragments he'd alluded to. Or, rather, what I picked up was *King Henry V*, to give it its full title, a copy of the old Arden edition, bought in 1977 in Madrid according to a note I had written on the first page, and at some point I had written in it, although I couldn't remember when—but before I would have met Luisa—and my mind was in no fit state to pay due attention to the text or to trawl back through the past, I merely glanced through it, looking at the underlinings left by the young reader I had been on some distant day, so long forgotten that it no longer existed. My mind was concentrating on one noise only, which is why I heard all the other noises too, my ear cocked and waiting for the sound that mattered to me, that of the elevator coming up, followed by the key in the door. I heard the first several times, but it always stopped at other floors and only once at ours, and on that occasion it was not accompanied by the second sound and wasn't Luisa returning.

Mercedes returned to the living room, looking happier and more relaxed. She was an attractive girl, but so excessively blonde and pale and cold that she appeared not to be. She asked if I would mind if she turned on the TV, and I said I didn't, although that was a lie, because the sound of the television would wipe out all other sounds; but I was there as a mere unexpected visitor, if not an out-and-out intruder, which I was more and more becoming with each minute I lingered there. The young woman used the remote control to flip through the channels and finally opted for a film with real animals in the main roles, it was as I realized at once, *Babe*, I recalled taking Guillermo to see it at the movie theater a few years before, it was mystifying why the moronic programmers should put it on at that hour, when most children would be asleep. I was happy to watch it for a while, it was less demanding than Shakespeare and the little pig was a great actor, I wondered if perhaps he had been nominated for an Oscar that year, but I doubt he would have won; I would buy it on DVD for Marina, who, having been born later, might not have seen it. I was just considering the sad fate of actors—anyone can do their job, children and dogs, elephants, monkeys and pigs, but, so far, no one has found an animal capable of composing music or writing a book; although, of course, that depends on how strict you are with your definition of animal—when I saw Mercedes spring to her feet, scoop up her things in a matter of seconds and, after addressing an abrupt 'Goodbye' to me, race to the front door. Only when Mercedes was already there did I hear the key in the lock and the door opening, it was as if she was endowed with extraordinarily acute hearing and had picked up the exact moment when Luisa arrived at the street door in a car or taxi. She, the babysitter, must have been in a tremendous hurry to leave, she clearly didn't want to stay any longer than it took for her to be paid and provided with her promised expensive transportation home, for it was nearly midnight, Luisa had been out for a little over four hours. Or perhaps it wasn't just that, perhaps she wanted to warn Luisa immediately that, contrary to her expectations, she wouldn't find herself alone: that I had insisted on waiting for her, against her wishes, or perhaps in disobedience to the orders that Mercedes had received and failed to enforce.

I heard them whispering for a few moments, I got up from the sofa, but didn't dare to join them; then I heard the door close, the Polish babysitter had gone. After that came the sound of Luisa's footsteps in the corridor—she was wearing high heels, I recognized the click-clack on the wooden floor—she always wore them to go out—heading towards the bathroom and her bedroom, she didn't even look in at me, she must be desperate for a pee, I assumed, as one so often is on arriving home; that seemed quite normal really, if she'd been with other people and not wanted to get up, for example, during a meal, either at someone's table or in a restaurant. Or perhaps she wanted to tidy up before showing herself to me, assuming she had spent the evening with my ephemeral replacement and was returning as women sometimes do return from such prolonged encounters, with her skirt all wrinkled and slightly askew, her hair disheveled, her lipstick erased by kisses, a run in her stockings and the signs of all that impetuosity still in her eyes. Or perhaps she was so angry with me that she had decided to go to bed without even saying hello and to leave me in the living room until I got fed up or until I understood that when she had said she wasn't going to see me that night, she had meant it. She'd probably decided to shut herself in the bedroom and not come out, to get undressed, turn off the light and climb into bed, pretending that I wasn't there, that I was still in London and did not exist in Madrid, or that I was a mere ghost. She was perfectly capable of that and more—I knew what she was like—whenever anyone tried to impose something on her that she didn't want. But she would have to leave the bedroom before she closed her eyes, at least once, and if the worst came to the worst, I could intercept her then, for it would be quite beyond her powers not to go in and see the children and make sure they were safe and sleeping peacefully.

I continued to wait, I didn't want to rush anything, still less go and pound on her door, beg her to let me see her, bombard her with awkward questions through that barrier, and demand explanations I had no right to demand. That would have been a bad start, after such a long separation, it would be best to avoid anything that smacked of confrontation or reproach, unnecessary and absurd and not at all what I wanted. From now on, the initiative lay with her, I had already made things awkward for her by refusing to leave, once the excuse of enjoying spending time with my children had lapsed. On hearing the key in the door, I had muted the TV, but could still see the antics of that porcine emulator of De Niro and John Wayne—he was an extremely polite little pig—and his co-stars: a few dogs, some sheep, a horse, a bad-tempered duck, all of them superb actors.

After a few minutes, I heard the door of her bedroom open and a few footsteps, she was still wearing her high heels, so she obviously hadn't changed her clothes, but she walked more quietly, trying not to make noise: she peered into Marina's room and then into Guillermo's, she didn't go right in or only a little way, just far enough to see that everything was in order. I still didn't want to get up and go and find her, I preferred for her to come into the living room, if she did, and when at last she did—her footsteps firmer, normal, now that she had breathed in the sound of the children's deep sleep, which had been enough to reassure her that she ran no risk of waking them—I thought I understood, despite any efforts at concealment she may have made in the bathroom that had once been mine, why she had wanted to avoid me, and that it hadn't been because she didn't want to see me, but because she didn't want me to see her.

At first sight, she looked very good, well-dressed, well-shod, although rather less well-coiffed, and yet wearing her long locks caught back in a ponytail suited her, gave her a youthful, naïve air, almost that of a young girl caught in flagrante on returning home late, but who was I to say anything, or even to feel surprised. Before I noticed anything was wrong, she had time to say a few words, with an expression on her face of mingled pleasure to see me and annoyance at finding me there, but also of fear that I had caught her out or perhaps it was embarrassment doing battle with defiance, as if I had surprised her doing something I wouldn't like or that would seem to me reprehensible, and, realizing that, she didn't know whether to strike her flag or to run it up the flagpole and stand and fight, it's odd how former couples, long after they have ceased being a couple, still feel mutually responsible, as if they owed each other a certain loyalty, even if that amounts only to knowing how they're coping on their own and what's going on in their life, especially if something strange or bad is happening. Things were happening to me about which I, being far away, had said nothing: I had clearly lost my footing or lost both grip and judgment, employed as I was in a job about whose consequences I knew nothing, not even if it *had* any consequences, and being paid a suspiciously large salary too; I had, by then, been injected with strange poisons and was leading an existence that grew ghostlier by the day, immersed in the dream-like state of one who lives in another country and is starting not always to think in his own language, I was very alone there in London, even though I was surrounded by people all day, they were just work colleagues and never really developed into pure friendships, even Pérez Nuix had turned out to be no different—not even my lover, which she wasn't, since there had been no repetition and no laughter—after that one night I had shared with her carnally, a fact we had kept concealed and excessively silent, from others and from ourselves, and when one pretends that something hasn't happened and it's never spoken of, it ends up not having happened, even though we know the opposite to be case; what Jorge Manrique wrote in his 'Lines on the Death of His Father' some five hundred and thirty years ago, and only two years before his own early death when he was not yet forty, wounded during an attack on a castle by a shot from a harquebus (even worse and more dishonorable than that of Richard Yea and Nay, felled by an arrow from a crossbow), 'If we judge wisely, we will count what has not happened as the past' is as true as the contrary position which allows us to count the past, along with everything else we have experienced, our entire life, as also not having happened. Then what does it matter what we do in our lives, or why it does it matter so very much to us?

'You just *had* to stay, didn't you, Jaime?' Luisa said before I could say anything. 'You just had to wait up to see me.'

Now, though, after that initial glance, I spotted what was wrong at once, it was impossible not to, at least for me. She had tried to cover it with make-up, to conceal it, hide it, perhaps in the same way that Flavia would have tried unsuccessfully, with the unlikely help of Tupra in the ladies' restroom, to make the wound on her face invisible, the mark of the rope, the weal left by the whip, the welt caused by De la Garza's clumsy lashings during his wild gyrations on the fast dance floor. That wasn't what Luisa had on her face, it wasn't *uno sfregio*, not a gash or a cut or a scratch, but what has always been known in my language as '*un ojo morado*'—literally 'a purple eye'—and in English as 'a black eye,' although since the impact or cause was not recent, the skin was already growing yellow, the colors that appear after such a blow are always mixed, there's never a single color, but several, which combine at every phase and keep changing, perhaps the disagreement between the two languages stems from that (although mine does lean more to English when it refers to such an eye as '*un ojo a la funerala*'—more or less 'an eye in mourning'), they always take a long time to fade, it was just our bad luck that not enough time had yet passed. When I saw it, I no longer had to respond to her words, nor to apologize. Unfortunately, I couldn't greet her either or give her a kiss or embrace her, I had waited so long for this meeting and now I couldn't even manage a smile or an '*Hola, niña*'—'Hello, love'—as I used to when we were still together and on good terms. I immediately went over to her and the first thing I said was:

'What's that? Let me see? What happened? Who did it?'

I took her face in my hands, taking care not to touch the affected area, she had clearly just been in the bathroom applying various creams, to no avail. Her eyelid was no longer puffy or only a little, but it obviously had been. I calculated that the injury must have occurred about a week or perhaps ten days ago, and it was the result of a blow, I was sure of that, dealt by a fist or a blunt instrument like a bat or a blackjack, I had seen such bruised eyes and cheekbones and chins years before, under the Franco regime, when students who had been arrested and beaten up would emerge from the police station, from the headquarters of the security forces in Puerta del Sol or from Carabanchel prison, my fellow university students who'd had much worse luck than I did during the small semi-spontaneous street demonstrations that we called '*saltos*' and at illegal rallies that were broken up with the aid of very long, flexible truncheons, which really hurt because the truncheon flexed on impact, they were used by the police or '*grises*' who charged on horseback, sometimes it seems incredible to me that it was only in the mid-seventies that we used to flee their hooves every few days or weeks, as we left our classes. Although, of course, everything can come back.

She moved away, avoided me, retreating two steps in order to re-establish the distance between us, smiling as if my questions amused her, but I could see that they didn't.

'What do you mean? No one did anything to me. I collided

with the garage door about a week ago. It was my wretched cell phone's fault. Someone called me, I got distracted and misjudged the distance when the door was closing. It hit me full on, it's really heavy, it must be made of solid iron. It's nearly better now, it looked worse than it was. It doesn't hurt.'

'Your cell phone? So you've got a cell phone now? Why didn't you tell me? Why didn't you give me the number?' And while, in my surprise, I was asking her all this, I thought or remembered: 'Reresby made me say the same thing to De la Garza, I had to translate it for him while he was lying motionless on the floor, bruised and beaten: "Tell him that if he has to go to the hospital, then he should give them the same line drunks and debtors do—that the garage door fell on him." Luisa has become neither of those things, neither a drunk nor a debtor, as far as I know. But Tupra was obviously aware that blows from garage doors are almost always inventions.' And thanks to him I was even more convinced that she was lying to me. She lacked the kind of imagination that a habitual liar develops, and so she had resorted to cliché, like any inexperienced liar who avoids the implausible, which is precisely the thing most likely to be believed.

'It's because of the kids,' she said. 'I realized that, however much we might hate cell phones, there's no sense in a babysitter or my sister, for example, or the school, not being able to locate me immediately if anything should happen to them.'—So the Polish babysitter could have called Luisa's cell phone from the kitchen and warned her that I was refusing to shift from the apartment, and also found out with some degree of accuracy when she would arrive.—'Especially since you're not here. I bought it for my own peace of mind. Now that I'm alone with them, now that I'm the only person anyone can contact in an emergency. And anyway why would you need the number in London? It's not as if we still spoke every day . . .'—Unfortunately, I sensed no reproach in these last words, I wished I had. I couldn't stop looking at her purple, yellowish, bluish black eye, the white of which was still slightly red, it would have been crisscrossed with red veins during the first few days after the blow. She was pretending that she wasn't even aware of it, but she could see me staring at it and this made her slightly nervous, as became apparent when she turned to look at the television so that she was in profile, to escape my scrutiny. And she tried to change the subject too. 'What were you watching, a movie about pigs? Is this some new interest of yours?' she added with the amiable irony that was so familiar to me and so attractive. She must have seen my fleeting smile. 'I'm sure the children would enjoy it. How did you think they looked, by the way? Have they grown a lot? Do they seem very different?'

While I did want to talk to her about the children, to tell her what impression they'd made on me after such a long time, I wasn't going to let myself be diverted so easily. I was the way I was, and now I had the examples of Tupra and Wheeler, who never let go of their prey as long as there was something to be got out of him or her, after all the digressions and evasions and detours.

'Don't lie to me, Luisa, you and I haven't changed that much. That business about the garage door is so old hat, they're always rebelling and hitting people,' I said, and again I noticed that I only called her by name when we were arguing or when I was angry, rather as she only called me Deza in similar situations, as well as in other very different ones. 'Tell me who did this to you. I hope it's not the guy you're going out with, because if it is, we've got a problem on our hands.'

'*Our* hands? Just supposing I was going out with someone, what's that got to do with you?' she said at once, parrying my remark not sharply, but firmly; and she had enough spirit to recover her irony and immediately soften the blow: 'If you're going to continue down that road, you'd better go back to watching your little animal friends while I tidy up, but once it's over, you leave; the children have to get up early, and it's already very late. We'll talk another day when we're both a bit fresher, but not about this. I told you what happened, so don't insist on seeing phantoms. And if that was just a way of asking me if I'm going out with someone, that's none of your business, Deza. Go on, finish watching your pig, and then go back to the hotel and sleep, you must be tired from your trip and from the children. They're exhausting, and you're out of practice being with them.'

She could always make me laugh and could always win me over. I still had a soft spot for her, and that hadn't changed during my time spent in London. This was hardly news—it was something that would probably never change—but being there with her only confirmed and made still plainer to me that I should, at all times, be careful not to allow myself unwittingly to be charmed, while she bustled around and took no notice of me. Quite apart from our conjugal life and our unforgotten love, Luisa was for me one of those people whose company you seek out and are grateful for and which, almost in itself, makes up for all the heartaches, and which you look forward to all day—it's our salvation—when you know you'll be seeing her later that evening like a prize won with very little effort; one of those people you feel at ease with even when times are bad and about whom you have the sense that wherever they are, that's where the party is, which is why it's so hard to give them up or to be expelled from their society, because you feel then that you're always missing out on something or—how can I put it—living on the margins. Thinking that such people could die is unbearable to us: even if we're far from them and never see them any more, we know they're still alive and that their world exists, the world that they themselves create merely by being and breathing; that the earth still shelters them and that they therefore retain their space and their sense of time, both of which one can imagine from a distance: 'There's the house,' we think, 'there's the atmosphere filled by her steps, by the rhythm of her day, the music of her voice, the smell of the plants she tends and the pause of her night; I no longer play any part in it, but there is the laughter, the wit and charm and the dear departed friends to whom Cervantes bade farewell when he was dying, "hoping to see you soon, happily installed in the other life." And knowing that therein lies all help, that we possess a memory not shared by everyone, which, as far as I'm concerned is the past, but not truly so, not in the absolute sense—that it's only by accident, or bad luck, or my own fault that I daily perceive it as the past—a place where others come and go and enjoy themselves without ever giving it much thought, just like us when we were part of that atmosphere and that rhythm, that wit and charm, part of the music of that house and even the pause of its quiet night. Knowing that it was not just a pleasant dream or something that existed in another imagined life.' And there I was, a witness to its permanence and not wanting to leave. There stood the person who was, for me, where the party was happening, with her good humor and her steadfastness and her frequent smiles, and even her high heels. That was enough, up to a point, knowing that she had not ceased to be, that she still trod the earth and still traversed the world, that she was not safe more or less in one-eyed, uncertain oblivion or already on the side of time where the dead converse.

And yet now there was a threat, or worse still there was an already visible wound that someone had inflicted and that might be repeated, possibly something worse next time, who knew (who knows when anything will stop once it's begun). What I did know was that nagging would get me nowhere: if she had decided not to tell me something or talk about it, there was no way I could twist her arm, I would have to find out by other means, but by what means, just then I could think of none apart from the kids, but I didn't want to use them, and then I was surprised to find myself thinking: 'I could always ask Tupra for help.' If, as I assumed, he had found out about the night Pérez Nuix had spent at my apartment and about the agreement we had reached behind his back; if, therefore, my favor to her had proved useless and Incompara had gained nothing from it, and young Pérez Nuix's father had received the inevitable beating for his recurring debts, a beating that Reresby had made me watch (the billiard cues—doubtless to inform me of my failure and to teach me a lesson), he would have no difficulty in finding out the name of the man Luisa was going out with, even though it was in another country and the wench, fortunately, was not yet dead. That had been one of my fears during my time in London, since my departure, when I thought about who would, sooner or later, replace me, and of the various possibilities that had always terrified me, the figure of the despotic possessive man, who subjugates and isolates and, little by little, quietly insinuates his demands and prohibitions, disguised as infatuation and weakness and jealousy and flattery and supplication, a devious sort who declines her first invitations to share her pillow in order not to appear intrusive and who reveals not a trace of any invasive or expansionist tendencies, and who initially appears always deferential, respectful, even cautious; until one day after some time has passed—or perhaps on a rainy night, when they're stuck at home—when he has conquered the entire territory and doesn't allow Luisa a moment's peace, he closes his large hands around her throat while the children—my children—watch from a corner, pressing themselves into the wall as if wishing the wall would give way and disappear and, with it, this awful sight, and the choked-back tears that long to burst forth, but cannot, the bad dream, and the strange, long-drawn-out noise their mother makes as she dies. In the face of that nightmarish scene, I had always thought, in order to dispel it: 'But no, that won't happen, that isn't happening, I won't have that luck or that misfortune (luck as long as it remains in the imagination, misfortune were it to become reality) . . .' Now I was faced by a real mark left by that imagined horror, in the form of a black eye or an eye of changing colors, and by the knowledge that in this area of reality there wasn't a single drop of luck, only a vast sea of misfortune drowning everything and driving out all trace of the imaginary, such a sphere would no longer exist, or is it just that it can never coexist with real danger: there are far too many poisonous cowards in Spain who, each year, kill their wives or the women who were their wives or who they wanted to be their wives, and sometimes they kill their own children as well in order to inflict more pain on the women, it's a plague that remains unquelled by persuasions, threats, laws, or even the most severe prison sentences, because such men take no notice of the outside world and they get carried away because they love these women so much or hate them so deeply that they cannot, like me, simply live without them, content in the knowledge that cheers me in my sadness (that consoles me as regards Luisa), that they continue to exist in the world and will be or are the past only for us, but not for everyone else. 'I can't take any risks in a country like this,' I thought. 'I can't take any risks with a black eye inflicted by a punch, I can't just leave the matter entirely in her hands and to her possibly weakened will and not get involved, it's enough that I know she's put herself in danger and therefore the children too, even if only because they might lose her, and they've already suffered a semi-loss with me leaving home.'

And so I took two steps back and decided not to ask her any more questions, I would ask elsewhere, I had two weeks, that should be time enough to investigate and to convince her, and perhaps, during my stay, she would receive another blow and then she wouldn't want to keep quiet and close her mind to my words ('Keep quiet and don't say a word, not even to save yourself. Put your tongue away, hide it, swallow it even if it chokes you, pretend the cat's got your tongue. Keep quiet, and save yourself.' But perhaps we shouldn't always do that, however much, in the gravest of situations, we are advised and urged to do precisely that).

'All right, I'll go,' I said. 'I won't take up any more of your time, you're right, it's late, I'll call you tomorrow or the day after and we can meet whenever it suits you. And don't worry about the pig, it was your Polish babysitter who started watching him, although, it has to be said, he is a wonderful actor, up there with the greats.' And at the front door, to which she accompanied me, smiling ever more brightly, as if the imminent absence of my gaze were already a source of relief, I added: 'But *te conosco, mascherina*.'—This was an expression I had learned a long time before from my distant Italian girlfriend, who had taught me her language, more or less; and that carnivalesque expression, known to Luisa as well, was tantamount to saying: 'You don't fool me.'

I wasted no time. The following day, I went to see my father, as I'd said I would; I had lunch with him and, while we were eating dessert, my sister arrived, she dropped in on him most days and since she knew nothing of my visit (my father had forgotten to mention it, 'Oh, I thought you all knew'), finding me there was a cause of great surprise and pleasure. And when my father went to lie down for a while, at the request of his caregiver, and left us alone, Cecilia brought me up to date on the medical situation, providing me with more details (the outlook wasn't good, either in the medium or more likely short term), and once she, in turn, had told me about her and her husband and I'd done my best not to tell her anything about myself beyond the innocuously vague, I finally got up the nerve to ask if she knew anything about Luisa: what kind of life she was leading, if they ever got together socially, if she knew whether or not she was going out with anyone yet. She knew almost nothing, she told me: they talked on the phone now and then, especially about practical matters involving their respective children, and they occasionally met up there, at my father's apartment, but generally only for a matter of minutes because Luisa was usually in a hurry, they would exchange a few friendly words and then Luisa would leave the children to spend some time with their grandfather or with their cousins, my sister's children or my brothers,' one or another of whom would usually be there on a Saturday or a Sunday; then, after a couple of hours, Luisa would return to pick up Guillermo and Marina, but, again, she was always in a rush. My sister understood, though, that Luisa sometimes visited my father on her own, on a weekday, to chat and keep him company, they had always got on well together. So it might be that she talked more with him, or about more personal matters, than with any other member of the family, even if only once in a blue moon. No, she had no idea what kind of life Luisa was leading in her spare time, not that she would have a great deal of that. There was no reason why Luisa would keep her up to date on her comings and goings, least of all the romantic kind. Her husband had bumped into Luisa one evening, about two or three months ago, coming out of an art gallery or an exhibition, she couldn't quite remember which, accompanied by a man he didn't know, which was hardly surprising really, it would have been far stranger if he *had* known him; they had seemed to him like friends or colleagues, by which he meant that they hadn't been walking along arm in arm or anything. The only thing he did say was that the man looked to him like an arty type. At that point, I interrupted her (my reflexes in my own language were beginning to go).

'You mean he's an artist? Why? Did Federico say what he looked like?'

'No, by "arty" he meant one of those people who like to look the part of the artist, the eccentric. They may or may not be artists, it doesn't matter. They dress in a way that gives that impression, it's a deliberate ploy, to fool people into thinking that they're very intense and, well, arty, it could be a black polo neck or a fancy walking stick with a ghastly greyhound head on the handle, or an anachronistic hat they never take off, or long wavy musician's hair, you know the sort I mean.'—And she made a corresponding gesture with her hands around her head, rather as if she were washing her hair without touching her scalp.—'Or a ridiculous Goyaesque hairnet,' I had time to think fleetingly. 'Or tattoos anywhere, especially on their heels'—'Or' she went on, 'women who wear caps, or those baggy stockings that reach just above the knee, or a sailor's hat or the kind of hat some smug sassy black woman would wear or else some ghastly rasta braids.'

It amused me to know that she hated that particular kind of

stockings. I had no idea, on the other hand, what she meant by 'the kind of hat some smug sassy black woman would wear' and I was curious enough to be tempted to ask. However, I couldn't afford to waste any time, my other curiosity was more urgent. 'I see. So what was the guy wearing? Or did he have the whole caboodle, polo neck, walking stick *and* hat?'

'He had a ponytail. Federico noticed this because he wasn't a particularly young man, your age or thereabouts. Our age.'

'Yes, in certain places, it's quite a common sight now. You get grown men wearing a ponytail, in the belief that it makes them look like a pirate or a bandit; or else it's a goatee, and then they think they're Cardinal Richelieu or a psychiatrist or someone's clichéd idea of a sage—there's a positive epidemic of them among professors; or they grow a mustache and an imperial and think they're musketeers. They're complete frauds, the lot of them.' With my sister I could allow myself to be as arbitrary and cranky and over-the-top as she herself tended to be, it was a comical family trait, shared by all of us except my father, whom we did not greatly resemble in terms of equanimity or good temper. I, for example, never trust men who wear those rather monk-like sandals, I figure they're all impostors and traitors; or anyone in bermuda shorts or clamdiggers (men, I mean), which nowadays means that in summer I trust almost no one, especially in Spain, that paradise of shameless ignominious get-ups. It may be that those intuitions-made-rules, those radical prejudices or defining superficialities, which are based solely on limited personal experience (as are all such intuitions), had helped me with Tupra in my now not-so-new job, even if only in the categorical way I sometimes pronounced on the individuals presented to me for interpretation and conjecture, once, that is, I'd acquired both the confidence to issue judgments out loud and the irresponsibility one always needs when handing down any verdict. Nevertheless, those generalizations are based on something, even if that something belongs only to the realm of perceptions: each person carries echoes of other people within them and we cannot ignore them, there are what I call 'affinities' between individuals who may be utterly different or even polar opposites, but which, on occasion, lead us to see or intuit the shadows of physical resemblances which seem, at first, quite crazy. 'Objectively speaking, this beautiful woman and my grandfather have absolutely nothing in common,' we think, 'and yet something about her makes me think of him and reminds me of him,' and then we tend to attribute to her the character and reactions, the irascibility and opportunism of that despotic ancestor of ours. And the surprising thing is, we're often right—if enough time passes for us to find that out—as if life were full of inexplicable non-blood relationships, or as if each being that exists and treads the earth and traverses the world left hanging in the air invisible intangible particles of their personality, loose threads from their actions and tenuous resonances from their words, which later alight by chance on others like snow on shoulders, and thus are perpetuated from generation to generation, like a curse or a legend, or like a painful memory belonging to someone else, thus creating the infinite, exhausting and eternal combination of those same elements. 'What else did he tell you? What was the guy like, apart from the ponytail? How was he dressed? Didn't Luisa introduce him? What was his name? What does he do?'

'How should I know? I've no idea. Federico didn't notice and anyway he only saw him for a moment. They just walked past each other and said "Hello," that's all, but they didn't stop. Besides, Federico and Luisa don't really know each other that well.'

'So the lovely couple were in a hurry, were they?'

'They all were, Jacobo, Federico didn't stop and neither did they. Now don't start going around giving funny looks to every guy with a ponytail you happen to meet. Besides, whoever he was, they've probably split up since then. And don't go calling them "the lovely couple" either, because there's no basis for that, not the slightest indication, I've told you what happened, but I obviously can't tell you anything much at all. You're just getting yourself all worked up about nothing.'

I prefered not to tell her about the punch, the unbearable blow, about the shiner, the black eye, it was best if I continued investigating on my own without alarming her, if Cecilia knew no more than she had told me, she wasn't going to be able to provide me with any further information, I didn't mind if she attributed my disquiet exclusively to feelings of jealousy, those were enough to justify my insistent curiosity and, after all, they did exist, perhaps as much as my concern that some poseur, some wretch, with ponytail or without, it didn't matter, was abusing Luisa: someone who was trying to take my place but who would have difficulty keeping it, because it wasn't his turn. Even so he must be gotten rid of. If he was violent, if he was dangerous, if he raised his hand to her, he must be ejected without delay, before he had a chance to settle in, because life is full of surprises and there's always the risk that something that seems to have no future at all could go on forever. And if she lacked the will, the strength, the resolve or the courage, I was the only one capable of attempting it, or so, at least, I told myself.

And so I waited for my father to get up (or for him to be helped out of bed and brought to the living room, to the armchair where he had always done his reading, beneath the pleasant light of the lampstand) and for my sister to leave, and then I could continue my investigations, or my soundings. I didn't really expect that he would know very much, possibly nothing, but if, of all the people I had to hand, he was, according to what Cecilia had said, the one who perhaps talked most to Luisa about her personal life—even if only now and then and given the natural constraints felt by a daughter-in-law and a father-in-law, or rather by two people with such a great age difference between them—I might be able to find out, if not about the man who aspired to my position—she wouldn't tell him anything about that; and there might well be several aspirants—at least about what most concerned me: how she saw me, now that I had abandoned the field and gently removed myself from her existence—and even from her practical life—and detached myself, unprotesting, from her time and from that of our children. I asked my father about her and again he said that she didn't often come to see him, although I was gradually discovering or realizing that he had grown rather bad at gauging the presences or absences of certain people, as if it seemed to him that his most pleasant or enjoyable visitors always visited him far too infrequently, although I knew that some of those people visited almost every day, as was the case with my sister and my older nieces; he had always enjoyed the company of women and now that he was so weak and in need of gentleness, this liking had become even more marked. I guessed that something similar was happening with Luisa, who would certainly not have been able to visit him quite that often, but who, given the familiarity with which he referred to her and the odd telling comment, clearly did so more often than he imagined or felt that she did. I pressed him ('What does she say, what does she talk about when she comes? Does she talk about me or does she try not to mention me? Do you think she has doubts, might she have regrets, or does my name on her lips sound always as if she had found a place for me from which I don't and won't move, a place that is far too calm and stable?'), and suddenly he looked at me with his pale eyes, without answering, resting his forehead on one hand, his elbow on the arm of the chair, his usual pose when he was thinking and preparing to say something, I had the impression sometimes that he mentally constructed his sentences before uttering them, the first few at least (but not the subsequent ones). He sat looking at me with a mixture of interest, slight impatience and slight pity, as if I were not his son exactly, but a troubled young friend, of whom he was very fond and in whom he found two things strange or perhaps disappointing: one, that I should take such pains over a matter involving the extent of someone else's feelings or, indeed, self-interest, neither of which one can do anything about; and the other, that, despite being a grown man, a father, and despite my years and experience, I had still failed to grasp the insuperable nature of such griefs, or are they perhaps merely disquiets, and their laments.

'You don't seem at all resigned to the situation, Jacobo,' he said at last, after studying me for a while, 'and you have to resign yourself. If someone no longer wants to be with you, then you have to accept it. On your own, and without always watching to see how that person is changing or always looking out for signs and hoping for some drastic change. If such a change occurs, it won't be because you're watching or asking me questions or sounding out someone else. You can't keep on at someone all the time, you can't apply a magnifying glass or a telescope or resort to spies, nor, of course, must you pester them or impose yourself on them. Pretending doesn't help either, there's no point in feigning indifference or politeness when you feel neither polite nor indifferent, and I don't think you feel either of those things—yet. She'll know that you're pretending. Remember, transparency is one of the characteristics of being in love and other related states, in all their many guises (love can often be confused with stubbornness in its first stages and its last, when one thinks that the love of the other person has not yet put down deep roots or is slipping away). It's very difficult to deceive the person you love, or who feels or has felt loved (who has known love), unless, of course, that person prefers to be deceived, which, I must admit, is not uncommon. But you always know when you're no longer loved, if you're open to finding that out: when everything has become mere habit or a lack of courage to bring things to a close, or a desire not to make a fuss and not to hurt anyone, or a fear for your life or your purse, or a mere lack of imagination, most people are incapable of imagining a different life from the one they're living and they won't change it for that reason alone, they won't move, won't even consider it; they patch things up, postpone, seek distractions, take a lover, go gambling, convince themselves that what they have is bearable, allow time to do its work; but it won't occur to them to try something else. Only self-interest can defeat feelings, and then only sometimes. And in the same way, you always know when you're still loved, especially when you would like that love to abate or to stop altogether, which is usually the case with a couple in the process of splitting up. The one who made the decision, if he or she isn't an egotist or a sadist, longs for the other person to leave, to disentangle themselves from the web, to stop loving them and oppressing them with that love. To move on to someone else or, indeed, to no one, but to wash their hands of the whole business once and for all.'—My father paused for a moment and again looked at me hard, the way one sometimes looks before saying goodbye. He seemed to be scrutinizing me, which was unlikely because his sight had deteriorated greatly and he found it hard to read or even to watch television, I think he listened to it rather than watched. And yet that look had exactly the opposite effect, those ever paler blue eyes fixed on my face seemed to see right through me and to know more about me than I did myself.—'I think you need to let Luisa go, Jacobo. You haven't done so, even though you've respectfully and courteously taken yourself off to another country and so on. But you still haven't let her go. And now you have no option, you have to do it whether you like it or not. Let her breathe freely, give her some air, don't stand in her way. Let her take the initiative. It's not in your hands to do anything. If, one day, she discovers she's unhappy without you, if she realizes that she misses you so much that it's making her miserable, I don't think she would hesitate to tell you so and to ask you to come back, if I know her as I think I do. She's capable of admitting she was wrong, she's not proud. If she doesn't do so, it's because she doesn't want to, and she won't change whatever you do or say or however you behave, here or at a distance; as far as she's concerned, you're transparent, as she will be for you if you're prepared really to see her and to recognize what you see. If you're not, then that's another matter, and I understand that. Just don't ask me something I don't know, but *you* do; she isn't transparent to me.' And he added at once: 'Do you have a girlfriend at all in London?'

Now it was my turn to sit thinking for a moment, but not because I wasn't sure. No, I didn't have anything remotely like a girlfriend; I'd merely had a few fleeting encounters, especially in the first few months of settling in and reconnoitering and weighing things up, but they had all lacked either continuity or enthusiasm: of the three women who had slept at my apartment during that period, only one had returned with my consent (another had tried but without success), and that relationship had soon foundered, after our third or fourth date. Subsequently, another woman had passed through, but without any consequences. Then there was young Pérez Nuix who, I could not deny it, had meandered through my imagination, and after the one night we spent together, she still did occasionally, but that strange encounter had become tinged with vague ideas of favors and payments, and such things quickly douse the imagination; and although ideas of secrecy and silence ignite it, they are perhaps not enough to counteract the former, which have more weight and force.

'No,' I replied. 'Just the odd fling, but at my age such things are no longer stimulating or particularly diverting. Or only to those who are easily flattered. Which is not my case.'

My father smiled, he was sometimes amused by the things I said.

'No, maybe not now. It was in the past though, when you were younger, so don't be so superior. It's not the case with Luisa either, of that I'm sure. I have no idea whether she's seeing anyone else. Needless to say, she doesn't talk to me about such things, although she will one day, if I live that long. She trusts me, and I think she would tell me about any serious relationship. What I do see is that she doesn't discount the possibility and might even be in a hurry for such a relationship to appear. She's in a hurry to get back on her feet or to remake her life, or however people put it nowadays, you'll know, I'm sure. I mean that I don't think she yet has doubts about her attractiveness, that's not the problem, although neither of you is as young as you were. It's more that she's afraid of starting "the definitive relationship" too late. For many years, she clearly thought you were that—"definitive" I mean—but realizing that you weren't hasn't made her think that such a thing doesn't exist, rather that you both made a mistake and that she has wasted a great deal of precious time. So much so that she must now make haste to find that definitive relationship, which she hasn't given up on, she hasn't yet had time to adapt her expectations, or her illusions, she must still feel quite bewildered.'—Now the look of pity on his face grew more marked, similar to the look one sees on the face of many a mother as she watches her small children and sees how ignorant they still are and how slow they are to learn (and therefore how vulnerable). Naïveté does, more often than not, provoke pity. My father seemed to see that quality in

Luisa, of whom he was speaking, but he may have seen it in me too, for asking him about her when he couldn't help me. All he could do was distract me and listen to me, that, after all, is what it means to take on another person's anxieties.—'It's rather childish, I suppose. As if she'd always had a particular model of life in her head and as if the enormous upset with you hasn't made her abandon that, not yet at least, and as if she were thinking: "If he wasn't the person I thought he was, there must be another one. But where is he, I must find him, I must see him." That's all I can tell you. She's not in need of flattery, nor, of course, of ephemeral conquests in order to bolster her confidence. Whenever she goes out with someone, if she does, she'll be looking at him as if he might be the definitive one, as a future husband, and she'll make every effort to make things turn out right, she'll treat him with infinite good will and patience, wanting to love him, determinedly desiring him.'—He paused and looked up at the ceiling, the better perhaps to imagine her at the side of some permanent imbecile, practicing her patience upon him. Then he added sadly: 'It doesn't look good for her. I'd say that such an attitude tends to frighten men off or else attract the pusillanimous. It would certainly scare *you* off, Jacobo. You're not the marrying kind, even though you were married for several years and miss being married now. What you really miss is Luisa, not matrimony. I was always surprised that it suited you so well. I was surprised, too, that it lasted so long, I never thought it would.'

I didn't want to go down that road, I certainly didn't feel any curiosity about myself or, as that anonymous report in the files at the office had put it, I just took myself for granted, or assumed I knew myself, or considered myself a lost cause upon whom it would be pointless to squander thought. And so I insisted on talking about someone I knew much better or, who knows, perhaps not that well:

'Do you think that in her haste she might end up with the wrong kind of man, with someone dangerous?'

'No, I wouldn't go that far,' he said. 'Luisa's an intelligent woman, and when faced with disappointment, she'll accept it, however reluctantly, however much she resists and however hard it is to do so . . . She might end up with someone merely average or with whom she feels only partially satisfied, or even someone who has qualities she dislikes, that's possible. What I do think is that whatever he's like, she'll give innumerable opportunities to that potential husband, to that project, to the person upon whom she's fixed her gaze, she'll do more than her share, she'll try to be as understanding as she can, as she no doubt tried to be with you until, I suppose, you overstepped the mark, although I've never asked you what exactly happened . . . She won't hand this man any blank checks, but rather than get rid of him, she'll use up almost the whole checkbook, little by little. Nevertheless, as far as I know, no such person exists as yet, or he's still not important enough for her to talk to me about him or to consult me. Bear in mind that I am now the closest thing Luisa has to a father, and that she still preserves a childlike attitude that makes her such a delightful person and leads her to ask the advice of her elders. Well, in some respects, but not, of course, in others. When did you say you were going back to Oxford?'

I could see that he was tired. He had made an effort, yes, an effort of translation or interpretation, as if he were me and I were Tupra in our office, and Tupra was putting pressure on him to talk about Luisa, I just hoped they never put her under scrutiny, there was no reason why they should, but the mere thought made me shudder. My poor father had done as I asked, he had tried to help me, as a favor to his son, he had told me what he thought, how he saw Luisa, what, it seemed to him, could be expected from her immediate future. Perhaps he was right in his estimations, and if Luisa *was* going out with someone who, at one fateful moment, on one fateful day, had gone too far, it might be that she was trying to excuse him or change him or understand him instead of distancing herself or running away, which is what you have to do while there's still time, that is, when you're not tied to someone, but only involved. It might be that she wanted to ignore or erase that moment, that she was seeking to relegate the fact to the sphere of bad dreams or to toss it into the bag of imaginings, as most of us do when we don't want that other face to fail us so soon, not today, without them even being considerate enough to wait until tomorrow to disappoint us. Many women have almost infinite powers of endurance, especially when they feel themselves to be saviours or healers or redeemers, when they believe that they will be able to rescue the man they love, or whom they have decided to love at all costs, from apathy or disease or vice. They think he'll be different with them, that he'll mend his ways or improve or change and that they will, therefore, become indispensable to him, sometimes it seems to me that for such women redeeming someone is a form—foolish and naïve—of ensuring the unconditional love of that person: 'He can't live without me,' they think without entirely thinking that or without quite formulating the thought. 'He knows that without me he would revert to his former self, disastrous, incompetent, sick, depressed, an addict, a drunk, a failure, a mere shadow, a condemned man, a loser. He'll never leave me, nor will he endanger our relationship, he won't play dirty tricks on me, he won't run the risk that I might leave him. Not only will he be forever grateful to me, he'll realize that with me he can stay afloat and even swim on ahead, whereas without me he would sink and drown.' Yes, that is what many women seem to think when some difficult or calamitous or hopeless or violent man crosses their path, they see a challenge, a problem, a task, someone they can put right or rescue from a little hell. And it's quite incomprehensible that after centuries of hearing about other women's experiences and of reading stories, they still don't know that as soon as such men feel sober and optimistic and healthy again—as soon as they feel real rather than mere specters—they will believe that they got back on their feet all by themselves and will very likely see the women as mere obstacles who keep them from running freely or from continuing their upward climb. It seems equally incomprehensible that the women don't realize that it is they who will be the most entangled or the most tightly bound and who will never be prepared to abandon those dependent, disoriented, irascible, defective men, because they will have made them neither more nor less than their mission, and if you have or believe you have a mission, you never give up on it, if you have finally found a mission and believe it to be an endless lifelong commitment and the daily justification for your gratuitous existence or for the countless steps taken upon the earth and for your slow, slow journey through the shrunken world . . .

I got up and placed my hand on his shoulder, it was a gesture that, in recent years, had always calmed my father, whenever he felt frightened or weak or confused, when he opened his eyes very wide as if seeing the world for the first time, with a gaze as inscrutable as that of a child born only weeks or days before, and who, I imagine, observes this new place into which he has been hurled and tries perhaps to decipher our customs and to discover which of those customs will be his. My father's sight must have been as limited as the sight of such newborn babies is sometimes said to be, he may have been able to make out only shadows, blotches, the familiar light and the blur of colors, it was impossible to know, he always claimed to see much more than we thought he could, possibly out of a kind of pride that prevented him from recognizing how physically diminished he had become. He knew who I was, and his hearing was as acute as ever, and so perhaps, more than anything, he saw with his memory. And that is why, in part, he accordingly located me in Oxford, where I had in fact lived, albeit many years before and from where I had, moreover, returned. As regards London, on the other hand, he didn't yet know for sure that I would return from there (I had returned now, but not for good). During my two-week stay I would, at some point during my visits to him, place my hand on his shoulder: I would leave it there for a while, exerting enough pressure for him to be able to feel it and know that I was near and in touch, to make him feel safe and to soothe him. I could feel his slightly prominent bones, his collarbone too, he had grown thinner since I left, and when I touched them they gave an impression of fragility, not as if they might break, but as if they might easily become dislocated, by a clumsy gesture or excessive effort; when his caregiver helped him up, she did so with great delicacy. On one occasion, however, he turned to look curiously at my hand on his shoulder, although in no way rejecting my touch. It occurred to me that he perhaps found it odd to be the object of a gesture that he had possibly often made when I was a child, when he was tall and I was growing only very slowly, the father bending down and placing his hand on his son's shoulder in order to tell him off or to instill him with confidence or to offer him some symbolic protection, or to pacify him. He looked at my hand as if at an innocuous fly that had alighted there, or perhaps something larger, a lizard momentarily pausing in its scurryings, as if hearing approaching footsteps. 'Why do you put your hand on my shoulder like that?' he asked, half-smiling, as if amused. 'Don't you like me to?' I asked in turn, and he replied: 'Well, if you want to, it certainly doesn't bother me.' However, on that first visit, he didn't really notice, as was usually the case, but was merely silently aware of that gentle, guiding, soothing pressure. I said:

'I don't live in Oxford any more, Papa. I only go there occasionally to visit Wheeler, I've mentioned him to you before, do you remember? Sir Peter Wheeler, the Hispanist. He's about your age, well, a year older. I live in London now. I'll be going back in a couple of weeks.'

Perhaps his wise interpretation of Luisa had taken its toll, he had made a great effort for me and now he was paying the price. It was as if he had grown suddenly tired of his own perspicacity and had again become confused about time, as he had the previous day on the phone. Perhaps he could no longer stand being himself for very long, I mean being his old self, his alert intellectually demanding self, the one who urged his children always to go on, to go on thinking, the one who used to say 'And what else?' just when we felt that an exposition or argument was over, the one who made us keep on looking at things and at people, beyond what seemed necessary, at the point when we had the feeling that there was no more to see and that continuing would be a waste of time. 'At the point,' in his words, 'where you might say to yourself there can't be anything else.' Yes, as I get older, I know how that wearies and wears one out, and sometimes I wonder why I should and why, to a greater or lesser degree, we *do* pay so much attention to our fellow men and women or to the world, and why we don't just ignore them, I'm not even sure that it isn't yet one more source of conflict, even if what we see meets with our approval. He was ninety years old. It was hardly to be wondered at that he should want to take a rest from himself. And from everything else too.

'Oh, honestly,' he said somewhat irritably, as if I had deceived him on purpose and for my own pleasure. 'You've always told me you were in Oxford. That you'd been offered a job there, teaching. And there was a man called Kavanagh, who writes horror novels and is a medievalist, isn't that right? And of course I know who your friend Wheeler is, I've even read a couple of his books. But didn't he used to be called Rylands? You always used to call him Rylands.' I didn't tell him they were brothers, that would have led to still more confusion. 'So which university are you teaching at in London?'

That is how the memory of the old works. He remembered Aidan Kavanagh or his name, and even the successful novels he used to publish under a pseudonym, a pleasant and deliberately frivolous man, the head of the Spanish department during my time in Oxford, but long since retired; he remembered Rylands too, although he confused him with Wheeler; and yet he didn't remember that I had gone to work for the BBC during my second English sojourn, so recent that it was still going on. There was no reason why he should remember what had happened subsequently: as with Luisa, I had told him very little—only a few vague, possibly evasive remarks—about my new job. It's strange how one instinctively hides, or, which is somewhat different, keeps quiet about anything that immediately strikes one as murky: just as I would say nothing to Luisa about meeting a woman with whom I had barely exchanged a word at a meeting or a party and with whom nothing could or indeed would happen, but to whom I had felt instantly attracted. I had possibly never even mentioned Tupra to my father or to Luisa, or only in passing, and yet he was, without a doubt, the dominant figure in my life in London (and after a few days I realized just how dominant a figure he was). It didn't seem to me, at that moment, worth disillusioning my father and telling him that I no longer did any teaching anywhere.

'I've got to go now, Papa,' I said. 'I'll pop in now and then, when I've got time. Do you want me to warn you? Shall I call before I drop by?'

My prolonged absence made me feel rather like an intruder and as if I needed to ask such a question, which was perhaps inappropriate in a son with respect to his father's home, a home that had for many years been mine too. I was still standing, still with my hand on his shoulder. He looked up at me, whether seeing me or guessing at my face or remembering me, I don't know. His gaze was, at any rate, very clear, surprised and slightly helpless, as if he had not quite grasped that I was leaving. His eyes were now very blue, bluer than they had ever been, perhaps because he no longer wore glasses.

'No, there's no need. As far as I'm concerned, you all still live here, even if you left a long time ago.' He fell silent, then added: 'Your mother too.'

I wasn't sure whether he meant that she still lived there as well or if he was reproaching her as well for having left, when she died, longer ago than anyone else. He probably meant both.

And I continued to waste no time. I didn't linger or delay or loiter or dally. I was longing to see my children again, not to mention Luisa and my sister, and, for the first time since my return, my brothers and a few friends, and to stroll around the city like a foreigner, but I felt I had something concrete and urgent to do, something to investigate and resolve and remedy. That was something I *had* learned from Tupra, at least in theory: Luisa was clearly in danger, and now I understood that sometimes one has no option but to do what has to be done and at once, without waiting or hesitating or delaying: I had to do this unthinkingly, like some very distracted, busy person, as if it were merely my job. Yes, there are occasions when one knows precisely what would happen in the world if no pressure or brake was imposed on what one perceives to be people's certain capabilities, and that if those capabilities were to remain undeployed, it was necessary for someone—me, for example, who else in this case?—to dissuade or impede them. In order for Tupra to adopt the punitive measures which he deemed necessary and appropriate, he simply had to convince himself of what would happen in each case if he or another sentinel—the authorities or the law, instinct, the moon, the storm, fear, the hovering sword, the invisible watchers—did not put a stop to it. 'It's the way of the world,' he would say, and he would say this about so many things and situations; he applied those words to betrayals and acts of loyalty, to anxieties and quickened pulses, to unexpected reversals and vertigo, to vacillations and torments and to the involuntary harm we cause, to the scratch and the pain and the fever and the festering wound, to griefs and the infinite steps we all take in the belief that we are being guided by our will, or that our will does at least play a part in them. To him all this seemed perfectly normal and even, sometimes, routine—prevention or punishment and never running too grave a risk—he knew too well that the Earth is full of passions and affections and of ill will and malice, and that sometimes individuals can avoid neither and, indeed, choose not to, because they are the fuse and the fuel for their own combustion, as well as their reason and their igniting spark. And they don't even require a motive or a goal for any of this, neither aim nor cause, gratitude nor insult, or at least not always, or as Wheeler said: 'they carry their probabilities in their veins, and so time, temptation and circumstance will lead them at last to their fulfilment.' And for Tupra this very radical and sometimes ruthless attitude—or perhaps it was simply a very practical one—was just another characteristic of the way of the world to which he conformed or adhered; and that unreflecting, inclement, resolute stance (or one based perhaps on a single thought, the first), also formed part of that way of the world which remained unchanged throughout time and regardless of space, and so there was, therefore, no reason to question it, just as there's no need to question wakefulness and sleep, or hearing and sight, or breathing and walking and speech, or any of the other things about which one knows 'that's how it is and always will be.'

I was feeling now as he did, that is, like someone who didn't bother to issue any prior warning, at least not always, someone who makes decisions at a distance and for barely identifiable reasons, or without the actions appearing to have any connection of cause and effect with those reasons, still less with the proof that such acts have been committed. Nor did I need proof of that arbitrary or justifiable occasion—who could tell which it was and what did it matter?—nor did I intend sending any warning or notice before unleashing my saber blow, I didn't even require any evidence of actions committed or proven, of events or deeds, or even certainty in order to set to and remove from Luisa's existence the man marring and threatening her life and, therefore, the lives of my children. First, I had to find out more about the man and then track him down. She wouldn't say a word to me about him, especially now that I had voiced my immediate suspicion that this as yet nameless, faceless man was the person responsible for her multicolored black eye. After my father's conjectures and his belief that my wife would be inclined to humor or encourage whoever she was attracted to or whoever she was focused on now ('Yes,' I thought, 'strictly speaking, she *is* still my wife. We're not divorced and neither of us seems in a hurry to get a divorce or has even suggested it,' and this confirmed me in my determination or in my first thought that admitted of no second thought), my next step was to go and see her sister or talk to her on the phone; and even though she and I had never got on particularly well or had much to do with each other and even though she led a very independent life with few family ties and saw myself and the children only infrequently, as mere extensions of Luisa, she did meet up with Luisa once or twice a month; Luisa would either go to her place without the kids and without me, her husband, or they would lunch together in a restaurant and tell each other about their respective lives, just how much I didn't know, but probably almost everything. If anyone knew what was going on, if anyone knew the identity of that man with violent tendencies, his face and name, that person was Cristina, Luisa's somewhat surly younger sister. And although her first loyalty was to Luisa and even though she considered me to be a mere dispensable appendage, I was sure that if something was worrying her—and if my deductions were correct, and even if they weren't, this guy was very worrying indeed—she would tell me and welcome hearing the views of someone who felt the same way about the matter.

I phoned her that evening, much to her surprise, for she didn't even know I was in Madrid, but then how could she unless she had spoken to Luisa during the day and Luisa had told her, she asked me how things were going in London, and I was amazed that she actually knew where I was currently living, 'Fine,' I said, without going into detail, after all, it was just a reflex question, and then I asked if we could meet up as soon as possible, 'No,' she said, 'impossible, I'm off on a trip tomorrow and I've got loads of things to do before I go,' 'How long are you away for?' 'A week,' 'It will be too late when you get back, I need to see you before you leave, I'm only here for two weeks, well, less than that now, what time are you leaving?' I asked, 'At lunchtime, but I'm really tied up until then, can't you tell me over the phone? Is it about Luisa?' 'Yes, it's about Luisa.' Then she fell silent for a few seconds and it seemed to me that she had sat herself down on a chair in readiness. 'What have you got to say, then? Come on, tell me,' 'What? Now?' 'Yes, now. If it's what I think it is, it won't take much time and I imagine we'll be pretty much in agreement on the subject. It's about Custardoy, isn't it?'

'Who?'

'Custardoy, the guy she's going out with. Or didn't you know? Oh, Jaime, don't tell me you didn't know.' She said this not as if she were afraid she had put her foot in it, but as if she couldn't believe I wouldn't know. Perhaps she had always thought of me as rather absentminded, or worse, a fool.

'I've only just got back. I didn't know his name.' Now, however, I did and knew of his existence in Luisa's life, so it wasn't all conjecture on my part. All I needed now was to know what he looked like and find out where he lived. Custardoy. It was an unusual surname, odd, there wouldn't be many in Madrid. 'I've been away for ages, and when you only talk on the phone, it's hard to know what's really going on. Who is he? What does he do?'

'He's a painter, a copyist, or both of those things. Some people say he's a forger too, but at any rate, he's in the art world. I'm glad you phoned actually, I've been really worried—although I'm not sure anything can be done, in this kind of situation there's rarely much you can do.'

'Worried? Why? What situation?'

'Tell me first why you phoned. Has Luisa told you anything?'

I wondered if I should pretend to know more than I did, but that seemed unwise, Cristina could be very touchy and, if she caught on to what I was doing, she might refuse to say another word. And that was the last thing I wanted, I was entirely dependent on her for help, and she had, inadvertently, already told me a lot, with no need for me to worm it out of her.

'No, not really,' I said at last. 'According to Luisa, what she does is no longer any of my business, and she's right of course. The thing is, I saw her briefly last night, I'd gone over there to see the kids, and she avoided me and left before I arrived, but I waited until she got back, she was away for several hours, I've no idea where she went, she left me with the babysitter, and I think the reason she was avoiding me was because when I did see her, her face was a real mess, and that was obviously the reason she hadn't wanted to be there. She claims she collided with the garage door, but she's got a black eye and it looks to me as if someone punched her, and I don't just find that worrying, I find it downright alarming, and it *is* my business, how could it not be? It would be the same if someone had hit you or any female friend. Do you know anything about it?'

'It wouldn't be the same if someone had hit me, Jaime, because you don't give a damn about me.' My sister-in-law's sharp tongue could not resist getting this comment in first. Then her tone changed and she said almost as if to herself: 'Not again. That's dreadful.'

'Again? You mean it's happened before?'

Cristina didn't respond at first. She paused as if she were biting her lip and weighing something up, but her hesitation lasted only a moment.

'According to her, no, nothing has ever happened, not what you suspect now nor what I've suspected in the past. Look, I'm telling you this because I'm worried, and even more so after what you've just told me, I didn't know anything about that, I haven't seen her for a couple of weeks, and she hasn't put any pressure on me to meet up before this trip of mine, presumably because she thinks the mark will have faded by the time I get back and then I won't ask any awkward questions. But I don't think she would be at all pleased if she knew I was talking about this to you. The only reason she hasn't told me not to talk to you is because it would never occur to her that you and I would be in touch. It wouldn't have occurred to me either, to be honest. Did she know you were coming to Madrid?'

'No, I phoned her when I arrived yesterday. I wanted it to be a surprise for the children.'

'She won't have had time to prepare herself,' she said, 'nor to worry about you finding out. She probably doesn't even want you to know she's going out with the guy.'

'What is it that you suspected?'

'Well, according to her, a couple of months ago or so she fell over in the street and hit her face on one of those metal posts the council have put up everywhere, which is perfectly possible, because the city's full of the things, bollards I think they call them, you have to make a real point of avoiding them if you don't want to fracture your kneecap. Did she mention anything to you about falling over?'

'No, nothing. And we talk at least once a week.'

'Well, I'm surprised she didn't. It was a really nasty cut, a superficial one, but it went from one side of her nose to halfway across her cheek, you couldn't miss it.'—'*Uno sfregio*,' I thought, that recently learned word sprang immediately into my mind, 'a gash.'—'And she had a graze on her chin. From the way she talked about it, I just didn't believe her, and it looked more like a scratch or a welt or as if someone had slapped her, I know a bit about these things because a woman I was vaguely friendly with some years ago used to get beaten up by her husband; in fact, he killed her in the end, after I'd stopped seeing her luckily, which is something.' I instinctively knocked on wood. 'So I asked her straight out if Custardoy had hit her, if he'd beaten her up. She denied it, of course, and said I must be mad, how could I even think such a thing. But she blushed when she said it, and I can tell when my sister is lying from years of watching her face whenever she lied as a child. And I've heard other things since.'

'What things? Do you know the guy?'

I realized that I preferred not to mention his name, although I had it stored away in my memory, as if it were a find, a treasure. It was a valuable piece of information.

'Yes, by sight. And by hearsay too. A few years ago, he was often to be seen drinking in smart bars like the Chicote, the Cock, or the Del Diego, or in others, he's an arty type, a nocturnal womanizer, although apparently he didn't restrict his activities to the nighttime only, he's the kind of man who can tell at once who wants to be chatted up and for what purpose, the kind who's capable of creating the necessary willingness and purpose in someone else, that is, in women. At least so I've heard. I don't know if he still goes to those places, because I don't go any more myself. You probably saw him once or twice there yourself, in the eighties or nineties.'

'What does he look like? Has he got a ponytail?' I asked, I couldn't help myself. I was burning to know this.

'Yes, how did you guess?'

'Oh, it was just something someone said. But in that case, no, I've never seen him. I mean, I can't remember anyone in particular with a ponytail. Then again, I pretty much stopped going out at night when Guillermo was born, and the guy probably didn't have a ponytail before that. And of course the surname doesn't mean anything to me either. What things have you heard?'

'Well, after seeing that cut on Luisa's face—which left me with a really bad feeling—I asked an acquaintance of mine, Juan Ranz, about Custardoy, who he's known since they were children. They never got on well and have had hardly any contact for years, but their parents were friends and used to leave them together to play and entertain each other, so he had to put up with his company quite often. He says Custardoy was one of those very grown-up kids, impatient to enter the adult world, as if he wanted to climb out of his as yet unformed body. Then, when he was older, Custardoy used to make copies of paintings for Ranz's father, who's an art expert (apparently, Custardoy's a brilliant copyist and can make a perfect copy of anything from any period, in fact, it's hard to tell them from the originals, which, of course, is where his reputation as a forger comes in), and so he still used to see him from time to time, through his father. Juan is an interpreter at the United Nations, and, as a matter of fact, his wife's name is Luisa too.'

'What else did he tell you?'

'The most notable or perhaps the most troubling fact, and

the one that most concerns us, is that, although he's a great success with the ladies, there's obviously something slightly sinister about the way he treats them because Ranz knows of some women who've emerged from a night with Custardoy feeling really scared, after having sex I mean (some of them were prostitutes, and so it was purely sexual). And afterwards, they didn't even want to talk about it, as if they needed to forget it as quickly as possible and shake off the whole experience. As if the experience, or even the mere memory of it, had burned itself into them and didn't lend itself to being turned into a story. And even when there were two prostitutes involved at the same time (apparently he's into threesomes, although always with women), both had emerged feeling equally scared and refusing to say anything about it. And inevitably, there are lots of other women, prostitutes or not, who feel an irresistible desire to know just what it is he does or doesn't do. There's no shortage of stupid women out there as you know.'

This was the worst possible news. A ladies' man who was also into whores, and who left his mark on women, even if that mark was only a mark of terror. 'A man like that won't even have to bury me or dig my grave still deeper, the grave in which I'm already buried,' I thought, 'because he will have erased my memory at a stroke, with the first terror and the first entreaty and the first fascination and the first command, and Luisa could already be under his thumb.'

'But Luisa isn't stupid, at least she didn't used to be, no, she's never been stupid,' I said. 'Perhaps he's different with women who aren't whores. Perhaps when he has more than one night at his disposal his behavior changes to the exact opposite, purely in order to ensure that there will be more nights to come. Or do you think that's precisely what is so sinister about him, that he beats up all the women he goes out with? I can't believe that. Someone would have said something, someone would have found out, the women he'd been with would have warned each other. You women talk about such things, don't you, I mean details? Spanish women do. In what sort of terms has she spoken to you about him? Is she in love or infatuated? Desperate, mad, distracted, flattered? Just how serious is she? She can't be in love. And how did she meet him? Where did he spring from?' The information provided by this Ranz fellow had perhaps made me even more uneasy than Luisa's now yellowing black eye. 'What else did this friend of yours say?'

'Nothing very good, except that he's brilliant at his job. According to Ranz, though, he's a slippery customer, not to be trusted under any circumstances. And he's not the sort to fall in love, or didn't use to be, he said. But who knows, love is an area in which people can change at any moment. When I told him that my sister was going out with him, he said: "Oh God" like someone heralding a disaster. That's why I was trying to find out more, well, because of that and her supposed collision with a bollard and that worrying cut. In fact, I asked him outright if he thought Custardoy would be capable of hitting a woman.' And Cristina paused, as if she'd completed that particular sequence of sentences.

'And what did he say? Tell me.'

'He wasn't categorical about it, but nevertheless . . . He thought about it for a moment and then said: "I suppose so. I don't know that he has, no one's ever told me he has and he wouldn't tell me so himself. It's not the kind of thing you boast about. But I suppose that, yes, he would be perfectly capable of doing so." You see what I mean. (Of course, Ranz doesn't like the man and so can't be taken as the oracle.) That was when he told me about the prostitutes and, well, I assumed it wasn't only prostitutes. Now you tell me that Luisa has another injury, one she hasn't even mentioned to me. If she'd bumped into a door and given herself a black eye, the normal thing would be for her to tell me about it, we may not have seen each other lately, but we've spoken on the phone. And she didn't tell you about the incident with the bollard. Yes, now I really am very worried. And Jaime, Luisa may not be stupid, but you've only known her in a stable situation, when she was with you. Apart from the last few months before you left, of course, but there was still a remnant of stability while you were at home, a kind of postponement, an inertia. But how long have you been away now? Nine months, twelve, fifteen?

That's a long time for the person left behind, longer than for the one who leaves. Neither you nor I know what she's like in that situation, and she was still very young when she met you. People are unpredictable when they've just split up with someone. Some might closet themselves at home and not want to see anyone, others might hit the streets and climb into the first bed that's offered. Some might do first one thing and then the other, or the other way round, I mean, who knows what foolishness *you've* been getting up to in London, fancy-free and with no family obligations. There are half-measures too, of course. Luisa won't have hit the streets because, to start with, there are the children to consider. But she won't simply have wept into her pillow. She must feel slightly impatient, excited, curious to meet another man and see how it works out, and curiosity leads to all kinds of silliness and to persisting in that silliness until the curiosity wears off. She hasn't told me a great deal, about her feelings, I mean, or her expectations; she probably doesn't have any great expectations and is simply letting time pass until she can see more clearly what she wants or, indeed, if she wants anything. From what Ranz told me, and given Custardoy's reputation, it's highly unlikely that he'll put any pressure on her to move in with him or to get divorced or whatever, if he isn't the sort to fall in love. Not that I've asked her much about it either, I suppose: you know what I'm like, I'll listen to what others tell me, but I'm not that interested really, unless things get serious. All I know is that she's going out with this guy, has a good time with him and obviously likes him. How much she likes him I don't know, possibly a lot, she might be crazy about him, which is why she's being discreet and keeping quiet about it. She doesn't try and hide their relationship, but she's not shouting it from the rooftops either. Not with me, I mean, and I would think with other people she says even less. She didn't announce it to me with a great fanfare, as if it were headline news. And I've only seen them together once, very briefly and from the car, so I haven't spent time with them or anything. I get a sense of reserve, modesty almost, as if after all those years as a married woman, she was embarrassed to have a boyfriend.'

'How did you happen to see them?' Even if it was as brief as she said, that would provide me with the only image I had of the two of them together, apart from the indirect and imprecise one provided by my brother-in-law via my sister. And I needed to be able to imagine them. It was odd to imagine Luisa being with anyone other than me. It seemed not so much repugnant or offensive as unreal, like a performance, a farce. Yes, it was more unreal than painful. Separations like ours make no sense, however commonplace they have become in the world and have been for a long time now. You spend years orbiting round a particular person, depending on her at every turn, seeing her every day as if she were a natural prolongation of yourself, including her in all your comings and goings, in your aimless thoughts and even in your dreams. Thinking of telling her the slightest thing seen or experienced, for example, a Romanian mother asking for a packet of baby wipes for her children. You are *with that person*, just as the Hungarian gypsy was *with her children* or Alan Marriott's dog was *without a leg*. You have a detailed, constant and permanently refreshed knowledge of her thoughts and preoccupations and activities; you know her timetable and her habits, who she sees and how often; and when you join her each evening you tell each other what has happened and what you've been up to during the day, during which neither of you has ever entirely left the consciousness of the other for a single moment, and sometimes those reports are quite elaborate; then you go to bed with her and she's the last thing you see that day and—even more extraordinary—you get up with her too, for she's there in the morning, after those hours of absence, as if she were you, someone who never goes away or disappears and of whom we never lose sight; and so on, day after day over many years. Then suddenly—although it isn't sudden, it just seems like that once the process is over and distance has been established: in fact it happens very gradually and both parties know when it began, even though they prefer not to—you cease to have any notion of what that person's daily thoughts, feelings or actions are; whole days and weeks go by with almost no news of her, and you have to resort to third parties—who used to know much less than you, well, nothing really, in comparison—to find out the most basic things: what kind of life she's leading, who she sees, how the kids are taking it, who she's going out with, if she's in pain or ill, if she's in good or low spirits, if she's still looking after her diabetes and taking her long prescribed walks, if anyone has upset or hurt her, if she's finding work exhausting, if it's getting her down or is a real source of satisfaction, if she's afraid of growing old, how she sees her future and how she views the past, how she thinks of me now; and who she loves. It makes no sense that it should go from all to almost nothing, even though we never cease to remember and are basically the same person. It's all so unbearably ridiculous and subjective, because everything contains its opposite: the same people in the same place love each other and cannot stand each other; what was once long-established habit becomes slowly or suddenly unacceptable and inadmissible—whether slowly or suddenly it doesn't matter, that's the least of it, someone who helped set up a home finds he's forbidden from entering it, the merest contact, a touch, once so taken for granted that it was barely conscious becomes an affront or an insult, it's almost as if you were having to ask permission to touch yourself, what once gave pleasure or amusement becomes hateful, repellent, accursed and vile, words once longed for would now poison the air or provoke nausea and must on no account be heard, and those spoken a thousand times before seem unimportant. Erase, suppress, take back, cancel, better never to have said anything, that is the world's ambition, that way nothing exists, nothing is anything, the same things and the same facts and the same beings are both themselves and their reverse, today and yesterday, tomorrow, afterwards and in the long-distant past. And in between there is only time that does its best to dazzle us, the only thing with purpose and aims, which means that those of us who are still traveling through time are not to be trusted, for we are all foolish and insubstantial and unfinished, with no idea of what we might be capable nor of what end awaits us, foolish, insubstantial, unfinished me, no, no one should trust me either . . .

'We'd arranged to have lunch one day,' Cristina said. 'This

was a few months ago now, before the business with the bollard and that ugly cut, I had no anxieties or concerns at the time, in fact, I really didn't care what she did or who with as long as it cheered her up a bit, she *is* the older sister, don't forget, and I've never tended to be very protective of her, although she is of me, which is only normal. Luisa had arranged to meet him afterwards, at his apartment or studio, I don't remember which now. Anyway, lunch went on longer than expected, and it got a bit late and she was really alarmed when she saw the time, because they hadn't arranged to meet actually in his apartment or studio or whatever, but outside in the street and they would then go up together or perhaps go on somewhere else, I don't know, but she was horrified at the thought of keeping him waiting. So I gave her a lift in my car, because she hadn't brought hers; she'd planned to take the metro, she said, which, normally, would have been quicker, but it was quite a way from the nearest station to his place and so would have taken too long, anyway, I dropped her off at the door. It's impossible to park in that part of town, I could barely stop, just long enough to let her out, I dropped her almost on the corner. She didn't introduce him or anything, although, as I say, I knew him by sight already from seeing him out and about in bars at night. I only saw them together from the car, for a matter of seconds, while I waited for the lights to change, from the corner.'

'What part of town was it? What corner?'

'At the end of Calle Mayor, just past Bailén, next to the viaduct. Just before you reach Cuesta de la Vega.'

'Can you remember which number?'

'No, I didn't notice. Why do you want to know?'

'Which side of the road?'

'The only one with houses. The eyesore's on the other side, if you remember, But why do you want to know?'

The 'eyesore' was the Almudena or museum of ecumenical horrors, the ghastly modern cathedral, largely the work of Opus Dei or so it seems, with a statue of the Polish Pope outside, *totus tuus*, with a bulging forehead, worthy almost of Frankenstein's monster, and arms flung wide as if he were about to dance a *jota*;

and this, though hideous, is perhaps the least of the uglinesses, because there are, among other monstrosities, some monstrous stained-glass windows made by an unimaginable artist called Kiko (Kiko something-or-other), well, nothing good can come from a man with a name like that.

'Oh, no reason. Just so that I can imagine them there. What did you see?'

'Well, not much really. Nothing. She leaped out of the car with the lights on red at the junction with Calle Mayor, she was in such a hurry, about ten minutes late. The one thing I did notice was that it had started to rain, and he, instead of taking shelter in the doorway (he only needed to step back two paces), was waiting for her on the sidewalk, getting drenched. Perhaps he was there so that he would be sure to see her arrive, out of impatience.'

'Or perhaps to have one more reason to reproach her for being late,' I said, wilfully misinterpreting the facts. 'That way he could make her feel even guiltier, by saying it was her fault he had got soaked or even caught a cold. How did he greet her? Did they embrace, did he kiss her, put his arm about her waist?'

'I don't think so, I don't think they actually touched. From her attitude and certain gestures, it seemed to me that she was apologizing profusely, she pointed to my car, to explain why she was late. What does it matter?'

'Did you see them go in?'

'Yes, just before the lights changed. Now that you ask, he might have been a bit annoyed, because he went in ahead of her rather than giving way to her, and Luisa followed behind, placing one hand on his shoulder, as if to soothe or placate him, as if she were still apologizing.'

'Ah, I see. A quick-tempered, artsy-fartsy, hysterical type. Well, certainly not a gentleman anyway.'

'I wouldn't go that far, I only saw them together for a moment, but he's definitely not the gentlemanly sort. He's well-dressed, mind, always wears a tie, very traditional. But his success, I suppose, comes from the roguish air he has about him and which lots of women find attractive. I don't myself, not at all, but maybe I'm odd or maybe I've met a few rogues already and know they're not worth the bother. That day, with his hair scraped back and all wet, he did look slightly menacing. He gives the impression of being a tense, self-contained, nervy sort, I mean, someone under constant tension. He's always seemed to me a rather somber figure. Friendly and seductive, but somehow somber too.'

'How old is he?'

'I don't know, he must be around fifty now, I should think. Although he looks younger.'

'Ten or twelve years older than Luisa. That's not good; he'll have authority over her, influence. Do you know his first name?'

'Esteban, I think. Wait. Yes, Esteban. Luisa has called him that occasionally, although she tends to refer to him more by his surname, as if she wanted to distance herself from him and make it seem as if they weren't that close.'—'I call young Pérez Nuix by her surname too,' I thought, 'but that's not the same thing at all.'—'As I said, sometimes it's as if she were embarrassed to have a boyfriend. Because of the kids and you and all that.'

'Esteban Custardoy. Are you sure? He's not known as a painter, then? I mean, his name doesn't appear in the papers, he doesn't hold exhibitions and so on?'

'Not that I know of, no; but I don't take much notice, to be honest; the last thing I would be interested in is modern art. I think he's more of a copyist. Luisa mentioned that sometimes he's commissioned to copy paintings from the Prado and that he spends hours there studying and copying. Or he gets commissions to copy paintings in museums abroad, in Europe, and then he goes away for a few days to study those paintings. Ranz told me that he learned the trade from his father, Custardoy the Elder as he used to be called, who made copies for his father, Ranz's father that is. And at first the son was known as Custardoy the Younger, but I don't know if he still is.'

I fell silent for a moment. I lit a Karelias cigarette, of which I had brought ten packs with me, knowing that I wouldn't be able to find them in Madrid.

'There's something that doesn't quite make sense, Cristina. I just can't believe that Luisa would put up with someone mistreating her, still less if she's only known him for a short time, a matter of months. If our suspicions are right, he hasn't hit her once, but twice. I don't understand why she would go on seeing him and going to bed with him as if nothing had happened, why she didn't break it off the first time, let alone the second. Only yesterday she denied anything was wrong; in a way she was protecting him or protecting herself, I mean her relationship with him, to make sure no one meddles or gets involved or sticks their nose in where it isn't wanted. It's understandable that I'd be the last person she'd want to talk to about her boyfriend, especially if relations with him are problematic, and even if he represents a danger to her. But she doesn't even talk to you! How would you explain such forbearance? And she's hardly the submissive type.' I suddenly realized that this was the first time I had spoken about or thought about or really imagined their relationship as something real and regular and ongoing; the words that came out of my mouth were: '. . . and going to bed with him as if nothing had happened.' Of course they went to bed together, that's one of the benefits of going out with someone, it's the norm. 'But that doesn't necessarily mean very much,' I thought at once in order to mitigate that fleeting image and those words. 'I've slept with Pérez-Nuix and with others too and it's almost as if it never happened. They don't occupy my thoughts, I don't remember them, or only very occasionally and without any feeling. Well, it's a bit different with Pérez-Nuix because I see her every day and each time I see her, I do remember or, rather, know, even though screwing her was an extraordinarily impersonal experience, performed, how can I put it, almost with eyes closed, almost anonymously, in silence. I've slept with other women in the past on a regular or continuous basis, Clare Bayes in England was a case in point, or my girlfriend in Tuscany to whom I owe my Italian. But so what, they're just data in an archive, recorded facts that have long since ceased to affect or influence me. No, those things don't really mean very much once they're over. The problem is that Luisa's affair is happening now and isn't yet over, and it's harming her and threatens us all, all four of us.'

Now it was Cristina's turn to pause and think for a few seconds. I heard her sigh at the other end of the line, perhaps she was weary of our conversation or felt she should be getting on with preparations for her trip.

'I don't know, Jaime. Perhaps we're wrong, and he hasn't done anything to her, maybe she did collide with a bollard and with the garage door, and is just having a run of bad luck. The trouble is that neither of us believes that. My feeling is that she's determined to stick to him, however much she may pretend not to know or care, and in that case anything is possible—when a person's set on loving someone then nothing circumstantial or external will dissuade them. People are much more long-suffering than we think. Once involved, they'll tolerate almost anything, at least for a time. I should know. They believe they can change the bad things or that the bad things won't last. And Luisa is patient, she'll put up with a lot, after all, look how long it took her to break up with you. I don't really know why we're talking about it. For the moment, as we've seen, she's not going to tell us anything, and even if she did, we wouldn't be able to persuade her. I don't see what we can do. Anyway, Jaime, I have things to do, I'm leaving tomorrow and this conversation is getting us nowhere, apart from feeding our mutual anxieties.' I said nothing, I was pondering what she had said: 'Once involved, they'll tolerate almost anything, at least for a time.' 'It's all a matter of involving the other person, of intervening, making a request, a demand, asking a question. Of speaking to him and interfering,' I was thinking, still saying nothing.

'Jaime, are you there?'

'We could try persuading him,' I said at last.

'Him? We don't know him, least of all you. What an idea! You can count me out. Besides, I'm off tomorrow. Anyway, if you did go and talk to him, he'd probably laugh in your face or punch you, don't you see, if he really is a violent man. Or were you thinking of offering him money to go away, like an old-fashioned father? Huh. For all I know, he may not even need the money, the art collectors he works for must be rolling in it. Then he'd go straight to Luisa and tell her, and exactly how would you justify such interference in her life? You are, after all, separated. She would never speak to you again, you know that, don't you? You're aware of that?'

But perhaps none of those things would happen after my attempt to persuade him. And so I ignored her objections and merely asked, as if I hadn't heard what she had said:

'Apart from the ponytail, what does he look like?'

I had learned a few things from Reresby and Ure and Dundas and even from Tupra, but I still wasn't like him, nor did I wish to be, except on the odd occasion, and this was just such an odd occasion. Perhaps it's not possible to imitate someone else only now and then and when you choose, and perhaps in order to act like your chosen model—even just once—you have to resemble him all the time and in all circumstances, that is, when you're alone and when there's no need, and for that to happen you must have more than just accidental reasons, reasons that come upon you suddenly and from without. You have to have a deep need, a profound desire to change, which was not my case. Initially, I behaved as I thought he would have behaved, but there came a point when I wasn't sure, or couldn't imagine exactly, how he would have behaved, or perhaps I preferred not to, or else couldn't imagine myself behaving like that, and I was filled with doubt, which he never would be; and so I went back to the idea that he might be able to help me, or at least give me advice and reassure me, or at least not dissuade me. I didn't phone Tupra until a few days into my stay and after my first visit to the children, my stolen glimpse of Luisa, my meeting with my sister and my father, my phone conversation with my sister-in-law Cristina Juárez, and after I had already taken a few steps in his imaginary wake.

I began by consulting the phone book and looking for that unusual surname, Custardoy. I discovered that I had been way off in my calculations, because there weren't a few Custardoys in Madrid, there was only one, who lived in Calle de Embajadores and whose initial, alas, wasn't E for Esteban, but a wretched R for Roberto, Ricardo, Raúl, Ramón or Ramiro and what use were they? His number must be under another name, possibly his landlord's if he was renting, although it seemed to me likely that he would own his apartment or studio or whatever it was, if those art collectors really did pay him well, doubtless for forgeries that could later be switched for the real thing in some ill-supervised church or sold as authentic to naïve, provincial museums, for I had already decided to myself that the man was a fraud, a con man. It might also be that he was listed under his second surname, some people do that to avoid being pestered, the ringing of the phone would disturb him when he was working, he would lose precision, concentration, he would jump and make the wrong brushstroke or put a hole through the canvas, the paint would run, he was, after all, an 'arty type,' but I couldn't think who would be likely to know that second surname, probably not even Luisa. I called directory assistance just in case, and asked for the number of someone called Custardoy living in Calle Mayor, but they had no one of that name, only the Custardoy in Calle de Embajadores. So I set off to the short stretch of Calle Mayor beyond Bailén and just before Cuesta de la Vega and the nearby park called Atenas, which I knew only from having driven through it once a long time ago, and I was in luck, because there were just two doors, and since one belonged to the offices of the nearby town hall, I deduced that it must be the other door, number 81. There were no names on the intercom—or *portero automático* as we call it in Spanish—only the numbers of the apartments, of which there were four and one on the ground floor. It was almost lunchtime—bad planning on my part—and the vast ornate carved door was closed, so there was no way of knowing if there was an actual flesh-and-blood doorman whom I could approach on another occasion. I thought of ringing a couple of the bells and inquiring after Custardoy, but if, by chance, I pressed the right bell and he answered in person, furious at this unexpected interruption to his fraudulent activities, I would have to invent some pretext, saying, perhaps, that I had a telegram for him and then not going up when he opened the street door for me, well, post office workers are so often unreliable and incomprehensible, he would wait for a while, mutter a few curses and then forget all about it, summoned back to work by his false art. I pressed a bell at random and no one answered. I tried a second one and, after a while, I heard a woman's voice.

'Is Don Esteban Custardoy there, please?' I asked.

'Who?' The woman was doubtless elderly.

'Cus-tar-doy,' I said slowly and clearly. 'Don Esteban.'

'No, he doesn't live here.'

'I must have the wrong apartment. Would you be so kind as to tell me which apartment he lives in? I have a telegram for him.'

'A telegram for me? Who from? We never get telegrams.'

'No, not for you, madam.' I realized that I would get nowhere with her. 'It's for your neighbor, Señor Custardoy. Would you mind telling me which floor he's on?'

'Which floor? This is the second floor,' she said. 'But there's no Bujaraloz living here. You've got the wrong address.'

The sound on those tinny intercoms is always dreadful, but the lady in question must, like Goya, have been both Aragonese and deaf for her to be able to trot out so blithely and so fluently the name of that rather obscure town in the province of Zaragoza. I apologized and thanked her, then left her in peace.

I decided to press a third bell, but there was no response, so many people have lunch out in Madrid. I tried a fourth bell and immediately heard another female voice, younger and more encouraging.

'Esteban Buscató?' the voice asked. That was the surname of a former basketball player, she must be a fan, I thought. 'No, I don't know the name. I don't think he lives here.' There was some creaking and the sound of the sea in the background, it was like having a seashell pressed to my ear and as if a ship somewhere out there was about to be wrecked.

'The name's Custardoy,' I said again. 'Cus-tar-doy. He's a painter. Perhaps you could tell me which floor he lives on or where he has his studio. He's a painter, Custardoy the painter.'

'We're not expecting any painter here.'

'No, *I'm* not a painter, Madam,' I said, fast losing hope. 'I have a telegram for Señor Custardoy. *He's* the painter. Don't you know of a painter living in this building? A painter, not a house painter, but a painter like Goya, do you know him?'

'Of course I know Goya. He's the one who painted *La Maja.*' And she sounded rather offended. 'But as I'm sure you can imagine, he doesn't live here, or anywhere else for that matter. You may not know this, but he's dead.'

I silently cursed the forger's outlandish surname and gave up. I couldn't stay there much longer, ringing every bell, or I could do so on another occasion (ringing two was enough at any one time, I shouldn't overstep the mark), or return at a different hour when the real-life doorman would be in, if there was one. Besides, it occurred to me that Custardoy might have rented or bought his apartment or studio under a false name, as befitted a criminal, or maybe under his own name, Custardoy being a pseudonym. In either case, no one in that building would be able to tell me where to find him.

I was almost certain I had the right place, which was promising, but I had to make sure and find out what floor he lived on and in which apartment; Tupra, I knew, would have had no qualms about stationing himself outside my house from early on—that is, outside Luisa's house—waiting for her to come out and following her as often as proved necessary, knowing that on one such sortie she was sure to head for that area near the Royal Palace and the cathedral-*cum*-eyesore, near Cuesta de la Vega and Atenas Park and the various other local parks and gardens, Sabatini, Campo del Moro, Viaducto and Vistillas or what remained of them (I had read that the Council and the Church were plotting to do away with them and use the land to build diocesan offices or semi-clerical housing or a parking lot or something), where the Madrid of the Habsburgs mingled with that of Carlos III, until she arrived at that or another door. I, however, did have qualms. It wasn't just that it seemed wrong and contemptible of me to shadow her like that, I feared, above all, that she might spot me and then all my plans would be ruined: she'd be on the alert, she'd be sure to get angry and forbid me from interfering in any aspect or area of her life, and then I would be unable to talk to Custardoy or influence him without her attributing to me any resulting change, and blaming me for any rupture with the con man or, indeed, his withdrawal, the thing I so desired, and then, as her sister had predicted, she would never speak to me again; well, perhaps not never, but certainly not for a long time. I had to save Luisa without her suspecting my intervention, or as little as possible. She would always have an inkling that there was some connection, because of my presence in Madrid: her boyfriend vanishing just when I appeared or shortly afterwards would be too much of a coincidence, and she'd be left with the conviction that I'd had something to do with it. However, if I performed my task well and kept out of the way as much as possible, that conviction would have no grounds, no proof, and, as such, would soon fade and end up tossed into the bag of suspicions and imaginings.

During the days that followed, I visited my children and took them out as often as I could, occasionally meeting Luisa when I picked them up or dropped them off, but usually encountering only the Polish babysitter. I avoided hanging around, as I had on the first night; I avoided asking Luisa anything more about her black eye, or, at most, ventured some neutral, indirect comment: 'I see it's getting better—but try to be more careful in future.' Nor did I insist we meet on our own one day, to go out to supper and talk in peace, it was best to see very little of her during that stay and concentrate on trying to extricate her from the unhealthy relationship she had got herself into, even if she didn't see the relationship like that or, worse, was drawn to it. And if she was bemused by my lack of insistence, I could always say chivalrously: 'You've got too much to do. I'm just passing through, almost like a tourist really. And it seems more appropriate to let you take the initiative. Besides, I need to spend time with my father, who's not at all well. He sends his love by the way, and always asks after you.' And so I tried to remove myself and not to coincide with her except where the coincidence was genuine, not to make myself too visible or to be always bumping into her, as would have been tempting, and as I might have tended to do had I not immediately taken on that unexpected, specific, urgent, vital task as soon as I arrived in Madrid. Not that I found it easy to maintain a discreet pose, especially when the first week had passed and Luisa showed no sign of regret at not being able to spend time with me nor—most woundingly of all—did she show any curiosity about my life in London, about the kind of person I was when I was there, about who I hung around with, nor if I had become someone else, even if only superficially, nor about my current job of which I had spoken so little over the phone, almost avoiding her occasional questions, perhaps asked only perfunctorily and out of politeness, but at least they were questions. Now there were no questions of any kind, nor did she seek the opportunity to ask them: during that first week she never made a single proposal to meet or get together, to go out to lunch, to linger a while in the apartment or have supper or a drink with her when I returned with Guillermo and Marina in the evening, having taken them to the movies or the Retiro or wherever. It was as if she had no mental space to think of anything apart from her relationship with Custardoy, or at least that was what I assumed must be filling it entirely, for what else could it have been? She seemed to me absorbed, preoccupied. It wasn't the absorption of mere excitement or of plenitude. Nor that of anxiety or torment or unease, but that of someone struggling to understand or to decipher something.

And I did, in fact, spend time with my father and see my siblings and a few friends; I also visited Madrid's secondhand bookshops and generally mooched around. In one of those bookshops I bought a present for Sir Peter, a large book of propaganda posters from the Spanish Civil War, some of which, I noticed, bore the same 'careless talk' slogan as had appeared in his own country, with very similar warnings—I'd had a vague recollection of seeing something similar in Spain, although he never had—and he would be intrigued to see these Spanish precursors, as would Mrs. Berry. I would go and see him as soon as I got back, without fail. And one morning, I returned to the area where Custardoy lived and, standing on the sidewalk opposite, looked at the street door leading to his apartment or studio in Calle Mayor. The door was still closed, so it may be that there was no doorman or only one who kept a very brief or idle or erratic timetable. In the end, however, I had decided that if I were ever to find him in, I would not approach the doorman; it was best that no one should see or identify me, still less associate me with Custardoy. If I were to go there in person to enquire after that copyist and forger, I might, depending on what happened later on between him and me, be putting myself in a vulnerable position, for you never know what might occur when two men come face to face and argue, or if one of them tries to get or demand something from the other, to force or convince or dissuade or repel. Standing on the same side of the street as the abominable cathedral, I looked up at the balconies, in the bizarre hope that I might have the great good luck that while I was there, Custardoy would appear on his—I would recognize him by his ponytail and from Cristina's grudging description—and I would know then, with no need for further effort or investigation, just where he worked or lived. There were balconies on all the floors until the fifth, where there were only the windows of what looked like an attic apartment. The balconies of the apartment immediately above the enormous door were made of stone and had little columns, while above that they were all fancy wrought iron, and every one had slatted shutters that stood open, an indication that each apartment was occupied and no one was away or traveling, and that Custardoy was in town. I studied each balcony and each window, trying to take in the fact—rather than imagine, which would have been a disagreeable and superfluous exercise—that behind one of them Luisa and Custardoy met and went to bed together, laughed and talked, discussed their day, that there they had perhaps argued and he had slapped her round the face with his open hand or punched her in the eye with his closed fist. He must be a very irascible fellow or perhaps not, perhaps he was utterly cold and had delivered both blows as a calculated warning, to remind her just what and how much he was capable of. And it might be that one night my wife would emerge from that ornate door opposite me, trembling with fear and excitement, simultaneously horrified and captivated. No, I didn't like that man or anything I knew or could imagine about him.

I also took to going to the Prado each morning, before I did anything else and as soon as I'd had breakfast, it was right across the street from my hotel. This wasn't just for my enjoyment and because I hadn't visited the place for ages. I also had in mind something my sister-in-law Cristina had said to me about Custardoy: '. . . sometimes he's commissioned to copy paintings from the Prado and he spends hours there studying and copying.' And so the first thing I did on the first day I went into the museum, and before looking at any pictures at all, was to search the place from top to bottom and from end to end, scrutinizing the copyists who were working in the various rooms, in case one of them was a fifty-something man with his hair scraped back in a ponytail, a man prepared to spend hours and hours before some painting not of his choice, whether good, bad or indifferent. Needless to say I spotted none of these characteristics, indeed, most of the copyists were youngish women, although not all of them young enough to be art students. Perhaps it's another of those professions, like art restoration, that the female population has appropriated and which they do very well. I saw no one answering that description on the second day either. I carried out that same preliminary patrol, although I was filled this time with less hope or was it mere superstition: copying is such a slow task that it was likely that only those from the day before would be there again, or so it seemed; it would have been an extraordinary coincidence if Custardoy had started work on one of his copies or forgeries on the very day I happened to be there, on the alert. This, however, did not prevent me from repeating what I had done the previous morning and striding round all the galleries, studying the few people who were sitting or, in some cases, standing at their easels, intent on reproducing what was there before their eyes, something that already existed and which had, usually, been painted better several centuries before.

On the fifth day, I got up late, after a relatively wild night with some old friends, and only arrived at the Prado around one o'clock, about two hours later than usual. I wanted to visit some of the rooms containing works by Italian artists that I hadn't seen for years, and since those in charge of the museum have the ridiculous habit of moving everything around every so often—as if they were running a supermarket—and I suspected that it would take me a while to find the current location of those paintings, I dispensed with my preliminary patrol and inspection of the copyists. And it was there and then that I noticed in passing, in one of the long galleries on the ground floor, a man with a short piratical or matadorish pigtail who wasn't copying anything, but taking notes or doing pencil sketches of a painting in a fairly sizeable sketch pad, although not so large that he couldn't hold it in one hand. He was standing quite close to the picture in question and therefore with his back to me or to anyone else who was not right next to him or who had decided to block his view. I was perfectly within my rights to do either or both of those things, it is, after all, quite common nowadays for rude tourists—almost a tautology really—or indeed the rude natives of any city to impatiently, inconsiderately interpose themselves between painting and viewer and even elbow the latter none too subtly out of the way in order to occupy his or her more central position, the way of the world of which Tupra spoke has become ill-mannered, especially in Spain, although it's now a near-universal phenomenon. I kept a safe distance from him and not only so as not to appear rude. Initially, I observed him from behind, but just as there was no space to his right, only a rope barrier and the side wall, to the left of the painting there was a high door and to the left of that another painting (there were only two on that end wall), and so I moved cautiously in that direction to get as clear a view as possible of his profile, at the same time doing my best not to enter, or only minimally, his field of vision. I realized at once that I needn't worry about him seeing me, for he was totally absorbed in the painting and in his sketchbook, his eyes moving rapidly back and forth between the two, with no interest in anything else, he wasn't even distracted by the continuous ebb and flow of tourists, mostly Italians (come to admire their ancient compatriots), who, curiously enough, did not insist on crowding round him and bothering him by looking at what he was looking at, rather, on seeing him so absorbed in his work, they walked past without stopping, as if intimidated by that tense motionless figure and as if prepared, for the moment, to allow him exclusive usufruct and enjoyment of it. I noticed that he had a mustache and sideburns, which, although not long, were somewhat longer than is perhaps considered the norm nowadays, or perhaps they were merely striking because, while his hair was straight and rather fair and with no visible grey in it, his sideburns were curly and much darker, almost black, but streaked with white and grey, as if old age had decided to begin its work from the sides, leaving the pale dome for later. He was quite tall and thin, with perhaps some evidence around his belly of having drunk too much beer, but the general impression was of someone gaunt and bony, and what I could see of his cheekbones and his broad forehead confirmed that impression, as did his swift active right hand, which had the long strong fingers of a professional pianist; alarming fingers, like piano keys.

Since I was unable to view him from the front, and so couldn't see his eyes or lips or teeth or facial expression (although I could see his nose in profile), it was impossible for me to interpret him, I mean, in the way I used to do at the building with no name when confronted by all those famous and unknown faces, whose voices I almost always heard as well, either in person or on video. From what I was able to make out (which was only his left side, whenever, that is, I pretended to be looking at the other painting separated from his by the high door and placed myself level with him, protected by the distance between us), everything seemed to agree with, or at least not contradict, Cristina's grudging but, as it turned out, accurate description of Custardoy. I had only asked her what he looked like at the end of our conversation, when she was already tired and eager to bring things to a close. 'Oh, I don't know,' she said, 'he's bony, sinewy, with a long nose like a flamenco singer, like the singer in Ketama, for example, you know the one I mean?' (I had an idea Ketama were some kind of semi-flamenco group.) 'And very strange dark eyes, I can't really describe them, but there's something strange, something peculiar about them that I don't like. Sometimes, he has a mustache and sometimes not, as if he kept shaving it off and then letting it grow again I suppose, because I've seen him with one and without.' 'What else? Tell me more,' I had urged her, just as Tupra or Mulryan or Rendel or Pérez Nuix used to urge me on, one more insistently than the others. 'That's all really. I can't think what else to say. Bear in mind that I only know him by sight. I've come across him over the years here and there, I know who he is and I've heard things about him as I have about a lot of other people (well, up until this business with Luisa, of course, since when I've heard rather more about him). But as far as I can remember, we've never been introduced, I've never been that close to him or exchanged a single word.' 'You must have noticed something more,' I had urged her again, knowing that if you press someone, there is always something more. 'Well, as I've said, he wears a tie on all occasions, as if he were trying to compensate for the slightly bohemian impression he makes with that ponytail and the half-grown mustache he sometimes sports: a contrast, a touch of originality. He dresses very correctly, very traditionally, he aspires to elegance I suppose, but doesn't quite make it. Perhaps because elegance is simply not compatible with the salacious look on his face, I don't quite know how to explain it, but he has one of those faces that oozes sexuality, absurd really, but maybe that in part explains his success with women, you can smell it on him. Even from a distance, you can tell what he's about. At least you can if you're a woman. He looks at you so brazenly, he sizes you up. He gives you the once-over, from head to toe, lingering shamelessly on your breasts and your ass, and, if you're sitting down, on your thighs. I used to see him do this, years ago, with loads of women at the Chicote and at the Cock, as soon as they walked in; and he's done it to me too, from a distance, because he doesn't care whether you're with someone or not. But he obviously didn't fancy me much or else could sense that he wasn't my type, because he never approached me. According to Ranz, he can tell immediately who is a willing prey, and he knows even more quickly whether he wants to sink his teeth in or leave well enough alone.' Given their present relationship, it had troubled me to think that he had spotted Luisa as a victim right from the start, as soon as he saw her. And I couldn't help but then go on to wonder if he would have seen the same thing in her had they met when she and I were together. The thought that followed was even worse: it wasn't impossible that they had met before I went off to London and before our official separation. That idea didn't bear thinking about, and so I did not pursue it.

In the man in the Prado I could see nothing of this, by which I mean his sexual voracity, although his gaze was intently fixed on a painting depicting a woman, a mother. Perhaps he had given her the once-over too, prior to any artistic, pictorial or even technical appraisal. Perhaps he had been put off by the fact that the woman appeared in the painting with her three small children; although not necessarily, if he was Custardoy, given that he was clearly attracted to Luisa and she, after all, was a mother of two. (True, the woman in the painting was a rather unattractive, matronly type, whereas Luisa kept herself very slim and, to my eyes, pretty and youthful, but I don't know how she appears to other eyes.) What I had noticed right from the very first instant was that he was wearing a jacket and tie and black lace-up shoes. They wouldn't have been made by Grenson or Edward Green, but they were plain and in good taste, with soles that were neither thick nor made of rubber, I couldn't object to his choice of clothes, except to say that they were too conventional. Not the ponytail, of course, although in recent years, that's become fairly common among men of any age (age no longer acts as a brake on anything and has lost the battle against fashion and vanity). It gave him a roguish look, which was the adjective Cristina had so aptly used to describe him, if indeed it was him.

Once when I walked past, always keeping a prudent distance so that he wouldn't notice me, I managed to confirm my first impression: he was making sketches of the four heads in the painting and, at the same time, taking notes, both at great speed. If he was Custardoy, he might have been commissioned to make a copy and was carrying out a preliminary study. Or, if he really was as good as they said, perhaps he didn't need to stand in front of the picture itself with easel and brushes for long hours and even longer days, and it was enough for him to capture and memorize it (maybe he had a photographic memory) and then work from a good reproduction in his studio, the fact is I know nothing about the techniques used by copyists, let alone forgers (he wouldn't be creating a forgery on this occasion, no one would believe that the work in the Prado wasn't authentic, wasn't the original).

However, I didn't want to spend too much time in his vicinity: the longer I stayed there like his shadow, the greater the risk that he would turn around or glance to his left and see me there, although it was highly unlikely that he would know me or recognize me from photos Luisa might have shown him, though I doubted that she had, and the probability was that he had never seen me. Anyway, I moved away a little and looked briefly at another painting, "Messer Marsilio Cassoti and His Wife" by Lorenzo Lotto, and then shifted closer again, I didn't want him to escape me now, to lose track of him; I ventured slightly further off and had a quick look at a "Portrait of a Gentleman" by Volterra, but was drawn back at once to the man with the ponytail, I didn't dare take my eyes off him for more than a few seconds; I wandered away again and studied Yañez de la Almedina's "St. Catherine"—all in reds and blues, resting a long sword on the wheel of her martyrdom—and that figure distracted me, so much so that after only half a minute's contemplation, I started in alarm and almost ran back to the painting of the mother and her children. In between all these comings and goings and periods of waiting, I managed to get a good look at that painting: it was average size, about three feet something long by three feet wide I reckoned; and the painting was a family portrait, according to the label, "Camilla Gonzaga, Countess of San Secondo, and her Sons" by Parmigianino, whose real name, I noticed, was Mazzola, like a famous soccer star from my early childhood who played against the Real Madrid of Di Stéfano and Gento, I seemed to recall he was a forward with Inter Milan. Against a dark almost black background stood the sturdy Countess, well dressed, discreetly bejewelled, holding in her right hand a golden, gem-incrusted goblet which looked slightly out of place

with so many children around her; or perhaps it wasn't a goblet, but the large tassel from her belt. She bordered on the plump, or maybe not (but she was certainly wide), her expression was rather absent and certainly not lively, although there was perhaps a remnant there of calm almost indifferent determination. She had slightly bovine, almost prominent eyes, very fine eyebrows, which looked as if they had been penciled in, and rather thin and unalluring lips; her best feature was possibly her lustrous un-lined rosy skin, so smooth and taut on her cheeks that it looked as if it might burst. More surprising was her lack of interest in her children, Troilo, Ippolito and Federico according to the label; she showed no signs at all that she was devoted to them, she wasn't looking at them or touching them, not even holding the hand of the child to her left, which was very close to her own inert left hand. The Countess was like an astonished statue sur-rounded by other smaller but similarly self-absorbed statues, be-cause the odd thing was that the children weren't paying *her* any attention either, although two of them were distractedly clasping the braided belt of her dress. Each figure was gazing out of the picture in a different direction as if each and every one of them was far more interested in people or elements beyond the frame than in each other in the case of the boys, or in her sons, in the case of the mother, who was the central figure. The oldest child on the right was the least attractive and resembled a foundling or an orphan, partly because of his ugly and excessively severe haircut, and partly because of the sad expression on his face; the youngest didn't seem very happy or very affectionate either, just vulnerable, and about to tug at his mother's belt like someone performing a purely reflex or habitual action; the boy on her left, the prettiest of the children and the one with the most alert eyes, seemed completely oblivious to the rest of the group, as if he were anxious to escape both the others and the enforced patience of his extreme youth.

The only gaze that one could follow or imagine was that of the Countess, given that, to her right, beyond the high door, which kept them still further apart (a whim of that month's reor-ganization), hung the portrait of her husband, at whom she was directing that distinctly chilly and possibly disappointed look, or perhaps it was a look that was wounded by the mere thought of him. 'They were painted separately,' I thought, 'husband and father on one side, wife and mother with the children on the other, two different portraits, in two distinct, isolated spaces rather than in one space common to them both: a bit like my now living alone in London, while Luisa stays here in Madrid with Guillermo and Marina, except that she's devoted to our children and they to her, at least that's how it has been up until now, it would be terrible if that Custardoy fellow were beginning to distance her from them, it happens with women sometimes, they suddenly have eyes and thoughts only for the new man they're chasing or for the old love they're losing—that's the only thing that can, very occasionally, create a rift and cause them temporarily to relegate their children to second place, just as the Countess perhaps has her gaze fixed on the distant soldier who is out of the picture and perhaps out of time, thus neglecting Troilo, Ippolito and Federico, who are accustomed now to the fact that their mother barely pays them any attention and lives obsessed with thoughts of her absent husband and perhaps sees them as a tie and an impediment and a hindrance, I don't think such a thing would ever happen with Luisa, although she does seem to have made frequent use of the Polish babysitter while I've been here, and there must be or could be a reason for that. And Luisa is clearly not obsessed with thoughts of me, however absent I might be. She, after all, was the one to expel me from her time and from the children's time, although I doubtless gave her some cause to do so.'

'Pedro Maria Rossi, Count of San Secondo. 1533–35,' said the label and then went on to describe him: "Pedro Maria Rossi (1504–1547) was a brilliant soldier who served under Francis I of France, Cosimo I de' Medici and Charles V' ('So he was a mercenary in other words,' I thought, 'as I am, too, in my own way'). 'The portrait was painted when he was fighting under the imperial flag, which explains the inclusion of the word "IMPERIO" and the many classical quotations.' The Count's blue-grey gaze was even colder than that of his wife, almost scornful, almost steely

and almost cruel, although it was harder to imagine that he was directing it at her than that she was directing hers at him. ('He could be Sir Cruelty,' I thought.) The long beard and mustache made him seem older (he would only have been about thirty when he posed for the portrait) and made it hard to know at first glance whether he was good-looking or merely elegant and severe, a second glance revealed that he certainly was (all three things, I mean). His noble nose was quite large, larger than mine but not as large as Custardoy's, which was, moreover, slightly hooked. Like St. Catharine and Reresby, he wore a sword, on his left side (which meant that he must be right-handed), but his sword was sheathed and you could only see the hilt and the guard, not the blade. He was wearing a fine costume trimmed with fur, and to his right was a statue of a helmeted youth also carrying a sword, presumably the god Mars. The Count had distinguished hands, with fingers that seemed too slender to be those of a warrior. But pretty much the most striking thing about him was the aggressive codpiece, seamed or stitched or whatever you call it (it must have been made of hard leather, not of reeds or wicker as they appear in most paintings), visibly and obscenely pointing upwards—a permanent reminder of his erection—far less discreet and modest, for example, than those worn by Emperor Charles V and Philip II in the full-length portraits, both by Titian, in the same museum. 'Perhaps this Count, this soldier, this husband, isn't like me at all,' I thought, 'the one who's leaving or has left, but like the one who is about to arrive or has arrived already and is a violent man who carries a sword, like that bastard Custardoy. Perhaps his wife's gaze then is one of devotion and fear, which is why she seems paralyzed and will-less, for devotion and fear are such powerful dominant feelings, whether felt simultaneously or separately it doesn't matter, that they can momentarily cancel out all other feelings, even love for one's children. I hope Luisa doesn't look at Custardoy like that, I hope she isn't afraid of him, still less devoted. But precisely how she looks at him is something I will never know.'

I again looked away from the portrait and glanced over at Custardoy or at the man who might be Custardoy and I saw that he was also looking in my direction; I was convinced that, for a couple of seconds, our eyes met, but so briefly that it was likely that we had, in fact, each merely glanced simultaneously at the painting that more or less matched the picture we each had before us, I that of Pedro Maria Rossi and he that of Camilla Gonzaga with Troilo, Ippolito and Federico, their children; since I first spotted him, he must have spent at least seven minutes there jotting down words and scribbling lines but he'd doubtless been there longer than that too, and that's a long time to look at a single painting. In that couple of seconds, however, I was able to see his face full on for the first time, and it immediately impressed me as being crude, rough and cold, with its broad forehead or receding hairline, its sparse mustache (dark like his sideburns) and its nose which appeared, as is only logical, less hooked than it had in profile (yes, he did suddenly remind me of a long-haired singer I had seen on television, probably the singer with that group Ketama), and two enormous very dark eyes, rather wide-set and almost lashless, and both those factors, the lack of lashes and the wide-apartness, must have made his obscene gaze unbearable or possibly irresistible when turned on the women he seduced or bought and possibly also when turned on the men with whom he might be competing. They were eyes that grabbed, like hands, and one night or one day, they had alighted on the face and body of Luisa and made her his prey. ('And very strange dark eyes, I can't really describe them, but there's something strange, something peculiar about them that I don't like,' according to the description I had coaxed out of a reluctant Cristina). And so, to give those eyes no time to fix on or grab me, I walked away from my portrait of the Count, retreated a few steps and went into the room next door, to the left and on a slightly higher level (a matter of going up three or four steps). From there I could peer in every thirty seconds or so to make sure Custardoy had not escaped without my realizing, and, at the same time, I was much less likely to re-enter his field of vision. In that first lightning glimpse of his face full on he had reminded me of someone else, not the singer, but someone I knew personally, but it was too brief a glimpse for me to be able to remember who, or if my memory was right.

The next room was dominated largely by German art. It contained Dürer's famous self-portrait, as well as his 'Adam' and his 'Eve.' However, my eye was caught at once by a long narrow painting I had been familiar with since childhood, when, as was only normal, it had shocked and filled me with a degree of fear tinged with curiosity, 'The Three Ages and Death' by Hans Baldung Grien, which, like the two portraits, has its counterpart in another painting of the same format and dimensions next to it, 'Harmony, or The Three Graces.' In the former, Death, on the right, is grasping the arm of an old woman or has his arm linked through hers and is tugging at her gently, unhurriedly, and the old woman, in turn, has one arm round the shoulder of a young woman while with her left hand she's plucking at the younger woman's skimpy raiments, as if she, too, were drawing her softly away. Death is carrying an hourglass in his right hand ('An hourglass figure,' I thought) and in his left hand keeps a loose hold on a spear twice broken (it almost resembles a thunderless flash of lightning) on whose point falls or rests the hand of a sleeping child who is lying at the feet of that group of three, though it may be a long time until he joins them, and he is quite oblivious to their dealings. To his right, an owl; in the background, a solar landscape that looks instead lunar, grim and desolate, with a ruined tower in flames; the inevitable cross hangs in the sky. I had always wondered, ever since I was a child,

if the young woman and the old were the same person at very different ages or if they were two separate women, I mean, if the older woman had always been tugging at herself from youth onwards and into old age, when she finally allows herself to be carried off by Death, for if that were not the case, the subject would be graver and more troubling. However, the two women looked very alike to me: the blue eyes, the nose, the rather thin lips, the somewhat sharp chin, the long wavy hair, the stature, the smallish widely-spaced breasts, the feet, the whole figure, there were even similarities in their facial expressions, or at least they were not entirely opposed. The young woman is frowning, either worried or annoyed, but not alarmed or frightened, as she probably would have been had the person drawing her away been a stranger, or just another person, or even her mother. She doesn't struggle or put up a fight or try to shrug off the hand on her shoulder, and at most, she tries to prevent her from removing all her garments. The old woman, for her part, focuses all her attention on the young woman and not on Death, and in her look there is a mixture of gravity, understanding, resolve and pity, but no ill will, as if she were saying to the young woman (or to herself when she was her age): 'I'm sorry, but there's nothing we can do' (or 'Come along, we have to go on; I know because I've already arrived'). As for Death, who has his arm linked through hers, she takes no notice of him, but neither does she resist or oppose him, she looks more towards the past than her future, perhaps because—despite the promises of the cross hanging in the air and the infernal tower in flames, with a large hole in the side as if made by a cannon ball—she knows that there is little or no future left.

'There's Sir Death,' I thought, 'as in the English and, generally speaking, the Germanic tradition: he's clearly male, *el Muerte* not *la Muerte*, because although he is cadaverous, a semi-skeleton with the skin clinging to bones it barely covers—like a disguise he's adopted to tread the earth, all the more so when you notice his eyes are more deeply sunken than the rest—you can see a few wisps of beard growing out of his chin, and other wisps, resembling tiny tentacles, more like the tentacles of a cuttlefish

or a squid than an octopus, peeping out where his penis and
his vanished testicles would have been, now there's only a hole
where once a codpiece doubtless stood erect. He's certainly not
like Sergeant Death in the Armagh ballad ("And when Sergeant
Death's cold arms shall embrace me"), who is a man in his prime,
a strong energetic warrior prepared to snatch lives away nonstop,
an experienced professional with his cold disciplined arms always
busy; this Death is the feeblest and most worn of the three figures, or of the four, with his meek broken spear, so meek that an
unwary child can almost touch it. And yet there is determination and energy in the scrawny arm that grips, and he is, above
all, the master of time, he holds the clock and knows the time
and can see when it's running out, the sand or water, whichever
it is that his hourglass contains and on which his red-veined eyes
are firmly fixed, rather than on the old or the young woman,
for time is his only guide, the only thing that counts for this Sir
Death, as naked and decrepit as our Latin hag with her scythe,
this Sir Death with neither helmet nor sword.' And I suddenly
remembered 'the loud tick-tock' in that small sepulchral living
room in the Lisbon cemetery of Os Prazeres, which, according
to the traveler who 'with a degree of indiscretion' discovered
and observed it, 'was to a normal tick-tock what a shout is to the
spoken voice'; and I recalled the enigmatic words suggested by
the sight of the alarm clock making the noise ('of the kind we
used to see in our parents' kitchens, round in shape, with a bell
like a spherical skullcap and with two small balls for feet'): 'It
seems to me that time is the only dimension in which the living
and the dead can talk to each other and communicate, the only
dimension they have in common.' Perhaps when all the sand or
all the water had trickled through, thus signaling the death of
the old woman painted by Baldung Grien, and who was perhaps
also the young woman, when he had finally sent them to join
'the more influential and more animated majority,' he would still
have to turn over the hourglass or clepsydra in order to begin
the countdown again, about which my compatriot the traveler
wondered: Was it the amount of time they had been dead or the
time yet to elapse before the final judgment? If it was measuring

out the hours of solitude, was it counting those that had passed or those still to come?

I kept peering in at the larger Italian gallery, then turning back to spend a little more time with the German painting, which while it no longer frightened me, still intrigued me. From the threshold I saw, too, 'The Annunciation' by Fra Angélico, an excellent full-size copy of which had presided over my father's living room for as long as I could remember, he and my mother had commissioned it from a friend who was a copyist, a Custardoy of the 1930s and '40s, Daniel Canellada was his name I recall; seeing that painting was, for me, like being at home. On one of my brief forays into the German gallery, I lingered too long in front of the Baldung Grien and, when I returned to the Italian gallery, the man was no longer standing before the Parmigianino, I mean, before the Countess and her children. I bounded down the intervening steps, looking anxiously to right and left, but, fortunately, I spotted him at once, his now closed sketchbook under his arm, on his way to the stairs that led up to the first floor and then to the exit. That's when I started to follow him, or where I became more like his shadow, not in quite the same way as I had been with Tupra on the journeys we made together, but in both cases I relegated myself to the background. Once upstairs, he went to the coat check, and I waited with my back turned until he reappeared, looking round every three seconds so as not to lose him again, and when he emerged, I discovered with horror that what he had left there and retrieved was a hat, possibly a fedora ('A man wearing a ponytail and a hat,' I thought, 'possibly a fedora. Good lord!'). He had the good manners not to put it on while he was indoors, but only when he went out into the street, and then I saw—although it brought me little relief—that it was broader brimmed than the aforementioned fedora, more the kind of hat a painter or a conductor or an artist would wear, and black, of course. Duly behatted, he set off down the steps outside the museum, opposite the Hotel Ritz, and I followed after, always at a safe distance. He strode along the Paseo del Prado at a good pace, then stopped outside a brasserie, studied the menu, peered in through the window, shielding his eyes with his hand against the reflections on the glass (wasn't the brim of his presumptuous hat enough?), as if he were considering having lunch there—although it was early for Madrid unless you happened to be a foreigner; perhaps I was wrong, and he was a foreigner; but he didn't look like one to me, I could sense something unequivocally Spanish about his whole appearance, especially the way he walked, or perhaps it was the trousers—and so I took advantage of that pause to look in the window of a nearby shop selling artifacts from Toledo, including swords—obviously aimed at tourists, but nowadays they wouldn't be allowed to take such swords with them on a plane, they'd have to check them, and even then a sword wouldn't easily fit in a suitcase; it wouldn't be permitted on trains either, and I wondered who the devil would buy such swords now if they couldn't be transported anywhere, a collector of decorative knives and swords like Dick Dearlove would presumably have them sent to him some way or other. Most would be made of our famous Toledo steel, very Spanish and very medieval, but I noticed that among those on display there were also a few that were apparently Scottish and even bore the name 'McLeod' engraved on the guard, an ignoble concession to the movie-mad Anglo-Saxon masses. It occurred to me that I might buy one, not right then, of course, but later, for I had learned from Tupra a little of the effect that such an archaic weapon could produce. Almost all of them, however, were much longer and larger, doubtless far more difficult and far heavier to wield than the 'catgutter' or Landsknecht or *Katzbalger*, they had really huge blades. They would cut off a hand at a blow. They would slice through and dismember. 'No,' I thought, 'it would be best if it were a sword I didn't have to get rid of, one that I could return to its place, used or not, it wouldn't matter, one that I wouldn't have to throw away or deliberately abandon for someone else to find later.'

The man who was now very probably Custardoy continued on along Carrera de San Jerónimo, past my hotel, where he peered in at the entrance and read the plaque there which states, incredibly, that the Palace Hotel was conceived, designed and built in the brief space of fifteen months spanning 1911 and

1912, by the Léon Monnoyer construction company, who were, I suppose, French or Belgian, I don't know how the builders of today—that plague, that horde—can hold up their heads for shame or indeed shamelessness; a little further on, more or less opposite the Parliament building, he paused momentarily by the statue of Cervantes—who also had his sword unsheathed—there were some police vans parked there, with five or six policemen armed with machine guns standing outside to protect the honorable members, even though there were none to be seen, they must all have been inside or off on a trip somewhere or in one of the bars. The man with the ponytail and mustache had clearly retrieved something else from the museum coatcheck, a briefcase with no handles, into which he must have put his sketchbook, and he was carrying said briefcase under his arm and walking quickly, confidently, head up, eyes front, looking frankly about him and at the people he passed, and I had quite a fright when, as he was passing Lhardy, he slowed his pace and turned his head to observe the legs of a girl with whom he had almost collided, possibly deliberately I thought. I was afraid he might see me and recognize me, I mean from before, from the Prado. His response to the young woman was very Spanish, one I often have myself, although whenever I turned round like that in London, I had the sense that I was the only man who did, less so in Madrid, although there are fewer and fewer men who dare to look at whatever we want to, especially when the person we're looking at can't see us and has her back to us, which means that we're not bothering or embarrassing anyone—in these increasingly repressive times the puritans are even trying to control what our eyes do, often quite involuntarily. His was a quick, appreciative, brazen glance, with those large dark marble-like eyes of his, intense and troubling, wide-set and lashless, which more or less coincided with what Cristina had told me about the way he visually grabbed at women; but perhaps that was an exaggeration, I myself sometimes look in a similar way at a passing derriere or a pair of legs as they move off, perhaps with less penetrating appraising eyes, more ironic or more amused. His eyes looked as if they were salivating.

If when he arrived at the ruined Puerta del Sol, he continued straight on, if he didn't go down into the metro and didn't catch a bus or a taxi, we would be on the right track, that is, heading for Custardoy's house or workshop or studio, and then there'd be no further room for doubt that he was he. I feared for a moment that he was about to deviate from that route when, at the beginning of Calle Mayor, he crossed the street, but I was reassured at once to see that he was merely going into a rather fine-looking bookshop, Méndez by name. From the other side of the street, through the shopwindow, I saw him greet the owners or employees affectionately (patting them on the arm; and he was again polite enough to take off his hat, which was something), and he must have made some funny comment because they both laughed, a burst of generous spontaneous laughter. He left after a few minutes, carrying a bag from the bookshop, so he must have bought something, and I wondered what sort of thing he would read, then he crossed back onto my side of the road, and I retreated a few steps, until there was the same distance between us as there had been since we left the museum. However, I had to stop again almost at once and make a slow withdrawal from an ATM, in order to gain time and not overtake him, because he met a female acquaintance or friend—I caught a glimpse of blue eyes—a young woman in trousers, with short hair and a fringed suede jacket, à la Daniel Boone or Davy Crockett or General Custer when they skewered him. She smiled warmly at him and planted a kiss on each cheek, he must live in the area; they chatted animatedly for a few minutes, she obviously liked him (he didn't take off his hat this time, but at least he touched the brim with his fingers when he saw the young woman, the classic gesture of respect in the street), and she laughed loudly at something he said ('He's the sort of man who makes people laugh, like me when I want to,' I thought. 'That could explain why Luisa likes him. Bad luck. Bad news'). No one would ever suspect that he hit women, or one particular woman, the woman who still mattered most to me.

He said goodbye and continued on his way; he walked with great resolve, almost fiercely sometimes when he increased the pace, he would never be bothered by any of the pickpockets or muggers who abound in that touristy area and who, for preference, fleece the Japanese; perhaps beggars would leave him alone too, his walk was that of someone who, however pleasant, is not open to overtures of that kind; and the duty of beggars and thieves is to recognize this at once and to sense who they're dealing with. He proceeded on past the San Miguel market on his left, where the road went slightly downhill. On the wall of a building I noticed a carved inscription which said soberly, gravely: 'Here lived and died Don Pedro Calderón de la Barca,' the dramatist on whom Nietzsche, in his day, was so keen, as indeed was the whole of Germany; and a little further along, on the other side, a more modern plaque indicated: 'In this place stood the Church of San Salvador, in whose tower Luis Vélez de Guevara set the action of his novel *El diablo cojuelo—The Devil Upon Two Sticks*—1641,' a book it had never occurred to me to read, not even when I was at Oxford, but Wheeler, Cromer-Blake and Kavanagh would surely have known it. Custardoy went over for a moment to a statue immediately opposite, in Plaza de la Villa, how odd that a painter should be so attracted to the three-dimensional. 'To Don Álvaro de Bazán' was all it said underneath, the Admiral in command of the Spanish fleet at the Battle of Lepanto, where Cervantes was wounded in 1571, losing the use of his left hand when he was only twenty-four, which meant that he could justifiably refer to himself as 'a complete man albeit missing a hand' in the same lines of farewell that I had quoted to Wheeler, even though he didn't want to hear them: farewell wit, farewell charm, farewell dear, delightful friends. There, too, was the Torre de los Luxanes, where it is said Francis I of France was held prisoner after being captured by the Spanish during the battle of Pavia in 1525; but since various other places in Spain also claim that he was held captive there, either a lot of people are lying or the Emperor Charles V trailed the French king round the country, exhibiting him like a monkey or a trophy.

Custardoy was still on the right track, the one that should lead him to his house, straight down Calle Mayor, and with me right behind, his rather distant or detached shadow. 'I've spent some time now being a shadow,' I thought, 'I have been and am a shadow at Tupra's side, accompanying him on his journeys and talking to him almost every day, always by his side like a subaltern, an interpreter, a support, an apprentice, an ally, occasionally a henchman ("No doubt, an easy tool, deferential, glad to be of use"). Now I'm playing shadow to this man whom I'm not even sure is the man I'm looking for, but as regards him, I'm none of those other things; I'm a sinister, punitive, threatening shadow of which he as yet knows nothing, as is usually the case with those walking behind, who cannot be seen; it would be better for him if he did not continue along this route, or if his route turned out not to be the one I hope for and desire.' Just after thinking this, I thought he might escape me, because when he reached the Capitanía General or Consejo de Estado (where soldiers bearing machine guns stood outside the first door), he again crossed the street as if he were about to go into the Istituto Italiano di Cultura, which is immediately opposite. Except that he didn't, he went down a narrow street just beyond that, and I felt really alarmed: surely, at this late stage, he wasn't going to turn out not to be he and not approach that ornate door before which I had stood on two occasions now. At the end of that street, very short and for pedestrians only, I saw him disappear to the left and I quickened my pace slightly to not lose track of him, and to find out where he was going, and when I reached that same point, he very nearly did see me: there, in the corner, was an old bar, El Anciano Rey de los Vinos, where he took a seat outside, looking obliquely across towards the Palacio Real; in Madrid, what with global warming, it's almost like summer for nearly six months of the year, and so there are tables and chairs set outside cafés and bars long after and long before the appropriate seasons. I immediately turned round to hide my face from him and pretended to read, like a tourist, another metal plaque just above me (and, of course, I did read it): 'Near this place stood the houses of Ana de Mendoza y la Cerda, Princess of Éboli, and in one of them she was arrested by order of Philip II in 1579.' She was the one-eyed woman, an intriguer and possibly a spy, who had doubtless in her day spread outbreaks of cholera, malaria and plague, as Wheeler had done, or so he said, and doubtless Tupra too, or perhaps the latter had merely lit the fuses that provoked great fires. (No age is free of such contagions; in every age there are people bearing flaming torches and people who talk.) The lady was always shown wearing an eye-patch, over her right eye I seemed to recall from seeing some portrait of her, and I thought, too, that I had watched a movie about her, starring Olivia de Havilland.

Out of the corner of my eye I noticed Custardoy placing his order with the waiter, and I walked back down the street as far as Calle Mayor, pondering what to do next, apart, that is, from keeping well out of the way. There was a ridiculous statue there, which Custardoy, showing excellent taste, had not stopped to look at; it was one of the many 'anonymous' pieces that fill our cities (in the name of 'democratizing' monuments, a contradiction in itself), but the fellow looked suspiciously like Hemingway, patron saint of tourists. And there was another plaque high up on the wall, that said: 'In this street, Juan Escobedo, secretary to John of Austria, was killed on March 31, 1578, on the night of Easter Monday.' Again this rang a bell with me, that murky murder; perhaps the Princess of Éboli had been involved, although it would have been very stupid of her to order an enemy to be killed right next to her house. (Later, I checked, and apparently it's still not known if the murder was carried out on orders from the Princess, from Philip II himself or from Antonio Pérez, his scheming secretary, who ended up being sent into exile; an as yet unsolved crime four and a bit centuries later, there in that narrow street which, at the time, was called Camarín de Nuestra Señora de Almudena. But why do I say 'still' or 'as yet,' in some cases the passing of time serves no purpose, so much remains unknown, denied, hidden, even as regards ourselves and our own actions.) 'What a lot of one-eyed, one-handed, hobbling people there have been in these old streets,' I found myself thinking, 'what a lot of deaths. They won't notice one more, should it come to that.'

I decided to take a few short turns about the surrounding area, so that I could return every so often to a point from which

I could keep an eye on Custardoy and his movements from afar, I couldn't risk missing the moment when he paid his bill, got up and set off again, from El Anciano Rey de los Vinos to what I presumed was his house, just steps away; he would only have to cross two streets. And so I moved a little way off and stopped before another statue in Calle Bailén, this time a rather rough bust of the admirable *madrileño* writer Larra, who committed suicide in 1837 by shooting himself in the head while standing in front of the mirror, before he was even twenty-eight (another member of the Kennedy-Mansfield fraternity, of which there are so many), perhaps over some unhappy love affair, but who knows; and then I stopped by yet another sculpture, slightly grotesque this time, of a certain Captain Melgar, all medals and curled mustaches—he reminded me somewhat of Tupra's improbable ancestor in the portrait by Kennington I had seen at his house— and who, according to the inscription, had died in the battle of Barranco del Lobo, in Melilla, during the African War, in 1909; it wasn't so much the actual bust of the Captain that was grotesque as a second disproportionately small figure—not so small as to be a Lilliputian or Tom Thumb, but certainly a midget—of a soldier dressed like Beau Geste and who was trying to climb up the pedestal or column with his rifle in his hand, whether to worship his Captain or to attack him and finish him off wasn't clear. And then I walked back the way I had come—although on the other side of the street this time, the same side as the Catholic monstrosity—and studied Custardoy where he sat outside the café. He had been served a beer, some anchovies and some *patatas bravas* ('So he treats himself to a proper aperitif, does he?' I thought. 'He obviously feels he's worked hard enough and he's in no hurry, he'll certainly be there for a while'), and had unfolded a newspaper, which he was sitting reading, legs crossed, now and then looking around with his huge eyes, which meant I had to be prudent, and so I again moved off, this time going as far as the Palacio Real, only to discover more hideous statues, a constant feature in Madrid: a whole line of Visigothic kings dressed like pseudo-Romans and each bearing a barely comprehensible inscription, especially for a foreigner, and I was feeling rather like a foreigner: 'Ataúlfo, Mu. A° de 415,' said the first one, and the same enigmatic inscription (meaning presumably *Murió Año de* . . . He died in the year . . .) accompanied Eurico, 'de 484,' Leovigildo, 'de 585,' Suintala, 'de 633,' Wamba, 'de 680' . . . Further on, stood a large monument, 'erected at the instigation of Spanish women to the glory of the soldier Luis Noval,' who must have been a heroic soldier and obviously the darling of the ladies, for he, too, was dressed like Beau Geste or Beau Saberur or Beau Ideal or all of them put together: '*Patria, no olvides nunca a los que por ti mueren, MCMXII*; My country, never forget those who died for you, MCMXII' (that word '*patria*' would have to be translated as 'country,' the word used by Tupra on the night we first met and which had made me wonder if he might, in spirit, be a fascist in the analogical sense). But my country forgets everyone, both those who die for it and those who don't, including that fellow Noval—why, no one in Madrid will have the faintest idea who he was or how he distinguished himself or what he did. Every time I retraced my steps, and the café terrace once more came within my field of vision, the more settled the man with the ponytail seemed to be, and so I decided to set off in another direction and walk down Cuesta de la Vega, 'Near here stood the site of Puerta de la Vega, the main entrance into Muslim Madrid, from the ninth century onwards' and 'Image of María Santísima de la Almudena, hidden in this place in the year 712 and miraculously rediscovered in the year 1085' ('They hid it in the year following the Moorish invasion,' I thought, 'presumably so that it wouldn't be destroyed.' But that very white effigy of the Virgin and Child, placed in a niche, didn't look remotely like something made in the eighth century or even a replica of one, but was a shameless fake; Custardoy would have known), and even got as far as Parque de Atenas, where the inevitable bust, almost hidden this time because of the isolated position in which it had been placed, was of no less a person than the jubilant Boccherini, who lived for twenty or more years in Madrid and died here in penury, never having been honored by this ungrateful city (it's not even known where his bones lie or if there was a grave to give them shelter); behind him was a stone plaque bearing the words of someone called Cartier which said: 'If God wanted to talk to mankind through music, He would use the works of Haydn; but if He Himself wanted to listen to music, he would choose Boccherini.' Yes, his music, like Mancini's, accompanied me wherever I went.

I had gone too far and hurried back up Cuesta de la Vega, fearing that I might be left not knowing what I needed to know, by a miscalculation or through carelessness. When I once again reached the point where Calle Mayor and Calle de Bailén meet— I glanced at the door to my right, but there was no sign of Custardoy going in—it occurred to me that the best place to keep watch over the café terrace, or part of it, without being seen, was from the top of the short double flight of steps that led directly to the statue of the Polish, *jota*-dancing Pope, and so up I went and stood leaning on the balcony, with my back turned on *Totus tuus*, yes, his really was the ugliest of the statues, but not through incompetence on the part of the sculptor; people would assume I was another devotee, a few of whom were taking photographs of the figure and imitating his invitation-to-the-dance posture. I could see my man from there, he wouldn't escape me when he got up. I waited. And waited. He was still reading the newspaper, still wearing his hat (he was, after all, in the open air); he had placed his handleless briefcase on the chair beside him, and he seemed to possess special antennae for detecting any good-looking women, because whenever one passed or sat down, he would look up and check her out, perhaps he just had a very good nose. 'Luisa hasn't shown much judgment in that respect either,' I thought. 'He's probably the kind of man for whom one woman is never enough.' I wished I had some binoculars with me so that I could observe him more closely. Even at that distance, there was something about him that reminded me of someone else, an affinity or a resemblance, just as Incompara had immediately brought to mind my old classmate Comendador, now a respectable building contractor in New York or Miami or wherever it was he had gone. But I couldn't put my finger on it, I couldn't identify the model, I mean, the first individual of that sort whom I had, at some point, met.

Finally, I saw him hold up his arm and click his fingers twice, a disdainful and now antiquated way of summoning waiters. 'He can't be about to order another beer,' I thought, 'there are two empty glasses on the table already.' Fortunately, he was asking for the bill; he took some notes out of his trouser pocket (I carry them like that too, loose, rather than in a wallet) and put one down on the table, as we *madrileños* always used to do: money should never pass from hand to hand, but via a neutral place. He obviously knew the waiter, which made his previous very classist finger-clicks even ruder; as the waiter put the change down, likewise on the table, Custardoy patted him lightly on the arm, as he had with the booksellers, perhaps he took his pre-lunch drink in El Anciano Rey de los Vinos every day. He made some comment to the waiter as he left and the latter laughed out loud, as had the people in the bookshop and the young General Custer or Davy Crockett with her fringed jacket; he clearly had a sense of humor. Soon I would know whether he was he or someone else. He didn't leave that corner café by walking back down the narrow street of the unsolved murder, but via Calle de Bailén, which was a good sign. As he walked along, he looked into the windows of the shop selling musical instruments which occupies that whole corner, strode quickly across Calle Mayor and paused by the traffic lights in Bailén, which were red. At that point, I lost sight of him and hurriedly retreated until I found a position from which I could see him again, to the left of the shop belonging to that ghastly temple, which was to the left of *Totus* (who on earth would want to buy anything there?). I could see the whole corner from there, from behind some railings, I was right in front of the door to his house—if it *was* his house—only on higher ground, where he wouldn't see me, because he was unlikely to look up, I felt like the Düsseldorf vampire lying in wait. Custardoy now only had to cross the street when the light turned green and go through the door towards which I was pushing him and which was, once again, closed. I could see him clearly now, he was unmistakable in his hat, I would see his footsteps too once he started walking. 'One, two, three, four, five . . .' I started counting in my head when the lights changed, he had small feet for a man his height, he followed the correct path, he wouldn't stop now, '. . . forty-five, forty-six, forty-seven, forty-eight, and forty-nine.' And he stopped outside the right door, his key ready in his hand. And then I thought with an ephemeral feeling of triumph: 'Got you, just where I want you.'

I waited for a few minutes more to see if a window opened, telling me what floor he lived on and confirming that he was home. There, however, I was out of luck. I walked down the steps, crossed the two streets that Luisa perhaps also often crossed, if, that is, she visited him much—she couldn't ever spend the night there—wondered briefly whether I should get a taxi back up to the Palace Hotel, but seeing none free, started to walk. When I reached Plaza de la Villa, I stopped to have a better look at the statue he had looked at, Don Álvaro de Bazán or Marqués de Santa Cruz, possibly the least ugly of the statues I had encountered. I walked round it and found an inscription at the back of the pedestal: 'I was the scourge of the Turk at Lepanto, the Frenchman at Terceira, the Englishman o'er all the seas. The King I served and the country I honored know best who I am by the Cross in my name and the cross-hilt of my sword.' 'We Spaniards are always such braggarts,' I thought, still feeling distinctly foreign, 'I should learn from them and convince myself that my enemies will all flee before me, saying: "I go, victorious Spaniard of lightning and fire, I leave you. I leave you too, sweet lands, I leave Spain and tremble as I go . . ." Spaniards are always boasting like that, even when confronted by a compatriot who will not be so easily frightened off. And Custardoy and I are compatriots.' The Admiral had one arm raised and was holding something in his hand. I couldn't quite see what it was, it could have been a rolled up map or, more likely, a General's baton. His other hand, the left one, was gripping the hilt of his sheathed sword, rather as the lone Count was in his portrait. 'What a lot of swords there are in these old streets too,' I thought.

7
Farewell

Sometimes we know what we want to do or have to do or even what we're thinking of doing or are almost certain we will do, but we also need it to be spoken about or confirmed or discussed or approved, a maneuver which is, after a fashion, a way of shuffling off a little of the responsibility, of diffusing or sharing it, even if only fictitiously, because what we do we do alone, regardless of who convinces or persuades or encourages or gives us the green light, or even orders or commissions the deed. On occasion, we disguise this maneuver as doubt or perplexity, we go to someone and play a trick on them by asking their opinion or advice—by asking or requesting something of them—and thus, at the very least, we ensure that the next time we speak, that person will enquire about the matter, ask what happened, how it all turned out, what we finally decided to do, whether their advice had been of any help, whether we took notice of their words. That person is then involved, entangled, drawn in. We have forced them to become a participant, even if only as a listener, and to consider the situation and to ask how it ended; we have foisted our story on them and they will never be able to forget or erase it; we have also given them a certain right, or perhaps duty, to question us about it later: 'So what did you do in the end, how did you resolve the problem?' they will ask us next time we meet, and it would seem odd, would show a lack of interest or politeness, not to refer to the case we'd laid out before them and to which we've obliged them to contribute with words or, if they declined to offer a view or to say anything, to listen to our doubts. 'I have no idea, I can't and shouldn't give an opinion, in fact, I really don't want to know about it,' they might well say, and yet they have still said something; with that response they have told us that they find the whole thing distasteful, poisonous or murky, that they want no part in it, even as a passive witness, that they would prefer to remain in the dark, and that they like none of the possible options, that it would be best if we did nothing and simply let it go or removed ourselves from the situation; and that we should certainly spare them the details. Even if you say 'I don't know' or 'I don't want to hear about it,' you've already said too much, and when you're asked that question, there's no easy way out, not even holding back or keeping silent is safe, because silence is in itself reproving or discouraging, and does not, as the saying goes, mean consent. Let us hope that no one ever asks us for anything, or even inquires, not for advice or a favor or a loan, not even for the loan of our attention. But that never happens, it's an entirely vain wish. There's always one almost final question, some laggardly request. Now it was my turn to do the asking, now I was going to make a request, one that would have proved compromising to anyone, except perhaps to the person who was about to hear it. I still had much to learn from him, a fact I found most troubling and that would perhaps bring me misfortune.

That evening, I phoned Tupra from my hotel room, for only he could advise me and, I hoped, give me instructions, make recommendations and serve as my guide, indeed, he was the ideal man to ask about matters in which talk was not enough; he was also the most suitable person, that is, the one I could rely on to confirm that I should do what I thought I should do or who would at least not dissuade me. I guessed that he would be at home at that hour, even though England was one hour behind, unless it was one of his convivial, festive days and he had recruited everyone, including Branshaw and Jane Treves, to go out together en masse. I dialed his home number and a woman answered, doubtless she of the attractive, old-fashioned silhouette (with her almost hourglass figure), whom I had seen at the end of that night of videos, outlined against the light of a corridor, at the door of his small study; if it was his wife or ex-wife, if it was Beryl, he would be able to understand my plight even better.

'How are you, Jack? How nice of you to call and keep me posted. Or were you calling to inquire about me and the others? That would be even nicer of you, especially in the middle of your holiday.'

There was a touch of irony in his voice, of course, but I noticed too a certain pleasure to hear from me, or was it amusement, for he still found me amusing. After the initial exchange of greetings, I preferred not to pretend or to deceive him.

'I have a matter to resolve here, Bertie. I'd like to know what you think or what, in your view, you think I should do.' I called him Bertie to please him, to put him in a good mood, even though he was sure to see through this, and then, without further ado, I summarized the situation: 'There's a guy here in Madrid,' I said. 'I think he's beating up my wife, or my ex-wife—or whatever—given that we're still not divorced—anyway, they've been going out for a while, I don't know how long, probably a few months. She denies it, but right now she has a black eye, and this isn't the first time she's accidentally—according to her, of course—banged into something. Her sister told me this, and she, quite independently, has reached the same conclusion. I really don't like the idea of my children running the slightest risk of losing their mother, because you never know how these things will end, so you have to nip them in the bud, don't you agree? Anyway, I haven't got many more days in which to sort it out. I'd like to have it all settled before I come back, anxiety is unbearable at a distance and very distracting if you're working. But neither would I want her to find out about my intervention, whatever form it takes. Mind you, she's bound to suspect something if—as I hope—the whole scene changes and that change coincides with my stay in Madrid. There would be no point in just talking to him about it, he would simply deny it. Besides, he doesn't seem the timid pusillanimous type, not at all; he's certainly no De la Garza. It would be equally pointless my trying to make her admit it, I know how stubborn she is. And even if I did get her to admit it, the situation wouldn't, in essence, be any different; after all, she's still with him despite what's happened.' I stopped. What I had to say next was more difficult: 'She must be really crazy about him, although they haven't been together long enough for that, I mean for her to be really crazy about the guy. That doesn't happen in a few months, feelings like that need time to take root. I suppose it's the novelty, the excitement of being with someone else, the first man she's been with since we split up, and the feeling won't last. But while it lasts it lasts, if you know what I mean. And it's lasting now.'

Tupra remained silent for a few seconds. Then he said, without irony this time, but not very seriously either, for he still spoke in a slightly frivolous tone of voice, as if my problem didn't seem that serious or as if he didn't see it as particularly hard to resolve.

'And you're asking me what you should do? Or what is it you're asking? What *I* would do in your place? Well, you know perfectly well by now, Jack, what I would do. I imagine the question is purely rhetorical and that you merely want me to reassure you. Fine, consider yourself reassured. If you want to get rid of the problem, do so.'

'I'm not sure I understand you, Bertie. I've already said that talking to him would get me nowhere—' But he didn't let me finish my sentence. Perhaps he was in a hurry or irritated by my slowness (he could have said to me as he did once before: 'Don't linger or delay, just do it'). Perhaps I had caught him in bed with Beryl, or whoever the woman was by his side, which is why she had answered the phone, because she was nearer, above or below, on her front or her back, I had probably interrupted them while they were screwing, we never know what is going on at the other end, or rather, what was going on just before the phone rang. I wondered how many times when I'd called Luisa from London she would have just got back from seeing Custardoy in his studio or how many times he would have been there in her bedroom, in my home, watching as she sat, half-undressed, talking to me, waiting impatiently for us to finish our conversation. If, that is, he visited her. It might be that he didn't or only at night because of the children. I hadn't asked them, but neither had they mentioned it spontaneously, in fact, they hadn't mentioned anyone new or anyone I didn't know.

'Look, Jack, just deal with him,' Tupra said. 'Just make sure he's out of the picture.' Those were his exact words in English, and I deeply regretted then that it wasn't my first language, because I don't know how they would strike a native English speaker, but to me they seemed too ambiguous, I couldn't grasp their meaning as clearly as I would have wanted; if he had said to me 'Just get rid of him' or 'Dispose of him,' that would have been clearer although, again, not entirely; there are a lot of ways of getting rid of someone, not all of which involve killing; or perhaps it would have been clearer to me if he had said 'Just make sure you get him off her back' or 'off your backs,' but I would still not have felt able to translate that expression into concrete unequivocal action, because there are also lots of ways of getting someone off your back. If only he had said 'Just scare him away, scare him to death,' then I would have understood that he was telling me to do what he'd done with De la Garza, nothing more, and to transform myself into Sir Punishment and Sir Thrashing, but not into Sir Death or Sir Cruelty. However, the words that emerged from his lips were: 'Just deal with him. Just make sure he's out of the picture,' and that word 'picture' could mean many things: a painting or a portrait, a panorama or a scene or even a photo or a film, although it was the first meaning of painting that I opted for, I had to remove Custardoy from the picture, to erase or exclude him, just like the Count of San Secondo in the Prado, who was cut off from his family, isolated, and would never ever be close to his wife or his children again. If I had heard that advice as a brief bit of dialogue in an episode of *The Sopranos* or in *The Godfather*, I would have understood perfectly that he was urging me to bump him off. But perhaps the mafiosi use pre-established codes, just in case they're being bugged, allowing them to be very laconic in the orders they issue and yet still be sure that their orders will be interpreted correctly and at once. Besides, this wasn't a dialogue in a film and we weren't mafiosi, nor was I receiving an order, as I had on previous occasions from Tupra or Reresby or Ure or Dundas, I was merely being given a little guidance, the advice I'd asked him for. Language, though, is difficult when you're uncertain as to what to do and need to know exactly what is meant, because language is almost always metaphorical or figurative. There can't be many people in the world who would say openly 'Kill him,' or in Spanish '*Mátalo*.'

I decided to press him a little, even though this might annoy him. Or rather, I got my question in quickly before he could put the phone down, because those last two utterances of his had sounded distinctly conclusive, dismissive almost, as if, after that, he had nothing more to add. Or as if he were bored with my inquiry, my little story.

'Could you tell me how, Bertie?' I said. 'I'm not as used as you are to frightening people.'

First, I heard his paternalistic laughter, brief and slightly scornful, it wasn't the sort of laughter we could have shared, it wasn't the kind that creates a disinterested bond between men or between women or the kind that establishes a bond between women and men that can prove an even stronger, tighter link, a profounder, more complex, more dangerous and more lasting link, or one, at least, with more hope of enduring, perhaps Luisa and Custardoy were joined by the bond of spontaneous, unexpected, simultaneous laughter, given that he seemed to be able to make people laugh so easily. Tupra's laugh, as I myself had occasion to notice, always sounded slightly disappointed and impatient and revealed small bright teeth. Then he said:

'If you really don't know how, Jack, that means you can't do it. Best not to try and just let events take their course—leave it be, don't try to change things, let your wife sort things out, it's her business, after all. But I think you do know how. We all know, even if we're not used to the idea or can't imagine ourselves doing it. It's a question of imagination. But I have to leave you now. Good luck.' And with that he brought to a close a conversation that I had managed to prolong only very slightly.

I didn't dare phone him back, I would have to make do with what I had. 'Let your wife sort things out, it's her business, after all,' those words had sounded like a reproach or a veiled criticism, as if what he'd really said was: 'You're going to abandon her to her fate, perhaps allow her to be killed one day and leave your children orphans.' Some other words of his had hit home too: 'It's a question of imagination.' What he probably meant by this was that the only way of imagining yourself doing something you have never imagined yourself doing is to do it, and then you have no trouble at all imagining it.

Next I called an old friend, well, a Madrid-style friend, namely, a fellow *madrileño* whom I had known superficially years ago and hadn't seen since: if there has been no friction or quarrel or dispute between you and such a friend, then, nominally, he can still be considered a friend, even though you might never have had a conversation alone with him, outside of the broad and ever-changing group of people that brought you together in that increasingly remote past. This friend was a bullfighter with a fanatical following, the sort of *torero* who retires, then returns to the ring every few years only to retire again—it wouldn't be long now before he would have to cut off his pigtail for good—and whom I had known slightly during one particular period of my life, with Comendador (who moved in all kinds of circles and had introduced me to him) and later on again, too, at the late-night card games that went on into the small hours and which the Maestro held at his house for members of his team, the odd colleague and all kinds of hangers-on like me; some bullfighters never spend a minute alone and will welcome anyone, as long as they come recommended by some trustworthy person, even at third hand: the friend of a friend of the person who really is a friend and not just a Madrid-style friend. He was a very amiable, affectionate fellow, and sentimental about anything to do with his past life, and when I asked if I could come and see him, he not only raised no objections or sounded remotely suspicious after that decade or more of silence between us, he even urged me to visit as soon as possible:

'Come today. There's a game tonight.'

'Would tomorrow morning suit you?' I asked. 'I'm only here for a few days. I live in London now, and I'd arranged to go and see my father today. He's getting on a bit and hasn't been too well.'

'Of course, say no more. Tomorrow it is then. But make it around one o'clock, for a drink before lunch. Tonight's game is sure to run late.'

'I want to ask you a favor,' I said, preferring to give him due warning. 'I need a loan, but not of money, don't worry. I have no problems in that department.'

'"Don't worry," he says,' he replied, laughing. 'You would never give me cause to worry, Jacobito.' He was one of the people who called me Jacobo, I can't remember why. 'Ask me for anything you like. As long as it's not my suit of lights.' I didn't really follow the bullfighting scene, certainly not from London, but I assumed from his comment that he was currently active. I had better find out before going to visit him, so as not to seem rude.

'You're getting warm,' I said. 'I'll explain tomorrow.'

'Just have a look around when you get here and take whatever you want.' These weren't mere empty words, he really was a very generous man. His name was Miguel Yanes Troyano, nicknamed 'Miquelín,' and he was the son of a *banderillero*.

The following morning, up to date now on his latest triumphs, thanks to the Internet, and bearing a gift, I arrived at his vast apartment in the area which, in my childhood, was known as 'Costa Fleming,' rather closer to Real Madrid's Chamartín stadium—which I prefer to call by its old name—than to Las Ventas, the bull ring through whose gates he had often been borne shoulder high. I would have preferred to speak to him alone, but that was impossible since he always had company. However, having been forewarned that I was going to ask him for a favor or a loan, he had been considerate enough not to embarrass me with too many witnesses, apart, that is, from his lifelong manager, who was always there, a discreet taciturn man of about the same age, and whom I scarcely knew at all even though I had known him since forever.

'I hope Señor Cazorla won't find our conversation too boring, Maestro,' I said tentatively, just in case.

'Not at all,' replied Miquelín, making a gesture with his hand as if sweeping aside such an idea. He had greeted me with a warm embrace and a kiss on the cheek, as if I were his nephew. 'Eulogio never gets bored, but if he does, he simply thinks, isn't that so, Eulogio? You can say whatever you like in front of him, because he'll neither tell on you nor judge you. Anyway, how can I help?'

I found it hard to begin, because I felt slightly ashamed of what I was about to ask. However, the best way to overcome this was to say what I wanted and get it over with. Everything seems more embarrassing before than it does afterwards and even during.

'I wondered if you could lend me one of your swords. I'd only need it for a couple of days.'

I saw that my request took them both by surprise and that Cazorla started slightly and tugged at one sleeve. He was wearing a suit, complete with a waistcoat, in rather too pale a shade of grey; he had a handkerchief in his top jacket pocket and wore a flower in his buttonhole; he was, in short, old school. But he would not speak unless Miquelín invited him to do so, and Miquelín managed to conceal his surprise very well and replied at once:

'As many as you want, Jacobo. We'll go and have a look at them right now and you can choose the one you like best, although they're all pretty much the same. But forgive me, if you'd wanted to borrow some money, it would never even have occurred to me to ask what you wanted it for, but borrowing a sword is a bit more unusual. Is it for a costume party?'

I could have lied to him, although a sword on its own wouldn't be much of a disguise. I could have invented some absurd excuse and said, for example, that I had been invited to a private bull-fight, but it didn't seem right to deceive such a kindly man, and I don't think I would have succeeded. I felt, too, that he would understand my reasons for borrowing it and wouldn't judge me either.

'No, Miquelín. I want to give someone a fright. It's to do with my wife, well, my ex-wife, we've been separated for a while now, although we're not yet divorced.' I always made a point of saying that, I realized, as if it were important. 'That's why I moved to London, so that I wouldn't be hanging around here while we gradually drifted apart. Given what I've found out, though, I'm not sure it was a good idea. We have two kids, a boy and a girl, and I don't want them to come to any harm. The guy's no good for anyone, least of all her.'

Miquelín understood, I didn't need to say any more, I could see this from the way he listened to me, as if he were in agreement. He didn't ask any questions, friends were friends and you didn't poke your nose into their business. Then he gave an affectionate amused chuckle, he was a man much given to laughter, and age had not changed that or made his laughter less frequent.

'And what are *you* going to do with a sword?' he said. 'Did you hear what he wants it for, Eulogio? Are you actually going to use it, Jacobo? Are you going to stick the whole blade in or just the point? Or do you simply want to wave it around a bit and scare the living daylights out of him?'

'I was hoping not to have to use it,' I replied. I had no idea what I was going to do with it; having heard Tupra on the subject, I had thought only of the effect it would have when I produced the weapon.

'You have to bear in mind two things, my friend. Firstly, the *estoque* only wounds with the point, by sticking it in, and that's why you need considerable momentum to drive it in really deep; the bullfighter's sword has almost no blade at all, so it won't be any use if you just want to cut someone up a bit. Secondly, if this sword can kill a bull weighing over 1,300 pounds when you stick it in up to the hilt—always assuming you don't hit a bone of course—just imagine what it could do to a man, one false move on your part and he'd be stone dead. Do you want to take that risk? No, Jacobo, the best way to frighten someone is to pull a gun on them. Preferably a clean one, because you never know.'

I hadn't made the connection until I heard Miquelín talking about what a sword could do to a man, but when I did, I felt a shudder of disgust run through me, although, oddly, strangely, not self-disgust; I must still have seen myself as quite separate from what I was planning to do, or felt that my plan was still empty of content, or was it just that one never experiences genuine self-disgust, and it's that inability that makes us capable of doing almost anything as we grow accustomed to the ideas that rise up in us or take root, little by little, or as we come to terms with the fact that we're really going to do what we're going to do. 'I would be like that vicious *malagueño*, that nasty piece of work, that bastard,' I thought, 'the one who killed Emilio Marés on the outskirts of Ronda some seventy years ago, helped and urged on by his comrades, the one who went in for the kill and cut off Marés' ears and his tail, held them up in one hand and with the other doffed his red beret as if it were a bullfighter's hat, there in those sweet lands. The one who brutally murdered my father's old university friend, who, as my father told me, was rather vain, but in a funny self-consciously frivolous way, a really lovely man, always in a good mood, whom he had very much liked and who had refused to dig his own grave before being shot, thus allowing his executioners to bait him like a bull as well as to kill him. And then they had, literally, baited him with banderillas and pikes and swords. It's fortunate that Miquelín, all unknowing, has alerted me to that connection.'

'Clean?' I asked. I didn't understand the term.

'Yes, a gun that no one knows about, that hasn't been registered, and, above all, that hasn't been used in any crime. As I say, you never know.' Miquelín, like all bullfighters I suppose, was all too aware that one never could know what might happen.

'What do you mean "you never know," Miquelín?'

'What do you think I mean, child? Listen to him, Eulogio!' And he chuckled again, he must have considered me a complete novice, which I was in such matters. 'Because if you put a gun in your pocket, there's always a chance you might end up firing it. You just want to give someone a fright, fair enough, but you never know how the other fellow's going to react. He might *not* be frightened, and then what will you do?'

'Fine, but where am I going to get a gun like that?' I knew that the Maestro owned various weapons, which he used when he went hunting on his estate in Cáceres, where he'd spend longish periods of time. And perhaps other kinds of weapons too, the shorter variety that are of no use for hunting. However, it was likely that he had licences for them all, and therefore no entirely 'clean' ones.

'I'll lend you one, man, just as I would have lent you the sword or whatever else you might want. But where were you going to put a sword, my friend, I mean, really, what an idea! A gun, on the other hand, fits in your pocket.' This hadn't occurred to me either, that I didn't own an overcoat with a sheath in the lining at the back or even a raincoat. And it wasn't the weather for overcoats. Miquelín added: 'I'll get you one now. Eulogio, would you mind fetching me my father's Llama. And the other one as well, the revolver.'

'Where do you keep them now?' asked Cazorla.

'They're in the library, behind *The Thousand and One Nights* and a little to the left, behind several books with brown bindings. Go and get them for me, will you?'

The manager left the room (I wondered what kind of library the Maestro would have—I had certainly never seen it during those nights spent playing cards; but he was, like other bullfighters, quite well-read) and returned shortly afterwards carrying two boxes or packages wrapped in cloth which he placed before Miquelín on the coffee table.

'Would you be so kind as to bring some gloves for Jacobo, Eulogio?' he said. Then turning to me: 'If you're going to use one of them, it's best you don't touch them. Not being used to handling guns, you might forget to clean it afterwards.'

Cazorla was as helpful as ever, his admiration for the Maestro being infinite, bordering on devotion. He again left the room and came back with a pair of white gloves, like those a head-waiter might wear, or a magician. They were made of very fine cloth; I put them on, and then Miquelín unwrapped the boxes carefully, almost solemnly, less perhaps because they were guns than because they had belonged to his father. Many fathers who had lived through the Civil War still had a gun or two, standard-issue and otherwise, indeed my own father had a Star or an Astra, of the sort that used to be made in Éibar. I had never seen it myself, however, and I wasn't going to ask him about it now or start rummaging through his apartment. 'He must have taken a risk after the War,' I thought, 'by keeping it and not surrendering it. Given that he was on the losing side and had been in prison.' Miquelín's father, who would, of course, have been older than mine, might well have been on the winning side, but we had never spoken about this, after all, it didn't matter any more. In fact, we had never talked about anything serious or personal. These Madrid-style friendships really are most unusual, often inexplicable.

'Is it all right to pick them up now?' I asked. They were very handsome objects, the revolver with its striated wooden grip, and the pistol forming almost a right angle.

'Wait just a moment,' he said. 'They both belonged to my father, and so those thieving bureaucrats have never got their paws on them. If they ever did, they'd probably sell them. The revolver dates from before the War, I think; it's English, an Enfield. It was a present from an English writer who was interested in bullfighting for a time, and my father persuaded one of the matadors in his group to let him travel around with them. He wanted first-hand experience for something he was going to write; his main character was called Biggles, a pilot I think, it was a series, and in one of the books the author thought he might send his hero off to have some adventures in Spain. My father was very proud of this, because apparently this Biggles fellow was very famous in his country.' There it was again, that word *patria*; perhaps it wasn't such a loaded word, Miquelín hadn't laid any special emphasis on it, maybe because he wasn't talking about his own *patria*, our country. 'The pistol dates from later on, a Llama, which is Spanish, an automatic. The revolver takes six bullets, the Llama ten. Not that this will matter to you if you don't foresee having to shoot. But if push comes to shove, you'll have more than enough with either gun: if not, it will be because you're dead. One magazine should be enough for the pistol. Here's your ammunition. Well-preserved and well-oiled, and all in working order, as my father taught me. The pistol can jam, of course, like all pistols. But on the other hand, look how big the revolver is, with the drum and the long barrel. I think you'd be better off with the Llama. Don't you agree, Eulogio, that a pistol is better for giving someone a fright?' Miquelín handled both weapons with ease.

'If you say so, Miguel. You know more about it than I do,' Cazorla replied with a shrug.

'Do you know how to use it?' Miquelín asked me. 'Do you know how it works? Have you ever held one before?'

'When I did my military service,' I said. 'But not since.' And I thought how odd that was, and how new, for there must have been many periods when it would have been unusual for a middle-class male not to have a weapon in his house, always close to hand.

'The first thing to remember, Jacobo, is never put your finger on the trigger until you know you're going to shoot. Always keep it resting on the guard, OK? Even if the pistol isn't cocked. Even if it's not loaded.'

He used what was to me an unfamiliar, seemingly old-fashioned word for 'guard,' '*guardamonte,*' but then Miquelín was himself in the process of becoming old-fashioned too, a relic, like his generosity. I didn't need to ask any questions, though, because he showed me what to do and I could see where he placed his forefinger. Then he handed the pistol to me, so that I could do the same, or copy him. I had forgotten what a heavy thing a pistol is; in the movies, they hold them as if they were as light as daggers. It takes an effort to lift one, and still more of an effort to hold it steady enough to aim.

And then the Maestro taught me how to use it.

I don't know, but I think perhaps by then I had absorbed Wheeler's dictum about how we all carry our probabilities in our veins and so on, and I was more or less convinced that I knew how to apply this to myself; I had, or so I thought, a pretty good idea of what my probabilities were, although not as clear an idea as Wheeler would have of his, given that he could draw on far greater experience: he'd had more time than me, more temptations and more varied circumstances in which to guide those probabilities to their fulfilment; he'd lived through and been involved in wars, and in wartime one can be more persuasive and make oneself more dangerous and more despicable even than one's enemies; one can take advantage of the majority of people, who were, according to Wheeler, silly and frivolous and credulous and on whom it was easy to strike a match and start a fire; one can more easily and with impunity cause others to fall into the most appalling and destructive misfortunes from which they will never emerge, and thereby transform those thus condemned into casualties, into non persons, into felled trees from which the rotten wood can be chopped away; it's also the best time to spread outbreaks of cholera, malaria and plague and, often, to set in motion the process of total denial, of who you are and who you were, of what you do and what you did, of what you expect and what you expected, of your aims and your intentions, of your professions of faith, your ideas, your greatest loyalties, your motives . . .

No, you are never what you are—not entirely, not exactly—when you're alone and living abroad and ceaselessly speaking a language not your own or not your mother tongue; but nor are you what you are in your own country when there's a war on or when that country is dominated by rage or obstinacy or fear: to some degree you feel no responsibility for what you do or see, as if it all belonged to a provisional existence, parallel, alien, or borrowed, fictitious or almost dreamed—or, perhaps, merely theoretical, like my whole life, according to the anonymous report about me that I'd found among some old files; as if everything could be relegated to the sphere of the purely imaginary or of what never happened, and, of course, to the sphere of the involuntary; everything tossed into the bag of imaginings and suspicions and hypotheses and, even, of mere foolish dreams, about which, when you awake, all you can say is: 'I didn't want that anomalous desire or that murderous hatred or that baseless resentment to surface, or that temptation or that sense of panic or that desire to punish, that unknown threat or that surprising curse, that aversion or that longing which now lie like lead upon my soul each night, or the feeling of disgust or embarrassment which I myself provoke, or those dead faces, forever fixed, that made a pact with me that there would be no more tomorrows (yes, that is the pact we make with all those who fall silent and are expelled: that they neither do nor say anything more, that they disappear and cease changing) and which now come and whisper dreadful unexpected words to me, words that are perhaps unbecoming to them, or perhaps not, while I'm asleep and have dropped my guard: I have laid down my shield and my spear on the grass.' What's more you can repeat over and over Iago's disquieting words, not only after taking action, but during it too: 'I am not what I am.' A similar warning is issued by anyone asking another person to commit a crime or threatening to commit one himself, or confessing to vile deeds and thus exposing himself to blackmail, or buying something on the black market—keep your collar turned up, your face always in the shadows, never light a cigarette—telling the hired assassin or the person under threat or the potential blackmailer or one of many interchangeable women, once desired and already forgotten, but still a source of shame to us: 'You know the score, you've never seen me, from now on you don't know me, I've never spoken to you or said anything, as far as you're concerned I have no face, no voice, no breath, no name, no back. This conversation and this meeting never took place, what's happening now before your eyes didn't happen, isn't happening, you haven't even heard these words because I didn't say them. And even though you can hear the words now, I'm not saying them'; just as you can tell yourself: 'I am not what I am nor what I can see myself doing. More than that, I'm not even doing it.'

What I had absorbed less well, or simply didn't know, was that what one does or does not do depends not just on time, temptation and circumstance, but on silly ridiculous things, on random superfluous thoughts, on doubt or caprice or some stupid fit of feeling, on untimely associations and on one-eyed oblivion or fickle memories, on the words that condemn you or the gesture that saves you.

And so there I was the following morning—the day was threatening rain—with my borrowed pistol in my raincoat pocket, ready to take some definitive action, but without really knowing what exactly, although I had a rough idea and knew what I was hoping to make clear: I had to get rid of Custardoy, get him off our backs, make sure he stayed out of the picture; not so much out of my picture, which was little more than a daub at the time or perhaps a mere doodle—'You're very alone in London,' as Wheeler used to tell me—but out of Luisa and the children's picture, into which that unwholesome individual was trying to worm his way and where he was perhaps about to take up long-term residence, or at least long-term enough to become an affliction and a danger. Indeed, he already was both those things, for he had already spent far too much time prowling round and circling the frame and making incursions into the picture or canvas, and he had already laid a hand on Luisa and given her a black eye and left her with a cut or a gash—I had been told about the second and had myself seen the first— and nothing would stop him closing his large hands around her throat—those pianist's fingers, or, rather, those fingers like piano keys—one rainy night, when they were stuck at home, when he judged he had subjugated and isolated her enough and little by little fed her his demands and prohibitions disguised as infatuation and weakness and jealousy and flattery and supplication, a poisonous, despotic, devious type of man. I was quite clear now that I didn't want to have the luck or the misfortune (luck as long as it remained in the imagination, misfortune were it to become reality) of Luisa dying or being killed, that I couldn't allow this to happen because once a real misfortune has occurred there's no going back and it cannot be undone, or, contrary to what most people believe, even compensated (and there is, of course, no way of compensating the person who has died or even the living left behind, and yet nowadays the living often do ask for money, thus putting a price on the people who have ceased to tread the earth or traverse the world).

As I walked along, I couldn't help touching and even grasping the pistol, as if I were drawn to it or needed to get used to its weight and to feel and hold it in my hand, sometimes lifting it up slightly, still inside my pocket, and whenever I did grip it properly, I always took great care to keep my finger resting on the guard and not on the trigger, as Miquelín had recommended me to do even when the pistol wasn't cocked. 'How easy it must be to use it,' I was thinking, 'once you've got one. Or, rather, how difficult not to use it, even if only to point it at someone and threaten them and just to be seen with it. Firing the thing would be harder, of course, but, on the other hand, it cries out to be brandished about and it would seem impossible not to satisfy that plea. Perhaps women would find it easier to resist, but for a man it's like having a tempting toy, guns should never be given to men, and yet most of those that are made or inherited or that exist will end up in our hands and not in the more cautious hands of women.' I also had a proud feeling of invulnerability, as if, as I walked past other people in the street, I were thinking: 'I'm more dangerous than they are right now and they don't know it, and if someone got cocky with me or tried to mug me he'd get a nasty fright; if I got out the pistol, he'd probably back off or throw down his knife or run away,' and I remembered the momentary feeling of pride that had assailed me on seeing the fear I unwittingly inspired in De la Garza when I went into his office ('You should feel very pleased with yourself: you had him scared shitless,' Professor Rico had said to me afterwords, neither mincing his words nor resorting to onomatopoeia). And I recalled, too, that immediately afterwards it had filled me with disgust that I could possibly feel flattered by such a thing, I had judged it unworthy of me, of the person I was or had been, of my face past and present, and which were both perhaps changing with the tomorrow that had now arrived. 'Presume not that I am the thing I was,' I quoted to myself as I walked. 'I have turn'd away my former self. When thou dost hear I am as I have been, approach me, and thou shalt be as thou wast. Till then, I banish thee, on pain of death, not to come near our person by ten mile . . .' These were the words of King Henry V immediately after being crowned and many years before the night when he disguised himself to go among his soldiers on the eve of the Battle of Agincourt, with everything pitched against him and at great risk of being misjudged, or, as one of his soldiers says to him, not realizing it's the King he's talking to, if the cause be not good, the king himself will have a heavy reckoning to make. Such words were unexpected coming from the man who, until only a short time before, had been Prince Hal, dissolute, reveler and bad son, especially when addressed to his still recent companion in revels, the now old Falstaff whom he was denying: 'I know thee not, old man,' for all it takes is a few words to abjure everything one has experienced, the excesses and the lack of scruples, the outrageous behavior and the arguments, the whorehouses and the taverns and the inseparable friends, even if those same friends say pleadingly to you, 'My sweet boy,' as Falstaff does to his beloved Prince Hal when the latter has just abandoned that name to become forever, with no possible way back, the rigid King Henry. Such words serve not only to mend one's ways and to leave behind the life of a debauchee or a *roué avant la lettre*, of a rake and an idler, but to announce that one is setting off along new paths, in new directions, or to announce a metamorphosis: I, too, could say mentally to Luisa and to Custardoy and to myself as I walked along: 'Presume not that I am the thing I was. I have turn'd away my former self. I am carrying a pistol and I am dangerous, I am no longer the man who never knowingly frightened anyone; like Iago, I am not what I am, at least I am beginning not to be.'

And so I stationed myself exactly where I had waited two days before, at the top of the short double flight of steps leading up to the monstrous cathedral, behind the papal statue that seemed always about to join the dance, and once there I paced back and forth between that point and a point nearby, behind the railings and to the left of that shop incomprehensibly selling souvenirs of the monstrosity; it was only a few steps between those two points and from both I could see the four corners formed by Calle Mayor and Calle de Bailén, as well as the ornate wooden door that was immediately opposite the shop, albeit lower down, and so whichever direction he came from I would be sure to see Custardoy arrive, although I was convinced he would take the same route as when I had followed him, if, that is, he had gone back to the Prado, though it was quite possible that he hadn't yet finished his note-taking or his sketches of the four faces painted by Parmigianino, each of them looking in a different direction, or that, on another occasion, he would have to study the portrait of the husband and father, in which the Count stands alone and isolated, like me, or that he would have to study other paintings for some other commission or project. And if he hadn't gone out that morning, it was likely that, just before lunch, he would stroll over to El Anciano Rey de los Vinos to enjoy his usual couple of beers and some *patatas bravas* (it was hardly surprising that, despite being thin, he had a bit of a belly on him), so I would be able to observe him there too if he went and took his usual seat. I would, at any rate, see him enter or leave his house, whenever he did that, and I would have time to go down the steps, cross the road—there wasn't much traffic along that stretch—and meet him at the front door as he was opening it. At first, I was surprised to see that, for the first time, the door stood open, and I deduced that there must be a doorman, but that could present me with a problem, a witness. However, after a few minutes, I saw the man come out and shut the door (he obviously lunched early) and this reassured me, because the seconds it would take Custardoy to put his key in and turn it and push or pull the door open and then give it a shove from inside or a tug from outside could prove vital, my idea being that he would complete neither action. I was trusting that he would not arrive or leave with anyone else, certainly not with Luisa. 'You'll never see her again,' I thought, 'unless she happens to be with you today,' it's odd how we address our thoughts to anyone we have it in for or whom we're preparing to harm in some way, addressing them familiarly as '*tú*,' as if what we were about to do to them were incompatible with any form of respect or as if any show of respect would, in view of our plans for them, seem utterly cynical.

I waited and waited and waited. I paced from one side to the other and back again, between steps and railings, looking down on each of the four corners and the eight stretches of sidewalk, Custardoy might come from the direction of the viaduct or pass beneath my eyes, staying close to the Cathedral or to the wall, or he might come from the direction of the Istituto Italiano or walk up Cuesta de la Vega from the Parque de Atenas; I kept a tight grip on the pistol hidden in my pocket and sometimes felt overwhelmed by nerves, I had a clear view of the whole scene, but there were too many fronts to keep watch over simultaneously and I constantly had to change my vantage point, I noticed that a few devotees were starting to eye me with interest—they didn't look Spanish, they were perhaps Lithuanians or possibly Poles, like their former boss—and, even worse, they were starting to copy me in my pacing back and forth as if they feared they might be missing out if they didn't do the same—people's tendency to imitate others' behavior is becoming an international plague—I felt slightly beleaguered and longed to be able to leave. And that was when I saw him in the distance, the unmistakable figure of Custardoy walking along Calle Mayor, on the same side as the Capitanía General and the Consejo de Estado, that is, on the same side as his apartment or workshop or studio. I stayed where I was, I didn't move, I waited until he had reached the traffic light, just in case he crossed over to take his usual seat outside the bar, but it was a cloudy day and not really warm enough for that. He was wearing a raincoat too, a good quality one, black and very long, almost like a dustcoat, and that, together with the hat he had chosen to wear that day, a kind of Stetson, but broader brimmed and cream or white in color like the hat Tom Mix used to wear in those ancient silent movies (the man really was a fool), gave him the appearance of a character out of the Wild West; he and his friend, the female Daniel Boone or Jim Bowie, would have made a fine pair. Fortunately, though, he was alone, striding along, the tails of his coat, and doubtless his ponytail too, beating the air (he was still a follower of fashion even at his age, with enough energy to try and keep up), walking as resolutely as I had done a short while before, but then I'd had a pistol in my pocket. 'He won't be easy to bring to heel,' I thought, 'he won't be easy to intimidate or even kill. Besides, he has the kind of strength that comes from pure energy and impatience and a desire to be many, this man accustomed to spending hours alone with his brushes, focused and still, concentrating on tiny details and staring at one canvas in order to make an exact copy of it on another canvas, and when he stops and finally gets up and opens the door and goes out into the street, he'll be filled by a vast amount of accumulated tension and be ready to explode. No, he won't be the kind to beg, he'll put up a fight, he isn't timid or easily scared, so one thing is sure, I have to instill him with fear, more fear than he might try to instill in me, he's not going to freeze and draw in his neck and close his eyes as De la Garza did, nor am I Tupra, who seems to instill fear whenever he wants to, quite naturally, nor am I the two Kray brothers Tupra told me about and who taught him the value of the sword, and to whom a cellmate had, according to Reresby, given a very condensed lesson in how to get what you want: "Now these people, they don't like getting hurt. Not them or their property. Now these people out there who don't like to be hurt, pay other people not to hurt them. You know what I'm saying. Course you do. When you get out, you keep your eyes open. Watch out for the people who don't want to be hurt. Because you scare the shit out of me, boys. Wonderful," that's what

Tupra had said,' I thought and remembered, 'in a fake accent which was perhaps his real accent, as he sat to the right of me in his swift silent car, in the lunar light of the streetlamps, with his hands still resting on the motionless steering wheel, squeezing or strangling it, he wasn't wearing gloves by then, but I've been wearing mine since I left the hotel and won't take them off until I return, having removed Custardoy from the picture, having done the deed.' 'That's the thing, Jack. Fear,' Tupra had added before urging me to go to his house to watch those videos that weren't just for anyone's eyes, and, after showing them to me, had asked again: 'Tell me now, why, according to you, one can't go around beating people up and killing them? You've seen how much of it goes on, everywhere, and sometimes with an utter lack of concern. So explain to me why one can't.' And it had taken me a long time to give him an answer, one that turned out to be no answer at all.

I hurried down the steps and very nearly collided with or, rather, almost flattened a devotee, Custardoy wasn't going to the bar, but to his studio, he had kept straight on and stopped at the traffic light on Calle de Bailén, and I knew that when the light turned green, it was only forty-nine steps from there to the door of his house, which was where we had to meet, not before he arrived and definitely not after, because afterwards the door would be closed again, with him inside and me outside. I decided to cross the road, taking advantage of the fact that the stoplight was in my favor; now we were on the same side of the street, I saw him set off when the cars stopped, one, two, three, four, five, I lurked for a few seconds behind a tree, not a very wide tree, hoping that he wouldn't see me *before* putting his key in the door, a matter of only a few moments, it would be best if he didn't notice me *while* he was putting the key in the door either, it would be best if I remained behind him for as long as possible and for him to feel as frightened as possible because he wouldn't know who it was threatening him, because he wouldn't be able to see his assailant's face, my face, and would wonder whether this was going to be a quick doorstep mugging or a slow ransacking of his whole apartment or a swift and then eternal kidnapping

Mexican-style, or whether I was alone or there were several of us, whether we were white, copper-colored or black (although our blacks don't go in much for mugging), or an unexpected settling of accounts, a tardy act of revenge on behalf of someone he didn't even recall, which, in a way, was the case with me, he probably didn't even remember that Luisa had, or once had, a husband, forty-six, forty-seven, forty-eight and forty-nine, and just as he put the key in the lock and the door opened, I stuck the pistol in his back without taking it out of my pocket (that way he wouldn't know if it was cocked or not, even if he spun round, which he wouldn't, not that it was cocked of course, and my finger was resting on the guard, I was very careful about that), but pressing the barrel of the gun hard against his spine, so that he would haven't any doubt that it was a gun and would feel it.

'Get inside, and don't say a word,' I whispered into the back of his neck with its stupid affected ponytail hanging there and which, at such close quarters, I found quite disgusting.

The door was half-open and he went in, we both went in, our bodies glued together, I slammed it shut with my free hand. Now he knew that there was only one of me.

'What bullshit is this?' he asked. 'Is this some kind of joke?' He still wasn't frightened, perhaps he hadn't had time to feel frightened or perhaps it wasn't in his nature. He sounded slightly cocky or at most uppity, but certainly not alarmed. 'It's going to be difficult to make him take me seriously, he's not the sort to lose his cool,' I thought at once. 'A bad beginning.'

'No, it's no joke, so be quiet. Let's go up to your apartment. We'll take the stairs. If we meet one of your neighbors, we're together. Take off your hat and hold it with your two hands. And don't drop your keys, you've got hands enough for both.' He didn't have his briefcase with him that day, so perhaps he hadn't been to the Prado. I was still talking into the back of his neck, perhaps Luisa had kissed that neck, I could smell his hair, it smelled of something, but nothing bad, he obviously washed it every day. He obeyed and took off his ridiculous hat. He would know now that I was a local, and not from Eastern Europe or the Maghreb or from South America, that my accent wasn't Albanian or Ukrainian or Arab or Colombian or Ecuadorian, it hadn't even occurred to me to put on a different accent or to disguise my own and I had said enough to make it clear that I was unequivocally Spanish, so he would know, too, that I was white, things remain hidden for such a short time, nor had I thought of addressing him in English, for example, a language I was used to speaking. 'You don't want a bullet lodged in your spine, do you? Well, get moving then.' Now he would know that I was a reasonably educated person too, because 'lodged' wasn't a word that would spring to everyone's lips.

'Look, if it's cash you want, we can talk and come to some agreement. We don't have to go upstairs and you don't have to keep that gun stuck in my back all the time. And there's no need to take that tone with me.'

He sounded less uppity now, but not afraid. He was addressing me as '*usted*,' not out of respect, but as a way of maintaining a distance. I was addressing him as '*tú*,' and his not doing the same to me was an attempt to appear superior despite his evidently inferior position, I was holding the pistol, I was holding the hourglass, like Death in the painting. I wasn't tugging at him, like the semi-skeleton of Sir Death, linking arms with the old woman, instead I was behind him and pushing him, which came to the same thing, I was the master of time and was propelling him up the stairs, he was trying to stop the flow of sand or water by talking, as have so many others, hoping to postpone events and save themselves, rather than remaining silent. He hadn't entirely lost his haughty manner, as indicated by the last words he spoke before I interrupted him. It was as if he had said to me: 'Don't you raise your voice to me,' except that wouldn't have made any sense because I was speaking in a whisper.

Then I took the gun out of my pocket for a moment and struck him hard on his right side with the barrel, as if I were slapping him except that I was striking him in the ribs and with the pistol, not across the face and with my hand, it made much less noise because he was, of course, wearing a raincoat. He staggered a little, but didn't fall. He didn't drop his hat either, but he did drop his keys.

'I've told you already, be quiet. Pick up your keys and get going.' I said this in the same calm whisper, which was, I thought, more frightening than a shout. I was surprised how easy it had been for me to deal him that blow and that it hadn't worried me to do so with a loaded weapon; usually, people who aren't used to carrying a gun are always afraid it will go off, however careful they are. My main concern was to frighten him, I suppose, or perhaps his last words had bothered me, either that or his use of the word 'bullshit' before, or perhaps I had remembered Luisa's black eye with its thousand slowly changing colors, an image I summoned up every now and then because I needed to, it filled me with reason and cold fury and strengthened my resolve. It seemed quite right that Custardoy should experience pain, some pain, he instinctively raised his hand to his side and rubbed it, but I told him at once: 'Keep your hands on your hat.' I realized, too, that everyone likes to give orders that must be obeyed. One part of my mind didn't like the fact that I liked that, but I wasn't in the mood to listen to it then, the rest of my mind was fully occupied, I had more than enough to occupy me, it wasn't possible now to leave half-done what I had already started.

We set off briskly, one step at a time, with me right behind him, holding onto his ponytail at each turn in the stairs so that he wouldn't take advantage of the one second when I stopped pointing at him full on to run up the stairs and shut himself in his apartment if, that is, he was quick enough putting the key in the lock (there was no way he would manage that, but I preferred him not to try), it must have been humiliating for him to have me touch his hair, I abstained from giving it a good tug, although I could have. We were lucky, that is I was and he wasn't, because we made it up to the third floor without meeting anyone; his was one of the apartments with a balcony looking onto the street.

'Here we are,' he said, standing outside his door. 'Now what?'

'Open the door.' He did so, a long key for the bolt and a smaller one for the lock. 'Let's go into the sitting room. You lead the way. But no funny business. I'm pointing at your spine, remember.' I could still feel the barrel of the gun against his bones, nice and central, if a bullet entered there it would take out his atlas vertebra.

We went down a short corridor and emerged into a spacious sitting room or studio with plenty of light despite the cloudy sky outside. ('Luisa has been here,' I thought at once, 'she'll know this room'). Then I saw the paintings lined up against the wall, in groups of three or four, their faces turned away, some might have been blank canvases, as yet untouched. Either he received a lot of commissions or he made numerous drafts before creating a final version; he was clearly in great demand and had no problem selling his work, for the room was comfortable, well-furnished and even luxurious, albeit slightly untidy; I particularly liked the fireplace. There were some paintings on the walls too, face out, of course, probably not his, although if he really was such a good copyist, who knows; I noticed a small Meissonier of a gentleman smoking a pipe and a larger portrait by Mané-Katz or someone like that, some Russian or Ukrainian who had spent time in Paris (if they were originals, they certainly wouldn't be cheap, although they weren't as expensive as the paintings I'd seen in Tupra's house). I noticed an easel, and the canvas resting on it was also face down, perhaps Custardoy always removed from his sight the thing he was working on as soon as he took a break, so as not to have to look at it while he was resting, perhaps it was the portrait of the Countess and her children on which he had already started work. Since I was the master of time and everything else, I could have looked at it. I didn't, though; I was otherwise occupied.

It was the moment for him to turn round and, therefore, to see my face. I didn't know whether he would recognize me from somewhere, from the Prado or from our shared walk or from photos that Luisa might have shown him; people are very keen on showing old photos, as if they wanted you to know them before the time when you actually met, it's something that happens especially between lovers, 'This is what I was like,' they seem to be saying to each other, 'would you have loved me then, as well? And if so, why weren't you there?' Before allowing him to turn round and before ordering him to sit down, I suffered a moment of confusion: 'What am I doing here with a pistol in my hand?' I thought or said to myself, and I immediately responded: 'There's absolutely no reason to feel surprised. There is a good reason for me to be here and even perhaps a real need: I'm going to rescue Luisa from anxiety and menace and from an unhappy future life, I'm going to ensure that she breathes easily again and can sleep at night without fear, I'm going to make certain my children don't suffer and come to no harm and that no wounds are inflicted on her, or, rather, no more harm, and that no one kills her'; and as I gave myself this answer, another quote came into my head, the words spoken by the ghost of a woman, Lady Anne, who slept so uneasily between the sheets of her second husband's 'sorrow-haunted bed,' cruel Richard III, who had stabbed her first husband at Tewkesbury, 'in my angry mood,' as he, the murderer, once put it; and so she, after death, cursed him on Bosworth Field at dawn, when it was already far too late to flee the battle, and in his dreams she whispered this: 'Richard, thy wife, that wretched Anne thy wife, that never slept a quiet hour with thee, now fills thy sleep with perturbations: Tomorrow in the battle think on me, and fall thy edgeless sword: despair and die!' I couldn't allow the same thing to happen to Luisa and for her never to sleep a quiet hour with Custardoy if, one day, he occupied my pillow and my still-warm or already cold place in her bed, I was the first husband, but no one in their angry mood was going to stab me or dig my grave still deeper than the one I was already buried in, my memory reduced to the first terror and the first plea and the first order, all of me changed into a poisoned shadow that little by little bids farewell while I languish and am transformed in London, expelled from her time and from that of my children (foolish me, insubstantial me, foolish and frivolous and credulous). 'No, she is not yet a widow and I am not yet a dead person who deserves to be mourned,' I thought, 'and since I'm not, I cannot so easily be replaced, just as bloodstains will not come out at the first attempt, you have to rub hard and diligently to remove them, and even then it seems as if the rim will never go, that's the most difficult part to remove, the part that resists—a whisper, a fever, a scratch. She probably has no wish and no intention of doing so, but she will find herself obliged to say to this present or future lover, or to herself: "Not yet, my love, wait, wait, your hour has not yet come, don't spoil it for me, give me time and give him time too, the dead man whose time no longer advances, give him time to fade, let him change into a ghost before you take his place and dismiss his flesh, let him be changed into nothing, wait until there is no trace of his smell on the sheets or on my body, let it be as if what was never happened." But I'm still here, and so I must have been before, and no one can yet say of me: "No, this was never here, never, it neither strode the world nor trod the earth, it did not exist and never happened." Indeed, I am the person who could kill this second husband right now, with my gloves on and in my angry mood. I have a pistol in my hand and it's loaded, all I would have to do is cock it and squeeze the trigger, this man still has his back to me, he wouldn't even see my face, today or tomorrow or ever, not until the Final Judgment, if there is one.'

In fact, it didn't really matter whether he saw my face or not; after all, I was going to talk to him about Luisa and as soon as I did, he would know without a shadow of a doubt who I was, and she would probably have told him about my sudden return to the city after so many months away, indeed, it was highly likely that he had already guessed it was her wretched imbecile of a husband who was pointing the gun at him, what a pain, what a cretin, what a madman, why hadn't he just stayed put where he was? 'Unless I'm the one who would rather not see his face and his eyes, his gaze,' I thought, 'nor say any more to him than I said at the front door, those were mere indifferent words, impersonal orders, not an exchange between two individuals. It's always said that killers avoid looking their victim in the eye, that to do so would be the only thing that might sow a seed of doubt or stop them slitting their victim's throat or firing a bullet or at least delay them long enough for the victim to say something or to try and defend himself, that's the only thing that can sabotage their mission or make them miss their target, so perhaps it would be best to finish the thing here and now, in keeping with Tupra's motto not to linger or delay, without giving any explanations or showing any curiosity, just as Reresby gave no explanations and showed no curiosity about De la Garza—without Custardoy even turning around, a bullet in the back of the neck and that would be that, goodbye Custardoy, out of the picture, guaranteed, and as with any deed once done, no going back, but if I speak to him and look him in the face, I'll find it harder and I'll start to get to know him and he'll become "someone" for me just as he is for Luisa, because he's important to her, someone for whom she probably feels a mixture of fear and devotion, so perhaps I should see him and hear him in order to imagine that, which is all I can aspire to, because I never will know how she looks at him, that's my eternal curse . . .'

The truth is I didn't know what I should do to be certain, to 'just deal with him and make sure he was out of the picture' as a scornful Tupra had told me with a paternalistic laugh; if only he had been more explicit or if only I were bilingual and had understood him with total exactitude, or perhaps such insoluble ambiguities exist in all languages. 'If you really don't know how, Jack, that means you can't do it,' he had said. I didn't know how, but I was in too deep by then. I couldn't just shoot Custardoy in the back and leave him for dead, not without first getting into my angry mood, not without being absolutely certain: Luisa had denied to me and to her sister that he'd hurt her, and I hadn't seen the act only the results, which, in a trial, wouldn't have helped me prove anything against him. 'But this isn't a trial,' I thought, 'or anything like it, men like Tupra, like Incompara, like Manoia and so many others, like the people I saw in those videos, like the woman who appeared in one of them, with her skirt hitched up and wielding a hammer with which she was smashing a man's skull, and who knows, perhaps like Pérez Nuix and like Wheeler and Rylands, they don't hold trials or gather evidence, they simply solve problems or root them out or stop them ever happening or just deal with them, it's enough that they know what they know because they've seen it from the start thanks to their gift or their curse, they've had the courage to look hard and to translate and to keep thinking beyond the necessary ("What else? You haven't even started yet. Go on. Quickly, hurry, keep thinking," my father used to say to me and my siblings when we were children, when we were young), and to guess what will happen if they don't intervene; they don't hate knowledge as do most of the pusillanimous people in this modern age, they confront it and anticipate it and absorb it and are, therefore, the sort who issue no warning, at least not always, the sort who take remote decisions for reasons that are barely identifiable to the one who suffers the consequences or is a chance witness, or without waiting for a link of cause and effect to establish itself between actions and motives, still less for any proof that such actions have been committed. Such men and women need no proof, on those arbitrary or well-founded occasions when, without the slightest warning or indication, they lash out with a saber; indeed, on such occasions, they don't even require the actions or events or deeds to have occurred. Perhaps for them it's enough that they know precisely what would happen in the world if no pressure or brake were imposed on what they perceive to be people's certain capabilities, and they know, too, that if they don't act with their full force, it's only because someone—me, for example—prevents or impedes them, rather than because they lacked the desire or the guts; they take all that for granted. Perhaps for them to adopt the punitive measures they deem to be necessary, they simply have to convince themselves of what would happen in each case if they or other sentinels—the authorities or the law, instinct, crime, the moon, fear, the invisible watchers—did not put a stop to it. They are the sort who know and adopt and make theirs—like a second skin—the unreflecting, resolute stance (or one based perhaps on a single thought, the first) that also forms part of the way of the world and which remains unchanged throughout time and regardless of space, and so there is no reason to question it, just as there is no need to question wakefulness and sleep, or hearing and sight, or breathing and speech, or any of the other things about which one knows: "that's how it is and always will be."

It was assumed that I was like them, one of them, that I possessed the same capacity to penetrate and interpret people, to know what their face would be like tomorrow and to describe what had not yet occurred, and as far as Custardoy was concerned I knew him inside out, I had no proof of anything, but I knew I was right: he was the dangerous, seductive, all-enveloping, violent type, capable of making someone dependent on the horrors he perpetrated and on his lack of scruples, his despotism and his scorn, and I mustn't give him an opening, I mustn't give him an opportunity to explain himself, to deny or refute or argue or persuade, not even to talk to me. Tupra was right: 'I think you do know how,' he had said to me before hanging up. 'We all know, even if we're not used to the idea or can't imagine ourselves doing it. It's a question of imagination.' Perhaps it was just a question of me imagining myself as Sir Death for the first time, after all, I had the pistol in my hand and that was my hourglass or clepsydra, and I had my gloves on, and now all I needed was to cock the gun, move my forefinger from the guard to the trigger and then squeeze, it was all just a step away and there was so little physical difference between one thing and the other, between doing and not doing, so little spatial difference . . . I didn't need certainties or proofs if I could convince myself that I was entirely, at least for that day, a member of Tupra's school which was the way of many and perhaps of the world, because his attitude was not preventative, not exactly or exclusively, but, rather, and depending on the case and the person, punitive or compensatory, for Tupra saw and judged when dry, with no need to get himself wet—to use Don Quixote's words when he announced to Sancho Panza the mad feats he would perform for Dulcinea's sake even before being provoked into them by grief or jealousy, so just imagine what he would do if provoked. Or perhaps Tupra understood them—the various cases—even though they were pages as yet unwritten, and perhaps, for that very reason, forever blank. 'But if I fire this pistol, my page will no longer be blank,' I thought, 'and if I don't, it won't be either, not entirely, after all the build-up and having thought about it and pointed the gun at him. We can never free ourselves from telling something, not even when we believe we have left our page blank. And even if there are things of which no one speaks, even if they do not in fact happen, they never stay still. It's terrible,' I said to myself. 'There's no escape. Even if no one speaks of them. And even if they never actually happen.' I studied the old Llama pistol at the end of my arm much as Death looked at his hourglass in that painting by Baldung Grien, the only thing by which he was guided, not by the living people beside him, after all, why would he be guided by them when he can already see their faces tomorrow? 'What does it matter then if things do happen? "You and I will be the kind who leave no mark," Tupra had said to me once, "so it won't matter what we've done, no one will bother to recount or even to investigate it." And besides,' I went on, still talking to myself, 'the day will come when everything is levelled out and life will be definitively untellable, and no one will care about anything.' But that day had not yet arrived, and I felt both curious and afraid—'And in short, I was afraid'—and had, above all, time to wonder as those familiar lines assured me I would: 'And indeed there will be time to wonder, "Do I dare?" and, "Do I dare?" Time to turn back and descend the stair . . .' Even time to ask the whole question that comes later in the poem—'Do I dare disturb the universe?'—the question no one asks before acting or even before speaking because everyone dares to do just that, to disturb the universe and to trouble it, with their small quick tongues and their ill-intentioned steps, 'So how should I presume?' And that's what kept my finger on the guard and my hand from cocking the gun, that is what happened, and besides I knew there would still be time to place my finger on the trigger and fire, having first cocked it with one simple gesture, as Miquelín had showed me.

'Turn around and sit down over there,' I said to Custardoy, pointing with my free hand at the sofa, a sofa on which he would probably often have sat or perhaps lain with Luisa. 'Put your hands on the table where I can see them.' In front of the sofa was a coffee table, as there is in most of the world's living rooms. 'Spread your fingers wide and don't move a muscle.'

Custardoy turned around as ordered and I finally saw his face full on and unimpeded, just as he did mine. He had a faint smile on his lips, which irritated me, and that long-toothed smile lit up his sharp-featured face and lent it a look almost of cordiality. He seemed quite calm, even amused in a way, despite that blow to his ribs, which must have hurt and frightened him. But, by then, he probably knew who I was, even if only by intuition or by a process of elimination, and relying perhaps on his own interpretative capacities, which were good enough for him to be sure that Luisa's husband wasn't going to shoot him, at least not yet, that is, without first speaking to him. (But then no one is ever totally convinced that someone is going to shoot him, not even with the gun barrel there before him.) His huge, dark, wide-set, almost lashless eyes really were most unpleasant and I immediately felt that grasping quality, how they quickly looked me over, with, how I can I put it, a kind of intimidatory intent, which, in the circumstances, was both strange and inappropriate. His half-smile, on the other hand, was perfectly affable, as if he were able to be two people at once. I couldn't understand how Luisa could possibly like him, even if there was something cocky and common about him—crude and rough and cold—a quality which, as I've seen and know, a lot of women find attractive. Before sitting down, he stroked his mustache, repositioned his ponytail with a gesture that was unavoidably feminine, threw his hat down on the sofa and said:

'May I light a cigarette? If I'm smoking, you'll still be able to see my two hands.' And then he sat down, taking care not to crease the tails of his raincoat. He had begun addressing me as '*tú*' now, and that confirmed me in my suspicion that he had identified me.

'Have one of mine,' I replied, not wanting him to put his hand in his pocket. I offered him a Karelias and took another for myself. I lit both from the same flame and we inhaled the smoke at the same time, and for a moment we resembled old friends, taking that first puff in silence. We had both suffered a fright, and a cigarette was just what we needed. But the fright was not yet over, and his must have been far greater than mine, after all, I had merely frightened myself when I saw what I was doing, and that always supposes a lesser, more controlled fear, one you can bring to an end yourself. The conversation that followed moved very quickly.

'What the fuck's up with you?' said Custardoy. 'You're Jaime, aren't you?' The use of a swearword denoted aplomb and a certain lack of respect, unless, of course, he always talked like that (after all, he had no reason to respect me and more than enough reason to be angry with me); regardless of whether such aplomb was feigned or real, it was clear, I thought, that I had not yet frightened him enough, and how was I to do that? I sat sideways on the arm of a chair, which meant that not only was I facing him, I was higher up as well.

'Who said you could talk? I didn't. I only said you could smoke. So smoke your cigarette and shut the fuck up.' I flung the swearword back at him so as to place us on an equal footing and I waved the pistol about a bit. I hoped he wasn't used to handling firearms or wouldn't notice that I wasn't. It's not easy to frighten someone if you're not in the habit of doing so. I knew I could do it (I had done so before on occasion), just as I knew or imagined that I would be capable, or at least not incapable, of killing; but to do both those things, I would—perhaps—need to be completely crazy, agitated or furious or gripped by a long-lasting thirst for revenge, and at that moment, I wasn't, not sufficiently; perhaps I had relaxed once the first phase of my unplanned plan had passed without mishap, intercepting Custardoy, going to his apartment and shutting myself up with him there. I had too little hatred. I had too little knowledge. I was too lukewarm. I lacked the necessary heat. And, unlike Tupra, I wasn't cold enough either.

'OK, talk. I haven't got all fucking day to waste over this kind of crazy nonsense. Why are you pointing that gun at me? Just what are you up to, pal?' And he attempted another of those smiles that revealed long shiny teeth and which made him look almost pleasant and his profile less aggressive. He still reminded me of someone, but I didn't have time just then to think who it might be.

Custardoy was either brave or overconfident. Or perhaps he didn't want to appear daunted despite the weapon pointed at his chest by this madman, or maybe he was convinced I wouldn't use it. He had spoken scornfully, as if he wanted to diminish us, me and my gun. He had gone so far as to address me as 'pal' (and I hate people who use such terms), trying to belittle me and make me feel like some ridiculous child with my antiquated pistol in my hand. If he *was* over-confident, I wondered what more I would have to do to puncture his arrogance: I had already hit him and hurt him, and he must have registered that if I was capable of that, I was capable of worse things. If he continued in that vein, he ran the risk of getting me seriously riled or, as Custardoy might have put it, of getting on my tits. So it suited me that he should continue in that vein. Or perhaps not, he might just make me see myself in that situation as grotesque and puerile.

'Listen,' I said. 'From today on, you're going to stop seeing Luisa Juárez. It's over. No more beatings or cuts or black eyes. You never touch her again, right?'

I thought he would immediately deny ever laying a finger on her and declare: 'I don't know what you're talking about' or some such thing. But he didn't, that wasn't what upset him:

'Oh, really? What? On your say-so? He's got some nerve.' The way he said this irritated me, as if he were not addressing me, but some invisible third party, some imaginary witness with whom he felt at liberty to mock me. 'That's up to her and me, don't you think?'

Yes, that was precisely what I thought. I had no right to involve myself in her affairs, she was free, she was an adult, she might even be very happy with him, she hadn't asked me for my opinion or my protection, she hadn't even deigned to tell me about her day-to-day life, that life no longer concerned me; of course I agreed. None of that, though, was relevant now—I had decided to involve myself and to use force and fear, and at that point you have to leave aside all arguments and principles, all respect and moral reservations and scruples because you have decided to do what you want to do and to impose that decision on others, to achieve your ends without further delay, and then, as with any war once it has begun, being right or wrong should neither intervene nor count. Once that line has been crossed, right or wrong no longer matter, it's simply a matter of getting your own way, of winning and subjugating and prevailing. He had hit her and must be made to stop, that was all. 'Just make sure he's out of the picture,' I repeated to myself. I had to leave that apartment with Custardoy suppressed and erased like a bloodstain, that was all. And my determination grew.

'Yes,' I agreed, 'it should be up to the two of you to make that decision, but that isn't how it's going to be. You're going to decide on your own. You're going to give her up today. Which would you rather give up—her or the world. Be quite clear about one thing though: either way you're going to give her up.'

For the first time, I saw him hesitate, perhaps I even caught a glimmer of fear. I thought: 'He's realized that it's not at all difficult to shoot someone, it's just a question of not being yourself for two seconds or perhaps of being yourself—one moment you're not a murderer and then suddenly you are and will be for all eternity—that anyone with a weapon in his hand might suddenly up and shoot you, all it takes is for him to forget for an instant the magnitude of the gesture, of a single simple gesture, or rather two, cocking the gun and squeezing the trigger, which might be almost simultaneous as it is in Westerns, cocking the hammer and pulling the trigger, put this finger here and that finger there, first one and then the other, up and back and there you are, it can happen to anyone, a slip of the hand or the finger, the hand that, in just one movement, puts the bullet into the barrel or the chamber and then the forefinger drawing back— this is a heavy pistol, quite hard to hold, but hand and finger act on their own as if no one were moving them, no consciousness or will, they caress and stroke and glide almost, you don't even have to make the effort that a sword inevitably requires, with a sword you have to raise it up and then bring it down and both movements require the whole strength of one arm or even both, which is why neither children nor many women nor feeble old men can wield one, but on the other hand, the pistol can be used by the weakest, most fearful, most stupid and most worthless of people—the pistol democratizes killing far more than the dishonorable crossbow—and anyone can cause irreparable damage with one, you just have to let things happen. And if I were to cock the pistol now, Custardoy would be terrified.'

And as soon as I thought this, and despite Miquelín's warning, I cocked the pistol. It was only a test and only for an instant, just to see a spark of panic in those strange dark eyes, it was only a spark, but I saw it. And then I immediately put my thumb on the hammer and lowered it and removed the projectile that had passed into the barrel or chamber or whatever it's called and put it away in my pocket; I uncocked the Llama. But he had seen how quick the pistol was to cock and how, once cocked, the bullets could fly out—a single gesture, then another and another—towards his head or his chest, towards an arm or a leg, towards his codpiece which would be reduced to a few fine hairs like the vanished codpiece of Death in the painting, or towards whatever part I chose to point it at. 'What a very odd feeling,' I thought, 'having a man at your mercy. Deciding if he should live or die, although it's not even really a matter of deciding.'

Custardoy, however, put on a brave face, or perhaps it was just that he wanted to be right, or, given that he had no weapon with which to defend himself, that he was trying to dissuade or terrify or destroy me, or to dig my grave still deeper with his ugly words and with his voice. His voice did not emerge cleanly, it was slightly hoarse, as if there were tiny pins in his throat similar to those on the revolving metallic disc or cylinder in a music box, which strike the tuned teeth of the comb and determine or mark the one repetitive melody. What he said emerged slowly, as if the spikes slowed down his speech. At any rate, he kept his hands on the table. He had finished his cigarette, but hadn't forgotten my earlier order, which was a good sign.

'Look, Jaime.' And it bothered me unutterably that he should call me by my first name, the name that Luisa used and which he had doubtless heard her say (how embarrassing) when she spoke to him about me. 'This is all total bullshit, and in a while, when you've left here, you'll be the first to see that. What is it that bothers you so much? Is it the fact that I screw her now and then? It's a bit late for you to be complaining about that. You probably do the same in London with whoever takes your fancy, and you're going to have to get used to it, if you aren't already, for Chrissake, there was whatever there was between you two and now there isn't. It happens all the time. But *this* I really can't believe.' He stopped and gave a short laugh, the laughter that made him almost pleasant and more attractive, he was still not fully aware of the danger, of the danger I represented. 'I mean, it's funny really, this is the last thing I would have expected. It's

like a scene straight out of an opera, dammit!' Again he said this
as if he were talking to a third party, to a ghost present in the
room and not to me, and that drove me wild. He was probably
looking forward to telling the story later on to a friend ('You
won't believe what happened to me today? Christ, it was weird')
or perhaps to Luisa herself ('I bet you can't guess who came to
see me today, and toting a gun as well. Fucking hell! You married
a really nasty piece of work there, he's nothing like you said, he's
a complete headcase'). But he wouldn't be seeing Luisa again, he
didn't know that, but I did. I doubted that he would talk quite
like that to her, although he did when she wasn't there, of course;
foul language came naturally to him, much more than it does
to me: I have no problem using swearwords when the situation
calls for it, but I lacked his fluency in that particular register,
with which I was as familiar as almost everyone else, but which
I didn't often use.

'You know exactly what bothers me. You know precisely
what I find unacceptable, you bastard. Like I said, from today on,
you'll never touch her again.'

He was still unbowed. He was playing a dangerous game. As
he must have noticed, he risked heating up my lukewarm blood
and provoking hand and finger into action. Perhaps this was a
useful stratagem: perhaps he was trying not only to show that he
was right, but also to show me that I was not, to open my eyes, to
rid himself of this stupid unexpected problem and get on with
his life by making me give in.

'What? Oh. The bruises,' he said, and each rasping word was
dragged out like the music from a music box, each one emerged
slowly as if it kept snagging on something, there was also perhaps
a little *madrileño* bravado in his way of speaking. Then he added
a trite remark, which, nonetheless, wounded me when I realized
what he was saying; it took me a few seconds because I found it
hard to grasp or preferred not to grasp what he meant, or maybe
it took me that amount of time to absorb the meaning. 'Look,
pal,' again that hateful belittling term, 'everyone has their own
sexuality, and with some partners it comes out naturally and
with others it doesn't. Didn't the same thing happen when she

was with you? I mean, what can I say, pal, I had no idea either. It just happened and you have to give people what they want. Or don't you think so? Look, I didn't do anything to her she didn't want me to. Is that clear? So don't damn well go blaming me for something I'm not guilty of, all right?'

Yes, it took me a few seconds. 'What *is* this guy saying?' I thought. 'He's telling me that Luisa enjoys being knocked around, he's telling *me* that? That's impossible. It's a lie,' I thought, 'I've known her intimately for years, although less so lately, and I've never seen the slightest suggestion of that, I'd have noticed it, however slight, a hint, a question mark, a glimpse, this guy's trying to slither out of it, trying to justify himself, to escape, he knows why I'm here and that my reason is a grave one and he's been thinking up this false explanation for a while now, he knows for certain that I'm not going to ask Luisa about it and he's taking advantage of that to tell me he only hurts women who want to be hurt, or something of the sort, but Cristina told me how frightened the women were who had slept with him, some at any rate, and their subsequent silence about or concealment of what went on, why wouldn't they speak, if he was a violent brute, they'd report him, they'd alert other women, they'd forewarn them, for example those prostitutes he goes with, sometimes two at a time. No, it can't be true, it's not,' I thought, shrugging off the idea. It's dreadful to be told anything, anything at all, it's dreadful to have ideas put in your head, however unlikely or ridiculous and however unsustainable and improbable (but everything has its time to be believed), any scrap of information registered by the brain stays there until it achieves oblivion, that eternally one-eyed oblivion, any story or fact and even the remotest possibility is recorded, and however much you clean and scrub and erase, that rim is the kind that will never come out; it's understandable really that people should hate knowledge and deny what is there before their eyes and prefer to know nothing and to repudiate the facts, that they should avoid the inoculation and the poison and push it away as soon as they see or feel it near, it's best not to take risks; it's understandable, too, that we almost all ignore what we see and divine and anticipate and smell, and that we toss into the bag of imaginings anything that we see clearly—for however short a time—before it can take root in our mind and leave it forever troubled, and so it's hardly strange that we should be reluctant to know anyone's face, today, tomorrow or yesterday. 'What face am I wearing now?' I wondered. 'And what about Luisa's face, one I thought I had plumbed and deciphered and knew, to all intents and purposes, from top to bottom, from past to future and from tomorrow to yesterday, and then along comes this son-of-a-bitch talking about her sexuality and telling me she likes him to get rough with her in bed, it's a joke, I mustn't believe him or think about it, but people do change and, above all, make discoveries, the kind of wretched discovery that takes those people from us and carries them far away, as with young Pérez Nuix when I discovered the pleasure of pretending that I wasn't doing what I was doing or of making believe that what was happening wasn't happening, which is not, I think, quite the same thing, that had been political, a tacit game, but that's what this bastard would say, damn him, that it's all a game, an erotic game, anything is possible, but it can't be true. Luisa's black eye wasn't the result of some game, like hell it was, and yet Custardoy said: "What? Oh. The bruises," why did he use the plural when I've only seen one bruise, perhaps there are more underneath her clothes, on her body, I haven't seen Luisa naked on this visit nor will I, I'll probably never see her naked again, but this bastard will unless I stop him and make sure he's out of the picture now and for good, with no going back and no further delay, don't ever linger or delay, just cock the gun again and squeeze the trigger, it's a simple matter of running my hand over the slide to release it and moving a finger, this and then this, forward and back and a bullet in the head and that will be that, I am, after all, wearing gloves, he'll be out of the picture forever and no more bruises, no more bed, no more wit or charm, it's in my hands to do all of that and I don't even have to listen to him or speak to him again.'

And so I did cock the pistol, and for the first time I moved my index finger from the guard to the trigger, remembering Miquelín's warning and believing that I was following his advice, 'Never put your finger on the trigger until you know you're going to shoot.' And for a few seconds—one, two, three, four, five; and six—I did know, but not afterwards. I have no idea what saved him that time, it wasn't his silence, perhaps there were several things—thoughts, memories, and a recognition—all crowded together into six or possibly seven seconds, or perhaps other things came to me later and so had more time to be thought or remembered once I was back in my hotel room. 'What face am I wearing now?' I thought again. 'It's the face of all those men and rather fewer women who have held someone else's life in their hands and it could, from one moment to the next, come to resemble the face of those who chose to take that life. Not Reresby's face, who did not, in the end, snatch away De la Garza's life, and who, if he has killed other people, did not do so in my presence, like Wheeler with his outbreaks of cholera and malaria and plague. But it would join the face of that vicious *malagueño* who baited and killed Marés, the face of that Madrid woman who boasted on the tram of having killed a child by smashing its head against a wall, of those militiamen who finished off my young Uncle Alfonso and left him dead in the gutter, even the faces of Orlov and Bielov and Carlos Contreras, who tortured Andreu Nin in Alcalá and possibly flayed him alive; of Vizconde de La Barthe, who ordered Torrijos and, according to the painting, seventeen of his followers to be shot on the beach as soon as they disembarked, but in reality and in history there may have been many more; the faces of the Czech resistance fighters or students who made an attempt on the life of the Nazi Protector Heydrich using bullets impregnated with botulin and the face of Spooner, the director of the Special Operations Executive, the SOE, who planned it all; the faces of the German occupiers who, in reprisal and with their hatred of place, destroyed the village of Lidice and killed either instantly or slowly one hundred and ninety-nine men and one hundred and eighty-four women on June 10, 1942; the faces of the thugs who machine-gunned those four unfortunates on another hidden beach, in Calabria this time, not far from Crotone, on the Golfo de Taranto, three men and a woman, a killing I myself watched; and the face of the man who screamed at another man in a garage, his mouth so close to the other's face that he sprayed him with saliva, and then shot him at point-blank range beneath the earlobe, as I could do now to Custardoy with no one here to cry out 'Don't!' as I did to Reresby and probably stopped him, I could put the barrel right there and that would be it, blood spurting out and tiny bits of bone; the face of the woman in green, her skirt all rucked up and wearing a sweater and a pearl necklace and high heels but with no stockings, who crushed the skull of a man with a hammer and sat astride him to strike his forehead over and over; the face of the European officer or mercenary who ordered the massacre of twenty Africans who fell in swift succession, like dominoes; the face of Manoia, yes him too, who scooped out the eyes of his prisoner as if they were peach stones and then, according to Tupra, slit his throat; and all those centuries before, the face of Ingram Frizer, who stabbed to death the poet Marlowe in a tavern in Deptford, even though his face is unknown and his name, too, remains uncertain; and, of course, the face of King Richard, who ordered his two little nephews in the Tower to be strangled, and had many others killed too, whether in his angry mood or not, including poor Clarence, drowned by two henchmen in a butt of disgusting wine and held by the legs, which remained outside the barrel and flailed ridiculously about in the air he would never breathe again . . . My face will resemble and be assimilated into that of all those men and rather fewer women who were once masters of time and who held in their hand the hourglass—in the form of a weapon, in the form of an order—and decided suddenly, without lingering or delaying, to stop time, thus obliging others no longer to desire their own desires and to leave even their own first name behind. I don't like being linked to those faces. On the other hand, I must remove Luisa from all danger and suffering and torment, so that her ghost will not one day say to this man what Lady Anne's ghost said to her husband on the eve of battle, nor hurl at him the curse that I am failing to carry out despite being in a position to do so: "Thy wife, that wretched Luisa thy wife, that never slept a quiet hour with thee . . . Let me sit heavy on thy soul, and may you feel the pinprick in your breast: despair and die!" Yes, it would be best to kill him while I still have time,' I thought, 'I might not have another opportunity in the future, perhaps there is no other way of removing him from the picture forever and this is the only way to make us safe.' That 'us' surprised me. And it gave me strength and encouragement to discover that I still thought of us as 'us.'

And although I was no longer at all sure that I would shoot him, I kept my finger on the trigger, and still more seconds passed. And as they passed and the risk remained that I might accidentally fire the gun, I was conscious that Custardoy was looking paler and less kempt, it was as if his immaculate appearance had somehow suffered a breakdown, his tie was crooked and he made the mechanical gesture of straightening it, reminding me of that other—unavoidably feminine—gesture he had made when repositioning his ponytail, then he obediently returned his hand to the table; his raincoat was creased now, the cloth seemed of poorer quality, and what I could see of his shirt looked grubby with sweat. As for his hair, it gave the impression of being plastered to his head and even his sideburns had lost their curl; he was trying hard to maintain his smile—obviously aware of its affable nature—but it no longer lit up his face; his nose had grown sharper, or perhaps it was simply that I had shifted position and the angle had changed; his eyes, I thought, were clouded and closer together, as if his whole being were striving to shrink and thus offer less of a target, a purely unconscious reaction, since, given the short distance separating us, it made no sense at all, for I certainly couldn't miss.

'Have you ever met my children?' I asked suddenly.

'No, I've never even seen them. I don't like getting kids involved.'

'How long have you been going out with her? How long have you known each other? And don't lie to me. I know her better than you do.'

The fact that I spoke to him and asked him civilized questions with no insults thrown in calmed him slightly, although he still kept glancing at the barrel of the primed pistol—'primed,' as I understand it, being another term for 'cocked'—with his large dark eyes, still cold and crude despite the fear in them, any roughness being attributable now only to his mustache and his nose.

'About six months.' And he allowed himself to add: 'Although longer isn't necessarily better. Look, why don't you just leave us alone? I've never liked a woman as much as I like her. You're out of the frame, we thought that was clear.'—'Ah, so I'm the one who's out of the picture now,' I thought. 'He's right. But that's going to change. He talks about "us" as well, meaning Luisa and him.'—'Anyway, that's clear to Luisa, and she assumed it was to you as well.'

'I don't know why you use the past tense. She's going to continue assuming that because you're not going to tell her anything about what's happened here.'

With a pistol in my hand, this sounded like a serious threat, although it wasn't, at least I didn't say it with that intention, but simply because I was sure they wouldn't be seeing each other again after that day. Custardoy was less mouthy now, I noticed, and was growing increasingly apprehensive. And then another thought or memory came into my mind, one that should have condemned him and yet, strangely, helped to save him: 'Good God, this man is my ġe-brȳd-guma, Luisa has made of him and me unwitting co-fornicators or co-fuckers, just as Tupra and I probably are as well through the intermediary or link of Pérez Nuix, and as I, all unawares, must be of many other men through other women; we never think about that the first time we have sex with someone, about who we're bringing together and who we're joining forces with, and nowadays, these phantasmagorical relationships, undesired and unsought, would be a story without end. But according to that dead language, this man and I are related, indeed, according to any language, we have an affinity, and perhaps for that very reason I should not kill him, yes, for that reason too, because we have something very important in common, I've never liked another woman as much as I like Luisa either, so what it comes down to is that we love the same person, and I can't blame him for that, or perhaps he simply has sex with her, it's impossible to gauge what his feelings are.' I could have tried to find out and ask him if he loved her, but the question struck me as absurd, and besides, with a pistol cocked and pointing at him, I knew what he would answer but not if that answer would be true. At that moment, the truth would be the last thing he would tell me, if he really thought the truth might kill him.

'I don't want anyone to disappear,' was my next thought. 'I don't believe in the Final Judgment or in a great final dance of sorrow and contentment, nor in some kind of rowdy get-together at which the murdered will rise up before their murderers and present their accusations to a bored and horrified Judge. I don't believe in that because I don't belong to the age of steadfast faith, and because it's not necessary: that scene takes place here, on earth, in a fragmented individual form, at least it does when the dead person knows or sees who is killing him and can then say with his farewell glance: "You're taking my life more for reasons of jealousy than justice, I haven't killed anyone, not as far as you know, you're putting a bullet in my forehead or beneath my ear lobe not because you think I'm beating up the woman who is no longer your wife, as if I were some vulgar wife-beater, although you can't and don't want to avoid that suspicion and at least part-believe it for your own momentary justification which will be of no use to you tomorrow, but because you're afraid of me and are going to fight for what is yours, as do all those who commit crimes and have to convince themselves that their crimes were necessary: for your God, for your King, for your country, for your culture or your race; for your flag, your legend, your language, your class or your space; for your honor, your religion, for your family, for your strongbox, for your purse and your socks; or for your wife. And in short, you are afraid. I died in my apartment on a cloudy day, among my paintings and without even taking off my raincoat, when I least expected it and at the hands of a stranger who intercepted me at the front door and gave me a last cigarette which I did not enjoy. I will no longer go to the Prado to look at the paintings, I will no longer study them or copy them or even forge them, I will no longer walk through Madrid with my ponytail bobbing and my fine hat on or drink another beer or eat another portion of *patatas bravas*, I won't go into the bookshop or greet my female friends or stop to look at statues or the legs of some passing woman, nor will I ever make anyone laugh again. You're putting an end to all of that. It may not be much, but it's what I have, it's my life and it's unique, and no one else will ever have it again. Let me sit heavy on your soul each night and fill your sleep with perturbations, may you feel my knee upon your chest, while you sleep with one eye open, an eye you will never be able to close." No, I don't want anyone to disappear,' I thought again, 'not even this man. I do not dare, and there will still be time to turn back and descend the stair, I do not dare disturb the universe, still less destroy anything in it, in my angry mood. There will be room for Custardoy in these streets for a while yet, they are already awash with blood and no one should tremble as they leave them, and they are perhaps already too full of men brimming with rage and with thunderless lightning that strikes in silence, I should not be one more such man. "We are all witnesses to our own story, Jack. You to yours and I to mine," Tupra said to me once. My face would become one with that of Santa Olalla and, even worse, that of Del Real, two names that have always been for me the names of treachery; because when they betrayed my father at the end of the Civil War, what they wanted was his execution and his death, that was the usual fate of any detainee, for they were the masters of time, they held the hourglass in their hand and ordered it to stop, except that it didn't stop and didn't obey them and, thanks to that, I am here, and my father did not have to say as he died: "Strange to see meanings that clung together once floating away in every direction. And being dead is hard work . . ." No, I will not be the one to impose that task on this unpleasant man for whom I feel a strange blend of sympathy and loathing, he is part of this landscape and of the universe, he still treads the earth and traverses the world and it is not up to me to change that; at the end of time there are only vestiges or remnants or rims and in each can be traced, at most, the shadow of an incomplete story, full of lacunae, as ghostly, hieroglyphic, cadaverous or fragmentary as pieces of tombstones or the broken inscriptions on ruined tympana, "past matter, dumb matter," and then you might doubt that it ever existed at all. Why did she do that, they will say of you, why so much fuss and why the quickening pulse, why the trembling, why the somersaulting heart; and of me they will say: why did he speak or not speak, why did he wait so long and so faithfully, why that dizziness, those doubts, that torment, why did he take those particular steps and why so many? And of us both they will say: why all that conflict and struggle, why did they fight instead of just looking and staying still, why were they unable to meet or to go on seeing each other, and why so much sleep, so many dreams, and why that scratch, my pain, my word, your fever, and all those doubts, all that torment.'

I took out the second bullet and put it away, I uncocked the pistol, removed my finger from the trigger and rested it once more on the guard, as Miquelín had advised me to do unless I was sure I was going to fire. I saw on Custardoy's face a look of contained or repressed relief, he didn't dare feel entirely relieved, how could he, when he still had the barrel of a gun pointing at his face and when the man holding the gun was wearing gloves and had just done something very worrying: he had picked up the two ashtrays with the two cigarette butts in them and their corresponding ash, his own and Custardoy's, the ash from the burned-out Karelias cigarettes, and emptied them into his other raincoat pocket to keep them separate from the bullets, just as, in the handicapped toilet, Tupra had put away his sodden gloves, wrung out and wrapped up in toilet paper, although he had done so only once his task was complete, while mine still lay before me. 'Now I do have his coldness, Reresby's coldness that is, now that I've recognized my similarity or affinity with this man, which is why he's going to emerge from this alive,' I thought, 'and now that I've thoroughly frightened him, even though he has barely shown it and put on a brave face, anything else I do to him will seem all right and of no account, he'll think himself lucky and find it perfectly reasonable. I will not be Sergeant Death or Sir Death or Sir Cruelty or even Sir Thrashing, I will be Sir Blow or Sir Wound or Sir Punishment, because something has to be done to keep him out of the picture, just as Tupra did with De la Garza.'

And while I was thinking (and much of this I thought later on), I realized who it was that Custardoy reminded me of; what, to use Wheeler's word, his affinity was; or his relationship, although in this case there was even a resemblance. And it was probably that very frivolous fact that saved him, truly and definitively, a nonsense, a mere nothing, a chance superfluous flash, an opportune association or a fickle memory that might or might not have surfaced; sometimes what we do or don't do depends on that, just as we decide to give alms to one beggar among many, whose appearance, for some reason, moves us: we suddenly see the person, see beyond his condition and function and needs, we individualize him, and he no longer seems to us indistinguishable or interchangeable as an object of compassion, of which there are hundreds; that's what happened to Luisa with the young Romanian or Hungarian or Bosnian woman and her sentinel son at the entrance to the supermarket, and about whom I had occasionally thought while I was far away in London, having first known of their existence through a story told to me. I associated Custardoy with my dancing neighbor opposite, with whom I had never exchanged a word, but who had so often cheered or soothed me with his improvised dances beyond the trees and the statue, on the other side of the square, alone or accompanied by his friends or *partenaires* or lovers. Yes, they had quite a lot in common: my dancer is a thin fellow with bony features—jaw and nose and forehead—but a strong athletic build, just as Custardoy is all sinew; he has a thick but well-groomed mustache, like that of a boxer from the early days, except that it's cut straight with no nineteenth-century curlicues, and he wears his hair combed back with a middle parting as if he had a ponytail, although I've never seen it, perhaps one day he'll reveal that he has one just like Custardoy, he also sometimes wears a tie as Custardoy always does, even when he's running and leaping about his empty living room, the guy's mad, but so happy, so contented, so oblivious to everything that wears the rest of us down and consumes us, immersed in his dances danced for no one, it's fun and even rather cheering to watch, and mysterious too, I can't imagine who he is or what he does, he eludes—and this doesn't happen very often—my interpretative or deductive faculties, which may or may not be right, but which never hold back, springing immediately into action to compose a brief, improvised portrait, a stereotype, a flash, a plausible supposition, a sketch or snippet of life however imaginary and basic or arbitrary these might be, it's my alert, detective mind, the idiotic mind that Clare Bayes criticized and reproached me for years ago now, before I met Luisa, and which I had to suppress with Luisa so as not to irritate her or fill her with fear, the superstitious fear that always does the most damage and yet serves so little purpose, for there's nothing to be done to protect ourselves from what we already know and dread (perhaps because we are fatalistically drawn to it and seek it out so as to avoid disappointment), and we usually know how things will end, how they will evolve and what awaits us, where things are going and what their conclusion will be; everything is there on view, in fact, everything is visible very early on in a relationship just as it is in all honest straightforward stories, you only have to look to see it, one single moment encapsulates the germ of many years to come, of almost our whole history—one grave pregnant moment—and if we want to we can see it and, in broad terms, read it, there are not that many possible variations, the signs rarely deceive if we know how to decipher their meanings, if you are prepared to do so—but it's very difficult and can prove catastrophic . . .

I had interpreted or deduced Custardoy and even had proof, and both those things had been enough to condemn him. But what bad or good luck—how I regret it, how I celebrate it— that he should remind me of my contented dancer to whom I was grateful from afar, which was doubtless why I felt for Custardoy that inexplicable sympathy mingled with profound loathing. Perhaps they were alike in other ways too, perhaps there were other affinities apart from the pleasant smile and the superficial physical likeness: when Custardoy was sketching and taking notes as he stood before that painting by Parmigianino he was, perhaps, as focused on that as my neighbor was on his dancing, as happy and contented, and when he painted at home, when he made his copies or forgeries, he may have been even more abstracted and oblivious to all that wears us down and consumes us. And the dancer was often accompanied by two women, just as Custardoy sometimes took two women to bed with him in his need to be many or to live more than one life. And it was that, above all, that made me give up the idea of killing him: a nonsense, a mere nothing, a chance, superfluous flash of thought, a doubt or caprice or some stupid fit of feeling, an untimely association of fickle memories, or was it, rather, one-eyed oblivion.

Without saying anything, I went over to his enviable fireplace and thereafter I acted very swiftly, as if I were distracted or, rather, busy, yes, my attitude was as businesslike as Reresby's had been when he walked into that immaculate handicapped toilet. 'Now I have his coldness,' I thought again, 'now I know how to frighten Custardoy, now I can imagine myself, because it *is* just a question of imagining yourself and only then can you rid yourself of problems; now I can calculate how hard the blow should be, can bring down my sword without severing anything, lift it up and then bring it down again but still cut nothing and nevertheless give him the fright of his life that will ensure he never comes near us again, near me or, above all, Luisa.' I picked up the poker and without giving Custardoy time to prepare himself or even to foresee what I was about to do, I struck him as hard as I could on the left hand that he had placed, along with his right hand, on the table. I heard the crunch of broken bones, I heard it clearly despite the simultaneous howl he let out, his face, no longer rough or crude or cold, twisted in pain and he instinctively clasped his broken hand with his other hand.

'Fuck! You've broken my hand, you bastard!' It was a perfectly normal reaction, he didn't really know what he was saying, the pain had made him forget for a moment that I still had a gun aimed at him and that my last words to him had been: 'you're not going to tell her anything about what's happened here.'

I raised the poker again and this time, applying less pressure—yes, now I could calculate how hard the blow should be—I slashed his cheek, gave him *uno sfregio* or a cut much longer and much deeper than the one Flavia Manoia suffered, although it barely touched bone. He raised his good hand to his jaw, his cheek, it was the right one, and stared at me with a look of panic, of fear, which was not so much visceral as atavistic, the fear of someone who does not know whether more blows will follow nor how many because that is the nature of swords, that is the nature of weapons that are not loosed or thrown, those that kill at close quarters and when face to face with the person killed, without the murderer or the avenger or the avenged detaching or separating themselves from the sword while they wreak havoc and plunge the weapon in and cut and slice, all with the same blade which they never discard, but hold onto and grip even harder while they pierce, mutilate, skewer and even dismember. I did none of those things, it was hardly the appropriate weapon for that, indeed, it wasn't a weapon at all, but a tool.

'Keep your hands on the table, I said,' and again I cocked the pistol, but this time I didn't place my index finger on the trigger.

He looked at me with stupefaction and renewed alarm, or perhaps a different kind of alarm, his eyes, having grown momentarily closer together, were once more wide apart. I know what was going through his head at that moment, he must have been thinking: 'Oh, no. This madman's going to break my other hand too, the hand I paint with.'

'No,' he said. 'Why? No, don't do it.'

And so I had no option but to press the barrel of the gun to his forehead, so that he would take me seriously, to his broad forehead, where his hair was beginning to recede, although I knew now that I wouldn't shoot him. He, however, couldn't know that, he had no idea, and that was my great advantage, that he could not interpret me, no one can in such circumstances, not even the best of interpreters. Not even Wheeler or Pérez Nuix or Tupra would have been able to, as the report on me said: 'Sometimes he seems to me to be a complete enigma. And sometimes I think he's an enigma to himself. Then I go back to the idea that he doesn't know himself very well. And that he doesn't pay much attention to himself because he's given up understanding himself. He considers himself a lost cause upon whom it would be pointless squandering thought. He knows he doesn't understand himself and that he never will. And so he doesn't waste his time trying to do so. I don't think he's dangerous. But he is to be feared.' Custardoy didn't know at that point that I wasn't dangerous, but he knew I was to be feared.

'Put your hands on the table.' I said this calmly, it seemed to me unnecessary to raise my voice or to swear. 'Or would you prefer me to put a bullet in your head so that then there'll be nothing at all? It wouldn't be hard, it would only take a moment.' Yes, how strange that someone should obey our every order and be at our mercy and do whatever we want.

He squeezed his eyes tight shut when he felt the cold metal of the pistol on his skin, this skin of ours that resists nothing, which offers no protection and is so easily wounded that even a fingernail can scratch it, and a knife can cut it and a spear rip it open, and a sword can tear it even as it slices through the air, and a bullet destroy it. (Blood was seeping from the wound to his cheek, but it wasn't running down his cheek, it was just coagulating along the wound itself.) I saw the look on his face, the look of someone who thinks or knows he is dead; but since he was still alive, the image was one of infinite fear and struggle, mental struggle, of desire perhaps; his face turned deathly pale, just as if someone had given it a quick lick of grey or off-white or off-color paint, or had thrown flour over him or perhaps talcum powder, it was rather like when swift clouds cast a shadow over the fields and a shudder runs through the flocks below, or like the hand that spreads the plague or closes the eyes of the deceased, because one is always instantly aware of any real danger of death and one believes in it and awaits the moment. Like De la Garza, he preferred to wait with eyes tight shut, they were trembling or pulsating—perhaps his pupils were racing about madly beneath the lids. And he put his hands on the table, you bet he did, the injured and the sound hand, the former he had difficulty placing flat. And again I acted quickly, I neither lingered nor delayed, I was sick of his company and wanted to get out of there fast; I was sick of his face too, despite its benign appearance, I used the poker to strike the same hand a second and a third time and just as hard, I think I broke the lower part of his fingers or some of them, between hand and knuckle, that's what it sounded like. He let out another two howls and clutched his left hand with his still intact right hand, he couldn't help but console the one with the other, his left was a terrible mess, but I tried not to look, I didn't want to see it or to contemplate my work as I had contemplated the broken hands of Pérez Nuix's father in that video as he tried in vain to protect himself as he lay sprawled on a billiards table, I didn't want to know exactly what damage I had done to him, if I didn't look, it would be easier for me to believe—later on, in years to come and, shortly too, when I went back to my hotel—that it had merely been one of those dreams one has abroad (I had a return ticket and abroad for me, at least in part, was Spain, and I was leaving). Despite the awful pain, Custardoy must have thought this nothing, a piece of good luck, when he had feared for his good hand and feared receiving a bullet in the brain at point-blank range. However, he still had sufficient courage to complain. Despite his panic, he remained unshaken, not at all like that dickhead De la Garza.

'What the fuck do you want,' he said, 'to cripple me?'

And then I told him what it was I wanted:

'I haven't touched your right hand, but I could give it the same treatment as your left hand or worse. And I can come looking for you whenever I want. I could hurt your right hand so badly that you'd never pick up a paintbrush again in your life.' And once more I couldn't help remembering Reresby again, when he gave me his instructions for De la Garza and I translated them to my compatriot where he lay on the floor. Tupra had issued a fluent list of orders as if he had thought it all out before, I must give the same impression of determination and wisdom and prescience, telling him what my pre-prepared plans for him were, telling him exactly what was going to happen and what he was going to do.

Custardoy had half-opened his eyes to gauge the damage done and I had not placed the barrel of the gun against his head again since dealing the second and third blow to his hand. His gaze was dull, stunned, almost oblique, but there was also a hint of vengefulness. Nevertheless, it seemed to me that any desire for revenge was muted and purely hypothetical, as if he understood that he would have to give it up however much he wanted it, or could see it only as a distant hope or postponed reward or deferred justice, rather as, during many centuries, people of steadfast faith would imagine and nurture the idea of the Final Judgment as something that would be given to them during their long death and which they could never have in life. I had removed the gun from his head when I struck him with the poker, and now it occurred to me that I didn't even need it, the threat of destroying his right hand had cowed him completely, overwhelmed him, especially as he didn't know if that was going to happen right there and then, and because he already had before him the vision of his left hand, and could feel it—the pain must have been terrible. In the state he was in, his ponytail looked even more ridiculous, as did his tie, his sparse mustache, his aspiration to elegance; at that moment he was an angry man, but fearful, too, almost imploring, his rage curbed indefinitely. However, I still didn't put the pistol away. And he did plead with me, although his tone of voice masked the fact. His words sounded more like a reproach than a plea, but they said what they said:

'For Christ's sake, don't do that. I earn my living with my right hand. Stop playing fucking games with me. What the fuck do you want?' Swearwords are good at masking feelings, of course, which is why almost everyone uses them in Spain—the most puerile, blustering country I know—in order to appear big and brave. But Custardoy had asked a favor of me ('Don't do that') and I did not, on that occasion, feel involved or enmeshed or entangled; on the contrary, I would happily have used a razor or a knife to cut the disagreeable bond joining us, him, Luisa and me, although she had created that bond of her own accord. All I had to say to the guy was: 'I want this in exchange.'

'I'm going to leave now and you're going to stay here quite still for thirty minutes from the time I leave, without moving and without phoning anyone, however much your hand hurts; you'll have to put up with it. Then call a doctor, go to a hospital, do what you like. It will take time for that hand to heal, if it ever does completely heal. Always remember that it could have been worse, and that we can always do the same to the other hand, or cut it off with a sword, I have a very clever friend in London who loves swords. While it's healing, leave Madrid, I know you've got enough money to be able to spend some time at a hotel, in a place that you like, somewhere with museums, and have a real rest. And if none of these ideas appeal, then do something else. I don't want Luisa to see you in this state; she must never ever associate what has happened to you with my stay in Madrid. You phone her and tell her that you've had to go away unexpectedly. Some important, urgent commission, copying or restoring some painting, or several, in Berlin, Bordeaux, Vienna or St. Petersburg, I don't care. Or better still, Boston, Baltimore, or Malibu, with an ocean between you, after all, there are famous museums aplenty over there with no shortage of cash to pay you for your work; anyway, I'll leave you to invent something. Call her from a cell phone or some number that can't be traced, just so that she can't find out where you really are. You can go and convalesce in Pamplona for all I care, but you must tell her that you're far away and very busy and that you'll phone her when you can, just in case, because if she thinks you're somewhere near, she might try and leave the kids with someone for a few days and come and join you.'

'She won't just let me go off like that without saying goodbye, especially if I'm going to be away for a while,' said Custardoy, interrupting me. I didn't mind because this meant he was accepting my plan and was prepared to obey it, and that I wouldn't have to damage his other hand or even consider doing so, because I would then have no other hold over him and would have to shoot him and that now seemed to me impossible. I had lost all my heat, what little I'd had. I had taken on Tupra's coldness only momentarily and half-heartedly. Perhaps not even Tupra was so very cold: after all, he hadn't, in the end, cut off De la Garza's head.

'Don't you understand? She won't be able to say goodbye to you, however much she wants to, because when you phone her, you'll already have left, you'll call her from somewhere else, do you see?'

'She'll think that very odd.'

'Try to make it seem perfectly normal. Emergencies do happen, as do unforeseen events. Besides, you don't see each other every day, do you? Or phone each other on a daily basis?' I wasn't expecting an answer, and I preferred him not to give one. 'While you're away, only call her now and then, and make those calls less and less frequent, until, in two weeks or so, you'll have stopped phoning altogether. After two weeks, you give no sign of life at all, none, and if she does manage to locate you, be evasive with her, impatient. And when your hand has healed and you come back (if that wretched hand of yours ever does heal after what I've done to it), you won't call her then either. Sooner or later, she'll hear from someone that you're back, and if she's still interested, she'll be the one to seek you out or phone you or demand an explanation. And you can tell her then, bluntly and arrogantly, it should come easily enough to you, you've probably done it hundreds of time. As far as you're concerned, you'll say, she's history, you never even give her a thought. Tell her that on the beaches of Malibu you've met the new Bo Derek or a lady security guard or Getty's daughter or whoever. Or an heiress from Boston whom you're about to marry. You make it clear to her that it's all over, that she should leave you alone, that you don't want to see her. And you won't see her. As of today, you've said your farewells, do you understand? And if you utter one word to her about what has happened here, about this visit, if you lead her to suspect or, however remotely, imagine what went on, now or later, even if it's in ten years' time, you can say farewell to your right hand as well.' The words of the 'Streets of Laredo' came into my mind: 'But please not one word of all this shall you mention, when others should ask for my story to hear.'

Custardoy opened his coarse eyes a little wider, he looked suddenly older, as if the weariness that follows immediately on relief had put ten years on him. He was cautiously stroking his crippled hand, he must have been impatient for this to be over, to be rid of me once and for all, so that he could go to a doctor or a hospital, where they could do something to take away the pain.

'I'm not the marrying kind, I'm not like you,' he said with a tiny, barely perceptible remnant of scorn, which I nonetheless noticed. It didn't matter, it afforded him some small compensation. He didn't know that I *was* like him, even though I had gotten married, contrary to my father's expectations. 'Anything else?'

'Like I said, you stay here for half an hour without moving and without phoning anyone. You never lay a hand on her again. You never see her again. I'll know if you don't do as I say, and London is only two hours away. It would be easy enough for me to fly over and cut off your hand.'

I flung the poker into the fireplace, it had a little blood on it, but I'd leave him to clean it off. I removed the third unused bullet, put the pistol in my raincoat pocket and headed for the door without taking my eyes off him, until he disappeared from my field of vision. There he was sitting on his sofa, with his clothes all rumpled, his hand shattered and a mark on his face. He held my gaze, despite his sudden tiredness, his abrupt senescence. No one has ever looked at me with such hatred. Nevertheless, I wasn't afraid that he would try anything, that he would grab the poker and hit me on the back of the head. The terror and humiliation he had experienced might have made him risk doing something like that. His hatred, however, was impotent, frustrated and without consequences, it was tinged with fear and shock; or it was like the hatred of a child condemned to remain too long in the incongruous body of a boy, obliged to endure a fruitless wait that consumes him, but which he will no longer remember when he does finally grow up. He was looking at me in the knowledge that I was no longer within his grasp and would not be for a long time, possibly never: like a furious adolescent looking out at a world slipping by before his eyes and which he's not yet allowed to enter; or like a prisoner who knows that no one is waiting or refraining from doing anything just because he's not there, and that his own time is disappearing along with the world rushing by him, and that he can do nothing about it; it's a common experience among the dying too, only far more tragic.

When I left the living room, he disappeared from my view. His eyes, dark with hatred, had followed me right until then, and he may have kept his gaze fixed for a few seconds more on the door through which my gloved figure had departed. It would take him a while to get used to the idea of what he had to do. And then he would find it hard to believe that what had happened to him had really happened, but he had a useful reminder, or two; now he would feel on his hand and cheek what Luisa had felt with her black eye and its thousand colors and perhaps before that, according to her sister, the cut, also on her face. He would have many days ahead of him to observe the evolution of his scar, and to hope that the small bones in his hand were knitting together under the cast or whatever it is they use now, although an operation might also prove necessary. He would look at his good hand and think perhaps: 'I've been lucky. At least this hand is still intact.' And he would remember the metal barrel against his forehead and then he would think: 'I've been lucky. He could have shot me, I thought he was going to. But we would always prefer it to be the person beside us who dies, every man for himself. I was saved and here I am.'

I hurried down the stairs ('"Do I dare?" and "Do I dare?" Time to turn back and descend the stair . . .'), anxious to leave the building and get away from there, to take a taxi and return Miquelín's old pistol to him as soon as possible, having first replaced the three bullets I had removed from the magazine, and to say to him: 'A thousand thanks, Maestro, I'll never forget this. Don't worry, here it is, there's not a bullet missing. It hasn't even got my fingerprints on it. It's as if you had never lent it to me, as if it had never left your apartment.'

None of the taxis passing by were free, the sky was still cloudy, full of thunderless lightning about to strike but never doing so, and so I set off, walking briskly, following the same straight route back, along Calle Mayor to my hotel, still with my gloves on, I wanted to get away from that place. I felt the lightness one feels on getting what one wants and a little of the conceit I had experienced when I discovered that Rafita was afraid of me, that, quite unwittingly, I filled him with fear. Seeing yourself as dangerous had its good side. It made you feel more confident, more optimistic, stronger. It made you feel important and—how can I put it—in charge. And, this time, that small rush of vanity did not immediately repel me. However, I also had a sudden feeling of heaviness, a feeling that can be triggered by various combinations: alarm and haste, the sense of tedium experienced at the prospect of having to carry out some cold-blooded act of reprisal, or the invincible meekness one feels in a threatening situation. I did feel something of that tedium, as well as haste, but my act of reprisal was over and done with. Only when I reached Plaza de la Villa and saw again the statue of the Marqués de Santa Cruz ('I was the scourge of the Turk at Lepanto, the Frenchman at Terceira, the Englishman o'er all the seas . . .' 'And in short, they were afraid') did I begin to think repeatedly, over and over: 'You can't go around beating people up, you can't go around killing them. Why can't you? You can't go around beating people up . . . Why can't one, according to you, go around beating people up and killing them? Why not? According to you.' And I remembered, too, what Tupra had said when we were at his house, after our session watching his store of videos: 'You've seen how much of it goes on, everywhere, and sometimes with an utter lack of concern. So explain to me why one can't.' And I gave myself the answer that I managed to give him just before we were interrupted by Beryl or whoever that woman was, the person at his side, his weak point just as Luisa was mine: 'Because then it would be impossible for anyone to live.' I had received no response to those words of mine, but by the time I reached Puerta del Sol, my thoughts had changed, and this was all they were repeating: 'What a lot of one-eyed, one-handed people there are in these old streets, but at least he's out of the picture. What a lot of cripples and what a lot of dead people there are in these old streets, but at least he's out of the picture. Yes, at least he's out of the picture and he'd better not try and climb back in.'

I didn't in fact think much about anything until I was in the plane on my way back to London, by which I mean that I postponed any form of ordered thought and, during the few days that remained of my stay in Madrid, restricted myself to feelings, sensations and intuitions. I devoted those days to the children and to taking them out and about (they were as insatiable as all children are nowadays, I suppose they've lost the habit of being at home, which feels to them like imprisonment, and require constant distractions in the exhausting outside world) and to visiting my father, who was getting very slowly, but perceptibly, worse.

The last time I went to see him, on the eve of my departure, he was, as he almost always was, sitting in his armchair, fingers interlaced, like someone who waits patiently without knowing what exactly it is he's waiting for—perhaps for night to fall and for day to come again—and now and then he would unconsciously raise his fingers to his eyebrows and smooth them, or use thumb and forefinger to rub or stroke the skin beneath his lower lip, a characteristic gesture of his, a meditative gesture. But I found it quite distressing to see him like that, in that strange waiting state, barely speaking to me, with me having to do all the talking and trying to draw from him the occasional word, racking my brain for questions and topics of conversation that might make him react and come to life—and without him putting into words or spontaneously offering me the results of his meditations, as he normally would; he had suddenly become as impenetrable as a baby, for babies must think about their surroundings, since they're equipped to do so, but it's utterly impossible to know what those thoughts are. At last, after various failed attempts to interest him in recent news and events, I asked:

'What are you thinking about?'

'About the cousins.'

'What cousins?'

'Whose do you think? Mine.'

'But you don't have any cousins, you never have,' I said, feeling slightly alarmed.

He looked somewhat taken aback, as if he were making a mental correction, then immediately adjusted his expression and did not insist, but answered again as if for the first time.

'About my Uncle Víctor,' he said. 'Ask him to please tell my father that I'm coming home.'

There had been an Uncle Víctor, but both he and my grandfather had been dead a long time, so long that I'd never even known them, either of them. This was the first time his mind had strayed like that, at least when I'd been with him. Although, perhaps that isn't the right way to put it—what had strayed was time itself, which, contrary to what we tend to believe, never entirely passes, just as we never entirely cease to be what we once were, and it's not that odd to slip back into the past so vividly that it becomes juxtaposed with the present, especially if it's the present of an old man, which offers him so little and is so unvaried, its days indistinguishable. Anyone who waits patiently or without knowing what exactly it is he's waiting for is perfectly justified in deciding to install himself in a more pleasing or more appropriate time; after all, if today chooses to ignore him, he's perfectly within his rights to ignore today— there's no room for complaint on either side.

'But your father's dead,' I said, correcting him again, 'he's been dead for years, as has your Uncle Víctor.'

Again he did not insist, but replied:

'I know they're dead. You're hardly telling me anything new, Jacobo.' And he gave an indulgent laugh as if I were the person whose mind was rambling.

Perhaps my father now came and went in time with great facility and speed. Perhaps he was now the master of time and held in his hand the hourglass or clock, of himself or of his existence, and while he calmly watched time advance he was traveling wherever he pleased. Maybe that's the only thing left to the very old, especially if they're not astute old men, as Wheeler is, and no longer struggle to fill the vacancies, to seek out substitutes or replacements for the many people they have lost throughout their life; and are no longer part of the universal, continual, sub-stitutional mechanism or movement—which, being everyone's lot, is also ours—and they stop accumulating and surrounding themselves with poor imitations, choosing instead to rediscover the originals in all their plenitude. They have no further need of flabby, pale, elusive life, only of thought, which becomes in them ever more potent and clear and all-embracing, since it only oc-casionally has to live alongside reality.

'You've got a pistol, haven't you?' it occurred to me to ask him then. It would turn up when he died, and I feared that his death would not be long in coming; and one of us, my brothers, my sister or myself, would inherit it as Miquelín had inherited from his father the Llama I had just held in my hands. Perhaps it would, in the future, be useful for me to know where to find an-other 'clean' pistol, without having to borrow it from someone.

A little surprised, he looked at me with those clear eyes of his that now saw only dimly.

'Yes. Why do you ask?' And this topic seemed to rouse him or return him to today.

'Where did it come from? Why have you got it?' I asked, not answering his question.

He raised one hand to his eyebrows, not this time in order to smooth them abstractedly, but in order to think or remember.

'Well, my father was very keen on guns. He wasn't just a hunter, he was a marksman. He loved that and was very good at it. He was a member of the National Shooting Club and owned a lot of weapons. A Mauser carbine; a Baker rifle; a very ornate Le Page target pistol; and even a Monkey Tail, although I can't recall now why they called it that; pistols and revolvers, some of them very old, from the Wild West era; there was an American LeMat and an English Beaumont-Adams and a couple of Derringers, one of them with a double barrel, and pistols from the seventeenth or eighteenth century, and I can remember him having a heavily gilded Blunderbuss, a Miquelet dueling pistol, and a silver-inlaid "Queen Anne," a really fine collection. And then there were knives and swords as well from exotic countries: gumias and yatagans, bolos from the Philippines, a Malay kris . . . As well as rapiers of course.' He paused and then remembered two more. 'Oh, and a Nepalese kukri and even an Indian bhuj, which was very rare, half-knife, half-axe, it was also known as an "elephant head," because it had a brass likeness of an elephant's head between blade and haft, which was long and narrow . . .' He was seeing it, I realized that he was actually seeing that bhuj from his childhood as well as all the other weapons, with that gaze so frequent in the old even when they're in company and talking animatedly, the eyes become dull, the iris dilated, staring far, far back into the past, as if their owners really could physically see with them, could see their memories I mean. It's not an absent look, but a focused one, focused on something a very long way away. And after a brief moment's absorption in thought, he went on: 'He passed on that enthusiasm to both my brother and me, but especially to me. He used to show them to us and explain all about them, and we got used to handling them with scrupulous care.'

'But what did he want with knives and swords? You can't shoot with them, can you? In the National Shooting Club, they don't let you fling a Malay kris at someone, do they?'

Now he was genuinely interested in the conversation, or at least in that remote reminiscence, and so he reacted quickly to my joke, amused but pretending not to be:

'Honestly, you are a silly lot, you never miss a chance to make some foolish remark.' He used the plural 'you' to encompass all four of his children, as he often did even when only one of us was present. 'Of course he couldn't use them to shoot with, he just liked them, I suppose. He was born in 1870, and people then had a liking for weapons in general. It was quite normal. And they were rarely put to criminal use as they are now.'

'Hm,' I said, 'although it doesn't seem very sensible to let children handle them. You and your brother could have blown each other's heads off or cut each other's throats. You say he owned rapiers as well. I know how sharp they can be. Nowadays, the authorities, no, what am I saying, the neighbors would have hit the roof over something like that. They'd have had your father locked up.'

The expression 'locked up' applied to his father must have annoyed him, even though I was the one using it and only jokingly.

'People do a lot of stupid things nowadays,' he replied reproachfully, as if I were one of those authorities or neighbors. 'Nowadays, everyone's afraid of everything, and people have very little freedom in their personal lives and less and less freedom in how they bring up their children. Before, we used to teach children all kinds of things as soon as they reached the age of reason, which is why it's called that, things that could be useful when they grew up, because in those days you never forgot that a child would one day be an adult. Not like now, it seems that adults are supposed to continue being children into old age, and idiotic cowardly children at that. That's why there's so much silliness everywhere.' He raised his fingers to his lips again and murmured: 'It's sad watching an era in decline, when one has known other far more intelligent eras. Where's it going to end? It will be one of the reasons I won't overly regret my departure, which, I believe, is quite close.'

'No, not that close, besides, who knows,' I answered, 'you'll probably outlive us all. No one knows who will die when, do they?' And when he didn't reply, I asked again: 'Do they?'

'No,' he agreed, 'but there is something called the calculation of probabilities, which works with some degree of accuracy. It would be an act of gratuitous cruelty if, at this point in my life, one of you were to die before me. It would be for all of you, but most of all for me. God forbid.' In his place, I would have touched wood. Not because I believe in wood, but simply as a gesture.

The conversation had taken a melancholy turn, which was

precisely what we tried to avoid with any topic or subject that might serve to distract him while he waited for the night and for the day, and for all the subsequent nights and days, until there were no more. This was my last visit before going back to London, and I would not be back in Madrid for a while. 'Perhaps I'll never see him again,' I thought with dismay. (And I realized as I did so, that I was *thinking* the Spanish word '*desmayo*,' meaning 'fainting fit,' but *meaning* the English word 'dismay.') And so I placed one hand on his shoulder, a gesture he liked and that calmed him, but this time I did so to calm myself, to feel his bones and to accompany his breathing.

'Anyway, what were you saying?' I went back to what had roused and entertained him a little. 'That your pistol is from your father's collection?'

'No, of course not. The whole collection disappeared years ago, when the lean times came. My father would make a few big business deals and in the ensuing euphoria spend all the profits and, as you know, invest them in foolish things. Then, when common sense returned, he'd more or less recover those losses, but there came a point when recovery was impossible. The few remaining pieces were sold at the start of the Civil War, and his collection of clocks and watches suffered the same fate. Some may even have been confiscated.'

'So where does the pistol come from?'

'I've had it since the War, it's a 7.65 caliber Astra De Luxe. It's quite nice for a Spanish pistol, rather ornate, with the barrel etched in silver and a mother-of-pearl handle. Why do you ask?'

'Oh, nothing, just curious. May I see it? I've never seen you handling it. Where is it?'

'I don't know,' he said at once, and it didn't sound like an excuse not to have to show it to me. 'The last time I had it in my hands, years ago now, I decided to hide it away somewhere, so that the grandchildren wouldn't ever stumble across it when they come here and start rummaging around in everything. You had your mother to keep a check on you, but she's not here any more. And I must have hidden it so well that I now have no idea where I put it. I've forgotten. It was complete with bullets, well-preserved and well-oiled. What do you want it for?' It's odd, it was as if he knew that I wanted it for myself. This wasn't quite true, I had done what I had to do with another borrowed weapon, and so I no longer needed it, but carrying a gun in one's pocket certainly gave a sense of security.

'No, I don't want it,' I said. 'I was just curious. Why did you take the risk of keeping it after the Civil War? If they'd caught you with it during the Franco regime, if they'd searched the apartment, you'd have had it, especially with your record. Why did you keep it? Why do you still keep it, even though you can't remember where it is?'

My father remained silent for a moment, as if, perhaps, it was hard for him to give an answer or as if he needed to ponder his reply, I'm not sure. Then he said succinctly:

'You never know.'

'You never know what?'

'What you might need.'

He had always told me that, during the War, he'd been lucky—in one respect—to be able to stay in Madrid, consigned to administrative duties because of his short sight. And although he wore the uniform of the Republican Army, he had never been sent to the front and never fired a single shot. And he used to say how happy he was about that, because he could also be absolutely certain that he had never killed anyone, that he had never been in a position to kill anyone. I reminded him of this:

'You've always said how glad you were that you could be certain that, in the War, you'd never killed anyone, that you never had the chance. That doesn't quite tally with hanging on to a pistol afterwards, when things weren't so bad. I mean when life was less exposed and less chaotic, although during a dictatorship, of course, no one is safe. Why didn't you hand it in or get rid of it?'

'Because after you've lived through a war, you never know,' he said again. And then he fell silent, his hands resting on the arms of his chair, as if he were gathering the momentum to say something more, and so I waited. And he did say something more: 'Yes, I'm very glad that I never killed anyone. But that doesn't mean I wouldn't have if there'd been no other option. If any of you or your mother had been under threat of death and I could have prevented that, I'm sure I would have done so. When you were small, I mean, because now it's different, you can look after yourselves. I don't imagine I would kill for you now. Apart from the fact that I'm hardly in a position to do so—I mean, look at me—you're perfectly capable of doing whatever might be necessary. You don't need me for that any more. Besides, I wouldn't know if you deserved saving now, you lead your own lives and I don't know what you get up to. Before, it was different, I knew everything about you, when you were little and living at home. I had all the facts in hand, but not now. It's odd how your children become semi-strangers, there are lots of parents who won't accept that and stand staunchly by their children whatever the situation, even against all the evidence. I know the person you were and I think I can still recognize that person in you now. But I don't really know you as I knew that child, not at all; and it's the same with your brothers and your sister. Your mother, on the other hand, I knew until the end, and I would have killed for her until the end.' Now both mind and time were working perfectly, and after the briefest of pauses to mark the parenthesis, he returned to what we had been talking about before. 'You never know, never, and it may be that one day you might have to use a pistol. Look what happened in Europe during the Second World War. For a long time, we had no way of knowing if it would spread to Spain, despite Franco's promises, as if we could trust those, and the endless evasions and delaying tactics he used with Hitler. I don't know if you realize it, but during that War they had to use every resource they had, whatever it was, no one could keep back so much as a cartridge, whether legally or illegally acquired. It was much worse than our war in one sense. In another way, of course, it wasn't so bad. In a qualitative sense, the war here was worse.' Again he stopped and looked at me hard, although I had the feeling then that he wasn't seeing me at all, that he was looking as the blind do, without calculating distances. I noticed that he was excited by what he was about to say. 'But the thing I feel happiest about, Jacobo, is that no one ever died because of something I said or reported. Shooting someone, during a war or in self-defense, is bad, but at least you can go on living and not lose your decency or humanity, not necessarily. However, if someone dies because of something you said or, worse still, invented; if someone dies needlessly because of you; if you could have remained silent and allowed that person to go on living; if you spoke out when you should or could have said nothing and by doing so brought about a death, or several . . . I don't believe that's something you could live with, although many do, or seem to.'—'That was perhaps how it was before,' I had time to think or thought later on when I was flying back to London and remembering our conversation, 'my father still imagines he's living in a world in which deeds left some trace and in which conscience had a voice—not always, of course, but for the majority of people. Now, on the other hand, it's the other way round: it's easy to silence or gag the majority, sometimes it's not even necessary: it's even easier to persuade them that there's no reason to speak out. The tendency nowadays is to believe that one is innocent, to find some immediate justification for everything, and not to feel one has to answer for one's actions or, as we say in Spanish, "*cargarse de razón*," I don't know how exactly one would say that in English, but it doesn't matter, I've lost the habit of speaking that other language all the time, although tomorrow I'll have to. Of course, people nowadays can live with that and with far worse things. People whose consciences torment them are the exception, as are old-fashioned people who think: "Spear, fever, my pain, words, sleep and dreams," and other similarly pointless thoughts.'—My father went on: 'And in our War there was so much of that, so much treachery and so much poison, so many slanderers, defamers and professional rabble-rousers, all tirelessly dedicated to sowing and fomenting hatred and viciousness, envy, and a desire to exterminate, on both sides, especially on the winning side, but on both sides . . . it wasn't easy to be entirely clean in that respect, perhaps in that respect least of all. And it was even more difficult for anyone who wrote for a newspaper or spoke on the radio, as I did during the War. You can't imagine the things that were read or heard, not just during those three years, but for many years afterwards. One sentence was all it took to send someone to the firing squad or the gutter. And yet I'm sure that I never said or wrote one word that could have proved seriously prejudicial to anyone. Nor later either, in the strictly personal sphere of my life after that. I never gave away a secret or a confidence, however small, I never told anyone about what I knew from having seen or heard something if that might do harm and if I didn't need to tell it in order to save or exonerate someone. And that, Jacobo, is what pleases me most.' My father was, I thought, drawing up a balance sheet of his life before he died. And for a second I wondered if it really was as he said or if he was deceiving himself like a man of my time rather than a man of his, and that he might perhaps have let something slip which, later, had terrible consequences. It was impossible to know. Even he couldn't know that, it's simply not possible to remember everything, as if you were the Judge of that old and steadfast faith. And sometimes we never find out about the consequences. I thought of those 'careless talk' cartoons that Wheeler had shown me: how could a sailor possibly imagine that something he had told his girlfriend could result in the sinking of a ship full of his compatriots? There's never any way of knowing this, that one is saying farewell with no weight on one's conscience. Then I remembered something else and it occurred to me that it was a memory that would help him to convince himself.

'You never wanted to tell me the name of that writer who took part in the baiting of your friend Marés, for example,' I said. 'And there was no reason why you shouldn't tell me or anyone.'

He looked slightly surprised, as if he had completely forgotten about that conversation we'd had a long time ago, when I was still living in Madrid. And from what he went on to say, it did seem that he'd forgotten I even knew about that episode.

'You know about that.' And this was a mixture of statement and question.

'Yes. You told me once.'

'And I didn't want to tell you, eh?' This was clearly a question. 'I didn't want to tell you the name, eh?'

'No. Because of his wife and his daughters. You said you didn't want to risk being the indirect cause of someone later dragging the whole business up and rubbing their noses in it. Even though, if I remember rightly, his wife is dead now too.'

'Yes, they're both dead. But that doesn't change anything.' And he said in a murmur intended more for him than for me: 'I didn't want to tell you, you say. Good, yes, very good . . .'

He sat there thinking, and his blue eyes took on the fixed intense gaze that did not, in a way, see me. And a few seconds later, I had the impression that the act of recalling those people had again transported him back to a distant time when my mother was alive, and the kindly cheerful wife of that infamous man was being so very very good to us and, in particular, to her. I let two or three minutes pass in silence. He was not speaking now and he looked tired. Perhaps I should leave, even if that might be the last time we would see each other.

'I'm going, Papa,' I said, and I got up and kissed him on the forehead.

'Where?' he asked in astonishment, as if he thought it utterly absurd that I or any of his children should go anywhere.

'To my hotel and then tomorrow I'll catch the plane back to London.'

'Oh, you're off on a trip. Well, have a good journey, son.'

'I live in London now, Papa. Have you forgotten?'

'Ah, so you live in exile,' he said, without giving that last word any solemnity at all. 'Like the Greek gods.'

'The Greek gods?' I didn't know what he was referring to or what that remark had to do with anything. But he never lost the thread, at least I never saw him do so. He might abstract himself from time and people and circumstances, but his mind and his memory were always working, albeit, at the end, very much after their own fashion. Then again, all minds and memories do that.

'Don't you remember that Heine poem?' he said, and immediately began to recite the lines in German, from memory. He had learned the language as a boy, at school, which was possible in the 1920s, but unimaginable now, and he had always prided himself on being able to recite whole poems, by Goethe, Novalis, Hölderlin, the giants of German literature.

'No, Papa,' I said, interrupting him, 'I can't possibly remember something I've never known, and, besides, I don't understand what you're saying. I never learned German, remember?'

'Honestly. You never learned German,' he replied with slight paternal scorn, as if not knowing German were an oddity, almost a defect. 'What kind of education did you have?' And he went on to explain, out of sympathy for my ignorance and out of enthusiasm for this poem from his youth: 'The poet sees a bank of white clouds in the middle of the night and these seem to him, as he puts it, like "colossal statues of the gods made out of luminous marble." Then he realizes that they *are* the gods, Chronos, Zeus, Hera, Pallas Athene, Aphrodite, Ares, Hermes, Phoebus Apollo, Hephaestus and Hebe, grown old and at the mercy of the elements, cast down and numb with cold in their exile. "No," exclaims the poet, "these are no clouds!"' And my father began translating the poem for me, drawing it slowly out of his memory. 'They are the gods of Hellas, the very gods who once so blithely ruled the world, but who now, supplanted and deceased, ride like giant specters the clouds of midnight . . .' But the words insisted on coming to him in the German of his childhood, or perhaps he found it wearisome having to translate, and so he lapsed back into German, and, at the time, I understood nothing more.

Later on, after his death, I tried to identify the words I had listened to without understanding them. I searched out a bilingual edition of 'The Greek Gods,' in German and English (I couldn't find one in Spanish), and it was doubtless this verse that he had translated into my language in tentative extempore fashion: '*Nein, nimmermehr, das sind keine Wolken! Das sind sie selber, die Götter von Hellas, die einst so freudig die Welt beherrschten, doch jetzt, verdrängt und verstorben, als ungeheure Gespenster dahinziehn am mitternächtlichen Himmel . . .*' I assume he had a good accent. And I also noticed two other brief passages that he must have recited in German that day. In one, the poet addressed Zeus and said to him, more or less: 'Not even the gods rule eternally, the old gods are driven out and supplanted by the young, just as you yourself once deposed your grey-haired father . . .' The other was an image applied to that troop of disoriented deities adrift in the dark, whom he describes as: 'Dead shadows who wander the night, fragile as the mist that the wind drives away.' Those words must have come from his lips when I was there with him, even though, at the time, I couldn't understand them. And I wondered what he would have thought then, as he spoke them.

While he sat, absorbed in his own recitation, I bent down and kissed him again before leaving, this time on the cheek, as if we were bullfighters, and I placed my hand once more on his shoulder for a moment, like a silent farewell, while he was walking into the mist that the wind drives away, or into that exile in which one has to leave even one's own first name behind.

I had also managed not to think too much about Luisa until I was on the plane, in business class, an Iberia flight, which was, characteristically and infuriatingly, an hour late in leaving. My not thinking about Luisa had been helped by the fact that she didn't once suggest we have lunch or supper together, and I didn't insist or protest or express regret; after what I had done, I preferred to avoid such a meeting—I didn't feel I deserved it, and although I very much wanted to see her, I found it easy enough to resist and to pretend. And so we only met briefly and occasionally at the apartment when I went to pick up or return the children or stayed with them for a while until they went to bed. And once they were in bed, she never offered me a drink or invited me to sit down for a moment to chat. She didn't eject me with excuses or with words, but by her attitude: she was constantly doing things, going back and forth, cleaning, washing dishes and glasses, answering the phone, tidying, picking up toys and clothes and notebooks and pencils—children always leave everything in a mess and never cease creating chaos—and it wasn't as it used to be when we lived together, when I would follow her from room to room, talking about something or other or telling or asking her something, as husbands often do trail through the house or apartment after their wives, who are more active physically and tend not to sit still in one place for very long, especially if they are mothers. I no longer felt I had that right, I mean, to go into just any room, not even into the kitchen, even accompanied by her or, rather, following in her footsteps. And so we would simply exchange a few words about the children or about my father's health, for she always asked after him, adding with feeling, 'I really must go and see him, I'll go this week without fail, be sure to give him my love,' and I would leave, having given her a discreetly affectionate, that is almost friendly, kiss on each cheek, to which she responded passively and rather mechanically, hardly noticing.

Her mind was elsewhere and I knew where. She seemed rather subdued on the last few occasions I saw her. I thought: 'She's heard that she won't be seeing Custardoy for a while, a great disappointment that's caught her unawares and which she's still trying to absorb, so there's one less incentive now, probably the biggest incentive, the one that helped her to get through the day, to wake up filled with hope and go to bed contented, but that incentive will be missing from her life for good—that's something she doesn't yet know, nor that she will never see the man again or only if they happen to meet by chance; that knowledge will come later, gradually, whole weeks will pass, or possibly even more, before she fully understands that it's all over, that this isn't just an extended absence, but a final separation, like the one she has been inflicting on me for a long time now. And then she will look out the window as I sometimes look out of mine at the lazy London night and across the square, its pale darkness barely lit by those white streetlights that imitate the always thrifty light of the moon, and a little further off, at the lights of the elegant hotel and of the houses that shelter families or men and women on their own, each enclosed behind a protective yellow rectangle, as Luisa and I would seem to be to anyone watching us; and beyond the trees and the statue at my carefree, dancing neighbor, who, from now on, will always remind me of Custardoy, because these resemblances and affinities work reciprocally, and no one is immune to them: I will no longer like that happy dancing individual quite so much: he may unwittingly have saved a life, but, in doing so, has become contaminated by that same life. And neither Luisa nor I will dare to think, when alone: "I'll be more myself," not now that we've seen each other again and brought each other a new sadness, although she doesn't know that her current sadness comes from me.'

Strangely, given that I was the cause of the newly begun solitude that would gradually grow, I allowed myself to feel slightly sorry, seeing her like that, in such low spirits, lethargic, apathetic, possibly in the early stages of a lasting period of languor and decline, the loss of someone we love marks us very deeply, much more than that of someone who loved us, and I was sure now that for Luisa, Custardoy belonged in the first category. At least I was not so cynical as to tell myself it was for her own good, although it certainly would be in the long term: I knew now that it was, above all, for my good, for my relative tranquility, my peace of mind while I was far away, so that I wouldn't have to worry too much about her or about my children, and so that I need not give up the fanciful hopes I still clung on to, despite all the time that had elapsed. And that was something I did think about in the plane with a clarity I had so far avoided: that I had been selfish and abusive and inconsiderate, that I had meddled in her life in the worst possible way, behind her back, without her knowledge, not just without consulting her on what could or should be done, but without her even having spoken to me about a problem that she didn't see as a problem, but possibly as a solution. I had acted like some nineteenth-century father with regard to his daughter, I had gone over her head as if she were a minor, not by approaching the lowlife in question and paying him to disappear, as had perhaps been the tradition of wealthy authoritarian fathers in that century, but by threatening him with death and by injuring him. I began to find the whole thing unbelievable, that I should have behaved like that, without a flicker of conscience, like a savage or as if I were a believer in the pragmatic idea that if something needs to be done then it's best just to do it, so that regardless of what happens next, the deed is done and there's no going back ('I have done the deed'). Officially, I knew nothing about Custardoy, at least not as far as Luisa knew, or indeed anyone else, apart from her sister Cristina, whom I would have to warn, by phone again from London, as soon as she was back from her few days away—I couldn't remember if she'd said it would be a week or longer, I had already tried phoning each day during what remained of my stay in

Madrid, just in case, but without success—I hadn't even been able to speak to her husband; and I kept calling during the first few days after my return, trying different times until I finally found her in.

'Cristina, it's Jacques, your brother-in-law, Jaime,' I said when she answered the phone, on my twentieth attempt. 'I'm back in London, but I wanted to bring you up to date on an important matter. Have you spoken to Luisa?'

'No, not yet, I've only just gotten home, my trip lasted longer than expected. Why? Has something happened?'

'Nothing bad, no. During my stay in Madrid I sorted out that business between Custardoy and her, at least I think I did, we'll probably have to wait a bit to be sure.'

'Really?' she replied, and there was curiosity and undoubted approval in her voice. 'How? What did you do? Did you speak to him? Or to her? Tell me.'

'That's what I wanted to say, that it's best if you don't know and absolutely essential that Luisa doesn't. I mean she must never even find out that I knew anything, or that you told me anything. That story's over now, or very nearly. What I absolutely don't want is for her ever to suspect that I had anything to do with it. As far as she's concerned I don't even know of Custardoy's existence, she never once mentioned him to me, and I want her to continue believing that. Now and always. If, one day, you were to mention our conversation, even if it's in ten years' time, she might still put two and two together and never speak to me again, despite the kids. She might never speak to you again either. I may have been the one who did the deed, but she would probably think that you were part of it too, that you had provoked or prompted me to act. You understand, don't you? If you betray me, I'd have no qualms about betraying you too.'

Cristina clearly did understand, but she was still curious.

'You *are* keeping your cards close to your chest. Whatever did you do to him? You needn't worry, if you've managed to get rid of him, I'll be the first to celebrate and safeguard your achievement. But surely if we're both going to keep quiet about it, it hardly matters if I know everything. What did you say to the guy? What did you do to him? Come on, tell me, given that it was all done at my instigation.'

'As I said, it's best not to talk about it. I prefer him to be the only one who knows, so that if by some stroke of bad luck they should meet later on and she should corner him, he'd be the only one who could tell Luisa what happened, not that I think he would, it wouldn't be worth his while and it would merely be his word against mine, with no way of corroborating the facts. It's not that I don't trust you, now, I mean. But you never know. One day, you might be angry with me for some reason and want to harm me. If something is best not known, then it's best that no one knows about it, not even your accomplice. Why else do you think criminals are always bumping people off?'

Cristina took this well, she laughed and didn't press me further. She said only:

'Don't worry, I won't say anything to Luisa. I hope you're right and that this story *is* over. I'll act surprised if she mentions it, the break-up I mean. She might be having a rough time and want to get it off her chest or just talk to someone. And if something has happened to Custardoy, I'll be bound to find out somehow, you know how people gossip.'

'No, I don't think you will find out. He's not in Madrid at the moment and he won't be around for several weeks at least. And when he does come back, he'll invent some tale, if, that is, he still bears the marks of our encounter. A garage door perhaps, or a bollard.' I realized that I had already said too much, it's so easy to let your tongue run away with you, especially when you're boasting, and I *was* boasting a little, even though several days had passed: I did feel slightly proud of my exploit, pistol in hand, and had no problem forgetting that the word 'exploit' is entirely misplaced when the other party was unarmed. I knew perfectly well that such private bragging was unforgivable, especially after what I discovered on my arrival in London, or just before. And yet that's how it was, and I couldn't help myself; I imagine it must happen to any otherwise nonviolent person who, when forced to use violence, meets with success. And so I added: 'Not that I'm saying I did anything to him, or that anything happened to him. Anything bad, I mean.' (In that brief conversation I had trotted out some of the classic lines recommending denial, ignorance and silence, appropriate to espionage and conspiracies and criminality, to the clandestine and the underhand: 'It's best if you know nothing; then, if they interrogate you, you'll be telling the truth when you say you know nothing, the truth is easy, it has more force, it's more believable, the truth persuades.' And: 'If you know only about your part of the job, even if they catch you or you fail, the plan can still go ahead.' Not to mention: 'Your ignorance will be your protection, so don't ask any more questions, don't ask, it will be your salvation and your guarantee of safety.' And even: 'You know the score, I've never spoken to you or said anything. This conversation and this phone call never took place, you haven't even heard these words because I didn't say them. And even though you can hear the words now, I'm not saying them.')

Cristina laughed again, perhaps because she was glad to think that her sister was now out of danger.

'You sound very mysterious and a touch threatening,' she said, half-serious and half-joking. 'This isn't the Jaime I know. It would seem that London and being alone there suits you. Just one thing, whatever you've done, I'm not your accomplice. So there's no need to bump me off.'

All this happened days later, when I was back in London again, and feeling more anxious and that the situation had changed for the worse. What I *was* thinking about on that return flight was that Luisa had still said nothing about herself right up until the last moment. On the final day, on the eve of my departure, I had gone to the hotel to change after visiting my father and then to Luisa's apartment to say goodbye to the children and, in passing, to her.

'So, when will you be back again?' Guillermo had demanded in accusing tones, even as Marina was insisting that I take her with me, up in the air.

'This time,' I had lied, unaware then that I wasn't lying, 'I'll be back soon, I promise.' And I had likewise promised Marina that, on my next trip, I would take her with me to that large island, knowing full well that small children barely remember what's said to them from one day to the next, one of their many privileges.

That was the sole occasion when Luisa seemed about to invite me to sit down in the living room for a while, as if she had suddenly realized that we wouldn't see each other again for some time and that we hadn't had a single proper conversation; that she hadn't asked me about my life in London or about my work, my habits, my prospects or my general state of mind or about my friendships or possible lovers (on that last point I could have declined to answer, just as she had done), not even about the slovenly, dirty, drunken or crazy—and definitely pantyless—women who had possibly dripped blood in my house or in Wheeler's house and who had caused her such amusement. Her lack of curiosity, her lack of interest in me, had been very marked during my brief stay, and were it not for what I had done behind her back, for my brutal interference in her life—in a way I had ruined or torn down the life she was trying to rebuild—and for my consequent feeling that I was in her debt, such indifference would have been more than enough reason for me to feel offended and to mutter darkly to myself about it. She, however, was so distracted and doubtless so immersed in her own story that she didn't even find it odd, my apparent resignation to the situation or my excessively discreet behavior. She knew me well, probably better than anyone. She knew I was respectful and certainly not inclined to make a nuisance of myself, that I accepted what was given willingly and did not fight for what was denied to me, that my pride kept me from pestering anyone and that I acted in a roundabout way to achieve my ends, lingering and delaying for however long it took. Whichever way you looked at it, though, it was very strange that with time to spare I hadn't made more of an effort to see her alone, that I'd left all the initiative to her and taken a back seat, that I'd let the days pass without making myself a more obvious or visible presence and without demanding that we meet alone. All of these things should have made her suspicious, and yet they didn't. Her mind was otherwise occupied, doubtless with Custardoy, first with the incomprehensible excitement he aroused in her, and perhaps, too, with the tension she felt between desire and distrust—she must have seen that choosing a man like him would always, at least in part, be inadvisable—then with her disquiet at his abrupt and unexpected departure with barely a word of explanation, with her growing unease over his delay in phoning her, for he had perhaps not yet, as I had ordered, given any sign of life since his disappearance. ('While you're away, only call her now and then, and make those calls less and less frequent'), and when you wait in vain for something it does take on a degree of urgency and occupies all your time and fills up every space: you expect the doorbell to ring at any moment and each moment becomes intensely long and oppressive, like a knee digging into your chest, like lead upon the soul, until exhaustion overwhelms you and gives you a slight respite.

Perhaps it was precisely that kind of truce brought on by weariness that allowed her to look around for an instant and to see me, to remember who I was and to realize that I'd be gone the next day, and that she would have allowed me to pass through without—so to speak—making the most of me; that I was still there that night and could serve as a way of killing time and diverting her for a few minutes—with my stories about London, with comments or anecdotes about a world of which she knew nothing—from her obsessive thoughts that continued unabated. She would probably only have listened to me with half an ear, not even a whole one, like someone vaguely aware of the murmur of a steady comfortable rain, so strong and sustained that, when he does finally look up, it alone seems to light up the night with its continuous threads like flexible metal bars or endless spears; or like someone sleeping with one eye open who thinks he can hear and connect with the languid murmur of the river that speaks calmly or indifferently, or perhaps the indifference comes from his own weariness and his own sleeplessness and his dreams that are just beginning, even if he believes himself to be wide awake; or like someone who allows himself to be infected and drawn in by an insignificant humming that reaches him from afar, across a courtyard or a square, or when he happens to go into a public toilet and hears a happy man humming as he carefully parts his hair with a wet comb ('Nanna naranniaro nannara nanniaro,' and then he can't help but add meaning and words to that catchy tune, if he knows it: 'For I'm a poor cowboy and I know I've done wrong.')

That is how Luisa would have listened to me, inattentively, if we had ever had the brief conversation she was on the point of proposing. I had already said goodbye to the kids in their respective beds, and left them, not sleeping, but about to fall asleep. I had closed their bedroom doors and said to Luisa, who was waiting in the corridor:

'Right, I'm off. I'm leaving tomorrow.' Then I had gently touched her chin so as to study her profile and added: 'Your black eye's nearly gone. Be a bit more careful in future.' The bruise was barely visible now, apart from one small area that was still slightly yellow, but only someone who had seen how it looked before would have noticed it.

'Oh, of course, you're leaving.' And judging from the slightly wistful tone in which she said this, it seemed to me that she would probably miss me in a vague kind of way, now that she would be spending more time with the children and have fewer distractions. 'We haven't really seen much of each other, you've hardly told me anything about yourself—you caught me at a bad time, with a lot of previous commitments and a lot of work, things I couldn't cancel or change, if you'd given me a bit of advance warning that you were coming . . .'

It was an apology of sorts, she was the one feeling slightly in my debt, but only slightly, because one does usually try to accommodate someone who's only going to be around for a few days, and she hadn't. She seemed sad and distracted, as if filled with bad presentiments or, worse, a prescience of bad things to come. She was quite serene in her despondency, like someone who has thrown in the towel before receiving a single punch, like someone who knows what's about to happen. She must have been convinced that something strange was going on with Custardoy, whom she would probably call Esteban; true, he did occasionally travel and spend days or weeks observing and studying paintings in various places, but such a sudden departure wasn't normal—without saying goodbye or seeing each other—nor was the ensuing long silence. I imagined with satisfaction that he must be following my instructions to the letter, or had perhaps gone even further: yes, it was quite possible that he hadn't phoned her again since that first time, after his supposed arrival in wherever it was he had told her he had gone. He might even had told her he was in Baltimore, when he hadn't, in fact, stirred from Madrid. I really didn't care, just as long as he did as he was told and disappeared for good.

'How are you?' I asked. 'You seem a bit down. Has something happened in the last few days?'

'No, nothing,' she replied, shaking her head slightly. 'A minor disappointment, nothing important. I'll get over it soon enough.'

'Can I do anything about it? Is it about anyone I know?'

'No, not at all. It's someone you don't know, someone new. And anyway, it's not his fault either, it was unavoidable.' She paused for a second, then added: 'It's odd; now there'll be more and more of my people whom you don't know, not even by name, and so there'll be no point in my telling you about them or mentioning them. The same thing will happen with your people. And that hasn't happened for years, or only rarely. It's strange, when you live with someone, you keep up to date without any difficulty at all, without making any special effort, and then suddenly, or, rather, gradually, you know nothing about the people who come after. I know nothing about your friends in London, for example, or about the colleagues you work with every day. You said it was quite a small group, didn't you? And that one of them was a young woman, half-Spanish, is that right? How do you get along with them? I'm not even entirely sure what it is you do.' And as she said this, she waved her arm in the direction of the living room, not in order to show me the door so that I could leave, but as if she were suggesting we go in there for a moment before I left so that I could tell her about my work, or maybe simply so that she could listen to me talking. Perhaps she had realized that I could help her get through a few minutes of her waiting or lift the lead that weighed ceaselessly upon her soul. I thought of asking about the young gypsy mother and her children, who were, in a sense, her people and whom I knew about from when she and I were still living together and sharing a daily life, and whom I'd thought about while in that other country.

We started walking in that direction, with her leading. We were about to sit down at home and talk, and, while it lasted, this would seem the most natural thing in the world, with none of the artificiality that would have surrounded an arrangement to meet at a restaurant or anywhere else. Then her cell phone rang, the phone whose number other people knew and I did not, and she hurried on into the living room, almost ran, she had left it there, in her handbag, and I had left my raincoat and gloves in the room too, draped on the back of an armchair. I let her go ahead, of course, I didn't hurry, but since we had been walking along together, I didn't stop or hold back either, my discretion being limited to not actually going into the room, to lingering on the threshold, looking at the books on a shelf, my books, which I might, on one not too distant day, have to take away with me, although where I didn't yet know.

'Hello?' I heard her say, her spirits suddenly buoyant, as if the voice at the other end had managed to drive away her melancholy (or was it sorrow?) with just a word or two. I was sure it was Custardoy, calling for the penultimate or antepenultimate time. 'Yes. Are you OK?' A pause. 'Yes, I understand. Although, to be honest, your leaving like that, so suddenly, did throw me a bit . . . And you've no idea how long you're going to be away? That's a bit odd, isn't it? Them not giving you a fixed deadline, I mean.' She instinctively moved away from me and lowered her voice, so that I would hear as little as possible. However, since she didn't want to be rude and close the door on me or go into another room, her murmured comments were still audible. I missed a few words, but not her tone of voice. She wasn't saying much, Custardoy was the one doing most of the talking, and the conversation was rather brief, as if he were in a hurry (he was obeying my instructions to be distant and abrupt and concise). 'But that just leaves me completely in the dark. And what am I supposed to do if I can't even call you?' said Luisa almost pleadingly and raising her voice, only to lower it at once and add by way of explanation: 'Look, Jaime's here at the moment, he came to say goodbye, he's flying out tomorrow, he was just about to leave, why don't you call me back in five minutes?' Another longer pause. 'No, I don't understand. You mean you've got to go out right now, this very minute?' For a few moments I couldn't hear what she was saying, only intermittent words and odd phrases. 'No, I don't understand the situation; first of all, that rushed departure and now all these difficulties. I'm perfectly aware that we haven't known each other very long, and I don't presume to think that I know you inside out or anything, but I'm not used to this kind of behavior from you, it's never happened before. And you sound strange, different.' She fell silent again, then spoke almost in a whisper, before raising her voice to say: 'Look, I don't know what's going on with you, it's as if I were talking to someone else entirely. It's as if you were suddenly afraid of me, and I'd hate to be any kind of burden to you.'—'It isn't you he's afraid of, my love,' I thought. 'It's me.'—'Fine. If that's how you feel. It's up to you. You're the only one who can know how you feel. I'm not a mind-reader.' And her last words, which followed immediately after, were spoken coldly. 'Fine. If that's what you want. Goodbye.'

In other circumstances I wouldn't have enjoyed hearing that conversation at all, hearing Luisa pleading with that other man, very nearly begging him, before reacting with wounded dignity to his evasiveness or indifference. But I had prepared that scene, almost set it up and dictated it, as if I were Wheeler, who doubtless devoted no small part of his time to the preparation or composition of prized moments, or, so to speak, to guiding his numerous empty or dead moments towards a few pre-planned and carefully considered dialogues in which he had, of course, memorized his own part. Except that I hadn't intervened in that conversation, or, rather, Custardoy had spoken for me, for he was, after all, not using his own words, but those which I, like an Iago, had led him to say or obliged him to pronounce. Knowing that I was there, close by, must have increased his fear as well as his hatred of me. My presence had been a complete coincidence, but he would not have experienced it like that, he would have thought I was watching over the whole process, keeping an eye on things. So much the better for me.

Luisa came over to where I was standing, the cell phone still in her hand, and the look on her face was a mixture of puzzlement, resignation and annoyance. 'You've still got a long way to go,' I thought, 'you'll know worse despair yet. And then you'll seek me out, because I'm the person you know best and the one who will always be here.'

'Right, I'd better be going,' I said, picking up my raincoat and gloves. She had initially asked the caller to phone back in five minutes, ready, at a moment's notice, to sacrifice our conversation, the one we had unexpectedly been about to have. Missing that conversation, having it or not, was only of secondary importance to her. And at that point, it was to me as well. My chance would not come on that trip, I would have to wait quite a while longer.

'I'm sorry,' she murmured. 'Problems at work. People behave in the strangest way. They say they'll do one thing, then forget all about it and disappear.' She didn't need to give me any false explanations. The conversation had clearly been of a personal nature, and nothing to do with work. I knew what was going on, and she as yet did not. I didn't mind being so far ahead of her, I didn't mind deceiving her. 'This isn't the Jaime I know,' Cristina would say to me later on, and I had already thought the same thing: 'No, I'm not. I am more myself.'

Luisa accompanied me to the door. We kissed each other on the cheek, but this time she embraced me too. I sensed that she did so more out of a feeling of vulnerability, or a sudden sense of abandonment and loss, than out of genuine affection. Nevertheless, I returned her embrace warmly and enthusiastically. I certainly didn't mind embracing her, I never had.

'Come, come back to me, I'll be patient, I'll wait; but don't delay very much longer,' I thought when I was on the plane, remembering that farewell. And then I quoted to myself a line from a recent poem in English that I'd read during one of my trips with Tupra, on a train: 'Why do I tell you these things? You are not even here.'

That was the last thing that happened before everything changed. I asked the stewardess for an English newspaper; I needed to get used to that other country again. I hadn't even looked at a Spanish newspaper that morning, I was still too involved in my own thoughts to bother with the outside world, although a copy of *El País* lay unopened on my lap. The stewardess offered me *The Guardian*, *The Independent* and *The Times*, and I chose the first two because I can't stand the dreadful decadence into which the third one has fallen under its present Antipodean regime. I glanced at the front page of *The Guardian*, and my gaze fixed instantly—familiar names always call to us, immediately attract our attention—on a report that must have made my eyes start from their sockets and which sent me straight to the front page of *The Independent* for reassurance and confirmation that this wasn't some absurd sick joke or a figment of someone's imagination. Both papers carried the story, so it must be true, and although it wasn't a headline or a long item, the report was given due prominence in both: 'Dick Dearlove Arrested Following Boy's Violent Death.' Obviously neither headline said 'Dick Dearlove'; Dearlove is just the name I have taken to calling him by.

I turned immediately to the relevant pages and read them fearfully, eagerly, then with a sense of horror and growing repugnance towards Tupra and myself—in fact, a feeling of self-disgust swept over me at once. The information was incomplete and the facts confused and did little to clarify the succinct, not to say hermetic statements made by Dearlove's spokesman and his lawyers, who were the people who had reported the incident to

New Scotland Yard on the morning after the night of the murder, which made one think that they must have had a few hours to weigh up the situation and prepare and agree the best line of defense, about which, on the other hand, they gave little or no detail. In England, as I understand it, unlike in Spain, where there's an irresponsible clamor of voices right from the start, or even a verbal lynching, they take the confidentiality of legal proceedings very seriously indeed and never release any evidence or testimony that will form part of a trial, and no one who might be called on to testify is allowed to give his or her version of events to the press prior to that trial. Lawyers and journalists were thus limited to making veiled hints and prudent, rather discreet speculations as to what actually happened. They suggested a possible kidnapping attempt, a possible burglary, or even a settling of accounts between lovers. The victim was seventeen and apparently either Bulgarian or Russian (no one knew for sure, nor if he had a British passport, although this seemed unlikely) and he was referred to only by his initials, which, curiously enough, were the same as those of his killer, let's say R.D. Whatever the truth of the matter—and I saw at once what must have happened—one thing was sure: two nights ago the singer had stuck a spear, one of several he had hanging in a room next to the dining room, into the chest and throat of that very young young man. This doubtless meant that televisions around the world, especially those in Britain, but in my own country too, not to mention the millions of anonymous or pseudonymous voices on the Internet, would already have had a whole day to dissect the affair. But I had seen neither television nor Internet.

I briefly regretted that the plane had no low, sensationalist rag like *The Sun* on board, *The Sun* belonging, of course, to the same Antipodean empire as *The Times* and being therefore more given to scandal, moralizing and rumor: such newspapers would be rubbing their hands with glee and prepared to risk breaking any law if it meant selling more copies. I had a glance at *El País*, just in case, but its treatment of the matter was sober and concise and revealed nothing more than its London colleagues claimed to know. My regret was short-lived or was, I should say, merely a moment of naïveté, because I didn't need to know the details or the circumstances or the background or the motives, or even the psychological explanations being pondered by journalists or whoever. It was clear to me that Tupra had projected onto that idol the maximum biographical horror, had plunged him into narrative disgust as if into a butt of disgusting wine, had lit a torch for him and inscribed him in letters of fire on the list of those afflicted by the K-M or Killing-Murdering or Kennedy-Mansfield curse, as it was known in our little group with no name and who knows, by a process of mimesis, in some other loftier place; that Reresby or Ure or Dundas had condemned Dearlove not just to a few years in prison, which, for someone as famous as Dearlove, with such a sordid crime behind him, would be a slow incessant hell—I mean slower and more incessant than for other people—unless, and this was the best-case scenario, those years were interrupted by a swift death at the hands of other prisoners; he had condemned him also to seeing his entire life story and achievements lost beneath a quick lick of grey or off-white or off-color paint, its whole trajectory and construction plunged into immediate oblivion, condemned him to knowing that whenever anyone mentioned or read or heard his name, he or she would always instantly associate it with that final crime. Mothers would even use his name to warn their unwary offspring and, even worse, the message they gave would become distorted and exaggerated over time: 'Be careful who you mix with and who you go around with, you can't trust anyone. Remember what Dickie Dearlove did to that young Russian lad—he took him to his house and slit him open.' And I was as sure of this as I was that Tupra would already have in his possession a recording, a film of these events about which the press were now hypothesizing and which were known to almost no one else; it would doubtless show the whole sequence, from the point where the young Bulgarian, R.D., arrived at Dearlove's house up to the furious, fearsome moment when the latter stuck a spear in him, causing his instant death, although it must have taken two blows—one in the throat and the other in the chest, or possibly the other way round—to silence him completely and put an end to him; and then, perhaps, still blinded by rage and gripped by a childish sense of triumph (a very short-lived emotion and one that he would deplore for the rest of his days), searching the young man's body for the cell phone or tiny camera with which he would have taken his compromising photos and which Dearlove had failed to find when he playfully frisked him on arrival, perhaps because Tupra had told the boy he wouldn't need to carry a phone or camera because a camera would have been hidden somewhere in the house prior to that amorous or commercial assignation, like the gun that was famously waiting for Al Pacino in a restaurant restroom in the first episode of that great masterpiece in three parts, each part better than the last.

Tupra wouldn't need to make use of that tape or DVD (he hadn't, on that occasion, recorded and kept it for future use) in order to persuade Dearlove later on to do or not do something; the important thing had been to make Dearlove aware of just one of the deceptions of which he was the victim and of the ir-reparable act he had committed in response, so irreparable and unconcealable that his punishment would not be long in com-ing. Tupra would keep that video simply in order to have it and to watch it when he was alone or to revel in the perfect execu-tion of his plan, the prize item in his collection. It wouldn't be of any further use to him, given that the main deed had been revealed as soon as it was done: Dearlove had done the deed, and the whole world knew about it. He had killed a young man with a spear.

In the final analysis, though, the person who had instigated that killing was me. Or perhaps not exactly: I had invented, con-ceived, described or dictated it, imagined the mise-en-scène. I had given Tupra the idea—no one is ever fully aware of how dangerous it is to give other people ideas, and it happens all the time, at all hours and in all places—and I couldn't help wonder-ing how many more of my interpretations or translations might have had consequences of which I knew nothing, how many and which ones. I had spent a long time passing judgment on a daily basis and with ever greater ease and unconcern, listening to voices and looking at faces, in the flesh or hidden in the station-studio or on video, saying who could be trusted and who could not, who would kill and who would allow himself to be killed and why, who would betray and who would remain loyal, who would lie and who would meet with failure or with only average success in life, who irritated me and who aroused my pity, who was a poseur and who I warmed to, and what probabilities each individual carried in his veins, just like a novelist who knows that whatever his characters say or tell, whatever is attributed to them or whatever they are made to do, will go no further than his novel and will harm no one, because, however real they may seem, they will continue to be a fiction and will never interfere with anyone real (with anyone in his right mind, that is). But that was not my case: I wasn't using pen and paper to write about those who have never existed or trod the earth or traversed the world, I was describing and deciphering flesh-and-blood people and pontificating and making predictions about them, and I saw now that regardless of whether I was right or wrong, what I said could have disastrous consequences and determine their fate if placed in the hands of someone like Tupra, who, on this occasion, had not restricted himself to being only Sir Punishment or Sir Thrashing, but Sir Death and Sir Cruelty and, possibly, Sir Vengeance. And I had not been his instrument, but something less common and perhaps worse, his inspiration, an innocent whisper in his ear, an imprudent and unwitting Iago. I didn't care nor was I particularly interested in what grudge he bore Dearlove or if he had laid that trap for him—my trap—on his own initiative or as part of some outlandish State mission or on the well-paid orders of some private private individual. That was the least of it. What troubled me most was the thought that he had put into practice my plan, which wasn't a plan at all, and that in order to ensure its success, he had shown no qualms about sacrificing the life of a young man: 'Strange to leave even one's own first name behind,' indeed, and the victim didn't even have a name, only the initials R.D. Worryingly or improbably, I hadn't until then noticed the most serious implication of all and—as I realized at once, with the three newspapers unfolded on my lap in that plane—the one that would torment me for the rest of my life. And however tenuous I tried to make and succeeded in making that link later on, and however tenuous it did in fact become—for that is what would happen, it would seem to me remote and accidental, on my part at least, and my feelings of responsibility would diminish, and it would all seem like a dream, and with luck I would deceive myself entirely and make it disappear, especially when the last stubborn rim was finally erased and I was able to say to myself one day: 'But that was in another country'—that young Russian man who did not even know of my existence, just as I had known nothing of his while it lasted, had died because of my prediction or hypothesis or fantasy, because of what I had said and reported, and now, in my head, I would always have the words: 'For I am myself my own fever and pain.'

The first thing I did when I walked through the front door of the apartment, which, for a while, came to be my home, ingenuously furnished by an Englishwoman I never met, was to dial Tupra's home number. It was the weekend and no one would be at the building with no name, at least in theory, for I knew I wasn't the only one who went there out of office hours, to finish off some task or report or to rummage around or investigate. As had happened when I phoned him from Madrid, a woman's voice answered. I uttered the name I found repellent to use, Bertie, in order to show my familiarity with him—not that I needed to; my knowing his home number was indication enough.

'He's out of London at the moment,' the voice said. 'May I ask who's calling?' I didn't have his cell phone number, which Tupra guarded jealously, and, besides, he was of the opinion that everything could wait 'as used to happen in the old days.'

'Jack Deza,' I said, and I unintentionally pronounced the 'z' as a Spaniard would, having got used to doing so again while in Spain, it would have sounded like 'Daetha' or 'Deatha' to an English ear. 'I work with him, and it's very important. Would you mind giving me his cell phone number? I've just got back from Madrid and I have something urgent and of great interest to tell him.'

'No, I'm sorry, I don't think I can. He's the only one who can do that,' replied the woman. And she added slightly impertinently, which made me suspect that she was Beryl, although I hadn't spoken to her for long enough at Wheeler's supper to be able to recognize her voice, which wasn't particularly young, although not old either: 'If you don't have it, it must be because he didn't consider it necessary.'

'Are you Beryl?' I asked, at the risk of causing my boss some domestic or conjugal upset if she wasn't. Not that I cared any more; he would soon cease to be my boss—I had made my decision. Or almost, nothing is sure until it's over and done with.

'Why do you ask?' was her reply. And in a tone of voice that seemed half-stern and half-mocking, she said: 'You don't need to know who I am.'

'Perhaps Tupra has forbidden Beryl, if she is Beryl and she must be,' I thought, 'from telling anyone that they're an item again, still less that they're living together, or perhaps they prefer to think of themselves like that, rather than as married, enjoying the clandestine nature of their situation.' I remembered her long legs and her unusual smell, pleasant and very sexual, which were perhaps the things that drew Tupra back to her again and again; sometimes our weaknesses are for the simplest of things, the things we cannot give up. I was about to say: 'If you are Beryl, we've met before. I'm a friend of Sir Peter Wheeler's. We were introduced at his house some time ago now.' I resisted, however, thinking that if I said any more, it would only make matters worse.

'I apologize, I didn't mean to be impertinent,' I said. 'Could you perhaps tell me when Bertie will be back?'

'I don't know exactly, but I imagine that if you work with him, you'll see him in the office on Monday. I assume he'll be there.'

This was a way of telling me not to phone him again at home on a weekend. I thanked her and hung up; I would have to wait. I opened the window to air the apartment after so many days away, quickly unpacked my bag, did a little dusting, examined the accumulated mail, and then, when evening was coming on and

I didn't really know what else to do—when you've just arrived home, life lacks its normal rhythm—I went over to the window and saw my neighbor opposite dancing, beyond the trees whose tops filled the center of that square: nothing had changed—why should it, time deceives us when we go off traveling, it always seems longer than it was. His usual two women friends were with him, the white woman and the black or mulatto woman, a well-matched trio, the women must be each other's *ġe-brȳd-guma*, with him as their link, another similarity with Custardoy, who enjoyed taking two women to bed with him at the same time, although not, I think, with Luisa—where would Custardoy have gone with his shattered hand, where would he really have gone, it was no affair of mine and I didn't care, just as long as he met my conditions and kept away from her and, most important of all, never told her of my intervention. The three dancers were performing some very fast steps, a kind of flamenco-style stamping or perhaps it was tap—I couldn't guess what loud music he would be playing in his living room on a Saturday—because they each had their right arm raised to hold something in place on their respective shoulders, some small and apparently living moving object, and this time I couldn't resist picking up my binoculars and when I managed to focus, I saw to my amazement that each of them did, in fact, have a very tiny dog draped around their shoulders, now I don't know anything about the different brands or, rather, breeds of dog, but the man's dog was snub-nosed and hairy, and the women's were more like rats, with pointed snouts, one of those scrawny dogs with a crest or bun or fringe or toupée on their heads, disgusting creatures whatever they were. The dogs certainly didn't look as if they belonged to them and I wondered where they would have got them from, perhaps they'd hired them especially in order to perform their eccentric dance, but whatever the truth of the matter, the poor creatures must have been feeling horribly dizzy, or indeed positively upset and desperate; the dancers' tapping would feel to them like a permanent earthquake or something similar. It was to be hoped that no member of an animal protection society, which are so fierce and so active in England, spotted what my neighbors were up to, because they'd doubtless be reported for the torture, harassment and bewilderment of small defenseless beasts. 'They must be mad,' I thought, 'they must think there's some special merit in being able to dance and, at the same time, balance a living being on their shoulders; one false move, and a dog could go flying off, hurled against a wall or a window.' I stood watching them for a few minutes until they all stopped abruptly amid urgent gestures of displeasure and alarm: the white woman's little dog had peed on her, spraying her face and hair, and because this had happened in the middle of some particularly frenetic stamping, it had sprayed the other two as well. Finding itself the object of such frenzied movements, the poor dog had doubtless judged that incontinence was its last line of defense. They released all three mutts—who tottered off—and began quickly and disgustedly taking off their soiled clothes, and just as the man was about to remove his elegant polo shirt, he looked straight across at my window and saw me. I immediately hid my binoculars and took two steps back, ashamed to be caught spying. However, they didn't seem angry at all, even though the two women had by then stripped down to their bras, a situation made worse—or better—by the fact that the mulatta wasn't wearing one. As on the previous occasion when they had spotted me, they waved cheerfully, beckoning me to come over. I had felt ashamed on that occasion too, but had managed to see an advantage in that reciprocal visual contact and thought that if one particular night or day proved truly desolate: I at least had the possibility of going in search of company and dancing on the other side of the square, in that happy carefree household whose occupant resisted all my deductions and conjectures, and inhibited or eluded my interpretative faculties, something that happened so infrequently that it bestowed on him a slight air of mystery. And the prospect of that hypothetical visit, that possible future contact, had made me feel lighter and less vulnerable, as if it provided a kind of safety net. That day could not have been more desolate, a whole empty Sunday stretched ahead of me until I could speak to Tupra, one of those desolate Sundays 'exiled from the infinite' or '*banni de l'infini,*' as I believe Baudelaire once wrote and as English Sundays tend to be; I knew them well from many years before, from the first time I had lived there, in Oxford, and I knew that Sundays in England aren't just ordinary dull Sundays, the same the world over, which demand that one simply tiptoe through without disturbing them or paying them the least attention, they are vaster and slower and more burdensome than anywhere else I know. So perhaps the moment had arrived to take advantage of the safety net offered by that jovial trio; what's more, the women had no compunction about showing themselves to me, especially the one I had always preferred and who had the most to show. I hesitated for a moment about whether to go downstairs, across the square and up to that other apartment, but instantly dismissed the idea. 'No, now it makes even less sense than ever,' I thought, 'in a few weeks or a month, at most two, I probably won't be living here or looking out on this square any more, and they will become merely a pleasant memory that will gradually fade. And now, alas, I can't help but interpret my dancer, because I can't help associating him with Custardoy and seeing an affinity between the two.' And so, smiling, I went back over to the window and wagged my forefinger at them to tell them 'No.' Then I opened my hand and raised it slightly in a friendly gesture, my way of saying 'Thank you' and perhaps also 'Goodbye.'

I shut the window and came back into the room. I decided to go out to a nearby grocery store and buy a few basic things to fill up the nearly empty fridge; the store also sold magazines and newspapers, but I no longer wanted to buy a copy of *The Sun* or any other paper of that ilk; and when I returned, I chose not to turn on the TV, sure that some program, if not most, would be discussing the horrible crime of Dr. Dearlove, former odontologist, now transformed into the new Hyde who could never go back to being plain Dr. Jekyll: he would be a lascivious murderer from now until the Final Judgment, at which, in other times—the times of steadfast faith—people would have expected a Bulgarian or Russian boy called Danev or Deyanov, Dimitrov or Dondukov to confront him and accuse him with the bitter words of someone who died too young. Or perhaps he would address Tupra or even me. I preferred not to know too much, about him or about Dearlove, mainly because I didn't need to and because it would only increase my sense of sadness. I already knew enough, and the press would be full of ghoulish, misleading speculations. What no one would know was that there was someone behind it all, an expert on narrative disgust or horror and on the Kennedy-Mansfield complex and its all too effective curse, and that the murder had nothing to do with chance or a bad night or a moment of mental derangement. Danev or Dondukov could no longer tell who had hired him or how, nor what he had been hired to do, and I was in no position to prove anything. Nor, indeed, was I even considering the possibility.

I phoned young Pérez Nuix, who was at home, told her I had just got back and asked if we could meet that evening or the following day ('It's urgent, important; but it'll only take a moment,' I said, as she had once said to me, and on that occasion, 'it' had lasted until morning; an experience that had not been repeated). She said that would be fine, made no attempt to find out in advance what it was about and was happy to come over to my part of town ('It'll do me good to get a bit of fresh air, I've hardly been out all day, and besides I need to walk the dog'), we shared a kind of unconfessed loyalty. We arranged to meet in the bar of the luxury hotel I could see from my window ('Give me an hour and a half, no more, long enough for me to take the dog out and then come over'), and when she was installed there, with a drink before her, I told her about Dick Dearlove and the interpretations Tupra had elicited from me after the celebrity supper in London and, later, in Edinburgh. I laid out to her my arrogant reports, my hypotheses, my theories, my mise-en-scènes, and my predictions. As things had turned out, they appeared to indicate a high degree of prescience on my part.

'It's too much of a coincidence, don't you think?' I added, and I did not for a moment imagine she would contradict me.

I noticed that she seemed slightly uncomfortable, as if for some reason she felt impatient with or displeased by my anxieties, and she took a slow sip of her drink as you do when you need to think a little longer about what you're going to say. Finally, she said:

'Coincidences do happen, Jaime, as you well know. In fact, I think they're part of normal life. But not, I guess, where Bertie is concerned. Where Tupra is concerned,' she corrected herself, 'you're right, it's unlikely. With him almost nothing is coincidental.' She fell silent for a few seconds, giving me, I thought, almost a commiserative look, then she went on: 'But what is it that you find so troubling? Giving him the idea to lay a trap that you don't like? That someone else was harmed, rather than the person who should have been hurt by that trap? That someone, an instrumental victim, died? Yes, of course, what else do you want me to say, of course I understand your unease. But we've talked about this before,' she reminded me. And seeing my bewildered expression, she added: 'Yes, I told you that what Tupra did or decided was not our responsibility. Everyone, regardless of who they work for, occasionally provides their boss with the occasional idea, and if he thinks it's any good, that boss then takes up the idea and, a mere two minutes after hearing it, believes he was the one who thought of it in the first place. Sure it's irritating, they don't even give you a pat on the back, but it also means that we're absolved of all responsibility. At the time, I said that worrying about what happened with our reports was like a novelist worrying about what potential buyers and readers of his book would understand and take away from it.'

I remembered that, and I also remembered saying that I didn't think the comparison worked. She had made further comparisons, none of which had convinced me. Again, she seemed to me more experienced and, in a way, older than me. She was looking at me as if she were idly witnessing the end of time, something that she had already experienced and left behind. Perhaps that was the origin of her impatience, displeasure or discomfort: it's disheartening having to explain to someone else what it took blood, sweat and tears to learn and with no help from anyone. Or perhaps she had been able to count on Tupra's help, who was no mean arguer.

'I didn't think the comparison worked,' I said. 'Besides, a novelist *should* take care what he puts in his book, don't you think?'

'I doubt that any writers do,' she said firmly. 'If that were the case, no one would ever write anything. It's just not possible to live that cautiously, it's too paralyzing. As you say in Spain, *son ganas de cogérsela con papel de fumar.* You just can't be that persnickety. And anyway, keep things in proportion. What do you expect, there are people in our field who do far worse things and get their hands dirty too. Or, depending how you look at it, perhaps they do better things because they're being of service to the country.' Since we were speaking in Spanish, I was grateful that she didn't use the word '*patria*' but '*país,*' but it nonetheless sounded horribly like one of the first things Tupra had said to me at Wheeler's buffet supper. Perhaps those who stayed longest by his side, of whom I would not be one, ended up adopting his ideas. Pérez Nuix, however, said the phrase in such a neutral tone that I couldn't tell if she was serious or quoting our boss or being sarcastic.

'Don't tell me that by arresting Dearlove, putting him inside for several years—if, that is, he doesn't get bumped off during his first few days there—has been of some service to this country. Or, for that matter, the death of that Russian boy; he'd probably only just arrived in England and was here illegally, thus ensuring that no one will dig too deep or kick up much of a fuss. What did you call him, "an instrumental victim"? I thought the usual term was "collateral victim," although in Spanish it should be "*lateral*" rather than "*colateral.*"' I couldn't resist adding this pedantic clarification.

'They're different things, Jaime,' she pointed out. '*Víctimas colaterales* or *laterales* aren't usually instrumental, they occur more by chance or by mistake or by mere inevitability. Instrumental victims, on the other hand, always perform a function. They're necessary for something to succeed.' She paused again, took another sip of her drink, and remained silent. It occurred to me that perhaps she had often been through what I was going through now. When she did speak again, she did so hesitantly: 'Look, I don't know, I simply don't know; Tupra doesn't confide in me anymore and hasn't for a long time now, and he didn't ever tell me much even when we were on better terms, I mean when he trusted me more or had more of a soft spot for me; he always keeps pretty much to himself. It seems unlikely that the State or the Crown or them,' and she pointed upwards, by which I assumed she meant the bigwigs in the SIS or Secret Intelligence Service, who, at least in the past, embraced both MI5 and MI6, 'would have ordered such a trap to be laid, such an operation, for a rock singer, a celebrity. But you never know: in America, declassification has uncovered the most ridiculous things—reports on people like Elvis Presley or John Lennon who were being kept under surveillance by the CIA or the FBI—so anything is possible. We don't know what Dearlove was doing, what he might have been getting up to, who he was involved with and who he might have blackmailed, who he could frighten with threats which, coming from him, would seem quite credible (insofar as someone like him can have any credibility, of course) or on whom he bestowed his favors. Insignificant, inoffensive and apparently purely ornamental people can prove to be full of surprises. Singers and actors often turn out to be real nutcases, they join weird sects or convert to Islam, which nowadays is no joke, as you know. One of the first lessons you learn in this job (although it's better still if you know it before you start) is that no one is insignificant, inoffensive and purely ornamental.'

'The time I talked to Dearlove longest was in Edinburgh,' I said, 'or, rather, I overheard him talking to an old friend of his, Genevieve Seabrook, which makes it more likely that he was telling the truth because, with her, there would be no reason for him to put on an act; anyway, it seemed to me that he wasn't involved with anyone, still less anyone desirable, that it wasn't even a possibility. He was complaining that in England he had no option now but to pay for sex. I doubt he could have been a serious threat to anyone, certainly not to anyone requiring the protection of the Secret Service. I had the impression that he was a man in decline, but eager to disguise that decline. In fact, he could already see himself disappearing, not so much from the world, but from people's memories. That worried him a lot, made him feel embittered and anxious.'

'As I said, it's highly unlikely that the State would have acted against him in this way. I'm more inclined to think it was a personal act of revenge by Tupra, some unfinished business—after all, they used to see each other socially quite a lot—unless Tupra did it as a favor to someone else. Or maybe it wasn't a favor at all, we shouldn't dismiss the idea of a contract.'

'You mean somebody paid to have it done?'

'Yes, why not, like I said before, this man Dearlove might to all intents and purposes be on the way out, but from what one hears, during his lifetime, he must have been with dozens of minors of both sexes, doubtless with some who were, in their day, desirable, to use your expression, either physically or socially or because of their family connections. Many of them will be adults now, some might be in possession of their own fortunes and would therefore have more than enough money to pay for such a contract killing. Then there are fathers and brothers too. I don't know, maybe Dick Dearlove ruined the life of Tupra's younger brother or sister. Perhaps he corrupted Tupra himself.' And she laughed at the idea.

'Is that possible, do you think? Tupra can't be many years his junior. And does Tupra have brothers and sisters?'

Young Pérez Nuix laughed again, this time at my naiveté or my literal-mindedness.

'No, of course not, I'm sure no one could ever have corrupted Bertie or done anything to him that he didn't want done. To be perfectly honest, I find it hard to believe that he was ever innocent and malleable. Besides, as I'm sure you realize, I was being ironic. I've no idea if Tupra has siblings or not, I've never heard him say a word about his family or his origins, I don't even know where his name comes from.'—'Peter didn't know either,' I thought, 'although he made fun of it.'—'No one knows much about him. It's as if he'd sprung into being by spontaneous generation.' Pérez Nuix had gone back to calling him Bertie and, in doing so, had adopted a slightly evocative tone, without realizing, without intending to; I wondered just what had gone on between them. However, she immediately returned to the matter in hand. 'What I'm trying to say is that the possibilities are at once limitless and secondary, so there's no point delving into it.' Again I noticed that faintly commiserative look and again I felt that it perhaps saddened her to see me going through a process she had already been through herself. It might also be that the subject bored her, even annoyed her. 'Who cares anyway, Jaime. It's none of your business. Even what happened is none of your business, although at the moment you think it is. Well, it isn't. You've got to get used to that fact. It won't happen often, but I suppose it's the first time it has since you joined. It might never happen again. But you have to get used to it, just in case, simply because of those possible exceptions. If not, you won't be able to continue in the job.'

'I don't think I am going to continue,' I said.

Young Pérez Nuix looked surprised, but my feeling was that she was only pretending, as if she thought that not affecting surprise would be rude and show a certain disdain for me. According to Tupra, she was the best, she would know me well, perhaps better than I did, especially since I wasn't interested and had given up trying understand myself—what was the point? ('No one can know you better than you do yourself, and yet no one can know himself so well that he can be sure how he will behave tomorrow,' that, I thought or remembered, is what St. Augustine had said.) Yes, she was pretending, a little:

'Really? When did you decide that, while you were in Madrid or since you got back? Are you sure?'

'I'm almost sure,' I said. 'But I want to talk to Tupra first. He's not in London today.'

'And all because of this Dearlove business? And what are you going to say to Tupra? What are you going to ask him: why it happened? That's his affair or possibly someone else's, but he'll never tell you. Sometimes even he doesn't know why; he gets an order, carries it out unquestioningly and that's that.' She looked at her glass. I raised a cigarette to my lips in the hope that she would continue talking, I would pretend ignorance of the hotel's no-smoking rule until someone protested. 'It's your decision,

Jaime, but it does seem a little over the top to me. As Bertie always says, it's the way of the world. Let things settle in your mind. Wait until it's sunk in that you have nothing to do with what happened to Dearlove and the Bulgarian boy. Ideas float, nothing is so easily transmitted. As soon as you put it into words, that idea was no longer yours, it was simply out there. And all ideas have the potential to infect others. Just wait a little, and one day you'll see I was right.'

'That isn't the only reason,' I told her. 'But it's definitely a contributing factor. I don't think I decided here or in Madrid, but in full flight, on the plane.'

'A man of firm principles, eh?' And her voice took on a slightly sarcastic edge, then immediately became more serious. 'They're not really so very firm, Jaime. No one who works in this field can afford to be that principled. You may be valiantly buckling on your principles now, but that's a different matter.' She sometimes used rather literary turns of phrase—'con denuedo,' 'valiantly'—due to her inevitably bookish rather than real-life knowledge of Spanish. 'I'm not criticizing you; it helps, it has its merits, we should all do it more often. But what you put on can always be taken off again.'

I remembered what Tupra had asked me the first time I was called on to interpret someone (the day when he had first urged me: 'Say anything, whatever comes into your head, go on'), when he asked me to stay behind in his office for a moment so that I could give him my opinion on General or Colonel or Corporal Bonanza or whatever he was, from Venezuela: 'Allow me to ask you a question: up to what point would you be capable of leaving aside your principles? I mean up to what point do you usually do so? That is, disregard it, the theory I mean?' he had asked me. And he had added: 'It's something we all do now and then; we couldn't live otherwise, whether out of convenience, fear or need. Or out of a sense of sacrifice or generosity. Out of love, out of hate. To what extent do you?' And I had responded: 'It depends on the reason. I can leave them aside almost entirely if it's in the interests of conversation, less so if I'm called on to make a judgment. Still less if I'm judging friends, because then

I'm partial. When it comes to taking action, hardly at all.' I had answered almost without thinking. When it came down to it, what did I know and what do I know? Perhaps Pérez Nuix was right in a way, and I *was* merely buckling on my principles or deciding not to set them to one side. However, she was not right about the last thing she had said: not everything that one puts on can be taken off.

'Not everything and not always either,' I said. 'You can't just take off a tattoo, for example. And there are some obligations that can't simply be unbuckled and discarded. That's why some are so difficult to buckle on in the first place and why others must be very firmly buckled on, so that there can be no turning back.'

There was not much more to say. I should have guessed that she would know nothing. Perhaps I had only phoned her as a way of stilling my impatience and sharing my astonishment with someone, giving vent to my feelings, possibly to convince myself, or at least to argue it through or to rehearse that argument. I stubbed out my barely smoked cigarette before anyone could call me to order. I paid for the drinks and we left. I offered to accompany her in a taxi to her house, but since we were just across the road from my apartment, she declined. And so I walked with her to Baker Street tube where we said goodbye. I thanked her and she said: 'Whatever for?'

'How's your father doing?' I asked. We hadn't mentioned him since that night in my apartment. She had told me nothing and I hadn't asked. I suppose I did so then because it felt to me as if we were saying farewell to each other. Even though we would see each other on Monday in the building with no name and perhaps on other days too.

'Not too bad. He doesn't gamble any more,' she said.

We exchanged kisses and I watched her disappear down into the underground, which is so very deep in London. Perhaps she envied my decision not to continue with the group, and that it was still possible for me to break away from it, having been part of it for far less time than her. There was, in principle, nothing preventing her from doing the same. But Tupra would certainly want to keep her at all costs, as he would the others, and me. He took whatever steps he deemed necessary and presumably hoped not to frighten us off in the process, and perhaps with that in mind he rationed and measured out the steps to be taken, gauging when we would be hardened enough to withstand certain major upsets. According to Wheeler, there were very few people with our curse or gift, and we were getting fewer and fewer, and he had lived long enough to notice this unequivocally. 'There are hardly any such people left, Jacobo,' he had told me. 'There were never many, very few in fact, which is why the group was always so small and so scattered. But nowadays there's a real dearth. The times have made people insipid, finicky, prudish. No one wants to see anything of what there is to see, they don't even dare to look, still less take the risk of making a wager; being forewarned, foreseeing, judging, or, heaven forbid, prejudging, that's a capital offence. No one dares any more to say or to acknowledge that they see what they see, what is quite simply there, perhaps unspoken or almost unsaid, but nevertheless there. No one wants to know; and the idea of knowing something beforehand, well, it simply fills people with horror, with a kind of biographical, moral horror.' And on another occasion, in another context, he had warned me: 'You have to bear in mind that most people are stupid. Stupid and frivolous and credulous, you have no idea just how stupid, frivolous and credulous they are, they're a permanently blank sheet without a mark on it, without the least resistance.'

No, Tupra would not be prepared to lose us so easily, the people who served him. I didn't consider that I as yet owed him any large debts or loyalties, nor had I established any very strong links, I had not become involved, enmeshed or entangled, I would not have to use a razor to cut one of those bonds when it ultimately grew too tight. I had tried to deceive him regarding Incompara, but now, with this Dearlove business, even if it wasn't quite the same thing, we were more or less quits. It was likely, on the other hand, that he had young Pérez Nuix caught from various angles, and that for her there could be no easy separation, no possibility of desertion. I remembered Reresby's comment when he froze the video image of her beaten father, the poor man lying motionless on the table, a swollen wounded heap, bleeding from his nose and eyebrows, possibly from his cheekbones and from other cuts, the broken hands with which he had tried in vain to protect himself—I, too, had broken a hand and slashed a cheekbone with apparent coldness or perhaps with genuine coldness, how could I have done that? Tupra had said: 'As I told you, nothing here gets thrown away or given to someone else or destroyed, and that beating is perfectly safe here, it's not to be shown to anyone. Well, who knows, it might be necessary to show it to Pat one day, to convince her of something, perhaps to stay and not to leave us, one never knows.' Perhaps he would show it to her, saying: 'You wouldn't want this to happen to your father again, would you?' 'How fortunate,' I thought, 'that my family is far away and that I'm all alone here in London.' But maybe he wouldn't need to go that far to convince Pat: after all, she may have been half-Spanish, but she was still serving her country. And I was not.

I slept badly that night, having resolved to get up early the next day. I had no intention of spending Sunday in London doing nothing but ruminate, with barely anything to occupy me (I'd dealt with any work pending before I left for Madrid), and with the television watching me while I waited for Monday to arrive so that I could talk to Tupra. I hadn't been to see Wheeler for a long time and, besides, there was the heavy present that I'd bought for him in a second-hand bookshop in Madrid and carted with me all the way to London: a boxed, two-volume set of propaganda posters printed during our Civil War, some of which—not only the Spanish ones and not all of them cartoons—used the same message as the 'careless talk' campaign or something very similar. And when you've taken the trouble to carry something with you, you feel impatient to hand it over, especially if you're sure the recipient of the gift will be pleased. It was a little late to call him on Saturday night when I returned from Baker Street, and so I decided to go to Oxford in the morning and tell him of my arrival there and then; it wouldn't be a problem, he hardly ever went out and would be delighted to have me visit him in his house by the River Cherwell and stay to lunch and spend the whole day in his company.

And so I went to Paddington, a station from which I had so often set off in my distant Oxford days, and caught a train before eight o'clock, not noticing that it was one of the slowest, involving a change and a wait at Didcot. During what was still more or less my youth, I had, altogether, waited many minutes at that semi-derelict station, and I'd been convinced on one such occasion that I'd lost something important because I'd failed—almost—to speak to a woman who was, like me, waiting for the delayed train that would take us to Oxford, and while we passed the time smoking, the hesitant pool of light surrounding us had illuminated only the butts of the cigarettes she threw on the ground alongside mine (those were more tolerant times), her English shoes, like those of an adolescent or an ingénue dancer, low-heeled with a buckle and rounded toes, and her ankles made perfect by the penumbra. Then, when we boarded the delayed train and I could see her face clearly, I knew and know now that during the whole of my youth she was the woman who made the greatest and most immediate impact on me, although I also know that, traditionally, in both literature and real life, such a remark can only be made of women whom young men never actually meet. I had not yet met Luisa then, and my lover at the time was Clare Bayes; I didn't even know my own face and yet nevertheless there I was interpreting that young woman on the platform of Didcot station.

The train stopped at the usual places, Slough and Reading, as well as Maidenhead and Twyford and Tilehurst and Pangbourne, and after more than an hour, I got off there, in Didcot, where I had to wait several minutes—on that so-familiar platform—for another weary and reluctant train to appear. And it was there, while I was vaguely recalling that young nocturnal woman whose face I soon forgot but not her colors (yellow, blue, pink, white, red; and around her neck a pearl necklace), that I understood what had made me get up so early in order to catch a train and visit Wheeler in Oxford without delay; it wasn't simply a desire to see him again nor mere impatience to watch his eyes when they alighted with surprise on those 'careless talk' posters from Spain, it was, secondarily, a need to tell him what had happened and to demand an explanation. I don't mean tell him about what had happened to me in Madrid, for which he wasn't remotely to blame (to be accurate, nothing had happened to me, I had done something to someone else), but about what had occurred with Dearlove; after all, Peter was the person who had got me into that group to which he had once belonged, the person who had recommended me; he had made use of my encounter with Tupra and submitted me to a small test that now seemed to me innocent and idiotic—and which in no way prepared me for the possible risks of joining the group—and then reported to them on the result. Perhaps he himself had written the report on me in those old files: 'It's as if he didn't know himself very well. He doesn't think much about himself, although he believes that he does (albeit without great conviction) . . .' He it was, in any case, who had revealed to me my supposed abilities and who had, to use the classic term, enlisted me.

Once in Oxford, I walked from the station to the Randolph Hotel and phoned him from there (now that I knew Luisa used a cell phone, perhaps I ought to get one too, they may be instruments of surveillance but they have their uses). Mrs. Berry answered and didn't even think it necessary to hand me over to Peter. She would ask him, she said, but she was sure my visit would make his day. A few seconds later, she was back: 'He says you should come at once, Jack, as soon as you like. Will you be staying for lunch? I'm sure the Professor won't let you leave before then.'

When I went into the living room, I experienced a moment of alarm—but not quite panic—because Peter's face had taken on the gaunt look of those whom death is pursuing although without as yet too much haste, not yet holding the hourglass in his hand, but keeping a close eye on it. That impression soon diminished, and I decided it must have been a false one, but it may also have been due to a rapid adjustment, as when we meet a friend who is much fatter or thinner or older than the last time we saw him and we are thus obliged to carry out a kind of rectification process, until our retina gets used to our friend's new size or new age and we can again fully recognize him. He was sitting in his armchair, like my father in his, with his feet on an ottoman and the Sunday papers scattered on a low table beside him. His stick was hooked over the back of his chair. He made as if to get up to greet me, but I stopped him. Judging from the way he was settled in his armchair, it seemed to me unlikely that he would find it as easy to sit down on the stairs as he had done very late on the night of his buffet supper. I placed one hand on his shoulder and squeezed it with gentle or restrained affection—that was the most I dared to do, for in England people rarely touch each other. He was impeccably dressed, with tie and lace-up shoes and a cardigan, as was, I believe, customary among men of his generation, at least I had noticed the same tendency in my father, who, when he was at home, always looked as if he were about to go out at any moment. Then, impatient to begin, I sat down on a nearby stool and the first thing I did, after exchanging a few words of welcome and greeting, was to remove from my bag the package containing *La Guerra Civil en dos mil carteles—The Civil War in Two Thousand Posters*—the next time I went to Madrid I would have to track down another copy for myself; it really was a marvelous book, and I was sure that Wheeler would appreciate and enjoy it greatly, as would Mrs. Berry, whom I urged to stay and leaf through it with us. However, she preferred not to ('Thank you, Jack, I'll look at it properly when I have more time'). And she left us on the excuse that she had things to do, although throughout the morning, she came back into the room several times, came and went, always near, always on hand.

'Look, Peter,' I said, opening the first volume, 'the book also reproduces various foreign posters too, and I've stuck post-its on any pages that have posters connected to the "careless talk" campaign. It seems that, as a recommendation, it was pretty much a constant in all kinds of places. The British campaign was imitated by the Americans when they finally entered the War, but theirs sometimes verged on the kitsch and the melodramatic.' And I showed him a drawing depicting a dog grieving for its dead sailor master '. . . because somebody talked!' or as we would say in Spanish: '¡ . . . porque alguien se fue de la lengua!'; another in which appeared a large hairy hand wearing a Nazi ring and holding a Nazi medal and the words: 'Award for careless talk. Don't discuss troop movements, ship sailings, war equipment'; and a third more somber one, in which a pair of intense narrow eyes peer out from beneath a German helmet: 'He's watching you.' 'And there are two English posters that I

...because somebody talked!

AWARD

FOR CARELESS TALK

DON'T DISCUSS TROOP MOVEMENTS SHIP SAILINGS WAR EQUIPMENT

HE'S WATCHING YOU

БОЛТАТЬ — ВРАГУ ПОМОГАТЬ!

Stärk
fronten här hemma-

Bygg dammar
för ryktena!

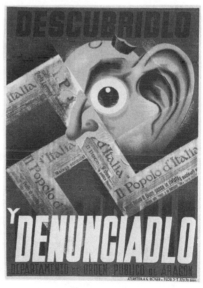

DESCUBRIDLO

Y DENUNCIADLO

DEPARTAMENTO DE ORDEN PUBLICO DE ARAGON

don't think you showed me, but that you're bound to remember.' And I turned to a page displaying a very succinct poster bearing only the words 'Talk kills,' the lower half of which showed a sailor drowning as an indirect or possibly direct result of someone talking; and another signed by Bruce Bairnsfather, which revived his famous soldier from the First World War, 'Old Bill,' alongside his son who has been called up for the Second. At the top are the words: 'Even the walls . . .' next to a swastika and above a huge ear; and underneath are written the young man's words: 'S'long Dad! We're shiftin' to . . . *Blimey. I nearly said it!'* And I pointed out to him a French poster, signed by Paul Colin: 'Silence. The enemy is listening in to your secrets' and a Finnish one, although the words were in Swedish, that showed a woman's full red lips sealed shut by an enormous padlock, and the text of which apparently said: 'Support our soldiers from the rearguard. Don't spread rumors!'; and a Russian poster in which one half of the listener's face and shoulders was much darker and had acquired a monocle, a mustache and a military epaulette (had taken on, in short, a very sinister appearance). 'And here are the Spanish posters,' I added, leafing through the second volume where most of them were to be found, although they were scattered throughout both. 'You see, these must have predated the British ones and the others too.'

Wheeler studied them closely and with evident interest, even fascination, and after a moment's silence, said:

'They're different. There's more hate in them.'

'In the Spanish ones?'

'Yes, if you look at ours and even those from the other countries, they were warning people above all of the danger and urging them to keep silent, to maximize discretion and caution, but they didn't demonize the hidden enemy or stress the need to hunt him down, to pursue and destroy him. It's odd, they hardly condemn him at all. Perhaps because we were conscious that whenever possible, we were doing exactly the same thing, spying in Germany and in occupied Europe and were aware that in wartime, it's only to be expected (and so, propaganda apart, one can't really be too reproachful) that each side will do whatever

DESCUBRID Y APLASTAD SIN
PIEDAD A LA 5ª COLUMNA

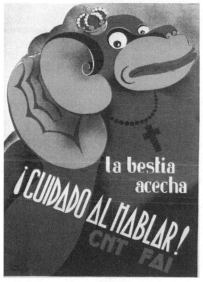

la bestia
acecha
¡CUIDADO AL HABLAR!
CNT FAI

cuidado con lo que haces

el enemigo te mira
un plano que traces,
un documento que
muestres,
puede ocasionar
muchos muertos

EL ESPIA
VE

it can to win that war, with no limits, or only those demanded by public opinion, which doesn't, of course, mean that the limits we're told, officially, that governments won't cross are never crossed, only that they cross them furtively, in secret, without acknowledging the fact and even denying it, if that's what's required. But look at this: "Find him out and denounce him," and they depict the spy as a monster with elephantine powers of sight and hearing as well as smell, and they associate him with Italian fascism, and I'm not sure, but he may even be wearing a priest's biretta on his bald head, what do you think that is? Not to mention this other one: "Find and ruthlessly crush the Fifth Column" whose members are shown as a handful of plundering, bloodthirsty rats caught in the light of a torch, with the sole of a giant shoe about to flatten them and a spiked bludgeon about to batter them. The poster was obviously published by the Communist Party, which was dominated by Soviet Stalinists, and they called for both the enemy and the halfhearted to be mercilessly hunted down and unceremoniously killed, just as the Francoists on the other side did. And look at this next one: they refer to the eavesdropper as "The beast": "The beast is listening. Watch what you say!" and the beast is wearing a crown on his head and a cross dangling from a necklace, which makes him look rather effeminate, don't you think? It's describing the ambushee, it's saying who he is and what he's like, it's pointing him out. The other posters, though, the ones by the celebrated artist Renau with the eye and the ear and the one published by the Dirección General de Bellas Artes addressed to militiamen, are more like ours, less aggressive, more to do with defense and prevention, more neutral perhaps. They are simply a warning against spies. The text of the latter could easily have appeared on one of the later British posters: "Don't give away any details about the situation at the front. Not to your comrades. Not to your brothers or sisters. Not to your girlfriends." Those wretched girlfriends again. One tended to confide in them and they, in turn, confided in you, too much really, at a time when no one could trust anyone. It really is a most fascinating book, Jacobo, thank you so much for thinking of me and bringing it all the way from Spain, especially given that it weighs a ton.' He thought for a few seconds, then added: 'Yes, that hatred is very striking. Quite different. I'm not sure we experienced it in the same way here.'

'Perhaps in our War it was necessary to describe and characterize the spy like that,' I said, 'because they had fewer distinguishing marks and it was easier for them to pretend and to hide. Don't forget, for example, that we all spoke the same language, not like here, where you were fighting the Nazis.'

Wheeler shot me one of those occasional looks of fleeting annoyance and displeasure—those mineral eyes, like two marbles almost violet in color, or like amethysts or chalcedony or, when narrowed, like the seeds of pomegranates—that made you feel you had said something stupid. That was when he most resembled Toby Rylands.

'I can assure you that most of those who spied here could speak English as well as you or I. In fact, probably better than you. They were Germans who had lived here since they were children, or who had an English father or mother. Some were renegade purebred Englishmen, and there was quite a large number of fanatical Irishmen too. It was the same with those who spied for us in Germany or Austria. They all spoke excellent German. My wife Valerie's German, for example, was impeccable, without a trace of accent. No, that wasn't the reason, Jacobo. I may have had only a very brief experience of your War, but I felt that hatred when I was in Spain. It was a kind of all-embracing hatred that surfaced at the slightest provocation and wasn't prepared to consider any mitigating factor or information or nuance. An enemy could be a perfectly decent person who had behaved generously towards his political opponents or shown pity, or perhaps even someone completely inoffensive, like all those schoolteachers who were shot by the beasts on one side and the many humble nuns killed by the beasts on the other. They didn't care. An enemy was simply that, an enemy; he or she couldn't be pardoned, no extenuating circumstances could be taken into consideration; it was as if they saw no difference between having killed or betrayed someone and holding certain beliefs or ideas or even preferences, do you see what I mean? Well, you'll know all this from your father. They tried to infect us foreigners with the same hatred, but, needless to say, it wasn't something that could be passed on, not to that degree. It was a strange thing your War, I don't think there's ever been another war like it, not even other civil wars in other places. People lived in such close proximity in Spain then, although it's not like that now.'—'Yes, it is,' I thought, 'up to a point.' 'There were no really big cities and everyone was always out in the street, in the cafés or the bars. It was impossible to avoid, how can I put it, that epidermal closeness, which is what engenders affection but also anger and hatred. To our population, on the other hand, the Germans seemed distant, almost abstract beings.'

That mention of his wife, Val or Valerie, hadn't escaped me, but I was even more interested in the fact that, for the first time, he should refer openly to his presence in my country during the War; it wasn't that long since I had first found out about his participation, of which he had never spoken to me before. I looked at his suddenly gaunt face. 'Yes, his features have grown sharper and he has the same look in his eyes as my father,' I thought or regretfully acknowledged, 'that same unfathomable gaze'; and it occurred to me that he probably knew he did not have much more time, and when you know that, you have to make definitive decisions about the episodes or deeds which, if you tell no one, will never be known. ('It's not just that I will grow old and disappear,' poor, doomed Dearlove had said in Edinburgh, 'it's that everyone who might talk about me will gradually disappear too, as if they were all under some kind of curse'; and who could say any different?) It is, inevitably, a delicate moment, in which you have to distinguish once and for all between what you want to remain forever unknown—uncounted, undiscovered, erased, nonexistent—and what you might like to be known and recovered, so that whatever once was will be able one day to whisper: 'I existed' and prevent others from saying 'No, this was never here, never, it neither strode the world nor trod the earth, it did not exist and never happened.' (Or not even that, because in order to deny something you have to have a witness.) If you say absolutely nothing, you will be impeding another's curiosity and, therefore, some remote possible future investigation. Wheeler must, after all, have remembered that on the night of his buffet supper I had asked him by what name he had been known in Spain, and that, had he told me, I would have immediately gone to look up that name in the indexes of all his books, in his War library, on his west shelves, and later on in other books as well. In fact, he was the one who had put the idea in my head, it hadn't even occurred to me until then: perhaps he had done so out of mere congenital pride and vanity, or perhaps, more deliberately, so that having once inoculated me with the thought, I would not be satisfied and would not let go of my prey, something which, as he knew perfectly well, I, like himself and Tupra, never did. Perhaps now he was ready to give me a few more facts and to feed my imagination before it was too late and before he would cease to be able to feed or direct or plot or manipulate or shape anything. Before he was left entirely at the mercy of the living, who are rarely kind to the recent dead. 'That's asking an awful lot, Jacobo,' he had said then in reply to my direct question. 'Tonight anyway. Perhaps another time.' Maybe that 'other time' had come.

'What did you do in Spain during the Civil War, Peter?' I asked straight out. 'How long were you there? Not long, I imagine. Before, you told me that you were just passing through. Who were you working with? Where were you?'

Wheeler gave an amused smile as he had on that earlier night, when he had played with my newly aroused curiosity and said things like: 'If you'd ever asked me about it . . . But you've never shown the slightest interest in the subject. You've shown no curiosity at all about my peninsular adventures. You should have made the most of past opportunities, you see. You have to plan ahead, to anticipate.' He raised his hand to the back of his armchair and felt around without success. He wanted his walking stick and couldn't find it without turning round. I stood up, grabbed the stick and handed it to him, thinking he was going to use it to help him get to his feet. Instead, he placed it across his lap or, rather, rested the ends on the arms of his chair and gripped the stick with both hands, as if it were a pole or a javelin.

'Well, I went twice, but on both occasions I was there only briefly,' he said, very slowly at first, as if he did not entirely want to release the information or the words; as if he were forcing his tongue to anticipate his actual decision, the not entirely definite decision to tell me all: he might want to tell me, but, as he had explained with some embarrassment, he might not yet be authorized to do so. 'The first time was in March of 1937, in the company of Dr. Hewlett Johnson, whose name will mean nothing to you. However, you might be familiar with his nickname, "the Red Dean," by which he was known then and later.' We were speaking in English. Of course I knew the name, of course I had heard of it. In fact, I could scarcely believe it.

'*El bandido Deán de Canterbury!*' I exclaimed in Spanish. 'Don't tell me you knew him.'

'I beg your pardon!' he said, momentarily disconcerted by that sudden intrusion in Spanish and by that strange way of referring to the Dean as 'the bandit Dean of Canterbury.'

'As you may well remember from what I've told you before, my father was arrested shortly after the end of the Civil War. And several false accusations were made against him, one of them, as I've often heard him say, was that he had been "the willing companion in Spain of the bandit Dean of Canterbury." Imagine! That strange cleric was very nearly responsible—albeit indirectly, unwittingly and involuntarily—for my not being born, nor any of my siblings either. I mean that in the normal course of events my father would have been summarily condemned and shot; they came for him in May, 1939, only a month and a half after the Francoists entered Madrid, and in those days if you denounced someone, even if you did so as a mere private individual, you didn't have to prove their guilt, they had to prove their innocence, and how could my father possibly have proved that he had never in his life seen that Canterburian Dean' (I was speaking in English again and so didn't need to resort to the strange Spanish equivalent '*cantuariense*') 'or the falsity of the other charges, which were far graver. He was immensely lucky, and after a few months in prison was acquitted and released, although he suffered reprisals for many years afterwards. But imagine . . .'

'It's certainly a striking coincidence,' Wheeler said, interrupting me. 'Very striking. But let me continue my story, otherwise I'll lose the thread.' It was as if he thought the coincidence to be of no importance, as if he felt coincidences to be the most natural thing in the world, as did Pérez Nuix and I myself. Or perhaps, I thought, he had been planning his next encounter with me for a while, hoping that it would happen, and that I would deign to go and see him, and so knew exactly what he was going to tell me, what partial information he was going to give me, and did not want to be forced to depart from his script by impromptu remarks or distractions or interruptions (he never lost the thread). He may not have wanted any interruptions, but he would have to put up with at least one, when I told him what had happened to Dearlove and demanded, if not an explanation, at least some pronouncement on Tupra's behavior. And so he set my father aside and continued, still slowly, rather like someone reciting something they have previously memorized. 'We were the first to break the naval blockade set up by the Nationalists (I always thought it scandalous that they should call themselves that) in the Bay of Biscay. We set sail from Bermeo, near Bilbao, in a French torpedo boat, and reached Saint Jean de Luz without mishap, despite the widespread and widely believed rumors that the whole area had been mined. That was a Francoist lie, and a very effective one, because it kept boats away and stopped provisions reaching the Basque Country. The Dean described the crossing in *The Manchester Guardian* and a few days later, a merchant vessel, the *Seven Seas Spray*, tried its luck in the other direction, leaving Saint Jean de Luz after dark. And the following morning, when it sailed up the river to the dock in Bilbao, having encountered neither mines nor warships en route, the people of Bilbao massed on the quay and cheered the Captain, who was standing on the bridge with his daughter, and cried: "Long live the British sailors! Long live Liberty!" It was terribly moving apparently. And we paved the way. It's just a shame we were going in the other direction. The Captain was called Roberts.' Wheeler, eyes very wide, paused for a moment, deep in thought, as if he were reliving what he had not actually lived through, but of which he felt himself, in part, the artificer. Then he went on: 'Before that, we'd witnessed the bombing of Durango. We missed being caught in it ourselves by about ten minutes, it happened when we were approaching by road. We saw it from a hillside, in the distance. We saw the planes approaching, they were Junkers 52s, German. Then we heard a great roar and a vast black cloud rose up from the town. By the time we finally drove into the town after nightfall, the place had been almost completely destroyed. According to the first estimates, there had been some 200 civilian deaths and about 800 wounded, among them two priests and thirteen nuns. That same night, Franco's general headquarters announced to the world by radio that the Reds had blown up churches and killed nuns in Durango, in the devoutly Catholic Basque Country, as well as two priests while they were saying mass, one when he was giving communion to the faithful and the other while elevating the Host. All of this was true: the nuns had died in the chapel of Santa Susana, one priest in the Jesuit church and the other in the church of Santa María, but they had been bombed, as had the Convento de los Augustinos. I remember the names or those were the names I was given. It wasn't the Reds who had done it, though, it was those Junkers 52s. That was on March 31st.'—He fell silent for a moment, a look of anger on his face, as if he were feeling the anger he had felt then, some seventy years before. 'That was what your War was like. One lie after another, every day and everywhere, like a great flood, something that devastates and drowns. You try to take one apart only to find there are ten new lies to deal with the next day. You can't cope. You let things go, give up. There are so many people devoted to creating those lies that they become a tremendous force impossible to stop. That was my first experience of war, I wasn't used to it, but all wars are full of lies, they're a fundamental part of them, if not their principal ingredient. And the worst thing is that none are ever completely refuted. However many years pass, there are always people prepared to keep an old lie alive, and any lie will do, even the most improbable and most insane. No lie is ever entirely extinguished.'

'That's why one shouldn't really ever tell anyone anything, isn't that right, Peter?' I said, quoting his words. It was what he had said to me just before lunch, on the Sunday of that now far-off weekend, while Mrs. Berry was waving to us from the window.

He didn't remember or didn't realize I was quoting him, or else he simply ignored it. He stroked the long deep scar on the left side of his chin, a gesture I had never seen him make before: he didn't usually touch or mention that scar, and so I had never asked him about it. If it did not exist as far as he was concerned, I had to respect that. I assumed it was from the war.

'Oh, I learned to lie as well, later on. Telling the truth isn't necessarily better, you know. The consequences are sometimes identical.' However, he didn't linger over that remark, but continued talking in this rather schematic manner, as if he had already drawn up a narrative plan for that day, that is, for the next time I went to see him. 'We were briefly in Madrid, Valencia and Barcelona, and then I came back to England. My second visit took place a year later, in the summer of 1938. On that occasion, my guide, or rather my driving force, was Alan Hillgarth, the head of our Naval Intelligence in Spain. Although he spent most of his time in Mallorca (in fact, his son Jocelyn, the historian, was born there, you've heard of him I expect), he gave me the task of watching and monitoring the movements of Francoist warships in the ports around the Bay of Biscay, on the assumption that I had acquired some knowledge of the area. Most, of course, were German and Italian ships, which had been harassing and attacking the British merchant fleet in 1936, both there in the Bay of Biscay and in the Mediterranean, and so the Admiralty was keen to gather as much information as possible about what kind of ships they were and their positions. I was traveling in the guise of a university researcher, on the pretext of delving into and rummaging around in Spain's old and highly disorganized archives, and I did exactly that—indeed some of the discoveries I made as a specialist in the history of Spain and Portugal date from that period: in fact it was in Portugal, when I was eventually deported there, that I started preparing my thesis on the sources used by Fernão Lopes, the great chronicler of the fourteenth century whom I'm sure you know.' The truth is I'd never heard of him. 'But that's by the by. I was arrested by the Guardia Civil when I was on the Islas Cíes, taking photographs of the cruiser *Canarias*, one of the few ships in the Spanish navy that had gone over to the rebels, as the Republicans called the Nationalists. They searched me, of course, and found compromising material, mainly photographs. Normally, as you can imagine, they would have executed me. We were, after all, in the middle of a war.' Wheeler paused. He may have been telling his story in that rather mechanical way, almost as if it had happened to someone else, but he nevertheless knew when to prolong the uncertainty.

'So how did you escape?' I asked, just to please him.

'I was lucky. Like your father. Like any survivor of any war. They took me in a launch to the Hotel Atlántico in the port of Vigo, and there I was interrogated by two SS officers.'—'It's always hotels they choose to convert into police stations or prisons,' I thought, 'like the one in Alcalá de Henares where they tortured Nin and possibly flayed him alive.'—'In 1935, I had spent part of the summer in Bavaria, at a Hitler Youth camp, for, shall we say, biographical reasons that are irrelevant here. When they found out and checked that I was telling the truth, they invited me out to supper with them. That saved my life. They consulted the Nationalist headquarters in Burgos and, as I understand it, Franco himself gave the order not to have me killed but simply to expel me. After a few minor hitches getting hold of an exit permit, I was taken to the international bridge at Tui where I crossed into Portugal. That was the slowest stretch of my journey, I mean the longest walk of my life, on foot and carrying a suitcase full of books. Two German machine-gunners had their guns trained on my back so that I didn't deviate from the path and ahead of me stood some armed Portuguese guards. And beneath me lay the River Miño. It seemed very wide, and perhaps it was. So, as you see, however disastrous Franco proved to be for the history of your country and for many, many people, he played a crucial role in my personal history. A paradox, eh?

And rather an unfortunate one for me, I must admit. Owing one's life to the clemency of someone who showed clemency to almost no one else is oddly unflattering. Being an ignorant provincial, he was, I suppose, impressed by educated foreigners like me.' He laughed briefly at his own mildly malicious remark, and I laughed too out of politeness. Then he went on. 'As I told you before, I merely passed through your War: I still use words precisely. I didn't stay there long on either occasion, and there would be no reason for either of my names to appear in the index of any of the books written about the conflict. What I did there is hardly worth telling and seems almost ridiculous now. As would my subsequent activities during our War, although some of the things I did were more spectacular or more damaging and, objectively speaking, more important. Toby was quite right when he told you years ago that in times of relative peace, wartime events seem puerile and, inevitably, resemble lies, conceits and fabulations. As I think I've mentioned before, even things I've experienced myself seem fictitious or almost fanciful. I find it hard to believe, for example, that I acted as custodian, companion, escort and even sword of Damocles to the Duke and Duchess of Windsor in the summer of 1940. That was one of my first "special employments" to adapt the term used in my *Who's Who* entry, if you remember. It seems like a dream now. And the fact that it happened abroad doubtless contributes to that feeling.'

I remembered the expression clearly, as I did every word I had read, urged on by Wheeler, in his entry in *Who's Who*. And I understood that dream-like feeling too: 'But that was in another country . . .'

'The Duke and Duchess of Windsor?' I asked. 'Do you mean the former King, Edward VIII, and the divorced woman he abdicated the throne for, that ugly American, Wallis Simpson?' Like almost everyone else, I had read about the couple who were, supposedly, deeply in love, and seen photos of both of them in magazines and books. She, if I remember rightly, was extremely thin, had a hairstyle like that of the housekeeper in Hitchcock's *Rebecca* and very thin red lips, like a scar. The exact opposite of Jayne Mansfield. 'And what do you mean: sword of Damocles?'

'Oh, she wasn't that ugly,' Wheeler said. 'Well, she was, but there was something troubling about her too.' He hesitated for an instant. 'I suppose I can tell you about it; it was a very harmless mission.' The word he used in English—'harmless'—means literally '*sin perjuicio*' or '*sin daño*' 'without harm or hurt.' 'Although it, too, sounds like a lie. I was charged with escorting them from Madrid to Lisbon, and, once there, to make sure that they embarked for the Bahamas. You may remember that he spent the War years there, as Governor of those islands—it was a way of keeping them far from the conflict, as far away as decorum allowed. Both of them had been through an embarrassing, shall we say, Germanophile stage, and had, it was rumored, visited Hitler incognito, before 1939 of course. There was no basis to the rumor, but the government feared like the plague the possibility that they might fall into the hands of the Nazis, that the Gestapo might kidnap them and take them to Germany, of course, but also that they might desert. That they might, in a word, go over to the other side. Churchill didn't trust them at all, and didn't dismiss the idea that if, one day, the Germans invaded us as they had the rest of Europe, the Germans would reinstate the former Edward VIII as a puppet king. Anyway, I and a naval officer from the NID (a very small escort, when I think about it, unimaginable now)'—I knew those initials, the Naval Intelligence Division—'were given a pistol each and told, albeit not in so many words, that we should make use of them if there was the slightest risk of losing the Duke and Duchess in unfortunate circumstances, and regardless of the couple's own wishes.'

'Use them against the Duke and Duchess?' I asked, interrupting him. 'Against an ex-King? Or against the Gestapo?' The whole business really did sound like a lie, although it obviously wasn't.

'It went without saying that we should use them against the Gestapo, although I don't think we would have stood much of a chance. No, we understood that we should use those pistols against the Duke and Duchess. Better dead than in Hitler's hands.'

'We understood? Not in so many words?' I was surprised by such expressions. 'Do you mean that they didn't give you clear orders?'

'MI6 was obsessed with never saying quite what it meant. But you soon learned to decode their orders, especially if you'd been at Oxford. I don't know if they still keep up the custom now. What they said to us, more or less, was: "Under no circumstances must they fall into enemy hands. It would be preferable to have to mourn them." The truth is that I would have interpreted this exactly as did he and the officer from the NID with whom he had shared responsibilities. And he went on to speak about the latter in an amused, almost jocular, gossipy tone: 'I bet you can't guess the name of the naval commander accompanying me.'

'No, I can't,' I said. 'How could I?'

'In fact, almost no one knows about this, not even his biographers.' Then he called out: 'Estelle!' And he automatically corrected himself: there was, after all, a witness present, even though I was a trusted friend and had occasionally heard him call her by her first name before. 'Mrs. Berry!' Mrs. Berry appeared at once, she was always close by, ready to be of service to him. 'Could you please bring me the Chocolate Sailor's passport? You know where I keep it. I want to show it to Jacobo.' That was what he said—'Chocolate Sailor.' 'Now you'll see, it will amuse you no end.' And when, after a few minutes, Mrs. Berry reappeared and handed him a document (I heard her go up the stairs to the top floor and then come back down again), he showed it to me with an almost childlike expression of shy pride on his face: 'Look.'

It was a safe-conduct pass or Courier's Passport as it said at the top, issued by the British ambassador in the city where I was born and valid only for a journey to Gibraltar and back, dated February 16, 1941, right in the middle of the Second World War, and then renewed ten days later and made valid for a journey to London via Lisbon. 'These are to request and require, in the Name of His Majesty,' it read, 'all those whom it may concern to allow Mr. Ian Lancaster Fleming *charged with despatches* to pass freely without let or hindrance and to afford him every assistance and protection of which he may stand in need.'

Courier's Passport.

777

Valid for a journey
to Gibraltar and
return to Madrid
16 February 1941.

Renewed and valid
for a journey to London
via Lisbon
26 February 1941.

Arthur Yencken.

By His Britannic Majesty's

Minister
at
Madrid.

Le Soussigné

Ministre de S. M.
Britannique à
Madrid

These are to request and
require, in the Name of His Majesty,
all those whom it may concern to allow

prie et requiert au nom de Sa Majesté
tous ceux à qui il appartiendra de laisser
passer librement

Mr. Ian Lancaster Fleming.

charged with Despatches to pass freely
without let or hindrance and to afford
him every assistance and protection
of which he may stand in need.

chargé de Dépêches, et de lui accorder en
toute occasion l'aide et la protection dont
il pourra avoir besoin.

Given at Madrid the sixteenth day of February 1941.

Arthur Yencken.

'Oh, I see,' I said, unmoved. 'Ian Fleming.' Wheeler seemed a little disappointed by my lack of surprise. He didn't know that I had already stumbled on the dedications that the creator of James Bond had written in copies of his novels (*To Peter Wheeler who may know better. Salud!*), which was why the fact that they were friends or acquaintances did not catch me entirely unawares. 'So they shared an adventure,' I thought, then said, in order to cheer him up: 'So the two of you shared an adventure in Spain, before he became a writer. How amazing.'

'This passport is from the following year. He gave it to me later on, when he was already famous, as a souvenir of our time in Portugal more than of our time in Spain. We were stuck there with that frivolous pair from June to August. Mrs. Simpson, I mean the Duchess, was not prepared to go into exile, which is how they saw it, without her wardrobe, her table linen, her royal bedlinen, her silver and her porcelain dinner service, all of which was supposed to arrive from Paris, via Madrid, in eight Hispano-Suizas hired by the multimillionaire Calouste Gulbenkian, a risky journey in those days. (Oddly enough, that was the same year in which Gulbenkian, who was Armenian in origin, was declared "Enemy under the Act" and thus lost his British nationality and became Persian instead; so when he helped the Duke and Duchess, I don't know if he was still a friend or an enemy.) Anyway, we had to wait in Estoril and accompany them each night to the casino, either Ian Fleming or myself or, more often, to be on the safe side, both of us. It's hardly surprising that there are so many casinos in the Bond novels: since the 1920s he had been a frequent visitor to the casinos in Deauville, Le Touquet, and later Biarritz; he loved to play, especially baccarat, which was a real stroke of luck because it meant the Duchess was kept entertained when he was around. (He never won very much and even lost, he was a fairly conservative player, placing low bets, not like the fictional character he created.) As for the Duke, at least he was a reasonable conversationalist. We had a somewhat bland but cordial relationship: he had studied here, at Magdalen, and so when I couldn't think how else to entertain him, I could always resort to telling him the latest Oxford gossip. He would listen in amazement, and with a touch of possibly feigned innocence, especially to news of any sexual shenanigans. But he didn't know how to laugh. A dull man and possibly not very bright, but worldly in a pleasant way and, of course, with impeccable manners: after all, there's no denying that he came from a good family.' And Peter laughed again at his little joke. 'Finally, we managed to send the royal couple off safe and sound, along with all the silver and porcelain and bedlinen, in a British destroyer that had been anchored in the Tagus, and it was with great relief that we saw them head off across the Atlantic, bound for the Bahamas. We parted company then, Ian Fleming and I, and didn't meet again until some time later. He was a personal assistant to Rear Admiral Godfrey and had a lot of contact with Hillgarth and with Sefton Delmer, I think he and the latter had been together in Moscow and they collaborated on the PWE's black game . . .'—'Black game,' he said. I had heard young Pérez Nuix use the term 'black gamblers' once, or was it 'wet gamblers'; it had made me think of cardsharps anyway. I didn't know what those initials, PWE, meant, but I didn't want to interrupt Wheeler.—'We lost track of each other, well, that was normal during the War, we were sent here, there and everywhere, wherever they chose to post us, and you always said goodbye to someone knowing full well that you probably wouldn't see them again. Not because it simply wouldn't happen, but because they or you or both of you might easily die. It happened every time I had to leave and say goodbye to Valerie . . . Every time . . .' His voice had been growing fainter and fainter until, when he spoke those last words, his voice was barely a murmur; he had probably worn himself out with speaking. He did not go on. He placed his two arms on the stick that lay across the arms of the chair, as if he had just engaged in some physical exertion and needed to rest. He looked tired, I thought, and his gaze was slightly abstracted. 'Yes, Sefton Delmer's black propaganda, that's what it was,' he added thoughtfully, then fell silent again. Perhaps he had remembered too much, mechanically at first and with great animation subsequently, but all memories lead to more memories and there is always a moment, sooner or later, when one comes upon a sad one, a loss, a nostalgia, an unhappiness that was not an invention. People then sit with eyes lowered or gaze abstracted and stop talking, fall silent.

'I don't know who Sefton Delmer was, Peter,' I said. 'Nor what PWE means.'

He raised his eyes and fixed them on me, wearily and with a certain bewilderment too. He said:

'Why are we talking about this? I don't know how it came up, I've forgotten.' The truth was I had forgotten too. 'Why don't *you* tell me something? You must have a reason for coming here today, without warning. I'm delighted to see you, but tell me, why *have* you come today?'

He was right. Wheeler still missed very little, even if his mind wasn't what it was and even though he now paid less attention to the outside world and was developing a form of loquacious introspection (or, I suppose, just introspection plain and simple when he was alone). Yes, I did have a reason for going to Oxford on that Sunday exiled from the infinite, to his house by the River Cherwell, whose quiet or languid murmur was just audible from where we were sitting, very faint, but still audible, and I recalled the words that my thoughts had attributed to it as they finally fell asleep, very late, on the night I had met Tupra there during a buffet supper: 'I am the river, I am the river and, therefore, a connecting thread between the living and the dead, just like the stories that speak to us in the night, I take on the likeness of past times and past events too, I am the river. But the river is just the river. Nothing more.' I had gone there to tell Wheeler what had happened to me or rather what I had done—after all, nothing had happened to me: other people had been the losers—and to ask him if he could have foreseen something like that happening when he first introduced me to the group to which he, too, had belonged; that is, in his role as intermediary, how far had he been aware of what he was getting me involved in and the risks he was laying me open to. He must have known about the possible consequences of our reports and about the uses to which they were sometimes put, to immediate and practical use or, in my case, to ruthless and criminal use. If, in times of relative peace, the result of one such report was a homicide and a scandalous arrest, the death of an innocent person and the ruin of another, tricked into being the guilty party, then, presumably, during the War, when the group had been created, and there would have been little margin for checking facts and when hasty decisions would sometimes have been made, the interpretation of people and the translation of lives or the anticipation of stories would inevitably have led to people being eliminated, to disasters and calamities. Although they would also have contributed to avoiding those things—I was sure of that. Wheeler would perhaps have found himself in a situation similar to mine now; he was not an unscrupulous person, and even though he might, in his day, have spread outbreaks of cholera and malaria and plague, that wasn't the man I knew. Perhaps his words had killed not one man, but many, some perhaps who should not have died. However, had that happened, he would always have had the consolation, the justification, the excuse that a war was on. I did not.

'Yes, I do have a reason for coming here today, Peter,' I said. And I put him in the picture and explained what had happened, just as I had with Pérez Nuix the night before.

Wheeler heard me out in silence, without interrupting me once, with his walking stick upright now, the tip resting on the floor, and the palm of one hand cradling his cheek in the gesture of one listening attentively. I told him about that first encounter with Dearlove and about Edinburgh, thus affording his weary tongue a rest. I spoke to him of my suspicions—or, rather, certainties—regarding the crime that had caused a frenzy of press speculation in the last few days and about which I assumed he would know.

'Yes, I read about it in the newspapers.' And he brushed the papers beside him with the tips of his fingers, as if he feared dirtying his hands. 'The contemptible Sunday papers are full of it, and Mrs. Berry, who watches television more than I do, told me how shocked and horrified she was. And very disappointed too: apparently, she enjoys this Dearlove fellow's music. I'm clearly not au fait with all her interests.' He paused and added, as if issuing a statement: 'It would never have occurred to me that you and your colleagues had anything to do with it. It's surprising really that the group can still surprise me. Although, naturally, things must have changed beyond belief.' He thought a little more, then said: 'I don't know, Jacobo. I don't know what Tupra is up to, he rarely calls me and confides in me still less. The older one gets, the more distant people become, not that I'm reproaching any of you for that.' But there was reproach, towards me as well, in those words. 'And of course it's very much Tupra's style when he doesn't act impulsively and takes his time; insofar as I know him, that is, which isn't very well. Toby knew him better. At least he knew the Tupra who was his student, the person he used to be. I find it hard to imagine what possible danger that singer could represent, to necessitate laying a trap for him and getting rid of him. But one shouldn't discount anything; in time one learns that, in theory, as people in our line of work come to realize, anyone can be dangerous. And our line of work, don't forget, is about protecting other people. And about protecting ourselves, because if we don't safeguard ourselves, we won't be able to protect anyone. It would seem, though, that you're quite right, given that they've carried out your predictions to the letter. The man was clearly a real danger, a madman. A murderer. You mustn't torment yourself overmuch on his account.'

'You don't mind if I smoke, do you?' He shook his head. I offered him the pack of cigarettes, he shook his head again, and I lit a Karelias. 'I'm afraid that they fulfilled those predictions only because I made them, Peter,' I said. 'It's not that easy. The thing didn't just happen naturally and spontaneously. Calculation and artifice played their part, as did machination and scheming; there was the interested party to whom I gave the idea, as if I were an Iago. Without my prognostications nothing would have happened, I'm sure, and Dearlove would not be a murderer. And a young man who had nothing whatsoever to do with it wouldn't have died. He may not even have received his payment for the job. I doubt that Tupra would have paid him in advance. I don't know how I'm going to be able to live with that.' Wheeler said nothing. He sat looking at me, his hand on his chin, attentive, thoughtful, rather as if I were new to him, or as if he were wondering what to do with me in a situation that was not so much unforeseen as insoluble. He didn't even say 'Hm,' but just sat there, looking at me. 'When I first got involved in this,' I went on, 'did you know that something like this might happen? That what you called my gift or my talent might be used for such things, with one person killed and another sent to prison? That it could lead to such drastic measures being taken, measures that could change lives so radically, and even put an end to one person's life? I don't think I can continue in this job. And I'd like you to know that before anyone else does, before Tupra knows. After all, you were the one who encouraged me, the one who first spoke to me about the group.'

Then I realized that he had got stuck again, that his voice or his words would not come out, that he had been assailed once more by that momentary aphasia, which, according to him was not physiological, but like a sudden withdrawal of his will: this was the third time I had witnessed this, so it obviously wasn't as infrequent as he had told me. As on the two previous occasions, it didn't happen in the middle of a sentence that I could then help him to conclude with conjectures, the way one does with people who stutter, but before he had actually spoken. This time, he was not pointing to anything that would help me orient myself (a cushion in the first instance, a cutting of an Eric Fraser cartoon in the second, when the helicopter flew over). He merely made a gesture with one hand asking me to be patient, to wait, as if he knew that it would soon pass and that it was best to leave him be and not add any more questions to those I had already asked him, best not to pressure him. His lips were pressed tight shut, as if they had suddenly become glued together and he could not open them. His face, however, remained unchanged, it was still attentive and thoughtful, as if he were preparing himself to tell me whatever it was he was going to tell me as soon as he could, once he had recovered the power of speech or liberated the word that had got stuck. This finally happened after about two minutes. He made no reference to his difficulty and answered me as if that silent hiatus had not existed:

'The problem isn't the group, Jacobo,' he said. 'You'll find this out for yourself, but leaving it won't necessarily prevent what you feel has happened to you happening again. It hasn't, in fact, happened to *you*. It has simply happened, and that kind of thing can occur anywhere. You can't control what use other people might make of your ideas or words, nor entirely foresee the ultimate consequences of what you say. In life in general. Never. It doesn't make sense for you to ask me if I knew or didn't know: no one can ever know, in any circumstance, what they might be unleashing, and everything can be put to use, for one purpose or for its complete opposite. The risk that you might trigger misfortunes was no greater here than if you had never moved from your home, from Madrid, from Luisa's side.' I thought of Custardoy for a moment, of my hand holding the pistol and of his shattered hand. Wheeler, with his now recovered voice, was still looking at me hard, as if he were analyzing me. I couldn't help but feel observed or more than that: spied on, decoded, laid bare. Then he added, as if, having examined me, he had decided to risk a diagnosis. 'Of course you can live with it. I can assure you that, unlike Valerie, you *can* live with what's happened to you or with what you think of as having happened to you. Strange though it may seem, in some respects I know you better than I knew her. We've studied you, but in her case, we were too late.'

I didn't know what to ask him about first, whether about the study that had been made of me or about Valerie, his wife, whom he had already mentioned; on that particular Sunday her name was haunting his tongue. I felt that if I showed too much curiosity about her fate, he might withdraw and say again: 'Ah . . . Do you mind if I tell you another day. If that's all right.' It was possible that there wouldn't be another day. It was best if that story arrived of its own accord, if it ever did.

'I know you've studied me,' I repeated. 'I've seen a report about me in some old files at the office. Who wrote that? Was it you?'

'Oh, no, it wasn't me, I've never written reports, I've only ever given them orally, you know, keeping to the bare essentials; writing reports would be too bureaucratic, too boring. No, that must have been Toby, during the time when you taught at Oxford. He was the one who discovered you, if I may use that expression. The first to speak of you to me and, I imagine, to the others.

The one who discovered your good gifts, as I think I told you, what, fifteen years ago? Twenty? No, it can't be that long.'

It didn't seem very likely to me. It was possible, but in that case, who were the 'you' and the 'her' alluded to in the report? '. . . It's almost frightening to imagine what he must know, how much he sees and how much he knows,' it said. 'About me, about you, about her. He knows more about us than we ourselves do. About our characters I mean. Or, more than that, about what shaped us. With a knowledge to which we are not a party . . .' Perhaps 'you' was Cromer-Blake, my other Oxford friend from that time and who was also a great friend of Rylands; and then 'her' had to be Clare Bayes, my former lover, from my youth, and whom I had never seen again. But that would mean that Cromer-Blake had belonged to the group as well, and that didn't fit at all; although, who knows, in Oxford everyone pretends all the time . . . I didn't believe Wheeler in that respect. I assumed that he didn't want to tell me who had written that report and it was easy to attribute it to someone who was dead. Or else he preferred not to confess it had been him, that was more likely. He was always reserved, except when he dropped his guard a little, as on that Sunday.

'What happened to your wife, what happened to Valerie?' And again I had that sense of abuse or sacrilege on my lips when I pronounced her name.

This time he raised his hand to his forehead, the same hand on which he had been resting his cheek and chin, while his other hand was holding, no, gripping his walking stick. He narrowed his eyes as we short-sighted people do in order to see into the distance and no longer directed them at me, but further off, at some point in the garden or the river, through the windows.

'We miscalculated, or, rather, it never even occurred to me that a calculation needed to be made. Had the group been formed earlier, if whoever had come up with the idea had done so a few months before (Vivian, Menzies, Cowgill or Crossman, or it might have been Delmer or even Churchill himself), she might not have been allowed to go so far. Or else I wouldn't have let her. *They* would of course: they would stop at nothing.' And here he used the Spanish expression *pararse en barras*. 'But I wasn't around much during the War, I was away on those "special employments." I only came back occasionally and then only briefly, and so I probably wouldn't have been able to prevent it anyway.' He stopped. He must have been thinking that he had started, but that he could still stop. But I think he decided not to make a dilemma out of it and simply to carry on. 'Valerie, like almost everyone then, wanted to make an active contribution, to help in some way. As I said, she spoke excellent German, because she had spent many summers in her childhood and adolescence with an Austrian family who were old friends of her parents, and the couple's youngest daughter was about her age; there were three other children, the eldest of whom was ten years older than her. She used to spend the summers in Melk, on the banks of the Danube, in Lower Austria, near the famous Benedictine abbey, you know, the Baroque monastery.' He saw my blank look, and added, as a parenthesis: '(It doesn't matter, there's no reason why you should know it.) And the girl who was the same age as her used to spend Christmas with her here in England. When war broke out, Val thought of volunteering as an infiltrator and being sent to Germany. However, she knew she wasn't very brave and would easily have lost heart and been discovered at once. She was very willing and intelligent, but she just didn't have the right temperament for a job like that. She lacked the necessary aplomb and the ability to pretend or, indeed, to deceive. She would never have made a good spy. Contrary to popular belief, most people wouldn't or couldn't spy. Besides, she was very young, only nineteen when the War began; I was seven years older than her at the time, but now the gap in our ages is much greater, and I oughtn't to let that gap get any bigger.' As if to confirm this, he looked down resignedly at his own veined, wrinkled, freckled hand. 'She worked as a translator and interpreter for the Foreign Office until, in August 1941, all the propaganda, both black and white, was handed over to the PWE, and they recruited as many people with a good knowledge of German as they could. The Political Warfare Executive,' he explained at last, and I immediately tentatively translated this to myself: '"*El Ejecutivo de la Guerra Política*,' I thought; or "*El*

Ejecutivo Político de la Guerra" or perhaps *"del Guerrear"* would be closer.' 'I thought this would suit her well. It was quite safe. I didn't want her running any risks, excessive risks, I mean, I didn't want her to be too exposed, because obviously everyone was running risks, as you know, at the front and in the rearguard. The PWE was a secret department and purely temporary, lasting only as long as the War, and began to be dismantled as soon as Germany signed the unconditional surrender on May 7, 1945. Its name or its acronym didn't become public knowledge until much later. A lot of the people who worked there didn't even know they were working for it and thought they were just part of the Foreign Office's PID, Political Intelligence Department, supposedly a small, non-secret section of the Ministry. The people who wrote the white propaganda (the BBC broadcasts intended for Germany and occupied Europe, for example, or the pamphlets that the RAF threw out of their planes on their raids, bearing the imprint of His Majesty's Government and all that) tended to know absolutely nothing about the existence of the black propaganda, or even the grey propaganda, which was being created by their colleagues, who were working in separate divisions and in utmost secrecy. The great advantage of the black propaganda was that no one ever acknowledged that it was British in origin, and we, of course, always denied authorship. As a consequence, the people involved had a completely free hand, with almost no restraints. Remember that officially we weren't doing certain things, even though we were doing them undercover. We never admitted it, because, among other reasons, hardly anyone knew that such things were being done. When Richard Crossman talked about the PWE in the 1970s, in a newspaper article about Watergate that had a lot of repercussions at the time (I remember that Lord Ritchie-Calder and others intervened), he admitted that during the War there had been what he called "an inner Government" with rules and codes of conduct that were completely at odds with those of the visible public Government, and he added that during total warfare, this was a necessary mechanism. Crossman was one of the key figures in the PWE, although not as important as Sefton Delmer, who was the genius responsible for creating a whole new concept of psychological warfare as purely destructive. Crossman had been a member of Harold Wilson's Cabinet in the 1960s and so his views were respected and what he said couldn't easily be contradicted . . .'

Wheeler stopped. I thought he must have grown tired again or that his mouth was dry from so much talking. It was incredible how fluently he spoke when his words did not get stuck, even if he had perhaps lapsed again into that strangely introspective loquacity. I wondered when we would return to the young Valerie, forever young and growing daily ever younger than him. I asked him if he would like something to drink, and he said, yes, a glass of water and told me to help myself to whatever I wanted, that I should ask Mrs. Berry to bring it, and he apologized for not having offered me anything before. I replied that I would go to the kitchen myself, preferring not to bother her. I brought him his water and, after opening a cold beer for myself, took the opportunity to satisfy a minor curiosity:

'Was black propaganda also called "the black game"? Are they the same thing? You used that expression earlier.'

'Yes,' he said. 'Well, it doesn't only refer to propaganda, but to all black operations. It may have been Crossman and Delmer who invented the term, I'm not sure. According to them, the Americans—who, in part, copied us when it came to subversion techniques and who have reveled in using them ever since (rather clumsily, it must be said)—never learned to apply them as we did, to play it as a game despite the gravity of the situation. Far worse, they didn't give it up in peacetime. There was a book published about twenty or twenty-five years ago entitled *The Black Game*. I read it, it's written by someone called Howe.'

'Was it also known as "the wet game"?' I was almost certain now that 'wet gamblers' had been the term used by Pérez Nuix on the night she visited me unannounced.

'It's not a term I've heard very often, but possibly, yes. Perhaps because black operations often involved blood being spilled. White operations, on the other hand, rarely did; they were dry. But where were we?' he added, slightly irritated. 'Why am I telling you all this? Oh dear me, I've forgotten again.' The Spanish equivalent of 'Oh dear me' would be '*Ay Dios,*' but in English there was no mention of God. Perhaps his memory could no longer stretch as far as it once could, from the beginning of a story to its end. Perhaps that was the one area in which his recent decline had become noticeable. He lost sight of the initial thread, although it took only the slightest of nudges for him to recover it.

'You were telling me about your wife,' I said to help him out. 'About what she did during the War.'

'Ah, yes, I was going to tell you how Valerie died, since you ask, and not for the first time either,' he replied. 'But it's important that you understand what the PWE was and how it worked, that you grasp precisely what she was involved in and what she became used to. In a sense, Sefton Delmer was the PWE's equivalent of Bomber Harris, except that he didn't have planes or troops at his command, just experts in deceit and forgery.' And when he saw that the name of Harris rang only a faint bell with me, he added: 'Arthur Harris, the Air Marshal, was the one who ordered the burning of fifty thousand Hamburg citizens and one hundred and fifty thousand Dresden citizens towards the end of the War on the cynical pretense that he was attacking military targets; he also flattened Cologne, Frankfurt, Düsseldorf and Mannheim; he was an implacable man with too much power, almost a psychopath really, willing to use any means at his disposal to crush the enemy and win.' Then I remembered him mentioning Harris before: 'A few months ago I read in a book by Knightley,' he had said, 'that the Commander-in-Chief of Bomber Command, Sir Arthur Harris, dubbed the members of the SOE amateurish, ignorant, irresponsible and mendacious,' the same men who had been behind the assassination of Heydrich using bullets impregnated with botulin and behind many other acts of sabotage, destruction and terror. 'Harris and Delmer were, according to Crossman, possibly the only ones who were allowed, in their respective fields, to wage total war—the total war that Göring and Goebbels had threatened but never carried out. Indeed, Delmer was allowed to outdo the Nazis themselves (that is, he plumbed still lower depths than they did) in lies and calumnies, in the manipulation and invention of news and information and in deceiving the enemy population. Black propaganda, like strategic bombing, was nihilist in its aims and purely destructive in its effects, as Crossman himself acknowledged. And it turned out to be an enormously effective weapon, which is why everyone uses it now and with no qualms at all. Sefton Delmer was a real genius, as no one would deny. He was born in Berlin of an Australian father.'—'Yet another bogus Englishman,' I thought, 'how many more?'—'He had studied there and later here in Oxford; before the War, as *The Daily Express* correspondent in Berlin, he had met Ernst Röhm and, through him, Hitler, Göring, Goebbels and Himmler. He had a perfect understanding of the German character and psychology; in fact, his background meant that, when War first broke out, he was initially eyed with great suspicion here and wasn't allowed to occupy any responsible post until the security services had observed him and given him the green light—imagine that. From the people who worked with him he demanded absolute secrecy, discipline and determination, in other words, a complete lack of scruples. He gradually began recruiting Germans to his team: former members of the International Brigades, emigrés, refugees, then a few prisoners of war willing to collaborate, an important deserter who had escaped to London after the failed attempt on Hitler's life in July 1944, and even a former member of the SS. He said the same thing to all of them as soon as they arrived in Woburn, where the department was based: "We are waging against Hitler a kind of total war of wits. Anything goes, so long as it serves to bring nearer the end of the war and the complete defeat of the Reich. If you are at all squeamish about what you may be called upon to do against your own countrymen you must say so now. I'll understand that. However, you will be no good to us in that case, and no doubt some other job will be found for you. But if you feel like joining me, I must warn you that in my unit we are up to all the dirty tricks we can devise. The dirtier the better. No holds barred. Lies, phone-tapping, embezzlement, treachery, forgery, defamation, disinformation, spreading dissension, making false statements and accusations, you name it. Even, don't forget, sheer murder."'—'Sheer murder' was the expression he used.—'Valerie heard him say this more than once. She became quite close to him.'

Wheeler paused for thought, perhaps remembering Valerie being close to Sefton Delmer. Now he raised his hand to his lips and gently stroked them. Then he again ran his thumb down the scar on his chin, it was odd that I'd never seen him make that gesture until then. I wondered if he was inviting me to ask him about that too. However, as long as he did not mention it himself, I would abstain.

'And what were these dirty tricks? What exactly did the black game involve?' I asked.

'Well, most of their activities we only found out about after the War was over. Needless to say, they forged everything. That was one of the things we really excelled at: radio broadcasts, every kind of document, including orders from Reich bigwigs like General von Falkenhorst who was in command of the troops in Norway; soldier's leave permits, entry passes into vital installations and buildings, circulars, satirical posters, postage stamps, rubber stamps, envelopes and letterheads, even packs of cigarettes, I remember seeing some called Efka—"Pyramiden," and everything had to be able to pass as genuinely German, or at least, when that proved impossible, as having been made in Germany or in Austria, which would create the uneasy sense that we had more infiltrators there than we really did, that we had far more people hidden in their territory, equipped with the infrastructure and the means and a tremendous operating capacity, which not only worried them, it made them waste a lot of time and effort pursuing and hunting down ghosts. We could reach everywhere with the radio, even submarines, whose crews had the demoralizing feeling that they were being watched by us and could not conceal their positions from us. But the most important thing was to stir up enmity among the Germans themselves and to work to their detriment, both at the collective and the individual level, so as to foment distrust among them and make them fear each other. And of course, when feasible, to eliminate or bring about the downfall of high-ranking officials both civil and military. The black section of the PWE printed wanted posters of SS officers who were accused of being traitors, deserters, impostors or criminals wanted by the authorities: they urged people to shoot these men on sight and offered rewards of ten thousand marks or more, and assured them that even the Iron Crosses the officers might be wearing were mere forgeries. It was all very calculated. Some of those posters, supported by a radio campaign, showed the Reichkommissar Ley, a Nazi Party heavyweight with a somewhat dissolute lifestyle, and accused him of hoarding ration coupons, and Dr. Ley was obliged to deny this indignantly: "I am a perfectly normal consumer!" he roared over the radio.' And Wheeler couldn't help chuckling, remembering something that Valerie herself might have laughingly told him, breaking the Official Secrets Act to which she would have been subject. 'They issued stamps bearing the image not of Hitler, but of that ambitious man Himmler, with the intention of setting them at each other's throats, giving more credence to the persistent rumors that the latter was hoping to replace the former as Führer and thus putting Himmler on the spot. But there were more serious things, too, much wetter things. A common practice of Delmer's was to have fake letters sent to the family members of German soldiers who had died of their wounds in military hospitals in Italy. They would intercept the uncoded cablegrams sent by the directors of those hospitals to the Party authorities in Germany and which contained all the information about the deceased and the address of his next of kin. The letters forged by Delmer's team, written in perfect German and on the hospital's headed paper, were supposedly penned by a distressed comrade or nurse who had remained by the dead man's side until the last, and what they usually said, in horrified tones, was that the soldier had, in fact, been killed by lethal injection on the orders of his superiors, when they were informed that he would no longer be available for active service. The Nazi doctors needed the beds for those soldiers who would soon be able to be sent back to the front, and so they got rid of the badly injured men without compassion or gratitude, cruelly and expeditiously, as if they were so much detritus. Delmer and his unit were perfectly aware that they were the ones who were practising real and extreme cruelty by making a grief-stricken widow or someone's aged parents or orphaned children believe such a falsehood (which was, on the other hand, quite believable). However, if this served to feed discontent and rancor among the population, to lower the morale of the combatants, spread disunity among the troops and encourage desertions, that was what mattered. Don't forget, Jacobo, the Second World War felt like a battle for survival. And it was, it really was. And in wars like that the limits on what one can acceptably do are constantly broadening out, almost without one realizing it. Times of peace judge times of war very harshly, and I'm not sure how far it's possible to make such a judgment. They are mutually exclusive: in time of war, for example, peace is inconceivable—and vice versa, a fact that tends to be overlooked. Nevertheless, there are still things that do seem reprehensible even while they're happening or being perpetrated in the most permissive of times, and you see, all those . . .yes, vile deeds, I suppose . . .were kept hidden at the time as well, when the War was being waged and no one knew how it would end. Sefton Delmer's unit didn't officially exist, and all its members were told to deny its existence (and, therefore, their own existence) both to the world as a whole and to other organizations that were almost (but not quite) as secret, like the SOE, or like us later on, silent and silenced for rather different reasons but mainly to do with secrecy and discretion. And do you know, after the War, not only was the PWE dissolved immediately, its black members were given more or less the following instructions: "For years we have abstained from talking about our work to anyone not in our unit, and therefore little is known about us or our techniques. People may have their suspicions, but they don't know anything for certain. And to keep it that way, we want you to continue as you have up until now. Don't allow anything or anyone to provoke you into boasting about the work we've done, about the tricks and traps we laid for the enemy. If we start to show off to people about the ingenious things we got up to, who knows where it will end. So, mum's the word."' And I remembered having seen that last expression on one of the 'careless talk' posters. "'Propaganda should, by its nature, be a subject one doesn't talk about.' This was doubtless out of prudence,' Wheeler went on, 'but also, I think, because the work was such that they couldn't feel entirely proud of it, and less so in the final stages of the War than at any other time. Valerie, *a fe mía*, certainly wasn't proud of it.' And he used that rather literary Spanish of his, *a fe mía*, the equivalent of the English 'forsooth.' 'When the German civilians were at their most desperate and confused, our phony radio stations heaped still more confusion and desperation on them. We warned, for example, that an enormous number of counterfeit German marks were circulating in the country, which meant that people could trust neither their own money nor what other people gave them. The worst, however, came after the brutal bombings by Harris and the Americans, and again when troops were already invading Germany, ours from the west and the Russians from the east. During air raids, the German stations stopped transmitting so as not to serve as beacons for the RAF and USAF planes. But in a matter of seconds, don't ask me how, Delmer and his colleagues managed to take over their frequencies, pretending, in their immaculate German, that normal transmissions had been resumed, and sending out bewildering, disorienting, counterproductive or contradictory messages that wreaked the maximum amount of havoc and spread chaos. Initially, survivors in the devastated cities (Hamburg, Bremen, Cologne, Dresden, Leipzig and so many others) were advised not to move, not to leave their respective cities and to wait for help to arrive. Delmer, apparently at Churchill's behest, ordered them to do exactly the opposite, via a communiqué that he passed off, of course, as an official statement from the Reich. His team informed the people that seven bomb-free zones had been set up in the center and south of Germany, to which refugees could go and where they would be safe from aerial attacks by the enemy. They were assured that neutral representatives of the Red Cross in Berlin had told the authorities of the Reich that Eisenhower himself was going to declare those seven areas to be safe, and that the banks were moving their securities there. This information was, of course, entirely false, but it had a tremendous effect. The roads were inundated with whole families fleeing towards those imaginary zones, with their ragged children, their wounded and their few household goods piled into carts, in dilapidated buses that ran out of gas, even in hearses, in whatever they could find to carry them away from their infernos. It was total chaos. Many roads were blocked by such large numbers of people that it hampered the defensive work of the German army, who didn't know how to avoid these hordes, nor where to put them or how to get them out of the way, or what to do with them. And it's likely that still more bombs fell on many of those terrified displaced persons who set off en masse in search of those phantom safe zones, and who would perhaps have survived among the ruins of their cities, if they'd sat tight, because there were no safe zones anywhere in Germany, or only in those places that had already been destroyed.'

Wheeler stopped speaking and eagerly drank some water, finishing the whole glass in one gulp or, rather, in several slow prolonged gulps, the way children drink when they're very thirsty, but, who, unable to cope with too much liquid at once, have to pause now and then to recover their breath, although without for a moment removing their lips from the cup, as if they feared that someone might snatch the glass from them. Then he summoned Mrs. Berry, asked her to bring him more water and a few olives as an accompaniment to my beer. 'That's how you still drink in Spain, isn't it, with something to nibble on so that the alcohol doesn't go to your head,' he said. 'I've got some Spanish ones, crushed olives with lemon, from Andalusia, I believe. They're very good. I understand you can buy them in Taylor's, almost opposite where you used to live.' I remembered that delicatessen well. It was a fairly expensive shop, but during my Oxford years, I had largely subsisted on its many frivolous products (I've never been much of a cook). I told Mrs. Berry not to go to any trouble on my behalf, there was no need, but Wheeler had asked her for them and she wanted to please him. When she had left the room and I had my olives before me—although she never really left the room entirely, she continued to come and go, always silent and busy—I asked Wheeler:

'And is that what your wife became used to, Peter? To what you called "those vile deeds"? At the time, I suppose, they weren't seen like that. And it might be that they *are* vile deeds now, but that they weren't then. Just part of the struggle.' I paused, slightly perplexed because I wasn't sure that I myself quite understood what I had just said, which is why I added: 'If, that is, it's possible for something to be fine when you do it, or at least justifiable, but not when you've done it, since the two things are one and the same. I mean, I don't know if it's possible for the same thing to be different when it's present and when it's past, when it's an ongoing action and when it's just a memory. Oh, ignore me.'

Wheeler looked at me as if he really had become lost in my confused thoughts, and didn't answer me at once; indeed, he seemed to be taking me at my word and ignoring me.

'In one of his volumes of autobiography,' he said, 'I can't recall whether it was *Trail Sinister* or *Black Boomerang* (I read them when they were published in the sixties, partly to see if Valerie was mentioned or alluded to at any point; she wasn't, nor was the affair in which she played the largest part, the leading role), Sefton Delmer described traveling to Germany towards the end of March 1945 and seeing the spectacle with his own eyes, the same spectacle he had seen before in Spain during the final days of your War (he had been there too, as a correspondent) as well as in Poland and in France: people aimlessly fleeing, trudging through a series of ruined landscapes, dragging with them all that remained of their possessions or that they had been able to pile into their broken-down vehicles, or walking along roads and across fields with very young children on their backs, their eyes empty or terrified, sometimes with dead children whom they couldn't bring themselves to bury at the roadside or whom they didn't dare to abandon, but continued pointlessly to carry as if they were effigies . . . And Sefton Delmer said that he didn't stop to ask anyone if, by any chance, what had first impelled them to set off along the roads and begin their aimless wanderings had been the messages broadcast on Radio Cologne or Radio Frankfurt, whose frequencies he had taken over. I remember that he wrote: "I didn't want to know. I feared the answer might be 'yes.'" So he did know. But he had done those things and would have done them again, just as almost everyone else was driven to do such things, just as almost everyone else does in time of war. During a war, very few ideas, even the most unlikely, fail to be put into practice. Almost anything that occurs to anyone as a way of harming the enemy finds an outlet, although it might not be publicly acknowledged afterwards. The trick we played with those radio broadcasts was so effective and had such grave consequences that the Nazi authorities were obliged to abandon the airwaves altogether as a way of issuing orders or instructions to the population. They had to fall back on the *Drahtfunk*, a wired diffusion network on which we could not intrude but which was much more problematic and restricted in scope. Yes, Delmer and his black game made a huge contribution. I don't know if he won the War for us, but he certainly contributed to our winning it more quickly.'

Wheeler really did seem weary now. At any moment, he might abandon his story, leave the rest for another day, fall silent or perhaps bring it to a definitive end. He might even regret having started, something I didn't want to risk, because I might never again find him in the same talkative mood, given that he normally kept himself to himself. 'Who knows, I might never find him again in any kind of mood,' I thought, 'if I'm going to leave here soon and go back to Spain. It's quite likely that I'll never see him again.' And so I decided to insist and even hurry him along.

'So what happened to Valerie?' I didn't mind pronouncing her name now. 'What was this affair in which she played the largest part? The leading role you said.'

Wheeler leaned forward slightly, rested both hands on the handle of his walking stick, which he had positioned upright between his legs, with his chin resting on his two hands, and I had the feeling that this was a way of gathering momentum or of preparing himself to make a major effort. His eyes shone and his voice sounded stronger, for it had grown weaker as he talked. It occurred to me that he might never have told, or only a long time ago and to very few people, what he was probably about to tell me. For I was still not certain that he would.

'Well,' he said, 'I'm not sure how familiar you are with the Nazi racial laws.'

'Not very,' I answered at once; I didn't want there to be any more pauses. 'Like everyone else, I have a vague general idea.'

'They were very precise, almost complex and, more than

that, from 1933 onwards, they kept changing. Their application also varied depending on the people and organizations who interpreted them. The Ministry of the Interior was less strict in applying them than Dr. Adolf Wagner, the Nazi Party's chief authority on the subject, and he, in turn, was less rigorous than, for example, the SS. However, the relevant point here is this: you were considered to be a Jew if at least three of your grandparents were Jewish, regardless of any other factors; a person with two Jewish grandparents and who either belonged to the Jewish religion or was married to a Jew at the time the Race Laws came into effect was also legally Jewish (and, apart from a few very rare exceptions, "half-Jews" ended up being treated as Jews); then there were *Mischlinge* of the first degree, crossbreeds, who had two Jewish grandparents, but who neither professed the Jewish religion nor had a Jewish spouse; lastly, there were *Mischlinge* of the second degree who had only one "contaminating" Jewish grandparent and three grandparents who were "gentiles," that is, "Aryans" or what the Nazis termed "Germans." The difference was crucial, because, generally speaking, *Mischlinge* of the second degree were left in peace, and some were even able to obtain a German Blood Certificate, once the application had been studied by Hitler himself, who apparently judged the matter to be of sufficient importance to merit his spending time poring over each and every file and deciding whether or not the applicant should be "reclassified," as several thousand were. He did so at his own pace, of course, and I imagine that, unlike the applicants, he was in no particular hurry to make those judgements: some were "Jews" asking to be promoted to first-degree *Mischlinge*, or first-degree *Mischlinge* wanting to be recategorized as second-degree *Mischlinge*, with those in the second degree aspiring to "Aryanisation" and the Certificate. Not a few committed suicide when they were relegated to "Jewry." People deemed to be doubtful cases were so panic-stricken that they often attempted, sometimes successfully, to forge, substitute, conceal or destroy their grandparents' birth certificates, especially between 1933 and 1939, after which this became virtually impossible. Many officials in town halls and registry offices, or wherever the documents were kept, removed compromising documents in exchange for outrageous sums of money or even property, sometimes even making use of convenient fires that broke out in certain parts of their archives or of plagues of highly selective mice. Or, if the forgery brought to them was perfect, written on old paper and everything, they would agree to do a swap and convert a Jewish grandfather or grandmother into a Catholic or a Protestant, with a change of surname included. This was a frequent occurrence in smaller towns and cities, where it was much easier. Of course, these officials almost never actually destroyed the document that had been replaced or removed, unless the payer demanded that it be handed over so that he or she could take personal charge of its disappearance. This wasn't usually the case, Jews not being in a position to lay down many conditions, and so the official would then keep the document just in case things changed in the future. The evidence, then, only vanished temporarily. Pour me a glass of sherry, will you,' added Wheeler, as if telling me all this had cheered him up. Talking about history often does have a cheering effect on the old.

"Do you have any preference?' I asked, pointing to a high shelf to my right, full of bottles.

'Any of those will do,' he said. I got up, poured him a glass and handed it to him; he took two sips and continued (and now I had no fear that he might stop): 'When, in time, a "quarter-Jew" was revealed to be a "Jew" or a "half-Jew" in disguise or else a second-degree crossbreed, or when an "Aryan" was shown to be a first-degree *Mischling* in disguise, it mattered little what the Laws said: their fate depended, above all, on who found them out and on what those people decided to do with the information and to whom they chose to give it. Taking the story to the local police or mayor wasn't at all the same thing as going to the SS or the Gestapo. It might be that nothing happened, the officials involved might turn a blind eye, or the guilty party, as punishment for his deceit, might be despatched to a concentration camp along with all his family. Apparently Göring or Goebbels—I can't remember which now—said: "I will decide who is a Jew." And when he said this, it wasn't in order to "judaize" someone, but because, on that occasion, it suited him to declare a particular person to be a non-Jew. Contrary to popular belief, and contrary to Nazi propaganda, there were many *Mischlinge* and even "half-Jews" who served the Reich loyally, even in the army and in positions of responsibility, both administrative and within the Party. A few years ago, a book came out entitled *Hitler's Jewish Soldiers*, by someone called Bryan Rigg—have you read it?—which gave an account of some of the more remarkable cases. The photo of a blond, blue-eyed "half-Jew" called Goldberg was used in the propaganda press as an example of "The Ideal German Soldier." Can you imagine? There were colonels, generals and admirals who were "half-" or "quarter-Jews," although Hitler conveniently declared them to be "Aryans." However, a Major General, Ernst Bloch by name, like the philosopher, and a veteran of the First World War, had to be discharged after Himmler made a personal protest. I don't know or can't remember what happened to him after that: perhaps he went from commanding troops to wasting away in a concentration camp, perhaps he fell from grace entirely. Much depended on chance, or on having the friendship or favor of someone high up. Field Marshal Milch, for example, was a "half-Jew," and his friend Göring provided him with false (forged) evidence that he was not, in fact, the son of his official "fully Jewish" father, but of his mother's "Aryan" lover; nobody knows, of course, what his mother, if she was alive at the time, would have made of this extraordinary revelation, or if she actually had such a lover. Milch was reclassified as "Aryan" and awarded the Ritterkreuz for his actions during the campaign in Norway. As you see, in the Germany of the time, it was a blessing to be a bastard." And Wheeler laughed again, in the mocking tone that always reminded me of his brother Toby's very characteristic laugh. "But how did we get on to this, Jacobo? I'm sorry about these memory lapses, it only happens with the immediate present. What with them and my moments of aphasia, pretty soon, I won't be able to tell anyone anything.'

'He's not so bad yet that he doesn't realize it,' I thought, 'which is some consolation, but he wouldn't have suffered such blanks a year or even a few months ago. It's as if he and my father were marching to the same drummer, at the same speed, although Peter is in better shape. Despite being a year older, he'll probably last longer. How sad when neither of them is here any more. How sad.'

'You'll know better than I,' I said, 'but I think it had to do with your wife, with her death. At least I believe so.'

'Ah, yes,' he said, 'it has a great deal, indeed, everything to do with my wife. Yes, yes.' And as he repeated that word, he seemed once more to pick up the thread. 'As I said, in the black section of the PWE, there were people who didn't even know they were working for it, who didn't even know of its existence. Valerie, of course, had no idea. However, there was a fellow who probably knew very well just who and what he was working for; he only turned up at Woburn or Milton Bryan occasionally, with a whole battery of ideas and, it would seem, enjoyed complete autonomy, even from Delmer. His name was Jefferys, almost certainly an alias, and he had a truly diabolical mind, or so Valerie told me when I returned from Jamaica or the Gold Coast or from Ceylon or wherever I'd been posted, and we were able to spend a couple of weeks or a few days together. Jefferys' mission was to create disruption, to invent problems which, however secondary or outlandish, couldn't be ignored by the Germans, who would be obliged to try and find a remedy. And he got the staff all fired up too, something he excelled at apparently.'

'To spread outbreaks of cholera?' I couldn't help asking. But he didn't pick this up as an allusion to himself, perhaps because he no longer remembered saying it.

'Exactly. Or even chicken pox. We were all convinced, in all the divisions, sections, units and groups, in the SIS in general, in the SOE, in the PWE, in the OIC, as well as in the NID, the PWB and, of course, the SHAEF, that any setback that might distract the Germans from what was really important, anything that hampered their war-time activities or took them away from or made them neglect their tasks, that even minimally diminished their efficiency, would be hugely to our advantage, and would help us to gain time while we waited for the Americans to make up their mind to enter the War (how tedious and hesitant they were; and then they have the nerve to boast about their contribution). It was a matter of keeping the largest possible number of men occupied with bothersome or seemingly dangerous minutiae. Each time the Nazis had to send a soldier or a member of the Gestapo to tackle some unexpected task that had nothing to do with the War proper, it helped a little and gave us some advantage, or that was our feeling, which, up until December 1941, after more than two years of resisting on our own, was one of absolute desperation. Anyway, this Jefferys fellow would arrive—a whirlwind of energy—and stay for a week, issuing all kinds of instructions and urging the people there to come up with their own tricks and dodges, all intended to cause the maximum amount of damage. He was an enthusiastic, hyperactive, febrile, infectious kind of man, who raised spirits simply because he treated everything as if it were really important. According to him, the smallest obstacle could prove useful, anything to make them trip or stumble. A city in Germany or occupied Europe, for example, might be plagued with murders or burglaries, with fires in buildings and hotels, or else an epidemic, even if it was only flu, might be declared, or the supplies of electricity, gas, coal or water were cut off; there might be a shortage of medicines in hospitals or foodstuffs left to rot; all those things could help. The accumulation of problems and calamities and crimes breeds insecurity, distrust and anxiety, and having to worry about many things at once is what most exasperates and wears people down. The more off-balance the Nazis were, the more burdened with nonessential tasks, the more chance we had of landing them a blow in the solar plexus.'

'You're not telling me that ordinary murders were committed that weren't ordinary at all? You're not telling me that you and your group planned and committed random murders of civilians?'

Wheeler made an ambiguous gesture with his open hand at forehead height, as if he were raising the brim of an imaginary hat.

'No, I don't believe so. Sefton Delmer may have been a *bon vivant* and a pragmatist, with few scruples about the subversive techniques used to undermine and destroy the enemy, a man who, in the middle of all this, was seen blithely eating, drinking and laughing as if entirely unaffected, but he did have a remnant of conscience. According to Hemingway, who met up with him in Madrid during our War, when both men were correspondents, he looked like 'a ruddy English bishop.' Others thought they saw a resemblance to Henry VIII, because he was a big man verging on the obese, with rather bulging eyes and a florid complexion. And since razors were in short supply during the War, he had let his beard grow too. Jefferys, on the other hand, did advocate encouraging or even actually carrying out non-political murders: nowadays, this would be termed terrorism. I'm sure they took no notice of him in that respect, and besides, the SOE, with its local collaborators in every country, had quite enough objectives of its own, in particular, military ones. When it came to acts of sabotage and torpedoings, most of his exuberant ideas were well received. And Valerie gave him an idea of her own. Yes, Valerie had an idea.' And Wheeler's tone, as he spoke those last two sentences, grew suddenly much more somber. He took another couple of sips of sherry, again rested his walking stick on the arms of his chair, gripped it with one hand, as if it were a bar to hold on to, and continued without further hesitation: he had decided to tell me this story and he was going to. 'Everyone wanted to help in those days, Jacobo. It was incredible how the whole country rallied round, first to endure, and then to destroy the Nazis. For those of us who lived through those times, what happened later on, in the Thatcher era, with the ridiculous Falklands War, when people got so fired up and cocky, was utterly shameful, a fake, a farce, a grotesque imitation of that other War. During the real War there was no cockiness and no vaudeville patriotism.' Wheeler pronounced 'vaudeville' with a French accent, as my father would have done. 'People simply resisted, but never bragged or boasted about anything. Everyone did what they could and, with a few rare exceptions, no one gave themselves a medal for it. They were real times, not phony, not sham. Jefferys was a stimulus, a spur during the days he spent in Woburn, or, rather, Milton Bryan, and Valerie wanted to help as much as she could, to make a real contribution. She worked hard. Anyway, her Austrian friend's older sister, the one who was some ten years older, Ilse by name, had had a boyfriend in the days when Valerie still used to spend her holidays in Melk with the Mauthner family, and so she got to know him over several summers. The boyfriend was already a convinced Nazi by then—I'm talking about the period from 1929 or '30 to 1934 or '35, which was when Valerie stopped going to stay with them and her friend stopped visiting her at Christmas, when they were both fourteen or fifteen. The older sister and the boyfriend finally got married in 1932 or '33 and moved to Germany, and the younger sister, Maria, with whom Valerie corresponded during the rest of the year and up until shortly before the War, had told her how worried the family were about that entirely expected marriage. The Mauthners always hoped it would never happen, that Ilse would break up with her boyfriend, as often happens with couples who meet very young. The man, whose name was Rendl—'

Here I couldn't help but interrupt him.

'Rendel? R-e-n-d-e-l?' I immediately spelled it out for him.

'No. In Austria, it was written without the second "e,"' he replied. 'But, yes, the Rendel you know and who works for Tupra is the grandson of that older sister and her husband. Not that I've ever met him and I only know his father slightly. I helped his father, Ilse's son, financially, so that he could come to England when he was still a child; afterwards, I preferred not to stay in touch. That's another story though. But let's not get ahead of ourselves. The husband, Rendl, and this was known by his in-laws, had a Jewish grandmother, who had died before he was born, and so he was a "quarter-Jew," a second-degree *Mischling*. As I said before, nothing tended to happen to such people because they were considered to be "German" and were assimilated, although they couldn't, in theory, aspire to holding any important post. However, that quarter of Jewishness worried the whole Mauthner family, the father, the mother and the other sisters. Not because they were Nazis—they were, it seems, apolitical, passive people, who did, later on, I imagine, become Nazified—what worried them was a fear of any "contamination," which was a very widespread fear at the time. Bear in mind that the Nuremberg Laws were passed in 1935, but in reality all they did was regulate many of the measures that had already been taken against the Jews unofficially (the whole business went back a long way) and to make official and legal an already existing situation, namely the intense social dislike of Jews and the discrimination against them. Now if Rendl hadn't been such a fervent Nazi, he could have lived a reasonably quiet life. However, he wanted to join the SS and achieved that ambition shortly after he got married. In order to do so, he first had to get rid of that Jewish grandmother, I assume by doing what so many others had done: offering a large bribe to the authorities in the place where she was born. And as a consequence of that concealment, that falsification, that imposture, the "stain" became a secret to be jealously guarded, and the Mauthner daughters were told as much as soon as the "cleansing" of the records had taken place. For one of them, however, it was too late.

'She had told Valerie, I mean, your wife, Peter.' This time I corrected myself at once.

Wheeler noticed my uncertainty. Very few things escaped him even now.

'It's all right, you can call her Valerie. And she wasn't my wife at the time. She was called Valerie Harwood then and could have imagined very little of what was to come. She couldn't even have imagined me because we hadn't yet met. But, yes, Maria Mauthner had told a friend who, a few years later, would turn into an enemy. Not a personal enemy, of course, but . . . how could you best describe it? National, political, patriotic? I don't know what kind of enemy one becomes in time of war. You hate complete strangers and old friends, you hate all-embracingly, hate a whole country or even several. It's very odd when you think about it. It makes no sense at all, and it's such a waste. Maria had not only told her about it just once, she continued to mention it in the years that followed, by letter. They had been friends since childhood, they trusted each other, they talked openly, they gave each other their news. Valerie learned that Ilse had three children, a boy and two girls, she even met the oldest, when he was just a baby, during her last visit to Melk, in 1934 or '35. She also learned that Rendl, whom she had always considered an imbecile when she'd met him during her summer visits, a kind of pre-fanatic, was rising fast in the SS; and when the two friends stopped corresponding in 1939, she knew that he had reached the rank of Major, or perhaps Captain, in one of the Cavalry Divisions of the SS. One of those divisions, by the way, the 33rd, met a sad (for us joyous) fate when it was wiped out at the Battle of Budapest in 1945, but I don't know if that was his division. Not that it matters, because, by then, Rendl wasn't in the Cavalry or in the SS, but, quite likely, in a concentration camp, in a mass grave or else incinerated.'

'What happened?' I asked so that he didn't get distracted recalling facts about the War.

Wheeler finished his sherry and hesitated as to whether or not he should have another. I encouraged him, got up to fill his glass, and he glanced across to where Mrs. Berry had been coming and going, but then we heard her begin to play upstairs, in the empty room where there was nothing else to do but sit down before the piano: perhaps it was her practice time, before lunch, at least on those Sundays exiled from the infinite. Wheeler pointed with one finger up at the ceiling and then at the bottle.

'You know already, don't you, Jacobo? You can imagine what happened. Valerie told me that she had doubts about the plan and would have liked to ask me my opinion. But I was away most of the time, and communications were difficult and brief, there wasn't time to discuss problems. When she told Jefferys about it, she hadn't had any contact with Maria for three or four years, and didn't even know if she was still alive. Besides, everything in the past fades and seems less intense, and childhood friendships are the quickest to blur, mainly because children cease to be children and they change, they cast off and deny their childhood until it's far far away, and only then do they miss it. Jefferys appealed to the inventiveness and to the remote, oblique, improbable heroism of his black gamblers, both those who knew what they were involved in and those who thought they were white gamblers; he'd say to them: "Don't keep anything back, however trivial and silly it may seem to you, tell us about it: it could prove vital, could save English lives and win this War." He demanded incessant activity, initiatives, plots, schemes, and always more ideas, and Valerie gave him hers, or he created one out of what she told him: "Hartmut Rendl, SS officer, with the rank of Major or at least Captain—if he's been promoted in the last few years—is a *Mischling* on his Jewish grandmother's side, and has, moreover, destroyed or falsified documents in order to expunge that information and be admitted to the SS, the most racially pure institution in the Reich and the principal perpetrator of atrocities." Rendl was a member of the SS, a criminal and an imbecile, so why have any doubts or scruples? It isn't hard to imagine the excitement that such a case would arouse in Jefferys and in Delmer himself when he was told about it. They couldn't wait to get the machinery up and running: they not only ensured that the information about Rendl reached the ears of the SS high command, and, if possible, the ears of his boss, the irascible and purgative Himmler, they saw in this a new opportunity for black propaganda. They began forging birth certificates and pages from the register of births, marriages and death, which accused other army officers, high-up government officials and even members of the Nazi Party of being "Jews," "half-Jews" or "first-degree *Mischlinge*." Not many, of course, they didn't want to overdo this "plague," they spaced out those reports, issuing just a few at a time, those that seemed most believable and had most basis in fact. It was no easy job, but the PWE was brilliant at forgery: thanks to a collector, they had German types and moulds (or matrices or whatever they're called, I know nothing about printing) of what are called *Fraktur* or Gothic print, dating from the seventeenth century to the twentieth. And even if sooner or later those forgeries were discovered (although not all of them were), while the Nazis were carrying out their investigations and checking each of those suddenly suspect files . . . well, it was worth keeping them busy over nonsense like that which had nothing to do with the War and making them waste time rummaging through the old archives of town halls and parishes (in the nineteenth century, many German and Austrian Jews had converted to Christianity, especially to Catholicism), and thus fomenting distrust towards their own kind, for as I mentioned before, one of Delmer's priorities was to bring the Germans into conflict with each other. And when the trick worked and brought with it the removal or fall from grace of a Colonel, a General, an Admiral, or a Party leader, that saved us a job and spread panic and lowered morale among the rank and file. It may seem idiotic to us now, but it was a real blow to them, the idea that there were infiltrators in their most select units, that the *Wehrmacht* was infested with "rats," and that no one, however loyal and whatever their merits, was safe from such "revisions." It was a pretty dirty trick. It was of course "black" in more than one sense, because what they did was to take advantage of the cruellest and most repellent aspect of the Reich and, by exploiting it, brought about the persecution of more Jews, whether real or imaginary. However, these "half-" or "quarter-Jews" were not your average Jew, they weren't poor innocents; they were, above all, convinced and active Nazis, who were either fighting us or hunting down "full Jews" or both, and so no one at Milton Bryan worried overmuch about the possible injustice of that tactic, based on false accusations or, worse still, on actual fact, as was the case with Rendl. No one lost much sleep over it. Nevertheless, Delmer, as I recall, chose not to mention it in his autobiography. I wouldn't have lost any sleep over it either, just as I lost no sleep over many of the other things I had to do and did. On the other hand, I did lose sleep over some of the things I *saw*, but that's different, it's easier to deal with what one has done oneself." He paused briefly, as if he were starting a new paragraph or opening a long parenthesis, and he turned to look outside, at the river. "I only disobeyed an order once, on a crossing from Colombo to Singapore. I was a Lieutenant Colonel at the time. I was accompanying an Indian agent who had first been recruited by the Japanese and who then, under threat of immediate execution, became a double agent for our side, a man whom I myself had interrogated and trained in Colombo. With the War nearing its end, I was told to dispose of him during the journey, since he was no longer of any use to us.' In that context, the words 'dispose of him' could, I understood, mean only one thing. 'It was suggested that I find him a watery grave.' And the expression 'watery grave' confirmed my first impression. 'His code name was "Carbuncle" and I'm sure that he, too, was expecting to meet his end on the crossing. Perhaps it was his conviction that he was going to die, and his apparent acceptance of the fact, that prevented me from finding the right moment. He had toyed with the Japanese and with us, as all double agents do, but then again, he had told a lie to the Japanese that had helped us intercept and sink the Japanese heavy cruiser *Haguro* off Penang, in May 1945. He had, after all, been instrumental in our laying that trap. I don't know why I did it, why I disobeyed. I didn't really see what reason there was to get rid of him, and, besides, the Secret Service was full of idiots. If he was no longer of any use to us, he would be of still less use to the Japanese: if he fell into their hands, they would soon find a grave for him, either watery or dry, or would leave him out in the elements to rot and be eaten by the pigs. I had seen what they had done in the Andaman Islands: part of the indigenous population piled into barges and shelled from the garrison, as target practice, when they were already far out in deep water; decapitations, terrible rapes, breasts not lopped off with a machete or a sword but crushed by repeated blows, a parade of soldiers in full array obeying the orders of a Commander whose years of atrocities, during the long Japanese occupation, I had to investigate when the Islands were liberated. I had had enough . . . Nowadays you hear or read that violence is addictive, or that once you've inflicted violence or seen it, it loses its impact, that you get used to it. In my experience this is totally false, a fools' tale told to fools. You can stand a certain amount, and possibly more than you imagined you could, but ultimately, it's not so much that you grow tired of it, more that it exhausts and destroys you. And it keeps coming back and you can't forget it . . . When we reached Singapore, I disembarked with "Carbuncle" still handcuffed to me, wrist to wrist, which is incredibly uncomfortable. Have you ever tried it? I shot a sideways glance at him from my great height, because he was much shorter than me. He seemed genuinely surprised to have reached his destination and to be on dry land again. Then I took out the key, unlocked the handcuffs while he stared at me in amazement, and then I said "Fuck off!" He took to his heels and I watched him disappear into the crowd filling the port. Yes, I'd had enough . . . But it wasn't over yet . . .'

He fell silent, looking out at the placid river that I had come to know years before in the house of his brother Toby Rylands, as if he could still see his prisoner 'Carbuncle' vanishing into the crowds filling that distant port. I had seen that look in my father's eyes more than once, and in Wheeler's eyes too when he had slowly followed Mrs. Berry and me to the foot of the stairs and I had pointed out to them the place at the top of the first flight, where, during a feverish night spent at his house and after sitting up alone consulting books, I had found the bloodstain; it was a wide-eyed look that gave him a contradictory expression, almost like that of a child who discovers or sees something for the first time, something that does not frighten or repel or attract him, but which produces in him a sense of shock, or else some flash of intuitive knowledge, or even a kind of enchantment.

Wheeler took another long drink of water, almost unconsciously; it was hardly surprising that he was thirsty, he had been talking for a long time and, towards the end, had drifted into that strangely introspective loquacity of his. Apart from just one moment, I had been afraid all the time that he would decide to stop, because of fatigue or a more prolonged attack of aphasia or because he suddenly regretted telling me so much. He had never before spoken in such detail about his former life, or indeed about anything. 'Why is he doing this now?' I wondered. 'It's not as if I had insisted or even cajoled or flattered him into it, nor have I been trying to draw him out. I must ask him before I leave, if there's time.' I found everything he was telling me fascinating, but if I allowed him to wander off to the Southeast

Asia of the special missions he had undertaken, there was a risk he wouldn't come back or only when it was too late, when Mrs. Berry was already calling us in to lunch, as a mother calls her children. Not that I thought Wheeler would keep quiet in her presence or that he would have many secrets from her, certainly not regarding Valerie's death, which is what I most wanted to know about just then, perhaps because I had recently seen my own wife and had felt her to be in danger; but one has to be careful with stories, sometimes they don't allow witnesses, not even silent ones, and if there are any witnesses, they stop. I could still hear Mrs. Berry at the piano, again she was playing some rather cheerful music—this time, I thought, pieces by the Italian Clementi, another exile, who had also lived in London for a long time, something from his popular piano exercises *Gradus ad Parnassum* or perhaps a sonata; he was another musician sidelined by Mozart (never, it seems, a good colleague), who had dismissed him as a mere *mechanicus* or automaton and with that remark had ruined him, perhaps because Clementi had dared to take part in a musical duel with him in Vienna before the Emperor, two virtuosi pitted against each other.

'What happened to Rendl?' I decided to get Peter back on track, but I didn't dare redirect him immediately to Valerie, although whatever I did, I might still end up losing her.

'Oh, yes, I'm sorry. That's why I don't like telling stories any more, especially in my current state. As you say in Spanish, I often go clambering about the branches—*voy por las ramas*—and I'm not sure how interesting those branches are. Ideally, they should be as relevant as the roots and the trunk, don't you think?'

'Oh, they're fascinating, Peter. The "Carbuncle" branch, for example, which, obviously, I've never heard before. It's just that I'm curious to know what happened to Rendl.'

'No one has heard this story before, not you or anyone. Until today,' he replied, and it seemed to me from the way he said this that he wanted to place due emphasis on the importance of this fact. 'Not even Mrs. Berry, not even Toby. Not even Tupra, who is always rummaging around in people's past lives. As I believe I told you once before, in theory, I'm not yet authorized to say what my "special missions" were between 1936 and 1946, and the same applies to some I carried out afterwards, and I've kept my word. Until today. Of course for me to say "not yet" about anything is rather ironic and even in bad taste, since permission to speak will arrive too late. There's another reason to keep quiet about the "Carbuncle" affair: my superiors never found out that I'd let him go. Not that anything very bad would have happened to me just because I'd disobeyed an order: we weren't like the Germans or the Russians, and I didn't put anyone's life at risk by doing so. However, I preferred to tell them that, as recommended, I had found him a watery grave during the crossing. After all, the fellow was as untraceable and as unfindable as if he were lying at the bottom of the Strait of Malacca with a ridiculous golf bag tied around his neck, a bag I had, in fact, forced him to carry throughout the voyage, and which I allowed someone to steal from me in that same port. (Oh, yes, there were some real idiots in the Secret Service, like the ones who lumbered me with the golf clubs.) Having played that trick on the Japanese, it was in his best interests to be presumed dead, and there wasn't the slightest danger of him going and presenting himself to some other British person, *ni en pintura.*' And he used the Spanish expression—meaning literally 'not even in the form of a painting,' but here meaning something like 'no chance' or 'no way'—perhaps because there is no exact equivalent in English, at least nothing quite as graphic. He'd had recourse to my language earlier when he'd referred to the expression '*me voy por las ramas*' and had then elaborated on the metaphor in English; such linguistic mixtures were commonplace between us, as they had been between Cromer-Blake and me in my Oxford phase. 'In Rendl's case, well, it wasn't just a matter of everything having its time to be believed, we were unfortunate in that the accusation wasn't false and that he wasn't in the regular German army, the *Wehrmacht*, let's say, where he might have received nothing more than a reprimand, a period of detention or a demotion, or all three. Even if he had been a Party leader, his deception, with luck—and depending on what friends he had and what influence—might well have been simply brushed under the carpet.' I noticed his use of the first person plural, '*we* were unfortunate.' 'It was said that the SS, on the other hand, demanded that its members should be able to prove purity of blood as far back as 1750, at least in theory and in principle. Himmler must have realized that this was an impossibilty for most applicants and that the number of men in his unit would rapidly diminish once they started to suffer any war losses. And so from 1940 on, the SS depended in large measure on volunteers from countries considered "Germanic," this being especially true of the Waffen-SS, the combat arm, which filled up with Dutchmen, Flemings, Norwegians and Danes. And later on still, towards the end, they also admitted "non-Germanic" volunteers, Frenchmen, Italians, Walloons, Ukrainians, Belorussians, Lithuanians, Estonians, as well as Hungarians, Croats, Serbs, Slovenes, and Albanians. There was even an Indian Legion and Muslim divisions, I recall a Skanderbeg and a Kama division (and there was a third one, too, whose name I can't now recall); so much for Aryan purity. And there was even a tiny British Free Corps, which really only served for propaganda purposes. But the initial severity of the 1920s and '30s gives you an idea of how unacceptable it would have been for a veteran officer to have a not particularly remote Jewish ancestor, a grandmother to be precise, and for him to have lied about it and paid for incriminating documents to be removed in order to conceal the truth and so "contaminate" the corps. While the War was on, we didn't know exactly what had happened to Rendl after we'd unmasked him, although we did know that it must have worked, because his name disappeared from the lists of officers that periodically fell into the hands of MI6 or the PWE. Jefferys, or Delmer, or the East Germans, used to pass the accusations on to the Nazi authorities through our infiltrators, and the Nazis, I assume, then carried out their own investigations. It was relatively easy to pass such information on, especially in the occupied countries, where we could count on local collaborators. It wasn't quite so easy afterwards to find out what the results had been, to know which of our false reports had "taken" and what had been the fate of those affected, which forgeries had been accepted as authentic and which not, or only by checking which counterfeit "Jew" or "half-Jew" remained in his post, and was not removed or demoted or anything. At least we knew that Rendl, without having been declared or presumed dead, in action or in the rearguard, had ceased to be a Major or a Captain, or whatever he was at the time. He no longer appeared on the list.'

'And did that please Valerie? I mean, did it satisfy her?' I asked, spotting an opportunity to remind him of the person I was most interested in. This was pure naïveté on my part, however, because she was also the person Wheeler was most interested in and he hadn't forgotten her for a moment. He never, in my presence, entirely lost the thread.

He raised one arm to his forehead—or it may have been his wrist to his temple—as if he were in pain or checking to see if he had a fever, or perhaps it was a gesture of horror. Whatever its intention, it was the same gesture he had made when he finally opened his eyes and uncovered his ears after the capricious passes of the helicopter that made a sound like a giant rattle or like an old Sikorsky H-5, 'the noise alone used to be enough to provoke panic,' on that other now distant Sunday in his garden by the river, as we sat on chairs with canvas covers the color of pale gabardine, on those chairs disguised as mammoths or tethered ghosts, when I wasn't yet working for the group and he recruited me and suggested that I join and become part of it. He took a while to respond, and I feared that he might have got stuck on some word again. However, it wasn't that, but rather—I thought a little later—because he preferred not to let me see all of his face while he was telling me what he had not yet told me, or that he needed to keep his arm or wrist near his eyes, so as to be able to cover them at once, just as I had been tempted to do several times—and as I had done, I seemed to remember, on more than one occasion—when Tupra was showing me those videos in his house. As if he wanted to be ready to hide or to put his head under his wing.

'Yes, it did satisfy her,' he said. 'I suppose you could say that. It had been her idea, and it was her first personal, individual, distinctive contribution to the development of the War or to the search for victory. She was congratulated by Jefferys on one of his subsequent visits. As I said, he would come for a week, leave a trail of ideas and then vanish, and not reappear again for a month or more. I've never heard him mentioned since or seen his name in any book, which is why I'm sure it was an alias. Sefton Delmer doesn't mention him, so who knows who he really was. But it also left her feeling unsatisfied, uneasy. She wondered what had happened to Ilse, Rendl's wife, what Ilse's situation would have been after her husband's downfall. He was our enemy and not just any enemy, not some poor recruit, but a Nazi volunteer, determined to join the SS. More than that, he was a complete imbecile; but he was also the brother-in-law of her old friend, and the husband of the older sister who had always been so kind and patient with her. The War, though, allowed little time for doubts or regrets. For that reason, some people remember times of war as the most vital of their entire existence, the most euphoric, and in a way they even miss them afterwards. War is the most terrible thing, but when you live through a war, you live with extraordinary intensity; the good thing about them is that they stop people worrying about silly things or getting depressed or pestering those around them. There's no time for any of that, you move ceaselessly from one thing to another, from anxiety to fear, from terror to an explosion of joy, and every day is the last day, no, more than that, the only day. You walk, you *exist*, shoulder to shoulder, everyone is busy trying to survive, to defeat the beast, to save themselves and to save others, and as long as panic doesn't spread, there's great camaraderie. Panic didn't spread here. You'll have heard your father and others talk about this, and your War was the same.'

'Yes, I have heard people talk about it, not so much my father, but mainly people who were still children at the time, because my father, although very young, was already an adult when the War began. I imagine, though, that you can only miss such times when your side wins, don't you think, Peter? It can't be the same for my father as it was for you.'

'Yes, you're right. I can't conceive what it would have been like if we'd lost, but if we had, I would probably only remember the horror, or have done everything I could to forget it, and perhaps, with great effort, would have succeeded. It's hard to imagine. I don't know, I can't know.' And Wheeler moved his arm away from his forehead and instead rested his cheek on his hand and sat pondering, as if the idea had never occurred to him.

'And what happened? What else?' That was what Tupra always used to say to me during our sessions together: 'What else, tell me more.' He would not do so again nor would there be any more sessions, that much was sure.

'The worst came after the end of the War, when the whole country raised its head to look around, and some, not many, started thinking about what had happened, what they had seen and how they had lived, and what they had been obliged to do. A few months after the surrender, Valerie received a letter from her friend Maria. They hadn't had any contact since 1939, since before war broke out. Maria didn't even know that Valerie was married and that her surname was now Wheeler. Val and I met in 1940 and got married in 1941, shortly before I turned twenty-eight and when she was twenty-one. The truth is that neither of them knew if the other was still alive. Maria sent the letter to Val's parents' address, and her mother forwarded it to Oxford, where we had moved after I'd been elected Fellow of The Queen's College in 1946. Val's father had died in one of the air raids on London. Valerie was overjoyed at first, but that feeling only lasted as long as it took her to open the envelope. That letter was our death sentence. Or rather, hers.' And when Peter added these words, some words Tupra had said came back to me, like a premonition, like an echo: 'While it isn't something any of us would wish for, we would nonetheless always prefer it to be the person beside us who dies, whether on a mission or in battle, in an air squadron or under bombardment or in the trenches when there were trenches, in a mugging or a raid on a shop or when a group of tourists is kidnapped, in an earthquake, an explosion, a terrorist attack, in a fire, it doesn't matter: even if it's our colleague, brother, father or even our child, however young. Or even the person we most love, yes, even them, anyone but us.' I wasn't there when she received and read it, but she showed it to me afterwards, or, rather, translated it for me: although Maria spoke English, Val's German was better, and that was the language in which they wrote to each other. It was a long letter, but not that long, I mean not enough for Maria to be able to explain all that had happened to her during the War years; she summarized the most important facts. She, too, had married and her name was now Hafenrichter; however, her husband had died at the Russian front, leaving her a widow. She was managing to scrape a living in the international zone of Vienna (as you know, Vienna, like Berlin, was divided into four occupation zones: American, British, Russian and French, and the center was international, that is, it was controlled and patrolled by the four powers simultaneously). She spoke about her current hardships, the same dire situation as in German towns and cities, although Vienna had suffered less devastation, and she asked for help, although without specifying what form that help might take, money, medicine, clothes, provisions . . . Her parents, Mr. and Mrs. Mauthner, had died, as had one of the four sisters, the third, and it was presumed that the oldest, Ilse, was also dead, for she had vanished along with her two small daughters. The only surviving Rendl was the boy, whom she had taken in and whom she now wished to send to England, and she was asking Valerie's help in that regard too, if possible: the child had had a terrible time, and in Austria he faced a bleak, poverty-stricken future, and she could barely manage to support herself. But the worst thing was . . .' Wheeler's voice faltered and he hesitated for a moment, then recovered. 'The worst thing was that she explained to Val what had happened: "I don't know how," she said, and those were the words that tormented Valerie from the moment she read them until her death, the words that killed her: "I don't know how," she said, but the SS had somehow found out that Rendl had a Jewish grandmother and had bribed officials to have her name removed from the records. The records in question, though, hadn't been destroyed, only moved elsewhere and replaced with false documents: the originals turned up and the accusation was found to be true. The SS were very strict on the matter of racial ancestry, Maria told Valerie (imagining that there would be no reason why Valerie would know about that), and it seems that the case reached the ears of Himmler himself, who was enraged by such deceit and determined to make an example of Rendl, mostly in order to wring confessions from any other SS officers who were in the same or a similar situation, promising them that if they did confess, he would treat them more leniently, or at least less severely, than their impostor colleague. The discovery, along with the rumors that followed Heydrich's death, that even he had been "half-Jewish"'—'Heydrich,' I thought, 'who died slowly and in great pain, from those bullets impregnated with poison'—'led him to believe, as I found out later, that his purer-than-pure body of men had, in fact, been transformed, since the enactment of the Nuremberg Laws, into a refuge for *Mischlinge* and even for "half-Jews," reasoning, as was proper to a mind as sick as his, that there could be no better disguise for the prey than to camouflage themselves as hunters. Well, perhaps his mind wasn't so very sick when you think of Delmer or, even more so, of Jefferys, who were both capable of dreaming up the most complicated plans and machinations. Or when you think of mine, perhaps, for we all had war minds, there are no healthy minds in wartime and some never recover. But returning to the letter: Maria had managed to learn what Rendl's exemplary punishment had been: to be sent to a concentration camp as a prisoner, even though he was only a "quarter-Jewish"; and not just that, but one day, the Gestapo turned up at his house in Munich, where he and his family were living at the time, and took the girls away. They didn't take the boy because he wasn't there when this happened, he was staying in Melk with his grandparents, and once the Gestapo had got over their initial rage, they didn't bother overmuch to seek him out. When Ilse, horrified, asked why they were doing this, all they would say was that the girls were Jewish, but that they had no proof against her; if she wanted to go with the girls, that was her business. Properly speaking, those girls were only one-eighth Jewish and would normally have been considered to be "German." But that was the reprisal, the punishment: making "full Jews" of the descendants of the man who had deceived and tricked them. After all, as Göring said, or Goebbels, or perhaps it was Himmler himself: "I decide who's Jewish." None of this became public, of course, it would have made a terrible impression, it was made known only to the officers of the SS, as a warning to them to tread carefully, and that is why the PWE heard almost nothing about it. The SS were very keen on secrecy and childish rituals. According to neighbors who witnessed the scene, Ilse got into the car that was about to carry her girls away and no more was heard of any of them. It was supposed that, once in a concentration camp, all trace of them would have been lost and their "origin," which was the reason they were there, quite forgotten, and they would have become, in effect, Jews or, at best, "dissidents"; no, there was no "best" about it: their fate would have been the same. Maria didn't want to deceive herself with fantasies, she had no hope that they were alive. She assumed they were dead, with no room for speculation or doubt, especially once information was published about the gas chambers and the mass exterminations. So that was what the letter said, Jacobo. Maria ended by saying that she didn't know if Valerie was still alive or if she would ever read those lines, but she begged her, if she *was* alive, to send her news and help as well, especially for Ilse's son, young Rendl. He would have been about eleven or twelve at the time.' Wheeler paused, took a breath and added: 'If only those lines had never reached her eyes. If only no one had ever told her. I wouldn't have seen her kill herself. I wouldn't have been left alone and sad.'

Wheeler remained silent and thoughtful and again raised the back of his wrist to his brow, as if to wipe away some sudden beads of sweat or as if he were again taking his temperature. 'Give me your hand and let us walk,' I quoted to myself. 'Through the fields of this land of mine, edged with dusty olive groves, I walk alone, sad, tired, pensive and old.' I had known this poem since I was a child, they were the words addressed by Antonio Machado to his already dead child wife, Leonor, who died of tuberculosis at the age of eighteen. Valerie hadn't died, she had killed herself when she was only slightly older, looking at her own hourglass and holding it in her hand. But she, too, had left Peter alone, sad, tired, pensive and old. Regardless of all the things he went on to do afterwards.

I should have expected this revelation after what Wheeler had been telling me, but I was so taken aback that, for a moment, I didn't know what to say. And when he did not immediately go on, I gave voice to a thought that slipped unavoidably into my mind, even at the risk of diverting his thoughts elsewhere and missing the end of the story:

'That's what Toby said had happened to him. I told you, don't you remember?' And I recalled, too, the look of irritated surprise on Wheeler's face when he had heard the story. 'Is that what he said: "I watched the suicide . . ."' he had repeated, taken aback, without completing the sentence. 'That he had watched the suicide of the person he loved.'

Wheeler responded at once, but this time he was more sympathetic than annoyed:

'Yes. It disappointed and angered me a little when you told me that. After all, how were you to know? Nothing like that ever happened to him, but he enjoyed playing the man of mystery and hinting at a more turbulent or more tragic past than he actually had; not that his past didn't have its moments, but that's true of almost anyone who lives through a long war. He must have stolen my story when he told you that, to make his own more interesting. That's the trouble with telling anything—most people forget how or from whom they found out what they know, and there are people who even believe they lived or gave birth to it, whatever it is, a story, an idea, an opinion, an anecdote, a joke, an aphorism, a history, a style, sometimes even a whole text, which they proudly appropriate—or perhaps they know they're stealing, but push the thought to the back of their mind and thus hide it away. It's very much a phenomenon of the times we live in, which has no respect for priorities. Perhaps I shouldn't have got angry with poor Toby like that, retrospectively.' Wheeler stopped, took a couple of sips of sherry and then murmured almost reluctantly, almost with distaste: 'Fortunately for him, he didn't ever have to see that. It's not a scene that is easy to bear, I can assure you. It's best to avoid tragedies. Nothing can ever make up for them. Certainly not talking about them.'

'What happened?' And out of politeness I added as I had on another occasion, although this time I had to force myself to do what I had been taught as a child, never to put the screws on anyone. 'If you don't want to tell me, Peter, don't.'

I was afraid that, at any moment, Mrs. Berry might close the piano and come downstairs and, so to speak, break the spell, although we could still hear her music; she seemed to have moved on to Scarlatti; she always played cheerful pieces, which that afternoon just happened to be by people who had changed countries, Scarlatti having spent half his life in Spain, although no one knows how or where he died or even if he had a grave, just like Boccherini: they probably both died in Madrid and both now lie in unmarked graves. A country indifferent to merit and to services rendered. A country indifferent to everything, especially to anything that no longer exists, or to matter in the past.

'It's not pleasant to remember, Jacobo, nor to hear either. But I think, nevertheless, that I can tell you. I suppose there comes a point when one has to tell things, after a lot of time has passed, so that it doesn't seem as if they simply never happened or were just a bad dream,' Peter answered. '"I don't know how," Maria had said in her letter, and Valerie, from the moment she read those words, kept repeating, even in German sometimes as if she were talking to Maria: "I know how, oh, I know how, I know very well, in fact, I was the one who told the SS." And she repeated over and over: "The children. How could I have forgotten about Ilse and the children? I should have thought of them, why didn't I? I didn't take them into account at all." She spent the last days of her life in torment, in hell, and at no point did she consider answering her friend's letter. "I'd rather she believed me dead," she said. "I couldn't possibly tell her what happened." "And what if you didn't tell her, but just helped her," I said, trying to convince her: "Perhaps we can do something for the boy, get him some kind of permit to enter the country and a scholarship, I don't know, I could talk to people about it and give him a hand financially." I've always had family money. My maternal grandfather, Thomas Wheeler, sold the newspaper companies he owned in New Zealand and Australia for a large profit, and Toby and I, when we were still very young, each received a large legacy when he died. I even suggested adopting young Rendl, even though I hated the idea myself. But Val was paralyzed with horror and grief, she didn't want to hear any of those ideas, and she didn't respond. She lay awake at night, and even if, for a moment, she did drop off out of sheer exhaustion, she would soon start awake, crying and drenched in sweat, and would say to me in distraught tones: "Those girls. If I had just found out what happened on my own, I might have had some right, possibly, although I don't believe so. But I found out through Maria, and I betrayed her without a thought; how could I have done that, why didn't I realize? And those girls, who died because of me in a concentration camp, they wouldn't have understood anything, and their mother who got into the car with them, what else could the poor woman do, oh, dear God . . .'" Wheeler stopped for a moment and bit his forefinger, thoughtful, tense. ('Sorrow haunted thy bed,' I quoted to myself.) Then he said: 'Treachery just wasn't in her nature, still less betrayal. More than that, those were the very last things she would have been capable of in normal circumstances. She was a fine person, someone you could trust absolutely. She was the antithesis of bad faith, of deceit; she was, how can I put, a clean person. But war turns everything upside down or creates irreconcilable loyalties. It wasn't in her nature either to spare any effort in helping her country when its very survival was at stake. She was still smarting because she had lacked the courage to infiltrate enemy territory, and so it would have been impossible for her to hold back that information about Hartmut Rendl once she was convinced that revealing it was important and could save English lives. Now, though, her perspective had changed, as always happens in peacetime, except for those of us who know that war is always on the prowl, always just around the corner, even though no one else believes it, and that what seems to us reprehensible, horrific and extreme in peacetime could happen again tomorrow with the consent of the entire nation. "War crimes" is the term they apply nowadays to almost anything, as if war did not consist precisely in the commission of crimes, which have, for the most part, received prior absolution. Now, though, Val couldn't see in what way the information she had given, the idea she had put forward, could possibly have contributed to victory. Or, rather, she was sure that if she had kept quiet the result would have been the same. And she was probably right in thinking that, as, with very few exceptions, would all the other Britons who had added their grain of sand. That's another thing that happens in time of war, Jacobo. You do everything that's necessary, and that includes the unnecessary. But who is capable of distinguishing one from the other? When it comes to destroying the enemy, or even merely vanquishing him, it's impossible to gauge what really is doing harm and what is merely a matter of shooting his horse from under him, or, as you say, lancing dead Moors or making firewood from a fallen tree.' And he said these last two expressions in my language: '*alancear moros muertos*' and '*hacer leña del árbol caído*'. 'I tried every means I could to make her see this: "Valerie," I would say, "it was wartime and in a war, soldiers sometimes even kill their comrades, you've heard of friendly fire, haven't you? Or those in command sacrifice their own troops, send them to be slaughtered, and that doesn't always serve any useful purpose either: think of Gallipoli, Chunuk Bair, Suvla, and you can be quite sure that in years to come we'll find out about similar and equally bloody cases in this recently won War of ours. In every war innocent people are killed, there are mistakes and frivolous, foolish acts, there are imbecilic or cynical politicians and military leaders. In every war there is waste. Do you imagine that I haven't committed repugnant acts, things which, if I think about them now or in the future, could perhaps have been avoided? I committed them in Kingston, and even more in Accra and in Colombo. They're repugnant to me now and will seem more so as time passes, the farther off they get, but they weren't then. And that's what you mustn't do, view these things out of context and coldly. You can't look back after a war, don't you see? Not if you want to go on living."'

Wheeler stopped again, this time, more than anything, in

order to catch his breath. He clearly needed to. He had a slightly faraway gaze, which was directed at the stairs, although without actually seeing them. He seemed to me simultaneously very tired and very agitated, as if he had relived the words he had spoken to Valerie rather too intensely, words spoken perhaps in their haunted bed, perhaps when she woke him with her crying and with her nightmares that corresponded all too closely to reality, and those are the ones no one can bear, when reality only echoes the dream. 'Let me be lead within thy bosom, may you feel the pin prick in your chest. Despair and die.' I waited and waited and waited. Finally, I said:

'I assume it was no use.'

'No, it wasn't, and the worst thing is that, by then, I knew nothing would be of any use, that her life had been twisted out of shape forever and could never be made straight again. I was already part of the group, which was created too late to save her life. Not that my gift, my capacity for interpretation was any less before I joined, of course, but you adapt your vision to the task in hand and you hone that vision; you grow used to deciphering and looking deeper into what tomorrow will bring. You must have noticed the same thing, that increase in perspicacity, since you've been with Tupra, or am I wrong?'

'No, you're right. I am more alert now. And I tend to interpret everything, even when I'm not working and no one wants me to report on what I've seen.' And I took the opportunity to ask him something that I couldn't quite understand, even at the risk of losing precious time and of Mrs. Berry interrupting us: 'If I remember correctly, Peter, the first time you talked to me about the group, you told me that Valerie was already dead when the idea was first mooted by Menzies or Vivian or whoever. I don't understand, given that the group was formed during the War.'

Wheeler looked bemused, perplexed. He sat thinking for a few moments and then his face lit up like someone who has found the solution to a minor enigma (right to the end, he enjoyed linguistic curiosities) and he said in Spanish:

'Ah, I see. It's a problem of ambiguity, or a misunderstanding on your part, Jacobo. If I said it as you said it now, "she was already dead," that would translate in your language as "*estaba ya muerta*," but in the figurative sense, I meant that she was already doomed, not that she had literally died.' And he moved back into English again, because by then, it was clear that speaking a foreign language tired him more. 'What I probably meant was that by then it was too late, that she had already done the thing that would later lead her to kill herself, that her fate was sealed. And that was the thing, you see; if the group had been formed before, someone might have decided, doubtless I myself with my watchful, trained, alert eye, that just as Valerie wouldn't have gotten very far as a spy, as she herself knew, neither was she equipped for black propaganda, which was too dirty for her scruples and for her dislike of deceit. Still less was she equipped to put at risk or sacrifice the lives of innocent people, however German they might be. As you know, step by step, you start doing things for which you have no stomach or aren't suited, and war stretches people a lot, or they themselves, without noticing, stretch themselves beyond their capabilities and only snap when it's all over. If someone had spotted her limitations in time, they would perhaps have withdrawn her from Milton Bryan. She would have been sent back to the Foreign Office maybe, or been restricted to working on white propaganda.' Wheeler ran his hand over his forehead, almost squeezing it this time. 'Sometimes I tell myself that I should have known anyway. But it's easy to be wise after the event or *a toro pasado* as you say—once the bull has passed—when you know all the facts. I wasn't altogether sure what kind of work Valerie was doing in the PWE, and we were thousands of miles apart most of the time. And she never even mentioned the term "black propaganda," so she may well have been engaged in it without knowing of its existence, or, rather, without even knowing the concept. She may also have been following orders and divulging nothing, not even to me. I don't know. If Delmer was diabolical, then Jefferys was Lucifer in person.' He paused very briefly, then added: 'I'll never know who he was, who was hiding behind that name. I have very little time left, Jacobo. Almost none.'

The music stopped, and after a few seconds, I heard Mrs.

Berry coming down the stairs. 'That's it, it's over,' I thought. 'I'll never find out how Valerie killed herself and why Peter saw her do it, even though, in principle, I have more time than him, and not almost none. And why, if he saw her kill herself, he couldn't have stopped her.' And I added to myself: 'But I can't complain. I've found out a lot today, and that isn't even why I came.' However, Mrs. Berry didn't come into the living room or call us in to lunch, but went straight to the kitchen, where I could hear her bustling about. Perhaps we would still have time if she was putting the finishing touches to lunch and if I hurried.

'How did Valerie kill herself, Peter?' I asked, this time with no show of tact. 'And how come you saw her do it?'

Wheeler shifted in his chair, trying to find a more comfortable position, and then he hooked one thumb under his armpit as if it were a tiny riding crop and he seemed to rest the whole weight of his chest on that thumb, at least that was my impression. It was as if he needed to lean on something, even something symbolic: a poor thumb, although he did have long fingers.

'We were living then in a house rather like this, but much smaller,' he said, 'with two or three floors, depending on how you looked at it, because the top floor was very small indeed, with only a *chambre de bonne* I suppose you'd call it, which we used now and then when we had visitors. It was and still is in Plantation Road, near where you lived. It cost a lot more than my salary could stretch to then, of course, but the money I had inherited allowed me such privileges, as it always has. Anyway, after four agitated nights during which she barely slept'—'Yes,' I repeated to myself, 'sorrow did indeed haunt thy bed'—'Valerie persuaded me to go and sleep in the little room on the top floor, so that I could get some rest until she calmed down; she hoped it wouldn't last very much longer, that vicious circle of nightmares and insomnia, of loathing herself when awake and being filled with panic whenever she fell asleep, of being unable to tolerate herself either awake or asleep. It worried me to leave her unaccompanied during those night hours, because they were doubtless the worst and the most difficult to get through, but I thought, too, that perhaps she needed to spend them alone in order to begin to recover, that it might be good for her not to have me by her side to talk to her and try to console her and ask her questions, to reason and argue with her, because this had served no useful purpose in the four days and nights she had spent awake, none at all. I don't know, when a situation doesn't change, you think all kinds of things. I remember feeling very uneasy as I got into bed, leaving the door open so that I could hear her if she called me, so that I could go to her at once—we were only separated by one floor, two brief flights of stairs. But such was my accumulated exhaustion that I soon fell asleep. Sleep must have proved utterly irresistible because I didn't even turn out the bedside light or close the little book I was reading and which lay on the counterpane. I only woke at dawn and I must have been lying very still because it was only then, and not before, that the book fell to the floor, with hardly any noise: it was *Little Gidding*, the last of the *Four Quartets*, the paperback edition published by Faber. I remember that clearly; it had only recently come out and I hadn't been able to read it during the War; books like that didn't reach Ceylon or the Gold Coast.' And he murmured what were doubtless lines or parts of lines: '"Ash on an old man's sleeve . . . This is the death of air . . . the constitution of silence . . . What we call the beginning is often the end . . ." etc.' Then he went on: 'So it wasn't the book falling that woke me. I don't know what it was. It took me a few seconds to realize that I was in the *chambre de bonne* alone and to remember why. I picked up the book and placed it on the bedside table, glanced at the clock—it was almost four—and automatically turned out the light, although not with the intention of going straight back to sleep, because that sense of unease had returned. I preferred or decided to look in at our room first, to see, without going in, if Valerie was sleeping or not, and, if she wasn't, to ask if she needed anything; or if she perhaps wanted me by her side. I put on my dressing gown and went very quietly down the stairs, so as not to wake her if she was asleep, and then I saw her sitting where she shouldn't have been sitting at all, at the top of the first flight of stairs, with her back to me.' Wheeler pointed upwards to his left, towards the top of the first flight of stairs in his current house beside the River Cherwell and not in Plantation Road. 'Just there, where you say you saw a drop of blood. It's odd, isn't it? She was still fully clothed, not in her nightdress or her dressing gown, as if she hadn't been to bed at all or was getting ready to go out, and that was what surprised me most of all, in the very brief instant during which I could feel surprise. But I didn't feel alarmed, the fact is that never, never, not during one of those fleeting moments or beforehand, did I ever suspect, did it even occur to me to fear that she was going to do what she did, not once. And there I failed. My gift or my faculty or my ability, whatever you want to call it, the gift that Tupra and you and that young half-Spanish woman have, the gift that Toby had and I have had regarding matters that were of no importance to me, failed me completely on that occasion. How could I not have guessed, how could I not have seen it, how is it that I had not the slightest glimmer? I've been asking myself that since 1946. How could I have been so stupidly optimistic, so trusting, so unaware, how is it that I saw no warning signs? That's a long time, isn't it? When it comes to the things that touch you most deeply, you never want to hear the warnings, but they're always there. In everything. One is never willing to think the worst.' Now Wheeler covered his eyes with one hand, placed it like a pulled-down visor, perhaps as I had done at some point while I was watching and not watching Tupra's horrific videos on that night when he was Reresby. 'I could understand her concern, her bad conscience, even her horror,' Wheeler continued to speak with his eyes covered, 'but I thought that sooner or later she would get over it or it would abate, just as almost everyone else got over what they had seen or done in the War, what they had lost or suffered. Up to a point, of course, enough to be able to live. It's one of the things that peacetime brings to people who are no longer at war, although it falls to some of us to continue and to watch. It brings forgetting, at least a superficial form of forgetting, or the sense that it was all a dream. Even if that dream is repeated every night and lies in wait during the day: just a bad dream. A terrible dream. But we had, after all, won the war. "Valerie," I said, and that was all I had time to say. She had her hair caught up. She didn't turn round, but I saw the back of her neck and her shoulders shudder and saw her fall violently backwards, and at the same time I heard the explosion. And only then, in the midst of my despair and my incredulity, I realized that she had been sitting there, for who knows how long, with the hunting rifle in her hands, pointing at her heart. Perhaps she had been hesitating or waiting until she felt brave enough, she who wasn't brave at all. I was probably the signal, my presence, my voice, hearing her own name.'—'Strange to leave one's own first name behind. Strange to no longer desire one's desires. Strange to see meanings that clung together once, floating away in every direction. And being dead is hard work . . .'—'She probably thought I would snatch the weapon from her and that there would be no more time later, I don't know.'—'And indeed there won't be time to wonder, "Do I dare?" and "Do I dare?" Do I dare disturb the universe? Time to turn back and descend the stair . . . And in short, I am afraid . . .' And so it would be best not to wait.—'She lay there.' And Wheeler again pointed up to the top of the first flight of stairs of his current house, where I had found the drop of blood and cleaned it up with such diligence and difficulty. 'It was very hard to get rid of that blood. It poured out, flowed out, even though I immediately staunched the wound with towels. I knew she was already dead, but nevertheless I covered the wound. She had gotten dressed and put on her make-up, she had put her hair up and put on lipstick to say goodbye to me, it was a matter of politeness, the age we lived in, her now very antiquated politeness, she never received a guest or went out into the street without her make-up . . . And even when there was no trace of blood, I could still see it.'—'The last thing to go would be the rim,' I thought; 'Although there would have been several, because there must have been more than one stain, and perhaps it made a trail.'—'And then I moved house, I couldn't stay there.'

'But you didn't come to this house, did you, Peter?' I asked.

'No, I went to my rooms in college and lived there for three years, I preferred to have people around me. But you see, the one night, the one and only night, that I failed to watch over her sleep or non-sleep, Valerie went and killed herself. She couldn't live with what she had done. And I didn't foresee it. It never crossed my mind, not even when she sent me upstairs to the *chambre de bonne*. It was a perfectly reasonable excuse, and I wasn't prepared: it was the first time she had ever deceived me. You can't imagine the times I've wondered if I would have gotten there in time had I only been quicker to realize where she was when I woke up'—'Don't linger or delay,' I thought—'if I hadn't picked up the book or turned out the light or put on my dressing gown or if I'd gone down those two flights of stairs more quickly or gone down them just as quietly but without opening my mouth, without saying her name, without letting her know I was there. All nonsense of course. But you think those things over and over.'—'Bloody and guilty, guiltily awake,' I remembered.—'Some time afterwards, I wrote to Maria Mauthner and introduced myself, because she knew nothing about me. I told her that Valerie had died, but not how or why. The War, I said, and that was enough. I helped her nephew come to England, but I couldn't bring myself to have anything to do with him, it would have been like looking at Valerie's rifle. And I've helped his son, too, the Rendel that you know: apparently he's pretty good, but not as gifted as Tupra or you, he lacks vision. At least he has a good job, though. My vision, I can assure you, has improved greatly since then. I promised myself that such a thing would never happen to anyone again simply because I couldn't or didn't dare to see. Not that anyone was ever as important to me again, of course: most of the people I observed and interpreted subsequently, on whom I reported, of whom I said whether or not they might be useful and for what, haven't mattered to me one jot in comparison. But now at least I can say to you, with no fear that I might be wrong, that you *can* live with what has happened to you, with what you came here to talk to me about, because, unlike her, you find it hard to believe that you were responsible.'—'Yes,' I thought, 'I will always be able to say to myself tomorrow: "Oh, I didn't intend to do it, I knew nothing about it, it happened against my will, in the tortuous smokescreens of fever and shadow and dreams, it was part of my theoretical, parenthetical life, of my vague parallel existence that doesn't really count, it only half-happened and without my full consent, in short, as it said in the report I found among those old files and which was headed *"Deza, Jacques,"* I don't see myself or know myself, I don't delve into or investigate myself, I don't pay much attention to myself and I've given up trying to understand myself. And besides, that was in another country." And then the judge would say: "Overruled, case dismissed."'—'And anyway, you're made of very different stuff and you belong to a different age, Jacobo, a much more frivolous age. No, don't worry, you're not like Valerie. In fact, no one ever has been, during all these years without her. Or only occasionally, in my dreams.'—'Give me your hand and let us walk. Through the fields of this land of mine . . .'—Wheeler removed his hand from his eyes and looked at me with surprise, or fright, as if he had just emerged from a long dream. Or perhaps it was more that he opened his eyes very wide, as if seeing the world for the first time, with a gaze as inscrutable as that of a newborn child, born only weeks or days before, and who, I imagine, observes this new place into which he has been hurled and tries perhaps to decipher our customs and to work out which of those customs will be his. He looked very tired and very pale, and I suddenly feared for his health. I felt like putting my hand on his shoulder, as I had with my father a few days earlier. He noticed the olives, picked up two and ate them both. Then he drank a little more sherry, and the color returned to his cheeks, maybe he had suffered a brief drop in blood pressure. When he spoke again and I heard a different tone in his voice, I felt completely reassured, realizing that the evocation, the story, was at an end: 'Go and ask Mrs. Berry if it's time for lunch yet,' he said. 'I don't know why she hasn't called us, she stopped playing a while ago now.'

I still live alone, not in another country, but back in Madrid. Or perhaps I live half-alone, if one can say such a thing. I think I've been back now for almost as much time as I spent in London, during my second English sojourn, which had been more bewildering than the first but less transforming, because I was of an age when it's harder to change, when almost all you can do is ascertain and confirm just what it is you carry in your veins. Now I am a little older. Both my father and Sir Peter Wheeler have died, the former only a week after that last Sunday in Oxford, not so much in exile from the infinite as from the past. It was his death, in fact, that precipitated my return to my home city, to be with his grandchildren, my brothers and my sister, and to attend the funeral. There was a space for him in my mother's grave. No one else will fit in there now. It was my sister who told me, she phoned me in London and said: 'Papa has died. His heart stopped half an hour ago. We knew his heart was weak, but it was still very unexpected. I was talking to him only yesterday. He asked after you, as usual, although he was convinced that you were in Oxford, teaching. You'll come, won't you?' I said that I would, that I'd come immediately. And so I went, I consoled and was consoled, I only saw Luisa at the funeral and there she embraced me in order to console me too and then I returned to London, to sort out that ingenuously furnished apartment and leave everything in order before my definitive departure, which it would now best be to hasten; a great many things required my attention in Madrid: house, furniture, books, a few paintings—that copy of the 'Annunciation'—my own bereft children, a modest or possibly not so modest inheritance; and the task of remembering. Both alone and in the company of the others.

There were no matters pending with Tupra, everything had been pretty much resolved and, indeed, settled the day after the Sunday I spent with Wheeler, in Tupra's office in the building with no name (and which, I assume, remains nameless). As predicted by Beryl or by the person who refused to tell me if she was Beryl or not, Tupra, having returned from his trip or weekend absence, was already in his office when I arrived on Monday. Our conversation was very brief, partly because it turned out to be a repetition, I mean that we'd had that identical conversation before, in the distant days when I still called him Mr. Tupra. I went straight to his door as soon as I arrived, saying a quick good morning to Rendel and young Pérez Nuix as I passed; I didn't see Mulryan, perhaps he was with Tupra. I knocked.

'Yes, who is it?' asked Tupra from inside.

And I replied absurdly:

'It's me,' omitting to give him my name, as if I were one of those people who forget that 'me' is never anyone, who are quite sure of occupying a great deal or a fair part of the thoughts of the person they're looking for, who have no doubt that they will be recognized with no need to say more—who else would it be—from the first word and the first moment. I suppose I confused my point of view with his, for we sometimes erroneously believe our own sense of urgency to be universal: I had spent many hours impatient to see him, to demand an explanation and even to confront him. But Tupra wouldn't be the least impatient, I was probably just another matter or another person to deal with, a subordinate returning to work after two weeks' leave in his country of origin, I think he often forgot that I wasn't yet English. When I didn't receive an immediate response, and suddenly aware of my own naïveté or presumption, I added: 'It's me, Bertram. It's Jack.' I accepted calling myself by a name that wasn't mine right until the end; it was the least important of the compromises I made while I was earning my living listening and noticing and interpreting and telling. But at least I didn't call him Bertie on that occasion.

'Come in, Jack,' he said.

And so I opened the door and peered in. He was sitting behind his desk, making notes or writing something on some papers. He didn't actually look up when I went in.

'Bertram,' I said, but he interrupted me.

'One moment, Jack, let me finish this first.' I waited for a minute or perhaps two or three, enough, in any case, to foresee that what did happen would happen. I sat down in an armchair opposite him, took out a cigarette and then lit it. He automatically picked up his Rameses II cigarettes, which were in their lavish red pack on the desk. In theory, smoking was forbidden in any of the offices, but I couldn't imagine anyone stopping Tupra inhaling and exhaling smoke, nor complaining about it. There had to be some advantage in the fact that neither the building nor our group had a name, and that we barely existed at all, more or less like the black propaganda group run by the PWE and Delmer and Jefferys during the War. When he finished his note-making, he took out and lit one of those exquisite cigarettes. 'So, Jack, how did it go?' There was nothing unusual in the way he said this, it wasn't even a question, more as if he were taking a routine interest in a simple little errand he had sent me on the day before. 'They told me at home that you phoned on Saturday about an urgent matter. Problems with your problem in Madrid?'

But I didn't answer his question, I got straight down to my own business—without delay:

'What happened to Dearlove and that Russian boy? What have you done?' I said. 'You really dropped me in it, I mean, it was me who gave you the idea, *joder.*' That '*joder*'—that 'damn it'—came out in Spanish because it was what my anger required me to say, even if I was speaking in English.

He sat looking at me for a few seconds with his blue or grey eyes—they were grey in that light—through his long eyelashes, dense enough to be the envy of any woman and to be considered highly suspect by any man, with those pale eyes that had a mocking quality, even if this was not their intention, eyes that were, therefore, expressive even when—as then—no expression was required, warm or should I say appreciative eyes that were never indifferent to what was there before them. And he responded in the same tone of voice, identical, with which he had said: 'Yes, I have,' when I had asked him in that same office, on another morning many months before, if he had heard about the failed coup d'état in Venezuela, and it had occurred to me that perhaps it had fallen through because we hadn't seen—because I hadn't sensed—sufficient determination on the part of General or Corporal Bonanza, who was the first person for whom I acted as translator with Tupra and on whom I improvised a report and offered my interpretation.

'What happened is in all the papers.' Perhaps he took advantage of that extemporaneous Spanish expletive, incomprehensible to him, to pretend that he had only heard my first sentence and to ignore the rest. No, he wasn't pretending, it was a way of telling me that the rest of what I had said seemed to him inadmissible and that he wasn't going to tolerate it. 'You must have read about it. Even in the Spanish press, I expect, didn't you tell me once how famous he was there? Especially . . . where was it now? In the Basque Country?' His memory never failed him. 'And you yourself warned me in Edinburgh that Dearlove was so concerned for his posterity that he might commit some barbarous act simply in order to be remembered. That having so little faith that his music would last, he might very well blot his own life and thus deliberately enter the ranks of the Kennedy-Mansfield clan, isn't that right? So you see, you were very sharp, it was clear he might come to a bad end. And on purpose too.' I had forgotten about that additional report of mine; he, on the other hand, had not and was now using it as an alibi. I realized that he was not willing to discuss the matter, that he wasn't even going to take part in the conversation, I was still just an employee who did my job and was paid well for it, but I had no right to ask about objectives or motivations, still less to demand explanations or make reproaches, at least that was how he saw it. Perhaps because he held me in a certain regard, because of his temporary fondness for me, he was putting me in my place only indirectly, almost tacitly, surreptitiously. And I understood this even more clearly when he added: 'Anything else, Jack?' It's what he had said on that other far-off occasion, after replying succinctly: 'Yes, I have.' No, he didn't usually comment on my successes and failures, or on his aims or motives, or on his pacts or transactions or commissions. He had said enough with the words 'you were very sharp.' In fact, I think that was the only time he complimented me.

'Yes, there is something else,' I said. 'I have to leave, I have to go back to Madrid. Things have got a little complicated there, I won't bore you with an explanation, it would take too long. But I can't stay here in London. I have no alternative but to resign. That's why I phoned you at home on Saturday, to let you know as soon as possible, in case you wanted to start looking for a replacement, although, obviously I can't help you with that.'

I played his same game, I resorted to an acceptable alibi, I preferred not to confront him, not to insist, after all, he would soon be merely the past for me, dumb matter, or perhaps a dream, as I would be for him. But I'm sure he understood the real reason for my leaving. It must have seemed ridiculous to him, but he didn't show it.

'As you wish,' he said coldly. 'It's your decision.'

'If you like, I can still come in occasionally, until I actually leave,' I added.

'Fine,' he said. 'That way some things won't be left half-finished. But it's not really necessary. You do as you like. Really.' There wasn't any spite in the tone in which he said this, but, rather, curtness or indifference, whether feigned or recently acquired, I don't know. It was, at any rate, new. He didn't care whether I came in or not.

'I'll see you around, then. If, that is, I do manage to come in on the odd day. Although I will have an awful lot of things to sort out.'

'Fine. Anything else, Jack?' he said again and picked up his pen as if intending to resume writing his notes as soon as I left his office.

And this time I gave the same answer as I had on that previous occasion:

'No, nothing else, Mr. Tupra.' That is how I addressed him.

I got up and went over to the door, and just as I was about to open it, his voice stopped me:

'Just out of curiosity, Mr. Deza.' When he addressed me in the same formal way, I realized that it amused him that I should have chosen such an odd moment to do so with him, just when we were saying goodbye. I turned round and thought I saw the tail end, just the shadow of a smile on that soft fleshy mouth, on those lips that were rather African or perhaps Hindu or Slavic, or even Sioux. 'Did you sort out that business in Madrid? Did you take care of that guy who's been bothering your wife? Did you make sure he's out of the picture?'

I stood still for an instant. I thought.

'Yes, I think so,' I replied.

And then he smiled broadly, waving his pen at me as if he were telling me off:

'Be careful, Jack. If you only think you did, that means you didn't.'

I didn't go back to the building, so that was the last time I saw him. But here in Madrid, I think of him more than I imagined I would. Despite that rather abrupt ending, despite the possible disappointment I must have caused him and the very real disappointment he caused me, I still feel that he is someone on whom I could always count. In a time of difficulty or confusion or trouble or even danger. Someone I could call one day and ask for advice or guidance, especially with the kind of situation I don't deal with very well. And now that Wheeler is dead, it's as if Tupra, strangely enough—possibly because of his link with Rylands, the brother whose student he was—were all that remained to me of him, even if only in my memory and imagination: his unexpected substitute or successor, his legacy almost, part of that permanent process of replacing the people we lose in our lives, of the shocking and persistent efforts we make to fill any vacancies, of our inability to resign ourselves to any reduction in the cast of characters without whom we can barely go on or survive, part of that continuous universal mechanism of substitution, which affects everyone and therefore us too, and so we accept our role as poor imitations and find ourselves surrounded by more and more of them.

Peter died six months after my father, although he was about eight months older than him. Mrs. Berry phoned me in Madrid; she was very succinct, belonging, as she did, to the thrifty generation and doubtless mindful that she was phoning abroad. Or perhaps that was just her style, one of extreme discretion. 'Sir Peter passed away last night, Jack,' she said, employing the usual euphemism. That was all, or, rather, she added: 'I just wanted you to know. I didn't think it fair that you should carry on believing he's still alive when he's not.' And when I tried to find out what had happened and the cause, she merely said: 'Oh, it wasn't unexpected. I had been expecting it for weeks,' and informing me that she would write to me later on. I couldn't even ask her to whom it would have been 'unfair,' to Peter or to me. (But presumably to both of us.) A few days later, I recalled that in England, in comparison with Spain, they take a long time to bury their dead and that I might still be in time to travel to Oxford and attend the funeral. So I phoned her several times and at different hours of the day, but no one answered. Perhaps Mrs. Berry had gone to stay with a relative, had left the house as soon as her employer died, and I realized that there was almost no one I could ask now to find out more information. There was Tupra, but I didn't turn to him: it was hardly a moment of difficulty, confusion, trouble or danger, and he hadn't himself deigned to inform me of Peter's death. I was assailed by the feeling—or perhaps it was a superstition—that I didn't want to waste a cartridge unnecessarily, as if with him I only had a certain number that would last as long as our respective lives. Young Pérez Nuix didn't bother to tell me either: she may not have known Peter personally, but she would have heard. I could have phoned one of my former colleagues, Kavanagh or Dewar or Lord Rymer the Flask or even Clare Bayes—the very idea!—but I had long ago lost touch with them. I could have tried The Queen's or Exeter, the colleges with which Peter had been connected, but their bureacracy would almost certainly have passed me fruitlessly from office to office. And the truth is I couldn't be bothered; memory and grief don't always chime with social duty. I was very busy in Madrid. I would have had to dust off my cap and gown. So I just let it go.

Mrs. Berry's promised letter took more than two months to arrive. She apologized for the delay, but she'd had to take care of almost everything, even the recent memorial service, a ceremony which, in England, tends to take place some time after the death. She was kind enough to send me a copy of the order of service, listing the hymns and readings. Wheeler hadn't been a religious man, she explained, but she had preferred to fall back on the rites of the Anglican church, because 'he always hated the improvised ceremonies people hold these days, the secular parodies that are so popular now.' The service had taken place in the University Church of St. Mary the Virgin in Oxford, a church I remembered well; it was where Cardinal Newman had preached before his conversion. Bach had been played and Gilles, as well as Michel Corrette's gentle, ironic *Carillon des morts*; hymns had been sung; passages from Ecclesiasticus had been read ('. . . He will keep the sayings of the renowned men: and where subtil parables are, he will be there also. He will seek out the secrets of grave sentences . . . he will travel through strange countries; for he hath tried the good and the evil among men. Many shall commend his understanding; and so long as the world endureth, it shall not be blotted out; his memorial shall not depart away, and his name shall live from generation to generation. If he die, he shall leave a greater name than a thousand: and if he live, he shall increase it'), as well as the Prologue from *La Celestina* in James Mabbe's 1605 translation and an extract from a book by a contemporary novelist of whom he was particularly fond; and his praises had been sung by some of his former university colleagues, among them Dewar the Inquisitor or the Hammer or the Butcher, whose eulogy had been particularly acute and moving. And this had all been arranged according to the very precise written instructions left by Wheeler himself.

Mrs. Berry also enclosed a color photo of Peter taken some years before ('I thought you would like it as a keepsake,' she said). Now I have it framed in my study and I often look at it, so that the passing of time does not cause my memory of his face to grow dim and so that others might still see it. There he is, wearing the gown of a Doctor of Letters. 'It's made from

scarlet cloth with grey silk edging or facing, and the same on the sleeves,' Mrs. Berry explained. 'Sir Peter's gown had belonged to Dr. Dacre Balsdon, and the grey had faded somewhat, so that it looked more like a dirty blue or a greyish pink: it had probably been left out in the rain. I took the photo in Radcliffe Square on the day he received that degree. It's a shame he took off his mortarboard to pose for the picture.' There is, of course, no word in Spanish for the untranslatable 'mortarboard.' Underneath his gown Peter is wearing a dark suit and a white bow tie, an outfit which is referred to as 'subfusc' and is compulsory at certain ceremonies. And there he is now in my study, fixed forever on that far-off day, in a photo taken when I did not yet know him. The truth is that he changed very little from then until the end. I can recognize him perfectly when he looks at me with those slightly narrowed eyes, and you can clearly see the scar on the left-hand side of his chin. I never did ask how he got it. I remember that I hesitated over whether to ask him on that last Sunday, after lunch, when I was about to go to the station and get the train back to London and he accompanied me to the front door, leaning more heavily than ever on his stick. I noticed then that his legs were weaker than they had been on any other occasion, but they were doubtless capable of carrying him about the house and the garden and even up to his bedroom on the second floor. But he looked very tired, I thought, and I didn't want to make him talk much more, and so I chose to ask him something else, just one more thing before we said goodbye:

'Why did you tell me all this today, Peter? Believe me, I found it fascinating, and I'd love to know more, but I find it odd that, after years of knowing each other, you should tell me about all these things you've never said a word about before. And once you said to me: "One should never tell anyone anything," do you remember?'

Wheeler smiled at me with a mixture of slight, almost imperceptible melancholy and mischief. He placed both hands on his walking stick and said:

'It's true, Jacobo, you should never tell anyone anything . . .until you yourself are the past, until you reach the end. My end is fast approaching and already knocking insistently at the door. You need to begin to come to terms with weakness because there will come a day when it will catch up with you. And when that moment arrives, you have to decide whether something should be erased forever, as if it had never happened and never even had a place in the world, or whether you're going to give it a chance to . . .' He hesitated for a moment, looking for the right word and, not finding it, he made do with an approximation: '. . . to float. To allow someone else to investigate or recount or tell it. So that it won't necessarily be lost entirely. I'm not asking you to do anything, I assure you, to tell or not to tell. I'm not even sure I've done the right thing, that I've done what I wanted. At this late stage, I don't know what my desires are any more, or if I have any. It's odd, towards the end, one's will seems to become inhibited, to withdraw. As soon as you go through that door and walk away, I shall probably regret having told you. But I can be sure that Mrs. Berry, who knows most of what happened, will never say a word to anyone when I'm gone. With you I'm not so sure, though, and so I leave that up to you. I might prefer it if you kept silent, but, at the same time, it consoles me to think that with you my story might even . . .' He again sought some better word, but again could not find it: '. . . yes, that it might still float. And that's really all it comes down to, Jacobo, to floating.'

And I thought and continued to think on the train back to Paddington: 'He's chosen me to be his rim, the part that resists being removed and erased, that resists disappearing, the part that clings to the porcelain or the floor and is the hardest bit to get rid of. He doesn't even know if he wants me to take charge of cleaning it up—"the constitution of silence"—or would rather I didn't rub too hard, but left a shadow of a trace, an echo of an echo, a fragment of a circumference, a tiny curve, a vestige, an ashy remnant that can say: "I was here," or "I'm still here, therefore I must have been here before: you saw me then and you can see me now," and that will prevent others from saying: "No, that never occurred, never happened, it neither strode the world nor trod the earth, it never existed, never was."'

Mrs. Berry also spoke in her letter about the drop of blood on the stairs. She couldn't have helped hearing part of our conversation as she bustled around in the kitchen and came and went, on that last Sunday when I visited them (the verb she used was 'overhear,' which implies that it was involuntary), and how Wheeler referred in passing to the stain as if it had been a figment of my imagination ('Just there, where you say you saw . . .'). She felt bad about having lied to me at the time, she said, to have pretended to know nothing, perhaps to have made me doubt what I had seen. She asked me to forgive her. 'Sir Peter died of lung cancer,' she wrote. 'He knew deep down that he had it, but he preferred not to. There was no way he would go to the doctor and so I brought one, a friend of mine, to the house when it was already too late, when there was nothing to be done, and that doctor kept the diagnosis from him—after all, what was the point in telling him then?—but he confirmed it to me. Fortunately, he died very suddenly, from a massive pulmonary embolism, according to what the doctor told me afterwards. He didn't have to endure a long illness and he enjoyed a reasonable life right up until the end.' And when I read this, I remembered that the first time Wheeler had suffered one of his aphasic attacks in my presence—when he had been unable to come out with the silly word 'cushion'—I had asked him then if he'd consulted a doctor and he'd replied casually: 'No, no, it's not a physiological thing, I know that. It only lasts a moment, it's like a sudden withdrawal of my will. It's like a warning, a kind of prescience . . .' And when he didn't finish the sentence and I asked him what kind of prescience, he had both told me and not told me: 'Don't ask a question to which you already know the answer, Jacobo, it's not your style.'

'In fact, the only symptom, during almost the whole time he was ill,' Mrs. Berry went on, using a term doubtless learned from her medical friend, 'was the occasional hemoptoic expectoration, that is, coughing up blood.'—And I thought when I read that paragraph: 'So much of what affects and determines us is hidden.'—'This used to be quite involuntary and only happened when he coughed particularly hard, and sometimes he didn't even realize; remember, although he may not have seemed it, Sir Peter was very old. So although it's impossible to be sure, that might be what you found that night at the top of the first flight of stairs and that you took such pains to clean up. I'm very grateful to you, because that, of course, was my job. On a normal day, it would have been most unusual for me to miss something like that, but I was so busy that Saturday getting ready for the buffet supper, with all those people, and, if I remember rightly, you pointed to the wood, not the carpet, where it would have been much more visible. Anyway, on your last visit, when I heard Sir Peter telling you about his wife's blood at the top of that first flight of stairs, sixty years before and in another house, well, I was afraid you might think you'd had a supernatural experience, a vision, and I had to let you know about this other real possibility. I do hope you'll forgive my pretense at incredulity, but I couldn't, at the time, mention something that Sir Peter preferred not to acknowledge. Well, the truth is he chose not to do so right up until the last. Indeed, he died without knowing he was dying, he died without believing that he was. Lucky him.' And then I recalled two things I had heard Wheeler say in different contexts and on different occasions: 'Everything can be distorted, twisted, destroyed, erased, if, whether you know it or not, you've been sentenced already, and if you don't know, then you're utterly defenseless, lost.' And he had also stated or asserted: 'And so now no one wants to think about what they see or what is going on or what, deep down, they know, about what they already sense to be unstable and mutable, what might even be nothing, or what, in a sense, will not have been at all. No one is prepared, therefore, to know anything with certainty, because certainties have been eradicated, as if they were infected with the plague. And so it goes, and so the world goes.'

Yes, now I'm living in Madrid again, and here, too, everything points towards that, or so I believe. I've gone back to working with a former colleague, the financier Estévez, with whom I worked for a few years after my Oxford days, when I married Luisa. He no longer refers to himself as 'a go-getter' as when we first met, he's grown too important for such nominal vanities, he doesn't need them. I contacted him from London, to sound him out regarding job opportunities, given my imminent return: I had saved quite a lot, but could foresee a lot of expenses on my return to Madrid. And when I told him briefly over the phone what I had been up to, I noticed that he was impressed when I said I'd worked for MI6, even though I'd been employed by a strange unknown group in a building with no name, which never gets a mention in any book—so ethereal and so ghostly that it didn't even require its members to have British nationality or to swear an oath—and even though I couldn't give him any proof, but only tell him what I knew. Not that I wanted to give him too many details, and those I did were invented. Anyway, he took me on at once to help with his various projects and he trusts my judgment, especially about people. And so I do still interpret people, just for him, now and then, and given my previous experience—given my record—he always listens to me as if I were the oracle. Thanks to him I earn enough money to be able to pay for Luisa to have some botox treatment, if one day she should ever want to, or indeed anything else that might improve her appearance, if she ever starts to get obsessed, although I don't think she will, it's not in her nature. To me it looks as good as before I left, before I left my home for England, her appearance I mean. And what I didn't see for a long time—but which was seen by another in my absence—that, too, seems just as good. And when I say I don't live alone but half-alone, that's because I either take the children out or visit them almost daily, and on some afternoons Luisa comes to my apartment, leaving the kids with another babysitter, not the stern Polish Mercedes, who has married and set up on her own—she's apparently opened her own business.

This is how Luisa wants it, with each of us in our own apartment, which is perhaps why she has never said what I wanted her to say or write to me during my solitary and, subsequently, troubling time in London: 'Come, come, I was so wrong about you before. Sit down here beside me, here's your pillow which now bears not a trace, somehow I just couldn't see you clearly before. Come here. Come with me. There's no one else here, come back, my ghost has gone, you can take his place and dismiss his flesh. He has been changed into nothing and his time no longer advances. What was never happened. You can, I suppose, stay here forever.' No, she hasn't said that or anything like it, but she does say other occasionally disconcerting things; during our best or most passionate or happiest moments, when she comes to see me at home as she must have gone to see Custardoy over a period of many months, she says: 'Promise me that we'll always be like this, the way we are now, that we'll never again live together.' Perhaps she's right, perhaps that's the only way we can remain properly attentive and not take each other or our presence in each other's lives for granted.

I haven't forgotten what Custardoy told me, not a single word; any information that the mind registers stays in it until oblivion catches up with it, and oblivion is always one-eyed; I haven't forgotten his insinuations or more than insinuations ('Everyone has their own sexuality,' he said with *madrileño* bravado, each rasping word dragged out like the music from a music box, 'with some people it's straightforward and with others it isn't. Didn't the same thing happen when she was with you? I mean, what can I say, pal, I had no idea either'), and on occasions I've been tempted to try hurting Luisa, just a little, as if unintentionally, distractedly, accidentally, to see how she would react, to see if she would accept it without protest, holding her breath, just to know how she would respond. But I've always stopped myself and always will, I'm sure, because that would be like accepting that Custardoy had been right and exposing myself to a new poison, and I'd had quite enough poison on that night with Tupra or, rather, Reresby. Also, it implied a danger, albeit remote: that of putting myself in the place of the man I had so feared, the devious fellow of my imagination, who might turn up one rainy night, when they're stuck at home, close his large hands around Luisa's throat—his fingers like piano keys—while the children— my children—watch from a corner, pressing themselves into the wall as if wishing the wall would give way and disappear and, with it, this awful sight, and the choked-back tears that long to burst forth, but cannot, the bad dream, and the strange, long-drawn-out noise their mother makes as she dies. ('While it isn't something any of us would wish for, we would nonetheless always prefer it to be the person beside us who dies,' Reresby had said that night. '. . . even the person we most love, yes, even them, anyone but us.') No, one mustn't slip or skate too close, one mustn't toy with the time, temptations and circumstances that might lead to the fulfilment of some probability carried in the veins, our veins, and my probability was that I could kill, I know that now, well, I knew it before, but I know it even better now. Best to shy away from it all and keep oneself at a distance, better to avoid it and not to touch it even in dreams ('Dream on, dream on, of bloody deeds and death'), so that not even in dreams could someone say: 'Your wife, that wretched Luisa your wife, Jacques or Jacobo or Jack, Iago or Jaime, that never slept a quiet hour with you because the names don't change who you are . . . Let me be lead within thy bosom and may you feel the pinprick in your breast: despair and die.' No, that won't happen, it doesn't happen. Best to keep away.

One day, I went over to his part of town, Custardoy's; normally I try to avoid it as much as I can, which isn't easy, given that it's so central. I don't avoid it for any real reason, it's just that places become marked by what you did in them, far more than by what they did to you, and then something happens which bears a very faint resemblance—a mere shadow, a poor imitation, nonsense, no comparison—to the grudge against place, the spatial hatred, that the Nazis felt for the village of Lidice which they reduced to rubble, razed to the ground and wiped from

the map, and for so many other towns in Europe, and the spatial hatred that Valerie Harwood felt perhaps for Milton Bry-
ant and Woburn, and Peter Wheeler for Plantation Road, that
pretty leafy street in Oxford, and I myself for the building with
no name near Vauxhall Cross and the indiscreet headquarters
of the Secret Intelligence Service by the Thames with its look
of a lighthouse or a ziggurat, where I never venture if I go to
London now, whether with Luisa or without her; I have a little
money in bank accounts there—well, you never know when
you might have to leave Spain in a hurry. But I did feel a kind
of spatial hatred for Calle de Bailén and Calle Mayor, quite unconscious, because I like the area, despite the fact that various
oafish mayors have done their best to ruin it. I was passing by
the Palacio Real, where I sometimes go to see an exhibition,
and, which is another building that can no longer be seen from
any other angle but from the front—one of the many views that
those same idiotic mayors and their town planners and venal
architects have inconsiderately and idiotically stolen from both
the inhabitants of Madrid and the people who visit it. I was
returning from some errands on the other side of Plaza de Es-
paña when I came across two policewomen on horseback—they
regularly patrol there now that all the traffic has been sent underground in this, the capital of tunnels—one white horse and
one black, and I passed so close to the white one that I almost
touched him and felt his breath—you only realize how tall they
are when you're next to them. I hadn't gone five steps beyond
the crossroads when I noticed at my back the horse's agitation
or anxiety: the dog belonging to a woman who happened to be
passing had started barking at the horses and harassing them, and
the white horse took fright, reared up and was about to bolt, and
did indeed try to make a run for it, although it only got a few
yards, while the dog—tis tis tis, aerial footsteps, it was a pointer
like Pérez Nuix's, except that this one had a spotted coat and a
brown head—got even more excited by all that reined-in skit-
tering and the almost galloping clatter of hooves and barked
more loudly. The policewoman regained control of the horse
at once, although not without some alarm and some effort: she

had to turn it in circles in order to to rein it in and calm it down, and the owner of the dog finally dragged her pet off and put an end to its incursions—the tis tis tis sounded much sadder now—and stopped its barking. The other horse, the black one, wasn't in the least perturbed, either by the pointer's threats or by its companion's attempted escape, he was clearly less delicate. The sound of clattering hooves soon slowed, and when the momentary commotion had subsided, the policewoman and her horse stood quietly for a while, silhouetted against the royal façade, while she soothingly stroked his neck, under the gaze of two guards in nineteenth-century costume, inscrutable and motionless in their sentry boxes by the Palace gates. We weren't far from the monument to Captain Melgar, with its disproportionately small legionnaire, a kind of dwarf Beau Geste trying to scramble up to the Captain's beard or mustaches.

Then, from among the people who had stopped to watch this minor incident (of whom I was one) I noticed a man step forward, the kind of spectator who is prone to jump into the ring at bullfights, who always seems to be around eager to take center stage, whenever there's an altercation, a bit of trouble, and whose whole posture seems to be saying: 'I'll have this fixed in no time' or 'I'll knock some sense into these madmen and restore peace and amaze the onlookers.' His intervention was entirely unnecessary because the policewoman had by now managed to pacify her mount, yet the man strode over to them and, as if he were a wrangler or something, was patting the horse's neck and stroking its muzzle and whispering mysterious or trivial words. The first thing that alerted me was the glove, the black leather glove that stood out against the horse's white coat; it was a spring day, overcast but not cold, and covering your hands seemed odd, and even odder to have just one hand covered, because when he reached out his other hand and placed it on the horse's back, I saw that it, the right one, was bare, and that made me think: 'What a lot of one-handed people . . . Perhaps his left hand never healed properly and that's why he wears the glove, to hide a deformity or scars, who knows, perhaps he never shows it to anyone.' Then he turned to face me just as I was thinking this, it was simultaneous—he didn't turn to look at anyone else, but at me, as if he had seen me before the incident with the horse and knew where I was, or perhaps he'd been following me—and he gazed straight at me with those unmistakable eyes, crude and rough and cold, two enormous, very dark eyes, rather wide-set and lashless, and both those factors, the lack of lashes and the wide-apartness, that make his obscene gaze unbearable or possibly irresistible when turned on the women he seduces or buys and possibly also when turned on the men with whom he competes, and we were not just rivals, he hated me with the same fierce intensity as when we had seen each other for the last time on the sole occasion that I visited his apartment, with an old Llama pistol and a poker in my hand and wearing gloves like the ones Reresby had worn in the handicapped toilet and like the single glove he was wearing now. But it wasn't the same hatred, not identical: there, in front of the Palacio Real, it wasn't old or impotent, frustrated and without consequences, it wasn't tinged with fear and shock; nor was it like the hatred of a child imprisoned in a childish body, nor like a furious adolescent who watches whirling past him the world he is still not allowed to climb aboard; nor like the prisoner who knows that no one is waiting or abstaining from anything because he is not there; and his gaze was no longer murky, but unequivocal and clear.

It had taken me a few seconds to recognize him because Custardoy wasn't wearing a hat now or a ponytail or even a mustache, or only the merest shadow of one, as if he were starting to let it grow again after a period of shaving it off. He was stroking the horse with his gloved left hand and murmuring short sentences, but I didn't know now whether he was addressing these to the animal or to the policewoman—who happily let him carry on, perhaps she was already won over, with her high leather boots like those of a distant English gypsy girl in Oxford—or to me, knowing that I wouldn't be able to hear what he was saying. And when I saw the way he was looking at me, with utter loathing, I saw that there was insolence in that gaze too, and a threat, not one that was in any hurry to be carried out, but one that was prepared to linger and delay for as long as he chose or needed to; my expression must have changed and I thought: 'Damn. I didn't remove him from the picture, not entirely, I didn't make absolutely sure. This man might come after me one day or after us both, after me and Luisa, or all four of us, perhaps the children too. I humiliated him, I hurt him, and I took from him the person he loved. I should have removed or erased him from the picture for good, as if he were a drop of blood.' And suddenly an image flashed into my mind—like lightning in its brevity but not its brilliance, for it was terrifying, nauseating and sordid; or like thunderless lightning that strikes in silence—an image I had seen in one of Tupra's videos, a tethered horse, a defenseless woman, and I couldn't help but associate Custardoy with those well-dressed men sitting beneath white, red and green awnings, sporting thick mustaches and Texan hats most of them, although Custardoy no longer had a hat or much of a mustache, but I had seen them and the marks left by his abuse. That's the trouble once you've been inoculated with any kind of poison, whether through the eyes or the ears, there's no way of getting rid of it, it installs itself inside you and there's nothing to be done and it comes back to penetrate and contaminate any thing or person, saying each time, repeating, insisting: 'Let this sit heavy on your soul.'

I stood there for a few seconds, before turning and continuing on my way. I don't know if I looked at him with equal hatred, but I might have, it's very likely, more than anything because what I saw him do next troubled me greatly, I didn't like it at all: with his right hand, his bare uninjured hand, his painting hand, he took from his trouser pocket a watch and chain and checked the time with strange intensity. At first, I thought this was just some new eccentricity; having given up his ponytail, he had to find some other way to underline the fact that he was an arty type, as my sister had described him before I had even seen him; and from his stupidly archaic bohemian point of view, carrying such a watch in the twenty-first century was doubtless in keeping with that. Then I thought of another possibility: 'Perhaps he doesn't wear a wristwatch for the same reason that he wears a glove,' I thought, 'because he would have to lift up his hand whenever he wanted to know the time. Perhaps his hand really is irrecoverable, ruined, although there's no sign of the gash I made on his cheek. Whatever the truth of the matter, I don't like the image of him holding that old-fashioned watch in his hand and studying it; he may be measuring out my time.' I didn't want to look at him any longer, and when I was already a few paces away, I thought again, perhaps to exorcise him from my mind or perhaps to raise my spirits: 'But now I know that in my angry mood, I, too, am capable of measuring out his time; I counted it once and stopped the count, and he knows that; he was lucky, but I very nearly counted him out. That will dissuade him from coming near. And if he ever does, we'll see then who will be the first to leave his own first name behind.'

You can live with a threat hanging over you because there is always the possibility that it will never be carried out, and that's what you have to think. Sometimes we see what is approaching and nevertheless we pay no attention, and perhaps not only for the reason Wheeler gave: because we hate certainty, because no one dares any more to say or to acknowledge that they see what they see, what is quite simply there, perhaps unspoken or almost unsaid, but nevertheless there; and because no one wants to know, and the idea of knowing something beforehand, well, it simply fills people with horror, with a kind of biographical, moral horror; because we all prefer to be utter *necios* in the strict Latin sense of the word that still appears in our dictionaries: 'Ignorant and knowing neither what could or should be known,' that is, a person who deliberately and willingly chooses not to know, a person who shies away from finding things out and who abhors learning. '*Un satisfecho insipiente*, a nincompoop,' as Wheeler had said with a pedantry I now often miss. No, perhaps it's also because we fear wasting our life on our precautions and suspicions and our visions and alarms, and because it is clear to us that everything will have its end, and then, when we say goodbye, when we are already the past or our end is fast approaching and already knocking insistently at the door, it will all seem to us vain and naïve: why did she do that, they will say of you, why so much fuss and why the quickening pulse, why the trembling, why the somersaulting heart; and of me they will say: why did he speak or not speak, why did he wait so long and so faithfully, why that dizziness, those doubts, that torment, why did he take those particular steps and why so many? And of us both they will say: why all that conflict and struggle, why did they fight instead of just looking and staying still, why were they unable to meet or to go on seeing each other, and why so much sleep, so many dreams, and why that scratch, my pain, my word, your fever, our poison, the shadow, and all those doubts, all that torment?

I had arranged to see Luisa that afternoon: we see each other two or three times a week in this long truce we are enjoying. Indeed, she has the keys to my apartment and, on occasion, arrives before I do and then she waits for me, exactly as Tupra believed someone was waiting for me in London on that night of poison and dance, when no one was ever waiting for me, when there was no one to turn off any lights in my absence, the lights I left on all the time so as not to be entirely in the dark. No one had my keys and no one was ever waiting for me there. The doorman said: 'Your wife, I mean, your girlfriend has gone up already. I gave her a package that arrived for you earlier.' The man senses something marital about us, but is uncertain quite what our relationship is, and so hovers between wife and girlfriend. I've told him that Luisa is my wife, but he still doesn't quite believe it, or perhaps he doesn't understand why, in that case, she comes and goes.

Before opening the door, I could hear her humming to herself inside, she often does that now and she laughs a lot too, with me and without me, I suppose; she no longer rations out her laughter, and I trust this will remain so, if possible forever, or so I think. Her return is nothing like Beryl's return to Tupra, according to my distant interpretations and always assuming they did, in fact, get back together, which was something I never found out: there's no self-interest, not a spurious self-interest, and there's nothing clandestine about it either. It's clear that Luisa benefits from and enjoys us seeing each other like this, just now and then, and not living together, although she might grow tired of that one day; she has already started leaving clothes here. And it suits me too. After all, in London, I got used to being very alone, as Wheeler paternally said to me early on, and sometimes I need to continue to be alone because I don't think I could bear someone's company all the time and never be able to look out at the world from my window on my own, the living world that knows where it's going and to which I imagine I still belong. I opened the door and saw on the coffee table in the living room the package that the porter had given to Luisa, who was in the kitchen, still humming and not aware that I had come in. I saw that it came from Berlin, shoes by Von Truschinsky, from whom, since they have all my measurements, I still occasionally order a pair, even though they are very expensive. I always think of Tupra when I receive them, but then he's always vaguely in my thoughts, as if he were a friend on whom I continue to count—which is odd—and to whom I could turn for help. I haven't done so yet.

That afternoon, he was even more in my thoughts after my silent encounter with Custardoy, with two or three animals as indifferent witnesses. On the way home, something else had occurred to me, I had thought: 'I didn't want to frighten De la Garza when I went to see him at the Embassy, and I was horrified to see the panic my mere presence instilled in him, but, on the other hand, I would have liked to see that same fear on Custardoy's face and in the way he behaved. He's completely recovered from his fright now or if a little remains—as it must—he doesn't show it. Nothing ever works out as we want or as we think, or perhaps I'm still too hesitant; such a thing would never have happened to Tupra, he would have removed him from the picture when he had him in the frame, and now I'll have to watch every corner, just in case he slips back in again, this time with sword or spear, although that might take some time, because once you've experienced fear, you never entirely lose it.' These thoughts continued to preoccupy me. Luisa noticed that I was quiet and was perhaps even a little worried because I wasn't responding much to her jokes, for she's gone back to poking gentle fun at me.

'What's wrong?' she asked. 'Has something happened?'

'What do you mean?' I replied, half-suspicious, half-distracted. 'What sort of thing?'

'I mean, something bad.'

Yes, something bad had happened to me, and no, nothing bad had happened to me at all. Nothing out of the ordinary anyway. Someone hurts you and you become an enemy. Or you hurt someone and create an enemy. It's as easy as breathing, both things happen much more frequently than we imagine, often by chance and without our realizing, it pays to stay alert and watch people's faces, but even then we don't always notice. I *had* noticed that afternoon, which is an advantage. But I couldn't say anything to Luisa, I couldn't talk to her about it, I couldn't tell her about that meeting. We have barely asked each other anything about our time of absolute separation, best not to. She has never spoken to me about Custardoy, nor have I to her, and I will never know how much she loved or feared him. That is perhaps the only thing about which I will never be able to say anything to her, not even when I am already the past or my end is fast approaching and already knocking insistently at the door, because I think I know her face and I stake everything on that, even the way she will remember me. Perhaps because of that, and also because I am usually perfectly content, I sometimes sing or hum to myself at times, as she does, and I have a tendency to sing or whistle that song of many titles, from Ireland or the Wild West ('Nanná naranniario nannara nanniaro,' that's how the melody goes), 'The Bard of Armagh' who forecast: 'And when Sergeant Death's cold arms shall embrace me'; or 'Doc Holliday' who first justified himself by saying: 'But the men that I killed should have left me in peace' and then lamented: 'But here I am now alone and forsaken, with death in my lungs I am dying today'; or 'The Streets of Laredo,' which is the version whose words I know best and which is therefore the one I sometimes sing out loud or to myself, perhaps, who knows, as a reminder, especially the last verse that ends by asking: 'But please not one word of all this shall you mention, when others should ask for my story to hear.'

'No,' I said, 'nothing bad.'

May 2007

Acknowledgments

Throughout the writing of the three volumes of *Your Face Tomorrow*, various people have helped me at some point or other: with a fact, an image, a foreign word, some piece of historical or geographical information, a medical query, a bullfighting term, a few lines of poetry, some advice that contributed to clarifying the narrative, or by looking after my only two copies of the original (I still use a typewriter) until it was completed. They are as follows: Julia Altares, John Ashbery, Antony Beevor, Inés Blanca, Nick Clapton, Margaret Jull Costa, Agustín Díaz Yanes, Paul Ingendaay, Antonio Iriarte, Mercedes López-Ballesteros, Carme López Mercader, Ian Michael, César Pérez Gracia, Arturo Pérez-Reverte, Daniella Pittarello, Álvaro Pombo, Eric Southworth, Bruce Taylor and Dr. José Manuel Vidal. To all of them, my heartfelt thanks.

Separate mention must be made of my father, Julián Marías, and Sir Peter Russell, who was born Peter Wheeler, without whose borrowed lives this book would not have existed. May they both rest now, in the fiction of these pages as well.

JAVIER MARÍAS

64

Polly's Angel

Katie Flynn has lived for many years in ___ ___ rth-west.
A compulsive writer, she started with ___ ___ ories and
articles and many of her early storie___ ___ oadcast on
Radio Merseyside. She decided t___ ___ er Liverpool
series after hearing the reminisc___ ___ amily members
about life in the city in the e___ ___ s of the twentieth
century. For many years she ___ ___ cope wi___ ME, but
has continued to write. Sh___ ___ es as Judith Saxton.

Praise for ___ ie Flynn:

'Arrow's best and biggest saga author. She's good.'
Bookseller

'If you pick up a Katie Flynn book it's go___ ___
wrench to put it down again.'
Holyhead & Anglesey Mail

'A heartwarming story of love an___ loss.'
Woman's Weekly

'One of the best Liverpool writers.'
Liverpool Echo

'[Katic Flynn] has the gift that Catherine Cookson had of
bringing he period and the characters to life.'
Caernarfon & Denbigh Herald

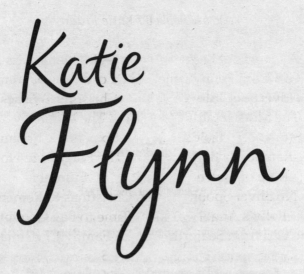

Katie Flynn

Polly's Angel

arrow books

3 5 7 9 10 8 6 4

Arrow Books
20 Vauxhall Bridge Road
London SW1V 2SA

Arrow Books is part of the Penguin Random House group of companies
whose addresses can be found at global.penguinrandomhouse.com.

Penguin
Random House
UK

Copyright © Katie Flynn 2000

Katie Flynn has asserted her right to be identified as the author of this Work
in accordance with the Copyright, Designs and Patents Act 1988.

First published in the United Kingdom by William Heinemann in 2000
First published in paperback by Arrow Books in 2000
This edition reissued by Arrow Books in 2016

www.penguin.co.uk

A CIP catalogue record for this book is available from the British Library.

Typeset by SX Composing DTP, Rayleigh, Essex

Penguin Random House is committed to a sustainable future for
our business, our readers and our planet. This book is made from
Forest Stewardship Council® certified paper.

MIX
Paper from
responsible sources
FSC® C018179

Printed and bound in Great Britain by Clays Ltd, Elcograf S.p.A.

Dear Reader,

Every time I write a book I find myself becoming very fond of one or other of the characters. Sometimes the feeling is so strong that the character positively demands that she should appear in another book, and this happened with Polly. She is a darling, totally well-meaning, totally loveable and most of all, totally innocent.

So when *Strawberry Fields* was finished, I found I could not get Polly out of my mind; her efforts to keep poultry in a flat surrounded by streets, and her curiosity over the connection between the cockerel and the eggs the hen produced, made me laugh and love Polly all the more. Thus it was that *Polly's Angel* came into being, only this time Polly has grown up and knows all about cockerels and hens!

When we were a good deal younger, Brian and I spent a lot of time in southern Ireland and I hope and believe that my love of the countryside comes from there. During the war, the Wrens' headquarters were at Holyhead, on Anglesey, and of course I love the island – we have a caravan there – and I do a lot of my research in that area, though things are very different now. The docks, which were so useful in wartime, have been allowed to fall into disrepair, though the memories of the importance of the port are retained in the Maritime museum, which I visit constantly whenever we are on Anglesey.

Also, various parts of the island have been named in English as well as Welsh, and I have often thought each one must have a story. Why is Turkey Shore so named? And Soldiers' Point must have some military significance, though nobody seems to know what it is; it's just Soldiers' Point. I'm sure there are many others.

As I sit here writing, the gales have reached us at last, blowing with a ferocity which is worthy of Anglesey, which I am sure is the windiest place in North Wales. Our caravan faces out into the Irish Sea and regularly gets a battering. Every time we return to it at Easter, we fear to find it has gone, but so far, so good . . .!

All best wishes,
Katie Flynn

For Nell Shepherd, whose lovely letters always make
me laugh and who keeps me up to date
with what's going on in Liverpool.

Acknowledgements

My thanks are due, as usual, to a great many people. First and foremost, Cyril Dodman explained the ramifications of becoming a yeoman signaller, the conditions experienced on the Russian convoys and in general life in the Royal Navy during the Second World War. He also checked the MS for me and corrected a couple of awful errors I had made – thank you, Cyril!

Regarding Liverpool during the Blitz, Rosemarie Hague gave me a child's eye view of this ghastly time and put me right on the transport conditions during early May 1941.

Information about Anglesey during the war came to me via Rhys Bebb Jones of the library service, who put me in touch with John Cave of the Maritime Museum, Holyhead, who, in his turn, told me who could help me most. Life in the WRNS was made explicable to me by Kathleen Roberts of Holyhead, who was actually stationed on the island and was thus able to tell me most of the things I needed to know. The late Captain Pritchard had told me about the ferries in wartime for another book, and his widow, Margaret, refreshed my memory, whilst John Emlyn Williams of Four Mile Bridge was kind enough to tell me of his own experiences on the Irish ferries. Information about RAF Valley was provided by Ken Grey, who also gave me titles of books likely to prove helpful to one wanting to know about Beaufighters.

I spent a good deal of time in the Maritime Museum in Holyhead, talking to people, looking at the exhibits and drinking tea in their excellent little cafe, so I'm very grateful to all the staff there, most of whom are volunteers, for the generous giving of their time. What could be nicer than researching in such surroundings and amongst such company!

Because I'm still suffering from ME this book has taken me nearly twice as long as usual to write and consequently, what with the time-lapse and my highly unreliable memory, I may have left someone helpful out, so I do apologise if I have done so.

Chapter One

1936

It was a warm Sunday afternoon in late October, with the leaves on the trees already turning from green to pale gold, crackly brown and deep, gleaming scarlet. Polly O'Brady and her small brother Ivan, each with a basket at the ready, were picking blackberries whilst the dog Delilah roamed ahead, occasionally raising a leg against a particularly inviting bush to a chorus of objections from both children. Polly, who adored her dog, nevertheless scowled at his scraggy, long-haired body as he pottered around the brambles, inhaling deeply whenever he found a new smell.

'Delly! Oh, Ivan, isn't he the worst dog in the whole world now? Why can't he understand not to widdle on the blackers, when we's still only half filled our baskets?' Polly stamped an imperious foot. 'Come back here at once, you tarble animal, or I'll tie a knot in your penny whistle, so I will!'

Delilah, unmoved by this dreadful threat, turned and grinned at them, gave a perfunctory wag of his undisciplined ginger tail, and suddenly whipped round and broke into an ungainly canter as his large nose caught a whiff of something he hoped might prove to be rabbit. Although he had yet to catch anything – apart from fleas – he was a grand chaser and was hopeful of meeting a rabbit one day which could not run quite as fast as the rest.

'You've got to catch him before you can do anythin' to him,' Ivan observed, watching Delilah's shaggy

1

backside disappear into a likely-looking bush. The children could hear his crashing progress gradually getting fainter as he charged up the hill. 'He's a bad feller, so he is, but we loves him, don't we, Poll? And anyway, Mammy washes the blackers, so it doesn't really matter who—'

'Yes, it does,' Polly interrupted, much shocked. She glanced around her. 'Besides, you shouldn't talk like that. It's rude, so it is. But we've picked the best berries here be now, so we ought to go further up the hill where the bushes haven't been touched yet, 'cos tomorrow's Hallow'een and that's when the girls at school say the devil overlooks the berries an' turns 'em bad, an' they give you bellyache. So if we don't get enough today, that'll be the end of our mammy's blackberry jelly, 'cos you can't pick 'em once the month's turned.'

'That's a lot of nonsense, so it is,' Ivan objected. 'What does the ole devil want wit' blackers, anyhow? I never heared he turned 'em bad in Ireland, so why should he do it here? Not that it matters, 'cos we'll fill our baskets well before teatime.' He sighed deeply and gave his sister a pathetic glance. 'Only me arms is achin' somethin' tarble, an' me basket's only half full.'

'They'll ache worse by the time we get home,' Polly said callously. She picked a couple more berries, popped them into her mouth, then set off up the hill in Delilah's wake. 'Come to think of it, the blackers will be better up there, out o' the trees, because they'll have had more sunshine on 'em.' She glanced back at Ivan, trailing well in her wake. 'Come *on*, will you, Ivan! Aren't you lookin' forward to eatin' Mammy's lovely jelly on a nice round of bread an' butter?'

'Ye-es, but me legs is achin' as well,' Ivan said in what was perilously close to a whine. 'An' don't you say yours is too, Poll, 'cos my legs is only seven, yours is great, twelve-year-old legs – almost a grown-up's. So just you go slower, or – or I'll tell Mammy on you.'

'Call yourself a boy! They say as girls are the weaker sex, but I'm stronger than you, *Ivy*,' Polly said mockingly, using a hated nickname which Ivan had had many a fight over in school. 'Now do stop moanin' an' come along, or it's me what'll be tellin' the mammy a t'ing or two.'

'You called names! Oh, won't Mammy tell you what a bad girl you are, Polly O'Brady!' Ivan said triumphantly. 'An' Daddy won't be too pleased wit' you either. Just wait till we get back to the crossin' cottage.'

Polly, seeing that she had gone too far, slowed and waited until Ivan caught her up, then she took his free hand, saying guiltily: 'It's sorry I am, Ivan – there, isn't that handsome of me now? I shouldn't have teased you, for you've picked like – like Bevin would have. Now I can't say fairer than that, can I?'

'No, you can't say fairer than that,' Ivan agreed, cheering up immediately: such comparison with elder brothers was always welcome. For he admired both of them greatly, as Polly well knew. Now she squeezed his small, grubby paw and smiled down at him. He was a broth of a boy was her little brother, and it was mean to tease him, so it was.

The trouble was, she was missing Grace. Grace Carbery had been her best friend ever since they had come from Dublin to live on the Wirral, and the two girls had been inseparable during holidays, which Grace had spent at the railway crossing cottage. But Polly would never have met Grace, she knew, had it not been for her eldest brother's wife, Sara, who had worked at the Strawberry Field Orphan Home, where

Grace had been one of the inmates. Sara had brought Grace to the cottage, and the two girls had become great friends, for all that Grace was some four years the elder. And then Brogan and Sara had married and gone to America, where they had speedily settled down and had a baby boy. They had named him James Peter, after Brogan's father, Peader, though they usually called him Jamie, and the young couple had kept an old promise – they had invited Grace over to America to stay with them and, hopefully, to find herself a better job than had been possible in Liverpool.

So eight months ago, Grace had set sail for the States, where she looked after the baby in the mornings, when Sara was teaching at the small private school where she had worked before Jamie's arrival, and worked at something called a delicatessen in the afternoons and evenings; Polly thought it was some kind of a shop. Grace and Polly exchanged frequent letters, but Polly missed her friend terribly, and found young Ivan a poor substitute, though she did her best never to show it.

But Ivan was a good kid and Polly knew it so she was about to offer to carry his basket for a bit when a shrill, excited bark came from higher up the hill and she and Ivan exchanged anxious glances. 'Come back, you tarble feller,' Polly shrieked, but was not surprised when the dog failed to reappear. Delilah was always chasing rabbits, squirrels and anything else that would oblige him by scuttling ahead, but suppose, just suppose, that he had actually caught something, or was about to do so? Polly knew she would find it hard to forgive Delilah if he killed a fluffy little rabbit – or a squirrel, come to that – but if he half-killed it . . . She closed her eyes tightly for a

4

moment in order to say a quick prayer for the safety of all small animals in the area, then she and Ivan dumped their baskets and set off at a run towards the barking, bursting out of the shade of the trees and into sunshine almost at once.

They saw Delilah immediately, emerging from a bramble patch and dancing across the rough grass and heather towards them, his dark eyes shining with excitement, his mouth open to show what looked like yards of pink tongue and a very capable set of white teeth. To Polly's relief, however, the teeth were his own; the rabbit had clearly escaped.

'Stay wit' us, Delly,' Polly commanded, almost breathless with relief. 'And if you go off after rabbits, me fine boyo, I'll – I'll marmelise you, so I will.' She turned to Ivan. 'Will you stay here, Ivan, while I fetches our baskets? You could pick some blackers to eat, for I've seldom seen bigger berries. Aren't they just great now?'

'You stay here, I'll go for the baskets,' Ivan said. 'And isn't it Delly we ought to be t'ankin', Poll, for bringin' us out o' the wood? 'Cos these are the best blackers I ever did see.'

He turned as he spoke and trotted into the trees and Polly, not to be outdone in helpfulness, followed him. They reclaimed their own baskets – Ivan's had a piece of blue ribbon tied round the handle and Polly's a piece of pink, in order that there should be no squabbles over who had picked what – and returned to the blackberry heaven at the top of the hill where Delilah, still recovering from his earlier pursuit, was lying in a patch of sunlight thoughtfully licking his front paws.

'You're a good feller,' Polly said approvingly, handing the dog one of the larger blackberries.

5

'Here's a treat I picked specially for you. Now no runnin' off, or Mammy won't let us take you out again.'

Delilah accepted the blackberry and ate it absently, more from politeness, Polly thought, than pleasure. Still, she could see he would stay where he was for a bit, because his sides were heaving from his recent efforts, so she moved away from him and began to pick, telling Ivan that she rather thought another ten or fifteen minutes' work would fill their baskets, so richly berried were the brambles hereabouts.

'Mine's nearly as full as I can carry,' Ivan said after a few moments. 'I'd better stop now, Poll, or I'll be fallin' over goin' down the hill, and blackers aren't so good when they've been scratted up off the ground. How are you doin'?'

'I've got enough as well,' Polly admitted. 'Oh, Ivan, I've only just t'ought but it must be gettin' on for teatime, an' Martin an' that horrible Monica is comin' for tea an' catchin' the last train back to Liverpool. The trouble is, if we're late we'll get in trouble, but if we're on time they'll make us wash an' change an' sit quiet while that Monica talks in her lah-di-dah voice an' Martin agrees wit' every word she utters. So the question is, shall we hurry, or take as long as we can to walk back?'

And this question, Polly could see, taxed her small brother. He frowned down at the toes of his boots, at the blackberry stains on his hands and then at Delilah's coat, sewn thickly with bits of undergrowth where the dog had forced his way into the brambles. After Mass this morning Mammy and Daddy had been talking to the Father and had mentioned Brogan, who lived in America, and Donal, who was a seaman aboard a merchant ship, to say nothing of Niall, who lived in Sydney, Australia. 'You've a far-flung family so you have Mrs O'Brady,' the priest had said, and Polly, having just remembered that Martin and his Monica were coming to tea, had thought to herself, *I only wish that Monica could be far flung – right out of the nearest window!* But she had said nothing aloud. The problem was, as Polly well knew, that none of them, from Daddy and Mammy through Donal and Bevin, right down to Ivan and herself, liked Martin's wife, who was the daughter of a successful baker and thought herself more than a cut above an Irish railway worker and his family. But families stuck together, and despite Martin having made Monica family without so much as a by your leave, family she now was so she must be treated as such.

But amongst themselves, of course, the children could say what they liked. 'If she says one word against me bein' allowed to get meself into a bit of a pickle wit' blackberry juice, I'll stand on her toe be accident,' Polly said disagreeably. '*And* I'll put Lionel in her lap when she isn't lookin', and doesn't she have a good screech when she sees the poor cat now?'

'So'll I, too,' Ivan said. 'I'll tug at her dress wit' my dirty hands, so I will, and then when she says we're mucky, I'll point to the stains on her dress and she'll be sorry.'

Brother and sister giggled together, making their way down the hill. Martin and his Monica were coming to tea, so if she and Ivan were late they would be in trouble and just as Polly made up her mind that it would be best to go home, Ivan turned a sunny face up to hers.

'We'd best stop coddin' and start hurryin' back, Poll,' he said seriously. 'For we do love Martin, don't we? And we wouldn't want to make him sad, because if he knew we didn't like that Monica, he'd be real sad, so he would. Isn't that right, Poll?'

Polly laughed and nodded. 'You're right, so,' she agreed. 'Let's hurry then, me brave feller! Come on, Delly, you can run faster than the pair of us, so let's be gettin' home!'

Deirdre was in the cottage kitchen, cutting bread for sandwiches, when she heard the children coming in. Knowing that they had been blackberrying she was not unduly surprised by the state of them, but she pursed her lips, poured hot water into a tall enamel can and sent the pair of them up the stairs to wash and change before Martin and Monica arrived.

'They're catchin' the three forty,' she said, pushing Polly's red-gold curls back from her forehead and tutting over the stains round the child's mouth and the dirt liberally smearing her hands. 'And you know how Monica will make remarks . . . God above knows why Martin doesn't tell her it's none of her business how I bring up me kids, but he'll not do it, he's still daft about the girl . . . so I'll not have the pair of ye coming in for tea like that.'

'Like what, Mammy?' Ivan said. Deirdre laughed down at him. Her precious little son looked, she told him, like a tinker's brat, and his sister . . . 'Well, words fail me,' she said. 'What a couple! Now, Polly, get those old rags off your little brother and give him a good scrub before you start on yourself; hear me? I'll take a brush to that horrid mongrel of yours . . . I put the cat out half an hour since, so's he'd not jump on Monica's lap like he did last time. Poor girl, she went white as a sheet. She's not a cat-lover, that's for sure.'

'She doesn't know Lionel,' Polly muttered, taking the heavy can of water and heading for the stairs.

'He's no *ordinary* cat I told her when first she came visitin'. But she squealed out anyway, and she'd have t'umped him but for me catchin' him up and takin' him out quick. So it's glad I am that you've put him out of harm's way, Mammy.'

'Ye-es, but it isn't Monica's fault that she doesn't like cats, alanna,' Deirdre felt bound to point out. After all, one must be fair, even to a daughter-in-law. 'It's a feelin' she can't help, like some people don't like spiders and others can't abide rats, or snakes.'

'I'm not too keen on spiders meself,' Polly admitted, turning back on the bottom step and raising her voice so that her mother could hear her. 'But a cat's a lovely t'ing to stroke, and it purrs, and winds round your legs givin' you love. A spider's a different t'ing altogether, wouldn't you say?'

Deirdre, who disliked spiders quite as much as Polly did, would have liked to agree, but it would not do to let Polly blame poor Monica for a dislike of cats which verged on real fear. 'Would you let a spider sit on your hand and gaze up at you with its little squidgy eyes and beg for a dead fly?' she asked. 'Some folk will.'

'Oh,' Polly said, taking this in. 'Right. Poor Monica. I'll keep Lionel away from her, Mammy.'

Deirdre waited until her daughter had thundered up the stairs, then crossed the kitchen and opened the door of the oven beside the fire. She took out a tray of scones, cooked to a turn, and carefully transferred them to a wire rack to cool, then went back to slicing and buttering the brown loaf. Beside her was a plate covered in the ham which Peader had cut for her before he left the house. Deirdre, cutting and buttering the bread and slapping ham between the pieces, reflected that Polly wasn't unreasonable, not when it came right down to it. She had taken her sister-in-law, Sara, to her heart long before Deirdre had realised that Sara was a fine person, and look how attached she had been to Grace Carbery! No two girls had been closer, and though she tried not to feel jealous of their friendship, Deirdre sometimes wished that Polly would hand her Grace's letters so that she could read them for herself, instead of just reading out odd bits. But it was fair enough, the girls confided in each other, she guessed, in a way which they would not want to share with any parent, no matter how sympathetic. In fact if only Monica were not quite so critical, not so demanding, the two of them would probably have got on fine despite the older girl's fear of cats. But there was no getting away from it; Monica was extremely pretty, she dressed fashionably and talked in a very refined sort of way, but you could not blame the O'Brady kids for finding her hard to love. She looked down on them, sneered at their achievements, thought herself superior, even thought Martin fortunate to have won her. And no one, except possibly the saints, Deirdre told herself, could take to someone who treated them like that.

A good deal of their – understandable – dislike of Monica was made worse, Deirdre realised, because back in Dublin Martin had been engaged to a charming girl, Kathleen Delaney, and when the rest of the family had crossed the water to join Peader in Liverpool they had confidently expected that Martin and Kathleen would be married quite soon.

But then Martin had come over to Liverpool for a job interview and had said, briefly, that he and Kathleen had had a 'disagreement', that their engagement was off and that he had decided to take the very good job which had been offered him as assistant to the chief clerk in the Liverpool branch of his bank. Questioning him further, what was more, had got them nowhere. He would not discuss what had taken place between himself and Kathleen, simply saying that they had been mistaken in their feelings, that it had been a mercy they had discovered this before marriage and not after, and had then thrown himself into city life with such enthusiasm that he had met Monica and married her within four months.

Deirdre and Peader, discussing their son's alliance in bed at night, when there was no one about to overhear, had long ago decided that Martin had met and married Monica on the rebound from Kathleen, but there was nothing they could do about it. Martin was hot-tempered and self-willed; he had decided he wanted a smart wife from a well-to-do family and he had got one. Whether he would ever be happy with her was another matter, but it was a matter in which his family had absolutely no say. They could not like his new wife, but they must put up with her for Martin's sake, and hope that, when the babies came, Monica would soften and become more likeable – and easier to live with, for her 'high standards' as she called them meant that every penny of Martin's salary disappeared either on to her back or into the tiny house in Nelson Street.

'And this house won't be good enough for long,' Martin had told his mammy soon after the wedding. He had sounded rather prouder of his wife's ambition than otherwise, Deirdre thought now. 'Soon Monica will be after something detached, out in the real suburbs. Still and all, she's an only child and her parents dote on her. No doubt between us, we'll manage to see that she lives in the style she so desperately wants.'

Deirdre and Peader, terribly worried that their boy would be taken from them by Monica and her parents, were reassured that in this one thing at any rate Martin seemed to be the master. Every other Sunday, the young O'Bradys came out to the crossing cottage, and once in eight weeks the rest of the O'Brady family got into the train on a Saturday and went into the city centre, where they looked at the shops and galleries, had tea with Martin and Monica, and returned – with a sigh of relief – to the cottage on the last train.

But it's no use my worrying over Martin and Monica, Deirdre told herself now as she busily sliced and buttered. He's a man grown and must please himself. As for Monica, she's very young yet. She'll mature, and change, and – and grow nicer, easier to get along with.

'Mammy, where's Daddy gone? Or is he waitin' at the station for the three forty?' Deirdre, with her back to the door, had not heard it open and jumped at the sound of her son's voice and Bevin chuckled and came right into the room. 'Sorry, did I frighten you?' He walked around the table and picked up a scone, bit into it, then hissed in his breath. 'Dear God in heaven, Mammy, that was *hot*!'

'And so I should hope,' Deirdre said severely. 'Wasn't it meself that just took them out of the oven? As for your daddy, he's gone along to the station all right, to have a bit of a crack wit' Mr Devenish. Then he said he'd walk back wit' Martin and Monica so I'm minding the crossing while he's away. And what might you be doing home so early?'

'I remembered you were cooking scones,' Bevin said, 'So I thought I'd come home, give a hand. And anyway, someone's got to stop our Polly going for

Monica's throat and stranglin' some sense into her.'

'You're no fonder of Monica than Polly is,' Deirdre said. She began to smear mustard on half the sandwiches; Polly and Ivan hated mustard, even with ham. 'So don't you go pretending to be a peacemaker, Bev! It's your daddy who behaves best, for I'll admit she gets me hackles up so high I'm surprised I don't growl at her, like that misbegotten mongrel your sister's so fond of.'

'Oh, Mammy, we all love Delly,' Bevin said, turning the subject rather neatly, his mother thought. 'Anyway, I'm home now, so I am. What do you want done?'

Deirdre put her knife down and looked up at her tall son. He was getting more like his father every day, she thought affectionately – and more like his elder brother, Brogan, too. All three of them had the same very dark, wavy hair falling across broad, placid foreheads, the same sweet smiles, the same nice natures. For Bevin's offer of help was genuine, as she knew well. The other boys might moan and try to evade household tasks, but Bevin was always ready to give a hand. Just as Polly was, though that, Deirdre told herself, was more upbringing than a family trait, because . . .

'Will I lay the table in the parlour, Mammy? It's a cold tea, isn't it? Sandwiches and cakes and a nice apple pie.' Bevin smacked his lips. 'I dream about your apple pie, Mammy, when I'm slaving away over me books.'

'That's about it,' Deirdre acknowledged. She glanced at the big clock which hung over the dresser and was kept accurate to the second by Peader, for a crossing keeper had to know the exact hour so he could be sure to open and close his gates in good time.'Would you get some eggs out of the pantry, Bev, and hard boil 'em for me? You can lay the table whiles they cook. There's a big bowl of eggs in the pantry.'

'I've got 'em,' Bevin called presently from the big, walk-in pantry by the back door. 'janey, Polly's hens must be laying well, Mammy, the bowl's full.'

'Your sister has a way wit' animals and birds, the same as you've a way wit' figures and examinations,' Deirdre said. 'I swear she goes out and talks to the hens and next day there's an egg or two in each nesting box. Put half a dozen on to boil, Bev; that should do us.'

'Right, Mammy,' Bevin said. 'Then I'll get that table laid.'

For a while mother and son worked contentedly together until a thundering on the stairs heralded the arrival of Ivan, with Polly close on his heels. Ivan was looking distinctly aggrieved.

'Mammy, Mammy, she near on scrubbed me ears off of me head, so she did,' Ivan shouted, hurtling across the kitchen and casting himself at his mother. 'Look how red they are – that wit' bein' pulled out sideways so's she could see the spuds growin' in 'em, she said. I told her I didn't want lugs restin' on me shoulders and she said: "Shaddup, you, or I'll tie a knot in—"'

'Mammy, don't listen to him, he's tale-clattin', that's what he's doin', and it's wrong to tale-clat, you've told me so many a time—' Polly was beginning breathlessly when she saw Bevin. Immediately she rushed round the table to hug him, saying: 'Bev! Oh, you're home early for to see that girl – and our Martin, of course. But there's a grand tea, so there is – Mammy always makes a grand tea when . . .'

14

'. . . your penny whistle!' Ivan finished his sentence at the top of his voice, glaring at his sister across the laden board. 'Mammy, she's a bad girl an' she needs a good smackin' for sayin' bad t'ings to her little brother.'

'Well, you shouldn't have kept pullin' away, and me only doin' what Mammy had said, makin' you respectable so that Monica wouldn't get a chance to talk about kids playin' in pigpens and things like that,' Polly said. She cast a guilty glance at her mother, standing with an arm protectively around Ivan's small shoulders. 'Oh, Mammy, I love Ivan, so I do, but he was strugglin' like a fish in me hands . . .'

Bevin held up a hand like a policeman and made shushing noises until both children had ceased their clamour. Then he spoke. 'Polly, the kid's little lugs look like beetroot, so they do. Say you're sorry for mauling the little feller.'

'I'm sorry I heaved at your lug then, Ivan,' Polly said. Deirdre thought she sounded rather half-hearted about it, but refrained from saying so. An apology was an apology, after all, and Ivan was smiling once more.

'That's all right, Poll,' he said with all his customary sunniness. 'I'm sorry I stamped on your toes, then.'

'Truth will out,' Bevin said. He grinned at his mother. 'Best clothes, I see. Was that orders too?'

Deirdre turned and looked properly at her two youngest for the first time. Polly was now wearing a pale green smock dress and white stockings whilst Ivan was in all the beauty of his Sunday suit. Deirdre clutched at her hair. 'Polly! Not your party dress, you silly young wan, nor Ivan's Sunday suit. Just something nice – your dark brown skirt wit' the pink blouse. And Ivan's grey shorts and blue shirt will do perfectly well. It isn't as if we're having the Queen to tea,' she finished.

Polly heaved a sigh and took Ivan's hand. 'Well, there's gratitude, when I put on our bestest t'ings special,' she said as they headed across the kitchen once more. 'I'm sure I don't know why I try so hard, when nothin' I do is ever right.'

'Nor me,' Ivan said in a lugubrious tone. 'You won't have to wash me lugs again, will you, Poll? I does hope not!'

Deirdre waited until they were out of hearing before she and Bevin caught each other's eye and began to laugh. After a moment, however, Bevin heard the eggs boil over and ran to take them half off the fire, and soon enough it was time to drop them into a bowl of cold water, then to crack the shells and peel them off, and to arrange them, each one cut in half on a plate, and to put it down on the big table in the parlour, between the bowls of tomatoes – grown by Peader, in the little lean-to greenhouse against the bicycle shed – and fine, floury potatoes, still hot from the pan.

'I'd best put on a dress,' Deirdre said resignedly, when all the preparations were finished and she had put the kettle on to boil and stood the china teapot patterned with roses near at hand. 'I'll put me pinafore over it, because otherwise I'll spill something down it, so I shall, but I just know Monica will be wearing something new and smart.'

Bevin said he would hold the fort for her whilst she changed, so she slipped up the stairs, meeting Polly and Ivan, now sensibly dressed, on their way down.

'Better, Mammy?' Polly said, holding out her brown skirt and doing a little bobbing curtsey. 'Will she find fault wit' me in this?'

'Oh, you poor lamb, fancy anyone finding fault wit' you,' Deirdre said mockingly, but she pinched her daughter's rosy cheek consolingly. 'You and Ivan both look fine, so you do. Tell you what, the train went past a while ago, why don't you and Ivan take Delly and walk up to the station to meet Daddy and the others? I daresay you'll enjoy that better than sitting quiet in the parlour until they arrive.'

'Oh, yes,' Polly and Ivan chorused at once. They galloped down the rest of the stairs and straight out of the front door, without even thinking about putting on a coat or a hat. Deirdre called after them, but was not surprised to get no reply. Well, it was a warm enough afternoon, they'd come to no harm. And the exercise would mean that they wouldn't fidget so much during tea, nor be so patently eager to make themselves scarce after it.

The train clattered into the small station and Martin stood up and pulled on the leather strap to let the window down. The train was still moving, though slowly, and the crisp, late autumn air came into the carriage, reminding him of the harvest fields, autumn woods, and the cropped grass of meadows where mushrooms grew at this time of year, spangling the grass with their neat white caps. Martin sighed. He loved the country, but he could not imagine Monica ever wanting to live anywhere but in – or near – the city. She was too fond of shopping, people and amusements to take kindly to country living, but privately Martin envied his parents and the young ones their rural home.

'Is anyone waiting? Your da said he might come down and meet us.' Monica squeezed into the window space beside him and they both looked along the platform. It was empty, save for the stationmaster's brown and white terrier and a couple of pigeons, pecking between the big, flat paving stones.

'No one about,' Martin said, and heard her draw in her breath with a little hiss of satisfaction. She had spent most of the journey telling him that his family did not like her, that she did not like them, that this visit, every other Sunday, was nothing but a farce. 'They'd sooner we didn't come, and I'm afraid I don't enjoy being where I'm not really wanted,' she had said in a drawling, self-pitying tone. 'We'll tell them once a month in future, eh, Martin? Then we can go to my parents' occasionally, or spend the day by ourselves.'

Martin had been looking out of the window; for a moment he let his eyes continue to roam over the stubble in the harvest fields, the leaves turning to gold and brown, tumbling down from the high branches, like falling stars from the blue arch of heaven. He had lifted his eyes from the scene beyond the glass and glanced at her briefly. So very pretty! Streaky blonde hair, light blue eyes, the full-lipped red mouth . . .

'We'll come every other Sunday,' he had said. Not as though he were arguing with her, more as though he were agreeing. Yet the words were not the ones she wanted to hear.

'Oh, but Martin, this just isn't fair, they're *your* family, not mine, and they resent me, you know they do. And I'm not used to children, I don't understand them – and they're so *dirty*, and then there's that huge dog, and the cat – you know I'm scared of cats – and all those hens pecking about the place . . .'

They had been alone in the carriage. Martin had said flatly: 'I like seeing them. I'm fond of me family.

18

As for the kids, you'd better get used to them, so when we have kids of our own—'

She had interrupted him, actually grabbing his arm, pinching it, her face white with temper save for a bright red spot on each cheek. 'Kids! I'm not going to have kids for years and years yet! I *told* you I didn't like kids, didn't want a family, not for years and years and you never said – I'm tellin' you, Martin O'Brady, that I'm norra gal what'll act pleasant if I find meself in the fam'ly way!'

He had looked at her, then smiled. He liked it when she forgot her smart accent, her posh school, and spoke as other Liverpudlians did. 'We're both Catholics, Monica,' he had said gently. 'You didn't think I'd been using rubber johnnies all these weeks, did you? Because I tell you to your head I've done no such t'ing.'

'No, of course not, but—' She had stopped, suddenly seeming to be aware of his sharpened look. She looked down at her feet, catching her full red lower lip with her very small, very white teeth. Then she had looked up at him through her thick, dark lashes. The breath caught in Martin's throat.

'But what, Monica? So why aren't you *in the family way* already, is that what you're going to tell me?' He had caught her hand in his, squeezing the fingers until she squeaked with pain, the pale skin reddening.

'Stop it, Martin! Don't you dare try to knock me about – if that's the sort of wife you wanted I'm telling you here and now—'

'What have you done to make sure we don't have kids, Mon?' His voice had been cooler now, faintly amused even. 'Women's magic, is it? Something us poor, ignorant fellers don't know about?'

She had looked at him doubtfully. 'Well, I – I went

to the clinic, and they gave me . . . It's what heaps and heaps of women use if they don't want babies, there's nothing *wrong*, it's not as if . . . It's not like doing bad things to yourself. It – it's just a – a thing, a sort of sponge thing . . . it doesn't *hurt* either of us, it just – just gets in the way, kind of.'

He had nodded. 'I see. But this is no place to talk about birth control and families. We'll discuss it later. And in the meantime, don't let me here any more talk about not visiting my parents. Understand?'

She had nodded, her lower lip trembling, tears misting her eyes. 'All right, Martin. And – and, Martin, don't be angry. I *did* tell you I didn't want babies yet; it was your job to make sure I didn't have them, only I was afraid you wouldn't bother, so I did it myself. I don't see that I've done anything wrong, honest to God I don't.'

Inside himself, Martin had sighed. He had known deep down even before he married her that he was not doing the right thing by her. He liked her looks, her parents' money and her air of fragility. He had not experienced the sharpness of her tongue nor her jealousy until the marriage was a couple of weeks old and then he had been dismayed. She was jealous of his parents and his siblings, of anyone in fact who Martin loved.

As to her not wanting babies, perhaps she was in the right of it after all. Babies need love, and two parents, and . . . He cut the thought off abruptly and jumped down on to the platform. He turned to help her to alight, then the two of them walked slowly, arm in arm, towards the stationmaster's office. It was a good twenty minutes' walk from here to the cottage, Martin told himself rather grimly; they had best spend the time in talking about the things which really mattered and which, to date, they had both avoided. Things like her feelings towards his family, and her reasons for not wanting babies of her own. Things like the money she insisted they put away every month towards a bigger house. For Martin, the only reason for wanting a bigger house was children, who would need more room. Surely, *surely* that must have been Monica's reason too? Why else would she want a bigger house, with a nice garden of its own? It crossed his mind, but fleetingly, that perhaps they ought to discuss their reasons for marrying one another too, but he dismissed it at once. There were some things, he told himself, that were best left unsaid.

'Martin? You said your father was meeting us, didn't you? Not that I mind having you to myself for a while, and the walk's awfully pretty at this time of year, with the trees turning and berries in the hedges.' Martin smiled down at her. She was doing her best, he supposed. 'We'll likely meet Daddy on the way. Come on, best foot forward.'

Polly and Ivan were good at first. Mindful of their decent clothing, they walked sedately along the lane, playing I spy and trying not to stir up too much dust, for they wore their best shoes as well. Delilah bounded ahead of them, not rushing off the lane for once but sniffing placidly at the verge and occasionally stopping to lift his leg. However, such goodness could scarcely last for long. Any time now, as Polly remarked, they would meet up with either Martin and Monica or with Daddy, and that would mean having to behave properly.

'So we might as well play somethin' interestin', whiles we got the chance,' she said brightly, looking

21

all around her. 'Not mud pies – well, it's been so dry there's almost no mud – but something we can do as we're walkin'.'

'Relievio,' Ivan said hopefully. His sister snorted and gave him a glance loaded with scorn.

'That's not a game you can play as you walk, silly, nor wit' only the two of us! How about hide an' seek?'

'That's not a game you can play as you walk either,' Ivan objected, but Polly sighed deeply and shook her head at him.

'Use your imagination, Ivan,' she said. 'Use that – that lump you've got on the end of your neck that you call a head! It just means you have to walk wit' your eyes shut whiles you count to fifty, an' I run ahead like lightnin', and hide. Then you come after me.'

'But we'll take hours to reach the station if we do that,' Ivan pointed out. 'Besides, why's you to hide an' me to seek? T'ain't fair!'

'It doesn't matter how long we take to get to the station, because we're not meetin' the perishin' train,' Polly pointed out briskly. 'It arrived . . . oh, ages ago. Go on then, you run ahead and hide and I'll count to fifty. Slowly,' she added, seeing her brother looking up at her doubtfully. 'Aw, c'mon, Ivan, we'll be bored to death else.'

'Right,' Ivan said. He cantered off in a cloud of dust and Polly shut her eyes and started to count. Presently she shouted: 'Coming, ready or not!' and charged up the lane, scanning the hedgerows, the autumn-tinted trees and any likely hiding place with an eagle eye. She very soon realised, however, that she should have set some sort of limit on the distance away from the lane which the hider could travel, since she could see no sign of her small brother. In fact she was about to give up when a stifled giggle above her head made her glance up into the boughs of the enormous pine tree around which she had been peering. Sure enough, there was her brother's rosy face hanging upside down and laughing at her, whilst the rest of him was laid comfortably along the large, rough-barked branch quite eighteen or twenty feet above the ground.

'Got you!' Polly squeaked, only to be immediately thwarted.

'You haven't,' Ivan said. 'Come up here if you can, an' then you've got me, but I'm safe from you else, Polly O'Brady!'

'Ivan, you're a perishin' liar!' Polly said indignantly after a moment's thought. 'This is hide an' seek, not Relievio. Come on down, or I'll come up and marmelise you, so I will.'

'I know it's hide an' seek,' the tree-dweller said tauntingly. 'But you can't get me, can you? So you've not won.'

'If I come up there I'll . . . I'll . . .'

'If you come up, I'll go higher,' Ivan declared boastfully. 'I'll go right to the top of the tree, an' – an' I'll be able to see the station, an' the crossin' cottage, an' the village . . . Why don't we both go up the tree, Poll?'

'Because I'm wearin' me decent t'ings, an' me best shoes,' Polly said primly, but she was tempted. Boys always thought they could climb better than girls, but in her experience this was not so at all. I can climb like a cat, so I can, she told herself, it's just – just that I'll likely tear me decent skirt and Mammy can't afford to keep buyin' me skirts. T'ings are a tarble price these days, so they are.

'And what am I wearin', Saint Polly?' her brother

23

asked mockingly. 'But I'm up the tree – and never a scratch on me, because I climb so well.'

'Right,' Polly said grimly. She hitched up her skirt, tucked it into her navy-blue knickers and then, after some thought, removed her shiny strap shoes and her white ankle socks. No point in asking for trouble, and she could climb just as well barefoot she was sure.

The difficult part was the beginning, however. For the first dozen feet or so there wasn't a branch to hang on to, you simply had to swarm up the trunk and though she was a good climber, swarming was something she had never tried. But she tried it now, and after a couple of false starts, during which Ivan jeered terribly, she managed to get the hang of it and humped herself, caterpillar-like, up the long, sloping, rough-barked trunk, seizing the first branch with hands which trembled. She hauled herself aboard it, realising with a sinking feeling that now that she was actually on the branch it was possible that neither of them might be able to get down. And it was horribly high, so high that she felt quite giddy when the tree swayed in the wind.

'Grand, isn't it, Poll?' her small brother said complacently. 'Are you comin' up to me or shall we both go higher?'

Polly swallowed. 'This is plenty high enough,' she said, trying to sound calm and matter of fact. 'Let's go down now, eh, Ivan? Me legs is tarble scratched from grippin' the trunk and me hands is *raw*.'

'Oh, well, I'll come down, then,' Ivan said airily. He swung off his branch on to the one below with an insouciance which brought Polly's heart thumping into her mouth. Dear God in heaven, don't let him fall, she prayed inside her head. Oh, it's ever so dangerous up here, so it is – let us get safely down to the ground!

But whether her prayers were answered or whether Ivan simply had no fear of heights she could not have said, for presently he thumped on to her branch, dusted his palms together, and grinned at her. There was a smear of dirt across his right cheek, Polly saw, and bits of bark and pine needles in his thatch of dark hair. His trousers had also attracted quite a lot of bark and the palms of his hands, like hers, were red-raw, but he seemed indifferent to such things. 'There y'are, easy-peasy,' he said nonchalantly. 'I say, Polly, what's that there?'

Polly looked down in the direction of his pointing finger, but could see nothing save for waist-high bracken and a tangle of brambles. 'Where?' she said crossly. 'There's nothin' there except bracken and old bushes, Ivan. Are you goin' down first?'

'If you like,' Ivan said. 'But there was something there, Poll. You can't see it from here, but up where I was—'

'I'm not goin' higher,' Polly said at once. 'It's a long way to the ground from here, so it is. I don't t'ink it'll be easy gettin' down, Ivan.'

'I didn't say to go higher,' Ivan assured her. 'I said from where I was I could see somet'ing glitterin' in the bracken. If I go first, though I'll have to get past you. Can you squeeze against the trunk?'

Not unwillingly, Polly got as close to the trunk of the tree as she could, and was impressed, against her will, by the casual way in which her little brother went past her, swung by his arms on the branch, then gripped the trunk with his knees until he had a good hold and could grab with his arms as well. Then, monkey-like, he descended the trunk until he stood once more on solid ground, looking up at her.

'C'mon, Poll,' he called. 'It's not bad – it's quite easy, so it is.'

Polly nodded, as though she thought it was easy too, then she glanced at the bracken and the brambles, at the pale grass which straggled between them and the beginning of the trees. Just for a moment she, too, saw something gleaming and glittering in the depths of the bracken but then she moved her head and the object disappeared. To distract Ivan, she called down to him. 'I see somet'ing in the bracken, Ive. We'll take a look when I'm down, so we will.'

Ivan nodded and Polly took a deep breath, turned towards the trunk and closed her eyes. Then she launched herself at the tree trunk, hanging on, limpet-like with desperate hands, knees and feet. She felt that, had she been able to do so, she would have hung on to it with her nose and eyelashes as well, but failing that, she decided she would simply stay here for ever – or until someone came along with a good, strong ladder. She dared not move for fear she would lose her nerve – and her grip – and plummet to the uncommonly hard ground far below.

'You've froze, like Bev said some fellers do when they first climb a pine,' a voice from below said with more than a trace of satisfaction. 'Me an' Bev practised climbin' a pine whiles you were goin' shoppin' wit' Mammy last weekend.'

The unfairness of it! He had climbed up and down pine trees before, been taught by Bev to do it, yet here was she, a true beginner, stuck here like a fool, like a monkey on a perishin' stick! Indignation – and a strong desire to clap her small brother's ears until they rang – got Polly's eyes open and, forcing herself not to look down or to remember the drop, she unclamped her hands, one by one, and moved them lower down the trunk, making her legs follow suit. The cheek of that young feller down there, saying that she, Polly, was froze wit' fear, when she was no such t'ing! Determinedly closing her eyes again, she repeated the movements over and over. She would not let him see how terrified she was!

It was Ivan's laughter which made her open her eyes. He was roaring laughing, and when she looked round at him she saw that there were actually tears of laughter on his cheeks. But it wasn't until her foot hit something, and she realised it was the ground, that she knew why he was so amused. She had been so busy concentrating on not looking at the drop that she had reached the foot of the tree whilst still imagining herself up in the air somewhere, above that perilous drop.

However, there was nothing she could do about it now except to act with what dignity she could. She stood up and began to brush bits of bark and pine needles off her clothing and out of her hair. Then, ignoring Ivan's gradually fading mirth she said: 'Where's Delly?'

As she had guessed it would, this took Ivan's mind off her tree-climbing. He looked around him. 'Delly? Oh, janey, he'll be off after rabbits again, Poll. Or else he's gone on ahead to look for Daddy. Shall I give him a yell now?'

Polly was about to agree when the dog burst out of the bushes which lined the lane and hurled himself at Polly, whining and trying to grab at the hem of her skirt. Polly seized his collar and began to try to tow him along the lane in the direction of the station, but Delilah resisted, his whines growing louder. 'What's up, old feller?' Polly said. 'What've you found?'

'It's probably something horrible,' Ivan said with relish. 'Oh, remember that flashing t'ing I told you about? He came from that direction, didn't he? Mebbe we'd best tek a look, Poll.'

'I'm not goin' to have much choice,' Polly panted as Delilah turned round and began to tow her in the opposite direction. 'All right, old feller, what is it, then?'

The children and the dog crossed the road, scrambled through the ditch – dry providentially – and out into a small hazel copse. Delilah, freed from Polly's grip, ran over to a recumbent figure lying face down on the ground and began to bark again, but Polly shushed him.

'Delly, shut your gob, will you?' she said, approaching the figure cautiously. She bent over the man's head, then straightened, her eyes rounding with horror, both hands flying to press against her small, flat chest. 'Oh, Ivan, Ivan, it's Daddy, an' he must have been hurt real bad!'

Despite the shock, neither child panicked. Ivan took one look at his father's white, set countenance and then turned back towards the lane. 'I'll go to the station an' fetch help, so I will,' he said breathlessly. 'I can run like the wind when I want to. You stay here wit' our daddy, Poll. You'd best keep Delly too. He'll give a bark if – if anyone comes near.'

'Well, all right,' Polly said tremulously. 'D-do you t'ink Daddy tripped over something, an' fell, Ivan? Should I try to sit him up, mebbe?'

'No. He's too heavy,' Ivan said simply. 'Shan't be long.'

He disappeared. Polly sat down beside her father and put a tentative hand on his cheek. It was cool, for the sun's rays had little power so late in the day, but it was not cold. No need, then, to try to get him warm. She put her head close to his and listened. To her enormous relief, she could hear his breathing, low and rasping. 'I knew he wasn't dead, so I did,' she whispered to Delilah, who had come and sat beside her on the ground as soon as Ivan had disappeared. 'Me daddy's the best daddy in the whole wide world, so no one would let him die. Not even God . . . because what'ud we do wit'out Daddy, eh, Delly?'

Delilah sighed deeply. Polly leaned over her father once more. She could not help wishing that she and Ivan had been accompanied by someone older – last year at this time it would have been she and Grace – but she would just have to do her best to be sensible and reassure her father. 'Daddy? It's your own little girl, so it is. I'm wit' you, an' Ivan's gone for help. Oh, Daddy, could you say a word or two? Did you fall an' bang your poor head, then? I know I ought to fetch water, like they do in books, to trickle between your lips, only . . . only I don't t'ink there's any water nearby and I don't want to leave you, so I don't.'

Delilah grunted and moved over so that he was leaning against Polly. He looked down at Peader, anxiety written all over his woolly face, and then bent his head and licked the unconscious man's cheek. Polly, despite her fears, chuckled. 'Sure an' isn't it just like our Delly to t'ink a kiss from him will bring you round, Daddy, just as if you were the sleepin' beauty an' Delly was the handsome prince? Oh, don't I wish it would too! But if you've had a bump on your head mebbe it's better for you to lie quiet a whiles. Anyway, Daddy, I'm goin' to hold your hand, so's you know I'm here, an' before you know it they'll come runnin', all the grown-ups from the station, an' you'll be took proper care of, an' better in no time at all, at all.'

It seemed a long while to poor Polly before the adults she longed for actually did arrive, and when they did the men did not waste time in examining the unconscious man or trying to work out what had happened. They lifted him with great care and gentleness on to the door they had brought and took him straight to the crossing cottage. Ivan and Polly had run ahead to alert their mother and a bed had been made up on the sofa, whilst the beautiful Sunday tea had been bundled out of the parlour and waited, unregarded, in the kitchen.

'The doctor's coming,' Martin told Deirdre as soon as they had settled Peader on the sofa bed. 'Mr Devenish telephoned him as soon as Ivan explained what had happened. He'll be able to tell us what's wrong wit' Daddy, Mammy. Maybe he just tripped . . . The doctor will know.'

And the doctor, when he had had a chance to examine Peader, looked grave. He told Deirdre that her man would have to be admitted to hospital and that his condition was serious.

'He's had a stroke, Mrs O'Brady,' he said bluntly. 'He's a very sick man and may not be well for some time.'

'But he will get well, won't he, doctor?' Deirdre said, her voice heavy with pleading. 'He was ill before, when the train near killed him, but he come to himself in the end.'

'He's a strong man,' the doctor said evasively. 'With good nursing he'll probably do well . . . I'll arrange for him to be admitted to the hospital in Liverpool which treated him last time. But strokes are funny things; you'll just have to wait and see.'

Chapter Two

A month later, Polly's entire life had changed completely. It was a Saturday morning and she was strolling along the pavement in Nelson Street, kicking at the scatter of leaves which had been blown along from the trees which lined Great George Square and half-heartedly watching the passing traffic, whilst from the main road ahead of her she could hear the occasional rumble as a tram passed by. She was wondering how she would ever get used to what had happened to them. Her daddy was still in hospital and Polly, her mammy and Ivan were uncomfortably squeezed into the spare room of Martin's little house, whilst Bevin had stayed in the country with his pal. Because Peader's stroke had proved to be a serious matter which would probably affect him for the rest of his life, they had had to agree to the railway company's insistence that they move out of their cottage so that another railwayman could take over the job of crossing keeper.

'I'm sure your married son will take you in until you can find a place of your own, and you'll want to be nearer the hospital,' the official who had come to discuss matters with them had said. 'Something like this is always a shock, but we'll see that you have some money to tide you over, since Mr O'Brady's original injury was a railway matter. What's more, if – I mean when – your husband recovers sufficiently he may be able to take up some sort of desk job in the city, but he's unlikely to be manning a crossing again. The disturbed nights, the importance of a clear head . . . In short, Mrs O'Brady, I'm sure you understand that a less demanding job would be very much better for your husband.'

Polly knew that Deirdre had agreed because in the back of all their minds there had lurked the horrible suspicion that the official did not think Peader would ever recover. And if this was so they would certainly have to leave the cottage. So because of these fears Polly had set off by herself a few days after the accident to visit the church in town and have it out with God.

'Sure and I love me daddy as much as I love me mammy, and that lots and lots,' she told Him earnestly, on her knees in the small Catholic church in which she and her family had worshipped ever since they had left Dublin and come to England to live. 'But me daddy's a special person, so he is, a wonderful feller; everyone says so. Why, if he hadn't dived at Grace Carbery that day and pushed her out of the path of the train, he'd never have been hit himself. And if he'd not been hit the doctors say the clot of blood that gave him the stroke wouldn't have been runnin' around loose in his head, so don't You go makin' me daddy a member of Your heavenly host when he's not had his fair share down here yet.'

She had paused for a moment to consider, and had then proceeded to tell God that much though she would like to do it, she couldn't promise Him that if He let her daddy get well she would be good for the rest of her life because she didn't think she could stick to it. 'But I'll be as good as I can,' she promised. 'And if it means givin' up me hens and me cat Lionel and me pig and me rabbits, and goin' to live in the city wit'

33

that – that Monica, then I'll do that too.' She had glanced consideringly around her. 'I'm tarble fond of Delly, but if you're set on really makin' me suffer for me daddy, then I suppose I'll have to let you take me dog too.' She gave a deep sigh and scrambled to her feet, bobbing a small curtsey at the altar. 'But if you make me leave me pals, and then take me daddy anyway . . . Well, I just wouldn't, if I were You,' she finished on a distinctly threatening note, 'because I can be bad as bad when the fancy takes me, so I can.'

But that had been a while ago, before the move to the city. Now, Polly knew just how much of her offer had been acceptable to God. The hens, the rabbits and the pig had been left behind with the new crossing keeper and his wife, and Lionel, Polly's ginger cat, had not seemed unduly perturbed to find himself left behind as well. And dear Delilah, though he would join them, Mammy promised, as soon as they did have a place of their own, was in the country, with Bevin and his friend Paul.

But now, with a fine Saturday morning at her disposal and no one to play with, for she knew none of the neighbourhood children yet, Polly was simply mooching, passing the time. If Grace had still been living in Liverpool, of course, it would have been very different. The two girls could have looked in the shop windows, discussed the clothes, imagined what they would most like to buy. Naturally, they would have talked too, discussing all their most intimate thoughts – that was one of the things about Grace which Polly missed most, someone in whom she could confide with the complete certainty that Grace would never breathe a word to a soul. And Grace would have made sure that Polly met all her pals, so that games would have been possible – though Grace, at sixteen, would not perhaps have liked games such as Relievo, which Polly still enjoyed. But the girls had been such close friends that Polly knew she would never have been bored in Grace's company.

In Dublin, too, she reflected gloomily, there would have been a *grosh* of things to do, and masses of friends to do them with. She had had her own particular pal, Tad Donoghue, who had seldom left her side and might have got her into all kinds of mischief but was still her best friend. They could have gone to the tuppenny rush at the cinema, or they could have fished in the Royal Canal, or played games with other kids in Phoenix Park, or walked along O'Connell Street looking in the smart shops and choosing what they would have had if they had found a heap of money lying in the gutter.

Because they had only been living with Martin and Monica for ten days or so – it felt more like ten *years*, Polly reflected bitterly – no arrangements had yet been made for Polly and Ivan to attend school. So they were like two little fish out of water, living on sufferance in Monica's spotless house and dreading the moment when Mammy would pile them on to a tram and take them right across the city to the Catholic school of her choice, for plainly she would not let them go to just any old school.

'Education's important,' she had said to Polly one night as the three of them lay squeezed into the inadequate bed in the young O'Bradys' spare room. 'I'll not have you pushed into the nearest school here just because it is the nearest. And anyway, we can't stay here for ever, we're bound to find a place of our own soon, so there's not much point in puttin' the pair of you in school just to take you out of it as you're settlin' in.'

Polly and Ivan agreed fervently with this remark, but realised that Monica did not. She could not wait to see the back of them, though they did their level best to keep out of her way, hanging round the quiet back streets and trekking across to the nearest open space to play games whenever Martin and Monica were at home.

This afternoon, however, Polly and Mammy and her brothers – Bevin too, for he came into the city each Saturday – would visit the hospital. It was no longer as worrying and frightening as it had been at first, for though Daddy could only mumble out of one side of his mouth at least his beautiful eyes looked at his little Polly with recognition and love. At first, when he had not seemed to recognise any of them, Polly had dreaded the visits, but now they were much nicer. She talked a lot and Daddy gave her his peculiar new lopsided smile, and when they went home Mammy always made sure there was something nice for tea because she said Polly did Daddy good, so she did, and never talked about the crossing cottage or her animals but only about cheerful or funny subjects, like the big fat woman in the sweetie shop who always popped an extra piece of toffee into their penny bag because their daddy was in hospital.

But right now Polly wasn't thinking as much about the hospital visit as about her lack of friends. She had always been popular with other kids and it seemed strange to suddenly find herself so alone. When she reached the cross where Nelson Street met St James Street she saw one or two other children, and looked after them a trifle wistfully, but they were all intent on their own affairs and paid no heed to her. Some were running messages, with money in their hands and bags or baskets full of shopping, and others were with their parents, walking along chattering. But none of them looked as though they needed a friend, or were in the slightest bit interested in Polly.

There were never messages for a child to run in Monica's house. 'We're here on sufferance, and don't we know it,' Mammy had sighed on their very first day in Nelson Street when she had bought meat and potatoes and other vegetables and made a big stew for the whole family. Monica had walked into the kitchen, looked at the big pot of stew, and silently taken from her neat little shopping bag two tiny chops, the makings of a salad and a bought sponge cake. A bought cake! 'And she wit' only one man to feed,' Mammy had said later, in the privacy of their own small room. But Monica worked in an office and didn't have the time to make cakes, Martin had said so. Still, she need not have pushed the stew to the back of the stove quite so disdainfully, telling Mammy grimly that she and Martin preferred a light meal, and that Mammy was welcome to make stew for herself and the two children, provided they ate it before Martin came home.

'I didn't understand . . . but surely, just this once . . .' Mammy had faltered, and Monica had heaved an exaggerated sigh and said that on this occasion the family might eat their stew in the kitchen later, since she and Martin intended to go out to the cinema.

'But there's enough stew here for all of us, dear,' Mammy had said, her beautiful eyes filling with tears at the snub. 'Surely just this once . . .'

Monica had not even answered. She had gone over to the stove and had begun to arrange her two little chops in the gleaming new grill-pan, behaving as though she were the only person in the kitchen – in the world, in fact, Polly thought crossly now. And after that, Mammy hadn't liked to cook anything after about four o'clock, since the smell of cooking made Monica wrinkle up her nose and glance around her as though she suspected them of harbouring a pig or worse.

'Polly me love! I thought I might catch up wit' you if I hurried.' It was Mammy, in her brown coat and hat, with her shopping basket in one hand and the other firmly gripping Ivan's small paw. Her cheeks were flushed and she looked bright-eyed and happier than she had done for some time. 'Oh, Poll, you'll never guess what! One of the nurses who's been lookin' after Daddy called round just now, to tell me of a house she's seen which is goin' for a reasonable rent. Me and Ivan's off to take a look at it right away – want to come along, alanna?'

Polly clasped her hands to her breast, just like all the heroines of her favourite storybooks did when they heard wonderful news. 'Oh, Mammy – you never said you'd asked anyone to look out for a house . . . Oh, it 'ud be so grand to have somewhere of our own again! Yes, please, I'd love to come. Where is it? I'm after hopin' it's near a school where me an' Ivan might go – and as far away from Monica as possible,' she added, grinning widely at Ivan, who was hopping up and down and looking every bit as excited as she felt. 'Will it hold the lot of us? Will it suit Daddy when he's better and can come out of hospital? Oh, janey, I'm excited, so I am!'

'I don't know anything about it, alanna, except that it's not far from the Scotland Road, because Nurse Fry had been shopping up there, and cut through Titchfield Street to visit an old aunt who lives thereabouts. That's when she noticed that one of the houses was to let. So now, if you've finished askin' me questions, we'll make our way to the tram stop.'

A couple of hours later, three members of the O'Brady family stood on the pavement outside the new house, for Deirdre, having closely examined every inch of the place, had talked to the landlord. After a little genteel haggling the two of them had agreed a rent and Deirdre had paid a week in advance and meant to move her family in as soon as possible.

'Of course Titchfield Street isn't as smart as Nelson Street, but wit' your Daddy not working and money being tight it's all we can afford,' Deirdre said half-apologetically, looking up at the terraced house which was to be their home. 'But sure and you'd have to look a lot further to find a house so convenient, and wit' room for us all! There's a jigger along the back so's we can reach the yard, and there's a decent Catholic school just up the road, on Silvester Street, right next door to St Sylvester's, so we shan't have far to go of a Sunday, and the best shops for bargains I ever did see are on the Scotland Road, no more than a brisk walk away. Why Monica went and chose to live out on Nelson Street . . . But there, we're all different, praise be to God, and no doubt she prefers the – the quieter side of the city. Now we'll catch a tram back to Nelson Street and tell Martin we're movin' out just as soon as I can arrange it.'

'There's kids next door,' Polly told Ivan joyfully as they crossed Limekiln Lane and dived into Tenterden Street. 'In fact, there's kids everywhere, round here. We're goin' to like livin' here, Ivan me lad!'

'You're right about kids everywhere,' Deirdre said rather dubiously. 'I don't know when I've seen more kids all in one spot,' she said, her voice sinking. 'Or dirtier ones, come to that. Why, that child's wearin' nothing but a petticoat.'

The children, however, treated this remark with the scorn they felt it deserved. 'They's playin' out, Mammy,' Ivan said reproachfully. 'No one wears good clothes when they's playin' out.'

Polly giggled. 'Mammy's got used to country dirt, she's forgettin' city dirt,' she said. 'As for petticoats . . . well, t'ink of Francis Street on a Saturday, Mammy. There was kids playin' around the stalls wit' only a vest to their backs. Remember Swift's Alley, and me pal Tad, and the awful old tenement in Gardiner's Lane that the Donoghues lived in?'

Deirdre laughed. 'Sure and I mustn't forget me past, for there was a deal of poverty in Dublin, particularly in the Liberties. But I'm after forgettin' the bad t'ings, because life's been better since we came over the water and moved into the crossin' cottage. But of course, life's goin' to be hard now, wit' your Daddy ill and me desprit for work. Now look at that, a tram goin' our way on the main road. We could have caught that if we'd walked faster. We'd best hurry.'

'Oh, trams seem to be comin' and goin' all the time,' Polly said, taking Ivan's other hand and beginning to step out. 'We'll not be long gettin' back to Nelson Street and tellin' them the good news. And I'll write to Grace and Tad this very day, so I shall, tellin' them what's been happenin'. I know Grace knows about Daddy, Mammy, because you wrote and told Brogan when Daddy was took bad, but Grace will want to hear all the very latest news, and you can't write every day, to everyone. Grace'll be ever so glad Daddy's gettin' better, because she always says he saved her life and she loves him nearly as much as I do, and even Tad was mortal fond of me daddy, so I'd best let him know what's been happenin',' she finished. But she was not too pleased with Tad. He had been her best, her dearest, pal in Ireland and when the family left the Liberties he had promised faithfully that he would write, and indeed, at rare intervals, had done so. Polly reckoned she wrote four letters to every one of Tad's, and usually the fourth letter had to be full of threats, or he'd not, she feared, have bothered to answer even that. Though his letters usually contained interesting news, they were short and laboriously written on shockingly poor scraps of paper. Several times she had warned him that she would never write to him again unless he mended his ways, but somehow she always gave in.

After all, as she had told her mammy, she and Tad meant to marry one day and that meant she could scarcely stop writing to him. If she did he might move away, or get himself adopted by a rich man and change his name, and then where would they be?

'That's right, you tell your pal what been happenin' to us,' Deirdre said now, as they emerged on to the main road. 'Oh look, there's a tram stop! And a tram goin' in the right direction! Put your hand out, Poll, so's the driver sees us and stops!'

Tad got the letter as he was setting off to take Dougal and Biddy to school, and recognised Polly's writing at once. Not that there would have been any doubt in his mind who had sent the letter, since no one wrote to him bar Polly.

Now Tad took the letter from the postman's hand joyfully and crammed it into his pocket. The postman winked at him. 'Sure and isn't your little Polly a broth

41

of a girl to write so regular to a chiseller like yourself?'
he said genially. 'I hope you write back as often,
young Tad.'

'Oh well, girls like writin' letters and chisellers
amn't so keen. We're more for doin' t'ings,' Tad said
rather obscurely. 'Still, I do write.'

'And since when's you taken to bein' a gaoler to
that chiseller, then?' the postman enquired next, for
Tad had a firm hand on the shoulder of young
Dougal. 'Poor feller, what's he done wrong?'

'Sure and he's not so keen on goin' to the brothers
to get his schoolin',' Tad explained virtuously. 'I
told him he'd need readin' and writin' one of these
days, but he t'inks a feller can manage very well
wit'out it.'

Dougal, who was seven and regarded school as an
unnecessary evil, sniffed. 'You was sellin' newspapers when you was eight, you often told us so,' he
pointed out. 'I'll be eight in the summer. And you
don't go to school no more. Why can't I—?'

'I'm too old for school, remember?' Tad said
smugly. 'Besides, summer's summer, but now
winter's comin' and you'll be a deal better off in
school than workin' the streets. C'mon, the pair of
yiz.' He took Biddy's small hand and, retaining his
grip on Dougal's shoulder, set off once more in the
direction of the school. When he had delivered his
charges Father Mac had given him a fearful, foxy grin,
reminding Tad uncomfortably that you learned a lot
more than reading, writing and arithmetic when
Father Mac was teaching you and he never meant you
to forget that. You learned to keep a fair distance from
an angry brother and the strap which he wore round
his wrist because of the quick temper most of them
had on them. You learned to dodge, and to take unfair

punishment stoically, and to speak the truth, if you were certain a good lie would be found out. Still, Dougal would thank him one day, if not today, Tad told himself as he turned away. But all the way, the letter had burned in his pocket and as soon as his errand had been accomplished he made for the quays. There was always plenty going on down there, but a feller could usually find a quiet corner out of the bustle, from whence he could keep his eye open for any paid work going, whilst reading a letter. And it was early still, too early to hope for much in the way of running messages or delivery work.

Now that old man Donoghue had left Dublin with the gypsy woman he had taken to hanging around with – and she'll regret it sooner than I will, Tad's downtrodden little mammy had said grimly when she first heard – Tad, Liam and Kevin simply had to do their best to earn what money they could. Tad had a number of jobs; sometimes he sold turves from door to door, or kindling wood when he could get hold of fruit boxes to chop up. At other times he ran messages for anyone who would pay him a penny or so, carried heavy shopping for the elderly, or went round the fish market, collecting odds and ends of fish which he could sell to dog and cat owners for a few pence. His brothers did the best they could, selling newspapers when all else failed, or helping at the cattle market when drovers were scarce and trudging into the countryside in summer to pick potatoes. But being younger than him they were both still in school, so they could not work all day, as he could. However, it was the mammy, Tad knew, who really kept the family going. She cleaned at the big shops and offices on O'Connell Street, took in washing, made neat brack loaves which she sold for a small profit and generally turned her hand to anything. And as she often said, life was not nearly as hard as when Mr Donoghue had been living at home. Mammy kept her wages tucked away from force of habit, but now there was no one crashing into the place drunk as a fish, to burgle Mammy's earnings for his next drinking bout. Now the rent was paid regularly, food appeared on the table each mealtime, no matter how sparse it might seem, and although the children did not own good boots or shoes, they all had a jealously guarded pair of what their mammy called 'rubber runners', which did very well for school and could be handed down to the next child in line when toes were threatening to come out at the end of the shoe.

Tad reached the quays and took up a position behind a large stack of boxes of what, from the smell, he took to be fish. Then, with pleasant anticipation, he opened his letter. He counted the pages before reading a word, though, like a miser checking on his gold. Yes, it was a four-pager, a good, long letter even for Polly, who once she got going tended to tell, in great detail, everything she had done since she last wrote. Grinning happily to himself, and seeing Polly's small, fair face in his mind's eye, Tad settled down to read.

Twenty minutes later, after reading through the letter twice, Tad shoved it back into his pocket and headed for Gardiner's Lane. He was horrified to hear of Peader's stroke and dismayed that the family had had to move from their country cottage – which sounded like heaven to Tad – back into the city, and felt that he must, for once, write back to his little pal immediately. But even in his sorrow for her, a certain excitement could not be altogether denied. They could come home! Back to Dublin! If Peader did not recover then the family would have a pension and would be no worse off – perhaps better off – in Dublin than in Liverpool; and if he did recover – and Tad sincerely and honestly hoped that he would, for Peader had always been good to him – then why should he not take up a desk job, whatever that might mean, in Dublin, where the family had friends and relatives, rather than in Liverpool, where they only had Martin and his snooty wife?

But halfway home, Tad reconsidered. There was no paper at home and probably no pencil, either, and he would have to earn some money to pay for the postage stamp too. Best go and get himself some work, then buy what he needed to write a letter. He turned his footsteps towards the fish market. Old Mrs O'Brien had a stall there, and since her husband's death she had been glad of a hand when she had plenty of customers. Wednesday and Friday were traditional fish days, and today was Wednesday, so Tad turned his footsteps towards the fish market and Mrs O'Brien's stall. He would write back to Polly this very evening, so he would furnish himself with paper, an envelope and a stamp before returning to Gardiner's Lane. And in the meantime he would consider how best to suggest to Polly that this tragedy might, at least, mean a return to Dublin at last.

It was getting dark before Tad left the fish market and headed towards Gardiner's Lane once more, but he did so with a good deal of satisfaction. He had sold a great deal of fish – his hands were raw and chapped from constantly dipping the fillets and steaks into the bucket of increasingly dirty cold water which Mrs O'Brien kept behind the stall – and he had enough in his pocket to buy paper and an envelope, besides his usual contribution to the household expenses. And what was more, he would not need to buy paper; he would nip into Merrick's, on the corner of Mark's Alley and Francis Street, and buy a screw of tea for his mammy. He well knew that if he mentioned he was about to write a letter to Polly, old Mr Thomas Merrick, who weighed out the tea and the sugar and the other dried goods whilst he kept an eye on his staff and other customers, would hand over an envelope. Polly had been a great favourite with the old man, who had beamed down at her over the top of his gold-rimmed glasses and always found a little treat for her – a few raisins, some nuts, or even, if all else failed, one of the strong peppermints which he sucked because he had a dry mouth.

This evening Mr Merrick was in his usual place and as soon as Tad had bought the tea and taken a half-pound of broken biscuits as well, he asked after Polly. 'Sure and wasn't she a grand little lass, and don't we miss her in here?' he enquired, carefully sliding Tad's pennies into the till. 'It was a sad day for us when she left – and her mammy always shopped here, you know . . . Only the best for Mrs O'Brady.'

Tad, who usually shopped round the markets or picked up unconsidered trifles from anyone selling cheap, tried not to look abashed. It was all very well buying the best, he thought crossly, but you'd got to earn the money to do it first. Polly's mammy had been one of the lucky ones; her menfolk didn't drink all the money away and expect the poor woman to manage on thin air, and she had a neat family, not a great big sprawling one, like his mammy. However, he leaned forward with the air of one about to impart a secret, and was amused to see Mr Merrick immediately lean forward too, and cup one thin, bony hand around his long, whiskery ear.

'Well, boy? Have ye news of the little 'un?'

Tad drew the letter out of his pocket. It was a bit crumpled now, and more than a bit dirty, for every time he had been free of customers or errands for a moment he had reread the letter, and in one corner a silvery huddle of fish scales was proof of his activities. But he held the letter out and Mr Merrick, after only the slightest of hesitations, took it, then glanced up at Tad. It was a questioning, almost shy glance, and Tad interpreted it at once.

'Sure you can go ahead and read it,' he said generously. 'See what you t'ink, Mr Merrick, sor.'

Despite the dirt and crumples, to say nothing of the fish scales, Mr Merrick read the letter a good deal more quickly than Tad had been able to do. Practice, I guess, Tad told himself. If I had a job where I had to write out bills and take down orders . . . But he would never rise to that sort of job and he knew it. There were too many bright boys chasing every halfway decent job which came along, he was lucky to be able to make a few bob the way he did.

'There's a Depression on, you know,' was a favourite remark of half Dublin – the rich half, usually. They addressed it to the poor half, Tad thought angrily, whenever anyone asked for a fairer wage, or a day off around Christmas. Still, there you were, it had always been the same. The rich got richer and the poor got poorer – wasn't that a song or something?

But right now, Mr Merrick was folding the letter up and looking enquiringly down at Tad. 'Well, and isn't it a sad t'ing that poor Mr O'Brady's been after goin' into hospital wit' a stroke?' he enquired. 'I scarce

47

knew the feller, but I'm real sorry for him. And they've lost their home . . . though they seem to have another all lined up to be sure. So you're after writing a letter, to tell Polly we're all t'inking of her? Is that it?' Already his hand was reaching into the drawer behind the counter where he kept paper and envelopes, billheads and invoices and so on. 'I'll give ye a nice bit o' lined paper and an envelope, so's you can write properly. And a stamp,' he added. 'And you'll send the family me regards, and tell 'em I'll be putting in a word for Mr O'Brady at Mass on Sunday?'

'Ye-es, Mr Merrick,' Tad replied. 'And aren't I goin' to do just that meself? Only – don't you t'ink they might come home to Dublin now? The O'Bradys, I mean. Polly an' all. 'Cos the cottage has gone, an' they're managin' on a pension . . . Wouldn't it be just as easy to live here? In Dublin.'

Mr Merrick gave this his consideration, which meant that he seized the end of his long, fleshy nose between finger and thumb and then rubbed them up and down for a moment, whilst pursing his lips, bringing his bushy white eyebrows together in a frown and half closing his eyes. Tad, repressing an urge to snigger, continued to look earnestly at him across the counter and was rewarded by Mr Merrick slowly nodding his balding head.

'You could be right so, young feller-me-lad. But they'll manage, because they've sons earning good money, wouldn't you say? Brogan in the United States, Niall in Australia and young whatsisname in the merchant fleet . . .'

Tad knew that Mr Merrick was right; sons always sent money home – daughters too, if you had any. That was why most young people emigrated to

America or went over the water to work; they could earn good money and send a fair amount home. But he also knew that the money would go on arriving whether the recipient lived in Dublin or England, so what difference would that make to whether the O'Bradys came home or stayed away?

'And the t'ing is, young Tad,' Mr Merrick continued, 'who is there in Dublin for them now? The young O'Bradys aren't here any more, they're either overseas or in Liverpool, and jobs are easier to find over the water, so they say.'

Tad could not reply 'They've got me,' because of course he was not family, but he knew he was dear to Polly – wouldn't that count? He sighed and held out his hand for his letter.

'Oh well, 'twas a nice t'ought, Mr Merrick,' he said, carefully folding the four pages and jamming them back into his pocket. He knew he sounded down, and tried to grin up at the older man. 'Mebbe they'll come back for a visit, eh?'

'Or mebbe you'll go over the water yourself one of these days,' Mr Merrick said kindly. 'You're a likely lad, you never know when a chance might come. So don't forget, now, to be after giving me best wishes to the O'Bradys when you write.'

'I will so,' Tad said stoutly. 'And, Mr Merrick, if you've ever a job goin', a job a feller like meself could do, I'd be mortal grateful . . .'

'We'll need an extra delivery boy come Christmas,' Mr Merrick said, and Tad's heart gave a joyful bound. It just went to show, one moment bad news floors you, and the next moment some amazing good news lifts you six feet above the ground. 'If you want to pop back here in a couple o' weeks mebbe we'll manage something. Got a bicycle?'

Tad shook his head, his face falling. Some chance of him having a bicycle – he couldn't even afford a bell!

But Mr Merrick was tutting to himself and frowning. 'No, no, of course not. 'Tis the regular boys who ride the bicycles, you'd have to manage on foot or by tram. Anyway, you call back here around the 15th. I'll not have forgotten.'

So Tad left the shop with his purchases and a light step; it looked as though things were looking up for him, even if Polly and the other O'Bradys would not be on their way home soon!

Halfway back to Gardiner's Lane, however, Tad remembered that if he was going to write to Polly he really should go round to Swift's Alley first and see what news and gossip he could pick up. On the grounds that it made his letters more interesting – and God knew, he found it hard to fill half a page, let alone four – he usually went round to Polly's old home and asked the neighbours if they had any snippets of news for the O'Bradys. Not only did it add interest to his letters, but he hoped that it would keep Swift's Alley, and Dublin, alive in Polly's mind, so that she really would come back here when she was able.

He turned his steps towards Polly's old home and very soon was climbing the first long flight of stairs. Or at least he climbed as far as the first landing, where he stopped because someone was coming down. He glanced up . . . and stayed where he was, with his mouth open and his eyes rounding.

A girl of about his own age was coming down the stairs towards him. She was wearing a blue and white checked dress, white cotton socks and light brown strap shoes, and as she got closer he saw that she had a pale oval face and a pair of very large, light blue eyes. But what really caught his attention was her hair. It was long, thick and shining, and it was the colour of – of moonlight, Tad thought reverently. It must have been recently brushed for it stood out round her head like a halo and indeed, for a moment as he looked up at her, he had a very odd sensation, because it was at this precise spot, long ago, that Polly had seen her guardian angel for the first time.

Tad had been with her though he had not seen the angel, had not believed Polly at first. But Mrs O'Brady had accepted without the flicker of an eyelid that Polly's guardian angel was a fact, and despite loudly pooh-poohing the whole idea of an angel who had nothing better to do than keep an eye on young Polly, Tad had, insensibly, begun to believe that the angel was there all right. He couldn't see it – only Polly said it was a girl, not an it – because chisellers didn't go in much for seeing angels, but Polly was the most honest person he knew, and she saw her angel all the time, so the angel had to exist.

And standing there, pressed back against the chipped and dirty tenement wall, looking up at the vision which seemed almost to float down the stairs, Tad really thought, just for a second, that this was Polly's angel, letting him see her at last so that he wouldn't tease Polly about it any more. Only then the girl caught sight of him and grinned, showing a chipped tooth, and then she swung the basket she was carrying and it caught in the banisters and she said a word – but quietly – which Tad knew full well that no angel would ever allow to pass its lips, and he grinned back, greatly relieved. He didn't mind Polly seeing angels if she was set on it, but he didn't want any truck with the supernatural himself, be it angelic or devilish. Life was quite tough enough without adding ghoulies and ghosties to the mixture.

But the girl, coming level with him, had stopped. 'Sure an' you don't live around here, or I'd know it,' she stated. 'I've been livin' here ten whole days and I know everyone in the block by sight, just about. What are you doin' here, then? Me family's on the next floor up an' you aren't after seein' me brother Mick, 'cos I know all his pals, so I do. And you're too young to be visitin' the poor girls on the top floor.'

'I was goin' up to see Felicity,' Tad said with dignity. He was not quite sure why she thought him too young to visit the poor girls, since he and Felicity were great pals, so they were, and often had great crack together. Indeed, Felicity was his main source of tenement gossip, for she had lived in this particular block for five years now and knew everyone and was, furthermore, well-liked. Tad knew, vaguely, that the poor girls were thought to be no better than they should be, but he was not at all sure just what this entailed. He only knew that Felicity was sweet and generous, that she sometimes gave him tuppence to run her messages and take her baby boy out for a couple of hours, and that Mrs O'Brady, Polly's mammy, had said that the girls were good girls, or if they weren't good girls then it was not their fault but the fault of their one-time rich employers. So now Tad stuck to his guns, even though the girl grinned more broadly than ever. 'She's a friend of mine, so she is,' Tad said reprovingly. 'And she knows all what's goin' on around here, you bet your life she does! So when I write a letter to me pal Polly, who used to live in the rooms you live in now, I come round here first to find out if there's any news the poor girls t'ink would interest the O'Bradys.'

'I've heard about Polly,' the pale-haired girl said. 'She sounds a great gun, so she does. I wish she was still here. There's no one my age livin' in this block. What's your name, eh?'

'I'm Tad Donoghue,' Tad said readily. 'I'm fourteen, I've left school. Who's you?'

'Angela Machin. Wish I were fourteen, but I shall be, come next summer,' the blonde girl said. 'Where d'you live?'

'Gardiner's Lane,' Tad said. 'I've got a tree growin' out of me bedroom chimney, so I have, an' – an' a huge brown an' yellow fungus on the wall above me bed. It smells somethin' tarble at this time o' year,' he added with pride.

'Truly? Cut your t'roat an' hope to die?' Angela asked. 'Can I come an' see it for meself?'

''Course, when I've been up an' talked to Felicity,' Tad said. 'Do you only have the one brother? No sisters?'

'That's right,' Angela said. 'I'll come up wit' you; I like the poor girls.'

She fell into step beside him and the two of them climbed the stairs together, passed the door behind which the O'Bradys had once lived, and up the next flight to the attic rooms rented by the poor girls. Tad kept giving quick little sideways looks at his companion. What a pretty creature she was! He just hoped that some of the fellers who'd been to school with him would see him with this girl, who was more like a film star than anyone else he had ever met. He decided, as they climbed the stairs side by side, that he would take her home and show her the tree growing in the crooked little fireplace in his bedroom, and the huge, evil-smelling fungus, and that he would tell her all about his daddy's defection and his

53

mammy's hard work and his large family of younger brothers and sisters. If, after that, she decided that she no longer wanted to be pals, that was that. But if she decided he was worthy of being a friend . . . Tad decided that when he next had some money he would take Angela Machin to the flicks, or to some other place of entertainment. She would be his as Polly had once been his – but was, he supposed sadly, his no longer. She was too far away, she would never come back to Dublin . . . And what was more, a description of Angela could easily fill up half a page of anyone's letter.

Thoroughly pleased with himself, Tad reached the attic landing, beat a tattoo on the door with one fist, and flung it open. Felicity was stirring something in a big black cauldron over a rather small and smoky fire.

'Hello, Tad,' Felicity said, looking round. Her smile included Angela. 'So you've met up wit' our Angel, have you? Isn't she a picture, then?'

Tad wanted to make some manly, disclaiming remark, but his traitorous mouth had its own ideas. 'Aye, she's as pretty as Polly,' he said rather thickly. 'Prettier.'

To the old Tad, this would have been almost blasphemy since he had made no secret of the fact that he thought Polly the prettiest girl in the whole of Dublin, if not the world, but Felicity just raised an eyebrow and then turned back to her pot-stirring. 'She's pretty in a different way, so she is,' she corrected in her calm, country voice. 'If you go to the crock on the sideboard, young feller, you'll find some oatcakes. Help yourselves. Now, Tad,' she went on as the two children settled themselves on the wooden table, swinging their legs and munching oatcakes, 'what can I do for you?'

54

*

By the time Tad and Angela parted company, Tad knew as much about Angela as she did about him, which was a good deal. Her elder brother, Mick, was a young man of twenty and worked in a shoe shop. He was courting, Angie said – she told Tad to call her Angie since everyone else did – and very much disliked being parted from his young lady, who was still in Limerick, but who intended to come to Dublin just as soon as she could. The Machins had come over from Limerick because Mr Machin had been offered the job of head sales assistant in the men's department of Switzers on Grafton Street. Mick, who had been working as a clerk in a solicitor's office, had been glad to leave and take his chance of a job in the capital city, for the wages in Limerick had been poor and the hours long, and sure enough he had been taken on by the shoe shop within a couple of days of arriving here. Mrs Machin, it seemed, was a dab hand with her needle and at home in Limerick had worked as a dressmaker, but her sight was failing, so they had seized the chance of a better paid job in order that they could manage on one less salary.

'I was a lovely surprise to me mammy an' daddy so I was,' Angela told him complacently as they sauntered towards Gardiner's Lane. 'Mammy had given up all hopes of another baby before I was born, so I were a lovely surprise and now they've got me, they want to see I'm brought up right. Which is why they're sendin' me to the convent school, though I dare say there's a lot of t'ings they'd rather do wit' the fee money.'

'I went to the national school; you don't have to pay there,' Tad said. 'Now me brothers go there. Ain't all schools the same, then?'

55

But he knew they weren't, not really. Polly had gone to private school, though she had grumbled about her eckers and the nuns just as much as Tad's sisters, who went to the free school, had done. But Angela was shrugging.

'I don't think it matters. I'm not clever, like some, but I keep me end up. I get good enough marks. And Mammy and Daddy think I'll get a good job when I leave, because I've been to private school.'

Tad nodded gloomily. He remembered Polly saying something of the sort now that he thought back. 'Where's your school, then, Angie? Miles away?'

'Well, I usually take a tram,' Angela said vaguely. 'I suppose I could walk, but it 'ud take me a while. I'm glad you came callin', Tad. I don't know hardly anyone in Dublin yet . . . now I know you!'

'That's the idea. We'll be pals, shall we?' Tad asked eagerly. 'There's all sorts to do in Dublin when there's two of you. Does your mammy give you money for the tuppenny rush at the cinema? I go to the Tiv, on Francis Street; I do love Sat'day flickers.'

'I do too,' Angela said. 'Me mammy used to give me a Peggy's leg or an ounce of rainbow caramels of a Sat'day, so's I don't fade away before me dinner, and I used to see the show and then go round to me cousin Kitty's, an' play Piggy Bed or Shop or skippin' until it were time for tea. But here . . . well, I don't know folk yet.'

Tad understood this completely. If you went to the free school you would meet your pals everywhere, but the small private schools took in children from a much wider area and the chances were that you'd not have a schoolfellow living within two or three streets of you. And Angie and her family hadn't been living in Swift's Alley for long enough to get to know people there, either.

As for Angela finding out about Tad, it wasn't hard to guess most of it once you had visited his home. Small and grubby brothers and sisters had greeted him as he crossed the courtyard and climbed the stairs, and in the kitchen, where the family lived, his sister Annie had been scrubbing a pan of potatoes for their tea whilst Biddy, who was getting to an age when she could be helpful, had been trying to chop cabbage with a knife which was rather too large for her to handle.

'Lemme do that,' Tad said, taking the knife. He put the screw of tea and the brown paper bag of biscuits down on the scrubbed wooden table and turned to Annie. 'Biddy's not old enough to use a knife, alanna. Don't let her chop t'ings or she'll be destroyin' her fingers entirely, so she will.' He saw his small sisters staring and stopped chopping cabbage for a moment to wave the knife towards his companion. 'Oh, Ann, this is me pal Angela Machin, what lives in Swift's Alley, in the O'Bradys' old place. Angie, the big 'un with the spuds is Annie an' the other's our Biddy. They's two of me sisters.' He finished chopping the cabbage, then headed for the door again. 'I'm just goin' to show Angie our tree, an' our fungus,' he added, and picked up a stub of candle and lit it from the lamp.

The boys' room was further along the landing and on the opposite side. It was a tiny room, only about four feet wide though it was a good deal longer. It smelt strongly of damp and the pigeon droppings which came through the missing roof tiles, but Angela, after one somewhat startled glance around her, made no comment. Instead, she admired the tree in the fireplace and the huge, leathery brown fungus with yellow patches, and only looked once at the beds, which were mostly piles of rags and straw, with one thin blanket apiece to pull over each boy.

'Where does your mammy and your sisters sleep?' she enquired, after Tad had pointed out which boy slept in which bed. 'I didn't notice another room.'

'They sleep in the living room,' Tad explained. 'It's a big room. They have to put their beds away before we go off in the mornings, though. Mammy as well.'

'Oh,' Angela said. 'And – and your daddy?'

'Left. He's been gone more than a year, thank the good Lord,' Tad said piously and with some satisfaction. 'Good riddance, Mammy says. He was a docker, and he could drink the Liffey dry, so he could. We's better off now than we was afore, 'cos he used to take Mammy's money off her. And mine too, if he could find it.'

'Oh,' Angela said again. 'But aren't you the lucky one to have all those brothers and sisters – you've always got someone to play wit' when you fancy a game.'

'Ye-es, only I'm the eldest, you see,' Tad explained. 'The eldest does the messages an' helps in the house an' finds firewood to light the fire, you know.'

'I don't, really,' Angela said. 'Micky's the eldest, but he's been workin' as long as I can remember, pretty near. And there aren't many jobs like fetchin' firewood when there's only four of you. But I get the messages for Mammy,' she added, clearly anxious not to appear too different. 'And I put the delft out on the table, and the knives and forks and that, and make my own bed and—' She stopped short. 'Well now, what'll we do next? Your sisters seemed to be managin' the supper wit'out too much fuss, even though they're young.'

Tad considered. He had meant to write to Polly, but he could do that any time, he told himself. 'What would you like to do?' he asked at last. 'You won't want to be too far from home as it's late or your mammy might worry.'

'I'd like to look in the shop windows on O'Connell Street,' Angela said longingly. 'But you're right, it's too late. Mammy's not workin' yet, so she'll be home. Would you like to come back wit' me and stay for a bit?' She added: 'Mammy wouldn't mind.'

'Well, I'll walk you home,' Tad said. 'But after that I'd best be gettin' back home meself. The kids'll see to the supper all right, but Mammy will wonder if I'm not there to give a hand. Only if you tell me where your school is I might meet you out tomorrer an' we could go on to O'Connell Street from there.'

'I t'ought you were workin',' Angela said artlessly. 'Suppose you've got a job tomorrer? No, you come round to Swift's Alley when you finish. If it's too late for window-shoppin' then we can always go up to my house and make ourselves toast before the fire or somethin' of that sort.'

Toast before the fire! Shades of Polly's mammy and the uproarious games the family had sometimes played whilst waiting for toast, or chestnuts to roast, or the cake in the oven to rise flickered temptingly in Tad's mind. He swallowed. 'That 'ud be grand,' he said. They had reached Angela's tenement now and they crossed the cramped little foyer and began to mount the stairs, but on the half-landing Tad paused. 'You can go the rest o' the way,' he said gruffly. 'See you tomorrer, then, Angie.'

But all the way home he thought about her. That

hair, fine as a dandelion clock and almost as pale. And her big blue eyes, and the nice clothes she wore! He wished he could get clothes like that for Biddy and Annie, but there was a world of difference between what two parents and an elder brother in work could afford and what one poor, hardworking mammy with a great many children could manage.

When he reached Gardiner's Lane it occurred to him that if Mrs Machin was a dressmaker she probably made Angela's dresses herself, which would mean they were cheaper than he had supposed. So no one could expect his poor ould wan to compete in the matter of dresses, he told himself, and was vaguely comforted. Besides, Angela had never stuck her nose up in the air and acted superior to him. In fact, she had been very nice. Not a word of reproach had passed her lips over the state of the boys' room, though she had mentioned that she made her own bed each day. He wondered just how one could possibly make a bed like his, though. Knowing Polly and the other O'Bradys had taught him that people with a bit of money had proper beds, with sheets and blankets over a mattress, and pillows on which one laid one's head, but he had supposed that Polly somehow wriggled into her bed without disturbing the neat, tightly tucked-in bedding. Now he realised that Polly – or her mammy, possibly – had had to retuck those sheets and blankets each morning after they got up.

He was just thinking that perhaps he ought to have drawn his blanket up over the pile of straw and rags when someone called his name and, turning, he saw his mammy coming across the courtyard. She was walking slowly, her shoulders drooping, and she carried a large bundle of what looked like bedding under one arm and a string shopping bag hung from the other hand. 'Tad, giz a hand, there's a good feller. These sheets are dry, pretty well, but they'll need ironin' before I can take 'em back to Mount Street tomorrer.'

Tad took the bundle and the string bag from her, tucked the bundle under his right arm and slung the bag on his wrist. Then he put his left hand under his mammy's small, skinny elbow and began to help her along. For the first time it occurred to him that his mammy could not be more than thirty-five or so, yet she was already grey-haired and carried herself like someone very much older. And Angela had said that her own mammy was very smart, with goldy-brown hair and pink cheeks, and didn't look her age. Life, he concluded, helping his mother up the first flight of stairs, was not a very nice business, particularly if you were poor and overworked and managing alone. It wasn't even that, either. His mammy had been knocked about by her bullying hulk of a husband for nigh on thirteen years, to his knowledge. She had had a broken arm, a broken nose, and her lip had been split more times than he cared to remember. Yet she had a lovely grin on her, though it was rather a toothless one, and she could laugh over something the kids did or said as though she hadn't a care in the world.

I believe me mammy's a real heroine, that's what I believe, Tad told himself as they climbed the stained and creaking wooden stairs. When I'm a man growed and earning decent money I'll pay her back all she's done for us, so I will. I won't run out on her like me daddy did, nor I won't let her down. She deserves better than she's had these past few years.

'You're a good boy, Tad,' Mrs Donoghue said

breathlessly as they reached the top of the last flight and Tad opened the living-room door for her. 'Oh, me loves, is that kettle just boiled now? And is that a teapot, heatin' up beside the fire? Eh, I'm a lucky woman . . . I'll just sit down for ten minutes and I'll be as good as I ever were. Annie, you're a grand girl to make your mammy a nice cup o' tay and serve it up so spruce, in nice delft!'

Annie, a tiny sprat of a girl with lank brown hair and small, twinkling eyes, grinned, showing that she was just at the age when teeth are neither all gone nor all there. 'There's a biscuit an' all,' she announced with a pronounced lisp, putting the cup down beside her mother, who had collapsed into one of the two sagging armchairs drawn up by the fire. 'Tad buyed some wit' his earnings, didn't you, Tad?'

'That's right. I got 'em from Merricks, 'cos if I send messages to Poll for him, he'll give me envelopes an' paper, so he will. An' today . . . you'll never guess what he said!'

'Have a lollipop? Did he say you could have a lollipop, Tad?' Eileen enquired. She was three and always hungry for something sweet; Tad knew she would already have had the only pink sugar biscuit in the bag but he grinned down at her anyway. She was pretty, round-faced and babyish, though Sammy, a year younger, was the baby now. 'Oh, I does love lollipops, so I does.'

'It were better than that,' Tad informed them. 'Go on, have a guess.'

Obligingly, everyone had a guess but no one was anywhere near, so of course Tad had to tell them, settling himself down on the kitchen table and swinging his legs as he drank the tea Annie poured for him and ate a broken custard cream. 'He said there might be a job for me come Christmas – a delivery job,' he told them proudly. 'I'm to call round once we're into December, an' Mr Merrick says if they need another lad it'll be me!'

'Sure and that's good news enough for a whole year,' his mammy said, clasping her cup with both hands to warm them. 'When I'm makin' me barm-bracks for sale I'll buy me dried fruit and me butter and flour from Merrick's, so I will. If they make you a delivery boy, that is,' she finished.

'And Tad brought ever such a pretty lady round to see us earlier,' Biddy said, lifting the lid of the pan on the edge of the fire and gazing critically at its contents. 'She had hair like pure gold, so she did.'

'She's goin' to be me pal,' Tad said contentedly, helping himself to another biscuit. 'She's called Angela Machin, Mammy, an' she's as pretty as Polly was – prettier.'

'No one could possibly be as pretty as Polly, nor as kind and sweet,' Tad's mammy said firmly and the girls nodded approvingly. Polly had a generous spirit and had often brought treats round for her pal's family. 'Still, I don't doubt this girl's a decint girl. Angela – that's not an Irish name, though.'

'No-o, but she's from Limerick,' Tad said, as though folk from Limerick were well known for outlandish names. 'Her fambly live in the O'Bradys' old rooms – ain't that a strange t'ing?'

'Aye, strange enough. And what do they do – the fambly?'

'Well, her daddy's in the men's department of Switzers on Grafton Street, and her brother's in a shoe shop, sellin' shoes. Her mammy's a dressmaker, but I don't think she's dressmakin' here yet. And that's all the fambly,' he ended.

63

'Ah. Well, wit' two of 'em in work they'll be well off,' Tad's mammy said. She heaved herself out of her chair and went towards the fire and the bubbling saucepans. 'You're a good girl, Biddy, to get the food a-goin' afore I'm even through the door. Is it nearly done? Tad, go down and shout the rest o' the kids, then we'll eat, 'cos I want to get this ironin' done this evenin' whiles the fire's hot and I'm not too tired. Then mebbe tomorrer I'll do some bakin'.'

'Sure I will,' Tad said, making for the door. 'Liam an' Kevin will be in soon, I 'spect. I wonder what they'll bring home wit' them?'

Chapter Three

Polly, having despatched her letters, waited in vain for a reply from Tad, and this both surprised and annoyed her. Sure, Tad usually took ages and ages to answer a letter, but she had told him that, in view of her daddy's illness, she expected a reply by return, and had added her customary threat about never writing to him again if he failed her in this matter. And to be fair to Tad, he was a kind-hearted boy and, though he hated writing letters and was a poor hand at it, would, she was sure, have done his best to comfort her in her affliction.

For Daddy's illness was an affliction indeed. Mammy was always off up at the hospital, where children were not allowed to go save with special permission on a Saturday afternoon, and Martin was grumpy.

'Anyone would t'ink he'd enjoyed havin' us to stay and didn't want us to move out to Titchfield Street,' Polly grumbled to Ivan, after an uncomfortable evening during which she and Ivan had done their eckers and then played a game of Snap and tried to ignore the fact that Martin sat in his chair staring at nothing and wouldn't answer when you spoke. 'When you t'ink how his old wife has grumbled and moaned and stopped us havin' meals wit' them and said we eat them out of house and home when Mammy pays for our food and not her or Martin . . . well, he *can't* want us to stay,' she ended.

The two children were in the cramped little spare room, getting ready for bed. Polly, already clean and nightgowned, was watching Ivan as he dabbed at his face with a wet flannel and then hastily rubbed himself dry on the towel which hung beside the wash-stand. When she saw that he had finished with the water she turned towards the tiny dressing table with its small square of mirror on top and picked up her hairbrush.

'Mebbe he doesn't fancy the t'ought of bein' alone wit' Monica again, when he's had us for her to grumble at,' Ivan said with surprising shrewdness. 'When we're here, she can nag about us. What's she got to nag about when we ain't here but him, eh?'

'They're married, so it's different,' Polly pointed out. She began to brush the tangles out of her curls, wincing and squeaking whenever the brush got stuck, which happened frequently. 'Mart's her husband, so he is, and husbands have to get used to bein' nagged at.'

'Don't call him Mart, he's got a decent Christian name and I like to hear all of it, please,' Ivan squeaked, in a very fair imitation of his sister-in-law's mincing vowels. 'Oh, jeez, Polly, I don't care what Martin wants, I want get to our new house this very minute if it means that Monica will keep whinin' at us.'

'And I've not heard a word from Tad, would you believe?' Polly said, as though her small brother had not spoken. She had got rid of most of the tangles in her hair and now began to brush steadily, counting beneath her breath as she did so. 'Forty-five, forty-six, forty-seven . . . and I telled him special to write back at once. Forty-nine, fifty . . .'

'He'll write,' Ivan said comfortably. 'Sure and doesn't he always, in the end?'

'Ye-es, he does,' Polly admitted. 'Ouch! Fifty-three, fifty-four . . . I 'spect he's busy, wit' Christmas comin' up, and them wit'out their daddy to help save up for presents an' that.'

'Their daddy spended all the money, I've heared you say so,' Ivan reminded her briskly. He sat on the bed to remove his last garments – his socks – and then struggled into his striped nightshirt. 'The fellers at the school in the village didn't wear nightshirts, they went to bed in their kecks,' he informed his sister succinctly. 'Wish Mammy would let me do that.'

'They never does!' Polly said, shocked. 'That ain't decent, Ivan.'

'Well, mebbe not, but it's warmer, an' they can dress quick as quick in the mornin's, because they're already in their school t'ings,' Ivan pointed out. He yawned, stretched, then snuggled down. 'Come on, Poll, it ain't fair if I warms the bed an' then you colds it again, comin' into my lovely warm part wit' your cold old feet.'

'Ninety-eight, ninety-nine, a *hundred*,' Polly shouted triumphantly. She threw the brush down on the dressing table and leapt the short distance on to the bed, heaving the covers off Ivan and then disappearing beneath them like a rabbit into its burrow. 'Well, if Mammy knew what those boys at our old school had told you, she'd have took us away from the crossin' cottage anyway,' she said in a voice muffled by blankets. 'I hope the new school's nicer than that.'

'Oh, it'll be grand,' Ivan said. 'Tell you what, Poll, I bet your letter comes tomorrer. I bet you a penny!'

'Haven't got one,' came the muffled reply. 'I'll bet you a ha'penny, though. Mammy gave me a ha'penny to spend for doin' a message for her. She said I could buy sweeties, only I'm savin' it for Christmas instead.'

Ivan began to speak, then his voice unaccountably stopped. And presently, Polly poked her head out of the covers to look at her small brother. As she had guessed, he was sound asleep, his lashes lying on his cheeks, his pink mouth a little open and tiny snores escaping from him now and then.

Lucky chiseller, to be able to sleep like that, between one word an' the next, Polly thought . . . and was asleep herself before Deirdre came stealing in to turn out the light.

If Ivan had remembered the bet next morning he would have been a ha'penny the richer, but as so often happened he had no recollection of what he had been saying just before he slept, so Polly, who wanted all the ha'pennies she could get to buy her daddy a Christmas present, kept her mouth shut on the subject.

'Me letter's arrived,' she said triumphantly, however, thinking that it was only fair to give Ivan a chance to get his money, but Ivan, up to his eyebrows in porridge and making a pathway across it which he promptly filled with buttermilk, merely grunted. Deirdre, who had put the letter down by Polly's plate, was more interested.

'You can read it when you've et your breakfast,' she said, eating her own porridge neatly, and not playing swamps and dinosaurs, as the children did. 'And come to t'ink, 'tis a lucky t'ing indeed that the letter's come today because we're movin' tomorrer.'

Polly started to speak with her mouth full, spluttered, and Ivan ducked as porridge flew everywhere. Fortunately Martin and Monica had departed for

68

their respective places of work some time before so Deirdre, clucking, went and got a cloth from the sink to clean up the mess whilst Polly and Ivan clutched each other and jigged around the table, their breakfast forgotten.

'Tomorrer! We're movin' out of here tomorrer!' Polly squeaked, picking up the envelope with Tad's writing – and a good deal of porridge – on it and waving it in the air. 'Aren't I just so glad, Ivan! Oh, a house of our own again, an' me darlin' Delilah an' me dearest Lionel back in me arms where they belong! An' school, instead of bein' stuck here all day tryin' to be tidy an' not make a mess or a muddle!'

'I didn't mind missin' school that much,' Ivan observed, taking his place at the table once more and beginning to spoon porridge furiously. 'But it'll be good to have Bev back, I agree wit' you there.'

'Oh, Bev's nice, but he's not like dear Delly. And now I'm goin' to read me letter,' Polly announced, putting a finger under the flap. 'You said I could, didn't you, Mammy?'

'I said after breakfast, so have you finished? Then you can wash the dishes, Polly, and Ivan can wipe them. And then you can read your letter, alanna, but not before.'

Polly heaved a huge, exaggerated sigh but obediently began to carry the dishes over to the sink. And presently Deirdre went up to tidy the bedroom and get their outdoor things and Polly and Ivan began to play a vigorous game in which the porridge spoons waged war on the delft, and a good deal of water got scattered on the floor and splashes appeared on Ivan's flannel shirt and on Polly's grey skirt.

But the game was over and all the washing-up done and put away by the time Deirdre came downstairs. She flicked a quick glance over the room, tightened her lips a little over the splashes, and then held out their coats. 'Play out for an hour whilst I do the floor in here, kids,' she said briskly. ''Tis chilly out, so keep movin' . . . Oh, if you want to read your letter first, alanna, take it through to the parlour. Monica won't mind you readin' it in there – well, she won't know. Off wit' you now.'

Almost reluctantly, Polly trailed through into the parlour where she sat in the window, slit open the envelope, pulled out the single sheet of paper it contained, and began to read.

Deirdre had washed the kitchen floor when Polly re-entered the room and was just polishing the taps over the sink with a wash-leather. She looked round and smiled as Polly tiptoed across the wet linoleum. She thought her daughter looked rather pink and wondered what Tad had said to upset her; clearly there was something wrong. 'Well, alanna,' she said carefully, 'what's Tad got to say, then? Any interestin' news?'

'He's got a new pal called Angie. She's got yellow hair – he doesn't say that, but that's what he means – and all he talks about is her,' Polly said in an injured tone. 'Mammy, Tad's *my* pal, what does he want this Angie girl for?'

'I guess he misses you, and is lonely for company,' Deirdre said gently. 'You had plenty of pals when you lived in the crossin' cottage, and you'll have friends again once you're in school and we're in our own house. You mustn't grudge poor Tad wantin' a pal too.'

'Ye-es, but when I write letters to Tad I don't go on about me other pals,' Polly said, pouting. 'Honest to

70

God, Mammy, you'd t'ink there never was a girl born like this Angela! She's come from Limerick because her daddy's got a job on Grafton Street and would you believe, the spalpeen lives in our old house in Swift's Alley, in the very rooms we had, Mammy, when we lived in Dublin!'

Deirdre turned away to hide a smile, then turned back to take both Polly's small hands in hers. 'Me darlin' child, what could be more natural than that Tad would make a pal of a child who lived where his best friend ever had lived?' she asked. 'I expect this Angie was lonely too, if she'd not lived in Dublin long, and was glad of Tad's company. Why, I daresay she's like yourself, and not even in school yet.'

'She's in school all right,' Polly said broodingly. 'She's at the convent, like I was . . . I guess she's probably Sister Andorra's favourite too, the same as me. Only – only she isn't me, Mammy, and – and I don't want Tad lovin' anyone else!'

'I don't suppose he loves her like he loves you,' Deirdre said rather helplessly. What could she say to comfort her little girl, who was taking her pal's defection so very hard? 'But she's a new friend, and he t'ought you'd be interested . . .'

'Huh!' Polly said crisply, but with a curling lip. 'He goes on about her yellow hair, an' her big blue eyes, an' her pretty dress . . . Mammy, he says when he first saw her he t'ought she was me guardian angel!'

The last words came out as a wail and Deirdre hid her involuntary smile by taking Polly into her arms and hugging her. 'Alanna, you're jealous! You should know better – you know what Tad's like wit' the letter-writin', he simply can't t'ink what else to say once he's said *Dear Polly, how are you, I am doing awright but missing you,*' she reminded her daughter.

'He's talkin' about this Angie for something new to say, not because he's t'inkin' much about her.'

For answer Polly wriggled out of her arms and thrust the letter into her hand. 'Read it,' she demanded. 'Just you read that letter, Mammy, an' then you can see if the eejit's in love wit' Angie Machin or not! And I'm goin' out to play wit' Ivan, an' *Mr Donoghue* can whistle for a letter from me, I'm tellin' you!'

And with that Polly grabbed up her navy coat and her pixie hood and slammed out of the house and could be seen running down the pavement and struggling into coat and hat as she went.

Deirdre sat down at the table and began to read the ill-spelt and extremely ill-written letter.

Dear Polly,

How are you, I'm doing awright but missing you. I's real sorry your Daddy's Ill, but glad he's Better an he Was. The ~~noo~~ new House sounds fine – is it a whole House, Poll, like the Cotage was a whole House? They's lucky in Liverpool to have whole Houses and not just bits, like we has over here.

When your letter come I went round to Swifts Alley for ~~noos~~ niws. And you'll never Gess! I were halfway up the Stairs, around where you saw your Guarjan Angel that Christmas, when I tought I saw One as well. It came down the stairs, it had a haylo of gold hair an very blue eyes. Well, Poll, it weren't a Angel at all. She's called Angie Machin an she lives in yore rooms!!! She's real nice, you'd like Her so you would. Her Daddy an Mammy brung her from Limerick – she told me how to Spell that, Poll – cos her Daddy's got a job on O'Connell. I'm that glad she's here, she's goin to be me pal, we're goin to the Satday Rush nex week, we went an watched the Big Fellers playin Pitch an Toss, She liked that.

Mr Merrick give me the stamp for the Letter when I bought Tea and Biskits, an he said if I come back soon I might be a Christmas Delivery Boy. I'll have Good Money then an me an Angie will go to the panto and mebbe more tings.

Well goodby for now, Polly, you are still me Best Pal an I wish you was still in Dublin.

Your friend Tad Donoghue

After she had read it through twice, Deirdre leaned her elbows on the table and seriously considered the letter. Tad was clearly smitten with this Angie, and Polly was obviously both upset and furious because of it. Deirdre admired many things about Tad and liked the boy too, but she had never taken the friendship as seriously as her daughter had. Polly was still a child so time, and distance, she had always believed, would mean that in a few more years the two would think of each other as old playmates rather than as the future bride and groom. But then she had never believed that Polly and Tad would continue to correspond for two and a half years, so perhaps the sudden advent of Angela Machin – he spelt that right as well, she thought inconsequentially – might be a very good thing, even if Polly found her old pal's sudden defection painful at first.

Having made up her mind on that point, Deirdre folded the page, put it back into the envelope, and got her own coat off the back of the kitchen door. She got her big marketing basket and her handbag and her hat, for it was still very cold out, and set off down the short garden path. Once in Nelson Street, she could see Polly and Ivan playing Piggy beds with a round tin filled with garden earth as the Piggy, the beds marked out in chalk on the paving stones. Even from a distance, Deirdre could see the dogged, mulish way that Polly kicked the Piggy along; she was still cross, then.

But when she reached them, Polly took her hand and gave a couple of skips before announcing: 'Well, I've made up me mind, Mammy! *I'm* goin' to have a pal of me own just as soon as I get to school – not a girl-pal, Mammy, but a boy-pal, because there's boys go to St Sylvester's school as well, in the boys' half – and I'm goin' to write to Tad an' tell him he needn't write back no more if he don't want to, because we'll mebbe never meet each other again in this life, so what's the point?'

Deirdre, who had been hoping for something like this, was startled at the sudden seriousness in her small daughter's face and said: 'Well now, alanna, you needn't go that far! But you can tell him you'll just be pals. How about that, eh? You wouldn't want to hurt his feelings, would you?'

'Yes I would,' Polly said emphatically. 'I'd like to give him a clout round the lug, so I would. Still, a letter will have to do. And won't I tell him all about me new pal when I've chose one,' she added dreamily. 'I'll teach the wicked chiseller! Oh yes, I'll show Tad Donoghue that he isn't the only one wit' a special pal!'

On Sunday, Polly, Ivan and Bevin all went to the hospital to see their father, though they were only allowed to stay on the ward for ten minutes apiece and then had to wait in the corridor for their mother.

Deirdre thought that Peader was looking a great deal better. There was colour in his face now, and when Polly began to chatter about the new house, and about Tad's letter and the wonderful golden-haired Angela girl, he actually smiled.

'Tad's a good lad,' he said dreamily. 'You won't go far wrong wit' Tad.'

'The nurse says you can come home for Christmas Day,' Deirdre told him, hoping to get him off the subject, for she did not want Peader encouraging Polly to forgive Tad for his behaviour over Angela Machin. 'They'll want you back by evening, they say, but sure an' you'll have had enough excitement by then. And you'll enjoy a day wit' us, won't you, me darlin'?'

Peader nodded, then said slowly: 'Yes, I'll enjoy that.' His voice was slurred, but stronger than it had been since the stroke and Deirdre beamed at him, grateful for every small improvement.

'We're havin' a real waggon to move our t'ings from the storage place to the new house, aren't we, Mammy?' Polly said excitedly. She did not seem to notice her father's halting speech, nor the effort it cost him to turn his cheek towards her for a kiss. 'Oh, Daddy, I'm longin' to see Lionel and Delly again, so I am. Mammy's afraid they may not like the city, but they will, I'm sure they will – they were happy in the Liberties, weren't they, Daddy?'

She would probably have enlarged on the topic, Deirdre thought, but at that moment Bev came in, accompanied by a nurse, who shooed Polly out whilst Bev told Peader how his exams had gone and assured his father that he was looking forward to moving back in with his family, even though it meant leaving the village behind.

'Sure an' no woman ever had better children, me darlin',' Deirdre told her husband as soon as they were alone. 'And when you're back home wit' us . . .

75

Oh, I can't tell you how I'm lookin' forward to havin' you home!'

But later, when she left the ward and went into Sister's office, that lady told her that Peader would be needing treatment for several months. 'He will need to be kept quiet once he goes home,' she told Deirdre. 'Will you be able to manage that, with the youngsters around him all day?'

'We've a front parlour; I'm t'inking he can spend most of the day in there, whilst the kids will be in the kitchen,' Deirdre said. 'But they're good kids, and if I tell them their daddy needs peace and quiet I'm after thinkin' they'd be the last to make a noise or worry him.'

'Oh, I'm sure. But . . . children can't help tiring an invalid, Mrs O'Brady. However, if you can see that he spends most of the day quietly, in your parlour, then I'm sure things will work out all right,' the sister said. 'He's beginning to fret over hospital routine, and that's a sure sign he's on the mend. I don't think it will be too long before the doctors discharge him.'

Walking home with her hand in her mammy's, with Ivan clinging on to her other hand, Polly was happier than she had been since Tad's letter had arrived. Daddy liked Tad, so perhaps she was wrong, perhaps Tad was not trying to give her the brush-off, but was merely being Tad. Probably by the next time he wrote the girl Angela would have gone from his mind and he would be boasting about his job of delivering for Merrick's.

And in the meantime there was a great deal to look forward to: the move, the reunion with Delilah and Lionel, neighbours to meet, friends to make, a new school to tackle, and best of all, Daddy back with them for good. Polly saw the future as bright once more, and danced along beside her mother, chattering like a starling and pushing Tad's defection to the back of her mind. It would all work out all right; things always did. So she might as well enjoy living here, and remember her time in the crossing cottage like a lovely holiday which had come to an end, as lovely holidays always do.

The move went like clockwork and almost before they knew it the family found themselves settled into the Titchfield Street house, with Bevin and his bicycle installed amongst them and Delilah accompanying Polly wherever she went – except to school, of course.

'But Lionel's better off wit' the Templetons, alanna,' Deirdre said sincerely. She hated to disappoint Polly, but she had thought the matter over and believed that the child would understand, given time. 'Cats like people all right, but 'tis places they become attached to, and Lionel knows every inch of the country around the crossin' cottage. I know he was a city cat once, and I know you t'ink he could be a city cat again, but, Polly me darlin', it wouldn't be kind to take him from the place he knows.'

Polly was a fair-minded child. She knew, really, that Lionel had infinitely preferred the country to the city, and feared that, should she insist that he come back, he would be run over by a tram or a horse and cart, having grown unused to such conveyances. Besides, at home in Dublin she had done her best to keep him in the flat. Now that he was older and knew the joys of the outdoors, she guessed he would slip out of the house the first chance he got. So she agreed, if rather sadly, that the Templetons should keep Lionel and threw herself, with considerable enthusiasm, into the life of the neighbourhood. She had always made friends easily, and knew that she would soon have plenty of pals and the sort of social life which she had enjoyed both in the village and in Dublin.

'There's a girl up the road the same age as me, in the same class,' she told her mother excitedly on her first morning at the new school. 'She's got a brother Ivan's age an' all. We're goin' to school together, the four of us, so you needn't fret we'll get lost or anythin' bad, Mammy. And we'll come home together too . . . Mebbe we'll be best friends by the time we come home,' she added hopefully. 'Her name's Alice and she has dear little red mittens to keep her hands warm, an' she takes a white bread roll for her carry-out at break-time each mornin' too.'

'Well, you can have two biscuits, because what wit' the move an' all I've not had time to bake this week,' Deirdre said. 'As for red mittens, won't your green ones do?'

Polly said they would do just fine and Deirdre decided to buy some red wool when she went marketing that morning. They're good kids, she told herself as she looked round her spruce new kitchen, with the furniture which they had brought all the way from Dublin in place round the walls, and a roll of cheap but colourful linoleum on the floor. Many a child would have insisted on her mother taking her to a new school for the first time, but not Polly. She's bright, brave and independent – aren't I a lucky woman to have her!

She left the house, abandoning Delilah to roam the new premises, trusting that he would know better than to splash his mark all over the interior of her home, and walked through to the Scotland Road. It was a good road, she decided contentedly, walking along in the pale, wintry sunshine with her good brown coat buttoned right up to the neck, for it was getting near Christmas and despite the sun it was bitterly cold. It wasn't as smart as Nelson Street, of course. Monica had definitely sneered at the idea of Titchfield Street but money was going to be tight now. Deirdre knew she would have to get a job as soon as she could but this was a good area if you had little money to spare. There were a grosh of shops, most of them selling goods reasonably priced, and if she went further to her right, to where the road divided, there was Byrom Street, with market stalls selling their goods even more cheaply than the shops could.

She found a bakery which looked respectable and went in and bought four large loaves and took a good look round whilst the shop assistant was wrapping them for her. Their new house did not have a baking oven so she would be taking her bread, cakes and pies to a local bakery once or twice a week to be properly cooked and she wanted to make sure the place she chose was clean. This one certainly seemed so, and the assistants were quick and smiled when they spoke, and what was more the shop was crowded, always a good sign. Yes, next week I'll bring me baking here to be done, Deirdre decided, though she could not help thinking wistfully of the bake-oven in the crossing cottage with its two bright metal shelves and the fire blazing up beside it so that it was the work of a moment to rake red-hot coals into position beneath it. The new house had a good closed-in fire on which pans, kettles of water and other such things could be cooked, but there was nothing quite so good as being able to do your own baking. Deirdre had heard about the new free-standing gas and electric stoves, of course, but with Peader still in hospital and only his pension coming in at present, she did not see them acquiring such a wonderful contrivance yet awhile.

Leaving the bakery, she continued down the road, looking in the shop windows as she passed. Christmas this year, she reflected, was going to be a lean one, but she had good kids, they would make the best of whatever she could provide. So she continued to look wistfully into each window as she passed, which was how she came to see the notice. It was not a large notice, and it was tucked into the frame of a window displaying some beautiful clothes, so when it caught her eye she stopped and looked at it more closely. *Wanted, sales assistant*, it read. *Extra help needed up to Christmas and until January Sales finish. Apply within.*

Deirdre had done a number of jobs in her time, but she had never sold dresses, and yet . . . You only got cleaning jobs when you were in the know, she reminded herself. And with the kids still at home she could scarcely tie herself up full-time, but for a month over the Christmas period, surely they could manage? It would make a world of difference to their Christmas if she was earning, and she knew that Peader would begin to worry once he was well enough to realise that his full wage was no longer coming in. She had worked hard in Dublin, until Peader and the boys had been earning enough to make it unnecessary for her to take a job, and she rather enjoyed work. What was more, the dresses in this window were beautiful, it would be nice even to be in the same shop with them – surely they would be easy to sell? Anyway, applying did not mean she would get the job. The proprietor might not want her, might need someone younger, or more experienced, might not like her Irish brogue – but she could at least try!

Deirdre pushed open the door of the shop and went in.

The shop was not a very big one, but it was absolutely full of racks of clothing, so that Deirdre did not at first see the small, skinny, black-clad woman behind the counter. The woman was putting blouses on to hangers – pink ones, yellow ones, white ones – whilst at the same time pinning small price tickets on each. She did not look up as the bell tinged for Deirdre's entrance, then as Deirdre neared the counter she did so, and smiled. Since she had been holding the price tickets in her teeth, this presented an odd appearance and Deirdre's returning smile was full of amusement.

'Don't stop work, sure an' I'm not a customer,' she said quickly, seeing the woman about to put down the blouse she was holding. 'There's a notice in the window . . .'

The woman's gaze sharpened. 'Oh aye, the notice,' she said. 'Done shop work before? In a dress shop, I mean.'

'No,' Deirdre said. 'But I'm a quick learner so I am. Me mental arithmetic's good, and I'm not afraid of hard work.' She paused, desperate for the job but aware that Peader had to come first. 'Only me husband's in hospital and I visit each evenin', so I'm real sorry but I couldn't work much after six o'clock.'

'Oh. Well, you've a nice appearance,' the woman said slowly, taking the tickets and arranging them in a fan shape on the counter, facing Deirdre. 'Can ye add them up and tell us what them prices come to?'

Deirdre did the sum in her head and announced

her conclusion. The woman looked pleased and a little surprised too.

'Quite right. Not that you'll be needin' to go to the till, queen, because that's me own job. I don't believe in purrin' temptation in young people's way.'

Deirdre would have liked to ruffle up – she knew she coloured – but the older woman was smiling at her as though she knew very well how she felt, and sympathised, but would nevertheless stick to her guns. So Deirdre just said, rather stiffly: 'That's all right, then. Is it a six day a week job?'

'No, I shan't be needin' you weekends, nor after six, because I've gorra schoolgirl comin' in each day after six, and all day Saturday. You'll work from nine in the morning till six, and you can eat your carry-out when we're quiet. You should be takin' home between eighteen and twenty-two shillin' a week for six or eight weeks, I suppose. It's more than I'd pay a permanent girl, but I expect to pay more for seasonal work. Would that suit?'

'Oh, yes indeed,' Deirdre said, relieved and delighted. The money would make the difference between a poor thin Christmas and a decent one. Perhaps they could even run to a bird. 'When do I start?'

'Monday, and you'd best come in at eight, your first day,' the woman said. She came round the counter and held her hand out. 'I'm Mrs Bechstein, I own the shop. And you are . . .?'

'Oh, sorry, I'm Deirdre O'Brady,' Deirdre said, feeling her colour rising once more. 'Thanks very much, Mrs Bechstein; I hope I give satisfaction.'

'If you don't, I give the sack,' Mrs Bechstein said, but Deirdre could see she was laughing. 'Shall we say a week's trial on both sides, O'Brady? If we don't get along I'll pay you off at the end of the week and no hard feelings. How about that, eh?'

'That's fine,' Deirdre said. She turned back towards the door of the shop. 'See you on Monday morning, on the dot of eight, Mrs Bechstein!'

The children were cautiously pleased about the job, though Polly, who had once been left in charge in Dublin whilst her mother was away, said mutinously that she did not intend to do all the work in Mammy's absence.

'Ivan's seven, he can flamin' well help,' she said, wagging an admonitory finger at her small brother. 'And Bevin, too. I don't mind puttin' the tea on, if you tell me what to cook, Mammy, but they can wash up an' clear away. I know they's boys an' I'm a girl, but fair's fair. Daddy wouldn't let them bully me.'

'Nor shall I, sweetheart,' Deirdre said stoutly. She did not add that she could never forget the state of affairs she had found when she had returned after her enforced absence. It had not, after all, been Polly's fault; a ten-year-old was not a woman grown and Polly, she acknowledged guiltily, had always been rather spoilt. 'I'll leave you a nice list written out of anything I want done. Will that help?'

'If you put what I'm to do and what Ivan an' Bev's to do as well,' Polly said cautiously. 'Why do you want to go to work, Mammy? Why can't you stay here, wit' Delly an' us?'

'Because though the boys are very good and send home every penny they can spare, and though Daddy's got a little pension, money is goin' to be tight until Daddy's better and can earn a proper wage again,' Deirdre said carefully. She did not want to frighten the kids into believing them to be paupers, but she wanted them to realise that things might be difficult for a while. 'This job is only over Christmas and up until the end of the January sales, so by the time Daddy comes out of hospital for good I'll be out of work again.'

'Oh, well, all right,' Polly said, leaning forward to take a piece of raw potato and beginning to crunch it up. Deirdre, who was scrubbing the potatoes and cutting up a large winter cabbage, swallowed. The things the young ate! 'I'm glad you isn't workin' for always though, Mammy. I like to have you home even when I'm not here meself.'

'I'm sure that's very nice of you,' Deirdre said. She finished the vegetables, tipped the potatoes into a pan and began to push the sliced cabbage into the steamer which she would balance on top of the potato saucepan as soon as the water boiled. 'Now then, I'm goin' to the hospital as soon as we've ate our tea so d'you want to come wit' me, for the walk, like, or do you want to take Delly for an airin' right now?'

'Both,' Polly said promptly. She missed the long country walks which had been a part of her life at the crossing cottage, Deirdre knew. 'And you've not asked me how I got on at school today,' she added accusingly.

'How did you get on?' Deirdre asked obediently, as Polly fastened her length of rope to Delilah's collar. Normally, none of them would have dreamed of putting the dog on a lead but Polly was mortally afraid that if not attached to her person Delly might leap on a tram bound for Lime Street, then get off it and leap on a train, and reunite himself with the crossing cottage.

'Oh, I got on fine,' Polly said airily. 'Me teacher's a great love, so she is, and she says I'm ahead of the whole class – the whole *class*, Mammy – in arithmetic an' history. She pinned me essay on "Nature's Ways" – I did from jelly in a ditch to frog – up on the board and she said that Maisie Lightfoot – she's got the longest hair, she can sit on it! – ought to try to copy my writin', because I'm so neat. And after dinner Father Ignatius came round to talk to us, and I asked him about his choir, and I'm goin' to do a – a audy-something-or-other on Sunday, after Sunday school.'

'Audition?' Deirdre suggested. 'What about Ivan?'

'Him too,' Polly admitted. 'I told the father about him bein' new too, an' he's goin' to audy-what's-it as well. And Ivan can sing in tune, Mammy, everyone can. He just doesn't because he's a bad boy, so he is.'

'He's tone deaf, alanna,' Deirdre said reproach-fully. 'No one can help being tone deaf. But mebbe the priest wants a growler wit' the face of an angel in his choir, you never know.'

'Oh, that reminds me! Mammy, you know I said I'd not seen me angel all the time we were in Martin's house? Well, she were in me room last night, just before I went to sleep. Smilin' at me, she was . . . She looked so beautiful!'

'Good,' Deirdre said. She never asked questions about Polly's angel because the child clearly believed she saw the holy creature and who was she, Deirdre O'Brady, to doubt her little girl, who had never, to Deirdre's knowledge, told a deliberate lie in her life? 'Off you go, then, alanna, or it'll be time for tea. And if you see Ivan outside, tell him tea in twenty minutes, would you?'

'Right, Mammy,' Polly said cheerfully. She let herself out of the kitchen door and banged it shut behind her. Smiling to herself, Deirdre finished off the potatoes, put them on the fire, and began to lay the table. What a lot I'll have to tell Peader when I reach the hospital tonight, she told herself as she worked. I'll say one thing for having kids; there's never a dull moment!

Sunday saw Polly and Ivan, neatly clad in clean clothes and hand in hand, making their way up to St Sylvester's church, where they would first attend Sunday school and then audition for Father Ignatius's choir. Polly, with her curls brushed till they shone and a red ribbon nestling amongst them, was looking forward to everything, but Ivan was frankly rebellious.

'You never should ha' mentioned me to the father, you bad gorl, you,' he grumbled, as they neared the huge bulk of the red-brick church and headed for the steps which led to the side door. 'I doesn't *want* to be in the choir; I'll only get shouted at 'cos me voice won't get up off the floor the way yours does.'

'Well, if you sing like you always does you won't get into the choir,' Polly said with all her usual frankness. 'So why grumble at me, Ive? Anyway, you'll like Sunday school.'

'I shall not,' Ivan said mutinously. 'The fellers in my class don't go to Sunday school, they say it's for girls and cissies, and I ain't either. When's we to play, anyway, if we go to the hospital to see our daddy after this lot's over?'

'After that,' Polly said, undisturbed. 'Sunday school's two to three, visitin' at the hospital's three to four, and we can play out four to six. Then it's tea. And after that I'm goin' to meet Alice Eccles and she's goin' to show me how to play a new skippin' game, and then we'll see if there's a game of Tag or Relievio goin' on that we could join.'

86

'Alice Eccles? Is her brother called Teddy? Teddy Eccles is in my class at school.'

'I expect so, and he'll be at Sunday school as well, I daresay. If you like, we could all play together when we come back from the hospital,' Polly said craftily, and was rewarded by a beam from her small brother.

'Could we? That 'ud be grand, so it would.' Ivan's footsteps, which had been lagging, quickened up. 'Come *on*, Poll, or we'll be late!'

Polly had always enjoyed Sunday school, but something happened to her just as she and Ivan were about to enter the building which, she later decided, had probably changed her entire life. A group of big boys was standing about on the corner of Rayner Street which led, Polly knew, between Silvester and Ashfield Streets. They did not look like good boys, she decided, after a long stare. For a start, they were all grouped round something on the ground, and when she looked more closely, she could see that they were playing cards . . . and that there were ha'pennies and farthings in little piles on the paving stones.

Gambling! Gambling, Polly knew, was bad, but gambling on a Sunday, right outside a church! That was so bad that the little soft hairs on her neck stood upright with outrage. Those boys would go to hell, so they would, and it would serve them right! But then one of the boys turned round and caught her eye and when he did he grinned, and Polly's heart did a most peculiar double somersault.

'Hello, blondie,' the boy said. Which was pretty good coming from him, Polly thought, since his own straight, shining hair was as yellow as – as a primrose petal. He looked her up and down, then turned back to his companions, and Polly, dragging Ivan by one

87

hand, began to ascend the steps at the side of the church which led into the Sunday school.

'Who was that, Poll?' Ivan asked as soon as they were inside the church. 'He were playin' cards . . . and smokin' a cigarette. Mammy would say he wasn't a nice sort o' feller, wouldn't she?'

'I dunno who he was, but you're right, he's probably not a nice feller,' Polly said automatically. She spied Alice in the crowd of children already gathered, and went over to her. Alice, like Polly, had a number of brothers, one of whom, Teddy, was with her now. Teddy and Ivan immediately gravitated to one another and Alice and Polly sat on one of the long wooden benches and talked about school . . . and Polly thought about the boy with the yellow hair. He had the sort of face that is so guileless and innocent that you just know he's a real devil, and the sort of smile, unfortunately, which makes it a matter of indifference to most girls whether he's a devil or not. He was also tall, and though his clothes were ragged and his runners had holes in the toes he still had an air of being *right*, as though because he was wearing such things they were automatically fashionable.

'So I told Sister that I'd done me best, only we're a big fambly, chuck, an' it ain't easy to get peace an' quiet when you've got bleedin' brothers banging about—'

'Alice,' Polly interrupted. 'There's a feller outside shouted out to me . . . He's got yellow hair. D'you know who he is?'

'Yaller hair? Oh aye, that'll be Sunny Andersen. His dad's Swedish or summat.' Alice touched her hair, pushing back one richly dark, heavy lock, then glanced towards the church door as though she thought that Sunny Andersen might come through it at any moment. 'Ain't he just the best-lookin' feller you ever saw? Everyone's crazy for Sunny.'

'Well, I'm not,' Polly said stoutly. 'He gambles, and he was smokin' too. My mammy says I shouldn't talk to fellers what gamble or smoke.'

Alice laughed. 'If you don't talk to fellers what gamble or smoke you won't be doin' much talkin' round here,' she said. 'Pitch an' toss is a fav'rite game, an' most of the fellers smoke when they gets work. Still, Sunny wouldn't tek no notice of *you*; you're too young by half.'

'Well, good,' Polly was beginning, when the teacher came in. She was young and pretty, and when she took off her long, fur-trimmed coat Polly saw she was wearing a fashionable dress with a fringed hem and a scalloped neckline. Around her slender white throat hung a necklace of gold beads, interspersed with tiny pearls. Polly decided that she was not only pretty, she looked nice, and her smile, as she turned to her class, was both open and friendly.

'That's Miss Rawlins,' Alice hissed. 'She's me fav'rite teacher – I'm goin' to be just like her when I grow up.'

'She looks lovely,' Polly said fervently. She decided to think about Miss Rawlins and her beautiful clothes and just hope that dreadful, gambling Sunny Andersen would get out of her head and stay out.

'Good afternoon, children,' Miss Rawlins said, having hung her coat and hat on the hook provided. She came and stood before the class, smiling at them all. 'Now I'm going to read you a story . . .'

Polly enjoyed the Sunday school class and came out with a coloured picture of Saint Elizabeth with her basket full of roses, given by the teacher to all who could correctly answer questions when her story had been read. The priest had come and given them a short audition and Polly was now a member of his choir, which would cut down her free time on a Sunday to almost nothing, as Ivan insisted on explaining to her. But Polly, who loved singing, said that it was worth it, and emerged from the church with a light heart. She had been immensely gratified to receive the Holy picture and had assured Miss Rawlins that she would take great care of it and would try very hard to win another, and as she and Ivan walked down the steps she told herself that she had forgotten all about the boy Sunny, but nevertheless when she glanced round and saw that the card school had scattered she felt a little pang of disappointment. However, she reminded Alice that she, Polly, would call at the Eccles' place when she was back from the hospital, waved a cheery goodbye to the children she had met that afternoon and set off in the direction of home, for Mammy and Bevin would be walking towards them, since they all liked to go to the hospital together.

Presently, they met Mammy and Bevin and the picture was shown and Miss Rawlins's charm and person described in minute detail whilst Ivan, looking bored, kicked a stone along ahead of them and occasionally broke into a gruff one-note song which only an experienced parent could have recognised as 'Pack up your Troubles'.

'So you got into the choir, alanna, but Ivan didn't?' Deirdre asked as they hurried along the pavement. 'I can't t'ink even the most desperate priest would put up wit' Ivan's flat notes.'

'I'm in,' Polly admitted. And chattered on, retelling Miss Rawlins's story and flourishing the Holy picture which she had won for her good answers. But presently, as they continued to walk towards the hospital, she began to feel she was being watched – perhaps followed. Out of the corner of her eye she seemed to see someone lurking, though the street was by no means empty and they were meeting other people, now, also heading for the hospital. So presently, she stopped to tie her shoelace, and glanced back and upside down though she was, she saw a boy with an unforgettably yellow head dodging into a shop doorway behind them.

Polly straightened, feeling puzzled. That Sunny boy was following them; he could have walked along the pavement in their wake without anyone minding, he could have caught them up and overtaken them . . . What on earth was he playing at?

But presently they arrived at the hospital and Polly pushed Sunny Andersen and his odd ways resolutely out of her mind. He would soon get fed up with hanging around the hospital and go home and leave her alone. She still thought him very handsome, but she did not like being followed one bit. It was stupid, so it was, and he was an eejit to play silly games and him at least three years her senior.

Peader was delighted to see them and he was looking better, sitting up in bed and smiling a lot, even speaking now and then, and obviously looking forward to emerging from the hospital for Christmas Day, even if he did have to go back in by evening.

When the visit was over Polly truly did forget Sunny Andersen and did not so much as glance round when the family emerged on to the pavement once more. They hurried home, because darkness had fallen and the cold was really beginning to bite, and went indoors to start making the tea.

'I'm goin' to call for Alice when me tea's ate, though,' Polly announced as she put the delft on the table and began to fish knives and forks out of the dresser drawer. 'We might play at her house . . . unless you'd rather we played here, Mammy?'

'I don't like you being out after dark, alanna,' Deirdre admitted. 'What does Alice's mammy t'ink?'

'Oh, Alice can play wit' me,' Polly said cheerfully. 'There's ten kids, only two growed, so her mammy won't mind at all if she comes round here. I'll ask her then, Mammy.'

But when she went outside, with her warm coat and scarf on and the heels of her best shoes ringing on the icy pavement, the first thing she saw, leaning idly against the wall of the house opposite, was a tall figure topped with that exceedingly yellow hair.

Polly gaped, then hesitated. What would he say if she asked him what he thought he was doing, following her around? Would he deny it, or give her cheek? But the only way to find out was to ask him, so she marched across the road until she was only a couple of feet away from him and then spoke. 'What are you doin' here, feller? Why's you been followin' me?'

He looked down at her from his superior height and grinned. It was a nice grin. It warmed his whole face and made his eyes, which looked unfathomably dark in the hissing gaslight, sparkle like diamonds. 'Oh, I just thought I'd see where you lived, blondie,' he said in a light drawl. 'Nice place!'

'Me name isn't blondie,' Polly said coldly, but with a fast-beating heart. 'Sure and no one's called that, except in the comic strips!'

'Ah, an Irish colleen,' the boy said, his eyes dancing. 'Now who'd ha' thought it! Well, queen, if

92

you aren't called blondie, what are you called?'

'I'm Polly O'Brady,' Polly said at once. 'And I know who *you* are an' all. Me pal told me in Sunday school. You're Sunny Andersen.'

He raised a hand in a sort of half-salute, acknowledging a hit. 'Right on the nail, Polly O'Brady. And what else did your pal tell you?'

'Nothin',' Polly said shortly. She certainly did not intend to tell this self-possessed but wicked boy that Alice thought him handsome!

'Nothin'? She didn't mention that I were the best footie player the Scottie ever spawned? Nor that I can ride a leckie wi' the conductor tryin' to knock me off, an' stay fixed on for miles like a bleedin' limpet on a rock? Nor that I—'

'Were the biggest boaster in the whole of Liverpool? No, she only said you were called Sunny Andersen,' Polly cut in waspishly. She would teach this boy not to play games with her!

'Oh-oh, who's gorra tongue on her like an adder, then?' Sunny Andersen said softly. 'Me little Irish colleen can snap like a bleedin' crocodile, I see. Well, I'm norra feller to take agin a girl wi' spirit, so let's you an' me have a chat, eh?'

'No, I don't t'ink so,' Polly said at once. 'You're older'n me, and – and me mammy doesn't like me talkin' to strangers. I'm off to me pal's house.'

She half-expected him to follow her, or to try to change her mind for her, but he did no such thing. She walked away and he continued to lean against the house wall, though she was fairly sure that he turned to gaze after her. She went round to Alice's house, which was not far away, and then the two of them came back along Titchfield Street, intending to play at number 8. As they came within sight of it, Polly automatically glanced across the road, to where Sunny had stood under the gaslight, but the roadway was empty. Sunny Andersen had gone.

'Good riddance,' Polly said savagely under her breath. But deeper inside her, where only she could hear, a little voice said: *What's the matter wit' you, Polly O'Brady? You liked that feller, you know very well you did. And you didn't have to be* quite *so nasty to him, did you?*

'What'll we play, Poll?' Alice said when the two of them were in the small bedroom which was Polly's very own. She looked enviously round at the white muslin curtains, the pink and white counterpane, at the curtained-off alcove where Polly kept her clothes. 'Ain't this just fine, though, queen? Wish I had a room all to meself like this.'

'Well, we'll start by pullin' the curtains, 'cos you never know who's out there, watchin',' Polly said darkly, suiting action to words. But though she stared very hard, the road outside remained empty. Sunny Andersen, despite his outward appearance of brash self-confidence, had clearly taken his dismissal well. And much later that night, when Polly was getting ready for bed and Alice had long gone, she pulled the curtain aside again to have, she told herself, one last look at the stars.

They were all there, twinkling in the heavens. But the roadway below Polly's window remained disappointingly empty of a tall, yellow-haired figure lounging against the opposite wall.

Well, that's a good t'ing, so it is, Polly told herself as she began to fold her clothes neatly over her chair. Still, it'll give me something to tell Grace when I write next. For Grace was growing up and enlivened her letters with talk of clothes, young men, and the fact that her bosoms, as she called them, refused to grow as quickly as did those of her friend and fellow child-minder, Kate. Grace's letters also mentioned such problems as underarm hair, which did not seem to flourish on her as it did on her more mature companions, and Polly thought that Grace would be the very person to advise on how she should behave should Sunny Andersen continue to haunt her. But it was only because she was new around here, she reminded herself as she climbed into bed and pulled the sheet up round her ears. It was always the same, anyone new in a neighbourhood always came in for extra attention.

So Polly closed her eyes, and began to think about her dear Grace, to wonder about little Jamie her nephew, and to wish fervently that Grace was not quite so far away.

Polly's big brother Brogan had written just as soon as he had got the news of Peader's illness, and had said that Grace had wanted to come home, but had realised, after they had discussed the matter, that her arrival would not make things any easier for the O'Bradys.

For she has a good job here, with us. And though the Depression's biting pretty deep here too, I guess there are still more jobs this side of the Atlantic than there are back home. And Grace isn't just highly regarded by us, the man who owns the delicatessen says he'll take her on full-time just as soon as young Jamie's in school. I guess Sara will go back to her teaching full-time then, but right now . . . well, I reckon we all need Grace, and she's happy here, Mammy, honest to God she is. What's more, Sara's teaching her all about keeping house, cooking and managing the money – some fellow's going to be very lucky to get our Grace. And in the meantime we're all of

*us thinking about you, so we are, and praying for
Daddy.*

You couldn't say fairer than that, Polly thought
sleepily now. Grace had been an orphan, living in the
Salvation Army children's home of Strawberry Field
when she and Polly had first got to know each other,
and Grace had been very happy to spend all her spare
time with the O'Bradys at the crossing cottage. Grace
had never complained, she had been happy at
Strawberry Field, but she knew she could not stay on
there for ever and Polly knew better than most how
her pal had longed for a real home of her own, and
loving parents. And then Brogan had written, and
Grace had gone . . . And from her letters, no one could
be happier than she, with a good home, the baby to
look after, and Sara and Brogan giving an eye to her
and seeing that all was well. What was more, she
enjoyed her job and liked meeting people, especially,
she told Polly, since they were all intrigued by her
accent and this made her feel special. She was
beginning to find her feet and to have a circle of
friends. The homesickness was not so bad, and she
was beginning to appreciate New York and to enjoy
her life there.

Coming back to Liverpool to no job and no prospects was not really a good idea. Brogan was right, as
usual. So Polly, who had so longed for Grace's companionship, had virtuously not included in her
prayers one for Grace's return. Fair was fair; you
could not pray for something which would upset
your dearest friend, no matter how happy it might
make you, personally.

But that doesn't stop me wishing a tiny bit, she
thought wistfully, as her eyelids grew heavy.

Chapter Four

At eleven o'clock that evening, climbing wearily up the four flights of stairs, Grace thought that there was not a vast lot of difference, really, between the poor here in New York and the poor back home. The weather had brought extra customers to the soup kitchen; a long line of wet, hopeless men and women took the bowls of nourishing soup and the hunks of bread which accompanied them in hands which shook with cold.

I thought America was a land of opportunity where anyone could rise to be the highest in the land if they had the intelligence, Grace thought. But it was all fairy tales really – there were men in this queue who once had well-paid jobs, motor cars, two or three homes. And there were professors, teachers, engineers, architects . . .

She knew better, however, than to let her depression show; it had been impressed upon her by other Salvationists, that one of the things they could do for the poor down-and-outs they fed was to smile and be cheerful, tell them that better times were bound to come, joke with them if they joked.

So she had worked cheerfully, done her best to cheer everyone up, and had taken heart when Sara had pointed out, in her quiet way, that the faces of those who had been fed and had spent twenty minutes or so in the warmth of the hall were a good deal brighter than those still waiting to come in.

Sara had left before Grace this evening, however. Sometimes they walked home together, but because Sara's job meant an early start, she never stayed later than ten o'clock and this evening the queue had still been waiting at that hour. So Grace had trudged through the emptying streets alone, and had entered their building conscious of enormous tiredness and, strangely enough, a great urge for a cup of tea. She had drunk a cup an hour or so earlier, but it had been weak and though it had quenched her thirst at the time, she was thirsty again now. So it was with considerable pleasure that she heard Sara's voice call: 'Kettle's on!' as she put her key into the front door and opened it. Hanging her damp bonnet, coat and scarf on the small hallstand and kicking off her boots, Grace called back: 'Grand, I'm just about dying of thirst,' and hurried into the kitchen.

Brogan was sitting beside the stove, his heavy boots off, his stockinged feet stretched out before him. He grinned at Grace as she entered. 'My, you've been busy, alanna! I meant to come out and meet you so I did but I fell asleep – bad cess to me – and only woke just this minute when Sara bawled out to you. There's sorry I am that you had to walk through the streets alone, a girl of your age. Was there no one coming your way, dearest?'

Grace shook her head slightly guiltily. 'No, not when I left. But it was all right, there was scarcely a soul about, and the down-and-outs, poor dears, know our uniform. I don't think they'd hurt us, honest to God I don't.'

'That's why they tell us to wear our bonnets when we're going to and fro late at night,' Sara said. She poured three large mugs of tea and handed Grace one, then went and sat in the chair opposite Brogan's, leaving the other chair for Grace. 'Well, it won't be long before I'm in bed, I'm telling you. Jamie decided he didn't want to go to bed, and then when I got him into his cot, he didn't want to go sleep. I wouldn't be surprised if he was cutting another tooth, poor little fellow.'

'What time did he settle?' Grace asked, sipping the hot brew. How good it was to feel warm again, right down to her toes . . . and how she pitied those trying to sleep on the streets tonight! She had done enough of that as a child to remember the way you tried to combat the cold, and the helplessness of it. The thick wads of newspaper underneath you, whatever warm rags you could get over the top of you, and the positioning, carefully thought out, of your makeshift bed so that your back was to the draughts and you had – hopefully – some sort of shelter from rain and snow descending. But then there were the scuffers – they were cops here, she corrected herself hastily – who would move you on if they got half a chance, though there were kindly ones, she knew, who would look the other way. The cops here, she reminded herself, were no better or worse than those in Liverpool. She knew from talking to the destitute there were those who would try to get them into one of the night shelters which had been set up for the vast army of unemployed who had descended on New York in the hope of finding work.

'What time did Jamie settle, Brog?' Sara asked. 'It must have been half past ten, I suppose. Oh well, perhaps he'll wake later in the morning,' she added hopefully. She drained the last of her tea, stood up and took the empty mug over to the sink. Rinsing it in cold water she dried it on a tea-towel and hung it back on its hook. 'Sorry, but I'm really very tired. See you in the morning, Gracie. What shift are you on tomorrow, Brog?'

'It's me day off,' Brogan said lazily, still sipping his tea. 'So mebbe I'll take Jamie out for the day . . . well, I'll bring him back for dinner,' he added hastily, 'Seeing as I'm no sort of a hand wit' the nappy-changing, let alone feeding him that pap you girls hand out. Now when he's on to the steak an' chips, I'm your man so I am.'

Sara, in the doorway, laughed back at him. 'I'm going to teach you to change a nappy if it's the last thing I do,' she declared. 'And it's no good you going green and saying you can't stand the sight of – of what he's just done. These days, with both Grace and myself so busy, you've simply got to have a working knowledge of minding a baby.'

'Oh, I can do it,' Brogan said, finishing his own tea and taking Grace's now empty cup over to the sink. 'But I can't say I like it and the little devil wiggles so I'm scared out of me life that he'll end up on the floor, or wit' a safety pin through his – his—'

Grace, laughing, said she quite understood and dried up the mugs when Brogan had rinsed them. 'Then if you're on a day off tomorrow I'll not wake you,' she said cheerfully. 'As for taking Jamie out, in this sort of weather a rush to the shops is about all he gets – and probably all he needs, what's more, so don't you worry about him. He's no trouble, you know, but a pleasure to be with,' she finished.

'Not when he's teethin' he's not,' Brogan said darkly. 'A bad-tempered spalpeen, that's what he is when he feels the teeth of him comin'. But don't throw me offer back in me face, Jess, or you'll find yourself saddled with him until you go off to work again.'

'I don't mind . . .' Grace was beginning, when she

stopped, a frown descending. 'What did you call me, Brog?'

'Je . . . I mean Grace, I suppose,' Brogan said. He went quite pink Grace saw. 'Now off to bed wit' you, Grace Carbery, or Sara will tell me off for keepin' you chattin'.'

'You called me Jess,' Grace said slowly, ignoring his words. 'And it's not the first time, Brog. Why Jess, though?'

'Oh . . . well, you've a likeness to your sister I suppose,' Brogan said in a mumble. 'Sorry . . . I can't think what made me . . .'

'But it was Sara who knew Jess, and baby Mollie, not you,' Grace said, staring at him. 'I never heard tell you'd met Jess, Brog.'

'You haven't? Well, of course I knew her, alanna,' Brogan said, the pink dying out of his face. He began to get cups, plates and cutlery from the dresser. 'I'll just lay the table for breakfast so I will, since we'll all be takin' it together for once.'

'How did you know Jess?' Grace demanded. She took the cutlery from him and began to arrange it around the table. 'I know Sara met her just – just before she died and – and the baby disappeared, but no one ever said you'd met my sister.'

'I – I guess I saw her hangin' round the railway from time to time,' Brogan said slowly. 'She – she usually had the baby with her – your sister Mollie I mean. She were a good girl were Jess, but I'm sorry I miscalled you, alanna. I think it's because you're gettin' more like her, now you've some flesh on your bones, but it – it doesn't mean anything, you know. Except that I'm liable to forgetfulness. Now off to bed wit' you, or I'll be gettin' a drubbin' from Sara for keepin' you talkin', I keep tellin' you.'

'It isn't the first time you've done it, though,' Grace said thoughtfully, turning towards the kitchen door. 'It isn't the first time you've called me Jess, I mean. Still, it's nice to think I'm even a bit like her; she was one of the best people I ever knew, though I was really almost a baby myself when she died.'

'Aye, four or five, you must have been I suppose,' Brogan said. He was beginning to look hunted, Grace thought, amused. But she was very tired, and what did it matter, after all, that Brogan had called her by her dead sister's name? On previous occasions when Brogan had called her Jess, Sara had always been present and had cut in so quickly that Grace had not liked to comment. But the answer was simple after all – Brogan, as well as Sara, had known her beloved elder sister. So she smiled up at him and opened the kitchen door.

'Do you know, I still miss her, in a way?' Grace said. 'When you think of all the Carberys, the whole great clan of us, and we all somehow lost touch. I don't know whether I've a brother living – or a sister for that matter – and though I'd still love to see Mollie again, if she's alive that is, I've no urge whatever to meet the boys.'

'Better not to meet 'em, from what I've heard,' Brogan said. 'Goodnight now, Gracie; see you in the mornin', and don't hesitate to wake me when you need a hand with the boy.'

Brogan entered the bedroom to find Sara sitting before the mirror, brushing her hair. She had undressed and put on her night-gown, and smiled at him through the mirror.

'I'm sorry, darling,' she said. 'But I was so tired! And then, when I had washed and cleaned my teeth I found I wasn't so tired any longer, so I checked on Jamie – he's sleeping soundly – and then decided to give my hair a really good brushing.'

She continued to attack her hair but Brogan, without preamble, took her shoulders, rested his chin on the top of her head and said flatly, 'I called her Jess again. Grace, I mean.'

'Oh, mercy,' Sara said, her brush suspended for a moment. 'Did she notice?'

'Certainly she did,' Brogan said gloomily. 'She asked me why, too.'

'And what did you say? Oh, Brog, you didn't spill the beans, did you? You know we all agreed not to do so until Polly was older . . . well, until they were both older.'

'Of course I didn't, no more I didn't tell her it was me stole her little sister away after Jess died and sent her to Ireland for me mammy to bring up,' Brogan said indignantly, then spoiled the effect by adding: 'but it was a very close run thing so it was. She asked me why I'd called her Jess and without really thinking I told her the truth – that she sometimes reminded me of Jess now she's growing up.'

'Oh, lor',' Sara said, beginning to brush her hair again. 'What did she say to that?'

'She said she didn't realise I knew her sister, though she was well aware that you did, of course. So I told her the truth, more or less. I said I'd known Jess as well, I used to see her about the railway when I worked in Liverpool.'

'And?'

'And she accepted it. Why not? And it isn't so far from the truth as all that. She does remind me of Jess. Why, she's got a likeness to Polly as well, don't you think?'

'I know what you mean,' Sara said after a pause for thought. 'But it isn't an obvious likeness. Polly's hair is very fair and curly, and Grace has straight brown hair. And Polly's got big blue eyes and dimples; Grace's eyes are grey and she doesn't have Poll's roses and cream complexion, either. I don't think their likeness to each other will ever be remarked on by anyone outside the family. And the family all know better than to say anything, don't they? After all, you stole Mollie and renamed her Polly, and your parents knew, and said nothing because they wanted a baby girl so much. Your mammy is still afraid that the authorities would punish her in some way if anyone ever found out how it was.'

'Aye, that's true,' Brogan said. He moved away from his wife and began to undress, then went over to the washstand and sluiced his hands and face in the water Sara had left. Sara, climbing into bed, giggled.

'I thought you'd not want to bother with fresh water, you horrid thing,' she said affectionately, pulling the sheet up to her chin. 'Now let's hurry up and get some sleep before young Master Jamie decides to start shouting the odds again.'

Tad did well as a delivery boy for Merrick's, because he was not afraid of hard work and was quite willing to continue tramping the streets of Dublin until midnight if necessary, to see that all the deliveries were done before Christmas Day. He was hopeful, of course, that Mr Merrick might see the justice of keeping him on, though his mammy thought this extremely doubtful.

'Just use your head, son,' she said kindly the first time Tad allowed his secret hope to surface. 'Christmas time, everyone eats, no matter how poor.

Well, I know the rich has meat an' pies an' all sorts, and the rest make do wit' whatever they can afford, but one way an' another, we all eat over Christmas. And what happens in January? Why, we all pay for it. Once the 6th of January is over, it's tightenin'-belts time, which is why January an' February are called the hungry months. Folk have spent all their spare cash and after Christmas they know they won't have much of anything until the spring comes again. And there's nothin' goin' free around then, either. No blackers on the brambles, no nuts on the hazels, no apples in the orchards. See?'

'So what?' Tad said, staring. 'D'you mean Merrick's won't sell nothin' after Christmas?'

'No, 'course not. But they won't need extra deliveries, will they? They'll manage wi' the lads they employ all year, so it's no use your gettin' your hopes up. Best start lookin' round for another job come the New Year.'

So when the New Year came and his mammy's prophecy came true, Tad tried very hard indeed to get another job, but he wasn't the only one. All over Dublin, boys who had earned money over the Christmas season were looking for jobs – any job. It was hard enough if you had some sort of training, but when, like Tad and his brothers, you had only sold newspapers, run messages or delivered goods, there were simply too many of you chasing every possible post.

And yet when Tad did get a job, it was largely because of his time with Merrick's, plus the most enormous stroke of luck.

Merrick's not only had delivery boys on bicycles and on foot, they also had an elderly van which did the out-of-town orders. And once or twice in early

December because the deliveries in the countryside were so heavy, Tad had been sent on the van with Mr McGrath, the driver, to help him with his deliveries. Tad had enjoyed the experience immensely; it was fun to sit beside the driver, fun to watch how he actually drove the old van – Tad had not, before, realised that a motor vehicle had gears, he had thought that a brake, a steering wheel and a horn were all that had to be mastered – and because he never complained when asked to carry great heavy baskets of food up long, tree-lined drives which had most town-boys thinking uneasily of ghosts, bulls and fierce dogs, Mr McGrath decided that he preferred 'young Donoghue' to the other delivery boys, and asked for him whenever his workload was heavy.

This, whilst pleasant for Tad, might not have had any repercussions but for the fact that three days before Christmas, when the van was so laden that Mr McGrath had crawled most of the way in second gear, it broke down on a long stretch of country road without any sort of immediate help in sight.

''Tis sorry I am, but you'll have to walk back to the city, young feller,' Mr McGrath said wearily, for it was raining briskly and the sky overhead was grey and lowering. 'It'll be dark soon, and I've no fancy to be stuck out here all night by meself, let alone tryin' to deliver this lot on foot.'

'Let's have a look in the engine before I go,' Tad had said, highly daring. He had discovered that he liked tinkering with motors when a neighbour with an old motorbike had stripped it down one afternoon the previous summer and had instructed Tad in the strange ways of the internal combustion engine. 'You never know, Mr McGrath, it might be somethin' dead simple.'

Mr McGrath had made discouraging noises, but it was cold and wet and as he had said, darkness was coming on. He was a city man himself and really did not like the thought of waiting out here whilst Tad tramped back into Dublin to fetch help. So he walked round to the front of the van, heaved up one side of the creaking bonnet, and surveyed, with a jaundiced eye, the mass of nasty, messy-looking odds and ends which constituted the engine.

'There's no sense in it that I can see,' he grumbled, peering in the fading light at the coils and boxes and pipes. 'I'm thinkin' you'd best be—'

'It's the fan belt. See . . . there,' Tad said coolly, peering into the engine and pointing at something, though Mr McGrath certainly did not know what. 'It's broke, Mr McGrath. If we can just find somethin' to tek its place while we make our way back home . . . there's the belt on me apron, but . . .' He eyed Mr McGrath up and down, then exclaimed: 'Your tie! Sure an' it's a fine tie, but it'll wash! Will ye give me a borrow of it, Mr M?'

Mr McGrath's first impulse was to clutch his tie and refuse to part with it, but as he glanced round he saw that it was already growing darker . . . and the van was still fully laden . . . 'Oh, all right, but don't you ruin it, young Donoghue. Me wife give it me for me birt'day last year,' he said, reluctantly beginning to unknot the tie from around his neck.

Tad had taken the tie, run it round the pulley-wheels, knotted it, and then told his superior to start the engine. Wonderingly, Mr McGrath had climbed back into the cab and watched as Tad went and fetched the starting handle, fitted it into the appropriate slot in front of the bonnet, and began to crank vigorously. He had very little faith in the ability of a delivery boy to solve the problem, but he had clearly underestimated Tad Donoghue. The engine coughed, stuttered and began to purr like a contented cat. Tad jumped into the cab beside him as soon as he was sure that the engine was really and truly all right and Mr McGrath, with a huge sigh of relief, had put the van into gear and set off once more.

''Tis only a temporary solution,' Tad said when Mr McGrath marvelled at his unusual knowledge. 'But it'll likely get us round and back and then you can get another fan belt – a real one, not just your tie.'

When at last they got back to the shop Mr McGrath took the van to a garage and then told Mr Merrick how 'the temp'rary boy' had got him out of a scrape and Mr Merrick was impressed. However, he thought no more about it until around the middle of January, when he was talking to a customer, a Mr Barnes, who owned a garage on Thomas Street.

'You say you're lookin' for a lad to train up in the trade of mending motors?' he said. 'Well, I may be able to help you there . . .' and he told Mr Barnes about young Tad Donoghue and the broken fan belt.

Mr Barnes screwed up his mouth into a silent whistle; he thought this sounded promising. He got Tad's address from Mr Merrick and when he had paid for the tea he was buying went round to Gardiner's Lane. He found Tad at home, getting a meal ready, and as was his wont, got straight to the point. 'I've been in Merrick's Grocery, and Mr Merrick was tellin' me that you'd got his van driver out of a scrape before Christmas,' he said to Tad's open-mouthed astonishment. 'I've a garage where we mend motor cars, motor bicycles and the like, as well as sellin' the occasional second-hand model, and I'm lookin' for a young feller to train up. There's not a great deal of money in it at first, but if you work hard and do as you're told, you'll find yourself in a good position. Why, I were just a young lad interested in the workin's of cars an' such, yet now I own me own garage!'

Tad would have scrubbed sewers for a chance like this! What was more, the wages of ten shillings a week sounded princely after the sort of money most of his pals earned. He agreed, breathlessly, to all the conditions Mr Barnes laid down – and they were neither many nor unfair – and said he would report at the garage prompt at eight the next morning. Mr Barnes said good, shook Tad's hand and as he was turning away suddenly turned back. 'You'll need overalls,' he said kindly, fishing some money out of his pocket. 'We'll have nothin' to fit you – you're our first boy, see – so buy yourself a stout pair tomorrer, before you come in. So, tomorrer I won't expect you in until nine.'

So by mid-January, Tad had a job he enjoyed and was already beginning to be useful to the garage mechanics who were training him.

'He's a practical lad, so he is,' Mr Barnes told his wife, after Tad's first week. 'What's more, he's willing. He'll make the fellers cups of tea, do messages for them, spend hours under a car trying to discover a broken connection . . . Oh aye, we did all right when we took on young Donoghue.'

And Tad, of course, was very pleased with himself and determined that he would write to Polly and tell her all about his new job just as soon as he could spare the time. He had sent her a Christmas card with some of his earnings from Merrick's, and after much thought had laid out a whole sixpence on a little yellow-haired angel for the top of a Christmas tree. It was a celluloid doll dressed in white cotton, with a halo and gold gauze wings. But what had really attracted him to it was its sweet expression, which had immediately reminded him of Polly herself.

It's the Nearest I could get to your Guarjan Angel, darlin Polly. So you put it on Top of your Xmas Tree an it'll keep you Safe for Me. I tought you might come bak to Dublin for a Visit, perhaps, but I no you can't now, not wit Your Daddy ill, so I've sent the Angel instead.
All Best Wishes from your lovin Tad Donoghue.

He posted off the letter, the card and the little celluloid angel and felt he had done well by Polly. She was, after all, a long way off. Besides, her letter answering the one in which he had told her about his new pal had been very peculiar, not like herself at all. She had asked several questions about Angela Machin – rather stiff, nasty questions, and it had put Tad's back up, so it had. So when it came to Christmas presents, instead of spending all he could afford on Polly he reminded himself that he had to split the money this year, and bought Angela a box of chocolates which also cost sixpence, and a penny card with a picture of the Holy Family on it.

He ignored Polly's questions about Angela too. If she wanted answers then she should have been nice and friendly, the same as he would have been had Polly got a new friend, he told himself. So when, just before Christmas, a letter, card and present had arrived for him – the present was a small dictionary with a faded blue cover and Tad rightly read a touch of criticism into such a gift and was consequently cross – he had opened the letter already prepared for some further nastiness and had read the contents with

110

feelings which were so contradictory and strange that even now he did not fully understand them. Polly had written in her neat, round hand:

Well, Tad, I've met ever such a nice feller, so I have. His name is Sunny Andersen and he's got lovely yellow hair and blue eyes, and he took me to the Saturday Rush last week and bought me a pennorth of popcorn and a Vanilla Ice. So you see I don't mind about That Angela no more, because I know you must of been lonely to turn to a girl like that.

(Like what? Tad thought, and felt even crosser with his Polly.)

Hope the enclosed Dicker is useful to you, because I always have one to hand when I write to you. It isn't Brand New, but it is almost, the feller on the stall said. If you know the first two or three letters it makes spelling a lot easier. My Daddy is better and comin home for Christmas Day so I must go now I have a great deal to do and lots of messages to do.
      Your loving Polly O'Brady.

But it was no use being cross with Polly over the dictionary because he knew very well that he was a poor speller. Mr Barnes, who was taking a great interest in his newest employee, had told him that one day he must learn to fill in job sheets, explaining what had been done to the car, which new parts had had to be fitted, and how much it had cost. At the moment such work was done by others, but one day, if Tad fulfilled his potential and got on as Mr Barnes had got on, he would need to be able to read, write and spell.

So Tad swallowed his indignation because his little

pal had given him such a prissy present and spent an hour or so each evening simply reading the thing. Since he was quite as bright as Mr Barnes thought him, he soon found this an absorbing exercise, for often he met strange and fascinating words with even stranger spellings, and what was more, he began to take pleasure in getting the words by heart. He set himself a target of three new words learned, with the correct spelling, each evening and it was surprising how they mounted up.

What was more, Angela Machin was proving to be a real pal, the sort that seems to want to help you and to spend time with you. Now that he was working he could not meet her out of school, but they usually met at some stage during the evening, either Tad going round to Swift's Alley or she coming round to Gardiner's Lane. She brought her homework and Tad, who had always been top of his class at mathematics as well as actually enjoying the subject, was able to help her a good deal, which gave him a great feeling of superiority. It did not seem to matter so much that he had a poor home and a great many younger brothers and sisters; he could do sums!

So the winter days passed much more pleasantly for Tad than he had ever believed possible with Polly so far away. He and Angela grew easy together. They, too, went to the cinema, though usually in the evening since Tad worked all day Saturday. Because Angela's mammy did not have to struggle to feed her family, with three of them earning, they usually went back to Swift's Alley for meals, and Tad's mammy grew used to Tad coming in late, and fed.

Then Tad had another letter from Polly telling him that her daddy was now at home with them all the time, but would not be working again just yet.

He'll be getting better little by little. But he can't work for a while yet, the doctor says, which means there won't be a special free house, not like the crossing cottage, nor much money coming in, but things should go back to normal in a few months, so they should . . . Mammy says. The boys are very good, and help all they can, and I'm helping to deliver papers so I don't need pocket money no more. And last week I found a poor ole feller of a tomcat, thin and bony wit a horrid patchy coat and his ears so torn they are like lace curtains, and I've called him Tom the Chimney Sweep, like in The Water Babies *– because he's black, of course – and I'm going to keep him instead of dear Lionel, who is very happy with the Templetons. It isn't selfish, because there are mice in this house, and Daddy said a cat was a good idea, so it was.*

I dressed the Christmas tree, as I telled you earlier, and my dear Christmas angel looked a treat, everyone said so. But now the holiday's over and she's come off the tree so I've put her in my bedroom on my dressing table, and every time I look at her I think of you, Tad. You were so good to me. My own real angel is still around, only you mustn't look right at her, only to one side and if you look straight – wham – she goes. I don't tell other people about her, though. Not even Sunny. Going to do my eckers before bedtime so cheerio for now.
Your loving Polly O'Brady.

Tad laughed over the scratty old tomcat – how typical of his Polly! – and nearly cried when he read that she hadn't told anyone else about her guardian angel, not even Sunny. But he knew that Polly was becoming somehow distant in his mind, a memory rather than a real, loving person, and regretted it very much. Only . . . well, he did have Angela now, and she was a great girl, so she was and they got on real good.

To be sure he didn't have the same sort of fun with her that he had once had with Polly, but he and Polly had been kids, exploring everything like a pair of inquisitive puppies and frequently getting into trouble for it. He and Angela were verging on being grown-ups, and grown fellers didn't take their girls boxing the fox in the apple orchards outside Dublin, or out to Booterstown to collect cockles on the sands.

The thought made him smile. Angela was beautiful, and kind, and sensible. She had chosen him out of all the fellers she could have had, and that made him a lucky chiseller – if he was still a chiseller, when he was working for his living and taking a pretty girl out to the cinema and – and thinking about her most of the time. But she wasn't his old pal, the one who had known him since he was a scruffy kid trying to keep out of his daddy's way and having a job, most of the time, to stay fed. But he supposed that one's life is divided into little parts, and you hop from one part to another as you grow older. He had hopped out of the chiseller's part, in which Polly had been the only person he really cared for, apart from his own family, and into an almost-grown-up part, in which Angela, who was nearly fourteen, was a more natural companion for him than a child of twelve.

Polly would be thirteen soon, of course. Only the trouble was, Tad couldn't think of her as nearly a woman. He still thought of her as the bright-eyed ten-year-old who had shed such bitter tears when she had been taken away from him, to live over the water with her mammy and daddy. And anyway, she had that Sunny Andersen – ridiculous name – to go about with now.

He – Sunny – was fifteen, according to Polly. Older even than Tad now was, although only by a few months. But he was too old for Polly, that feller, Tad concluded uneasily. Then again it was her business now – she was too far away, and too distant, somehow, for him to meddle in her affairs.

Tad had been reading the letter, and thinking his thoughts, whilst sitting on a broken-down piece of wall in Gardiner's Lane as twilight turned slowly into dusk. Now he stood up. I love Polly like a sister, he told himself, and I'm beginning to love Angela in a – a *different* way. That's all there is to it. And he shoved the letter into his pocket and ran across the court towards his home.

Chapter Five

Sunny Andersen was strolling down the Scotland Road in the beautiful June sunshine, idly kicking a tin can along the paving stones in front of him and wondering what he should do next. He was having a day off; he had a lot of them. Although he was now sixteen years old he was still not in regular employment. However, because of his looks and charm he had had a good many jobs, though he had never stuck to any of them for long. Or perhaps it was not that he had not stuck them, but that they – his employers – had not stuck to him. He did not see why he should work on a sunny day, when he might get out his fishing rod and skip a leckie out to Seaforth and try his luck there. Neither did he see why he should work on a wet day, when it was nicer to stay in bed. Or a snowy day, when considerable fun was to be had making a slide down one of the steep streets which led on to Netherfield Road.

Sunny always pretended to be sorry when employers gave him his cards, but he wasn't really. Of course he enjoyed the wage-packet part of a job and sometimes he quite enjoyed other parts of it too, but this was a rarity, the exception rather than the rule. Ambling along the pavement, he remembered one job that he had enjoyed, though. For a couple of months last summer he had been employed by a firm of ice-cream manufacturers to sell their products in New Brighton. He had been given a stout and reliable bicycle with a cart attached, and all he had to do all day was cycle up and down the New Brighton promenade, stopping whenever he saw a customer.

The job of selling ice cream had been grand, he thought now, whistling a tune beneath his breath as he strolled along the dock road, an eye cocked for anything of interest. But when you ran out of ice cream you had to cycle back to the depot for a refill, and whilst you were doing that you weren't earning. And the bicycle was a heavy old thing, and he had not always enjoyed being at everyone's beck and call. He should have stuck it until the season was over, he realised that, had realised it at the time, but then his mam had come home, having been generously rewarded by someone for something, he did not enquire what, and handed him a big white fiver. That had been the end of the job – a fiver can last a good long time if you're careful and make it work for you. Sunny bought a quantity of powder and lipstick which weren't quite what they should have been from someone he knew on the fringes of the make-up trade, and went round the big offices about once a month, selling the stuff for a nice little profit. But when both the fiver and the make-up ran out, he had not bothered to get another job because Christmas was coming, and a boy with good looks and charm could always find himself a good little job over Christmas.

And then he had met Polly. Sunny had never quite understood what had happened to him upon setting eyes on that small, wide-eyed face surrounded by all those bright, primrose curls. But whatever it was, it had changed things. He wanted to be with her all the time, only she was in school, so it became essential that he get the sort of job which allowed him

117

weekends and evenings free. And he soon realised that he must ingratiate himself with her mam and dad and her brothers, those that were living in the city, anyway, because Polly was still a schoolgirl, although she was only just over two years younger than Sunny, and if he did not have parental approval then he knew instinctively that they would break the friendship up. Polly was very dear to them, and because they loved her they guarded her against anything – or anyone – which they thought might hurt her.

Sunny agreed with this, naturally. He guarded her himself, when they were together. And fortunately, Mrs O'Brady was a nice woman and did not seem to worry unduly that he had not, at present, got a job, particularly when she saw how hard he worked over Christmas – and what nice times he and Polly had together.

'Sure an' you'll get a job when the better weather comes, Sunny,' Mrs O'Brady had said reassuringly when the Christmas job finished. 'Work's always hard to find – harder when there's a Depression, but you're intelligent, always clean and neat . . . Why, you'll be after gettin' a better job than most of your pals, I'll be bound.'

Mr O'Brady, however, had begun to look rather thoughtfully at Sunny lately, so Sunny supposed that he would have to get himself into work again. The trouble was, when his mam was doing well she gave him money and work simply seemed an unnecessary unpleasantness. On the other hand, though, Mr O'Brady had said once or twice, in his deep, slow way, that sure and wasn't Mrs Andersen a fine woman, to keep a lad of Sunny's age and not drive him out to work, and there was something in the way he said it which made Sunny fear that Mr O'Brady had rumbled him. Or worse, had rumbled *them*, for he had no desire for the O'Bradys to look too closely at the way in which Mrs Andersen made her living.

For Sunny had known, ever since he had reached years of discretion, which, in his case, was the age of eight, that his mam earned money from having various gentlemen friends. Now that he was fully grown he knew that this meant she lived on what the priest would have called 'immoral earnings', but he did not put it quite so plainly even to himself; he wrapped it up, telling himself that his mam was 'a theatrical', or, even better, 'a receptionist'. Indeed, she undertook a variety of legitimate jobs when she needed to do so, but he knew, really, that most of the money she made came from men who bought her favours.

And doing such work could be dangerous too. Women who pleased men sometimes had their throats slit as they lay in bed, or were robbed of their takings by other men – shiftless and greedy ones. Some women worked for men called pimps, who took the lion's share of their money, but Cecily Andersen was far too clever to get mixed up with anyone like that. She was a tall, handsome woman, blue-eyed and yellow-haired, but it was from her that Sunny had inherited his casual attitude to the task of earning a living. Cecily liked pretty clothes, cinema and theatre, and her bed. When she was working as an usherette at the cinema – a favourite job, because she met men there – she could have a nice sit-down in the back stalls and a zizz if the film was boring, but when she was doing receptionist duties she had to be – or at least appear to be – alert and ready to help, so although her good appearance and charm might get her into a job, her idleness very soon got her out of it.

However there were always men, she said, when washing her hands of her latest job. Cecily's most regular friend was Sunny's father, Bjorn Berkesmann, a Swedish officer on a timber ship which called every two or three months at the port of Liverpool. He came to the small house close by the Wapping dock whenever his ship was in port, so although Sunny did not have a full-time father in the accepted sense of the words, he saw Bjorn as often as most children of sailors saw their dads.

Bjorn was tall, blond and handsome. He was very like Cecily, so like her that once or twice they had been mistaken for brother and sister, and of course no one who had met Bjorn ever doubted Sunny's paternity. He was proud of his son furthermore, openly acknowledging him, and when Sunny had been small he had helped Cecily financially so that she had not had to work too hard or too often. Now that Sunny was a man grown, however, his father's attitude towards him had hardened somewhat.

'You a good job should hev,' he had said accusingly only a couple of months ago, sitting in the big fireside chair whilst Cecily cooked them a meal and Sunny sorted out his shore lines, for he intended to go fishing next day. 'You should your mudder be helpink to support, not still expectink her to support you.'

'I've had good jobs, but they all get tired of me, an' gi' me me cards,' Sunny had answered, casting his father a mournful look. At least, it was supposed to be a mournful look, but Sunny saw by his father's expression that it had not been mournful enough. 'Now summer's comin' I'll be gettin' somethin', Bjorn,' he said in a wheedling tone. 'You know me, I like a bit of a change, an' a challenge, an' all.'

'You're lazy, like your mudder,' Bjorn had said flatly. 'But it vill not do, Sunny. Why not try the sea? It to me good hes been.'

'It has been good to me,' Sunny had corrected automatically. His father's English was very good, but he sometimes got his sentences the wrong way round and appreciated being reminded. 'I don't think mam would be too pleased if I went off to sea, would you, Mam?'

But to Sunny's astonishment, his mother had let him down. She was stirring something in a large saucepan and her spoon had stopped for a moment whilst she considered the question, then she had replied seriously, as though she had been thinking about it for some time. 'Well, I'd miss you, natural,' she had said thoughtfully. 'But I agree wi' your dad. You'd be better off at sea than idlin' round the docks gettin' into mischief. 'Sides, you've gorra girlfriend, haven't you? Well, she's goin' to expect things like trips to the cinema, an' the seaside, to say nothin' of little gifts when her birthday comes round. Oh, I know I've always done me best for you, but I'm not gerrin' any younger, chuck. It's time you fended for yourself, did your own courtin'.'

Sunny had been so taken aback that for a moment he could only stare disbelievingly at his parent. Then he had said sulkily: 'I don't idle round the docks gettin' into mischief. I've had lots o' jobs and while I'm in 'em I work damn' hard . . . but they bore me after a bit, all of 'em. And as for goin' to sea – what d'you think me young lady would say to that, eh?'

Bjorn, who was always fair, had admitted that a girl liked a feller to be ashore with her, though most girls appreciated that a man must get work in order to keep her. 'So you must a good job find, and soon,' he had insisted. 'Or you will get bad name for unreliability.'

So of course Sunny had promised to mend his ways, and had done so in a manner of speaking. He had kept out of the house during normal working hours and had kept some money jingling in his pocket with a variety of small jobs.

But right now it was a sunny day and yesterday he had worked from dawn until dusk, moving a large houseful of furniture from Rodney Street to Southport for a delivery man he was supposed to be working for, so he had money in his pocket and nothing to do until school came out, when he would be seeing Polly. At the weekend they meant to go over to New Brighton for a day on the funfair and some time on the beach, but today was Wednesday and an evening did not give them sufficient time to go far. Knowing that he would not be working he had suggested last evening that she should sag off school next day, but Polly had frowned on this, reminding him that she would be looking for a job in a year and a good school report was something she could not afford to whistle down the wind.

'But you could say you had a sore throat, queen,' Sunny had said in his most coaxing tone. 'A sore throat's easy to fake . . . An' if them teachers at your school are fussy about such things, I'd write a note for you, pretendin' it were from your mam.'

They had been sitting on the wall which surrounded St Martin's recreation ground, desultorily chatting whilst watching a group of lads playing a forbidden game of football amongst the flower beds. Polly had shaken her head, then turned large, reproachful eyes on him. 'Sunny, you're a divil straight from hell, so y'are, and I'll not risk me immortal soul tellin' huge *lies* just so's you can have someone to mess about wit' when you're out of work. Anyway, what happened to the job on the furniture van?'

Sunny had grinned and caught hold of Polly's small neck, pulling her closer to him so that he might drop a kiss on the end of her nose. Polly who, while she sort-of liked it sometimes, found such behaviour embarrassing in the extreme, gave Sunny a playful punch in the stomach. 'All right, all right,' he had said, laughing. 'There's no need for violence, Poll, it were only to show you how I feel about you. Just a – a lovin' gesture, like.'

'Lovin' gestures aren't needed,' Polly had said sharply. 'Just you remember that if one of the teachers should happen to look out of me school, they'd be starin' straight across at us. And what would they think, eh, if they saw you maulin' me about and kissin' me nose? And the presbytery is even closer . . . Why, if the priests saw what you were doin' they'd probably want you to *marry* me, and what would you be after sayin' then, clever clogs?'

'Can't marry someone of thirteen,' Sunny had said happily. 'Anyway, I don't see why you're so goody-goody. Your Ivan said that in Dublin you were a right hell-raiser, and—'

'What a thing to say!' Polly had gasped, clearly outraged. 'I am *not* a goody-goody, nor I aren't a hell-raiser, neither. Ivan's just cross because when me daddy was ill and me mammy put me in charge of the house, I sometimes made him work a little bit, idle chiseller that he was.'

'He scrubbed the spuds, cleaned the cabbage, mended the fire, brushed the floor . . .' Sunny had muttered beneath his breath, and had turned to grin at Polly, who had grinned back, unrepentant.

'Oh well . . . mebbe I wasn't an angel, Sunny, but I never did tell lies . . . All right, I took apples from orchards an' spuds from the fields . . . Once we sold holly to the big houses round Phoenix Park – and it were their own holly, what we'd robbed from their hedges. But that's just – just mischief, not real badness.'

Sunny, who agreed with her, had still pulled a doubtful face. 'Stealin's stealin', queen, no matter how you try to cover it up. Still, if you won't sag off school I'll call for you when you leave off, and we'll have a ride on the overhead railway down to Seaforth and back. I'll gerra couple o' tickets from somewhere.'

Polly had known, of course, that he was extremely unlikely to pay for the tickets, but apparently her strict code of conduct did not wince at this, so here he was now, walking towards the overhead railway terminus, which was down by the Pier Head. If you were quick, clever and lucky, it was often possible to pick up a ticket which someone had not handed over to the ticket collector, smarten it up, fill in the bit which had been punched out, and use it during the rush hour, when the railway staff were too busy to peruse each ticket separately.

So Sunny strolled on, and thought about getting a part-time job selling ice cream up and down the Pier Head; ices would go down well there on a hot day like this one. He could sell the ha'penny wafers, most folk could afford a ha'penny. In fact, he could make his way to the warehouse now, see if there was a spare bicycle and cart not in use . . . After all, what good was a lovely sunny day when you were alone and hadn't got your fishing rod handy? And he knew Polly – she would enjoy the ride on the docker's umbrella a good deal more if it was accompanied by a bag of popcorn or an orange or two. Sunny jingled the money in his pocket and decided to go down to the ice-cream factory. And if they didn't have a spare bicycle, perhaps they would sell him one of those big metal cases of the stuff; he reckoned he could shift a deal of ice cream on a day like this even without the bike.

Polly sat in the classroom with her books spread out on her desk, her friend Alice on one side of her and her friend Sylvia on the other, regarding Miss Witherspoon seriously with eyes which followed the teacher's every movement as she wrote on the blackboard and turned occasionally to explain something to her class. But despite her apparent deep interest in the lesson, Polly's thoughts were elsewhere.

It was a lovely day, the nicest one of the summer so far, and far from listening to Miss Witherspoon, who was teaching them to analyse a sentence, Polly was thinking wistfully that if only she had not been such a goody-goody, as Sunny had put it, she might at this very moment have been skimming stones across the River Mersey or searching for four-leaved clovers in Princes Park or paddling in the little waves on Seaforth shore.

'Now we need a subject, a verb, an object . . . Which of you would like to come up and mark out this sentence?' Miss Witherspoon said, turning back to her class. 'Polly O'Brady, can you show the class the adjectival clause, please?'

Polly dragged her happy mind, up to its ankles in cool seawater, back to the hot and stuffy classroom with its smell of girls, cabbage and chalk dust. Fortunately the teacher had said her name before the question and not after it, so she stood up, went to the board, and after a short hesitation, during which time subjects, objects, predicates and various other parts of a sentence whirled in her head, she marked the adjectival clause firmly with the piece of white chalk Miss Witherspoon held out.

'Correct. Thank you, Polly,' Miss Witherspoon said. Rightly taking this for dismissal, Polly returned to her seat whilst another girl took her place to find the subject and object of the sentence.

'Considerin' you was half-asleep . . .' Alice whispered as Polly sat down. 'Still, ole Withers don't usually prose on like this. I wish she'd forget all this rubbishy stuff an' let us read *A Tale of Two Cities*. We was up to an excitin' bit when the bell rang last time.'

Miss Witherspoon, despite her nickname, was an energetic young teacher with black hair arranged in the popular pageboy cut and a trim figure clad in grey and white poplin. She was a great favourite with the girls and her lesson, English, was easily Polly's best subject yet somehow, today, even had the class been reading the Dickens classic, it would have seemed a waste of time. But she had refused to sag off school because she wanted a good report at the end of the summer, so she really ought to concentrate on the lesson.

For a few minutes, indeed, she did so, but then her mind began to wander again. What would Sunny be doing? He wasn't working, that much was certain, so he could be doing almost anything, she supposed wistfully. He loved to fish, probably because he usually fished either sitting down or standing still, and he liked the cinema too. Polly remembered trips to the Grand Canal in Dublin, with Tad importantly hefting a hazel wand and carrying a tin filled with a quantity of writhing, bug-eyed maggots which he would examine with masculine pride every five minutes, just so that he could make her squeak with dismay, and that made her wonder what Tad was doing as well. It would be a lovely day in Dublin of course, that went without saying. She could hardly remember any dull days in Dublin, either the sun was shining or the snow was falling in her dreamy recollections of her home town, and now she visualised Tad setting off to catch himself a few minnows in the canal, or maybe going down to the quays to see what he could pull out of the Liffey . . .

'So if we're left with only that phrase . . . Polly, would you like to come up and mark the last words, please?'

Miss Witherspoon was so nice, so polite, Polly thought dismally, making her way to the front through the rows of desks. Other teachers ordered, threatened, shouted, but Miss Witherspoon treated them like the young ladies they thought themselves, and never forgot to say 'please' when she asked one to do something, and 'thank you' when it was done. Now, Polly looked across at the board and saw at once that the unmarked phrase was an adverbial clause . . . as if it mattered! She stopped short, a couple of feet from the board, and turned to face the teacher. She could feel boredom and rebellion rising in her chest like the River Mersey rose when the tide began to come in, and suddenly she did not like school at all, or lessons. Not even Miss Witherspoon seemed worth the waste of this lovely day.

'Well, the t'ing is, Miss Witherspoon – what does it matter? I mean, who's goin' to ask us to analyse a sentence once we've left St Syl's?'

It wasn't a fair question, she realised that as soon as she saw the colour rise up the white neck and invade the face of her favourite teacher, and she was suddenly shocked that she had asked it. But having asked it she did not intend to let such a thing as fairness cause her to back down so she stood there, politely smiling, her eyebrows still raised.

'Well, unless you're intending to be a traveller, Polly, I don't suppose that geography will be of much use to you in your future life, do you?' Miss Witherspoon said with a very slight edge to her voice. 'As for mathematics, well, since you don't intend to become a chartered accountant I suppose one could argue that mathematics, too, has little use for a young person such as yourself.'

No one laughed. The class, to a girl, thought that Polly's question was fair and Miss Witherspoon's answer was not. Polly went on waiting. Miss Witherspoon sighed. She pointed to the board. 'Don't you know the answer, dear? Then I'll ask someone else to come up, so if you'll return to your place—'

'I do know the answer as it happens, but you're not after answerin' me question, Miss Witherspoon,' Polly said obstinately, keeping her eyes fixed on the teacher. If she had been a bad girl, the sort of girl that Sunny would clearly much have preferred, she would not be here at all, on this hot and delightful day, standing in front of the board in a stuffy classroom whilst the teacher tried to evade giving her a straight answer. 'You could say that it's kind o' useful to know that the Chinese grow rice, I suppose, or good to know Paris is the capital of France – for them cross-word puzzles – and even bein' able to add two and two is useful if you're workin' in a shop. But analysin' a sentence . . . well, I don't see the *use* of it, no matter how hard I try.' And in a final burst of bravery she added, 'Which makes this lesson seem a waste of time, so it does.'

Someone giggled. Someone else gave a muffled snort. Miss Witherspoon turned from a delicate shade of rose-pink to the dark red of a boiled beetroot. She pointed her chalk at Polly in a very decided sort of way, though her hand trembled a little. 'In that case, since my lesson's useless to you, you'd best go and call on Miss Rutherford,' she said in a voice which she strove to keep even, but which climbed a trifle. 'No doubt she will be able to convince you that I'm not analysing sentences just to waste either your time or my own,' she finished.

Polly had never been told to go to the headmistress before, but she found that she did not care in the least, and once outside the classroom door, decided that she would *not* go to Miss Rutherford to get told off for asking a perfectly respectable question. Instead, she would go quietly off home . . . No, she would go off to Sunny's home, and see if he still wanted to go to Seaforth for the day.

It was not hard getting out of the school – in fact, she just walked across the playground, through the gate and into the road. And she felt free, and lovely, and not in the least guilty. I'm thirteen years old, so I am, and that's too big for stayin' indoors on a hot day whilst a teacher writes on the board and won't answer questions, she told herself, padding along the pavement. She rather wished she had taken her carry-out with her, but that would have made Miss Witherspoon suspect that something was up. No, she would go round to Sunny's house and he would doubtless find her something to eat – and he would praise her for being sensible for once – and then they could set off for Seaforth, or wherever they decided they most wanted to spend the rest of the day.

Whistling a tune beneath her breath, Polly stepped out.

It took a good deal longer to catch up with Sunny than she had supposed it would, because when she reached his house no one was in at all, but a neighbour, an old lady who spent most of the day sitting on her front steps watching the life of the waterfront go by, had seen Sunny setting off earlier in the morning and had asked him where he was bound.

'He said somethin' about the Pier 'ead,' the old lady said. 'I wondered if he'd tek off to New Brighton, bein' as 'ow he's rare fond o' the seaside. This time a year ago, he were sellin' ice cream over there, wi' a bicycle an' cart.'

So Polly, though a little daunted by the vagueness of the neighbour's suggestions, set off for the Pier Head, and it was here that she found him, leaning on the handlebars of a stop-me-and-buy-one bicycle whilst he studied the goods set out in the window of the small shop which huddled beneath the docker's umbrella.

'Sunny, I'm out o' school,' Polly had shouted, running across the roadway and grabbing his arm. 'Where d'you get the bike?'

'From the factory, of course,' Sunny said. He sounded rather cross. 'Honest to God, Poll, what a girl you are for messin' a feller about! I'd not have hired the bleedin' bike if I'd known you was goin' to sag off school after all – now what'll I do?'

'Whatever it is, I'll do it as well, so I shall,' Polly said peacefully, turning to stare into the shop window which seemed to be interesting Sunny so much. 'What does it matter about the bike, Sunny? You can push instead of ride, when I'm out o' breath wit' runnin'.'

Sunny's frown disappeared and he grinned at Polly, all his annoyance seeming to melt away. Then he turned round and began to wrench open the metal container which was strapped to the rear part of his bicycle. 'It don't matter about pushin', queen,' he said. 'Here, I'll mek you up a wafer. I were goin' to sell this lot round here, where there ain't no one else sellin' it, so I could earn us some spare money for Sat'day . . .' he went on, gesturing to the ice-cream container, which was now open and sending a delicious smell and wreaths of white vapour into the warm air, '. . . only I didn't know they'd mek me hire the bike, so I've no money left. Still, you can have all the ice cream you can eat until I've sold some of the stuff an' made some gelt,' he added with his customary generosity. 'Eh, look, a customer!'

Polly, standing beside him and licking her wafer, saw very soon that Sunny's instinct had been right about selling the ice cream. Within five minutes he had a small queue of people waiting, within ten minutes a long queue. After an hour he was regretfully scraping the bottom of the container and the old leather bag slung round his chest and one shoulder literally bulged with pennies and ha'pennies.

'Come wi' me to tek the bike back,' he suggested presently, having closed the lids of the container and turned the bicycle back towards the main road. 'I'll gi' you a seater; hop on!'

Nothing loth, Polly hopped, and very shortly the two of them, having concluded their business with the ice-cream factory and handed back the hired bicycle, were jumping aboard a tram and heading for the overhead railway.

'Seaforth Sands, here we come,' Sunny said blissfully, as they got off the tram at the Pier Head and went to buy their tickets. 'Eh, you won't regret it, young Poll – and I called you a goody-goody! Yet here you are, saggin' off school wi' the best of 'em.'

'I know,' Polly said. 'And I don't feel at all guilty, I just feel happy.'

'So you ought,' Sunny said decidedly. 'Two returns to Seaforth, please, mister.'

When, tired but happy, Polly got home that evening she waited for Mammy to start asking her just what she had been up to, leaving school in the middle of the morning, but Deirdre said nothing. She had taken Peader in his wheelchair to Princes Park, and the two of them had wandered amongst the flower beds and the lawns, and admired the lake and the ducks, and it had put Peader in mind of the crossing cottage and how he had enjoyed his life there. The two of them, Deirdre told Polly, had spent a wonderful day planning how they would go back to the country when Peader retired and how, until then, Peader would potter about the house and maybe take on a simple little job like stuffing envelopes, or helping someone with their books, whilst she worked outside the home for a while. This meant that they could, she hoped, save up sufficient money for a place in the country again.

'Not to buy,' Deirdre added hastily, seeing her daughter's eyes widen. 'Just to rent . . . but we'll need money to live on, and though the railway pension's a help, we'll need a bit more earned if we're to put anything by for a rainy day.'

'Do – do you really think Daddy will work again?' Polly asked, as Deirdre cleaned lettuce and sliced tomatoes whilst she herself cut and buttered the bread. 'Only his walkin' doesn't seem to get much better, no matter how hard he tries. And sometimes I've wondered whether he could stand bein' in some ticket office all day, so I have.'

Deirdre looked all round her, clearly checking that Peader was still reading his book in the front room and not about to appear in the kitchen, then lowered her voice. 'Sure an' you're a sensible girl, Polly me love, so I don't mind tellin' you that it'll be a long job, if it happens at all. But if he's here, at home, wit' something to take his mind off himself, then I t'ink he'll get better quicker. I don't mind telling you there's days when I don't know which way to turn for the rent, let alone extras. Ivan seems to go through trousers like nobody's business. We managed while me little job lasted but since then . . . If only I could get another job . . . But work's hard to come by.'

So Polly went to bed with a good deal to think about despite not having had to pay for her day's illicit pleasure. She wished that Deirdre did not have to work, but being a practical person, she realised that every family needed a wage-earner. So if Mammy works now, then as soon as I'm fourteen I'll get a job and she can go back to being a housewife again, she told herself, snuggling under the covers. And though it's grand, so it is, that no one at home knows about me day out, tomorrer I'll probably get a good scolding, if nothing worse.

Yet when she went into school next morning she was neither seized upon nor punished. 'Miss Witherspoon said you'd been unwell in class, and had probably gone home rather than risk upsetting the lessons,' her class teacher, Miss Chardwell, had said. She had stopped Polly as the girls were streaming past her after a history lesson, heading for the playground and twenty minutes of comparative freedom.

'But another time, Polly, just tell me you're feeling poorly and want to go home. As your class teacher I'm responsible for your well-being, you know. What exactly was the matter?'

'Sorry, Miss Chardwell,' Polly said. She decided to buy Miss Witherspoon a bunch of roses and bring them in to school the following day. What a sport old Withers was, not to give her away – and she had behaved awful bad, she knew it. 'It was women's troubles, miss,' she added with relish, since her class teacher was still looking at her enquiringly. She knew that there were such things as women's troubles, she had heard her mammy talking about them, but as yet they had not troubled her. But having been bad yesterday, a little lie to keep the stick from her back seemed only sensible.

'Oh . . . I see,' Miss Chardwell remarked, turning away. She went rather red as she did so and Polly, fascinated, wondered what she had said. Mammy and Alice's mam, Dora Eccles, talked about women's troubles in hushed voices when the men were about, but loudly enough in all-female company. Still, Miss Chardwell was a teacher, not entirely a woman, so perhaps that made a difference, Polly decided, returning to the playground and her pals.

Out there, she asked Alice and Sylvia about women's troubles but though they both giggled and said it wasn't something you should talk about to teachers, they seemed to have very little more idea than Polly. 'When you get 'em, you're a woman growed,' Sylvia said, and so not unnaturally Polly thought that it must have something to do with having to wear a bust bodice because your chest bounced about otherwise, and then forgot it. Why should she worry, after all? She had always been

134

taught that badness was always found out and that only goodness was rewarded, but Sunny had laughed this notion to scorn and he had been proved right. She had been downright wicked, now that she thought about it, but she had enjoyed a marvellous day out and was clearly not going to suffer for it. Perhaps, Polly thought, it's just a waste being good. Perhaps a little wickedness now and then added spice to life. Or perhaps she was beginning to grow into a different girl, the sort of girl Sunny liked, but her mammy and daddy – and Tad – might not like at all. As for her guardian angel . . . Polly gave a superstitious little shudder. She decided she would have to think very hard before she risked mitching off school again – her angel might not approve!

Deirdre had decided very soon after Peader got home from hospital that she would have to think about getting another job. She had enjoyed working in the dress shop, but it had been a long day and she knew the children had not liked being left with so much to do. What was more, though the money had been useful, with only four weeks' work it had been impossible to put any money aside, so another job it would have to be, whether she liked it or not. She had always worked as a young woman – until Polly had arrived, that was. Then her menfolk had seen that she had sufficient money to stay at home, and she had been glad to do so, not from laziness, but because she had always felt that children needed at least one parent in the home. So from the moment Polly had arrived Deirdre had concentrated on being as good a mother and housewife as she could possibly be. Oh, she had done small jobs from time to time, taking in washing and ironing to earn something extra towards

Christmas, fruit-picking in summer when she could take the children with her, even 'obliging' a woman in one of the big houses with a few hours' cleaning when Polly and Ivan had both been in school. But that had been casual work, and in a city she knew like the back of her hand. Liverpool was still strange to her; she did not even know in which direction to walk if she wanted to find the sort of houses which would employ staff, and the staff themselves would be strangers to her. She knew herself to be clean, hardworking and of good appearance, but would that be enough? She was in her late forties and thought that was too old to try for shop work. There was, as everyone kept reminding her, a Depression on, and she guessed that shopkeepers would rather employ young girls that they could underpay and overwork rather than a mature woman like herself who would expect at least a show of fairness.

Cleaning in some large private house was the obvious choice, but she was afraid that it might involve taking a long tram ride, which would mean being away from Peader for more hours than she needed to be. Then there was taking in washing, but although she knew some women still did this, the pay was poor, the work incredibly hard, and in winter, Peader would be sitting in a room which was full of the steam of drying sheets half the week, and she was determined not to do anything which might undermine his chances of a complete recovery.

So a couple of weeks after her talk with Polly, when she had despatched the children to school, Deirdre helped Peader to dress and to eat his breakfast, settled him in a chair by the back door with the morning paper, and told him she was going shopping.

'Shan't be long, me darlin',' she assured him, and

he never queried her best hat, a jaunty lilac-pink pill-box with a tiny veil, or her navy coat and skirt with the matching shoes. He just smiled his slow, sweet smile and told her to be as long as she liked, for hadn't he the paper to read now and the good fresh air coming in through the open back door?

'I'll come out with you this afternoon,' he said in his slow, careful voice which had grown, alas, slower and even more careful since the stroke. 'If you'll not mind wheelin' me a way?'

Deirdre dropped a kiss on the top of his head and squeezed his shoulder. 'I love to wheel you, so I do,' she assured him. 'We'll go down to the docks and watch the shipping if the sun goes on shining. You'll enjoy that.'

'I'm not so keen on all them handsome sailors watchin' you, alanna,' Peader said, making her smile. 'I'll peel some spuds for you while you're out gadding.'

Deirdre thanked him, trying to ignore the stab of dismay which went through her. The trouble was, Peader found the knife difficult to handle and sometimes she ended up with what looked more like marbles than spuds. But there you were, trying his hand at small tasks was all part of him getting better, the doctor said so.

'Well, only if you're bored wit' the paper,' she said as she went out through the back door. She crossed the yard with a brisk step, opened the gate into the jigger and turned and waved, only Peader was already holding the paper very close to his eyes and squinting at the headlines and didn't look up. I'll have to get him some spectacles, she told herself as she made her way down Tatlock Street. But I'll leave it until I've fixed meself up wit' some work, then I won't have to worry about the cost.

It was a fine morning, however, and Deirdre, who had a naturally optimistic nature, found it difficult to remember that the family had fallen on hard times, that she had to work. The truth was, she had been rather lonely since moving from the crossing cottage into the city, and had frequently longed for the women friends she had had in Dublin, and in the village on the Wirral. Her conscience had kept her close to Peader's side, but if she worked, and brought in money, then Peader would realise that she was not being selfish at all, at all, but doing no more than her duty. And if working led to her making friends – Deirdre smiled to herself – then that was just a bonus, so to speak, a piece of good luck for her.

So Deirdre made her way to the Scotland Road and browsed along, keeping a weather eye on the windows for any sign that a worker was needed. And she had not gone far before she came level with a large cafe with the legend *Mathilda Ellis's Dining Rooms* written in fancy gold letters across the very large bow window. And beneath it, tucked into a corner of the frame, was a small white card. Heart beating with excitement, Deirdre bent and read it.

Wanted, a reliable Woman to assist with dinners and teas at Busy Times and to Wait on; supply own Overalls but aprons provided. She read it, with some puzzlement. That sounded odd! You had to bring your own overalls, that was clear, but they would provide you with aprons. Yet surely, if you were swathed in overalls, you were not likely to need an apron as well. However, it was the first job she had seen – and that meant the nearest to home, so checking her appearance in the window and finding that she still looked neat, Deirdre took a deep breath, squared her shoulders, and entered the Dining Rooms.

It was mid-morning, so a few women were sitting at the small tables in the window drinking coffee and talking, but the rest of the very large room was empty. However, there was a till behind a glass panel in one corner and a woman in a navy dress with her grey hair pulled back from her face into a neat bun and a pair of small gold spectacles halfway down her thin nose, was sitting there, head bent, writing in a large ledger. When the bell rang to announce Deirdre's entrance she looked up, then looked down at her work again. She thinks I'm a customer, so she does, Deirdre thought with some dismay. Oh dammit, she won't like it when I tell her it's after the job I've come!

But here she wronged the lady at the till. When Deirdre walked across towards the till and stammered that she had come about the card in the window she half-rose to her feet and gave a very thin, lemony smile. 'Ah, the job,' she said, with a world of satisfaction in her tone. She raised her voice. 'Miss Collins, can you come and take over the till for a moment?' she called. 'I'll go through to the office; I'm interviewing.'

In response a thin, harassed-looking woman came out of the swing door to one side of the room, eyebrows raised. She was clad in rather stained white overalls, had a white cloth tied around her head from which stray locks of grey streaked hair depended, and looked to be about fifty.

'Yes, Mrs Ellis?' she enquired in a voice in which Deirdre unerringly detected a touch of Irish brogue. 'Were you after wanting me? I t'ought I heered me name called.'

Mrs Ellis, for she was clearly the owner of the Dining Rooms, raised her eyes to heaven and said: 'Yes, I did call you, Miss Collins. This – this person has come about the job. Will you keep the till for me whilst I have a few words with her?'

No brogue there, Deirdre thought. Only sharpness and impatience. Oh dear! But the older woman was speaking again. 'Right you are, Mrs Ellis,' she said, wiping her hands down the sides of her overalls. 'But who's to finish making me Yorkshire I don't know, for you're no hand wit' eggs and flour as I've telled you a t'ousand times.'

'I don't pretend to be a cook,' Mrs Ellis said, lowering her voice but not abating the sharpness of it one bit. She jerked her head at Deirdre. 'Follow me.'

Half an hour later Deirdre emerged from the Dining Rooms. Despite some private doubts, she felt on top of the world. She had got the job, which seemed to be just the sort of work she could do. She would go in at eleven thirty each weekday morning and remain there until six thirty, when what Mrs Ellis described rather grandly as the 'evening shift' came on. On a Saturday she had schoolgirls, she said, from the local convent, eager to make some money in their spare time, so Deirdre guessed that the 'evening shift' was probably made up of the same young girls.

Her own work would consist of laying, clearing and wiping down tables and serving the customers, and when not doing this she would assist with the cooking, which was in the capable hands of 'my junior partner, Miss Collins'. The washing-up, she was told, was done by a cheerful, cross-eyed woman, who must have weighed ten stone though she was less than five feet tall. Her name was Naomi, and whenever she caught Deirdre's eye she grinned and winked, which, combined with a squint, was somewhat confusing, though Deirdre realised that it was a friendly overture.

Deirdre had been told that she must provide herself with three overalls, preferably white but Mrs Ellis was willing to accept colours until her new worker had earned enough money to purchase the white ones.

'Skirt and jumper, or a dress, it doesn't matter which provided they are black, clean and in a good state of repair,' Mrs Ellis had told her. 'We provide the aprons. You will wear your black skirt and top with the white frilly apron round your waist when you are waiting on tables and the overalls whilst doing kitchen work.'

Deirdre had agreed meekly to all this, for the money was a little better than she had imagined; she thought that this was probably because she would be doing the work of two or three people, but reasoned that beggars could not be choosers.

'Can you start tomorrow, Deirdre?' her new employer had asked. She pronounced the name English fashion, as though it were spelt 'Deirdree', but Deirdre decided not to correct her. Not yet. Mrs Mathilda Ellis, she had already guessed, was not a woman to take correction lying down. No point in getting her back up before I've even started the job, Deirdre had thought, and was then told by Mrs Ellis that the customers would call her 'miss', and that she was not to tell them she was married.

'We are all referred to as miss, except myself,' she said grandly. 'As the proprietor, I am respected more as a married lady, I feel.'

She had introduced Deirdre to the other waitress too, the one who came in early for the breakfasts and morning coffees and then came back at five thirty to help out with the evening rush. Her name was Trixie and she was a pretty redhead of thirty or so with a roguish twinkle in her green eyes and a ready smile which endeared her immediately to Deirdre.

'Regardin' your clo'es, if you can't find nothin' black, chuck, we're abou' the same size, so you can always borry from me,' Trixie said in a thick Liverpool accent, lowering her voice when Mrs Ellis had returned to the till to take a customer's money. 'It ain't a bad job, if your feet'll stand up to it an' you're strong, 'cos the fellers who come in for dinners tips good, 'specially if you're quick. Of course, ole Ellis is a drawback—' She broke off as Mrs Ellis turned away from the till and came towards them. 'Well, see you in the mornin', queen,' Trixie said cheerfully, raising her voice. 'Don't forget, I live over the greengrocer's three doors along, so pop in tomorrer if you wanna borry some blacks.'

'Trixie's a hard worker, but common, very common,' Mrs Ellis said, as soon as the other girl had disappeared. 'That accent! But she's quick, and the gentlemen like her.' Deirdre must have looked startled for Mrs Ellis went quite pink and immediately began to talk again, faster than before. 'Not that I'd dream of encouraging . . . I mean, my girls must be above reproach . . . It don't do to get a name for employing flighty young pieces . . .' The older woman seemed about to lose herself in a maze of half-sentences, but Miss Collins came to her rescue.

'They're all good gorls, so they are,' she said soothingly. 'You've got to have a way wit' you, though, Deirdre, if you're going to make a good waitress. A ready smile, no offence took if a feller makes a bit of a pass, but he's got to be shown you aren't interested in that sort of t'ing . . . It takes tact, so it does, but you'll know what I mean.'

Deirdre thought she could guess, but simply smiled, agreed to be in at eleven next morning so that Trixie could show her the ropes before going off, and went proudly home to tell Peader that she was now an employee and would be bringing in an extra eighteen and sixpence a week, plus tips, and might sometimes be given leftovers into the bargain.

Polly and Sunny were walking up the Scotland Road, arguing hotly over what they should do that day. Sunny wanted to go fishing at Seaforth Sands but Polly, who had had some of that, said it was boring and why could they not catch the next ferry to Woodside and go into the country for the day? Sunny had a proprietorial arm about Polly's shoulders and Polly was snuggled against him when they stopped for a moment to look into a cake-shop window.

'Do we have enough pennies for a bag of sticky buns?' Polly was saying longingly when a voice which turned the marrow in her bones to ice said: 'Polly O'Brady, what in the good God's name are you doing here in the middle of the morning? I sent you off to school wit' your little brother and what do I find? Don't you try to tell me you aren't mitching, Polly, because I'll not believe you, not if you swear it on a stack of Bibles!'

'Mammy!' Polly gasped, thunderstruck. 'Oh, Mammy!'

'She felt unwell, Mrs O'Brady,' Sunny said at once, giving Deirdre the benefit of his most charming smile. 'Poor kid, I met up wi' her outside her school an' said I'd walk her home, but I thought mebbe she'd feel better wi' some food inside her, so . . .'

Polly might not have been the Saint Polly her

brother had called her, nor the goody-goody Sunny had taunted her with, but she was not a liar and she would have been ashamed to shelter behind the lies of another. She pushed Sunny's arm off her shoulders and faced her mother, very pink-cheeked and hot-eyed, but straightly, as was her wont. 'I am mitchin', Mammy,' she said in a very small voice. 'I didn't feel even a little bit ill, only it was such a sunny day, and—'

'It's all my fault, Mrs O'Brady,' Sunny said, charming again. 'I talked her into it, she wasn't at all keen at first . . . If you want to blame anyone, blame me.'

'I do,' Deirdre said steadily. 'She's always been a good girl has my Polly, and would be still if she'd not met yourself. Oh, I know a bad, idle feller when I see one, Sunny Andersen, and I'll t'ank you not to try to turn my good daughter into just such another.' She put her arm around Polly, so that she and Polly faced Sunny across the pavement. 'Leave her alone, d'you hear me, lad?' She swung Polly round, taking her hand in a firm grip. 'You go off home, as Polly and meself will. Then I'll go up to the school and see what the teachers have to say.'

'But it ain't Poll's fault, Mrs O'Brady,' Sunny said, sounding agitated now and almost running along beside them to keep up with Deirdre's fast pace. 'I told her to sag off school, I told her we'd have fun . . . it's all my fault!'

'Oh? You went into the schoolroom, did you, and dragged her out by one arm and a leg?' Deirdre enquired frostily, still keeping up her fast pace and not allowing Polly to hang back. 'And she does what you tell her, eh? When you say mitch, she mitches. Is that the story you're trying to get me to believe? Well, all I can say is, what next will you say to me daughter?

Will you tell her to take flowers from the graves in Anfield Cemetery, and sell them around the streets? Will you suggest that she goes into Mrs McKenna's and helps herself to a quarter of aniseed balls and two ounces of liquorice? Oh, go 'way, Polly's not afraid of taking responsibility for the wrong she's done.'

'Oh, but . . . please, Mrs O'Brady, it were all my fault,' Sunny said desperately. 'I just want to explain . . . want to tell you how sorry I am . . .'

Deirdre stopped short and turned to face him. She longed to give him a hard slapping, to march him home to his own mother and tell that lady just what she thought of her good-for-nothing son, but she knew that Sunny was too big, too old for such treatment and anyway, she knew better, she told herself, than to slap another woman's child. But she did not intend to have him trailing along behind them all the way to Titchfield Street. 'Go home, boy,' she said, in a quiet tone which nevertheless had ice in it. 'Go home and don't come near me daughter no more. I'm telling you I mean it, and if I catch you hanging around her it'll be the scuffers who'll come knocking on your door; hear me? Because as God's me witness, I mean to stop you seeing Polly. She's only thirteen still, so I'll have right, and the law, on me side in getting rid of you. I've telled you once, now I'm telling you again. Clear off.'

Sunny scuffled with his feet in the dust, then turned to Polly. 'Ah, I were only sayin' it weren't your fault, queen,' he began, but Deirdre did not wait for any more arguments. Further up the street she could see a policeman, strolling along in the bright sunshine with his helmet tipped back a bit and his white gloves in one hand. She pointed and Sunny, after a startled glance, sighed, shook his head, then turned on his heel. The last Deirdre saw of him was his back view as he hurried away down the pavement.

'Oh, Mam, he was only tryin' to say he was sorry—' Polly began, only to be told to hold her peace until they got indoors.

'For this sort of behaviour has got to stop, and I'm the woman who's after stopping it,' Deirdre said briskly to her daughter's downbent head, for Polly was staring at her sandals as though they were the only interesting things for miles. 'Not another word now, miss, until I've got you indoors.'

It was late before Polly got to bed that night. The row had lasted, on and off, all through the afternoon and into the evening, but at last she had capitulated, and now that she had done so, had agreed not to see Sunny again, she found that she was almost relieved. Ever since she had started her life of sin, things had been going wrong. Her angel, who was usually on the half-landing when she made her way up to bed, had not so much as appeared, no matter how hard she tried to peep out of the corner of her eye. Ivan had realised that something was going on and though he was too good a kid to tell on her, he had begun muttering that she would be in big trouble, so she would, when Mammy found out, and she had known that this was true. What was more her friends, Alice and Sylvia, thought she was being a proper fool, and had begun to count her out of evening entertainments because she was so often with Sunny.

And she had known, with increasing conviction, that what she was doing was really wrong. She had mitched off school whenever he asked her to do so, that was certainly true, but her conscience had begun first to whisper, then to mutter and, this past week, had been positively shouting. She knew it was wrong to mitch, to catch trains and ferries using tickets skilfully 'doctored' by Sunny. Even more wrong was going into shops and picking up any sweets or biscuits handy when the staff were serving someone else. She had refused to do it at first, but then it had seemed awful mean to enjoy the stuff that Sunny prigged in that fashion and never to do her share.

Of course, Mammy hadn't known about the used tickets or the sweeties, but it was almost as if she guessed that such things were a regular part of Sunny's days when he wasn't working. Polly had tried to defend herself against the only known sin, which had been mitching off school, but it hadn't worked.

'You've not got a leg to stand on, Polleen,' her father had said, his voice so sad and so loving all at once that Polly had had hard work not to start crying again. 'You lied to the teachers, you took in false notes to say you'd had a family bereavement, you simply let that young feller lead you round by the nose, so you did. And it isn't as if your mammy wanted to punish you for these t'ings, because she's said a dozen times she won't do so. All she's doing is trying to see that you behave properly in future. And she's doing that by askin' you to promise, on the Bible, that you'll not see that young feller again. After all, alanna, he's t'ree years older than yourself, he should be workin', not idlin' round the streets corruptin' a child still not even in the top class at school.'

So Polly had promised, with her hand on the Bible which Mammy had fetched out of the parlour, that she would not see Sunny again, although she didn't think that Peader's comments about Sunny's age were very fair – he was only a little older than her pal

Tad, and Polly herself would be fourteen next year.

'Only I can't stop him speakin' to me, Mammy, and it's awful rude not to answer, so it is,' she had pointed out in a small and shaking voice, for it had been a gruelling row in which she had done little but cry and protest that Sunny was all right really, so he was, and that she would never mitch off school again.

'I'm afraid you'll have to be rude then, alanna,' Deirdre had said firmly. 'You've made a promise, a serious promise, remember.' She had patted Polly's shoulder, then bent and kissed her tear-streaked face, rumpling the soft, untidy curls. 'Don't worry about it; he'll soon find someone else to go around wit', especially if he gets himself a job.'

So Polly, having given in and agreed not to see Sunny again, had sat down with her parents and her two brothers, eaten a meal, washed up and cleared away, and had then come up to her room, where she sat on the edge of her bed, slowly taking off her clothing, and wondering why, after such a dreadful time, she was actually feeling almost better. A peacefulness which she had not known for weeks and weeks was slowly taking possession of her. She supposed, as she pulled her white cotton nightie over her head and began to brush out her hair, that it was because at last her conscience was clear. She had known all along that Sunny had encouraged her to be a bad girl, she had even known that her guardian angel was so disappointed with her that she – her guardian angel was definitely a she – had taken herself off somewhere. She had stopped saying her prayers before bed each night, not because she wanted to do so but because she was afraid of what God would think if he took a peep at her and saw all the sins weighing down her soul.

And now all that was over. As she had been wearily climbing the stairs she had seen, on the edge of her vision, a shadow, a shade which she had been almost sure was that of her guardian angel, almost visible but not quite, in the very corner where she had always appeared to Polly.

I'm meself again . . . though I'm goin' to miss that Sunny tarble bad, Polly thought drowsily as she said her prayers and then climbed into her little bed. It were fun while it lasted, but I t'ink not seein' Sunny again is for the best.

Just before she fell asleep, she thought of something else too. She thought of the friendship of Tad Donoghue, far away in Dublin, Tad who had taken care of her and given her Lionel as a kitten and teased her and played with her, but had never led her into bad or sinful ways.

It was a pity, she thought, that Sunny was so handsome and Tad so plain. Of course, everyone knew that it wasn't looks which mattered, it was character, but she'd been awful proud to be seen out wit' Sunny, so she had, and now she would have to go around wit' girls again. And write to Tad and tell him . . . Or was it really necessary to tell him anything, save that she still thought about him all the time? She had boasted about Sunny's friendship, of course, but she need not actually admit that she didn't see Sunny any more. She would just write a nice, friendly letter . . . and with Tad she could be a little girl again, because he didn't expect anything else. Sunny's arm round her in the cinema, his habit of kissing her nose and tousling her hair, was something she would not miss at all. It was all a bit worrying and grown-up, and was one of the reasons, she realised now, that she had not been too dreadfully unhappy over her promise not to have anything to do with him in future.

She had not yet dropped off when her bedroom door opened softly and she saw her mammy. Once, she would have feigned sleep but now, because of the guilt she felt, she stirred and opened her eyes to smile at the figure in the doorway.

'Not asleep yet? Well, it's been a long day so it has but it's over now, and forgotten. Tomorrow's a fresh day for a fresh start. All right, acushla?'

'I'm fine, Mammy,' Polly whispered. 'Will you come and give me a butterfly kiss now, and tell me you aren't still in a bate wit' me?'

Deirdre with Peader, hovering behind her came and gave Polly the required butterfly kiss and then a cuddle. 'Oh, Polly, I can never be in a rage wit' you for more than a few minutes,' she said. 'Go to sleep now and forget all about today. As for tomorrow, it's another day as they say in the song. Goodnight, alanna.'

'Goodnight Mammy, Daddy,' Polly whispered. 'I'll sleep good now – I've said me prayers and I saw me guardian angel as I come up the stairs . . . just a shadow, you know, but she's there again so she is.'

Deirdre smiled, then bent and kissed her. 'All's right wit' the world, then,' she said softly. 'Sleep well, me darlin' daughter.'

Chapter Six

DECEMBER 1939

It was a cold day and Polly, emerging from Blackler's with her arms full of packages, paused for a moment on the pavement to put down her burdens whilst she straightened the belt of her navy-blue coat and pulled on her knitted mittens. As she did so her breath fanned out like fog round her and she gave a little shiver, then glanced up at the lowering sky. It wasn't snowing yet, but it was cold enough; they might have a white Christmas.

Someone else came through the swing doors and stopped short just behind Polly's packages. It was Ivan, also heavily laden, saying in a plaintive voice: 'Hey, our Poll, wharrabout that cup o' tea you said we'd have, eh? And them iced buns, an' all? It's hours an' hours since me dinner an now I'm that hungry me belly thinks me throat's been cut!'

Polly turned and surveyed her small brother. He was right, she had promised him tea and a bun if he came Christmas shopping with her, and he had been remarkably patient for a ten-year-old, waiting whilst she searched the big store for suitable presents for everyone. He had not suggested that they tried elsewhere either, knowing as he did that Polly, who worked part-time at Blackler's on a Saturday, got a staff discount which meant that she could buy the best without having to pay top prices. During the week she was an office junior in a very large firm of accountants on Sir Thomas Street, and on a Monday, Wednesday and Friday she went to evening classes to learn shorthand and typewriting, so no one could have said that Polly did not work hard. What was more, she gave Ivan tuppence a week pocket money, so she felt entitled to ask for help from him now and then.

'Oh aye,' she said vaguely now, however. 'But where'll we go, Ivan? It looks to me as if the whole world and his wife are out Christmas shoppin' this afternoon, and I don't fancy fightin' me way into one of the posh teashops and then havin' to wait hours to get served. How about if we go straight home and I make you a nice butty and a cuppa?'

She hefted her parcels again but Ivan was shaking his head. 'No, Poll,' he said obstinately. 'You *said* we'd go to a teashop, an' I've gorra thirst on me that can't wait till we's home. Can't we go to Cooper's, on Church Street? They do lovely cakes an' buns . . . doughnuts, an' all.'

Polly thought about reminding Ivan that there was a war on, but she had had it said to her so often now, that it was beginning to lose a good deal of its menace. Back in September, when war had been declared, they had all been very frightened indeed; Mammy had talked about going back to Dublin and Martin had joined the Navy whilst Bev, who had been about to go back to university, had thrown it all up and joined the Air Force. Only there had been a hold-up – too many young men trying to join the forces all at the same time, Peader had said wisely – and though Martin had got a ship and left his nice new house and Monica – quite quickly – Bev was still mooching around at home, neither one thing nor the other, he said gloomily, waiting for his papers to arrive.

'Poll? Aw, c'mon, it's only fair, I've done what you said, haven't I?'

Polly, who fancied a cup of tea herself, capitulated. 'You're right, Ivan me boy,' she said, turning in the direction of Church Street. 'We'll go to Cooper's – why not? Mammy won't be home yet, and Daddy will be havin' a nice sit-down before he puts the kettle over the fire and the spuds on to boil. Anyway, we'll probably have to walk home – look at the tram queues!'

'I don't mind walkin' if I've had me tea first,' Ivan said equably. 'And you're used to walkin', ain't you, Poll? You often walk to work an' back when you want to save your tram fare.'

'That's right,' Polly admitted. 'But I'm not usually all hung about wit' parcels, like a bleedin' Christmas tree. And don't tell the mammy I swore,' she added hastily, 'or you'll not have one iced bun, let alone a doughnut!'

'It's funny how cross the mammy gets over swearin', ain't it, Poll?' Ivan enquired, trudging along beside her. He was wearing a stiff navy coat much too big for him, grey socks which hung wrinkled around his ankles where they tended to end up if he forgot to put on his garters, and a large checked cap. When war was declared Blackler's had decided to do a half-price sale and the O'Bradys had been at the head of the queue which had formed on the first morning, thanks to Polly's advance information, so Ivan was now wearing on his back clothing which, his mammy had said gloomily, might have to last him for several years if the shortages being predicted came to pass.

'Swearing's wrong,' Polly said judiciously. 'Only what with the war, an' all, Ivan, us young folks have to relieve our feelings somehow. Only not in front of mammies and daddies,' she added. 'Come on, best foot forward!'

The pair of them turned into Church Street and headed for Cooper's, but before they had reached that haven of tea and buns, Ivan gave a squeak. 'Polly, you 'member that feller Mammy told you never to go out with again? The feller wi' the yaller hair? That's him, ain't it?'

Polly stopped short and followed the direction of his pointing finger. Ahead of them, a tall figure strode jauntily along the pavement, a figure topped with a good deal of wheat-coloured hair, though some of it was hidden beneath a sailor's hat.

'I think you're right, so I do,' Polly said, suddenly beginning to snatch the parcels from her young brother's arms. 'Yes, I'm sure it's Sunny . . . Oh, give me the stuff you're holdin', Ivan, and then you run and stop him for me! 'Cos I can't get up any real speed wit' all these bleedin' packages in me arms!'

'Oh! But Mammy said—' Ivan began, only to be abruptly cut short.

'When Mammy said that I was only a kid, and there wasn't a war on! He's in uniform – a sailor's uniform – if I don't stop him now I might never see him again! Run, Ivan, there's a good feller!'

Ivan accordingly dumped the rest of his parcels in Polly's arms and set off at a canter along the crowded pavement, dodging the people and shouting apologies as he went. Polly, with bumping heart, leaned against the nearest shop window and prayed that Sunny would not suddenly disappear as abruptly as he had done over two years ago, after the row with her mammy.

He had not disappeared at first, of course. Despite her promises, she could not simply shut her eyes to the tall, yellow-topped figure which lounged outside the school, popped up when she was doing Mammy's messages, appeared in church, head devoutly bent, eyes fixed burningly upon hers. But although she shed many tears over it, she had been true to her promise. Not a word had he got out of her for all his pleadings, and whenever possible she had avoided him altogether. And then one day she realised that she had not seen him for a week ... two ... three. She had asked her friend Alice to find out what had happened to Sunny Andersen and after a while, Alice had reported back that he had left the 'Pool. No, she did not know where he had gone, but she had been told that he and his mother had moved out of the old house. Did Polly want Alice to go round and ask the people who lived there where the Andersens had gone?

But Polly's conscience, which had been extremely uneasy over her tentative enquiries, had made it clear that asking for news of his whereabouts from his old school pals was one thing, cross-questioning the neighbours quite another. So Polly said no, it didn't matter, that it was best left, and Alice, greatly relieved – for she had never thought Sunny a good influence on her friend – had put the whole matter of Sunny's whereabouts out of her mind.

But right now Polly could see Ivan haring along the pavement and the yellow head bobbing along, the distance between the two lessening, and it occurred to her that after so long, the feeling between herself and Sunny must have changed. In the time since her mammy had put a stop to their friendship Sunny would undoubtedly have had several other girl-friends. And she had been friendly with several boys, though she knew that none of them had come any-where near being as good a friend as Sunny had once been. So what would happen when they met up again? Would they seem like two strangers, or would they fall immediately into the happy friendship – no, it had been warmer than mere friendship – which they had once shared?

But it seemed she was not to find out, for suddenly she realised that Ivan had turned round and was heading back towards her – and that the yellow head in the jaunty sailor's hat had disappeared.

'The bloody feller must have gone down a side street, or into one of the perishin' shops,' Ivan panted, coming up to her once more and beginning to reclaim his parcels. 'Cripes, I never run so hard before . . . not through a crowd o' people doin' their Christmas shoppin', that is. Sorry, Polly, but I did me best.'

'So you did, Ivan,' Polly said, realising that she was not sure whether to be glad or sorry that her brother had not caught up with her old friend. 'Oh well, mebbe it weren't him, after all. But I've not forgot me promise and after all that runnin' I reckon you deserve an ice as well as a couple o' cakes. Let's get into Cooper's and bag a table before they're all taken.'

But seeing that glimpse of someone who might well have been Sunny Andersen had definitely started something so far as Polly was concerned. She ate an ice and two doughnuts and drank several cups of tea and she laughed and joked with Ivan and marvelled at his ability to eat her under the table, but all the time she was wondering, wondering. She was almost sure that it was Sunny she had seen which meant that he had come back to Liverpool, even though, since he was in uniform, this might well be only a flying visit. And she was fifteen, going on sixteen – surely that was old enough to meet up with a young man who had once been her good friend? She had promised her parents that she would avoid

Sunny, have nothing to do with him, but she had only been thirteen then, and in school. Now she was working, earning her own living. That must mean, surely, that she could choose her own friends?

'Poll, is there another cup o' tea in that pot?' Ivan suddenly shouted, his face only inches from hers. 'Dear God, girl, is it deaf you're goin' now you're gettin' old? Because I've asked you ten times if I've asked you once!'

'Oh . . . sorry, I was just thinkin',' Polly excused herself, reaching for the pot and taking off the round brown lid. 'I'll get the waitress to bring some more water, then we can both have another cup.'

'I t'ought you must be thinkin' about that Sunny feller, moonin' across the table wit' a soppy smile on your 'ole face,' Ivan observed, when the waitress had supplied them with another jug of hot water. 'And I 'membered Mammy hadn't liked him overmuch. Mebbe I shouldn't have chased him for you, Poll.'

'It's ages since Mammy said she didn't like him,' Polly said, pouring tea. 'Anyway, it probably wasn't him at all – you know what it's like when you t'ink you know someone – when you catch them up it's always someone else altogether. Thanks for tryin', though, Ivan. You're a good little feller, so you are.'

'Tha's okay,' Ivan said magnanimously. He smiled hopefully. 'D'you want the last doughnut, Poll? Only there's a chink left in me belly just about the size o' that doughnut!'

Tad was saying goodbye to Dublin and the life he had known there, standing on the station platform and waiting to board the train which would take him across the water to join up. He looked wistfully at Angela as they stood in the pale wintry sunshine, hand in hand and neither far from tears, because their friendship had become a precious thing to them and they both, he thought, dreaded the separation to come. But for him there was the consolation of seeing Polly again – a Polly almost full grown and not the ten-year-old who had left Dublin almost six years ago – whereas for Angela there was nothing like that to look forward to. She would be terribly lonely – though he hoped that she might make more girl-friends, for he had always been aware of her lack of them. Polly, he also remembered, had had a *grosh* of girlfriends as well as a great many young fellers like himself, but that had been Polly the child, of course. He could not imagine her as a young woman, but he reflected that he could once have said the same of Angela, who had only been a kid, really, when they had first met. Now she was a beautiful, rather serious girl, seventeen years old and she had never wavered in her affection for him. Polly, on the other hand, he reminded himself sternly, had not just wavered, she had taken up with some English feller, and though she scarcely ever mentioned him now, Tad had not forgotten Sunny Andersen, even if she had. So he would meet Polly, he hoped, and renew their friend-ship, but it would not – could not – be the same sort of friendship that he shared with Angela, for he and Angela meant to get married one of these fine days, when they were old enough and when he could afford it, of course.

Affording it might not have been all that far away either, had it not been for the war, for in the years since he had joined Barnes's garage Tad had become a first-rate mechanic. What was more, Mr Barnes told anyone who would listen that Tad had flair. 'He ought to be workin' wit' a racin' team, 'cos there's no one in Dublin can mend a puncture faster, and he's the quickest worker I've ever had on the oil changes. But there you are, it's happy he is wit' us, thank the good Lord.'

Only then the war had started, and Tad had got restless. Polly's letters, which had continued to come across the Irish Sea with great regularity, even when Tad's replies were less reliable, constantly referred to the war. They had a blackout over there, and the government said that food would be rationed, though it had not happened yet. But they had closed all the places of entertainment – picture houses, theatres, ballrooms – which seemed uncommonly mean to Tad – and to Polly as well. She had written discontentedly:

There's nothing for me and the mammy to do but knit for the soldiers and sailors and airmen. It's all right for the boys, they've joined up – Bev's going into the Air Force and Martin's in the Navy – but I'm too young for everything that's fun. Mammy says I should be thankful I can't be called up, but I'm not. I'd look nice in the WRN uniform, so I would, except for the horrible hat, which is just like the one they wore at the convent school – ugh! But I'll maybe go for to be a WAAF when I'm old enough; the colour would suit my eyes. Only they want girls on the land and I do love the countryside, so I do – they might let me take Delly!

Tad thought it highly unlikely that anyone would encourage a Land Girl to take a dog along to her place of work but wisely did not voice such thoughts in his next letter. He had learned, the hard way, that a quarrel which takes place in correspondence takes a long time to sort out and can leave lasting scars. Instead, he told Polly that she should come back to

159

Ireland. *'Your daddy's been poorly for a long while and would be better here,'* he wrote. *'And you're Irish, Polleen. Why should you stay over there and talk about fightin their war? We don't have this here blackout, nor we haven't closed cinemas. Come back, an bring your family.'*

But this had apparently been defeatist talk. Polly wrote back indignantly to say that only a coward would run away when the country she lived in was in trouble, and whatever she might be she was no coward, as she hoped Tad would acknowledge. Even Angela, to Tad's dismay, talked wistfully of uniforms, and she had a good job now working as a secretarial assistant in the Pensions Office. She constantly reminded Tad that one day she would be a secretary, earning even better money, so he considered that she should not be thinking of uniforms, and a war which was not her country's own. Advancement, for Angela, meant staying just where she was, whereas for himself . . .

'I dunno about this blackout, an' rationin',' Tad's mammy said when he read her bits out of Polly's letters. 'But I don't see how we'll be after managin' to stay out of the war once it gets goin', for sure an' if enemy ships blockade British ports to starve 'em out, how will the food get to us? I'm after tellin' you, son, that t'ings won't be no easier here than over there, once the Germans get theirselves organised.'

But Tad did not believe it. The Irish and the Germans were *friends*, weren't they? Ireland and Britain had been at loggerheads for ever, so why should anyone expect Ireland to make things difficult for themselves just to please the ould enemy? Only . . . well, Polly was there, and several other O'Bradys, and he had a good few pals who had gone over to join up and fight against the Jerries. In the last war they had

called them Huns, Tad had thought inconsequentially, but now they were usually referred to as Jerries.
Like the pot under the bed was called a jerry, though
Tad had no idea why this should be so. But he
supposed that to each generation their own enemy,
and what had sounded right in 1914 was not quite
right in 1939.

He might have stayed in Dublin, enjoying his work
at Barnes's Garage, taking Angela to the cinema or the
theatre, going dancing on a Saturday, but for Phil,
who also worked in the garage.

'Me big brother Albert's joined the English Air Force,
an' it's desperate keen they are to get more fellers what
know a t'ing or two about engines an' the like,' he told
Tad eagerly one freezing afternoon when the two of
them were down in the inspection pit, trying to change
a shattered exhaust system for a new one. 'And the
engines in aircrafts is just like cars. Some of them are
even made by the same firms. They need mechanics –
fellers they can train to work on the aircraft engines an'
make sure they run sweet. Fellers like us, Tad.'

Tad stood up and banged his head against the old
exhaust which was covered in rust and mud yet
refused to budge. It was one hell of an impact, and a
good part of the exhaust shifted, covering Tad's hair
in rust. Tad cursed and gave the exhaust another
heave, causing it to wobble hopefully, then repeated
the remark. 'Aircraft engines? But we don't know
anything about 'em, Phil.'

'No, but nor do most fellers; that's why the Air Force
is willin' to teach you, if you join up and put down for
to work as a mechanic,' Phil said eagerly. 'I tell you
what, Tad, it'll help us in our trade when the war's
over, if we know a t'ing or two about aeroengines. I
t'ought if you'd be willin' to go, I'd go too.'

'To England?' Tad said doubtfully. He could not personally remember the Tans when they had rampaged through Ireland, but he could remember the stories about them all too clearly. They had killed this one and hung that one, fired buildings, raped women . . . But that had been a long while ago, and to wear a smart uniform and yet still work with engines was an ambition which burned in most of the mechanics who toiled in garages. And I've nothin' against the English now, Tad had reminded himself magnanimously as he and Phil heaved at the recalcitrant exhaust system. Some of them are grand, Polly says so and she should know. She's lived amongst 'em now for years and she's a girl what knows a bad 'un when she sees him. Oh aye, you can't pull the wool over our Polly's eyes!

So the long and the short of it had been that he and Phil had taken a day off and bought themselves train tickets to Belfast, where they had gone into a recruiting office to join the Royal Air Force. Time passed, and then on the very same day they both got letters telling them to make their way to England and to appear at Cardington, where they would be kitted out and sent for further training. So they gave in their notice to Mr Barnes and packed their bags and now here they were, Phil with his family clustered round, Tad with his hand warm in Angela's, having positively forbidden the Donoghue clan to come down to the station to see him off, for they had to make their way to England via Dundalk and Belfast, where they had been accepted by the RAF.

'It'll be hard enough sayin' goodbye to Angela,' he had told his mother and his younger brothers and sisters. 'But sayin' goodbye to you, wit' half Dublin lookin' on – well, I couldn't do it, I'd be blubberin' like a five-year-old. So I'll say goodbye at home and save me blushes.'

They had agreed, therefore, not to come, and he was glad, yet when departure time arrived and Phil's family surrounded him, he realised that he was also a little sorry. However, he hugged Angela, kissed her, and then told her to go; no point, he said, in hanging around, it would only make it harder for both of them.

He slogged his way on to the train and into a crowded carriage beside Phil, lugging his canvas bag. It held all his worldly goods and was, Tad reflected with grim humour, uncommonly light. Once he had slung his bag on to a seat he stood up and looked out of the window to give one last wave to Angela and one last look at as much as he could see of Dublin – and saw a small group of people coming on to the platform where they stood in a bunch, staring towards the train and waving desperately. He stared again, and all in a moment he realised that it was the kids – Liam, Kevin, Dougal, Annie clutching Sammy's dirty little paw, and Biddy, Meg and Eileen. Angela had not seen them, she was still gazing up at him where he stood, waving . . . he could see tears running down her cheeks. But somehow, at that moment what really mattered was that despite his strictures the kids had come to wave him off – and the mammy! She stood a little apart from the kids and she waved and waved . . . and now and then put up a hand to her cheek. And Phil, beside him, was shouting something, and the porters were running along the train slamming doors, someone was waving a green flag, Angela was standing back, dabbing at her eyes . . . and Tad felt tears on his own cheeks and waved and waved and waved, and didn't care that he was crying – so was Phil, so was everyone within eyeshot. And presently the train gave a long, sad-sounding whistle and began to move and then the station began to recede, Dublin grew smaller and smaller, the people could no longer be distinguished, one from another . . . and the train whistled again as it picked up speed and the little houses they were passing became fewer and fewer, further and further apart. Tad and Phil were on their way to war!

They didn't talk much as the train ambled its slow way across the Irish countryside. When they reached Dundalk however they had to leave the train and queue up for customs and for the first time a nagging doubt assailed Tad that the customs officers might guess they were leaving Eire for the war.

'What'll we do if they turn us back,' he muttered to his friend as they shuffled forwards. 'We'd never live it down, so we wouldn't.'

'We'd have to try again tomorrow,' Phil said philosophically. 'Oh janey, I wish I didn't have this old suitcase. Suppose they make me open it?' However such doubts soon proved groundless. There were a great many young men crossing over, mostly armed with bags or suitcases, and though Tad and Phil both told the official that they were taking outgrown clothes to a younger cousin living in south Belfast the officer merely grinned at them, marked their cases with a chalk cross and sent them back to the train to continue their journey across the border.

'Well, that's a relief,' Tad said as he sank once more into his corner seat. 'Another few hours, Phil and we'll be seeing England for the first time. It was hard leavin' me fambly but I know we're doin' the right thing!'

164

*

Despite himself, Tad was impressed with Liverpool. Come to that, he told himself, as the ferry passengers began to descend at the Pier Head, he had been impressed by Belfast, which was a larger city than he had expected to find north of the border. But the waterfront, with the huge buildings lining the edge of the River Mersey and the great Liver birds with their half-open wings outlined against the noonday sky, was awe-inspiring. So this is where my Polly lives, Tad thought as he and Phil joined the others making their way down on to dry land once more. I hope I'll be able to find her in this scrimmage – but then I know the address, I can see a grosh of trams waiting alongside the dock . . . I'll find her all right!

'Let's book into a boarding house first, though, Tad,' Phil said when Tad asked him if he could amuse himself whilst he, Tad, went and visited his pal. 'If it's all the same to you I'll come along too. I don't fancy bein' left in a foreign city all by meself.'

'All right,' Tad agreed with assumed reluctance – assumed because he suddenly realised that it could take him quite a time to find this Titchfield Street place of the O'Bradys. They were on the Goree Piazza now, and Tad remembered Polly telling him, in one of her letters, that it had been here that the slaves had been sold long ago. 'Look, there's a pub – the Vaults – see it? We'll try there, most pubs can put a feller up for a night or so.'

'It'll probably be noisy, but it's only for the one night,' Tad said as the two of them went into the beer-smelling, sawdust-floored barroom. The bar was deserted but the two young men could hear voices coming from the back somewhere. Tad dropped his bag on the floor and rapped on the counter, shouting:

'Anybody home? You've got customers!' He lowered his voice again, and addressed his friend. 'Eh, I can't wait to find Poll again – it's been five *years*, Phil. She'll have changed a good deal, I daresay.'

'You've changed a good deal yourself,' Phil said just as a fat, slovenly-looking woman came through from the back and grinned at them, showing a fine array of black and broken teeth. 'Oh, mornin', missus. We're after wantin' a room, just for the night, you understand. And we'll be off early in the mornin', so we will, for we're bound for the station.'

'One betwixt the two of ye?' the woman said. 'I'm the landlady, by the way – Mrs Collett. Folly me, fellers – just off the Irish boat, are ye? I've relatives across the water meself.'

'That's it; we're headed for Cardington, to join the Air Force,' Tad said. 'I expect you can tell us the way to Lime Street Station?'

'Oh aye,' Mrs Collett said. She crossed the bar, her downtrodden slippers scuffing two clear patches in the sawdust on the floor, and headed for a blackened open staircase in a corner of the room. 'The Air Force, is it? Most of 'em's joinin' the Navy, I'd ha' said.'

'We're mechanics,' Tad told her. 'I say, missus, you don't happen to know Titchfield Street, I suppose? It's near St Sylvester's church, I know that much. Can we walk there, d'you suppose? Only I've a pal lives thereabouts – several pals. I thought I'd look 'em up whilst I'm in the city.'

The woman stopped at the head of the stairs to consider the question with a wrinkled brow. 'Titchfield Street. Oh aye, that'll be one of them roads near the Scottie, I don't know exactly which one it is. Well, lads, you could walk but your best bet will be to catch a number 43 or 44 tram from the Pier Head and get off at Burlington Street and then ask again. There's folks which will be able to tell you all right and tight once you get that far.'

'Thanks very much,' Tad said gratefully as she flung open a door and gestured them inside. The room was quite large with a lofty ceiling and a big sash window overlooking the Piazza, and the bed was a double one with a sagging mattress and a darned white sheet folded down on to a faded pink cotton bedspread. The washstand was old-fashioned and marble-topped and the wardrobe looked large enough to house a regiment of soldiers, but despite Mrs Collett's unkempt appearance the room was clean and the bedlinen fresh enough. 'And this looks fine, so it does. What d'you say, Phil?'

'How much?' Phil said immediately and the woman grinned again, then pushed a lock of lank brown hair off her forehead with a fat, pink-palmed hand. 'Half a crown each,' she said, adding hastily: 'There's a war on an' call for me rooms, you see. That includes breakfast, an' I'll do a dinner at seven for one an' six a head.'

'That'll suit us,' Tad said. 'Shall we have a dinner, Phil, or would you rather get some fish an' chips?'

'A dinner,' Phil said at once. He slung his own bag on to the washstand and held out his hand. 'Can we have the key, please?'

'Oh aye, when I've 'ad me five bob,' Mrs Collett said, chuckling. 'I waren't born yesterday, fellers.'

Tad and Phil handed over the money and closed the door behind their landlady, then grinned at each other. 'She's all right,' Tad said. 'But we'd better get a move on, old feller. Are you sure you want to come all the way out to Titchfield Street, though?'

'I won't come all the way, but I've heard about the

Scottie – that's the Scotland Road, isn't it?' Phil said, going over to the washstand and pouring water into the blue and white china basin. 'There's shops galore, all sorts . . . I've an uncle in the Navy and he says he never leaves Liverpool without visiting the Scottie – and somewhere called Paddy's Market, an' all. So if we go up together, we can come back separate.'

'Right. And look, Phil, if me luck's in I'll get asked in for me tea, very like, so if I'm not back by six, just explain to Mrs What's-her-name, will you?'

'Sure I will, so,' Phil said peacefully. He began to wash his face, not bothering with soap, ducked his head under the water briefly and then smarmed his hair flat to his scalp with both hands. 'Your turn now, Tad.'

Tad found Titchfield Street without difficulty, but as he had feared, the house was empty. He knocked as hard as he could, and even went round the back, but then, shrugging, he did the only thing he could. He wrote:

Dear all,
   I'm off on the train to Bedford tomorrow morning, early, but thought I'd just nip in and see you whilst I was in Liverpool. Will come back later, and hope there's someone home. All the best,
   Tad Donoghue.

He shoved this brief epistle through the letter box in the front door and then headed back to the Scotland Road, where he met up with Phil almost at once, since he had been such a short while away.

'I'm coming back this evening, around eight,' he

168

told Phil. 'They're all out so I left 'em a note, but at least this means that Poll can make sure she's in when I come back. Now what'll we do?'

'Take a look around,' Phil said. 'There's a grosh of shops and stuff's cheap compared with home, so it is. We'll ask the way to Paddy's Market presently — that's good, I've heard a thousand fellers say so.'

'Right,' Tad said. He was happy to do anything which would occupy the time between now and eight o'clock. 'There's some dining rooms just up the road, I passed 'em on my way back to you. We might get a meal there, or at least tea and a bun.'

Phil agreed and the two young men began to examine the shop windows.

At a quarter to eight Tad was walking along the Scotland Road once more, anticipation tightening into knots in his stomach. Very soon he would be seeing Polly after rather more than five years, and he found that her old magic was still at work. Angela might be his girlfriend, but he suspected that Polly would always have a special place in his heart.

So Tad trod the pavement with the palms of his hands damp and his heart beating overtime. His hair had been Brylcreemed to his head but because of its tendency to curl, it had not remained fashionably sleek for long. Still, Polly wouldn't mind, she wasn't a girl, Tad knew, to be taken in by appearances. Nevertheless he had done his best. A brand-new tie, checked in red and blue, was definitely eye-catching and the white of his brand-new shirt could have scarcely been surpassed. He had polished his best black shoes until he could see his face in them and despite the cold he had not worn his overcoat, which was a sight too small for him, though he carried it over one arm – no point in getting caught in a downpour and half-freezing to death.

It was very dark in the street now without any shop windows blazing and with what traffic there was showing only the cold, dim blue light of the special lamps the regulations allowed. People, mainly dark-clad, passed him, the pale ovals of their faces just about visible once your eyes got used to the gloom. Good thing there was a moon, Tad reflected, otherwise God knows how folk in cities managed to make their way about. And you took your life in your hands when you crossed the road; bicycles, for the most part, did not bother with lights at all and dashed along at a good old rate, the riders trusting to speed and their ability to swerve to save themselves from becoming killers or corpses.

He was about to cross over himself, in fact, when he saw a small group of people coming towards him. One of them, a girl, had primrose hair of such fairness that you could see it gleaming silver in the moonlight, and although he could only see the blur of her face, there was something familiar . . .

'Sure an' wouldn't I get out early when it's your last leave, me dearest?' the girl said, as she and the young man on whose arm she swung came alongside Tad. 'Nothin' would have made me stay late tonight, not if they'd been willin' to pay me a fortune!'

'Polly?' Tad said uncertainly. 'Is it yourself, Poll?'

The girl half-turned her head. Her face, in the moonlight, was all white and silver, the eyes hidden in the deep shadow, her mouth half-open still in speech. She said: 'Who's you when you're at home?'

The young man on whose arm she hung, however, had no intention of allowing her to stand in the street exchanging small talk with a stranger. He gave her arm a sharp tug, pulling her past Tad. 'She's me girl, an' she don't know you, no more'n I do,' the young man said sharply. 'Wharrer you think you're doin', accostin' a young lady in the street? Come on, Poll,' and he pulled her sharply away.

Tad stood for a moment, sick with horror. His Polly, behaving in such a way! Well, she had changed and no mistake – she'd not recognised him, her old playfellow, for a start off, and wasn't that a dreadful thing, for she should have been expecting him, having, he assumed, read his note when she got home.

For a moment he stood, irresolute, on the edge of the pavement. Then, very slowly, he turned back the way he had come, feeling more miserable than ever before. She had looked at him and not recognised him! She had allowed herself to be pulled away from him by a young feller she must, clearly, think pretty highly of to have treated her old friend so. Well, no point in going round to Titchfield Street now, he might as well take himself back to his lodgings and go to bed. They had an early start in the morning, best get a good night's sleep.

By the time he reached the Vaults, of course, he was beginning to have second thoughts. He sat in the downstairs bar drinking beer and playing poker with Phil and a couple of lads who had just signed on as ratings in the Navy, puzzling over the nasty little encounter. He was no longer at all sure that it had been his Polly – Polly O'Brady – that he had met in the darkened street. There must be a hundred girls called Polly in Liverpool, and probably a good few of them lived on or near the Scotland Road. And as for the hair, there were hundreds of blondes in Dublin which probably meant thousands in this great city. Most of them were bottle blondes, he knew, but he could not always tell the difference between bleached and natural even in daylight, and moonlight was the trickiest light there was, just about.

He had not said too much to Phil, only that he had missed Polly, who had gone out, but now he got to his feet a little uncertainly. 'Could you go on wit'out me, fellers?' he said rather thickly, for he did not normally drink more than a pint in one evening and now his score was at least three. 'I think I'm after going back to Titchfield Street to see if me pal's back yet.'

'You can't do that, Tad,' Phil said. 'It's after ten o'clock, so it is, and the family will be in bed and won't thank you for disturbing them. Besides, after this hand we'd best make our way to bed ourselves. We don't want a black mark against us at the very start because we've missed the bloody train!'

So Tad had sat down again, and presently the game finished, with Tad, oddly enough, four shillings the richer, when you thought how far his mind had been from the game, and the four of them made their way to bed. Tad decided, as he pulled the blankets up round his ears, that he must write to Polly first thing, and make some excuse for not turning up in Titchfield Street. The more he thought about the encounter, the more he became convinced that the girl he had met had not been Polly.

But a letter will explain it all, he thought sleepily, trying to keep to his own half of the bed, for Phil, already snoring, kept kicking and heaving at the covers. I'll write before I have my breakfast tomorrow, so's she'll understand.

'I waited in all evening, so I did, and not a bleedin' sign of the feller did I see,' Polly told her friend Alice next morning as they waited for the tram which would take them into the city centre. 'But something must have come up – Tad's very reliable as a rule. Or he was when we all lived in Dublin. I can't imagine him letting me down, not if he was able to come.'

'Oh well, once they're in the forces their time ain't their own,' Alice agreed cheerfully. 'He'll write and explain, I daresay.'

'Sure to,' Polly agreed, but she was rather cross with Tad no matter how she might excuse him to others. This was the first time they'd been within shouting distance of one another and he had failed to turn up – and he'd missed out on a treat too, so he had. Mammy had cooked a lovely supper and she, Polly, had baked a load of fruit buns. She had cooled them and parcelled them up and had meant to give them to him to eat on the train, and even this morning she'd not had the heart to hand them round to the rest of the family. Who knew, he might have meant this evening, he might yet turn up on their doorstep, stammering and apologetic, explaining how the mistake had happened. She would save the buns for one more day and if he did not come tonight, she and Ivan would eat them, which would show him!

All through the rest of the day, every time the office door opened, Polly glanced up hopefully, but there was no sign of a square figure with close-cropped hair and an anxious expression, so that evening the buns were ceremoniously served after tea and Polly got out a book and began to read, though in fact she was listening so hard for a sound on the doorstep and a knock on their door that she scarcely turned a page all evening.

'You know Tad, he'd not let you down,' Deirdre said comfortably when Polly put aside her book and said she might as well be off to bed. 'He'll write and explain, alanna, never you fret.'

'Oh, it doesn't matter,' Polly said with elaborate casualness which, she suspected, would not deceive her mother in the least. 'There's other times. Tad'll get leaves, I expect. Bedford isn't far away, like Dublin. He'll turn up again, like a bad penny.'

'So he will,' Peader said heartily. 'I must have stepped down to the Post Office when he come knockin' the first time. It's a pity, but there'll be other times.'

Agreeing, Polly trailed up the stairs . . . and saw, out of the corner of her eye, that the slight shape of her angel was not in its usual position at the bend in the stairs. Oh well, I'm growing up, so I am, Polly reminded herself, climbing the rest of the stairs and pushing open her bedroom door. Besides, she can't be there all the time . . . Oh, janey, I can't write to Tad, I've not got an address any more! Still, he'll write to me, I know he will. And with that she began her preparations for bed, pushing Tad's strange behaviour to the back of her mind, or trying to do so. Instead, however, she found herself thinking defiantly that Sunny would not have behaved so; if he had been able to come and see her he would most certainly have done so, even if he had got into the most awful trouble as a result.

Much comforted by this thought, Polly climbed into bed and presently slept.

Chapter Seven

Despite the war, the O'Bradys intended to have a good Christmas, and it certainly began well, Polly thought on Christmas Eve, as she joined the rest of the family round the fire. Peader was roasting chestnuts on the coal shovel, Bevin was whittling a whistle out of a smooth piece of pine, and Polly and her mother were knitting. Polly worked laboriously, Deirdre with precision and speed, so that the wool seemed to spin through her fingers and the needles clicked so rapidly that she sounded like a sewing machine, Polly thought enviously. Her own needles clashed together ever slower and Polly noticed, with annoyance, that she had dropped a stitch at some time or other and the resultant hole had now formed a small ladder which did little to add to the attraction of the khaki scarf she was making.

Sitting comfortably in the living room, Polly could hear an occasional gust of rain hitting the window panes and knew a moment of intense happiness – there is nothing like foul weather outside and a good fire inside to warm the cockles of your heart, she told herself, reaching for a roasted chestnut. Another gust made her think of Martin out on a tossing ocean with no warm fire, no chestnuts and precious little Christmas cheer. I'll write to him later, Polly told herself, and I'll work harder at the knitting. Earlier, she and Ivan had dressed the tree, with Polly's Christmas angel sitting demurely on the topmost bough and candy walking sticks, shiny silver and gold balls and small, gaily-wrapped presents hanging from every branch, and Polly was just covertly admiring it and wondering which of the little presents was for her when someone knocked at the front door. Ivan, who was nearest, pulled a face but got to his feet. 'It'll be bleedin' Alice, for you,' he muttered to his sister, but he kept his voice down, for although Deirdre and Peader both realised the inevitability of their younger son losing his Dublin brogue and picking up the local accent, they did not approve of the local swear words which were frequently on that same son's lips.

'It won't be Alice,' Polly said, but she turned towards the door nevertheless. 'Alice's mam was takin' her to see her gran tonight; they won't be back until ever so late, so they're goin' to Midnight Mass. Then they won't have to mess up Christmas mornin' by goin' to church. I wouldn't mind goin' to Midnight meself, so I wouldn't.'

Peader, fishing hot chestnuts from the ashes, said mildly: 'Communion doesn't mess up your Christmas mornin', alanna, it gives meanin' to it,' but Deirdre, still furiously knitting, looked up and smiled at Polly, though she shook her head a little reprovingly too.

'It's a period of calm in a busy day, so it is,' she said. 'And if you'd cooked as many Christmas dinners as I have, Polleen, you'd appreciate that quiet time more. If it's not Alice . . .'

But any more conjecture was banished by the sound of steps in the hallway, the door opening and Ivan ushering Monica into the room. In the years which had elapsed since they had left the crossing cottage nothing which Monica had said or done had endeared her any further to the family and Polly endeavoured to see as little as possible of her sister-in-law. Furthermore, when Martin had joined up Monica had moved out of their house and back in with her parents, who now lived in Southport, so there was a moment of astonished silence before a babble of conversation broke out.

'Monica, my dear! What in heaven's name are you doin' miles from home at this hour on Christmas Eve? What's happened? Is there – is there news of – of—' That was Deirdre, who had jumped to her feet at the sight of her daughter-in-law. She sat down suddenly, white to the lips. 'Oh my God!'

'Come in and sit down, girl,' Peader said comfortably. He turned to his wife. 'Don't you worry, alanna, Martin's fine; I'm sure that's what Monica's come to tell us, isn't it, eh?'

'What are you doin' here, Monica?' That, of course, was Polly, straight to the point as usual. 'I thought you'd moved back in wit' your mammy an' daddy. I thought you were all in Southport.'

'Sit down, girl, an' have a roast chestnut. Daddy's got a grosh of 'em ready.' That was Bevin, always the most phlegmatic of young men. 'Mart's all right, I'm sure of it. I'll go and put the kettle on, Mammy.'

Monica, who had listened to the babble of talk without uttering a word in reply, shook her head rather feebly when Peader proffered the nut and began to struggle out of her coat, talking as she did so. 'It – it's all right. I'm sorry I frightened you, Mrs O'Brady, I didn't mean to. I – I've heard from Martin and everything's fine. But me mam and dad took it into their heads to go up to Scotland to have Christmas and to see the New Year in with my aunt Pearl and uncle Alfred, and I – I didn't want to be so far away . . . I got the idea that Martin might be gettin' home for Christmas, you see, and Southport's a long way from Liverpool, and so I thought . . . I thought . . .'

'He's written? Oh, thank the dear Lord for that,' Deirdre said passionately. 'We've not heard . . . but I know it's difficult when a feller's at sea. When did you hear?'

'A letter come yesterday,' Monica said, shivering and holding out her hands to the blazing fire. Polly saw that her sister-in-law was very pale, without a trace of make-up for once, and that her usually smooth, carefully cut hair hung in rats' tails round her face. 'He s-said it didn't matter that I'd moved out of the house, he was sure I'd have a good Christmas, though it was unlikely, even if he got leave, that he could get all the way to Southport in the time he had ashore. So I thought . . . if you didn't mind . . . you see it's much easier for Martin to come to this house . . .'

'Of course we don't mind,' Peader said in his slow, placid voice. 'You'll have to share wit' Polly, but no doubt you realised that. And as you say, when Mart gets home he'll want to see you right away, an' if you're stayin' wit' us you're a good deal nearer than if you were wit' your own parents. Did you bring a few clothes? A bag?'

'It's outside,' Monica muttered. Polly saw that the colour was beginning to return to her cheeks and that her trembling hands were lying more quietly in her lap. 'In case . . . in case you couldn't fit me in, an' I had to go to a hotel . . . I'll bring it in.'

'I'll gerrit,' Ivan said. He sounded resigned rather than pleased, and Polly quite understood why. This would have been the first Christmas since Martin's marriage that they had not had Monica and Martin to stay and had had to struggle with Monica's obvious

178

urge to be anywhere but with her in-laws over the holiday, and they had all been looking forward to it. Of course, Ivan would be very sorry that Monica was in such a taking, but that didn't mean he was any fonder of her now than he had been ten minutes earlier! 'I'll take it up to Polly's room, shall I, Mammy?'

'Yes, please, Ivan. You're a good feller,' Deirdre said. She stood up and took Monica's coat, then frowned. 'It's wet – is it rainin', Monica?'

'It's pouring,' Monica said. She shivered again, and rubbed her hands over her wet face. 'Oh, I feel ever so odd, Mrs O'Brady, I think . . . I think . . .'

'She's goin' to faint,' Peader said, and tried to jump to his feet as Monica sagged sideways in the chair, but his movements were still slow and his wife was before him. She reached Monica in one bound and pushed the younger woman's head between her knees, then shouted to Bevin to make a cup of hot, sweet tea and bring it through as quickly as he could.

'The girl's wore out an' frightened half to death, what wit' the blackout an' the journey from Southport and her parents goin' off wit'out her,' she declared roundly, pushing Monica's wet hair away from her eyes. 'What's more she's soaked to the skin. Polly, go up and fetch down a decent dressin' gown, your red one will be just fine, an' some warm clothes – socks, a jersey, stuff like that. We'll warm her up an' get her right in a moment.'

Polly pulled a face, but knew better than to say what she was thinking. She stomped off up the stairs and by the time she returned to the living room, carrying the clothing her mother had requested, Monica was stripped down to her brassiere and pink, embroidered cami-knickers whilst of Peader, Ivan

179

and Bevin there was no sign. Polly raised her eyebrows at her mother as she handed over the clothing.

'In the kitchen, so's we could make the girl decent,' Deirdre said, reaching for the thick grey jersey which Polly had taken out of Bev's room. 'She's all floppy-like – giz a hand, Polleen, to get her into these warm t'ings.'

In ten minutes Monica, dressed in her borrowed finery, was sitting in the chair nearest the fire, sipping a hot cup of tea and explaining what had happened in a far quieter and more coherent fashion than she had been able to do earlier. 'Me mam and dad didn't realise I were going to try to stay in Southport alone,' she said between sips. 'I said I'd gerra friend in, only I don't know many folk in Southport yet. And – and it's a lonely house, or it seemed lonely once they'd gone. Only I'd ha' been all right, except that Martin's letter arrived. And – and I thought of him gerrin' home, and findin' his way here . . . and me up there in Southport all by me lonesome . . . Oh, Mrs O'Brady . . . Mam, I mean . . . I just couldn't bear it! So I put some things into me Gladstone bag and come as fast as I could, only I forgot me umbrella, and I missed the first bus . . . the feller wouldn't wait, though I waved and shouted . . . and a course I got awful wet an' cold . . .'

'Never mind, alanna, you're here now,' Deirdre cooed. 'Well, you're a lovely Christmas surprise, so you are, and Martin will be pleased as punch to find you here when he gets home. Now don't you worry about a t'ing, darlin', I'll get you a bite o' supper and then it's a warm bed for you, and sleep until mornin'. Polly, go an' make your sister some cheese on toast, wit' me homemade chutney on the side. Are the sheets on your bed clean?'

This was too much! Polly had often thought what fun it would be to have a sister, but Monica? Anyone but Monica! 'The sheets are clean enough for me,' Polly said, shooting a darkling glance at the new arrival. 'Whether they'll be clean enough for Monica I couldn't say, I'm sure. But I'll make the toasted cheese the best I can,' she added hastily, seeing a martial sparkle in her mother's eyes.

'Good. Now come along wit' me, Monica,' Deirdre said. She had dropped her knitting upon Monica's entrance but now she picked it up and put it on her chair, then took Monica's arm. 'Will toasted cheese suit you, me dear?' she enquired solicitously. 'It won't give you nightmares? Cheese can be after causin' nightmares, I forgot that when I told Polleen to make you some.'

'It'll be just fine, Mrs— Mam,' Monica said, still in the small, faint voice which Polly scarcely recognised. 'Oh, you're so good, and I've been so—' She began to sob and Polly, feeling self-conscious, slipped past her and into the kitchen, closing the door behind her. Once there, she took a long, hard look at her feelings. Sure an' she didn't want Monica sharing her room, no she didn't, but the girl *was* Martin's wife, and she, Polly, was mortal fond of Martin, so she was. And it wouldn't be for long; Monica wouldn't stand being cooped up in the little house for longer than necessary. Then there was her job. Monica had got a good job in an expensive gown shop when she had moved to Southport – she would not want to whistle that down the wind, Polly was sure. Apart from anything else, Monica liked spending money, and Polly knew that the small amount which the Navy sent home to her from Martin's pay would scarcely help towards the rent, let alone provide for such things as stockings, lipstick or a few sweeties.

Much heartened by this thought, Polly set to with a will and very soon she had laid out a tray with an embroidered traycloth and put upon it a mug of hot cocoa, the toasted cheese, some chutney and a little dish of stewed apple and custard. She added a white table napkin in a bright red ring, knife, fork and spoon, and set off up the stairs, mounting each one carefully so that she should not spill anything on the cloth.

She went into her own small room and there was Monica, tucked up in her bed, with her hair now brushed, her face shining with soap and water and a smile back in position. Not that she smiled at Polly – not she! Her smiles, it seemed, were all for her mother-in-law, who she had treated so badly in the past.

'Here's your supper, Monica,' Polly said softly, putting the tray down across her sister-in-law's knees. 'I hope it's all right for you, so I do.'

'It looks very nice,' Monica said. 'Thank you, Polly.'

'It's a pleasure,' Polly said politely if untruthfully. 'Will I be goin' to bed soon, Mammy? Will I be head-to-tailing it wit' Monica, then?'

'No, not tonight,' Deirdre said. 'You can sleep downstairs tonight, on the sofa in the living room. You'll do very well there, just for one night.'

Polly drew in a breath to expostulate. It wasn't fair that she should have to give up her bed, and on Christmas Eve too, when heaven knew what angels and magic might be abroad, for even if she no longer believed in Santa Claus, she believed in the magic of Christmas. Then she let out her breath in a long, quiet sigh. 'Yes, all right, Mammy,' she said. 'What did you do wit' me nightie when you tucked Monica up? I'd best take it downstairs if I'm to sleep in the livin' room.'

'Oh, I feel so guilty, putting you out of your room, Polly,' Monica said, and she sounded almost as though she meant it. 'Oh, and cocoa – just what I like before I go to sleep.'

'Your nightie's here, on the chest of drawers, alanna,' Deirdre said, passing it over. 'Now we'll leave Monica to her supper. Mind you eat it all up, me dear, because you've had a tiring day by the sound of it.'

Oh, so Monica's been telling her what a rotten old day she's had, has she? Polly asked herself grimly as she made her way down the stairs again with her mother close on her heels. Well, she's not done much for my day either, turning up here and putting me out of me bed! But there was no use repining, it was the sofa for her tonight. And it would, Polly reflected, be rather fun to sleep downstairs, and to watch the lovely bright fire gutter and die, and to sneak into the kitchen and let Delly in with her, so that they could cuddle up on the sofa together. Old Tom the cat might like to join them – sleeping downstairs wouldn't be so bad, and she would be first to see the tree in the morning too.

Back in the living room again, she saw her parents exchange a speaking glance and reflected that happy though they would be to have Martin back with them, they, too, were not as thrilled about Monica's unexpected arrival as they had pretended. Indeed, once the boys had gone to bed Mammy came down again on the pretence of checking that the fire was damped down and bent over Polly to give her a kiss.

'I know you must feel a bit put-upon, alanna,' she whispered, carefully tucking the covers in on the makeshift bed. 'But we're doin' it for Martin's sake, remember. May you have sweet dreams, me darlin' girl, and wake to a good Christmas!'

Polly lay awake for a while, enjoying the novelty of being downstairs when the rest of the family were in their rooms, asleep. And presently she began to think how lucky she was, and to wonder how Tad felt, in his barracks or whatever it was, down in Cardington.

He had written, explaining that thanks to a misunderstanding he had been unable to come to the house as his note had promised; the forces, his letter had said vaguely, were like that. And Polly had written back at once, of course, telling him how sorry she was to have missed him and reminding him that the O'Bradys were almost always to be found in Titchfield Street, and he must not hesitate to come and see them if he ever had enough leave to make the journey possible.

He had not replied to the latest letter yet, but a pal of hers, Nobby Taylor, had told her that the first few weeks in any of the armed services were pretty hard, and that Tad would not have much time for letter-writing until he got his first posting, so that was all right.

Grace kept writing, though. She had been horrified when war had been declared and had written at once, to say she was coming home just as soon as she could make the necessary arrangements. *'I don't intend to stay safe over here while my country fights these Huns,'* she had written fiercely – Polly could almost see the frown on her face.

I'm coming home and I'm going to fight as well, in whatever way will help most. After all, I'm a Salvationist and we're all soldiers, fighting evil and trying to do right. But I can't leave Sara and Jamie in the lurch. I must make arrangements. As soon as I've got a passage booked, though, I'll write and tell you, so's I can come to stay. The Strawb would have me – Matron writes almost as regular as you, Poll – but I'll come to you first. The O'Bradys have been as good as family to me, and that's the honest truth.

At first, Polly had waited daily for the letter to arrive, telling her when her dearest and best friend expected to be on British soil once more, but the weeks had passed and Grace had not been able to 'make arrangements' as easily as she had hoped, so Polly was still waiting.

I'll be glad when Grace is home, Polly thought sleepily to herself, eyes shut now but knowing, even through her closed lids, that the firelight still flickered. It would be fun if we could both join one of the services together – but then I'm not old enough, not yet.

Presently she fell asleep, and presently, too, she dreamed. She seemed to awaken in the early hours to find the fire out, the air chilly, and the Christmas tree looking shadowy and rather frightening in the darkened room. But she was snug enough in her blankets and merely looked about the room in a wondering sort of way, until she noticed Tad's present, the angel on the top of the tree, and it seemed to her that it would be sensible to climb out of bed and go over to have a word with her angel, now that it was almost Christmas morning.

She looked up at the little angel, with its golden hair, long white gown and gauzy wings. 'Merry

Christmas, angel,' she whispered up to it, and was sure that it smiled down especially for her. 'There's something I'd like to ask you, if you wouldn't mind.'

The little angel inclined her head very graciously, which Polly took to be a nice way of telling her to get on with it, so having thought for a moment she said slowly: 'A long time ago, me mammy and daddy told me I wasn't to see Sunny again. He was me pal, but he got me to wag off school, so he did, and I did some pretty bad t'ings.'

The angel looked sorrowful yet encouraging, and it suddenly occurred to Polly that though her own guardian angel was neither golden-haired nor clad in gauzy white, the two of them shared, at this moment, very similar expressions. So Polly, who often talked to her guardian angel when she was unhappy or puzzled, went on. 'But that was ages ago, angel, when I were just a kid. Now I'm almost growed, and me and Ivan t'ought we saw Sunny a little while back, in naval uniform, walkin' along Church Street just the way he always did. So Ivan chased after him, but he got away. Now d'you t'ink it would be wrong of me, angel, to try to see him again?'

The angel bent down, lower and lower, and she no longer looked like the little Christmas angel but just exactly like Polly's own guardian angel. She began to answer Polly's question, speaking very low indeed, saying that surely Polly's mammy . . . And Polly reached up and reached up so that she might be near enough to catch every precious word . . . and woke, to find pale sunlight streaming through a crack in the curtains and her mammy softly brushing the piled-up ash off the top of the fire and lifting the coals with a poker to let the air in underneath so that it would blaze once more.

Polly must have stirred or muttered, for her mother turned round and smiled lovingly at her. 'Happy Christmas, Polleen – did you sleep well?' she whispered. 'There's only you an' me awake in the whole house, for I t'ought I'd let the fellers have a lie-in, and Monica's curled up like a dormouse and snorin' like a lion. Do you feel like gettin' up and helpin' me to make some breakfast?'

'Happy Christmas, Mammy,' Polly said, keeping her voice very low. 'You'll never guess what! I woke in the night and me angel leaned over me an' said—' She stopped short. It had been a dream, of course, and now that she thought about it, she had only caught a few of the words that the angel had addressed to her in the dream. Besides, she was fifteen and three-quarters and should be too old for chatting to any angel, either the one on the Christmas tree or the shadowy figure she sometimes saw on the extreme periphery of her vision. She sighed; how difficult it was to know what was real and what wasn't, even if she was fifteen and three-quarters.

'What did your angel say?' Mammy asked. She sometimes looked a bit apprehensive when Polly talked about her angel, but she never even hinted that there was anything odd about a child who conversed with someone no one else could see. 'I trust she gave you good advice, and telled you to be kind to Monica?'

Polly giggled. 'I don't know what she was goin' to say, Mammy, but I t'ink what she *meant* to say was that I should tell you about me problem, an' not herself. The truth is, Mammy, Ivan an' me saw Sunny a few days ago. Just in the street, you know, not to speak to at all.'

'Sunny?' Deirdre said as though she did not know what Polly was talking about. 'Sunny what?'

'Sunny Andersen, the feller you said I wasn't to see again, and I haven't,' Polly explained, sitting up in her couch bed and hugging her knees. 'Only I'm old now, Mammy, and Sunny's in the Navy – at least he was wearin' that uniform – and I t'ought, if I bumped into him . . .'

'If you do, bring him home, acushla,' Mammy said gently. 'As you say, that other business was a long time ago, and I wouldn't want you to be upsettin' a feller what's fightin' for his country. Only bring him home, eh, alanna?'

'Oh, Mammy, I do love you!' Polly exclaimed. She hurtled off the sofa and flung herself into her mother's arms. 'I don't suppose he'll mind if I talk to him or not, because he's past eighteen now, and a man growed. But he was nice, and I'd like to bring him home, so I would.'

'Then that's settled,' Deirdre said. She pushed Polly gently towards the doorway. 'Can you wash in the kitchen, alanna, and dress there too? Then we'll make breakfast together once I've cleared this bed away and made the room neat.'

And presently Polly, washed, brushed and dressed, was slicing bread and laying the table and singing a carol as she did so, whilst upstairs various bumps and bangs seemed to intimate that the other members of the family were also getting up. She felt very happy, and at ease with herself in a comfortable sort of way. She *had* liked Sunny, and now that he was in the Navy he could scarcely get her into hot water – come to that, now she was working and not at school, surely the same applied?

So Polly continued to slice bread and sing and think happily about Christmas and wonder about the little packages on the tree, and the memory of Sunny's back vanishing into the Christmas-shopping crowds disappeared from her mind. Time enough to wonder what had been happening to him, time enough to plan how she would bring him home and introduce him to Mammy, Daddy and the rest of the family when they met up once more. For now, it was Christmas, her sister-in-law would be waking up and coming downstairs any time, and she must be really nice to the girl, for Martin's sake.

Oh the holly and the ivy, when they are both full grown
Of all the trees that are in the wood, the holly bears the
crown.

So sang Polly, working happily away in the kitchen, on the first wartime Christmas she had ever lived through. The blackout curtains were pulled back and the thin wintry sunshine streamed into the room and Polly, at peace with the world even if the world itself was not at peace, was suddenly sure that Martin would come home safe and sound and that Sunny and she would meet up again, as friends. Nothing but good could come of such a day as this.

Martin's ship had docked at three on the Christmas afternoon and by four o'clock he was walking across the almost deserted, frosty dockside and thinking peacefully that he and the rest of the crew of the frigate *Campion* had been extremely lucky. Their engine had gone on the blink a couple of weeks back and the captain had turned back to port as soon as he could. So now most of the crew had five days' leave – and over Christmas too.

Martin had been as pleased as anyone when he had been given this break whilst the *Campion* was checked and repaired. He had applied to join the Navy in April, believing, despite Chamberlain's 'Peace in our time', that war would come all too soon, and had comforted Monica over his departure by telling her that at least, when war did come, he would be trained to face it. She had not been pleased, of course, had said that he was too eager to get away from his city job and their small house, had accused him of becoming tired of her, of marriage, of his life in the city. Because she was not so far out he had explosively denied all her accusations and what had started out as a discussion had speedily become a full-blown row, with the result that they had parted awkwardly, both aware, he supposed, that their relationship was less strong, after more than three years of marriage, than it had been when they first met.

But now, knowing that she was safely tucked away in Southport with her parents, he was preparing to reach Titchfield Street with almost boyish excitement. It would be good to see the family, good to hug Mammy and Daddy, to buffet the boys on the shoulder, and to kiss Polleen. Of course he had seen them on a previous leave, but never alone, always with Monica either literally or figuratively clutching his arm, making it plain that he was hers, all hers, and was only on loan to his family.

What was more, the night alone in whatever makeshift bed his mammy could offer him would give him some much-needed thinking time. He knew that he was not being fair to Monica, criticising her because she was so possessive, but he did resent her obvious intention of keeping him away from his family. He had married her knowing that she was possessive and clinging so should not have expected her to suddenly become an independent and generous person. What was more, he had known for two years that she did not want children of their own, yet he was still annoyed by such selfishness – he saw it as selfishness, recognising it as a desire to have all of his affection for herself.

However, this was one Christmas Day, he told himself as his footsteps rang out on the icy pavements, which he would have with his family. He did not want to have to lie to Monica, to pretend that he had not had time to reach Southport that day. Now, it was no lie but a reality; dusk had already fallen and the streets were dark and difficult. A couple of trams had passed him, black, blue-lit ghosts with windows papered over and no headlights, but he had not attempted to hail them. The walk would do him good. He changed his kitbag from one shoulder to the other and stepped out, smelling the city smell of burning coal, cats and the contents of dustbins, almost enjoying it after weeks and weeks of the frowstiness of a small vessel crowded with men who found washing in such confined quarters difficult. Soon be home now! Soon have his mammy's arms round his neck, his daddy's hand in his! Tomorrow would be time enough to face Monica, give her the present he had brought, listen to her various woes.

As he reached Titchfield Street Martin felt his heart give a joyful thump at the sight of number 8 and, guessing that they were in the parlour though no glimmer of light showed through the blackout, he decided to go round the jigger and across the yard, then creep softly through the kitchen and the narrow hall and burst into the parlour, to surprise them.

Accordingly, he went round the back, opened the door and stepped in, basking for a moment in the warmth of the kitchen. The fire glowed, there was the most marvellous smell of roast meat and other good things and, although the lamp in here had not yet been lit, he could see in the firelight that preparations had been made for a high tea. The long wooden table had a checked cloth laid upon it, the cutlery was spread out and the best plates were ready to be piled with food.

As it's Christmas there will be cold ham left over from dinner, Martin thought longingly, taking off his duffel coat and hanging it behind the kitchen door. He began to struggle out of his boots, standing them neatly to one side of the back door, then picked up his ditty bag and slung it on one shoulder. Food on HMS *Campion* was doubtless as good as the Navy could manage in wartime, but it was still pretty dull stuff. For obvious reasons everything – or almost every-thing – was dried or canned, and although the frigate was rarely at sea for longer than a month, the crew had still got extremely tired of corned beef, mashed potatoes and the sort of peas to which you added a fizzy tablet in order to turn them from off-white to a more appetising green. There was the rum ration of course but it scarcely made up for the hardships and constant danger of being on the *Campion*.

As Martin crossed the kitchen he remembered the luscious taste of his mammy's Christmas cake and risked a side trip into the pantry just to reassure himself. There it was, standing on the slate slab, a white and scarlet edifice, as yet uncut. Martin, mouth watering, turned away and opened the door into the passage, his socks soundless on the red linoleum. He paused outside the parlour to adjust the ditty bag, since it contained the small gifts he had brought home for everyone. Right at this very moment, he had never loved his family so well. They were the salt of the earth, so they were; Mammy and Daddy the best parents a feller ever had, Poll and the boys the best sister and brothers. He grabbed the door handle and pushed it wide, grinning from ear to ear, shouting, 'Hello-ello-ello, here's Santy come to bring you what you most wanted at Christmas! And just in time for tea, so he is!'

Someone hurtled across the room and into his arms and Martin, fielding the girl, thought for one startled moment that a total stranger had mistaken him for someone else. Then all in a moment he recognised her. It was Monica, and he had thought her thirty miles away, in Southport!

He should have kept his mouth shut, of course. He meant to, but it wouldn't be silenced. Before he knew what he was saying he had spoken. 'Monica! What in God's name are you doin' here, when I t'ought you safe in Southport?'

His mother had jumped up as he entered, rushing to his side almost as quickly as Monica had, and now she said quietly, gripping his arm warningly: 'Isn't it a wonderful t'ing, me darlin' feller? Monica t'ought you'd likely be home for Christmas so she's come to stay – well, I can see for meself you're thrilled as can be, almost wit'out words!'

'Oh, I am, I am,' Martin said quickly, hugging Monica so hard that she squeaked in protest. 'Darling girl, you're the last person I expected to see here – I – I thought I'd have a quick word wit' me family and – and then mebbe get to Southport tonight, or tomorrow if I couldn't make it. I've got five days' leave – imagine that, five whole days ashore!'

By now Polly was hanging on to his arm and Peader was shaking his shoulder and grinning at him, whilst Bevin and Ivan were on their feet and crowding close, their faces alight with excitement. 'Me boy, it's the best Christmas present any of us could have asked for, to have yourself amongst us,' Peader said in his slow way. 'Come to the fire – we're eatin' in ten minutes or so, but until then sit yourself down and tell us how you come to be here.'

'Oh, we berthed this afternoon, so I got meself ashore as soon as I could and come on home,' Martin said. He still hadn't got over the shock of finding Monica in his parents' parlour, but had himself well in hand now. 'If I'd only had a forty-eight I'd have gone straight to Southport, of course, but since it's five days I thought I'd stop off here first . . . and now I don't need to rush off anywhere,' he added hastily, with Monica still pressed against him, her face hidden in his seaman's jersey. 'Well, I thought I'd give you all a surprise, but you've given me a better one.'

'So we have,' Deirdre said equably. 'Monica, you sit right down by Martin. Boys, go and wash up ready for tea and you, Polly love, go and warm the pot. Your daddy and meself will start slicing ham and buttering bread . . . because these two will have a great deal to say to one another, that I do know.'

Martin obediently sat down in one of the fireside chairs and as soon as his family had left the room Monica came and sat on his knee. Martin put his arms round her and gave her another hug, a gentler, more genuine one this time, and then turned her in his arms so that she faced him. 'Sweetheart – what a wonderful surprise! But you said you were living with your parents . . . I never dared hope to see you today . . . not unless I managed to – to make it back to the station . . .'

Monica heaved a huge sigh and snuggled into his

arms. 'Oh, Martin, I've missed you so! And – and your mam's been really nice to me, though that Polly . . . but never mind that. She's had to give up her room, and . . . well, I suppose I've not tried very hard with her. But I will now, really I will. I'll really try to gerron with your family.'

Martin kissed the side of her face and then bent down and rummaged in his ditty bag. 'Got something for you,' he said. And he pulled out the little square parcel which contained the box with the thin gold chain in it and held it enticingly before her. 'Want it now or later?'

'Oo-oh,' Monica said longingly. 'Only I'd better purrit under the Christmas tree, Martin, with all the other presents. It wouldn't be fair, else.'

And Martin, saying that he understood, put the parcel under the tree and began to tell his wife about his latest voyage and the course in gunnery which he would take, starting in the New Year. And he tried not to be glad when Polly popped back to tell them to come through to the kitchen for tea.

Grace was going home. As soon as war had been declared she had written to the Admiralty offering her services to the WRNS and had started to enquire about a passage to Britain, but it was not until mid-January that things began to happen.

The Admiralty had not replied, but she had been offered a passage by two Salvationists who were also keen to return to their native country. Mr and Mrs Carewe needed someone to help with their two small children, and who better than Grace? So she had cabled to the O'Bradys that she was coming home and now, with tears running down her cheeks, she stood by the rail of the SS *Queen of the South*, waving to Sara,

Brogan and Jamie, and trying not to wonder whether she would ever see them again, or whether she would see England for that matter, because it would not be an easy voyage, everyone aboard knew that. A great many vessels had fallen victim to the magnetic mines which now infested the seas, though Grace thought they would probably account for as many friends as foes, since no one could tell where they would turn up next. Then there were the U-boats, skulking below the waves, aiming their torpedoes at any ship they did not recognise as one of their own. Civilian ships owned by countries which had no part in the conflict had been sunk, so everyone on board knew the risks, and knew also that the voyage was unlikely to be an entirely peaceful one.

But it was no use dwelling on the dangers ahead. Being a member of the armed forces would not be all smooth sailing, she supposed. So Grace dried her eyes and led her young charges down to their cabin. She was here to do a job so the sooner she started the better.

'Let's have a game of "Happy Families",' she said brightly, getting out the pack of cards. 'Who'll deal, children?'

Because of her mother's words, Polly began to search for Sunny as soon as she could after the Christmas holiday was over, but she did not find him. Remembering what Alice had been told she went to his house, or what had once been his house, feeling very silly indeed and hoping that she would not make a fool of herself. At Sunny's old address she found a stringy, hatchet-faced woman with dyed black hair who told her, in the strangest accent that Polly had ever heard, that the Andersens had moved out some time previously and that she herself had been the tenant for nigh on eighteen months.

'Wh-where did they go, do you know?' Polly quavered. She felt sure the woman thought she was pursuing Sunny like some sort of common Mary-Ellen, but having come this far she was determined to get what information she could. 'Sunny was me pal, only we – we've not seen each other for a while. He was at school wit' me brother,' she added untruthfully, and imagined the woman's sharp black eyes softened a little.

'Oh aye? Well, his pa vas a sailor, so folk hereabouts kind o' thought that the lad vould have follered in his footsteps. Then it vould have been natural that the boy's mother would have headed for Pompey,' the woman said, having given the matter some thought, with her dyed black head cocked to one side like a blackbird, and her little eyes taking Polly in from top to toe. 'Pompey's a good place for sailors, and sailors' vives.'

'Yes, I expect so. I believe Sunny has joined the Navy, so perhaps his mother has gone to this – this Pompey to keep house for him,' Polly said, and was rewarded with an even sharper look, an abrupt crow of laughter – and the door slammed almost in her face, though the woman did have the grace to say: 'Try Pompey,' as she disappeared from sight.

Polly went thoughtfully home and got out the old *Atlas of the World* which countless O'Bradys had turned to for geographical advice from time to time. She found Great Britain with its principal cities, ports and harbours, but she could not find Pompey, no matter how she spelt it. Finally, she concluded that the woman had just been taking a rise out of her, put the atlas away and decided to think no more of

Sunny. Indeed, if he no longer lived in the 'Pool, she might as well forget him, because she was unlikely to walk into him again by accident. For by now she was even more certain that the naval back view she and Ivan had seen on Church Street had been Sunny, probably visiting Liverpool en route for somewhere else.

Martin and Monica spent the first two days of his leave at number 8, but then they went off to Southport, and it was not until they came back again, Martin walking into the house to say goodbye to everyone, that it occurred to Polly to ask her elder brother whether he had ever heard of Pompey.

'Yes, 'course I have,' Martin said indignantly. 'So should you, Poll. It's an Italian city out of Roman times, it was buried when one of the Italian volcanoes erupted – Etna, was it? Or was it Vesuvius? Any road, it's an Italian city.'

'Oh,' Polly said, confounded. 'Is it a port, Mart? Only someone told me that there are lots of sailors in Pompey and . . .'

Martin gave a little choke of laughter and put a brotherly arm round her shoulders. 'I thought you meant *Pompeii*, the ancient city,' he said kindly. 'Pompey's another kettle of fish altogether, so it is. It's a sort of nickname that sailors have given to Portsmouth, God alone knows why. And there are certainly a great many sailors in Pompey. All right, alanna? Does that answer your question?'

'It does,' Polly said with great relief. You never knew, if she decided to join the WRNs when she was older she might easily go to Portsmouth one day, though if there were really hundreds and hundreds of sailors there, she had not yet worked out how she might find Sunny and his mammy. But having discovered the possible whereabouts of the family, she decided that she would do nothing, for now – there was little enough that she could do, after all. 'Thanks, Mart.'

So now, knowing that in all probability Sunny was unlikely to be in the city, she decided to put him right out of her mind. Besides, she wasn't at all sure she wanted to join the WRNs; joining the WAAF might be more fun, because Tad was in the Air Force and she kind of liked the thought of meeting up with her old friend again.

So Polly continued to work, and study, and to help her mammy and write letters to anyone, just about, who would write back. And waited for the months to pass until she, too, could help to fight this war which seemed so slow in getting started.

Chapter Eight

Years ago, when it had first happened, Sunny had been deeply upset and angry that Polly had suddenly stopped meeting up with him, but even in his disappointment he knew better than to blame her. It was her stuck-up, stupid parents, that's what it was, and he was fairly sure that if he could just get Polly alone . . .

The trouble was, he could not. He had been baulked at every turn, not by Mr and Mrs O'Brady but by Polly herself. With her blue eyes sad instead of smiling, she had turned away from him, ignored him, moved if he came near her, until he was forced to realise that this was serious. He had done wrong to encourage Polly to mitch off school and now he was being paid out for it. They would not let him see her and since they had clearly abstracted some sort of promise from Polly, he knew that she was far too honourable to break her word and would consequently have nothing at all to do with him.

It was sad, but Sunny was young and on the brink of a new adventure. He was very soon fed up with skiving round Liverpool picking up bits and pieces of jobs when he could, and without Polly, life suddenly seemed dull indeed. So Sunny Andersen, son of a sailor, went and joined the Navy, because he saw a life on the ocean wave as being very much to his taste. He joined the Royal Navy as an ordinary seaman, of course, the lowest of the low, but he was bright and rapidly rose to able seaman and then he was sent on a course to learn to be a signaller, and when he had successfully completed the course he was posted to the sloop *Poppy*, whose home port was Portsmouth.

War was coming; everyone in the armed forces knew it and Sunny was no exception. He also realised that he was likely to be carrying out his duties on various ships anywhere in the world and it was unlikely he would be able to return to Liverpool often, since his ship's home port was in the south of the country. It was sad, because he loved the city, it was his home, the only one he had known until he joined the Navy, but as soon as he had moved away his mam had moved down to Portsmouth, 'to be near your dad,' she had said, though Sunny took that with a pinch of salt. Now when he was ashore it was convenient to move into the small spare room in his mam's warm, untidy little house and he supposed that he would be spending his leaves in Pompey now, so that he could see his mam and, when he was in port, his dad. A pity, because he had lost touch with Polly, and he still thought of her with affection and just a touch of desire, but he had had a good few girlfriends since he joined up and no longer thought of Polly as often as he once had.

He thought of her, however, when he found himself, just before Christmas, with a five-day leave – and a pal, also with five days off, who still lived in the 'Pool. Dempsey was a cheery lad, one of a big family, and when Sunny had explained that he could no longer spend his leaves in the 'Pool because his mam had moved – he did not say where – Dempsey had immediately told him that the entire Dempsey family – especially his three sisters – would be delighted to entertain him.

'Any pal of Reg Dempsey's a pal o' theirs,' he said lavishly. 'You come along o' me, Sunny, an' you can look up your old mates whiles I do the same.'

So Sunny had got himself a rail warrant and arrived in Liverpool on a cold afternoon just before Christmas.

Naturally, Sunny was rather pleased than otherwise to find himself, in all the glory of his uniform, back in Liverpool for a short spell. His first thought was that now he should get in touch with Polly again, since she would be a working girl by this time and no longer quite so much under her parents' thumbs, so at the first opportunity he left the Dempsey household, telling Reg that he was going to look up old friends, and then began to make his way across the city towards Titchfield Street.

He was nearing the turning he wanted when he thought he saw a girl he vaguely remembered from school, Edith something-or-other. He took a long, hard stare before approaching her, however; she was so different from the scruffy kid in her worn plimsolls and ragged clothing he remembered. Yet there is always something about a person which never changes, and there it was, in Edith's sharp, knowing little face despite the smart black coat and matching hat with violets on the brim, the high-heeled shoes on her feet and the liberally made-up face.

'Edie? D'you remember me, queen?'

The girl – only she was no longer a girl but a young lady – turned and smiled coquettishly up at him. 'Sunny! As if anyone could forget you! You ain't changed at all, chuck – you're in the Navy now, then? Eh, I've gorra yen to join the WRNS or the WAAF meself, but I'm makin' guns in a factory on Long

Lane, an' it's too well paid to throw over just 'cos I fancy meself in a uniform!'

'I'm sure you'd look very nice in it, but no nicer than you do now, Edie,' Sunny said, taking her arm. Suddenly he felt he needed time, and a bit more information, before he approached the house in Titchfield Street. 'Tell you what, I'm longin' to hear all the news; what say you an' me go an' get some char an' a wad – that's a cake to you, gorgeous – an' you can fill me in on what's been happenin' since I left.'

Edith was willing; clearly she had no objection to being seen with as personable a young man as Sunny. He took her to the nearest cafe, bought her what looked to him like a very sickly cake and a cup of tea, and then settled down opposite her to gather what news he could.

'What's been happenin' to the rest of 'em? Dougie Saunders, Bet O'Flaherty, Sid Smith? Oh, and young Polly O'Brady, what's she been gettin' up to?'

'Oh aye, you went around wi' her at one time, I remember,' Edith said. She took a bite out of her cream cake, then dabbed at her mouth with a paper serviette. It came away red with lip gloss, Sunny saw with mild amusement. He only had one use for lipstick himself – to see how quickly he could kiss it off – but he knew girls liked the stuff and this one clearly put it on with a trowel, judging by the fact that her mouth was still blood red, as was the serviette.

'That was when we were both kids,' Sunny pointed out virtuously. 'Tell me about Dougie, an' Bet, and Sid, then. Polly's a deal younger'n you, I suppose.'

This seemed to catch Edith on the raw. She looked up quickly, a martial sparkle in her eyes. 'Younger'n me? Well, no more than a twelve-month, if that! She don't change much, what's more – her mam an' dad and all them older brothers make sure she don't wear nothin' decent, nor run about wi' the fellers like the rest of us. She's workin', of course – I seen her in Blackler's t'other week – but she still looks like a school kid. No make-up, hair just the same, plain sort o' clothes . . .'

'An' Bet?' Sunny asked. He did not want to rouse Edith's suspicions and have her going round and telling the O'Bradys that he had been asking questions about Polly. Besides, he now knew quite enough to be going on with. Despite the fact that she was now fifteen years old, getting on for sixteen, in fact, it seemed that her parents were still babying – and bossing – his Polly. Better not go to the house then, particularly as he now knew where she worked. Blackler's was a big place but he was here for two more days; he could haunt the store for pretty well the whole of that time.

I'll lay siege to the bleedin' place, he vowed as Edie prattled on beside him. I'll kip down on the bleedin' floor if I have to, but I'll see Polly, and talk to her before me ship sails if it's the last thing I do!

But when the two lads set off back to the *Poppy* once more, Sunny's bright and optimistic hopes had suffered a hard knock. Despite the most exhaustive search, he had failed to run Polly to earth in Blackler's, and assumed that she must have had a couple of days off, possibly for Christmas shopping. Several times he thought he saw her – once, he walked all the way to Titchfield Street and actually hung about near number 8 – but no Polly appeared. It was a Friday, and since he had to return to his ship on the Saturday morning Sunny decided that he had done all he could, and would have to give up the search until his next visit.

I'll write to her, Sunny told himself, and spent the best part of the train journey plotting a letter which would sound like innocuous friendliness to Polly's parents but which would somehow manage to prove to Polly that he still wanted her to be his girl. He wanted Polly's friendship, he was still very fond of the kid, but he did not want anyone, either Polly or her parents, thinking he was . . . well, serious. He wanted her as his girl all right, but had no desire to 'go steady' if it meant cutting out the delightful interludes with other young ladies which he had come to think of as his due. After all, when there were so many pretty girls falling over themselves to be seen with a handsome blond sailor it would be a dull sort of chap who would get tied to a kid. So he decided not to overdo the eagerness, and as the *Poppy* set out for Londonderry and convoy duties in the North Atlantic he began to write the letter.

Grace reached Liverpool as afternoon was turning into dusk on a rainy February day. She looked up at the Liver birds as the big ship passed slowly up the Mersey and felt the sting of tears in her eyes, and then the warmth of them as they ran down her cold, rain-wet cheeks.

Home! New York had been grand, Sara and Brogan wonderful, but this – oh, this was home! But despite these feelings she went down to the cabin she shared with the two Carewe children and began to gather up their baggage. Presently, Mrs Carewe, with her small daughter in her arms, joined her there and soon enough the five of them were on deck, waiting their turn to descend the gangplank.

'I can't tell you what it's meant to us to have you with us, my dear,' Mrs Carewe said as they reached terra firma once more. 'You're efficient and kind and good, and a credit to the Strawberry Field Orphan Home, and we shall all miss you most dreadfully. But we can manage now; we'll get a taxi to Lime Street and book ourselves into a hotel, or a guesthouse, then catch the first train south tomorrow. And don't forget to write to us to tell us how you're going on.'

'I won't,' Grace said. 'Umm . . . some of the hotels near the station . . . well, they aren't very – very nice, you know.' She did not quite know how to tell these good, kind people that Lime Street was frequented by the sort of women that decent people tried to keep away from. 'Some of them . . . there are all sorts come up from the docks, and . . .'

'Don't worry, Grace,' the major said, smiling at her. 'We've not worked amongst the very poorest people in New York without knowing that hard times sometimes produce a desperate reaction. Poor souls, just to keep body and soul together . . . But there, we'll go to a respectable place, don't you fret.'

'Oh, I know you will,' Grace said hastily, hoping she wasn't blushing but knowing that she almost certainly was. 'And don't think I'll ever forget you, because I never could. I'll write as soon as I'm settled . . . but I don't know whether the forces will accept me, if they don't . . .'

'Any of the women's services would be glad to get someone as competent and experienced as yourself, Grace dear,' Mrs Carewe assured her. She took the baby's pudgy fist in her own and flapped it up and down. 'Wave bye-bye to Gracie, dear one.'

Grace watched the little family until they had found themselves a taxi cab, got their luggage and themselves aboard, and set off down the street, then she turned her feet towards the nearest tram stop with a great warmth beginning to flood through her. She would soon be at the house she had never yet entered – number 8, Titchfield Street – yet still felt would be her home. The O'Bradys had assured her, over and over, that since they now lived in the city she must stay with them, and she meant to do so. Until she joined up, that was. For Grace was determined that she would do her duty by her country and right now, her country needed all the help it could get, even if she only scrubbed potatoes or mended the uniforms of those more able to fight.

A tram came clanking up the road and stopped alongside the small queue of people waiting at the stop. In the dusk Grace could not see the destination board clearly but said breathlessly to the short, elderly woman directly in front of her: 'Excuse me, does this tram go along the Scottie, ma'am?'

The slight Americanism of the last word made the woman turn and stare, then she grinned. 'Aye, tharrit does, queen,' she said in the familiar, nasal accent which Grace had once used herself, until the years with Sara had made her almost forget it. 'What stop does you want? I'm gerrin' off at St Martin's Street meself.'

'That'll do me too,' Grace said as they both climbed aboard. She wedged her bulging suitcase in the gap under the stairs and began to push her way further down the vehicle in the small woman's wake, for it was crowded with home-going workers at this hour. 'I'm going to Titchfield Street – that's the best stop for me as well.'

'Right, chuck. When you see me shovin' me way out, jest you folly,' the woman said. She settled herself with her broad bottom wedged against an occupied seat and clung on to the back of the next one with both fat hands. 'Hold very tight, please,' she said in imitation of tram-conductors the world over. 'We're off, queen. You goin' home? In the forces, are you?'

'Not yet,' Grace said, smiling at the other's open curiosity. 'I'm just back from the States, where I've been working for a while. But I've come back to join up, though.'

'Good for you,' her new friend said heartily. 'We'll give old Hitler the runaround, so us will! What'll it be, then? ATS? WAAF? WRNS?'

'Well, I've applied to become a WRN,' Grace said, grabbing for a strap as the tram suddenly lurched to a halt, presumably at another stop. 'I wrote several times, from the States, but I've not had a reply, so I suppose I'll just have to see who wants me.'

'Hmm. Can you drive? Type? Or are you the domestic sort?'

'I can't drive,' Grace said at once. 'Wouldn't mind learning, though.'

'Well, there you are, then,' the woman said as triumphantly as though Grace had just admitted that she could drive, type and also steer battleships through minefields unaided. 'D'you favour brown? Or is navy more your style? Or that sort o' grey-blue?'

'I think I look best in dark colours,' Grace said, wondering where the question was leading and thinking of her Salvation Army uniform, which she secretly thought very becoming.

'Then that's settled,' the woman said. 'You done the best thing when you applied for the WRNs. Their uniform's navy like the fellers. So that's settled.'

Just as she spoke, more passengers began to climb aboard the tram led by a group of girls who, pushing and giggling, got between her and her erstwhile companion making it impossible for them to exchange any further conversation.

Deirdre was still working in the cafe, though her hours had been cut; no one wanted to pop in for a nice high tea when it meant struggling home through the blackout so she only worked, now, until three in the afternoon. Naturally, this affected her wages and made her think of changing her job because it was common knowledge that those working for the war effort were extremely well paid. In a way it was a pity, Deirdre thought as she cleaned down tables and brushed crumbs up off the floor, because she loved the work. The customers were friendly, Mrs Ellis wasn't bad once you got used to her odd little ways, and Miss Collins was all right as well, though despite her cuddly appearance and soft Irish voice she was capable of considerable malice and you always had to take what she said about others with a pinch of salt.

However, it was not war work and Deirdre thought that as soon as it was possible she would apply for a job which would help with the war effort. For the time being, though, she simply spent more time at home, cooking, knitting, and occasionally helping Peader to sort his employer's coupons. Peader, doing his books or rather his employer's books – in the front room was glad of her occasional help but happier still, she knew, because it meant he had company. He had always worked with other people and found being alone in the house all day dull work.

'All right if I go now, Mrs Ellis?' Deirdre enquired when she had finished cleaning down the dining room. 'Only it's a quarter past three and it's that dull and rainy outside that you're not going to find yourselves rushed off your feet.'

Mrs Ellis, who was counting out the float which she would leave in the till so that next morning they had some change for early customers, nodded silently, her fingers still busy amongst the ha-pennies, pennies and threepenny bits but Miss Collins, polishing glasses with a nice piece of wash-leather, said almost in a whisper: 'Want a sultana cake, luv? Well, most of one, anyway. It'll be too stale to sell tomorrer and I don't hold with using fruit cake in trifles.'

'Thanks very much, if you're sure no one else wants it,' Deirdre said rather nervously. It would be just like Miss Collins to offer her the cake and then to tell Mrs Ellis that Deirdre had asked for it, and with butter and sugar now on ration, making cakes at home was almost impossible. But Mrs Ellis, despite her preoccupation with small change, had obviously heard since she turned round for a moment and said: 'You take it, Deirdre. Rose can have the bit of meat and potato pie that's left over; she's no hand at cooking, I feel downright sorry for that husband of hers sometimes.'

Rose's husband, Dick, had suffered from TB as a young man and though he had been discharged by the sanatorium as cured, he was painfully thin and weedy and had a hollow cough which made the older ladies exchange significant glances. Deirdre could imagine her own mother looking at Dick and saying, in the sepulchral voice she kept for such occasions, 'There's a feller that's not long for this world,' whereas Peader's mammy, well known for her cheery and optimistic nature, would have announced bracingly that creaking gates lasted longer than sound ones.

'Right you are then, Mrs Ellis,' Deirdre said now,

taking the piece of cake and wrapping it in greaseproof paper. She put the small parcel into her capacious handbag, then turned to smile at her employer. 'Peader will be grateful – he dearly loves a piece of cake with his cup of tea. What time shall I come in tomorrer?'

Mrs Ellis cocked her head to one side. 'Well, what with January being one of the coldest months ever, and February not being much better, business doesn't seem to start until nearly mid-morning. Best be in by ten thirty, though, dear.'

'Right,' Deirdre said with unimpaired cheerfulness, though her wage packet at the end of the week, which had been so thin all through January, did not look as though it would improve much now. 'Cheerybye, all.'

She had been putting on her coat, hat and gloves as she spoke and now she went briskly out through the cafe and into the Scotland Road, putting her umbrella up as she came on to the pavement for Miss Collins, who had a superstitious streak, would have announced that the war was as good as lost had Deirdre erected it indoors.

Outside, the rain was falling steadily, and there was a raw chill in the air. Deirdre thought gloomily that if it froze tonight they would all be in a pickle tomorrow, and wondered whether to walk home or go for a tram. But it was growing dusk and the thought of hanging about in the cold waiting for a tram that might take almost as long to arrive as it would take her to walk, settled the matter. She sighed and set off, head down, umbrella lowered against the driving rain, trying to concentrate on what awaited her – the warm fire, the kettle on the hob, and Peader's welcoming smile.

She was almost at the Bevington Arms pub on the corner of St Martin's Street when a tram rattled up behind her and stopped in a shower of spray, decanting several passengers, all of whom either tucked their heads low into their coat collars and set off up the road or erected their umbrellas and followed suit. Deirdre glanced sideways, to see whether a friend or neighbour was aboard, and was struck by something about one of the girls who had alighted last from the tram, carrying a sizeable suitcase and a canvas bag. She had turned her coat collar up and pulled a dark red felt hat well over her face but due to the things she was carrying she could not use an umbrella – indeed, she did not seem to have one. The girl set off ahead of Deirdre, walking purposefully, and there was something about her, something familiar . . .

Deirdre quickened her pace. It was difficult to take in any details in the driving rain but she rather thought she had seen the girl somewhere before. She was overhauling the girl fast and presently they were side by side on the pavement, so Deirdre glanced sideways. A tall girl, and very slim, though her dark coat hid her figure pretty effectively. She had shoulder-length hair darkened by the rain which was probably quite a light brown under normal circumstances, and a pale face with a small straight nose and eyes whose colour was hidden but whose long, light lashes were beaded, now, with raindrops, though the rain itself seemed to have stopped, for the moment at least.

A neighbour? No, not a neighbour. Someone, Deirdre decided, folding down her umbrella, that she had known long ago and so now could not immediately recognise. Someone from Dublin, probably, that was why the girl carried a suitcase. They reached Limekiln Lane where Deirdre had to turn left and she stretched out a hand to stop the other, but the girl turned left as well, and as she did so, glanced at Deirdre. Immediately she stopped short, a smile breaking out.

'Oh, it's Auntie Deirdre, isn't it?' The girl dropped her suitcase and her canvas bag and grabbed Deirdre's hands, causing her to drop her umbrella and to clutch desperately at her handbag. 'You don't recognise me, do you? I can't have changed that much – I'm Grace Carbery, and you're Polly's mam! Why, I'm making my way to your house this moment!'

Deirdre squeaked and stood on tiptoe to give Grace's cheek a hearty kiss, then bent to retrieve her umbrella. She scooped the canvas bag up at the same time and slung her own bag over her shoulder to give her a free hand. 'Grace! Well, and haven't you changed now! You were just a slip of a thing when you left for New York, now you're a woman, and a very pretty one at that! Just wait until Peader sees you, he'll think I'm bringing a visitor to stay, and a very smart one too.'

'How *is* he?' Grace asked, picking up her suitcase. 'Now don't you go carrying my bag, Auntie Deirdre, you've got your own handbag. Let me do it, I'm very strong, you know.'

Deirdre, however, hung on to the canvas bag. 'No, no, my dear, me bag's doing very well hung from me shoulder, it'll do me no harm to give you a hand,' she insisted, beginning to walk forward once more. 'I'm so sorry no one met your ship, but with you not being able to give us any sort of definite landing time . . . My goodness, how thrilled everyone will be to see you at last!'

'I'm thrilled to be home,' Grace said quietly. 'I've had a grand time living with Brogan and Sara, and I dearly love Jamie, but . . . Oh, Auntie Deirdre, England's me home, Liverpool especially. Why, I've been gone years but I can still remember every street, every pub, every shop, just about. Oh, and I've brought you some photographs . . . Brogan's got a pal who takes pictures all the time so he took the apartment, the street, the park, and lots of Jamie. I'll get them out just as soon as we're indoors.'

'It'll be grand to see some snaps,' Deirdre said as they turned into Titchfield Street. 'We've had a shockingly cold winter, so we have, but spring will be on the way soon, and then you'll be able to enjoy being home again.'

'Ye-es, only I'll not be home for very long,' Grace said rather apologetically. 'I didn't come home just to *be* home, you know. I'm going to join one of the women's services, if they'll have me. Brogan thinks that the US will join the war quite soon, but I'm not so sure. There's a strong lobby for neutrality and although they've heard the stories of Nazi atrocities, same as you have no doubt, they're still holding back. And a good many of them have German roots which makes them unwilling to interfere in a war which they still feel needn't touch them.'

Nodding her understanding, Deirdre noted the slight American accent and smiled to herself. No doubt Sara and Brogan had that trace of an accent as well, and little Jamie who she had never met too.

'Right. So maybe we'll have to fight on alone, but judging from the people in the street, they're prepared for that. And you've come back to help us, you good girl, you.'

'Brogan wanted to come back too,' Grace said

quickly. 'But Sara remembers . . .' She hesitated. 'Well, they left because it seemed best and I don't suppose things like that have changed much, have they?'

'No, the feeling would still be strong,' Deirdre admitted. 'Oh, not from the family, nor our good friends. But a good many people don't like mixed marriages, and— Why are you smiling?'

'You sound like some of the folk in the States,' Grace said, smiling down at Deirdre. 'Only over there, mixed marriages don't really mean religion so much as colour. There's a lot of feeling against whites marrying coloureds, and of course you can tell at a glance when a man is black . . . I don't know, Auntie Deirdre, there's a lot of prejudice in this world against people who can't help what colour they are, or what religion they follow.'

Deirdre, who knew very well that anyone who was not a Catholic was doomed to spend eternity regretting the error of their ways, returned some non-committal answer just as they reached number 8 and went down the jigger and round to the back yard. The front door, which would have been the usual way to bring in a visitor, would have meant getting Peader up from his chair and she wanted to surprise him.

'Well now, and won't Peader be delighted to see you safe?' she said as they crossed the back yard. 'For he's known better than any of us the dangers of sea voyages in such times as these. I wonder if he'll recognise you? You've grown into a really pretty young lady, that's what, our Grace! And just wait till Polly sees you! She'll be tickled pink, so she will.'

Polly came in from work in the best of spirits, full of stories of what had happened to her during the day. She burst into the kitchen in her usual impetuous manner and for a moment did not recognise the tall young woman with the bun of light brown hair on top of her head who sat opposite Peader beside the fire and turned a smiling face towards her.

'Hello, Polly,' the girl said, getting to her feet and holding out her arms. 'Haven't you a hug for me, then?' And all in a moment Polly knew her and with a squeak of excitement hurled herself across the kitchen and into Grace's arms.

'Oh, Gracie, Gracie, aren't you smart and lovely? Oh, and you're a real grown-up lady, just like Mammy said you would be, only I couldn't believe . . . I love your hair done like that, and isn't it smooth as satin now, and you've not a spot to your face – wish I didn't have spots – and that dress . . . Oh it's lovely, so it is.' Polly began to drag her own coat and hat off, dancing across to the back door and hanging them on the hooks before turning back to her friend. 'How long have you been here, me darlin'? Did Mammy meet you off the boat? Have you had your tea yet? How's Brogan, Sara and Jamie? I've a million questions to ask you, I don't know where to begin.'

'Glory be, Poll. Glory be, Poll,' Grace said, picking up the scarf which had slid to the floor, handing it to the younger girl. 'You've grown up a good bit yourself but you haven't changed in other ways; you're still my dear little Polly. Don't you ever stop asking questions, honey?'

'Honey! That makes you sound like a real American,' Polly said, flinging the scarf on to the nearest chair regardless of the fact that it contained her father. Peader unwrapped the scarf from around his head and smiled across at Deirdre, who was quietly laying the table for tea.

'What a terrible girl she is,' he said fondly,

indicating his daughter. 'Now, stop motherin' Grace, Polly. Or she'll up and leave before she's arrived, so she will. And stop shootin' questions at her like a machine gun.' He turned to his wife. 'If tea won't be ready just yet, Deirdre, should the girls take a jug of water and go up to their room to wash? They'll be head to tailin' it same as they always did, though I daresay it'll be a bit of a squeeze because both of 'ems tall and neither of 'ems skinny.' He turned back to Polly. 'An' while you're up there, alanna, Grace'll tell you all about your brother and sister and the little lads and you can catch her up with our news. Grace took her case up earlier so she knows where she's headin'.'

'That's a grand idea, so it is,' Deirdre said. She went over to the stove and began to pour hot water from the kettle into a white enamel jug. She handed the jug to Polly who had begun to chatter again and pointed sternly to the stairs. 'Off wit' you,' she said with eyes that smiled though her mouth was grave, 'and be sure to be down in half an hour with all your questions answered and all your news given so we can enjoy our tea without bein' driven crazy by your brangling.'

Polly took the jug and headed for the stairs with Grace close on her heels. 'Thanks, Mammy,' she called over her shoulder, 'but half an hour's not long enough for all my questions! Still, we've got all night, once tea's done.'

It was true that the two girls had had a good deal of catching up to do, Polly reflected next morning as she crept out of the bedroom, having washed and dressed in almost total silence, without once causing Grace so much as to stir in her sleep. But despite having talked non-stop from ten o'clock or so until well after three, there was still a good deal she wanted to know. Oh, Grace had told her all about Sara, Brogan and Jamie. Sara and Brogan, she had said, were as eager to come home and help with the war effort as she, but they felt it would be deserting their adopted country. 'If America enters the war, however, they'll come back,' she assured Polly. 'Poor Brogan really envied me, I know it.' But she had not said a great deal about her own social life or what her plans were, apart from the fact that she had come home to join up.

'Which service will you join?' Polly had asked eagerly, and Grace had not been evasive – but not too keen to decide either.

'I wrote to the WRNs,' Grace had said rather crossly. 'I wrote two or three times – maybe four – but I never once got an answer. Oh, I'd like to be one of them, all right, but someone on the boat said they're the senior service and not nearly so keen on recruiting as the younger services. So I'll have to see.'

'But you'll try the WRNs first, won't you?' Polly had said eagerly. 'I'm goin' to join them, Gracie, just as soon as I'm old enough. And it 'ud be nice if we was both in the same service, don't you think?'

'Yes, it would,' Grace had said. 'Only they won't let the girls go to sea, will they? Did I tell you, Poll, that when there was a storm I was just about the only person on the ship that wasn't sick?'

'You did mention it,' Polly admitted, smiling to herself in the dark. 'Monica – she's Martin's wife, me sister-in-law – said she'd join the WRNs if only they'd let her go to sea wi' Martin. But she's ever so wet, not a bit like us. I mean, we'd like to go to sea all right but not so's we could be with our relatives!'

'No-oo,' Grace said cautiously. 'But some of the

sailors are awful nice, our Poll. Ever so friendly. One of 'em asked me if I'd like to go to the flicks with him one afternoon.'

'Did they have a cinema on the ship?' Polly had asked, wide-eyed at the thought, only Grace told her that Sam – that was the sailor's name – had actually meant her to go to the cinema in Liverpool, before the ship sailed again.

'Oh, I see,' Polly said, rather disappointed. 'Well, you could go, of course. When the war first started they shut all the cinemas and theatres and that, but they soon opened 'em again. I expect I told you in one of me letters.'

'You did mention it,' Grace said. She chuckled. 'Sara said if anything persuaded you to go to America it would be the cinemas shutting, I remember. But they changed their minds in time to keep you, I guess.'

'That's right,' Polly said. She laughed too. 'I were that mad – oh I *do* love the flicks, Gracie – that I'd have blowed up the houses of parliament if I'd had the chance. I love dancing, and going on walks wi' me pals, and going to the theatre now and then, but the flicks is best.'

'Why? Because you can hold hands without any-one knowing?' Grace asked curiously. 'Or because of the stories?'

'We-ell, it's a good place to go with a feller, all right,' Polly admitted after a moment's thought. Over the past four or five months she had gone about with a good many boys, though none of them had been particularly important to her. She was saving her real affection for her old friends, she told herself vir-tuously – friends like Sunny, or maybe even Tad – but the other fellers were great fun, and good company after a day spent dancing attendance on customers in the shop or taking dictation from dull old men, because all the young ones had been whipped into the armed forces. 'But it's the stories really, Gracie. And – and the acting, and all the girls so beautiful and all the fellers handsome . . . Oh, I don't know. It's me best thing, anyhow.'

'Yes, I know how you feel, 'cos I'm fond of a good film myself,' Grace acknowledged. 'But . . . well, with so much – well, reality going on, it seems a bit daft to go meeting guys at the cinema. And besides, I scarcely know Sam, not really. So I said I didn't think I'd have time, because I meant to join the forces at once, so that means I should really go along to the recruiting place first thing tomorrow, I suppose.'

'Guys? And first thing *tomorrer*?' Polly almost wailed. 'Oh, but they might send you away from the 'Pool right away and then what 'ud I do? I've been looking forward to you coming home so much, Gracie! I've a heap o' pals you've not met yet, girls and fe— guys, I mean, I've told them all about you and they're really looking forward to meeting you. Don't go away too soon, there's a luv!'

But Grace, though tired, was adamant. 'I think I ought to go along to try to join up tomorrow,' she said obstinately. 'They won't take me at once, Poll, that much I do know, so you'll have plenty of time to introduce me to your pals.'

So now, with this in mind, Polly did wonder whether to wake Grace up. Might it not be kinder, perhaps, to do so? But Grace looked so tired, and was sleeping so soundly, that eventually she decided that like it or not, Grace should lie in this morning, and went quietly down the stairs.

In the kitchen, Deirdre smiled at her daughter and

put a large plate of porridge down in front of her place, then poured her a mug of steaming tea. 'They've mebbe rationed bacon and butter and sugar but you can still have a nice plate o' porridge and a big mug o' tea,' she said, 'to say nothing of a pile of toast and margarine. Now get eating, or you'll be late for work, and that 'ud never do. Where's our Grace? Comin' down in a moment?'

'No. I've left her to sleep,' Polly said, sitting down and beginning to spoon porridge. 'She wants to join up today, Mammy, but I said she should get used to being home a bit first. Only you know what? She's that determined she'll probably take no notice of what I said, and there's me longing for her to meet me new pals, which wouldn't mean a huge delay in her joining up.'

She sounded so injured that her mother laughed. 'Never you mind, alanna,' she said, taking her place opposite her daughter. 'She'll mebbe go to the recruiting office, but I doubt they'll send her straight off to wherever she's to go. They'll have to go into her credentials first. Why, she's just got back from America – she could be a German spy for all they know.'

'Huh, not our Gracie,' Polly said. She finished her porridge and reached for the topmost piece of well-browned toast. 'She sounded ever so American when she first came home, but by the time we fell asleep she were talking just as ordinary and nice as I do!'

'Well, that's all right, then,' her mother said comfortably. 'Now you go off to work, me darlin' daughter, and I'll see that Grace is still around when you get home.'

With breakfast finished, Polly put on her green coat, wrapped her striped blue and fawn scarf around her throat, and set off for a day's work at the Reliant Insurance Company. She did not go willingly – like her mother Polly wanted to do war work – but for the time being Mr Slater of the Reliant would have to do.

She reached Exchange Flags and went slowly through the big oak doorway, up the stairs and in through the door marked *Reliant Insurance Company – Reception; please Enter*, where she found the receptionist, Sadie, already behind her desk, polishing her long, filbert nails with the little wash-leather buffer which was part of her manicure set. Polly envied her the little leather case with her initials – S.P. for Sadie Phelan – on it in gold, but she knew her chances of owning such an object was slight. Sadie was twenty-four and had been earning for years, whereas Polly was very much the office junior and was paid accordingly.

Sadie looked up as Polly entered and smiled. 'All ready for another day of glamour and excitement?' she asked, fitting the buffer into its place on the cream suede which lined the small case and extracting a spade-like object with which, Polly knew, she pushed down her cuticles – cuticles, Sadie had explained, being highly unfashionable this year. 'I don't know how you stand old Slater, chuck. What wi' his bad breath an' his terminal dandruff, to say nothin' of his whiney voice,' Sadie remarked eyeing Polly quizzically. 'I reckon he's old Hitler's secret weapon. Guaranteed to send any halfway pretty girl mad after workin' for him for a week, let alone months an' months.'

Polly took off her coat and scarf and hung them on the coatstand, then perched on the edge of Sadie's desk and eyed Sadie's small telephone exchange enviously. Lucky Sadie, she met all the people who came into reception, sent them to the appropriate departments or offices, and no doubt, knowing Sadie, made eyes and light conversation with any feller who took her fancy, whilst Polly was either stuck in the typing pool, or sat opposite Mr Slater, taking dictation and praying she would be able to read her shorthand outlines when she returned to her own desk. The trouble was, if she got sufficiently bored she simply stopped listening to what Mr Slater was saying, though her obedient hand continued to write neat shorthand across the pages of her notebook. If she had been listening, reading the work back was easy enough, but when she had not been listening, her own shorthand outlines looked more like Chinese characters to her, and she could usually only make a vague stab at their meanings.

'Oh, old Slater isn't that bad,' she said vaguely now. 'Besides, Sadie, I'm waiting for you to move on, so's I can take over in here. Aren't you longin' to join the forces, queen? Me pal Grace came back from America yesterday, docked in the early evening, and she's going to join up just as soon as she possibly can. The WRNs, I guess.'

'I've gorra lorra responsibilities,' Sadie said primly, and winked at Polly. 'To say nothing' of a nice wage packet – they don't pay you much to be a WRN or a WAAF, you know, queen. But tell me about your pal – she's been in America a while, hasn't she? I bet she's as fashionable as anything – how old is she? What about fellers? Don't say she left a feller pinin' for her in America! Oh, it's me dream to go over there some day – I got cousins . . . But the war's purra stop to all that. Bleedin' pity, but there you are.'

'I don't think Grace has any particular feller,' Polly said slowly. 'Which is odd, now I come to think, because she's got rather pretty in an – well, an unusual sort of way. She's got light brown hair which curls under when it reaches her shoulders, and a straight little nose, and really nice blue eyes, as well as a wizard figure, so you'd think she'd have the fellers swarming round her like bees after the honey. But it's a good thing she didn't have one over there, since she's come home now, to where she belongs. I expect she's hoping to meet one when she's in the WRNs – I would, anyway. A sailor . . . Oh, I do like sailors!'

Sadie chuckled. 'Don't we all, queen? Now you'd best get to your desk before old man Slater—' She broke off as the outer door opened. 'Good morning, Mr Slater!'

Polly promptly fled and joined her fellow-workers in the large, chilly room which had once contained eighteen young ladies, and now held only six. The other five were already there – Miss Highes, the senior typist, who worked as secretary to Mr Richards, the managing director, and occasionally unbent enough to go down to Claims and take dictation for the solitary man still working there, and Gladys, Paula, Anita and Jane, who were already clattering away on their elderly typewriters, although Polly knew very well that they could not actually be working yet, because it was only five to nine and none of the men would have sent for a typist yet.

'Where've you been?' Jane asked as Polly heaved the black cover off her old Remington and snatched her shorthand notebook out of its drawer and her pencil from the handleless mug which held an assortment of different writing tools. 'Chatterin' to that Sadie, I daresay?'

'Sadie's all right,' Polly said rather breathlessly. 'Look out, though, old Slater . . .'

The door opened and Mr Slater, coatless now and with his black bowler in one hand, came into the room. He gave them a brief, meaningless smile and then fixed his eyes on Polly. 'Good morning, ladies! Miss O'Brady, bring your notebook through, would you? I have to go to a meeting this afternoon so this morning will be a busy one – we had better start work at once.'

Polly got slowly to her feet and took an extra pencil out of its mug, in case the other one broke. Mr Slater got very cross if she was not prepared for such emergencies. If only he had been a trim, soldierly major with a blond moustache and laughing eyes! Or – or a sailor, with lots of gold braid, or a nice flight lieutenant . . .

'Miss O'Brady, why are you staring into space? Don't say you've forgotten your pencil again! If I've told you once . . .'

Mr Slater's whiney voice brought Polly back to earth with a jolt. She heaved a sigh and flourished her pencils at the old horror, noting with evil satisfaction that despite only just having arrived at the office, Mr Slater's shoulders were already well speckled. Thank the good God I don't have to get near enough to smell his breath, she reminded herself reverently as she took her seat opposite him. Now concentrate, Poll, or you'll regret it later. And anyway, when I join the forces I shan't work in a perishin' office, not me! I'll be something exciting, and outdoors, I'll not . . .

'Miss O'Brady, I said take a letter to Mr French of the Plymouth branch, but I've not seen your pencil so much as touch the paper. Really, if it wasn't for the fact that most of our staff have left to join the armed forces . . .'

'Sorry, sir,' Polly said with another sigh. 'It's just

that me pal – my friend, I mean – came back from America last night and we had a lot of talking to catch up on, so I'm a bit—'

'I'm not interested in your private life, Miss O'Brady, just in getting my letters typed,' Mr Slater said with unnecessary sharpness. He looked spitefully at her and Polly knew that if it had been in his power to do so, he would have sacked her on the spot. But fortunately she was a quick typist and, when she was not dreaming, an accurate one. So he knew he would have to put up with her for a while, anyway.

'Sorry, sir.'

'Right. Now are you attending? Good. Then a letter to Mr French, if you please . . .'

Grace woke late and lay in bed for a few moments, wondering where she was and why the ship seemed suddenly so still. Then she opened her eyes and saw the Sacred Heart on the wall above the bed and the edge of the pink and white checked counterpane which Deirdre had laid lovingly over the pair of them once they had settled, Polly at the foot of the bed and herself at the head, and remembered everything. She also glanced at the alarm clock on Polly's little bedside table, and gave a squeak. Half past eleven, the morning was almost gone and she had done nothing but sleep! But then she remembered the previous day and how very tired she had been and settled back on her pillow. It wouldn't hurt to lie in just this once . . . and although it was getting on towards lunchtime, she could join the WRNs just as well in the afternoon. Indeed, she would get up presently and go down to see if there was any hot water for washing and then she could make her plans. Auntie Deirdre would advise her what was best to do.

But ten minutes later, reaching the kitchen with her blue dressing gown on over her striped pyjamas, Grace realised that quite a lot had changed since she had last been in the O'Brady house. Deirdre had gone to work, Peader told her, pulling the kettle over the fire and getting out the loaf, but he was to be her deputy until his wife came home at around four.

'Your Auntie Dee said you'd have a bowl of porridge and a boiled egg for your breakfast, alanna,' he said, pouring cold water into an enamel jug, adding hot from the kettle, and handing it to her. 'And I t'ought the pair of us would have a couple of kippers at midday. But as you're late up, how about missin' out breakfast and havin' a nice hot bowl of vegetable soup first and then the kippers? Would that suit you?'

'Kippers! I haven't tasted a kipper since I left the 'Pool,' Grace said, her mouth watering at the thought. 'What about me cutting some bread and butter, Uncle Peader, while you put the soup on the stove? When I'm up, that is – and you may depend upon it, I shan't be long, not with kippers waiting.'

And so it was a comfortably full Grace who finally left the house at about half past one, bound for the recruiting offices. Peader had reassured her that she could perfectly well join up without having to leave them immediately; indeed, he said he'd told Polly over and over that it took at least a couple of weeks to get all the paperwork done when a body joined the services. Then she would have to wait until there were sufficient girls ready to undertake their basic training.

'Don't you worry your head that you'll be sent off to somewhere like a little parcel as soon as you sign on the dotted line, Grace me darlin',' he said with a comfortable chuckle. 'You'll be wit' us for a while yet.'

So Grace found herself heading with a quiet mind for Canning Place, where Peader told her she would find the Naval Recruiting Office. She was wearing her best navy-blue coat with a matching velour hat perched at what she hoped was a becoming angle on her smooth and shining hair, a pair of neat, navy lace-up walking shoes on her feet and a bounce of delighted anticipation in her step. As she walked, she glanced around. It was a fine, bright February day, with more than a touch of frost in the air so that her breath fanned out round her like a cloud, but the sunshine, though pale, was cheering and Grace, who had so enjoyed New York, still found herself remarkably glad to be home again. It was odd, she mused as she walked, that she remembered Liverpool with such fondness considering that the first dozen or so years of her life had been spent in this city in poverty and fear. But it had been Liverpudlians who had fed her and given her affection, and there had been pals, a good many of them, amongst other kids ... Oh yes, Liverpool was home all right, and one that still had the power to bring tears of affection to her eyes.

But best of all, the Liverpudlians, she reminded herself as she turned on to the Scottie, were the Salvationists. It had been Sara who had recognised her as Grace Carbery when she had first entered the Strawb, and she was a Salvationist. From then on she had had her own place, and that had been as a loved child of the Strawb. The Army had taken her in, and she had suddenly found herself with two families – the O'Bradys, and the Strawb. From being a child alone, with no brothers or sisters who acknowledged her, she had had a dozen sisters, and as the home grew, so did these wonderful new relatives, until by the time she was sixteen and able to go out into the world and earn her own living, Grace had had confidence, and friends galore.

She was thinking this, telling herself that as soon as she had cleared up the matter of joining the WRNs she must go back to the Strawb and tell them she was home, when a voice hailed her. She glanced across the road and saw a plump, yellow-haired girl heading in her direction, a wide smile spreading across her face.

'Gracie! Well, wharra turn-up for the books, eh, our Gracie! I reckernised you at once, you've not changed at all – where you been these past few years? Ooh, if that ain't the smartest coat I seen . . . You a member of one of the services yet? The coat's awful like a uniform one, only a bit too smart . . . I did hear as you'd gone to America . . . now who told me that, I wonder? . . . But I see I were wrong. Oh, Grace, give your old pal a hug!'

Grace squeaked and threw her arms round the other girl, hugging as tightly as she could, pressing her cheek to the plump, pink one so close to her own.

'Fanny! Oh, Fan, it's so good to see you! You were right, I have been to the States – I mean America – but I'm back now, and on my way to join up! This was my nannying coat – I was a nanny in New York – but I couldn't stay over there when dear old England was at war, and things weren't so good. How about you? What've you been doing all these years?'

Fanny stood back, then caught hold of Grace's hand and began to pull her along the pavement. 'Look, we've gorra deal of talkin' to do, our Gracie, so we might as well do it over a cup of char! There, that's Army slang for you, not that I mean to join the ATS, because I don't like that sludgy-brown uniform – the same colour as a baby's nappy when the baby's been feelin' poorly, I always say.' Fanny threw back her head and laughed uproariously, then continued to drag Grace along the pavement. 'Here, Miss Young's place is all right, we'll catch up a bit and then what say we join up together? Things is always more fun if there's the two of you in it. I've a mind to try the WAAF – what d'you think?'

'Oh . . . but I've applied for the WRNS,' Grace said slowly as they sat themselves down in the small tearoom. 'I – I wrote from the States, but—'

'The WRNS? But they say they've gorra waiting list, believe it or not,' Fanny told her. 'Besides, they don't let the WRNs go to sea, you know, or do anything much other than office work or cookin'. Now if you're a WAAF you can be a driver, or a mechanic, or you can pack parachutes . . . Oh, there's all kinds of thing you can do, queen. And then the WRNS are a bit kind o' snobby about gals from orphan homes, I daresay. Did they answer your letters, eh?'

'No, but—'

'Oh well, we'll talk about it when we've catched up on each other,' Fanny said with all her usual unimpaired cheerfulness. 'Oh, yes, two teas, please, miss, an' a couple of iced buns.'

Grace ate her bun and drank her tea and listened to Fanny telling her the story of her life so far. She had always greatly admired Fanny's easy ways and friendly attitude and when the two girls had become seniors they had shared a small bedroom and talked of all the things sixteen-year-olds talk about – young men, work, their dreams and aspirations. Now it was no hardship to talk to Fanny of her own wishes and dreams, and to listen, too, as Fanny shared hers.

'But I think I'll probably try the WRNS first, all the same,' she said finally, as the two of them prepared to leave the tearoom. 'Why don't we both go to the WRNS recruiting place? You might find you wanted to join them, after all. Think of the black silk stockings!'

'And them 'orrible school prefect hats.' Fanny laughed. 'Still, an' all, I'll give it a go, queen. And when we've done the deed, how about us goin' back to the Strawb, tellin' them all that we've joined up? Come on, we can catch a tram a bit further up the road that'll take us to the Pier Head. It'll save us quite a walk.'

When Polly burst into the little house in Titchfield Street that evening, full of curiosity to know how Grace had spent her day, she found her friend settled in front of the fire with a round of bread on a toasting fork, held out to the flames. Grace turned round and smiled rather guiltily at Polly.

'Oh, you're back, Poll! I've had a grand day, but I did miss you, though I did meet up with an old friend . . . Do you remember me telling you about Fanny Meeson, when we were at the Strawb? We shared a bedroom when we were seniors.'

'Oh, aye, the girl with yaller hair,' Polly said, casting her coat and hat on to the floor and hastily picking them up again as Deirdre turned from the sink to give her a reproachful look. 'Sorry, Mam . . . Well, go on, Gracie! Tell me the most important thing – have you joined up?'

'Yes, I have, and as your dad and mam said, it'll be a week or three before I hear anything further, but I've signed and now I'm . . . well, guess!'

'You're a WRN!' Polly shrieked, diving across the kitchen to give Grace an exuberant hug. 'Oh, aren't you the luckiest girl? Oh, don't I wish I were a bit older, so's I could be a WRN too!'

To Polly's surprise, Grace's cheeks went bright pink and she glanced rather guiltily across the kitchen, to where Deirdre, at the sink, was clearly amused by the conversation.

'Oh . . . well, I did go to the Navy, but . . . and anyhow, they didn't seem at all interested in my letters, said they were being besieged by applicants . . .'

Her voice trailed away and Polly's mother turned away from the sink and began to dry her hands on the roller towel which hung on the back door. 'She's a WAAF, Polly me love,' she said gently. 'Our darlin' Gracie's been and gone and joined the Women's Auxiliary Air Force!'

There was no denying that Polly was delighted to get Sunny's letter, particularly as it proved that she and Ivan had not been imagining things – Sunny had been in Liverpool just before last Christmas. Once she had an address for Sunny, Polly wrote regularly – as regularly as she wrote to Tad, who had joined the Air Force and had trained to be an aero-engine mechanic and was now attached to a squadron based in Lincolnshire. She looked forward to the post each morning, though, once a letter came, she naturally had to reply to it, which was not so easy now that she was working so very hard. 'Me war's passin' in letter-writin',' Polly grumbled to Deirdre one day as she sat at the kitchen table scribbling away, whilst outside the May sunshine fell on the kids playing in the jigger and Ivan and his pal Boz, kicking a bundle of rags up and down and ferociously screaming 'Goal!' every time one or other of them let the 'ball' get past him. 'It's not as if me life was full an' excitin' either, Mammy . . . not like Sunny an' Tad, to say nothin' of our Grace. She's up there, on an airfield full of fellers, payin' them their wages and dancin' with them and all sorts, whereas you don't even let me go to the hops, in case I meet someone interestin' who isn't a Catholic and might . . . well, might be – be interestin',' she finished.

'We're not against you going dancing, provided you go wit' a group of friends,' Deirdre said mildly. 'And what about the letters you get from Sunny and Tad? Both of them young fellers is probably holdin' a torch for you. Yet here's you, wantin' to gad off every night and have an exciting life . . .'

'I don't! It's just . . . well, Sunny says in his letters that he's a signaller now, and not just an ordinary seaman – he wasn't too keen on bein' down in the bowels of a ship, said he were rotten seasick – and Tad's with his squadron, messin' about with the innards of aeroplanes and probably getting covered in grease the way he always liked to be. Not that any of 'em's allowed to write much about what they're doing, because of walls havin' ears, but their letters are more interesting than mine. Once I've said I earned a bonus for typin' Mr Slater's private letters I've said it all, just about.'

'What private letters?' Peader said. He pushed his spectacles down on his nose and looked at Polly over the top of them. 'I didn't hear nothin' about this, not a word did I hear. I t'ought he was such a dull, pernickety old feller, too, but now you tell me he has a private life, and private correspondence, to boot! Not that it can be very private if he lets you into his secrets,' he added thoughtfully.

Polly giggled. 'Well, I'd never have thought it, but he's the father of six kids, Daddy, four of 'em in the forces. They write home, so he has to write back, of course, and he suddenly realised that if he paid me a bit extra and worked half an hour late in the evenings he could get 'em typed, which is a whole lot easier than handwriting.' She glared at her own correspondence, then rubbed her aching wrist. 'I wonder if I could type my letters in me lunch hour? she enquired plaintively. Not that there's anything much to tell 'em,' she concluded rather bitterly.

'Never you mind, love,' her mother said serenely. She was making bread for the week, pounding the great lump of dough as though it were alive and dangerous, Polly thought with some amusement. 'I dunno about Tad, but I reckon Sunny's life isn't all that easy; life aboard ship never is. I reckon your letters bring him a lot of pleasure.'

'Tad's still got that Angela girl writin' to him,' Polly muttered. She tried to write another word but her pen seemed empty so she shook it and was rewarded with a blot. 'Oh, damn!'

'Language,' Peader said mildly from his place opposite her at the kitchen table. 'If it were me, Polly me darlin', I'd write one letter and then copy it out twice more. After all, alanna, you've only the one life! They're leading their own lives, so why shouldn't you ease your trouble a little? Answer me that now.'

'No, that wouldn't work, Daddy,' Polly said firmly. She frowned over her letter for a moment and then signed off with a flourish and reached for the blotting paper. 'When I write to Grace I write like a girl, and when I write to Sunny . . . Oh well, I think I write a different side of me, so I do, If you see what I mean.'

'I do,' Deirdre said at once, when her husband

234

merely went on with his own work of addressing envelopes, though he did give his daughter a puzzled look before bending once more to his task. 'But never mind, love. Your letters give a lot of pleasure, I can tell you that without ever having read one word of them. You're a good girl, Polly.'

'Oh well,' Polly said. She heaved a sigh and glanced across at her father. 'Could I give you a hand wit' them envelopes, Daddy, seeing as I've finished me letter-writing for this week? I can do it without having to think too much, unlike letters to me pals.'

Chapter Nine

AUGUST 1940

Sunny leaned on the rail and stared towards the outlines of the Devonport dockyard as the ship nosed its way into its berth. The *Poppy* was coming in for repairs, since she had been nipping round a convoy when she had been attacked by Stuka dive bombers and holed just above the waterline, as well as losing some of her superstructure, for the attack had been a vicious one. They had been lucky, however; one of the anti-aircraft gunners had suddenly found one of the diving planes in his sights and had poured enough lead into her for the attacker to suddenly become the victim, as it fell, corkscrewing madly, into the sea. They had been even luckier, Sunny reflected now, that the bloody plane hadn't hit one of the convoy, but although they had managed to get the ships with their precious supplies safely home, they would have to go into dry-dock for repairs.

Which was why they were now steaming slowly into Devonport dockyard but although this might make things difficult for some members of the crew Sunny realised that it did not worry him at all. He was studying hard and knowing he would be given some leave while the ship was undergoing repairs he was considering staying at the sailors' home in Plymouth instead of returning by rail to Portsmouth and his mother.

The truth was that Sunny had begun to find his mothers 'guests' an embarrassment when he returned home unexpectedly, as he so often did. To find a boy of his own age or even younger at the breakfast table was somehow humiliating and though Sunny avoided such encounters whenever possible it did not make his leaves either easy or comfortable. But if he stayed in Devonport he could have some leave and get stuck into his books. He had another exam ahead of him and he was determined to pass, because he was beginning to enjoy his job. Signallers had to do a great many things other than learn how to read and send morse and to use the big Aldis signalling lamps for ship to ship messages. Folk thought it was all done by radio these days, but unless you wanted the enemy to know your every move – and secrecy was particularly important with the slow-moving ships in a convoy – you had to maintain radio silence once you were out of port. This meant that a signal, which could ideally be seen only by the ship to which it was addressed, was of the first importance, and Sunny had begun to realise that he relished the nature of his job and the standing which it gave him amongst the ship's crew. So he had studied on board ship whenever he was not actually on watch, and meant to pass this particular exam with flying colours so that he might, in the fullness of time, become a yeoman signaller, the right-hand man of his captain and someone who would indeed be of vital importance to his ship.

'Hey'up la'! Dreamin' of your sweetheart or a nice cool pint?'

Sunny jumped and turned to face the speaker. 'Dempsey! Warra' you trying to do, give me a bleedin' heart attack? I was just wondering whether to stay on Devonport and get some studying done. I've got an exam coming up and there's too much coming and going in me Mam's house for me to work. She won't know I've docked so there'd be no hurt feelin's although a week or so in the sailors' home ain't much bleedin' fun. If we were still livin' in Liverpool it would be different; I've a heap of pals there what'd let me work in their parlours if I were desperate but I don't know anyone in Pompey apart from me Mam – she's always busy . . .'

'Why not come back wi' me, old feller, same as you did last Christmas an' you can see all your old pals. Jest ask for a warrant to the 'Pool, 'stead of one to Pompey. The skipper won't notice where you're bound unless you're not back in time. What say, old pal?'

It was a generous offer, but Sunny had no doubt that Dempsey meant every word and after only the slightest of hesitations he accepted.

So thus it was that Sunny left the *Poppy* later that day with his old friend Dempsey – both Liverpool bound. It had been a while since he had been to Liverpool and he was looking forward to seeing his old friends, particularly Polly. He had written to her at least once a week and she wrote back with great regularity, though the letters could only be sent and collected when he was in port which made the correspondence a somewhat jerky one, but it wasn't the same as meeting, he reflected now as he and Dempsey strode towards the station. Meeting Polly would be wonderful – he just hoped she could arrange for some time off so that they could see more of each other.

There were his old friends, too. A good few of them had joined up, mostly going in the navy, as he had, so maybe there would be others on leave, too. And he liked the Dempsey family though he appreciated that with the overcrowding in their small house, studying for his exams would be difficult. However, Mr and Mrs O'Brady seemed like the sort of parents who would want a feller to get on. It was quite possible that when he told them he needed somewhere quiet to study, they might offer him the use of their front parlour, which would naturally enable him both to see more of Polly and to win her parents over.

On the station he and Dempsey learned without surprise that their train was running four hours late, so they decided to go back into the town and get themselves a meal – in fact they were on their way out of the station when something else occurred to Sunny. He would send Polly a telegram telling of his imminent arrival so that she might prepare her parents and, possibly, even meet him. He told Dempsey what he meant to do and the two young men went straight to the nearest Post Office where Sunny wrote and discarded half a dozen telegram forms before deciding that brief was best.

'Coming back to Liverpool as ship in dock stop. Arriving tonight stop. Will call tomorrow stop. Sunny.'

'That took you long enough,' grumbled Dempsey as Sunny rejoined him on the pavement. 'You and your girlfriends, old feller! Now let us get ourselves some grub.'

Polly was home from work and making tea when the knock came at the door. Since her mother now did war work, slaving away at Littlewoods, off Hanover Street, making parachutes for the Air Force on a huge commercial sewing machine, Polly and Peader between them quite often made the tea.

'I'm not as young as I was,' Deirdre would say as she came across the kitchen, to drop wearily into a chair and accept the proferred cup of tea which either

239

her husband or her daughter would be sure to make as soon as they heard the latch on the gate click. 'I tell you, war work pays well and we have some fun, the girls and meself, but I'm fair wore out by the time I catch the perishin' tram home.'

So what with the hard work and the tram journey on a vehicle crammed with other tired workers, naturally it was a relief for Polly's mammy to find that the potatoes had been peeled, vegetables such as cabbage or carrots prepared, and some sort of main dish got ready by Polly. Peader was handy about the house and getting handier, but most of the actual cooking was done by Polly. A day sitting behind a typewriter and running messages was not particularly tiring, and besides, she liked to make a meal. The shortages of almost everything unrationed made meals a challenge although Polly was glad she rarely had to do the marketing. If one saw a queue outside a food shop one joined it so Peader was largely responsible for the shopping since he had more time to spare. It gave her a far greater sense of achievement than typing boring letters for old Mr Slater.

So when the knock sounded Polly ran to the door and took the small yellow envelope and found it was addressed to herself. For a moment her heart did a very peculiar tap dance of fear, for did she not have brothers in the forces, and friends, and a mammy who worked the other side of the city and could easily be in some sort of trouble? So without delay she tore the little envelope open whilst behind her, Peader said anxiously: 'What is it, alanna? Not bad news, I hope to God.'

Peader had been sitting in the front parlour, with account books spread around him and his glasses perched on his nose. Naturally, Polly realised, he would have seen the telegram boy through the front window, and would have wondered, as she had.

But right now it was easy to reassure him. 'It's all fine and dandy, Daddy,' she said, popping into the parlour and waving the short telegram in the air as she entered the room. 'It's from me old pal Sunny, so it is. He's coming home on leave, should be in the city tonight, he just dropped me a wire to let me know.'

Peader's anxious look vanished at once and Polly realised that the telegram had done Sunny a good turn, even though he had probably not thought of it in quite that way; because he was so relieved that nothing bad had happened to any of his sons, Peader positively beamed at her.

'And he's goin' to visit us, no doubt,' he said heartily. 'Well, there's a thoughtful way to behave, alanna. And telegrams cost money, so they do. I hope he'll come round and see us as soon as he's able.'

Polly, assuring her father that no doubt Sunny would do so, returned to the kitchen and her work of dipping slices of liver into seasoned flour prior to frying it in the big pan with the onions she had already sliced and wept over; she smiled gleefully to herself.

It would be lovely to see Sunny after all this time. Oh, and Grace might meet him, because she would be arriving back for her leave the day after tomorrow. Polly frowned at the thought. She wondered how long Sunny's leave would be. She was longing to see him again, of course she was, but she could scarcely expect Grace to want to play gooseberry to the pair of them, and Grace was her best friend. If it came to a choice, Polly would plump for Grace every time. Still, what was the point in meeting trouble halfway? Grace had a week's leave but Sunny's was bound to be shorter. They might meet – that would be rather nice – but then Sunny would go back to Portsmouth and she and Grace would be able to enjoy themselves together as they had planned.

Sunny, knowing nothing of Polly's thoughts, however, took his time getting ready to go and see Polly the following evening. He knew from her letters that she worked for the Reliant Insurance Company during the week, which was on Exchange Flags, and had decided that it would be safer to meet her out of work, because you could never tell with parents. They might let bygones be bygones and treat him in a friendly fashion, or they might decide that they still did not want their little girl mixing with the likes of him and treat him coldly. In which case, he thought now, brushing his best bell bottoms with Dempsey's clothes brush, it might be as well to have a word with Polly first. If she gave him the go-ahead he would walk home with her and suggest going to a flick; but if she said her parents were still doubtful of him, they would at least be able to discuss what best to do.

Fortunately, Sunny was so eager to see his young friend that he arrived at the offices at four thirty, believing that she left off work at five, but he underestimated Polly's excitement at the thought of seeing her old pal again. Polly had got special permission to go at four thirty and as he arrived at the statue in the middle of Exchange Flags there was Polly, tripping down the steps of her office, not even looking around for him but heading in the direction of the tram stop.

For a moment Sunny stood staring, taking in the changes. His little Polly had been a lively and affectionate girl; now she was a young woman. She wore a white blouse and a navy skirt and carried a dark jacket of some sort over one arm, for it was a warm afternoon. She was bare headed, but the delightful bouncy curls that he remembered were pulled back from her face and tied into a bun at the nape of her neck with a piece of black velvet ribbon. She did not even glance round her as she crossed the flags so Sunny shouted.

'Hoy, Poll!' he called, and as she turned towards him, it suddenly seemed the most natural thing in the world to fling his arms around her, lift her off her feet, and give her an exuberant hug. 'Oh, Polly, ain't you grown up! And aren't you still the little smasher I remember! Give us a kiss!'

Polly, blushing a most becoming shade of rose-pink, laughed up at him and kissed his cheek, then pushed him back a bit so that she, in her turn, could take a good look at him. 'You're taller,' she said in a rather awed tone. 'And . . . and your hair's even more gold and you're brown as brown . . . Oh, Sunny, it's just wonderful to see you, so it is.'

'It's nice to see you too, beautiful,' Sunny assured her. He took a quick look round, then drew her close again and bent to kiss her mouth, though she wasn't standing too much of that, he realised as she shoved heartily against his chest. 'Oh, Polly, don't keep me at arm's length! It's been so long, and I've thought of no one but you ever since—'

'Liar, liar, kecks on fire.' Polly chanted the old school taunt in a hushed but laughing tone, but she blushed even deeper as she did so, Sunny was pleased to notice. 'I bet you've had twenty or thirty girlfriends since you and me went our separate ways. Not that it matters. It's now that matters, isn't it, Sunny? And you're coming home to tea, of course . . .

Don't worry about Mammy and Daddy, they'll be right pleased to see you, they were so happy when your telegram arrived.'

'Happy?' Sunny said wonderingly. He could not for the life of him see why a telegram from him should have made Polly's parents happy, even if they had quite forgiven him for his previous misconduct.

'Well, yes,' Polly said. She dimpled up at him, mischief clear in her glance. 'You see in wartime, everyone thinks that a telegram would be bad news, and I've brothers in the forces and me pals and all . . . so when I read your telegram out, they were just as pleased as could be. And Daddy said you were thoughtful to have sent it! So you'll come home with me, won't you, and have your tea wit' us?'

'Thanks very much, I'd like to,' Sunny said, really gratified by Polly's words. They weren't bad old sticks, the O'Bradys, he decided, glancing down at Polly's animated face close to his shoulder, and they had the prettiest daughter although he didn't approve of her new hairstyle.

He said as much as they walked towards Tithebarn Street where they would catch a number 16 tram for home. As he spoke he put a hand up and tried to loosen her hair but it felt as though the ribbon had been glued into place and Polly, though she laughed, pushed his hand away and shook her head at him. 'It takes me half an hour to get me hair flattened and tamed,' she said severely. 'I've growed it and growed it but it won't go straight, it just loves to curl and curls aren't right for working in an office, or me boss doesn't think so at any rate.'

'Well, I'm not your boss,' Sunny said as he put his arm round her and squeezed her waist. She really was a cuddlesome armful and the soft blonde hair so near his face smelled of sunshine and primroses. 'Wish I was, though – why don't you join the Navy and come aboard the sloop *Poppy* so's we could be together all the time? You could be me cabin boy when I'm captain of the ship, like I will be one day.'

'Oh you!' Polly said as they crossed Tithebarn Street and headed for the tram stop. 'I *am* goin' to join the Navy – the WRNs, I mean – when I'm old enough but they won't let me go to sea, and well you know it. Oh Holy Mother of God, look at the length of that queue! Still an' all, it's not as bad as it would have been at five o'clock which is why I got out early. I kind of thought you might come round to Titchfield Street this evening and I wanted to get ahead with the tea. Mammy's working at Littlewoods making parachutes and she's dead tired by the time she gets home so I usually gets the tea to save her the work. Or did I mention that in me letters?'

'You may have mentioned it,' Sunny said gloomily, 'but that's one bit the censor would have chopped. Some of your letters come through to me lookin' more like lace doilies than correspondence. Though I love gettin' them,' he added hastily.

'Yes, yours have holes cut in 'em too,' Polly said, having thought the matter over. 'But one of the gals at work – she's a woman really, quite an old one, I reckon she must be thirty at least – she says she and her old feller have worked out a code, so he can tell her where he's going and what he's doing, without the censor – or the bleedin' Huns, come to that – finding out where our Navy is. Although I don't see how letters can fall into enemy hands. I mean, if they torpedo one of our ships letters would be the last thing they'd fish out of the drink, wouldn't you say?'

'I dunno,' Sunny said. 'You'd think so, but there's

gorra be a reason. Anyway, most of your letters wait in Pompey until the *Poppy* docks, though one or two have follered me around,' he finished. 'Hey up, gal, is this 'un ours?'

The tram bearing down upon them was crowded, but the conductor seemed to have a knack of getting his passengers to move up, and presently Polly and Sunny found themselves on the step and then being pushed by the folk behind until they were halfway down the car.

'Reckon that feller used to pack sardines before he started tram conductin',' Sunny said in Polly's ear. 'It's real nice squeezin' *you*, Polly O'Brady, but I dunno as I'm particularly fond of bein' squeezed by a fat mary-ellen! What's more, her basket's diggin' into me best bell bottoms. I hope I don't get caught up on her wickerwork.'

Polly giggled. 'Well, it won't be for long, only half-a-dozen stops,' she told him. 'Oh, what'll we do tomorrer, Sunny? Only I've took a some days off work, and tomorrer's one of 'em. We could go to New Brighton on the train, or over to Eastham on the ferry and walk in the woods. Ivan and me used to do that a lot when we was kids. We could take a picnic – or what about Seaforth? We could go on the docker's umbrella, that's a nice trip, so it is, especially if the day's fine.'

'Anything would be grand,' Sunny said. He was pleased and flattered that Polly had taken some time off, obviously because he was coming home. 'Whatever we don't do tomorrer we can do the next day, though, if you're off work for a bit.'

'Ye-es,' Polly said, with considerable doubt in her tone. Sunny was about to ask her why this should be so when the tram stopped with a jerk which sent all

the passengers staggering into one another and somehow the two of them got separated. The mary-ellen
once more jammed her vengeful basket into Sunny
whilst people fought their way out of the crush. Then
the tram started up again and Sunny, staggering in
the other direction, found himself pressed up against
a couple of giggling girls and a thin woman whose
string bag smelled strongly of fish.

Sunny would have liked to reach Polly once more
but when he made the attempt the fat mary-ellen told
him to stop shovin' or she'd end up on someone's lap,
very probably breakin' their bleedin' legs wi' her
weight, and since this was clearly no idle threat he
heaved a sigh but stayed where he was. After all, he
and Polly were going to have almost a week to themselves, ten minutes apart should not bother them.

And presently, they reached the corner of Tatlock
Street and the tram jerked to a stop once more. This
time the mary-ellen, Polly and Sunny joined forces to
squeeze and batter their way off the tram, landing on
the pavement with triumphant grins – and crushed
clothing, Polly said, surveying her once neat jacket
and skirt with some dismay.

'Oh, a bit of a crush don't matter, but is me bum all
scratched?' Sunny asked rather anxiously as he and
Polly began to walk along Tatlock Street. 'Take a look,
there's a good gal. I hope I haven't ruined me best
kecks.'

'You're fine,' Polly said, giggling again. She linked
her arm with his and fell into step beside him. 'Only
. . . well, there's one thing I've not mentioned . . .'

'You must have asked for leave as soon as you got
me telegram,' Sunny said. He squeezed her arm.
'Clever little Polly!'

'We-ell,' Polly said again, and cast him what

seemed to be a conscience-stricken look as she spoke. 'We-ell, the fact is, Sunny, that me old pal Grace is comin' to stay tomorrer, and since she's in the WAAF and has only got a week's leave, and two days of it, almost, will get used up in travelling, I thought it only fair to get some time off.'

'Grace? Who's Grace when she's at home?' Sunny said. 'But anyway, why does she stay at your place, eh? Wharron earth's wrong wi' her livin' at her own home, or wi' one of her other pals?'

Polly shook his arm and pulled him to a halt on the corner of Titchfield Street. He could see her house from here, the neatly painted green gate, the jigger down which he had once run when calling for his little pal. He turned to look searchingly down at her; suppose . . . well, suppose she was going to cast him aside for this Grace person? But she wouldn't, Polly wasn't like that. Only he had rather hoped . . .

'Grace is Grace Carbery, and she's been me pal for years and years – until she went to New York, in fact, to live with me brother Brogan and his wife, Sara. She's an orphan, she was brought up in the Strawb, you know, out Calderstones way, and though I suppose she could stay with them on her leaves, she'd much rather come to us. Sunny, she were like a sister to me when we was kids, I – I couldn't expect her not to come to us.'

'But – but you're me best gal, our Poll, and there's a war on! No one, not even this Grace girl, would expect us to spend our precious time with someone else playin' gooseberry, when all we want is to be together. Together alone, I mean!'

Sunny looked down at her rosy, determined face. She seemed unmoved by his impassioned words, and he sighed inwardly at what might easily be the death of all his bright plans. It had been going to be such a marvellous leave, with he and Polly off by themselves all day and, he had hoped, him catching up on his book work in their front parlour of an evening. He had even indulged in the unlikely dream that Mrs O'Brady would beg him to stay over, to share with Ivan, perhaps, so that he and Polly could be together for his entire leave, even sharing the same roof. And now this – this Grace person was about to spoil it all! But surely he was clever enough to circumvent this in some way? He pulled Polly to a halt and took hold of both her hands, swaying them gently from side to side. Girls, he had discovered, seemed to like this gesture, to consider it romantic. But apparently Polly was not to be numbered amongst them, for she snatched her hands away and addressed him quite crossly.

'Don't, Sunny, you're making me feel seasick! As for Grace playing gooseberry to you and me, it's no such thing! Oh, I like you quite a lot, I suppose, but don't you tell me you've never taken a girl out since we split up all them years ago! It's grand to see you, and I want us to get to know one another all over again, but don't pretend I'm *that* special to you, or you'd have perishin' well come home and seen me before.'

'But I tried! At Christmas I tried! I hung about outside Blackler's because that silly mare – I can't even remember her name, now – said you worked there . . . I came round to your place too, only I didn't have much time and I missed you . . . Oh, Poll, don't pretend you weren't glad to see me, because I saw your face light up, and your eyes sparkle . . .'

Polly tucked her arm in his once again and pulled gently. 'Come along, Sunny, it's daft to quarrel, so it is! I *do* like you, I like you ever so much, but you don't understand about Grace. When we lived in the crossin' cottage she came to stay most weekends and we never had a cross word . . . Anyway, it's no use, because it's all cut and dried. Grace is coming to stay tomorrer evening and the only twosome there after that will be me and her! I can't let her down now.'

Sunny had always known when to back down and accept defeat gracefully, and he knew, instinctively, that if he continued to object he would lose Polly as well as his beautiful dreams of being alone with her. So he said remorsefully: 'Awright, Poll, that's fair enough. We've got tomorrer, after all, and after that I'll have to make do with me own company. Unless that is . . .' Sunny pretended to be struck with a bright idea, clapping his hand to his head and momentarily closing his eyes as if in deep thought and then opening them again to say triumphantly: 'What about this, Poll? Say I bring Dempsey along to make up a foursome? Dempsey's me shipmate and a grand feller – you'd like him and so would Grace. Unless she's got a pal of her own in the 'Pool. How do you know she's not got a feller in the RAF, or someone who she was friendly with at the Strawb? Or d'you know of any feller she seemed to fancy?'

He glanced hopefully at Polly, and was glad to see that the frosty look in her eyes which had warned him not to go too far was beginning to dissipate; instead, she was thoughtful. 'I don't think there was anyone special, not a feller, anyway,' she said after a moment. 'But look. I'll have to think about it and talk to Gracie. After all, she's never met yourself, the poor, unfortunate girl, nor your friend Dempsey! Now, let's forget all that and talk about tomorrer.'

Sunny grinned but made no comment, and

presently, Polly said brightly: 'Well, if there's no one home from the war stayin' at the Strawb, you could always take Ivan so you's got someone to go about with. Don't pull a face, Sunny, or I'll t'ump you one, so I will! But we'll see what Mammy says when she gets in; she's full of good ideas is me mammy! I don't want you to be lonely either. Oh, if only things had been different . . .'

By now, they had reached the jigger and were making their way round the backs of the row of houses. Polly pushed open a tall, green-painted door in the crumbling brick wall, led Sunny across a tiny, brick-paved yard and in through the back door. They stepped into a pleasant kitchen with a table laid for a meal and a kettle steaming on the hob. As they came in Polly said: 'Daddy, here's Sunny come to meet me! Oh, Daddy, was it a little doze you were having? I'm that sorry to waken you!'

But the tall, heavily built man got up out of his chair and limped across to Sunny, holding out one large, work-worn hand. 'Well, and how are you, me dear feller? Isn't it a grand t'ing to see you again, after so long?' He shook Sunny's hand, smiling all the time into Sunny's eyes, clearly bent on making his feelings clear. 'And wasn't it angry we were wit' you, all them years ago? But that's all over, old feller. You're our Polly's good friend and our guest, so sit yourself down and I'll make the tea.'

Sunny was much touched by the generosity of Peader's welcome, but could not find words to show his own feelings. Instead, he took the proferred chair and, presently, the cup of tea, and said he hoped that both Peader and his wife were well, and all the rest of the family, and allowed the talk to turn, as talk usually did these days, to the war.

By the time that his hostess came home, tea was made and Sunny, feeling quite at home, was buttering the bread which Polly sliced. He almost gave Mrs O'Brady a hug, so charming was her welcome to him, but decided against it at the last minute and shook her hand very heartily instead.

'It's grand to be back in Liverpool,' he told her honestly. 'I'm stayin' wi' me pal Dempsey, though it's terrible crowded. Still, they're friendly folk and I'm used to living in a crush. Once the hammocks are slung there isn't much room inside a sloop, I can tell you.'

'How'll you study then, Sunny?' Polly asked, almost as though coming in on her cue, Sunny thought gratefully. 'I know you've got an important exam coming up because you said so in one of your letters.' She twinkled up at him. 'And the censor let it come through too,' she added.

'Oh, I'll manage somehow, Poll,' Sunny said immediately. 'Though it won't be easy. I could go down to the library on William Brown Street, I suppose, but that's a way off. Still, it 'ud be quiet, and—'

'Sure and why shouldn't you use our parlour, Sunny?' Mrs O'Brady said at once, also as though she had learned the script, Sunny thought. 'Peader likes to work on his books wit' them all spread out on the kitchen table, but if you can manage on your knee in the parlour – and there's one or two little tables in there – well, you're very welcome.'

And Sunny, graciously accepting her kind invitation and thanking the O'Bradys for making him feel so at home, reflected that though he clearly could not expect an invitation to stay, not with another guest due late the next evening, at least half of his hopes had been realised, and with his usual optimism Sunny was sure he would not find himself alone – even after Grace's arrival.

Sunny and Polly had a marvellous time the next day. It was another fine, warm one, and they caught the ferry to Eastham and walked, talking constantly of their lives, their work, their friends. They ate their picnic in a little glade with a stream running through it, and later had tea in a farmhouse garden, where Sunny ate enough, Polly told him, to keep a normal feller alive for a week.

It was not until they were making their way back to the ferry in the early evening that the subject of Grace – and the morrow – cropped up again.

'Grace is arriving tonight. She and her pal Fanny have had their posting,' Polly said as they strolled down the road towards the landing stage where the ferry would presently dock. 'But first thing tomorrer we'll go off up to Beaconsfield Lane and see if we can find one of her pals. I know they probably won't be staying at the Strawb,' she added hastily, when Sunny looked doubtful. 'But everyone will go along to see the staff and the kids. Grace will; she said so. And that way, we may discover whether she's any pals in the 'Pool right now.'

'Why can't I come?' Sunny said at once. 'I've never been in the Strawb; I don't see why I can't come. And anyway, poor Grace won't want to spend the first day of her leave trailin' across half Liverpool! No, the three of us can find something to do tomorrer, and then we can all go up to the Strawb the following day.'

'No, Sunny, stop trying to boss me around,' Polly said vehemently, stamping her foot and glaring at him. 'You haven't changed a bit, have you? All those years ago when I was just a kid you told me what to do and got me into big trouble and listen to you now! No, don't shake your head, you're doing it again! I'm tellin' you Grace and me's goin' to the Strawb tomorrer and if you don't watch out you'll find yourself doing a whole lot more studying than you'd planned – and not in our front parlour either! Why, you're as bad as Ivan. He pestered to be taken with us today if you remember and we had to disappoint him. I can't have two people bothering me like that.'

'I'm sorry, Polleen,' Sunny said humbly. 'Honest to God I didn't mean to boss you about. It were only a suggestion and I take it back. If you and Grace are set on goin' to the Strawb tomorrer, *of course* you must go, only I haven't ever been there and I thought . . . I thought . . .'

He did his best to look thoroughly ashamed of himself and must have succeeded, for Polly's face softened as she squeezed his hand remorsefully. 'It's me that should be sorry, shoutin' like a fishwife at you when you're only tryin' to see everyone enjoys their leave. Look, you come round to my house tomorrer about dinnertime. I'll have had a chance to talk to Grace and see how she feels – we might even have been up to the Strawb by then – and I'll be able to tell you how things stand.'

'That'd be grand,' Sunny said, squeezing Polly's hand in his turn. 'I wouldn't spoil your friend's leave for the world. I suppose Dempsey and me could amuse ourselves somehow – we could even take Ivan at a pinch, get him out of your hair – though I'll miss you something awful, Poll, and it'll be harder somehow knowin' you're so near.'

'Let's not talk about it now,' Polly said, smiling up at him. 'Just you come tomorrer like I said and no more shouting or bossing from either of us.'

Agreeing, Sunny felt downright amazed at himself. Here was he, the popular, much in demand Sunny Andersen, who always had a couple of girls yearning for him, suggesting he wanted to see the inside of a children's home just so that he would be constantly with Polly, and then pretending he would take her kid brother around with him just to keep in her good books. What on earth was the matter with him? She was a pretty girl all right, but why should he go to such lengths just for a pretty girl? There were dozens of 'em about, he reminded himself, and most of them were a good deal more willing to let a chap have a bit of a kiss and a cuddle than Polly was. Delightful though the day had been, she had kept him at arm's length from the very start, and no doubt intended to do so for what remained of the day too.

But they were approaching the Mersey, and Sunny remembered that there was a cafe down near the ferry's landing stage where they could get a cup of tea, or a bun, or both, whilst they waited for their craft to arrive.

He reminded Polly of Mrs Jessie O'Brien's Refreshment Rooms and suggested that they should wait there and get themselves some tea instead of hanging about by the water. Polly shook her head, laughing at him, her eyes teasing. 'Sunny Andersen, we had tea – and a good one – just now, so we did. What can you be wantin' with another tea so soon?'

But Sunny, consulting his wristwatch, told her that their farmhouse tea had been two whole hours ago and added that he would murder a cuppa and Polly agreed that she, too, was thirsty.

'So we'll go inside and watch for the ferry from there, and have us tea and cakes,' Sunny said in his most masterful manner. 'And then, whiles you O'Bradys have your own meal, I'll be gettin' back to Dempsey's and studyin' for me exam. I know your mam said I could use your parlour, but I won't do it tonight, not wi' your pal comin' home and all the greetin' to be got over.'

Polly, following him meekly into the refreshment rooms and agreeing to tea and cakes, also agreed that Sunny had best go straight home when they crossed the river. 'For welcome though you'd be, everyone's attention will be on our Grace,' she admitted. 'But – but you'll come at around one o'clock tomorrer, won't you? You see, the three of us will be waitin' for you.'

'Three?' Sunny began, then his brow cleared. 'Oh, I forgot Ivan. Ah, there's a cream doughnut and an eclair. Which one would you like, queen?'

'It may be only mock, but it's still delicious,' Polly said, her hand hovering over the plate of cakes. 'Ooh, I do love doughnuts, but there's chocolate on eclairs. I think I'll just close me eyes and grab. This is a real treat. I don't get cakes like this often.'

This caused a good deal of hilarity, especially since Polly's small hand missed both eclair and doughnut and landed upon the only fairly plain cake on the plate, a Viennese whirl. Sunny tried to persuade her to eat both doughnut and eclair and they ended by cutting the two rich, squishy cakes into four more or less even pieces, and having half a doughnut and half an eclair each.

In fact, so merry was their tea and so happy were they that they missed their ferry and had to hang on for the next one, which meant that Polly fairly tore up to the tram stop and implored him not to waste time by coming all the way to Titchfield Street, but to go straight back to the Dempseys' place.

'If you take me home, Mammy and Daddy will feel they ought to ask you to stay,' she pointed out as the two of them climbed aboard an already heavily laden tram. 'But if you get off this tram and go straight to the Dempseys', then we'll meet up tomorrer, as we'd planned.'

It made sense, Sunny could see that, so he leaned over and gave Polly the only sort of kiss possible when you are both standing up on a crowded tram, and then jumped down, waving until the vehicle was out of sight, though he could see no answering movement from within.

And presently, back home in the Dempseys' crowded little house, he was glad he hadn't gone all the way back to Titchfield Street with Polly. You're makin' a complete fool of yourself, Sunny, he told himself severely as he sat himself down on the window sill in the boys' room and got out his books. Before you know it, she'll be talking about weddin' bells and gettin' engaged. And there's no sense in that, particularly in wartime.

But he knew, really, that there was little chance of Polly doing any such thing. She liked him, but it was a much cooler and more sensible liking than that usually shown him by girls he flirted with and took notice of. He was going to have to play his cards very carefully indeed to retain a place in Polly's affections without committing himself more than he wanted to do – and the thought of losing her still sent such a stab of dismay through him that he could scarcely believe the pain.

Still, all this wouldn't get his exam work learned. Sunny opened a large manual of seamanship and began to con the pages.

*

Grace woke and lay for a moment looking up at a low white ceiling just above her head, on which the sunlight played dappled shadows. She knew where she was, of course, having been looking forward to this leave for a week, but it was still rather nice to wake of one's own accord instead of being shouted out of sleep by reveille, and it was nice to feel the soft warmth of the bed around one, and to know— Good gracious, where was Polly?

The answer to that particular question came smiling into the room even as Grace began to sit up on her elbow. Polly, fully dressed, came through the doorway, a laden tray in her hands. 'Tea, bread and butter an' a lightly boiled egg, Miss Airwoman,' Polly said. 'Mammy thought we should spoil you today, just for once. My, you got in awful late! You must have been perishin' tired – you came up to bed and you were asleep before I'd finished gettin' me clothes off.' She settled the tray comfortably across Grace's knees and then plumped herself down on the foot of the bed, causing the tea to rock none too gently. 'Hey up, drink it quick, Gracie, before I spill it all over Mammy's clean sheets! Oh, but it's good to have you back after so long!'

'It's good to be back,' Grace said gratefully, sipping the tea. 'Well, this is the life, Poll! I'm sorry I was so worn out last night but that journey! It should have taken about four hours and it actually took nearly ten. Well, the engine broke down twice, which didn't help, and then there was a goods train on the line . . . I can't remember all the excuses, but there were lots. I was so tired I nearly wept when a porter told us we'd missed the last tram, but a few of us – all services – clubbed together and took a taxi, or we'd have been later still. What time was it when I finally staggered up to your door?'

'Midnight,' Polly said, satisfyingly round-eyed. Mammy kept trying to send me to bed, but Daddy said I'd a right to wait up for you, bless him. And of course I'd got holiday so I didn't need to get up early for work. Only you know how it is, the sun peeped through the window and I was awake, so I got dressed as quietly as I could and sneaked down to get you some breakfast. And here we both are. Do eat your egg before it goes cold and hard,' she added. 'Daddy's got an allotment, though it's a long way off, but he's got six hens, so we get extra eggs sometimes.'

'We do all right in the WAAF, though most of the eggs we get are dried,' Grace said, beheading the large brown egg and dipping a finger of bread and butter into the orange yolk. 'Oh, this is so good, Poll! I do love a runny egg.'

'So do I—' Polly was beginning, when there was a perfunctory knock on the door and Ivan appeared. He grinned at both girls and then said, all in a rush: 'Hi, Grace! Will you be long? Only that feller of Polly's is downstairs, and Mammy's gone to work so Daddy's put him in the parlour until you come down.'

'I told him dinnertime,' Polly said, her cheeks beginning to flush. 'I told him Grace and me would have things to do this morning. My goodness, I—'

'He says as how he thought you might like him to take me out today,' Ivan said, grinning from ear to ear. 'I don't believe a word of it meself, but that's what he said.'

Polly sighed. 'I forgot – we did say something like that,' she admitted. 'But I didn't really think . . . Oh well. I'll come down in a minute, Ivan, and have a word with him.'

Grace put a hand to her mouth and went to jump out of bed, but Polly pushed her back again. 'Sure an' there's no hurry,' she said breezily. 'It's just me pal Sunny's home on leave an' all, Grace. I did tell him to come round at dinnertime so you and he could meet, so he's only jumped the gun by a couple of hours. The thing is, he's at a loose end so he thought we might like his company if we go along to the Strawb later. He's never seen a children's home, you see, so he was quite curious about it.'

To tell the truth, Grace was more than a little dismayed by this information. She had gathered from Deirdre's letters to her son and daughter-in-law that Sunny had been a bad influence on Polly, had caused her to sag off school and generally misbehave, and did not much enjoy the thought of being forced to spend time with someone she scarcely knew and of whom she could not approve. But on the other hand, she could not expect Polly to cast off her friend for someone who had been out of the country for several years. However, she had no intention of making her feelings known.

'Why don't we go up to the Strawb right now, then, Poll? As soon as I get up, I mean,' she said, busily despatching the egg, the bread and butter, and several cups of tea. 'Come to that, why not let me go up to the Strawb? I could take Ivan, if you like, leave you and – and Sunny a bit of time to yourselves.'

But this Polly would by no means allow. 'Me and Sunny had all day yesterday,' she said, her eyes widening with dismay. 'It's *you* I want to spend time with, Grace, not Sunny. Sunny's a good chap, so he is, but you're me oldest friend and it's you I've been missin'. Oh, I know he's me friend, but he's a *feller*. You can't talk to them the same as you can to your bezzie, and you're me bezzie, honest to God you are.'

Grace laughed. 'You sound a real little scouser,' she

said teasingly. 'Look, you and I will go up to the Strawb this morning, because I do want to see if any of my pals are back on leave as well. And then there's others . . . they may be working in the city, I'd like to get in touch with them again for old time's sake. The staff always know where everyone is – the Army's a small world and you stick by your friends. I've got another six days before I'll have to do that awful journey again – not that it will be the same awful journey, come to think, me and Fanny Meeson will be heading south in a week, we've been posted – so whilst I'm looking up me old pals you can see Sunny. Isn't that fair enough? It means I shan't have to play gooseberry, but we'll both have plenty of time together. What d'you say?'

'That sounds very good to me,' Polly said, going over to the door. 'You get yourself dressed and ready then, Gracie, and I'll go downstairs and tell Sunny to slope off. He and Ivan can go down to the Pier Head or – or off somewhere, and come home here like I said in the first place, for a snack at one o'clock.'

Sunny, with his kitbag slung over one shoulder, was walking to Lime Street Station, on the first stage of his journey back to his ship. He and Dempsey had had a telegram saying that the *Poppy* was due to sail in forty-eight hours and requesting their presence. Or at least, if the telegram had not been worded quite like that, it was what it meant.

Dempsey had set straight off for the station that morning, although they both guessed their train would be late, but Sunny had nipped round to Titchfield Street first, because he wanted to thank the O'Bradys for making his leave such a good one. He had arrived, unfortunately, after Polly and Deirdre had both left for work, for Polly had only taken five days off from her job since that was all the time that Grace had been able to spend with her, but Peader was in. Sunny thanked him with real sincerity and told him that he would be writing to Polly, of course, and hoped that she would write to him too.

'But she's a great hand wi' a pen, unlike meself,' he said cheerfully, shaking Peader's outstretched hand. 'I know she won't let me down, not your Polly.'

'I daresay Polly isn't the only one you'll be gettin' letters from,' Peader said in his slow, amused way. 'The t'ree of you got on so well I'd be amazed if young Grace doesn't write an' all.'

'Well, the more the merrier,' Sunny had said, but he hadn't really believed that Grace would write to him as well. He had left after that, striding along the pavement in the brilliant August sunshine, beginning to remember just how good this particular leave had been – and he had not been exaggerating either – from the first moment that he had met up with Polly to last night, when they had said what they thought was a brief goodbye until next day, he had thoroughly enjoyed himself.

Despite the fact that there were three of them most of the time as well. Oh, at first he had had to be very careful not to get on the wrong side of Polly, but Grace was a real little smasher, for all he hadn't thought so at first. At first he had thought her rather plain, but after a day in her company, he had begun to see that she was a very pretty girl indeed, only beside Polly's bright blonde hair and vivid eyes, her own paler colouring seemed insipid. Grace was tall and slender, with light brown, shining hair which she wore in the popular fashion, curled round a piece of hair ribbon with the front of it swept up. But once

Polly had pointed out severely that she was no longer in uniform and could relax a bit, Grace had let her hair fall from a centre parting into a long, soft page-boy style, which suited her very well indeed. And though her skin was pale and her eyes hazel, that skin was very clear and those eyes very bright. Oh aye, Sunny considered that Grace was a pretty girl, and a pleasant companion too.

There had been one afternoon, furthermore, when he and Grace had gone off together, because Polly had been called back to the office. Grace had announced her intention of going up to the Strawb to say good-bye to Matron and the rest of the staff and Sunny, because he'd never been to the Strawb, had decided to go along. Sunny remembered various institutions he had visited as a youngster, the chill of the places and sheer soullessness that filled them, but the Strawb – well, no wonder Grace liked going back to the Strawb, he told himself now, remembering that visit. The staff were mostly quite young and very friendly, talking and laughing with Grace and himself as though they had known each other all their lives.

The kids had been fun too, swarming all over Grace and not saying a word when she gave the sweets into the care of a member of staff. They all knew that the sweets were meant for them and would be given to them at the appropriate time. One little girl in par ticular had taken a great shine to Sunny. She was about seven, he guessed from the gaps in her front teeth where the baby ones had fallen out but had not yet been replaced by the grown-up ones, and her name was Suzie, only due to the lack of teeth she called herself 'Thuthie', which amused him very much. Suzie had proved to be very good at Grand-mother's footsteps and when Sunny consented to be

Grandmother (to delighted shrieks from the children and broad smiles from the staff and Grace) she managed to sneak up on him without his once seeing her move, so that her final quick dash, and her climbing all over him and breathing stickily into his face was a great triumph. Cooing like a contented little pigeon, she had pressed her hot little face against his cheek and told him in a breathy whisper that when she was growed up, she meant to marry him. Sunny, laughing, had told her that he would be an ugly old man in his thirties or forties before she was in a marrying mood, but Suzie had just shaken her head and continued to clasp his hand and climb on to his lap whenever she could.

But now he was entering Lime Street Station, and began to look around for Dempsey.

'Sunny! Over here! So you made it, me ole pal – the next one in is supposed to be ours, so look lively, feller! I've kept a place for you by me.'

It was Dempsey of course, in what Sunny now realised was a vast queue. 'Thanks, Demp,' he said. 'It looks like we'll soon be on our way, ole mate.'

'Yeah, this is goodbye to the 'Pool for a time,' Dempsey agreed.

'Hope it still looks as good next time we come home,' Sunny said.

Dempsey, pushing his way ahead shoulder to shoulder with Sunny, turned and grinned. 'You comn' up this way again?' he asked. 'Wharrabout the disturbed nights then, la'? I thought you'd be glad to get some peace, in Pompey.'

There had been fairly constant enemy activity over the city for a couple of nights, but though the docks had been bombed in Wallasey and Birkenhead there had been no actual raids on the city itself. Sunny, battling through the crowd towards an emptying carriage, snorted. 'If you think the jerries are goin' to leave Pompey alone once they get goin', you're a bigger fool than I thought you were, Demp,' he declared. 'I reckon they'll home in on the south of England and start givin' us hell any time now.'

'Only we shan't be there,' Dempsey panted. 'Gerrin this first carriage, Sunny, then at least we're aboard. We can worry about gerrin' seats later.'

Chapter Ten

Grace and Fanny soon settled into their new station, and Grace began to enjoy her new job, for though Fanny was still on cookhouse duties Grace had been promoted. She would be tried out as an RT operator, which meant that she would be working in the control tower, talking the planes off and back, would be doing shiftwork, and would most definitely be learning new skills.

'The jerries were talking about invasion at the time of Dunkirk,' the officer who began to train Grace told her. 'Everyone believes that will be their next move, but before they can carry it out without the risk of being wiped off the board they'll have to gain air supremacy. That means we'll need every plane we've got to fight them off, and every girl with enough intelligence to help in the fight must use her wits and strain every nerve to see our chaps get down safely. Savvy?'

He was probably no more than forty, with a huge blonde moustache and a sprightly way of walking which the girls imitated when he was out of sight, but he was talking sense and Grace knew it, so she threw herself into her training with the greatest enthusiasm and very soon was as useful as any other WAAF RT operators on the station. 'It stands for radio telephone operators,' she said in a letter to Polly. 'I think that's because we hear the chaps over their radio sets, but we talk back to them on a sort of telephone thing which hangs down just by our mouths. I really feel I'm being useful, Poll, at last. This is a million times better than adding up columns of figures and paying a queue of men their wages.'

She wondered whether the censor would start clipping out half of this letter, but did not worry overmuch. She would see Polly when she next got a decent leave and would be able to tell her in person much of what was happening to her.

And what was happening was a great deal more exciting than just being a RT operator. For the first time in her life, Grace had met a young man who really mattered to her, though the fact that he was Polly's boyfriend might have taken the gloss off Grace's feelings for Sunny had she ever considered herself as being in competition with her young friend.

For Grace, who had dreaded meeting the dreadful young man who had set her darling Polly's feet on the road to wickedness, found that she liked Sunny more than any other young man she had met. He was incredibly handsome, she had guessed that he would be, but that he was kind, understanding, sympathetic and good company had come as a total shock to her. Most of the handsome young men she met – and she met a good few now that she was in the WAAF – were not in the least bit interested in a tall, shy, rather plain WAAF, but Sunny had not even seemed to notice that Grace was no looker, that compared to Polly's bubbly prettiness she was plain, gawky and shy. Sunny had simply seen someone who could share in the fun of a brief leave in the city.

But he was Polly's feller. That was understood, and funnily enough it did not worry Grace in the least. After all, she did not have the slightest intention of trying to wrest Sunny from Polly; she knew it would be impossible for a start, and would not have dreamed of doing such an unfriendly thing in any circumstances. What she felt for Sunny, she supposed, was a sort of hero-worship, combined with gratitude because he was so nice to her and never made her feel left out.

She had thought, however, that it was no use her writing to him. He would not reply; she might only make a fool of herself. Nevertheless she had written, just a funny, jokey sort of letter about the journey down from Liverpool to her present station, how she and Fanny had managed in the train and a little bit about her new job. She had sent the letter off immediately on arriving at her new station and had not expected much of a reply, if any, for months, but instead had got one from Sunny within the week which had clearly crossed in the post with hers. It was a nice letter too, telling her of his experiences on the train returning to Devonport and all about the friends who had joined himself and Dempsey before they had gone very far on their journey.

The good old Poppy *is sailing almost at once, so this is just a short note to let you know I got back safely and trust that you did the same, and I hope that one day you'll drop me a line. I expect we all like letters, and though mine are likely to be scrappy – and short – and probably full of holes where the censor has snipped bits out, I hope you'll write to me whenever you've got a spare moment.*

Grace had gone around in a daze of happiness, almost unable to believe her own luck. And oddly enough, it must, she thought, have given her confidence a boost, because next time she, Maria and

Annette, who were all budding RT operators, went off to one of the RAF dances together, she got quite as many partners as they did and, what was more, found it easier to talk and laugh naturally with the young men instead of becoming tongue-tied and awkward.

Next time she wrote to Polly, she told her about Sunny's letter and said how happy it had made her feel that Sunny, who was Polly's feller, still wanted her to write to him as a friend. Polly's reply was warming, too: *Of course Sunny liked you; anyone who doesn't is plain daft.*

Her letter went on to describe the fun she had had, dancing with a very motley assortment of young men at Daulby Hall and making it plain to Grace that much though she liked Sunny, she did not consider the two of them in any way tied to each other.

Not that I've the slightest intention of being serious about Sunny, Grace told herself that evening, as she prepared for bed in the long, blacked-out Nissen hut which was the nearest thing to a home the girls had on the station. He is awful nice, I like him a good deal, but even if he wasn't Polly's – and he is, whatever she may pretend – him and me would never do together. I'm too serious and he's too – well, unserious, I suppose. I'd begin to bore him and I expect he'd go back to his old ways, like when he led Poll astray, and then I wouldn't be able to respect him, and respect's ever so important. You have to respect someone before you can love them . . . not that I'm thinking of loving anyone, not yet . . . And Grace's thoughts broke down in confusion, leaving her with only two really coherent ideas. It was good that she and Sunny could be friends without any strings, and better that she was now finding it easier to mix with people of both sexes.

And then Grace forced her mind back to RT operating and the way the war was going and she thought about the fighter pilots, and the girls who loved them, and the number of planes that she and her fellow-operators saw off as they scrambled from their stations, and the number – quite often less – which came back. And she thought about the dangers which faced sailors, all sailors, and the bombing of Liverpool docks, which had taken place soon after they had left the 'Pool. And she remembered that those dangers were faced every day by Sunny, and she found, suddenly, that she was glad that she was just his pal, that if anything bad happened it would not be her tragedy, her gut-wrenching, pain-filled loss.

She turned over in bed and buried her face in the pillow. She wanted to be friends with fellows, of course she did, but she suddenly realised that real involvement, the sort that poor little Polly had with Sunny, was a cruelly sad business in wartime.

And presently she went to sleep, telling herself firmly that it was better to be uninvolved, fancy-free. And woke in the middle of the night to the terrible knowledge that if anything happened to Sunny – who was just a friend, and Polly's fellow – she would carry the scar of it on her heart to the end of her days.

Tad, up on his Yorkshire bomber station, was as aware as Grace of the loss of life – and the loss of aircraft – which was the sad result of even the most successful bombing raid, but although he knew the crews and the pilots a good deal better than she did, his main preoccupation, at this stage, was with the planes which he serviced. He had been a con-scientious motor mechanic when he worked at

Barnes's garage in Dublin, but now he was obsessional about the engines which he worked on. Men's lives depended on him and he was sharply aware that nothing, absolutely nothing, was more important than sending the fellers off in a machine they could depend on. He could do nothing if they were caught in the flak or gunned down by enemy aircraft, but he could make sure that their engines, their machines, were as perfect as he and his mates could make them.

Once away from his job, however, Tad had other tasks, amongst which was letter-writing. Never too keen on such an occupation, he now found himself with a number of letters to write each week – except that it was usually each month – and in order to ease matters he had taken to writing one letter, sometimes to Angela, sometimes to Polly or his family, and then copying it, with minor alterations, to his other correspondents.

'One of these days you'll be in a rare ole mess, cheatin' on folk the way you do,' his pal Smiffy told him one afternoon when he came into the billet and saw Tad, with four sheets of paper spread out on the table before him, the laborious script already completed upon the first page, whilst he copied it first on to one sheet and then on to the others.

Tad, looking up from his work, grinned. 'This is nothing, old feller. Last month I paid young O'Mara a packet of Woodbines to do the copying for me,' he said. 'Me writing's so bad that he just scribbled 'em down anyhow, and not one squeak from me family or friends did I get to say why was I writin' so fine all of a sudden! I'd do it again,' he added, 'except O'Mara's gone into town and no one else needed fags that badly.'

Smiffy heaved an exaggerated sigh and sat down at

the table, pulling the completed letter towards him. 'What've you said this time?' he asked accusingly. 'Not a great deal, by the looks of this. Dammit, Tad, you've only covered one side of the page, and I've seen the letters that you get back from your girlfriends, they write you sheets and sheets.'

'They've got nothin' better to do, so they haven't,' Tad said righteously. 'Oh, I know they both work, but it's not like our work, Smiffy. No one's life hangs on whether Angie sells some woman a silk dress or Poll makes mistakes when she's typing out an insurance policy. You an' me, now, we can't afford to make a mistake or one of our squadron could pay wit' his life. And put me letter down,' he added. 'Didn't no one ever tell you 'twas rude to read letters not addressed to yourself?'

'You don't write letters, you write round-robins,' Smiffy said absently. He screwed up his eyes, held the letter at arm's length, and read slowly, '"Dear blank, many thanks for your last. Glad you are well, as I am. We're well fed up here, but I miss blank. Last week I went into Lincoln to see a flick, and I wished you could have been with me. Only you couldn't, so I went with one of the lads. After, we had tea and a bit of sawdusty old cake at a little teashop down by the river. It was a sunny day and the sins . . ." No, swans . . . God, Tad, your writing is appalling, to say nothing of your spelling! "The swans were begging for bread and hissing at us if we didn't throw them any . . ."'

He threw the letter back on the table as Tad made a lunge for it. 'How you manage to keep one girlfriend, let alone two, I can't imagine! If they only knew what you did with your letters – but I reckon they must suspect something of the sort. And why the blanks, anyway?'

Tad heaved a sigh. 'Because you can't say exactly the same t'ing to your mammy and your girlfriends,' he said patiently. 'So I leave blanks and fill in the little odds and ends separately. Polly's real keen on animals, so at the end of her letter I'm goin' to put in a bit about Sergeant Smiler, but Angie wouldn't be interested, so at the end of her letter I'll tell her a bit about the fillum I saw last week. And me mammy likes to know I'm being fed right, so I'll tell her what we had for supper last night. See? It's simple if you use your brain.'

'You'll be caught out one day and get what you deserve,' Smiffy announced, having strolled round the table to look at the other pages, almost identical, which Tad had spread out round him. 'One of 'em's in England, isn't she? Why don't you go and see her, instead of all this letter-writing? You're bound to get a decent bit of leave one of these days.'

'Oh, you mean Polly,' Tad said, reaching for the nearest letter. 'She's more like a sister to me than a girlfriend, so she is. We was brought up together, like, when we was just a pair o' kids livin' in the Dublin slums. Now Angie – she's a real girlfriend, the sort you've got, Smiffy. She's pretty as a picture, smart as paint . . .'

'And waiting for you, I suppose, with no thought of any other feller,' Smiffy interposed, grinning. 'Yet you send her the same letters as all the others. Oh, what a peculiar bloke you are, Donoghue!'

But Tad, putting the first letter into its envelope, merely grunted. He could see nothing peculiar about his method of letter-writing and Smiffy, he well knew, did not have a great many younger brothers and sisters who liked a line occasionally, to say nothing of friends back in Ireland. Sometimes, his conscience gave a twinge when he posted off two very nearly identical letters to Angie and Polly, but they would never know and anyway, he reminded himself reasonably, a feller only had one life. He was merely simplifying a task which, had he tried to write individual letters to each one, would have kept him busy from dawn to dusk on any day that he happened not to be working.

Still. The thought of visiting Polly when he had sufficient leave had occurred to him several times, though in a way he felt guilty about even thinking about it. She was his dearest pal, they had shared so much when they were kids, but he had a feeling that she had never fully understood about Angie, that she thought him shallow and in some way fickle for having found himself a girlfriend other than herself. But this was clearly not the case, could not be the case, since she, on her side, had told him that she was seeing a feller by the name of Sunny, wrote to him, went around with him . . . Oh well, Poll would simply have to understand about Angie. What's sauce for the goose is sauce for the gander, Tad thought to himself, but Polly was a darling, he would really love to see her again.

He would, he decided, go to Liverpool the next time he got enough leave and spend a few days getting to know Poll all over again.

Sunny was soon engrossed in life aboard ship once more, though this time he was not aboard the sloop *Poppy* with the men he had sailed with for many months. It had not been possible, it seemed, to finish the repairs to the sloop in the time at their disposal so he had been drafted to the *Felix*, a destroyer. Rather to his dismay Dempsey was not with him but he knew from past experience that he made friends easily so had few worries on that score.

When first he came on board he was met by the ship's coxswain who took his draft documents and called a seaman to take Sunny forward to the starboard fo'c'sle where he would mess. He was told that eighteen men including himself would eat, sleep, stow their gear and live in an area about sixteen feet by twelve, but he was used to the cramped conditions aboard the *Poppy* and thought that this was fair enough. Life in a destroyer was clearly going to be a matter of cramming the maximum number of men into a tiny space as in all warships. On that first day, therefore, he found somewhere to sling his hammock and then followed the seaman back out on deck, and thence to the flag deck below and on either side of the bridge, where he would work when on watch.

'We've been told we're on convoy escort duty,' the leading signaller told Sunny later that same day. 'I hear the slops is full of tropical kit so's I reckon it'll be the arctic but we'll go where we're sent, as usual, and discover our destination when we arrive. That's the navy for you.'

Sunny knew that he would miss his pals aboard the *Poppy*, particularly Dempsey, but a destroyer, he considered, was a ship worth boasting about, and the chances of promotion were possibly even better than they had been aboard the *Poppy*, since he had passed his recent exam with flying colours. And although he had believed himself friendless aboard the *Felix*, he realised when he went below for his first night's sleep that he was not the only scouser aboard.

They were a mixed bunch, he could see that at a glance, and was slinging his hammock and shaking out his blankets when something about the able

275

seaman nearest him caught his attention. The man was putting up his own hammock, frowning in concentration, and when he became aware of Sunny watching him he turned and grinned.

'Hello – you're part of the new draft, aren't you? First time aboard a destroyer?'

'That's right,' Sunny said. 'I was on the sloop *Poppy* before, but she was badly knocked about so they've re-drafted a good few of us, I think. None to the *Felix* except me, though, worse luck. Wharrabout you?'

'I was on the corvette *Campion* before I joined,' the other said. 'They're grand ships, but a bit on the cramped side. Not that I've sailed with a destroyer before, mind, this'll be my first voyage with the *Felix*. But I can tell from your accent that you're a scouser, like me, though Liverpool's my adopted home rather than my birthplace. I'm from Dublin.' The older man glanced at Sunny's arm, but he had stripped to his white top in the heat of the fo'c'sle. 'Do you have a trade? I was made up to able seaman aboard the *Campion*.'

'I'm a signaller. I've just passed me latest exams okay, so mebbe I'll be made up to leading signaller soon,' Sunny said with more than a little false modesty. 'One thing you can say about the war, promotion comes quicker than in the peace. But I reckon you're norra a regular, like me?'

'No, I'm a Hostilities Only man,' the other said, grinning. He held out a square, capable-looking hand. 'O'Brady. And you're . . .?'

Sunny stared, too surprised to hold out his own hand. He stared very hard at the older man and it occurred to him, for the first time, that he had seen him somewhere before – or someone very like him. 'O'Brady?' he repeated. 'I've gorra pal in Liverpool . . .

now I come to think . . . you've gorra look of Peader . . . an' I reckon you're a bit like Ivan, an' all. Is – is your first name Martin? Only I've just spent me leave with the O'Bradys, they've gorra house in Titchfield Street, and—'

'You wouldn't be Sunny, would you?' the other man said, his grin widening. 'Dear God, if you are this is the strangest coincidence! Yes, I'm Martin, and I'd bet my bottom dollar that you're Sunny, who caused poor old Polly such grief when she was a little 'un.'

The two men shook hands, Sunny grinning now with more than a shade of embarrassment. 'Put it there, Martin,' he said. 'Me mam's always telled me *be sure your sins will find you out*, and by and large she's been right. But I'm a welcome visitor in your mam's house now, honest to God I am, me an' your Polly's still good friends.'

'Yes, Mammy did say you and Poll exchanged letters,' Martin admitted. 'I seem to remember Polly saying that you'd joined up back in '38. I wish I'd done the same,' he added rather bitterly. 'If I had done so, I'd have stood a better chance of promotion myself.'

'But you're an accountant, aren't you?' Sunny asked. He began once more to shake out his blankets and Martin, two feet away from him, followed suit. 'I seem to remember you were in an accounts department somewhere. And you're a married feller – you wouldn't have wanted to be at sea before the war, would you?'

'I dunno,' Martin said. He finished making his bunk and sat down on the Rexine cushion which lay across his locker and began to pull off his soft-soled shoes. 'My wife's gone back to live wit' her parents for the duration, which means that when I do get back for a forty-eight, I have to muck in wit' her parents. They're nice enough folk,' he added hastily. 'But it's not the same as having your own place.'

'I reckon sailors shouldn't marry too young,' Sunny said, sitting on his own locker. 'When you're fancy-free you can tek your pick, just about.' He was stripped down to underpants and vest and flicked himself into his bunk. 'What's it like being a gunner, anyhow?'

'We're just like everyone else – unless they pipe action stations we do any job that needs doing, just about. What was it like in your sloop?'

'The same, only signallers spend most of their time on watch on the flag deck,' Sunny said. 'Rushing backwards and forwards, reading signals, hauling pennants up the halyards. We aren't as important as the yeoman signaller, of course – he's our chiefie – but no one can afford to make mistakes, especially if they want to get on in the Navy. Still, we clean and scrub and sweep, good training for a housewife, that's wharr I always say.'

'Except that these days,' Martin observed, 'housewives seem to spend most of their time having fun, going to dances, entertaining the troops you might say.'

Sunny, rightly interpreting this embittered remark to apply to Martin's wife, was silent, having nothing to say, but after a short pause, Martin continued. 'Oh, I shouldn't moan, Monica does write . . . but her letters are so short and mostly she talks about dances, helping in the NAAFI, that sort o' thing. I suppose she doesn't know much about the Navy, so she thinks we're livin' it up in exotic foreign ports, or at least that's how she makes it sound. She actually asked me, in one of her letters, if I ever got a chance to buy pretty materials, because she'd like to make herself a new dance dress!'

'You want to put her right,' Sunny suggested. 'Poor gal, she'd be rare ashamed if she knew what your life was really like. I mean, I reckon the Navy's the hardest of all the services, don't you?'

'Yup,' Martin said briefly. 'Monica's all right, really – I shouldn't have criticised her to you, it wasn't fair. It's – it's just that she's got no relatives in the Navy, no uncles or brothers or anything like that and her daddy wasn't in the last lot so she's got no idea of what it's all about and I suppose I – I underplayed it a bit, so's not to worry her. Given time, she'll work it out and mebbe, when I'm home next, I'll tell her a bit more.'

'Right,' Sunny said equably. 'G'night, Mart. See you in the morning.'

It took several days for the convoy to assemble and during that time Martin and Sunny found that it was comforting to have a pal aboard. They talked a good deal about Polly, the O'Brady family and Sunny's parents and by the time the convoy finally went to sea they were good friends.

'Me dad encouraged me to go to sea,' Sunny told Martin as they prepared dinner for their mess, chopping vegetables and dried beef. 'I joined in '38, so he saw me in me uniform before war was declared. But I can't write to him or anything like that. Or perhaps I could, if I posted the letter when we are in port for refuelling,' he added thoughtfully.

The early part of their voyage was fairly uneventful, apart from a practice attack by the RAF during the course of which bags of flour were dropped on the ships by the attacking 'planes, putting 'out of action' a large number of the escort.

279

'Good thing it wasn't for real,' Sunny grumbled to Martin. 'The trouble is, Mart, that you couldn't tell if any of your guns hit an aircraft, so it was all a bit one-sided.'

'You say that because you got a flour bag right on the flag-deck,' Martin grinned. 'Did you know we're stopping at Gibraltar? It might give us the chance of an hour or so ashore.'

'It'll give me the chance,' Sunny said smugly. 'I'm the buffer's assistant that day. Of course they might let us all go ashore, but somehow I doubt it. Tell you what, Mart, if I get a chance, shall I get some material for your old woman? You can pay me in "sippers", or in fags if you'd rather.'

All men over twenty got a rum ration each day and it was a common practice to swap goods for either 'sippers' or 'gulpers' of your rum, if you didn't mind losing just about all your ration.

'I'll pay you for the service in fags and for the stuff itself in money,' Martin said promptly. 'Would you really buy it for me, Sunny? It would be kind of you so it would. And just how did you get a cushy job like that, come to think?'

'Oh, I heard the bo'sun sayin' he was going ashore to get fruit and that,' Sunny said airily. 'He said he'd not been ashore in Gib for years, and would like to go again. So I said I knew just the place for fruit and vegetables, good alright, but cheap, too. So he said I could come along if I liked to give him a hand.'

'How come you know the Rock so well?' Martin asked suspiciously. 'The bo'sun's been on the andrew for years.'

'Yes, but not on the med. runs,' Sunny said. 'As for knowing Gibraltar, I've only been there a couple of times meself. But mostly, it's one long street that winds up from the foot of the rock itself to near enough the top of the town, so I reckon we'll find a shop selling fruit along there somewhere.'

'You're a bit of a skate, aren't you?' Martin said, half-admiringly. 'Telling the bo'sun a load of tosh to get yourself a trip ashore. And anyway, we may all get shore leave; you never know.'

'That's true enough, la'. Wi' the Navy you never do know,' Sunny said. 'And I wasn't taking no chances, so do you want me to buy you some silk for your missus or don't you?'

'I'd be grateful, so I would,' Martin said promptly. 'She's not a bad girl, my Monica, just a bit thoughtless. And . . . and I daresay I've not been much of a husband to her in some ways. Will you be able to get some silk, d'you think?'

'Sure to,' Sunny said. He remembered the wonderful, colourful shops on Main Street, with the delicate embroidery, the fashionable gowns and the brilliant jewellery displayed in the shop windows. 'If you knew her size you could get her a dress, come to that. Would she rather have a dress, d'you suppose?'

But Martin, after only a second's thought, shook his head. 'No, she'd rather have material to make one up for herself. She's good wit' her needle, and if I can get enough stuff it'll keep her busy for a night or two.'

Sunny grinned. 'Right you are, ole pal,' he said cheerfully. 'A bolt o' silk it shall be!'

By the time Sunny and the Bo'sun set off on their expedition, Sunny had collected little commissions from a good half of his companions, for their stay in Gibraltar was to be a short one, and most people wanted something which they could not get aboard the *Felix*. On his own account, he decided he would buy a pair of pretty earrings for Polly, or perhaps a necklace; something pretty but inexpensive.

So it was with a light heart that Sunny set off with the Bo'sun, walking up through Irish Town towards the main shopping centre. It was a brilliant day and very hot in the narrow street, however, and presently Sunny began to realise that he felt rather odd. The money in his pockets seemed to be weighing him down, and when he glanced up at the whitewashed buildings, they seemed to dazzle and change shape before his eyes.

However, he said nothing until they entered Main Street and began their shopping, and even then he only told the Bo'sun that he thought he ought to walk on the shady rather than the sunny side of the street, since he was beginning to feel very hot indeed.

The Bo'sun made some joking remark about how odd it was that a feller known as Sunny should want to keep out of the sun and then they went into a shop selling the most marvellous materials, and Sunny began the serious task of choosing, for his pal, something that would both keep his wife indoors and before her sewing machine whilst at the same time making her think of her absent husband with warmth and affection.

In the end he chose a very beautiful cream-coloured silk covered with bronze poppies, which took up almost all Martin's money, and then the two of them went back into the hot and dusty street once more.

Out there, Sunny realised that he felt very peculiar indeed. Now, the buildings did not merely dazzle, they swooped up and down, seeming immense one moment and tiny the next. What was more, his skin felt as though he were being roasted, and also as though he had been attacked by a thousand fleas – his skin actually *crawled*. He had heard people say their skin crawled often enough but had never understood what they meant until this moment.

He turned to the Bo'sun with the intention of suggesting they went into a pub for a drink, but realised he did not even feel capable of speech, so merely continued to trail in the older man's wake, the steepness of the street seeming suddenly like Mount Everest, though the stifling heat gave the lie to this fancy.

Afterwards, Sunny could not remember what they bought or how they arranged things, but he realised they must have done most of their shopping when the Bo'sun steered him into what he dimly realised must be some sort of graveyard, right at the top of the town, and sat him down on a bench beneath a shady tree.

'You're not lookin' so good, young feller-me-lad,' the Bo'sun said. His voice sounded concerned, but not only concerned; it sounded hollow and echoing, and very strange indeed. 'If you don't buck up in the next half-hour I'm thinkin' I'd best get you back . . . Whoa up, hold up, young feller!'

Sunny wondered what on earth the other man was on about, but just then his mind was taken off the Bo'sun and his behaviour by the even odder behaviour of the land around him. It seemed to tip, tilt and slide sideways, so that though he was unaware of moving himself, he presently found that the burning blue sky was above him, and that he was seeing it through what appeared to be large, dark bars.

And then, as he tried to struggle up, to tell the Bo'sun that he would be all right in a minute, he found that everything was rushing away from him very fast, getting smaller and smaller until it disappeared into very unpleasant, roaring blackness.

Sunny came round, groggily, to find himself being carted over the cobblestones of what appeared to be a courtyard. He groaned and the Bo'sun's voice said breathlessly, close to his ear: 'All righty, young feller, soon have you where you belong.'

'Back . . . the ship?' Sunny asked dizzily. He was suddenly aware that he had not bought Polly's earrings – or had he been going to get a necklace? He tried to struggle free, to say he was all right, it was just the heat, and found that his arms were apparently tied to something, that he could scarcely move. He gave a squawk of alarm and forced his eyes open and realised that he was between two sturdy men – the Bo'sun was one, the other was unknown to him – being carried along with his feet trailing, his arms across their shoulders.

'We're takin' you up to the horspital, mate,' some-one said. 'You'll be awright there – you seem to 'ave got yourself a touch of fever, you're burnin' hot, so y'are.'

Another sailor, Sunny thought. It's another sailor, from another ship, and he's helping the Bo'sun to carry me . . . where? A hospital? But I don't need a hospital, all I need is – is a nice cool bath and then my own hammock. I'll be fine after a sleep.

He tried to say this but found it was simply too much trouble, and, without remembering how he got there, he found himself being divested of his clothing by what sounded like a couple of girls, dressed in some sort of nightgown, and thrust, gently but firmly, between snowy sheets whose brilliance was so extremely painful to his burning eyes that he shut them with great determination and kept them closed.

He was horribly thirsty now, though, and said so in a cracked, painful voice, and presently the soft-voiced girls brought a cup with a sort of pipe thing which they put between his lips and lovely cool liquid trickled across his parched tongue and down his burning throat.

He had barely finished the drink before a man came to the bed and addressed him in a voice of determined cheerfulness whilst heaving Sunny into a sitting position and beginning to fiddle with whatever garment – if felt like a large shirt – he was now wearing.

'Sorry to maul you about, old fellow,' the man said heartily. 'Dear me! Nurse, have you seen his chest?'

'He's covered in it, doctor,' a girl's voice said. 'His eyes hurt . . . Is it – can it be measles?'

'My own diagnosis exactly,' the doctor said. 'Here's one little rating who won't be sailing with his ship later today.' He turned back to Sunny, gently lowering him down the bed once more. 'Been in contact with any sick children lately, lad? Got younger brothers and sisters, have you?'

Sunny groaned. 'Oh my Gawd,' he mumbled disgustedly. 'I took me girl up to the Strawb, doc, and one of the kids were all over me. I said to me pal she were burning hot – the little gal – and somehow I never did get the measles, as a sprog.'

'Well, you've got 'em now,' the doctor said cheerfully. 'And you'll be in quarantine for two weeks, so you can forget sailing with . . . what is it? Oh yes, the *Felix*. She'll be going on without you, if she hasn't already gone, but the captain sent a message up to say she'd call for you on her way back, when she's taken the convoy to its destination.'

'Gone without me? Oh, but I were buyin' stuff for

me pals, the fellers aboard,' Sunny said, trying to struggle up the bed once more. 'I don't remember much . . . I'd not gorra pair of earrings for my girl . . . there was silk for me pal Martin . . .'

'Don't you worry about a thing, or you'll be here a lot longer than a fortnight,' the doctor said reassuringly. Sunny risked a peep and found that he was a large, cheerful-looking man with very short gingery hair and a pair of amused, grey-green eyes. 'You're going to feel pretty bad for a couple of days – measles once you're fully grown is no light matter – but you'll get excellent nursing and be up and about after a week, you mark my words. You're in a room by yourself because we've no one else with a contagious disease in at present, so make the most of the quiet to have plenty of sleep. Nurse Whitaker had measles when she was young so she will take good care of you, and mind you do what she says. Take your medicine – it's only aspirin dissolved in water, there isn't a great deal else we can give you at this stage – and you'll be fighting fit by the time your ship returns. Good day to you.'

Sunny risked another peep out of his sore and aching eyes. Nurse Whitaker was young, fair-skinned, freckled. Definitely pretty. He tried to smile at her and found, to his own astonishment, that he was tired, really tired. Seconds later, he slept.

The doctor was soon proved right. Sunny thought afterwards that he must have slept a good deal that first week, but at the end of it he was taking notice, eating whatever food was put before him and probably driving the nurses crazy by trying to persuade someone to let him go outside.

'We've no gardens, unfortunately, space being at a

premium on the Rock,' Sister told him when he fretted and fumed over being shut up indoors in his small private room all day. 'And you're still infectious, so we can't let you go wandering about the town or the dockyards. Just be a little patient, young man. And anyway, since you spend your life cooped up on board your ship . . .'

'That's different,' Sunny said, and was then unable to explain why. But the nurses provided him with jigsaws, copies of the English papers several days, or even weeks, old, and as much fruit as he could eat, and at last the doctor pronounced him free from infection and told him he could go to the Royal Naval Barracks and sling his hammock there until the *Felix* came back for him.

'Which shouldn't be long,' Sunny told Nurse Whitaker as she helped him to pack up his personal effects. To Sunny's joy, Martin had thoughtfully sent his shaving kit, clean underwear and various other bits and pieces to the hospital by messenger as soon as he heard what had happened to his pal. He had included a note thanking Sunny for the silk which had eased Sunny's conscience considerably. It was the first real proof that the Bo'sun had got all their shopping back on board the *Felix* before she sailed, and it had comforted him in his illness to know that at least he had not let his shipmates down.

Once in the Naval Barracks, with the companionship of other men, Sunny soon recovered his full health and although he was impatient for the *Felix* to return, he made the best of her absence. He went all over the town, made friends with some of the soldiers stationed there to guard the dockyards and thus got taken round the amazing defences which, long ago, other servicemen had tunnelled and blasted out of the limestone of the great face of the Rock. He also wrote letters to Polly, to Grace, reproaching her for giving him the measles, albeit second-hand, so to speak, and to his mother. He went up to the top of the rock where the Gibraltar apes lived and reassured himself that they were still very much there and in good health, since an old proverb said that when the apes left the Rock then the British would do likewise, and he stared out to sea, to the constantly changing face of the ocean and the various craft making their way into the enormous spread of naval dockyards below him.

But the *Felix* did not come. And one morning he was met by a seaman, also waiting for a ship, who told him that the pair of them had been drafted.

'Drafted? Where to? Why?' Sunny said, astonished. 'But I've gorra stay here, mate. Me ship's comin' back for me!'

'Oh aye?' the other man said, disinterested. He was also from Liverpool and had been brought ashore with a ruptured appendix some three months previously and had almost forgotten the name of his previous frigate. 'Well, we're to report to the *Pursuer*. She's a destroyer, so you'll know your way around.'

So Sunny got his gear together once more and went down to the dock and aboard the *Pursuer*, to find himself hailed with considerable glee by Dempsey, who had been with his present craft ever since Sunny had joined the *Felix*.

'It's grand to see you again, Dempsey,' Sunny said, going below and taking possession of his new locker. 'But why hasn't the *Felix* come back? Have you heard?'

Dempsey shrugged. 'The convoy could have been slower than they thought,' he said. 'Or she could have been sunk.'

Sunny stared, his heart sinking into his boots. 'Not – not sunk, surely?' he said incredulously. 'Someone would've telled me. Someone would have known!'

Dempsey looked embarrassed. He began to heave Sunny's hammock up on to its hooks and to spread out the palliasse. 'The convoy was about ten days outside Gib when they were attacked,' he mumbled. 'I – I don't reckon they fished anyone out, ole pal. You must have known something was up when she didn't come back for you earlier.'

But Sunny was staring at him, round-eyed. 'Polly's brother was aboard her. He was me bezzie,' he said slowly. 'Are you tellin' me he's drownded? Oh, Jesus, Dempsey, what'll I be telling my Polly?'

Martin had known they were going to have a sticky time as soon as he saw the Fokker-Wolf reconnaissance plane with the black crosses on its wings approaching the convoy. 'Action stations – clear away for battle,' had been piped as soon as the skipper saw the plane, a mere dot in the bright evening sky. The plane he knew could be the forerunner of an attack which they had feared ever since the plane had appeared in the sky the previous day. Then, the first enemy ships had been seen approaching over the horizon converging fast on them. Martin knew the German destroyers had 5-inch guns, heavier than their own 4.7s, but this need not affect the outcome of a battle at sea. Luck, the ability to move fast and to change direction quickly and above all, accuracy of fire, would more drastically affect the outcome.

He climbed into his gun trainer's seat in the turret where the guns were loaded and pointed skywards, ready to fire as soon as the order was given. Settling himself comfortably, he glanced at his companions.

They were standing as steadily as if this were just a practice, but like him they were ready to fire, knowing that everyone's life depended on the speed with which one's guns could retaliate.

Martin settled his anti-flash helmet and tightened the wrist-straps of his gloves. If there was a flash-back from one of the rounds then helmet and gloves, with vaseline liberally smeared on his face, could save him from nasty burns. The gun captain reminded them that they should keep the gun firing once they started, making sure that the ammo was handy.

The order had been given that no one was to leave his position and now Martin settled back in his seat and gripped the training wheel, watching as the two white pointers drew into line. They were on B-gun, and Martin could see through the opening in the gun-shield that the enemy were fast approaching, and that they were approaching, what was more, in force. It was easy to tell oneself that it was the wallowing merchantmen that the slim, deadly destroyers would be aiming for, but it did not take a great deal of intelligence to realise that the merchant fleet would be a good deal easier to attack if the enemy could first sink their defenders.

There was a commotion on deck; Martin could visualise what was happening as the officers watched the approaching destroyers through their binoculars, calculating the moment when they would come within range of the *Felix*'s guns. He risked a quick glance round and saw the crew of B-gun, shells at the ready for the reload. Martin was aware of a sickly sinking sensation in his stomach and a sweat breaking out on his forehead. As always of late, just before they went into battle, he saw Monica in his mind's eye, pretty in a summer dress, her adoring eyes fixed on his, anxious only to please him. He had not been fair to her, he had acknowledged it some time ago. He had tried to turn a little Liverpudlian girl with a head full of nothing but lovemaking and pretty clothes into the sort of woman he had wanted to marry. And when, in despair, she had stopped trying to please him and begun to rebel, he had been angry, hurt . . . but he had not gone about convincing her that he loved her, that their marriage, which had been at least half-play for her, could be real, earnest. And now they were going into battle and he might be killed, might never have the chance to tell her that he did love her, did value her, and was determined to make their marriage work. Why, he might never be able to give her the silk, which was so beautiful, which her clever fingers could make into a dance dress of such beauty that the fellers would vie for her attention – but other fellers would not matter, because she would know, by then, that it was Martin she loved.

He swallowed hard and despite his thoughts the sick feeling began to recede. It would be all right, he would have another chance, get back to Liverpool and see his poor, pretty little wife, show her how he felt about her, talk to her of serious matters. Get her a nice little house somewhere, where they might be together without her parents only a thin wall away so that even their lovemaking was circumscribed.

Fire! The order had been given, Martin's work had started. As he heard the first salvo, heard the clatter of spent shells on the deck and the snap of the closing interceptor, fear receded, thoughts of home became something which might take his whole concentration from the job in hand. Outside, the din of battle was enormous, and in the slight lull between broadsides, Martin risked a peep through the opening in his gun-shield. The light was fading from the sky and the dusk made the bursts of fire from other shipping seem even more brilliant. Screeching shells, whether from friend or enemy he could not tell, were falling all around and the pom-poms on deck, their noses turned to the sky, blended their clatter with the flash and thunder of their own guns.

Martin lined up his pointers and B-gun belched forth fire once more. In the pause, Martin could hear the sobbing breath of the men passing the shells up from the magazine and knew, amazingly, a moment of calm and confidence. They knew their jobs, they all did, so how could they fail to come out of this, to be the victors?

As night came down, the battle continued to rage and the sea grew rougher so that the ships, which had drawn close, were buffeted apart. The guns had blazed constantly until the ammunition in the magazines ran out and only then, when they were more or less defenceless, did the *Felix*, battered but still relatively uninjured, draw back a little from the fight. It was at that moment the explosion came. Martin, in his gun turret still, for they were still at action stations and would be until the battle was resolved, heard a tremendous bang and saw a sheet of flame appear before his eyes, the heat of it so strong that he was flung back, scorched.

He must have lost consciousness for a few moments for the next thing he knew he was out on the open deck, being supported by one of A-gun's crew, a Scots lad called Hamish.

'I think it was a torpedo, it hit us below the waterline and blew up our magazine – good thing it was empty,' he said, managing to give a short crack of laughter despite the conditions, the dark, the flames, the list of the deck which made Martin think for a moment that he was climbing some great hill. 'You got a chunk of metal on the head, we all thought you were a goner, and then, just as I was about to get the hell out o' there, I heard you groan and begin to come round. We should be okay, though we're a good way from the rest of the fleet . . . They're dropping boats, but the sea's very rough . . . You'll not have heard the pipe to abandon ship.'

It was now that Martin realised for the first time that it was quiet; they could hear, distantly, the sound of battle, but their own firearms were silent and apart from the roar of the waves and the hiss of the wind, the *Felix* might have been on her own in the great ocean. He looked around him; men were lining up, an officer was going from group to group, checking that they all wore life jackets, that they knew what to do.

He and Hamish joined one of the queues, and then suddenly it was as though Martin came completely back to life. That was it! They were in the *Felix*, heading for home albeit by a roundabout route, and he was taking Monica home a present of silk – cream-coloured silk covered with bronze poppies. It was the most beautiful thing he'd ever seen or imagined, his pal Sunny had chose it, and he would get it back to Monica if it was the last thing he did. He looked round wildly. A nearby companionway led down into the bowels of the ship – to his fo'c'sle, in fact. It looked very like the descent into hell, but . . .

'Come back . . . Martin, you fool, you can't go down there!'

'I've got to go, there's a present I bought for me wife . . .'

And he had gone, was fighting his way down the

steps into that strange darkness which smelt of gunpowder and charred wood and worse. It was like a vision of hell, and God alone knew how he found his own locker, wrenched it open, seized from it the soft thickness of the material and began to blunder out again, the stuff in his arms. But after only a few paces he realised he would need both his hands free for the clamber back to the deck, up the companionway, so with difficulty he heaved his life jacket away from his chest, pushed the material down the front of it, and struggled on, with water now above his knees. And presently, he heard a rushing and a crash behind him and felt the ship tilt more violently yet, and when he battled his way back along the narrow corridor and reached the companionway water, sizzling like frying sausages and churning and tearing apart anything in its path, roared to meet him. Martin seized the bannisters and for a moment imagined that he would be all right, that he could fight his way out on to the deck once more.

Then another, larger wave roared down upon him, snatching his hands from the rail as though he were a year-old child, and threw him back even as another huge explosion caused the ship to open up like an oyster to the knife. Martin caught a muddled glimpse of a dark sky blazing with stars, flames shooting skywards, and then it was just water, water, everywhere he looked. Heavy, salty, and icy cold it threw him down, overwhelmed him. Snuffed out the stars.

'If you ask me, I'm the only person in this war who's spending it writing bleedin' letters,' Polly said crossly, sitting at the kitchen table with her writing materials set out all around her. She pushed the pad away and stared mournfully across at her father, counting coupons on the opposite side of the table. 'First, I just wrote to me brothers, then it was to Tad, then to Sunny, now it's Grace as well . . . Oh, it isn't fair! If I were in the WRNs people would have to write to *me*, which would be more like it, so it would. Besides, I'd be doing interesting things, which would make letters far easier to write. Still, Grace writes pretty regular, and her letters are really interesting. She's met a lovely feller . . . and Daddy, d'you know she writes to Sunny? Isn't that the nicest t'ing, now? She's ever so kind, is our Grace.'

Deirdre, knitting socks beside the kitchen fire, smiled encouragingly across at her daughter. 'Your letters are lovely, and give a deal of pleasure,' she said. 'It's a hard life aboard ship, we know it, so Martin and Sunny are thrilled to bits when your letters arrive. But I didn't know Grace wrote to Sunny; did she tell you in that last letter?'

Polly nodded so vigorously that her short yellow curls danced on her forehead. 'Yes, she did so. She said she'd gone and given Sunny the measles, or good as, anyway, so he wrote and told her he was in hospital and she wrote and said how sorry she was. Well, she was sorry, because she'd been cuddling the little kid who was sickening for measles too, only Grace thinks she had it when she was six or seven. She said all the Carbery kids did, or at least she thought so.'

'Dear me, measles can be nasty,' Deirdre said, finishing off a row and flicking her work around to begin the next. 'Oh, me darlin' Polly, war work comes in a lot of different forms. Don't fret yourself; in the not very distant future you'll be joining the forces – the WRNs, I mean – I've no doubt of that. But until you do, keep on with those letters and little parcels, and don't forget that if you didn't have your good job you wouldn't be able to buy treats for Mart and Sunny.'

'Good job!' Polly said witheringly, but she pulled the pad of paper towards her again. 'I know I'm almost the only one left in the office wit' decent shorthand and speedy typing, the only one young enough to run messages over half Liverpool, but I'm not one whit appreciated, Mammy. Mr Slater would sack me tomorrer if he thought he could replace me with someone else.'

'Well, you've the satisfaction of knowing he can't—' Deirdre was beginning when someone knocked on the kitchen door, at first feebly and then with such a rattle that Polly fairly flew across the room to open it. It was November, and a wild night, with a high wind howling along the narrow street and when she wrenched at the door it was not only a slender, storm-battered creature who tumbled inside, but a miniature gale, as well as a good few dead leaves and a gust of rain. The girl in the dark coat began pulling off the garment even as Polly said hospitably, 'Evenin', Monica! You're quite a one for making an entrance, aren't you! I thought you were living it up in Southport, what on earth are you doing here?' She began to help her sister-in-law out of her wet coat. 'Oh, don't say Martin's coming home again!' she exclaimed, remembering the last time Monica had come rapping on their door. 'When did you hear? He and Sunny are on the same ship, you know, which means they'll both be back!'

Monica gave a moan and pulled off hat and gloves, dropping them on the floor with a complete disregard for the linoleum, which had been brushed and mopped clean directly after the family's high tea.

Then she produced a crumpled half-sheet of yellow paper and held it out to Peader, who had stood up to greet her with his customary hug and whose face, at the sight of that piece of paper, lost all its colour and looked suddenly haggard and old.

'H-he's missing,' Monica said brokenly. 'H-his ship went down . . . There was a battle . . . It was weeks ago, but the Admiralty waited . . . Oh Dad, I can't bear it!'

Chapter Eleven

MARCH 1942

Polly put the rest of her gear into her canvas issue kitbag and took a last, leisurely look around her, at the room where she and her friends had spent a good deal of their lives over the last six months. She was sorry to leave it in a way, but Scotland was a very long way from home, and though she had enjoyed herself well enough, learning her job, getting to know the other WRNs, she had often been homesick for Liverpool, for her family and friends.

She remembered her many moans in civvy life about letter-writing; how her letters to her brothers, to Sunny and Tad and Grace, had seemed so dull, with nothing very much to say. Yet she soon realised that life in the services, fascinating though it might be, did not take away her letter-writing chores, and because of the censor, her service letters might well be as dull as her civvy ones had been, for though the scenes in which they were set were more interesting to her, they concerned people that her correspondents had never met, with only occasional remarks about Liverpool, or her parents, to make them more personal.

What had really changed her life first of all, of course, had been Martin's ship going down, and Martin being lost. With the first real tragedy that she had ever suffered, the war had become personal to her. She thought of Martin with a deep and painful grief, because they had not been as close as they might have been, because she had not liked his wife, had

298

disapproved of his marriage. So it was partly guilt that had sent her marching into the insurance office to tell Mr Slater what to do with his job – that had given her enormous satisfaction – and then she had gone along to the parachute factory in Hanover Street where her mother worked and signed on with them. Making parachutes had been fun, she had enjoyed the company, the chatter, and the feeling that she was doing her bit to kick old Hitler in the goolies – not her own expression, Bev's – but it had not quite made up for the impersonality of it. For many weeks after the news of Martin's fate she had felt angry, felt that she wanted to see some damned Jerry suffer the way her parents – and Monica – were suffering because of what they had done. Munitions might have been better, knowing that the shells and bullets would actually go to kill the hated enemy, but munitions dyed your skin the most awful yellow colour which would not, Polly had decided judicially, have gone very well with her yellow curls. So she had stuck to making parachutes, putting a great deal of care and enthusiasm into the task, until the May Blitz.

Deirdre had been working at the time in the Hanover Street parachute factory in the old Littlewoods building, and she and Polly had been on the night shift with high explosive bombs and fire bombs raining down on the city, when it was considered too dangerous to allow the workers to stay at their machines, but it had been no joke trying to make their way home, either. The streets had been chaotic. Walking to work together earlier that evening Polly and her mother had talked about the destruction caused the previous night: Lime Street Station had been hit, so trains were no longer running from there and fire bombs had landed on the Crawford Biscuit

Works, totally destroying it. 'Not that they were making biscuits,' Deirdre had said darkly. 'Oh, I wouldn't mind a nice packet of custard creams, right this minute.'

But that had been before half past ten when this raid had started with a ferocity that Liverpool had never known before. It had been bad enough when they were both working, with other girls chattering to distract them from the mayhem outside, but walking through the streets lit by fires from buildings which only hours before had looked impregnable was truly terrifying. It did not seem possible that their factory could possibly escape, but neither did it seem likely that the two of them would reach home safely.

However, they had done so, and Peader, fire watching in the city centre, had also been unhurt, though he had not returned home until lunchtime the following day.

It had been the worst eight days of Polly's life. The destruction had seemed to be total. The overhead railway had been hit two or three times as had ordinary rail lines, making travel by such means impossible. Blackler's, where Polly had worked as a schoolgirl, and Lewis's, where she and her mother had shopped, were no more. Bankhall Bridge was destroyed, effectively cutting off the city from the north, and there had been considerable loss of life. Despite the fact that St Sylvester's had been razed to the ground, that her old school had been bombed almost out of existence and that Silvester Street itself had been gutted, the O'Bradys and their neighbours had suffered no fatalities. The barrage balloon site at the end of their road had been a casualty, though; none of the cheery RAF personnel had lived when the bombs had started fires which had destroyed their accommodation, their supplies of hydrogen, and their vast, inflated charges, which had taken to the air, casting flames on everything below, until they had burned out. Polly had got to know the Bops – balloon operatives – pretty well, and hated to think that those bright-eyed young men were all dead, but she had not known them as she had known Martin.

So when the May Blitz ceased, the O'Bradys had been left with a windowless, doorless, almost roofless house and no means of making it whole again, not whilst the shortages of building materials lasted. Peader, however, said that they had got their lives, which was what mattered, and shortly after the house had been pronounced unfit for occupation had calmly moved them out to a small, draughty bungalow on Morton Shore, owned by an elderly woman whose husband had been killed on his way home from a night-shift in the city and who was nervous, she said, of living alone through such times.

'It's her house, the place she and her husband saved for and bought when they were first married, so the good God alone knows how we'll all get on together, because two women into one kitchen usually don't go,' Deirdre had said doubtfully to her daughter, when Peader had announced the plan. 'But anything's better than this.' She had gestured around her, at the church hall where they had been told to stay until they found somewhere better. 'It's bedrooms which will be most difficult, because it's a two-bedroomed bungalow, which means one for Mrs Marshall and one for the rest of us. But you can have a bed on the couch in the living room, I daresay, and when the boys and Grace come home we'll manage something. Besides, you know how practical your daddy is – he'll find some way of getting the

Titchfield Street house put right before too long, you mark my words.'

But Polly had had enough of being a dutiful daughter and doing her best to please parents who, she had long ago realised, had no intention of going off to some safe haven, either in England or Ireland, and who were perfectly capable of looking after themselves.

'I'm going to join the WRNs, Mammy, so count me out when you come to dividing up the bungalow bedrooms,' she had said airily. 'I'm old enough, so I am, and I've been wantin' to do me bit ever since . . . well, for a year or more. I wouldn't have left you and me daddy whilst you were living in Titchfield Street, in the heart of the city, but out at Morton Shore you should be safe enough – as safe as you'll let yourselves be, that is.'

So Polly had joined the WRNs, had agreed to serve anywhere she was sent, and was duly despatched to Scotland, where she and her fellow-entrants had been trained for the work they were to do. Now she had a long and complicated train journey ahead of her, which would no doubt be further complicated by the heavy snow which still lay thick on the ground here in the north, but at the end of it there would be an interesting new posting – and who knew what she might have to learn when she reached Holyhead, on the Isle of Anglesey?

Once the train was on the move and was crowded with service personnel and a few civilians, mainly mothers with small children, going about their normal business, Polly got out her writing pad, albeit with a martyred sigh. She had best write to everyone she knew, telling them about her posting, so that she might receive letters when she got to Anglesey. Life, she mused as she got out her fountain pen, had a way of giving with one hand and snatching back with the other. Letters must be written no matter what.

It was not easy to write letters on the train, but fortunately in one sense at least, there were a good few hold-ups, when Polly's pen fairly sped across the page. Tad was still in Yorkshire with his beloved Beaufighters, but Grace had moved to Norfolk, where she seemed to spend a good deal of her time trying to keep out of the wind which, she said, blew constantly across the great flat expanses of the countryside. Polly knew she would have to write to them both – and Sunny – and send them her new address but decided that, for once, she would write them just the one page. To Tad first. Tad who she hadn't seen since her childhood, but who she still missed.

Despite himself, for he was a man grown now, Tad thought a good deal about Polly, though he usually thought of her as she had been when he had last seen her, a child of ten with a mop of primrose-coloured curls and such sweet and loving ways that she had been universally adored. She had been a little imp, but everyone had loved her and when she left Dublin to go with her parents to Liverpool, in England, how horribly he had missed her! There had been no one like Polly for sticking by a feller, no one like her to share in your adventures.

He thought about Polly more because of Angela's defection, of course. Poor Angela. She had hated having to break it to him that she'd met someone else but thank the good Lord she had had the courage to do it. The world was full of pretty girls eager to make an airman's life happier and Tad did not intend to deprive them of his charms. Polly was an old mate but she was not here. And truth to tell, he had been finding it hard, for some time, to bring Angela's face into his mind's eye when he wanted to remember her. It got muddled up with his memories of Polly – so much stronger, even after their long parting – so that Angela's pale, well-tended face with its elegant little nose and light blue eyes became confused with Polly's rosy, wickedly dimpled smiles; whilst Polly's sturdy ten-year-old body got equally muddled up with Angela's slender waist and firmly jutting breasts. Tad supposed somewhat doubtfully that Polly, too, would have a proper waist, and nice, rounded breasts by now, but somehow he could not imagine it. He could only see *his* Polly, the one he had teased and tickled and bawled at and comforted all those years ago. She had asked him tearfully to help her when she needed help and had shouted rudely at him to leave her alone now and bleedin' well buzz off when she was cross. And, peculiarly enough, he missed her.

There was his work, the most absorbing, exciting, challenging work that Tad had ever embarked upon.

He serviced the engines of the Beaufighters which flew from his station. He treated every plane as though it was the most important piece of machinery on the station, and not only that, as though he felt personally responsible for the slightest failure. He knew, to the last note, how an engine should sound.

Because of this, the pilots in his squadron began to offer him short trips in the planes, whenever a test-flight was needed after he had done a repair. And because of his interest, they began to show him how they flew the planes. As a result of this, no sooner were they off the ground than Tad would take over the controls, and he grew daily more expert, even landing – and taking off – more than once.

Sometimes it was suggested by one of the young airmen that he might like to change over and become air crew but much though he enjoyed flying, Tad knew that if he once agreed to fly, that would be the end of his close and loving association with the aero engines which were his abiding passion. He also knew that though he might become a pretty good pilot, he would never become a top-flight one. And he was a top-flight mechanic.

So though Tad enjoyed the company of pretty girls, right now, he was a Beaufighter man, and was well content to work in their service. So he did not repine unduly over Angela's defection. He wrote to his brothers and sisters and to his sweet-faced, long-suffering mother, and to Polly, of course. And he coaxed and coddled and cosseted his Beaufighters and was, though he probably never thought about it, that rare thing, a happy and contented young man.

Deirdre and Peader had been sad to leave the bungalow on Moreton Shore behind them, but it was a long way out when it came to getting into work each day, and Peader, though he joined the ARP there, as he had in Liverpool, found it less exciting than being with a big city force. So when Deirdre got chatting with Mrs Ayton from Snowdrop Street who worked alongside her in Hanover Street, she was interested to hear that Mrs Ayton's neighbours had recently moved out of their house three or four dwellings further along the road, and gone to live with relatives near Mold, North Wales.

'Will it be goin' up for rent?' Deirdre asked with

seeming casualness as the two of them drew the soft parachute silk through the maw of their machines, checking every stitch though the stuff fairly flew along, for was it not a matter of life and death to see that the silk was not bunched up or had gaping seams? 'I'd like to be nearer the city, so I would, and it's a long trail home at nights, when I'm tired half to death. What's more, my Peader's frettin' out there wit' so little to keep him occupied. Oh, he likes the gardenin', and he gets on well wit' Mrs Marshall, our landlady, but he'd see a lot more of me if we could move into somewhere like Snowdrop Street.'

She did not add, which she could have done with perfect truth, that Mrs Marshall, now that the worst of the bombing seemed to have calmed down, had made it clear that she was no longer afraid to be alone. She liked having Deirdre and Peader and made no objection to the occasional bursts of having a house straining at the seams when members of their large family got leave and came to stay, but she knew that Deirdre was itching to have Brogan to visit them when he got leave. Brogan had come over as a member of the American Army and was stationed at Burtonwood and though it was fairly near Liverpool he had not, so far, managed to get away from the camp.

So when Mrs Ayton came into work a couple of days later and told Deirdre that the house was indeed to be let, the O'Bradys had been delighted. Peader had joined his wife on the train into work that morning, she having arranged to have a morning off, and they had inspected the house. It was not newly decorated and needed a good deal of work, but Peader had seen at once that with a bit of help they could make it into a nice home.

306

'Building materials are hard to find,' the landlord had said doubtfully when Peader pointed out some of the faults – the back kitchen roof was leaking and there was no plaster on one wall and the privy in the back yard was full of cobwebs and had a large hole in the door and no bolt on the inside, either. 'You might get hold of some old roof slates from some of the bombed buildings, but I dunno about stuff like plaster – you need permits for that kind o' thing, to say nothin' of wood. Why, I've even had to go down on me benders for a few nails!'

But he agreed to a slightly reduced rent provided that Peader saw to such things himself and did not expect the landlord to perform miracles, and so in February, after a tearful farewell with Mrs Marshall, the O'Bradys had moved into Snowdrop Street.

'We'll tell the children right away, so's our post keeps coming straight to us,' Deirdre had planned busily, putting a couple of buckets in the main bedroom where the front of the roof persisted in leaking despite Peader and a pal having put a number of uncracked slates over the gaps.

But right now, it was Saturday morning and Peader and Deirdre had enjoyed a nice lie-in, since Deirdre did not work on a Saturday, and then they had got up slowly and gone downstairs to the kitchen to have a nice leisurely breakfast before deciding what they should do that day.

'Not that there's all that much choice, alanna,' Peader said ruefully as they sat down to toast and gooseberry jam and two good, strong mugs of tea. Deirdre had made quantities of gooseberry jam from the fruit in Mrs Marshall's garden, and that good lady had insisted that the O'Bradys should take a good half of the jam back to Liverpool with them. 'If we do some shopping this morning, though, we might go to a flick this afternoon. What d'you t'ink of that, eh?'

'It depends what's on,' Deirdre said, turning the pages of last night's *Echo* as she bit into her toast. 'I wouldn't mind taking a look in at TJ's this morning, though.'

TJ's was still managing to do a good job for their poorer clientele despite wartime shortages and Deirdre, who had thought the big store a regular heaven when she had first been introduced to it, was a frequent shopper there still.

'That suits me, we can catch a tram and mebbe do all our shopping up an' down London Road—' Peader was beginning when they heard the post come rattling through the front door and Deirdre jumped to her feet and ran to fetch it. She came back with a good handful, two air letters amongst them, and sat down again, abandoning the newspaper but beginning to crunch toast once more.

'Thank the good Lord we can still buy bread, and isn't this Sample's loaf twice as good as the stuff poor Mrs Marshall got, even though it's only a national loaf, same as hers?' she said, staring at the envelopes and putting them into the middle of the table one by one. 'There's a couple from the boys, one from Grace – what a good girl she is, Peader! – and one from Polly. Ooh, which shall we open first?'

'What's rare is precious; open the letters from the boys first,' Peader said, grinning. He loved his sons but acknowledged that letter-writing was not their forte, any more than it was his.

'One of them is from Niall,' Deirdre confirmed. She hesitated, twisting the letters in her hands. 'Oh, all right, I'll start wit' the boys.'

'It won't take you long,' Peader said comfortingly,

as she began to open the airmail letters. 'A minute, no longer, and you'll be free to start readin' what's been happenin' to your ewe lamb.'

Deirdre tutted and began to read, and he was right. Neither of the missives took longer than thirty seconds or so to read. Both Niall and Bev were happy. Niall had joined the Australian Air Force and was being trained at somewhere which the censor had seen fit to clip out. Bev was in the Air Force and was training to be a navigator. He seemed to relish the active life after his years at university, but like his brother, seemed to have very little to say save that he had met a very nice girl and might bring her home with him on his next leave.

'Good, good,' Peader said approvingly. 'Now let's open Polly's.'

'It's been an age since we've had our Poll under our roof,' Deirdre said wistfully. 'I wonder if she's getting leave soon. Wouldn't it be nice if she and Grace managed to have a few days at home together?'

'I wouldn't count on Polly gettin' leave at the same time as Grace, alanna,' Peader said mildly. 'Will you read me the letter now, Dee.'

'It's a long one,' Deirdre said joyfully. 'You know our Poll, she can't stop having a crack whether it's on paper or in person. Why, even her phone calls go on rather, though she can't afford long ones. Good thing they don't charge for letters by the page, or—'

'Oh, read it, woman,' Peader said, losing patience. 'Or I'll snatch it from your hand and read it for meself, so I will.'

'Right,' Deirdre said. She began reading.

It was, as she had anticipated, a good, long letter, filled with news, with scraps of information about her work, her friends, and her social life. It also contained her new address. 'Well, would you believe it, she's going to be working in Holyhead, where the boats go to Dublin,' Deirdre broke off to remark. Her eyes filled with tears. 'Oh, Peader, isn't she the lucky one, then? To be within spittin' distance of Dublin, where she was brought up! Why, she might even go over, on a visit. Oh, Peader, there's a bit here about her angel. Listen, whiles I read it to you.'

I don't see my angel as often as I did when I was smaller. But that doesn't mean I don't see her at all, because I do. Only it's strange, Mammy and Daddy, that she's a girl-angel, or so everyone else in my billet seems to think. Not that they know about her, for never a word would I speak to anyone. Not even Grace knows. But we got to talking about angels in the billet one night, and they all said angels were fellers. Only they're not Irish, like meself, so maybe 'tis only colleens that have girl-angels. Anyway, I wanted to tell you that I never see her full-on any more, the way I did when I was a kid. I don't even see her in the corner of my bedroom, or on the half-landing, like I did before I joined up. Now I see her if I'm out on the sea in one of the small boats in the darkness, and then it's just a shape and a sort of knowing she's there, rather than actually seeing her lovely little face. I suppose she couldn't come in to the billet, with so many other girls around me, but when I pad over to the ablutions sometimes she's right at the end of the building, where it's all dark and hardly anyone goes. She'll only be there for a moment, mind, but I'd not like to lose her altogether. Maybe, when I'm really old, she won't let me see her. But I reckon I'll always know she's there, somewhere, just out of sight, watching out for me.

'Now I wonder what brought that on?' Peader said mildly. He reached for the last piece of toast and spread margarine on it, then dabbed on some goose-berry jam. 'She's not mentioned her guardian angel for a long while, not when I'm about, at any rate. Do you t'ink it's because she's feelin' a bit strange over leaving' that Scottish island?'

'Probably because she's so near Ireland,' Deirdre suggested. 'It set her thinking about home, that's what. Now quiet or I can't finish.'

Peader, a quiet man, raised his brows but said nothing and presently Deirdre, having given him a severe look, continued.

I've just now written to Grace, to tell her where to send letters in future. Oh, I do love Grace, Mammy, she's as good as a sister to me – I wish she was my sister, so I do! We're going to try to get leave at the same time, because she's the best person to go about with, apart from you and Daddy, and the best person to share a secret. Sara's lovely, my favourite sister-in-law, but she's a deal older than me so it's not the same. Besides, she's married, so she's a woman growed, whereas me and Grace are still getting there. Sunny writes when he can, but sometimes I get a grosh of letters all in the one post and then I go without any for months and months. It's always the same with the Navy, everyone says, because they can only post their mail when they're in port, which doesn't happen all that often when they're on convoy duty. I miss Sunny a lot, but I expect I'll soon make other friends in Holyhead.

The letter ran on in Polly's usual bright, inconse-quential way and Peader waited until his wife had finished reading and put the letter down beside her plate with a satisfied smile before raising the question which, he thought, must be in both their minds.

'Deirdre, d'you t'ink this is the best moment to tell her? Tell Grace too? After all, so far as we've been able to find out they're the only two Carberys left. They should know that they're really sisters.'

He was watching his wife's face as he spoke and saw the bright colour drain from her cheeks, saw the way her hand flew to her throat. 'Oh, Peader, I can't bring meself to say a word about all that – isn't it dangerous, still, to let anyone know, this side o' the water?'

'I'm not suggesting we should broadcast it to the whole city, alanna,' he said gently. 'Polly's a good girl, and Grace is another, despite their background. When we'd explained how we'd taken Polly for our own to keep her from a drunken and violent father and an indifferent mother, then she – they – would both understand that we meant no harm by it. We thought, then, that it was for the best and we think so now. But Polly does so long for a sister, and one of these days someone is going to ask why she's so fair when the boys are all so dark . . . and there's a look, I can't explain it, but there *is* a similarity, put it no stronger, between Grace and Polly. Wouldn't it be better to tell them now, rather than to have them find out from a chance remark? Remember, the boys do know she's not our child, though they've never so much as mentioned it since we told them not to, all those years ago.'

Deirdre was silent, remembering. Her son, Brogan, coming into the kitchen and opening his coat to show them the bright-eyed baby nestling against his chest. The boys had crowded round – Bev had been the baby then – whilst Brogan told them how he had found the baby in a snowstorm, and had decided to steal her for his mammy when her older sister, who had had the care of her, had been killed by a train.

She had told her sons that they must pretend the new baby had been left behind by a cousin from the country who could no longer keep her, but within a very short space of time Polly had been accepted by everyone as an O'Brady. Deirdre had guessed the child to have been eight or nine months when Brogan had brought her to Ireland, and by the time she was two she very much doubted whether the boys ever thought about her arrival, or the secret that they all shared concerning her. She was their adored and spoiled little sister and they would have dealt harshly with anyone who had indicated otherwise.

The angel episode had shaken Deirdre, though. When Polly had told her about the girl with the raggedy shawl who had appeared in the dark stairwell, smiling at her, she had felt terrified. Did this mean that Polly was going to start remembering that other, darker life which she had lived before she came to Dublin? She had told Polly that the girl must be her guardian angel . . . Then Polly, when taunted by the little friend who had been with her at the time, had said that the angel's name was Jess . . . it could still turn Deirdre's skin to gooseflesh thinking about it, for had not Polly's sister, who had kept the little girl alive, been called Jess?

But right now, there was Peader's question to be answered. She sighed, took a deep breath, let it out slowly, shook her head. 'I can't tell them, Peader. I just dare not. We *stole* that baby, there's no two ways about it, stole her from her rightful parents. If we were still in Ireland, now . . . but we aren't, we're here, in Liverpool, in the very city where it all happened nigh on eighteen years ago. I *dare* not tell 'em, not yet, not whilst the war's on, and there's all this uncertainty.'

'Well, it's up to you, so it is,' Peader said equably. 'But don't say I didn't warn you, alanna. There's a likeness, I'm tellin' you.'

'I can't see it, meself,' Deirdre said obstinately. 'Why, our Polly's pretty as a picture and though I love Grace dearly . . . well, her hair's mousy, she's tall as a stalk and thin too, and she's shy, there's no – no *glow* about her. I can't see anyone thinkin' them alike, honest to God, Peader.'

'It's not the hair colour, nor the height, nor the figures of 'em that's alike,' Peader said slowly. He scratched his thick, greying hair. 'I couldn't put me finger on it no matter how hard I tried, but I – I'm *aware* of it, me love. Still, mebbe it's only because I'm close to the pair of them that I notice. Mebbe it's that.'

Deirdre opened her mouth to say, pretty sharply, that she was closer to Polly than anyone else could possibly be, and then closed it again. No, she couldn't say that, or Peader would expect her to notice this mythical likeness which she honestly could not see, though she had tried often enough. She did think that from Polly's description it was quite possible that Grace and Jess had been rather alike, but Jess had been dead a long time now, and she doubted very much whether Grace could remember the older girl at all, let alone clearly. So she would let sleeping dogs lie, for the moment, at any rate.

Finishing her breakfast and beginning on the washing-up, she said as much to Peader, who nodded resignedly. 'Oh aye, alanna, I thought that's what you'd say and mebbe you're right. Anyway, it doesn't look as if Poll's due for any leave for a while, not now she's been posted. So it can wait.'

'I know you're right, Peader, I know we've got to tell Polly one of these days,' Deirdre said, eager to agree with her husband now that the immediate danger seemed to be over. 'Only I've – I've got to prepare meself before I can work out how to do it.'

'Sure, I'm after knowin' you'd tell Poll, all in good time,' Peader said with all his usual good humour. 'And now let's wash up the delft and clear it all away so's we can go shopping!'

Chapter Twelve

It was a warm June day with the sky blue as a blackbird's egg and the breeze coming off the land for once, and smelling of the country, instead of the sea. Polly had soon settled into her new life, though it was very different from the life she had lived on her Scottish island. She had always loved the sea and the beach, and she found Anglesey an enchanting place. Unlike her Scottish island, where it had seemed to be dark nine-tenths of the time and cold and rainy ten-tenths, here she had come straight into spring, into peace almost, you could say.

Not that peace was all that obvious, since the island swarmed with uniformed members of the armed forces. So far, she had just acted as a messenger here, taking documents from the naval headquarters at Llys-y-Gwynt down Llanfawr Road and on to Turkey Shore, from whence it was flat pretty well all the way to the quay where the ships were moored. She and a dozen other WRNs were billeted on London Road, in a tall, elderly house overlooking the railway line so that washing hung out in the narrow garden was apt to come indoors a good deal dirtier than it had gone out. However, a great many items of uniform could be laundered, and stockings and collars, issue brassieres and the respectable knickers which they were supposed to wear were taken into the kitchen of the rambling old house where they could be hung on a drying rack which was hauled up to the ceiling so that wet clothing was out of the way. An elderly woman called, predictably, Mrs Jones, acted as part-housekeeper part-chaperon to the twelve girls, but she was only on duty from eight in the morning until two in the afternoon, which left the WRNs pretty free to look after themselves.

Not that they minded. In fact, they much preferred it that way, for Mrs Jones was a tight-mouthed strait-laced little woman who thought that a girl in uniform was heading fast for hell anyway. Today Polly walked slowly along Lands End, looking alternately at the tall houses which lined it on her left and the blue water in the harbour on her right. It was her afternoon off and since she and Diane, her best friend in the WRNs, were going to a dance in the old lifeboathouse on the promenade that evening, they had planned to go up and down Market Street to see if anyone was selling lipsticks. Both girls had long ago used up the small amount of make-up which they had managed to acquire before the shortages reached epic proportions, but everyone knew that it was the early bird which caught the worm, and most WRNs went into town at least once a week to see if the shops had got supplies in whilst they were not looking, so to speak.

'Not that I care much about lipstick, if I'm honest,' Polly had told Diane the previous evening as they ate mashed potatoes and a rather grey-looking stew in the canteen. 'But I could do with some face-powder. It 'ud cover my freckles; no sooner does the sun come out than freckles pop up all over me.'

Diane had looked at her friend critically. She was older than Polly by a couple of years and a good deal more sophisticated; in fact, Polly thought, they were an ill-assorted pair. Diane came from a rich county family, the male members of which were all something very high up in the Navy. She had a beautifully tailored uniform and never lacked silk stockings or pretty underwear and was on nodding and smiling terms with every officer in the place. She was very pretty, with shoulder-length black hair, china-blue eyes and the very white skin which frequently goes with such colouring. She was also easily the most disruptive element in the wrennery, always getting herself – and others – into trouble and falling into absurd scrapes from which she somehow managed to extricate herself just before news of it got through to the hierarchy under which they lived. She and Polly had formed what the other girls called an unholy alliance from the first day they had met and stood by one another through thick and thin. They followed each other's lead and enjoyed a deep and satisfying friendship which not even their many boyfriends could spoil.

'I don't want a permanent relationship until the war's over,' Diane said, and Polly agreed with her – though this did not stop either of them from going to every dance which they could get to and giggling over the lovesickness of their many swains.

The trouble was, the other WRNs told them severely, that they were both spoilt. One by having everything she wanted from the day she was born because she was the only girl in a family of boys, the other because her parents had all the money and position anyone could desire and doted on their youngest child.

'You're two of a kind,' the other girls said gloomily. 'You get away with murder just now, but it won't last. You'll get your comeuppance, the pair of you.'

So far, however, Polly concluded, they had not got

into any trouble from which they could not extricate themselves, or each other. And tonight they would go to the weekly dance held in the old lifeboathouse and have a marvellous time. If they were a little late getting home, they would climb up on to the roof of the scullery and from thence to the landing window, which was always left a little open for just such an emergency. Then before anyone had realised they were out after hours they would be padding quietly up the long flight of stairs to the attic room which they shared as the two newest members of HMS *Bee*.

In the end, Polly and Diane couldn't find a single lipstick in their whole afternoon of shopping, but the dance to which the girls had so looked forward was as good as they had anticipated and led, in fact, to a new friendship for Diane. Polly noticed that her friend was spending a good deal of time dancing with one of the local lads, and rather wondered at it; uniforms were what most of the girls went for and usually Diane was no exception. What was more, there were some American Air Force men and everyone in the room knew that they came over with their pockets full of nylon stockings and chewing gum and bars of chocolate which they insisted on calling candy. But Diane was sticking mostly with a tall, dark-haired Welshman called Meirion, and turning down what appeared, on the surface, to be more attractive offers.

When the dance ended, Polly waited for Diane and got quite annoyed with her friend when she was still hanging about at past midnight. The doors of the wrennery would have been locked a good while, and a wind had got up, coming straight off the Irish Sea and making Polly clutch her jacket round her and rather wish she had brought her lovely warm overcoat. What was more, a strong wind made climbing the slate roof of the scullery extension rather fraught, especially when the slates were wet, and there had been a shower just before the wind got into its stride.

In fact, it was a quarter past twelve and the streets were deserted as the two girls made their way back towards London Road. All the available buses had gone long since and taxis, though they might meet the ferries and the London trains, did not hang about in order to give WRNs a ride back from the harbour to their nest. So it was foot it or sleep on the beach and accordingly, the girls set out at a brisk pace.

'What was so fascinating about Meirion?' Polly shouted rather resentfully as the two of them bent their heads against the force of the wind and began to slog up Victoria Street. 'And why didn't you come straight out after the dance was over? It's not like you, Di.'

'He's nice, but it wasn't just that,' Diane said breathlessly. 'Oh Lord, if you want the full story we'd best stop in a doorway; this wind is trying to get back down my throat and blow my lungs up until I burst!'

'Better not, we're late already,' Polly shouted. 'Tell me once we're indoors.'

So they used all their energy to battle against the wind and were delighted to find themselves turning the corner into the backs of the houses on London Road.

'We should have come back at the same time as the others, Di,' Polly said breathlessly as they gained the shelter of the high wall which separated their houses from the railway sidings. 'It'll be pretty horrid on that roof in this wind . . . and the rain makes the slates slippery too. Shall I go up first?'

'Perhaps you'd better,' Diane said, then gave a squeak of dismay. 'Oh, dear heaven, where's the box?'

In order to gain the roof of the scullery the girls stepped first on a solid wooden box and then scrambled on top of the rainwater butt and from thence to the roof. Now, one glance was enough to tell them that the box had been blown away by the wind, and the most careful look around the back yard did not reveal its whereabouts.

'Unless it's that pile of broken slats in the corner it must have blown out over the railway sidings,' Polly said. 'Oh, isn't that just our bleedin' luck! But you can make me a back, I suppose?'

For answer, Diane crouched beside the water butt and Polly, giggling, climbed nimbly on to her friend's back and then sprang to the top of the barrel with such suddenness that Diane was knocked clean over, landing on the cobbles on all fours whilst giving vent to the sort of language which nice little WRNs, Polly told her, should not even understand, let alone use.

'I'm wounded, you horrible little bogtrotter,' Diane moaned, tottering to her feet whilst Polly clung to the edge of the gutter and braced herself against the wind. 'First you kick a great hole in my back, then you knock me on to the cobbles – my lovely stockings are in shreds, you toad – and it's just occurred to me that I've given you a bunk up but who's going to do the same for me?'

'I'll sneak down and unlock the kitchen door,' Polly said. 'See you in a minute,' and with that she began to scramble up the roof, not daring to stand up but clinging grimly on to the roof ridge. And presently she looked up and saw, to her horror, that the landing window, always left a little ajar, was closed. Someone must have thought the wind would slam it shut and shatter the glass, she supposed bitterly, sitting astride the scullery roof ridge now and reaching up to give a half-hearted tug to the clearly closed window. Oh dear God above, now what should they do? They could not possibly hope to wake anyone, not with the wind shrieking and moaning the way it was, and besides if they woke some of the more hidebound girls they would be in as much trouble as if they had handed themselves over to an officer.

But . . . Lilly Sumner slept in the bedroom nearest to the landing and she was a sport all right. If Polly knocked on the glass, was it possible that Lilly would hear, and come to her rescue? Polly got so close to the glass that her face was almost resting on it and raised a hand to knock. The blackout curtains were drawn across, of course, but if only Lilly woke, and realised that someone was still out . . .

Polly's hand was about to descend on the window when there was a sudden commotion and a hand, startlingly white against the blackness, came out from between the curtains and, seizing the window catch, pushed the window out with considerable force. Polly felt the wood of the window hit her squarely on the nose and then she lost her rather precarious balance and found herself bouncing down the tiles and across the gutter, to land heavily on the cobbles below.

In fact, she landed on Diane and not the cobbles, or the story, she reflected later, might have had a very different ending. As it was, Diane's startled *woof* as all the air was suddenly expelled from her lungs was so funny – or so Polly thought – that it completely took Polly's mind off her sudden descent and made the bruises from the encounter seem of little account.

'Sorry, Di, but the window was shut, and just as I was about to knock on it someone shot it open and it banged me on the nose and I fell,' Polly explained as soon as she and the older girl had untangled themselves. 'Will I climb back now, and get in? Oh jay, I'd better, it must be one in the morning, and we'll be in awful trouble if we're caught now, so we will.'

'Well, you aren't climbing on my back,' Diane said, breathing heavily and still clasping her skinned knees as she sat on the cobbles, leaning against the water butt. 'I'm very sorry but this time I'll climb the bloody roof and you can make me a back. Tell me when you're ready.'

'You're heavier than me,' Polly said doubtfully, getting to her feet. 'I didn't knock you over on purpose, Di, honest to God I didn't.'

'Well, I shall knock you down deliberately if I possibly can,' Diane said grimly. 'I'm a mass of cuts and bruises thanks to you, O'Brady.'

'I suppose it is my turn,' Polly said peaceably, bending down and gripping the water butt as tightly as she could. 'Go on then, up with you!'

Diane reached the top of the water butt and set off across the tiles whilst Polly sat on the cobbles and laughed as silently as she could at the sight of her tall, slender friend climbing like a huge daddy-long-legs across the slippery roof. Presently, Diane reached the now wide-open window, slung a leg over the sill, paused a moment, and then disappeared inside. And after only a very short time, during which Polly wondered apprehensively whether whoever had opened the window had lain in wait for Diane in the darkness and was now marching her off to bed in disgrace, the back door creaked open and Diane beckoned her friend inside.

'What a bloody awful night,' Diane said as the two of them threw their clothes off in their attic room and hurled themselves into their little iron beds. 'Oh, the dance was all right, I know you're going to say that, Polly, but the rest! Well, it beggars description.'

'So describe it,' Polly said from her cosy bed. 'Oh damn, I forgot to pull back the blackout curtains and open the window. It was my turn, wasn't it?'

'It was,' Diane said, but leaned over and jerked back the curtains so that the windy night could peer in at them and they could see the ragged clouds scooting across the star-drenched heavens. 'But I don't think we ought to open the window, the gale will probably set every door in the house slamming. Now are you ready to hear just why it was that I wasted – I mean spent – my entire evening in the company of Meirion Williams?'

'Won't it keep?' Polly said drowsily. Her nose hurt and all the various bumps and bruises collected on her descent from the roof were beginning to make themselves felt. 'I'm ever so tired, Di, and you can't be feeling all that good. I mean, I landed on you when I fell, so you got a double lot of bruises. Can't we talk in the morning?'

'We could, but I want to get it sorted out tonight,' Diane said stubbornly. 'Poll, has it ever occurred to you to wonder where the fellow in that little shop gets his supplies from? And why there are girls on this island with silk stockings and others who haven't anything better than lisle?'

'Ours are silk,' Polly mumbled. 'But what does it matter where the feller gets his stuff from? Black market, I suppose.'

'He gets all sorts from Ireland,' Diane said in a

thrilling whisper. '*Your* Eire, Poll, not this island. And the ferries go over there every other day!'

'So what? And as for the ferries, don't we all know it? We must watch them sail several times a week. I think they're very brave, the men who take the ferries across, because everyone knows that there are wolf packs of U-boats in the Irish Sea, just waiting to torpedo anything they can reach. Only of course our chaps go out at night and try to bag U-boats themselves, I've heard the sailors saying so. I say, Di, I wonder why the ferries don't sail at night, when our chaps are out U-boat-spotting, instead of during the day when there's no one to defend them?'

'Polly, will you stop rambling and *listen* for once?' Diane said, exasperated. 'Meirion told me that some girls go over on the ferry and buy stuff in Dublin, stuff that we can't get over here. And others take stuff the Irish need – tea is very popular, he said, and we have loads of tea in the stores – and swap for . . . well, for stockings, and lipsticks, and cheese . . . It seems a long while since I've had my way with a great, crisp pile of toasted cheese.'

'They go over to Dublin, *my* Dublin?' Polly asked, suddenly forgetting to be sleepy and sitting up on one elbow. 'But I thought you'd need special papers and all sorts to go over there.'

'Nope,' Diane said, shaking her head. 'All you need is a ticket. But of course it must help if you know the city, because you'd know where to go to find the sort of things you were after. Stockings and lipstick and so on, I mean.'

'Ye-es, but it can't be as simple as that,' Polly said. 'How d'you buy a ticket?'

'Meirion said that if I gave him the money he'd get you a ticket, and then—'

'Me? Oh no, you aren't getting me into that sort of a scrape, Diane Burlington,' Polly said roundly. 'Go yourself!'

'I can't, can I? I wouldn't know where to go for things, and I'd stand out like a sore thumb over there, as English as anything. But you, Poll, you could go over and be safe as houses!'

'I don't know,' Polly said gloomily, but in her heart she was beginning to get excited at the thought of seeing Dublin again. 'What about my uniform, though? I'm not a rich member of the Burlington family. All I've got is me uniform. You know very well that if I tried to go over in me uniform I'd be thrown in the Tower or something.'

'I'll lend you some civvies,' Diane said. 'And I'll give you the money, of course. Oh, and pay for the ticket and so on. Don't you want to go home? You're always talking about Dublin and how wonderful it was when you lived there.'

'Yes, and so it is,' Polly said stoutly. 'But I was only ten when I left . . . not that I've forgotten so much as a paving stone, for I've not, indeed. Kids always run the messages in Dublin, same as they do in Liverpool, so I know all the best shops for this and that. There's a dairy on Thomas Street where they sell the most wonderful Irish cheese . . . oh, it makes me mouth water just to think of it! But that doesn't mean I'm prepared to get into the worst trouble of me life, and get thrown out of the WRNs in disgrace, just so you can have a new lipstick.'

'Oh, it won't come to that,' Diane promised. 'If the worst comes to the worst I'd say it was all my fault. Besides, you'll never be found out; why should you? No one's interested in a girl going over for a few pairs of silk stockings. Come on, Poll, be a sport.'

'It's too risky,' Polly said obstinately. 'I'd love to see Dublin again, I don't deny it but—'

'Oh, come on, Poll, I know you can do it,' Diane said eagerly. 'You'll have to put in for some leave, of course, but they're pretty good about that sort of thing, and it isn't as if you'll need a week or anything like that. A forty-eight will be plenty.'

'A forty-eight? Why would I need that long? If I catch the— What time does the *Hibernia* leave tomorrer? She's on this week, isn't she?'

'Yes. She leaves at two o'clock, so you won't even have to get up terribly early. Not that you'd want to go tomorrow, because you'll need to get some supplies packed up carefully, so folk won't notice them. We said tea, didn't we? And I believe parachute silk's awfully popular over there. I can lay my hands on a nice big piece if you give me a few days.'

'Well—' Polly began, then frowned. 'Hey, the *Hibernia* leaves here at two o'clock in the afternoon, but what time does she get back?'

'Ah! Well, that's another good reason for yourself going over, Polly,' Diane said in a honeyed tone. 'She comes back in at noon the following day, so—'

'Oh! So I'd have to stay overnight,' Polly said. 'Why, all I'd have time for would be to have a night's sleep and then it would be time to get back to Dun Laoghaire for the ferry home! You're an idiot, you are—'

'That's another good reason why I can't go myself, Poll,' Diane said, keeping her voice low. 'No matter how willing, because I'd have nowhere to spend the night, and I wouldn't want to be cashiered or whatever they do to WRNs found sleeping rough in a foreign city. But you, Poll, you must have a thousand pals in Ireland, all panting to put you up for the night, especially if you took them some tea and some of those nice little sugar lumps they use in the officers' mess. Well? What do you say?'

'I say no way, not if I have to be there two whole days,' Polly said firmly. She lay down again. 'It 'ud all go wrong, I just know it would, plans you make always do. Come to that, plans made by me don't always go too smooth,' she added honestly. 'So something we've cooked up between the pair of us is doomed, positively doomed! As for me wearing your civvies, can you imagine what a figure I'd cut? You're a foot taller than me and about twice as broad – I'd get taken up for a vagrant, or a spy. Because me pal Tad's mammy told me that the city's stiff with bleedin' Jerries, you can't hardly step a pace in the big shops without treading on one of them. No, Di, I'm afraid your plan isn't going to include me!'

'It'll take some arranging, I grant you that,' Diane said as though her friend had not spoken. 'But I'm a good organiser; you won't be left without a plan of action, trust me for that. As for clothes, I said I'd lend you some but I didn't say they would be mine, did I? Flicky Andover is about your size and she got a lovely white pullover from her boyfriend and an old grey duffle coat . . . We'll fix you up so that your own mother wouldn't recognise you, Poll. I know you won't want to take a kitbag over, either, so I've arranged to borrow one of those knapsack things that you sling on your back when you go camping. Some of the fellers go over to the mainland to climb in Snowdonia whenever they've got a forty-eight, and Jimmy says we can borrow his whenever we want it.'

'It strikes me,' Polly said slowly, lying down in her bed again but fixing her friend with a round, reproachful eye, 'it strikes me that you've done a divil of a lot of planning without so much as consulting meself. How long have you been hatching this?'

'Only tonight, guide's honour,' Diane said promptly, lying down herself and pulling the blankets up over her exposed shoulder. 'All the loans – the knapsack and the clothes, I mean – were promised ages ago, when I talked about going climbing too. Lots of people owe me favours, I'm just calling in a few of them, that's all.'

'Well, the answer's still no. If you want someone to go over to Dublin, go yourself,' Polly said firmly. 'Goodnight, Diane; sweet dreams.'

A week later Polly found herself getting off the train at Tara Street Station in Dublin and walking briskly along Luke Street. Home! This was home to her in a way which Liverpool had never really become, because her happy childhood had been spent here. It was here that she had first gone along to the small convent school where her mammy and daddy had decided she should get her education, but it was also here where what she felt was her *real* education had begun, what you might call her street education. Here she had kept nix for her brothers when they were up to some mischief or other, had run messages for the mammy and had gone in and out of the shops, both big and small, as of right. She turned into Townsend Street and immediately left into College Street, remembering now the many times she had trodden this way when the family had gone off on the train for a day's cockling down at Booterstown beach, or had been meeting someone off the train at Tara Street Station.

Every twist and turn of the narrowing streets which led her into the heart of the Liberties held a memory for her, almost all nice ones. Street games, marbles, tops, Piggy beds, she had played them all, mainly in company with Tad, who had been such a good friend to her. Yes, she could scarcely look around her now without getting a mental picture of Tad, small, square, sturdy despite the fact that he was always hungry, helping her, protecting her, codding her about ghosts and boggarts, taking her boxing the fox in the orchards on the outskirts of the city, teaching her to swim in the canal, half-drowning her in the Liffey . . . The memories swarmed into her head, bringing tears to her eyes and a lump to her throat. Oh janey, but she'd been a lucky kid to live here, to have had such a pal!

Still, all that had been a long time ago, and she had not heard from Tad now for . . . well, it must be getting on for a year. She had continued to write to him at first, doggedly determined to keep their friendship alive, but finally his lack of response had got to her. If he cared so little for her then he might whistle for her letters! She had continued to write to Mrs Donoghue, though, because she guessed that Tad was a poor correspondent to his mammy as well as his best friends, and Mrs Donoghue wrote back from time to time, though they weren't an awful lot better, if Polly was forced to be honest, than the letters – grubby notes – Tad had sent on the rare occasions when he had bothered to write at all.

That was now, and the Tad she was remembering was a boy of twelve or thirteen, a boy who mitched off school more often than he attended, who worked like a slave to keep his mammy in pennies and his numerous brothers and sisters at least fed and moderately clothed in the cold weather. He had had, in those days, to battle against a drunken father who beat his wife and knocked his kids about when he could get hold of them. Tad had been good at avoiding the older Donoghue, but every now and then he would do his best to defend his mammy and would be seen on the streets the next day with a black eye, a split lip or an arm held awkwardly.

Polly sighed at the memory. Perhaps she had been wrong to stop writing to Tad but a good deal he must have cared, she reflected bitterly now, since he had not even written to reproach her for her silence.

Right now she was too excited at the thought of what was to come to worry about her old friend's behaviour. She had heard from his mammy or one of her other friends, that Angela had given Tad the go-by. Anyway, she would soon get all the gossip because she meant to spend the night with Tad's mammy, knowing that her old friend would welcome her.

Glancing around her as she walked, she realised she had reached the Cornmarket and now turned left into Francis Street, a place redolent of her childhood. As always, the street was busy, with chisellers playing games and small girls running messages. Threading her way between them, seeing the bare feet and ragged clothing, Polly realised sharply how different her life had been since crossing the water. There was poverty in Liverpool, she knew that, but because of rationing, perhaps, things were more fairly distributed now. The rich bought luxuries on the black market, everyone knew that, but at least the poor got the food to which they were entitled, and though some did sell their clothing coupons, they managed to clothe their children better than they had done when things were more easily available. Also, wages were very much better now, with men being provided with clothing and food in the forces, and having an allotment taken out of their wages and sent home to their wives and children whether they wished it or no. And then there was the money paid to women working in factories and shops; it had got better and better as labour became scarcer. Yes, things were definitely looking up in England, but here in Ireland, where there was no war, nothing seemed to have changed. Barefoot children queued for the family's bread, women in long black skirts with shawls wrapped around their heads stood and gossiped, shrieking to their children to 'Get away outta that,' and men lounged on street corners playing toss ha'penny and melting into the shadows whenever anyone in authority – a guarda or a priest – appeared.

But they've not got to fear the thrum of an aero-engine overhead and the whistle of descending bombs, nor the whizz and clatter of machine-gun fire, Polly told herself stoutly, pausing alongside a group of small boys who were obviously about to try their luck at one of the street stalls. The stalls, she noticed, were not so well-provided as they had been when she had lived here. Oranges and bananas were no longer available, though there was locally grown fruit and vegetables in plenty. She saw a whole stall covered in round, shining brown onions and determined to take some back with her and send them to Liverpool. Deirdre was always bemoaning the lack of onions, and Peader had said that when he tried to grow them on his allotment he had to keep a nightly vigil over them or they would be stolen by some wide-boy who would promptly sell them for ten times their worth.

As she watched, amused, it occurred to Polly that it might be a nice thought to take her unwitting hostess a gift of something other than the tea, sugar and bottled coffee which bulged through her knapsack. She glanced around her, and then dived into a fish and chip shop which seemed to be doing a roaring trade. Kids, she knew, would always eat fish and chips. It was a pity that she would have to queue, but the men behind the counter, sweating freely, were working like demons to get their customers served so she should not have long to wait.

She was halfway up the queue when she noticed that one of the lads behind the counter – he could not be more than fourteen or fifteen – was wearing a curious badge made out of some shiny silvery metal pinned or stuck to the breast of his grease-stained overall. She stared . . . and saw, with a frightened bump of the heart, that it was a swastika, with the German eagle above it. Horrified, she glanced about her, and realised that several of the boys in the queue wore badges, some of them the hated swastika and others cheaply made imitations of Air Force wings and roundels.

It was odd how it affected her, she thought now, trying not to stare too obviously at the badges. She had known, because Tad's mammy had told her, that some of the boys were making a game of the war, taking sides, swearing that they wanted the Germans to win because 'that would teach ould England a lesson, so it would!' But Polly now realised that it was one thing being told a fact, and quite another seeing it with one's own eyes. She felt hurt and rage combining; thoughts of Martin, dying at sea and leaving his wife a widow, thoughts of all the other young men . . . But it was no use blaming these boys for their ignorance and prejudice, they were just kids, chisellers who knew no better, who considered that if one were a true republican then it was Germany who one should back. And anyway, wasn't it just a game, hadn't Mrs Donoghue said as much?

Polly was at the head of the queue now and ordering her fish and chips. The youth behind the counter with the swastika badge on his shirt had a bright, cheery face and a pleasant manner. 'Will you be wantin' some vinegar?' he asked, holding the parcel open whilst glancing enquiringly at her. 'Will I put some on for yez?'

'It's all right,' Polly muttered, taking the parcel and folding the newspaper tightly round the delicious contents. 'I'm taking 'em to me friend's house, so I am – there'll be vinegar and salt there.'

She turned and walked out of the chipper, unable to throw off completely her feeling of distaste over the swastikas, but reminding herself that some of the boys had worn Air Force wings and RAF roundels. It didn't mean anything, really, not to them. Safe out here, watching a war going on as they'd watch the pictures and newsreels on a Saturday morning in the cinema, scarcely differentiating between what Tom Mix did in the big feature and what was happening on the other side of the Irish Sea.

Regaining Francis Street, she began to hurry on her way, anxious to get to Gardiner's Lane before the food got cold when someone drew level with her, turned to give her a casual glance and then grabbed hold of her by both shoulders, swinging her round to face him.

'Well, by all that's wonderful, if it isn't me own little Polly O'Brady! Poll, what in the divil's name are you doin' here? Last I heard . . .'

Polly's heart sank into her boots for a moment. She was wearing civvies and had pulled a truly hideous felt hat down over her curls. She had also borrowed a pair of 'props' – spectacles from one of the local amateur dramatic groups because they had plain glass in their lenses, but would help, she thought, to disguise her. And now here was this tall, broad-shouldered young man, his face difficult to see against the late sun which shone directly into her eyes, greeting her as though he had no shadow of a doubt who she was! Accordingly she pulled away from him, scowling.

'Sure an' it must be mad you are,' she said frostily, clutching her packet of chips to her bosom and wishing she could see her companion's face more clearly. The voice sounded familiar, but that was probably simply because he was using the brogue which, after so long in England, had begun to die out of her own voice. 'Who *are* you, anyway?'

'Don't tell me you don't recognise me, Poll!'

'I can't perishin' well *see* you,' Polly said irritably. 'The light's in me eyes, and you're in shadow.'

The man moved so that the light fell on his face. Polly gasped, then very nearly let go of her parcel of fish and chips as she moved involuntarily closer. 'Tad! Oh, Tad, you're just the same only a bit taller, and it's great to see you, so it is, but how can you ask me what *I'm* doin' in Dublin when you're in the Roy—'

'Ssh, Poll, do you want to get the pair of us hung up from the nearest lamp post?' Tad said in an urgent whisper. He took her hand in a large, warm palm and his touch sent a thrill through Polly, though she told herself severely that it was no way to feel, especially when, for all she knew, Tad might have become a deserter. 'Look, where are you rushin' off to, anyway? I'll walk along wit' you until we get off the main street.'

'I'm going to Gardiner's Lane,' Polly said, her voice reflecting more than a trifle of foreboding. 'I knew you were in England – well, you were a year ago, when you last deigned to write me a horrible little scrap of a note in answer to one – more likely a dozen – of me lovely letters. So I thought there'd be room for me to kip down on the floor somewhere.'

'Oh, there's bound to be,' Tad said. He then walked along, still holding her hand but saying nothing until they were in a comparatively deserted street, when he turned to her once more. 'Polleen, me darlin' girl, whatever brought you back to Dublin? All your family's in England, aren't they? And last I heard, you were in Scotland.'

'Oh, so you did get my letter?' Polly said sarcastically. 'No, I shan't tell you a word until you tell me what *you're* doing here, Tad Donoghue! Why, for all I know you might be a deserter, and if you're after bein' one of them, I'm none too sure I want to walk along beside you.'

Tad laughed. 'No, I've not left me pals in the lurch,' he said serenely, 'any more than you would, Polleen! I've come over wi't some stuff for me mammy and the little 'uns, and to make sure they're all right. Oh, I know everyone says that Dublin's got it easy, but apart from the money I send, Mammy doesn't do that well, not bein' able to afford the black market. So I pop over now and then wit' whatever I've managed to get hold of which will help her. Besides, I like comin' home, it's the big bonus of workin' in Valley instead of Yorkshire. Now what about you?'

'Valley? You mean Valley on Anglesey?' Polly gasped, quite overcome at this coincidence. 'Well, would you believe, Tad, I'm on HMS *Bee* in Holyhead! We're neighbours, as good as. How long have you been there? What are you doing? Do you come into town much? I've only been there a couple of months, but you'd have thought we'd have bumped into one another, wouldn't you?'

'Oh, I dunno. I don't go into town that often, except when I'm on me way over here,' Tad said. 'What really *is* odd is that we didn't spot one another on the ferry. I take it you've just come over on the *Hibernia*?'

'That's right,' Polly said. 'But it was very crowded and I got meself a spot up near the bows and sat down on me knapsack and just looked out over the sea and dreamed of home. Oh, and I'm here on a buyin' spree. I've brought tea and sugar and parachute silk and I'm hopin' to get butter and cheese, lipsticks and silk stockings. The girls paid me fare over and then gave me a list.'

'Trust you, Poll,' Tad said. He looked at her newspaper parcel. 'Though that looks more like fish and chips than tea or sugar or silk. Still, don't you know the trouble you could get into for coming over here when the country's at war? Mind, I'm not one to talk, I do it as well and I've not been caught out yet.'

Polly turned and looked at him. He was wearing grimy overalls over a dark grey shirt and wellington boots. He could have been a farm hand or a garage mechanic, she supposed. Certainly one would not have connected him with the Royal Air Force. 'No, you don't look much like an airman,' she admitted. 'And I don't look anything like a WRN, we're always smart, you know. So mebbe the pair of us will get away with it. I certainly hope so. But you've not got a knapsack, Tad. Where's your stuff hid?'

'I'm only bringing stuff for the family, don't forget,' Tad said as they turned into Gardiner's Lane and headed across the filthy paving stones for the tenement block in which the Donoghues lived. 'I bring a bit of sugar and some tea, they're in me pockets, and I've got three or four jumble-sale jerseys tied round me waist, but I'm not tradin', like you are.'

'I'm not,' Polly said rebelliously. 'Not much, anyway. Don't you take butter and cheese back, then, Tad? Only if you did you could finance your next trip, couldn't you?'

'I could. I do take stuff back,' Tad admitted. He squeezed her hand. 'Well, I can't get over it – me little pal, growed up, and growed up pretty, an' all.'

'Don't be so rude,' Polly scolded, but she did not pull her hand out of his. She eyed him covertly as they began to mount the stairs, side by side. He was tall, probably as tall as Sunny, and broad shouldered, and his taffy-brown hair had been cut neatly, so that you could see the nice shape of his head, but he was really very little altered from the boy she had once known so well. He still had a blunt nose, square chin, and the sort of grin which made him look as though there was not much he wouldn't do, given the chance. He wasn't handsome, she knew that all right, but he had a look of self-reliance and a sort of pride in himself which she had noticed before amongst members of the forces. Before, Tad had been scruffy, a bit spotty, but now, though he was wearing greasy old clothes, you could tell, somehow, that the dirt was not even skin deep. It was something which you could tell instinctively would be washed off every night . . . Other than that, he's just the same, Polly told herself. He's my friend and I'm fond of him, though he has let me down rather, over the writing business.

Up the stairs the two of them went to the familiar landing, only it, too, had changed. It was clean, the floorboards actually polished, and the door to the

Donoghue flat had been painted a bright, dark blue. A small brass lion's head hung in the middle of the door and Tad lifted it and let it bang down before pushing the door open and bellowing at the top of his voice: 'I'm home, Mammy, and guess who I've got wit' me – only you never will!'

Polly stood in the doorway, her eyes rounding with astonishment even as her lips curled with pleasure. The room that she remembered as dirty and drab was shining clean and bright, the furniture polished, the big table in the centre of the room spread with a decent checked tablecloth, the fire burning brightly in the hearth and a large pot suspended over it, sending out delicious smells. There were three or four young people in the room, all neatly dressed, and Mrs Donoghue was dishing up potatoes from a pan which had been stood on the side, and turned a beaming face towards her son and his friend.

'Polly O'Brady, by all the saints! Well, no colleen could be more welcome, alanna! Come in, come in – where did you find her, Tad me boy? What's that you've got? Don't say you've been to the chipper, spendin' your money like water when I've a pot full of taties on the stove and a fine stew on cookin'. But I know someone who'd rather have fish an' chips than the best stew in the world, so I do! Meg, go an' fetch up the little 'uns and tell them we've a visitor, and she's been to the chipper on her way back!' She turned, still smiling, to Polly. 'Eh, we've missed you something sore, alanna, but you're here now, so take off that jacket an' hat, it's crushin' your curls, and come and sit down. The kettle's on the hob, I'll have a cup o' tay in your hands in one minute flat, then you can tell us why you're here! Tad, it's grand to see you, so it is, you sit beside our Polly and you'll be suppin' tay before you're a minute older. Then you can both tell us how you came to arrive together this day!'

Lying on her improvised couch later that night, when the fire had died down and the others had all gone either to their beds or off on errands of their own, Polly thought over her day. From the moment of meeting Tad, she reflected, all the fears and uncertainties which she had been suffering from had fled. She had felt at once, as she had felt as a child, that Tad was to be trusted; he would take care of her. And when, after they had eaten their evening meal, he had taken her off for a stroll around the familiar streets, they had talked over her errand. Tad had promptly solved all her problems regarding the things the girls craved.

'Sure an' haven't I been doin' these deals for the past six months, meself?' he said cheerfully, tucking her hand into the crook of his elbow and grinning down at her. 'What's more, alanna, there's no need for you to hang about in Dublin all day and then to spend another night wit' the mammy, glad though she would be to have you. We'll get up early – the mammy does so anyway, she's still cleaning in Switzers – and get all your shoppin' done and be back in Dun Laoghaire in good time for the ferry, never you fear.'

It had sounded impossible, but Polly had thought of the many times that Tad had managed to get her out of scrapes, and did not doubt that he could solve her problems now. If he said she would be on the ferry tomorrow morning, with all her wheeling and dealing done, then he was right. All she needed to do was to put her trust in Tad; he would not let her down.

But though she might tell herself that he was simply her old friend Tad, grown a little taller and a great deal stronger, she knew that this was not really the case. They were almost like strangers, and in the eight years or so which had passed between their last meeting and this one, they had lived different lives. If we're to go on being pals we've got to get to know one another all over again, Polly told herself just before she fell asleep. Tad's a grand feller, so he is, but when it comes down to it, I only know the chiseller he was, not the grown man he has become. Why, I know Sunny a good deal better now than I know Tad. Only Sunny's so far away, and letters aren't the same . . . Still an' all, Tad's me best friend, and it'll be grand being near one another on the island, and grand getting to know each other all over again too.

And on this happy thought she fell asleep at last.

'Here we go, then! Give a wave to me little sisters, Poll. It were grand of them to come to see us off . . . Bye, Meg, bye, Biddy!'

Tad and Polly stood at the rail of the ferry, with their loaded knapsacks at their feet, waving lustily as the ferry drew away from the quay and the tiny figures of Meg and Biddy grew smaller and smaller. When they had melted into the distance, however, Tad took Polly's hand and lifted up both their knapsacks, slinging them over one broad shoulder. 'Come on, there's coffee below decks. Might as well wet our whistles since we missed breakfast. Are you hungry, alanna?'

'I am that,' Polly admitted, following him down the companionway to where a good smell of cooking came wafting up to greet them. 'Tad, you've been a real pal to me, so you have! By the time I was halfway across, yesterday, I was beginning to realise I'd bit off more'n I could chew, and then along you came an' rescued me! I thought I'd find someone standing on the dockside waiting for me to offer him tea and sugar, I think, or I thought your mammy would tell me where to go and how to set about swapping one thing for another. Tell me, when did you do it all?'

'Last night, after you were in bed,' Tad said, grinning. 'Sit yourself down whiles I fetch us some food . . . Will you be havin' coffee, or is tay more your tipple this early?'

'Coffee, please,' Polly said, and watched him shoulder his way to the counter, give his order and presently return to her, bearing two mugs of steaming coffee and two hefty-looking bacon sandwiches. 'Oh, that smells so good!'

'Yeah, no rationing aboard the *Hibernia*,' Tad said, taking a large bite out of his sandwich and sitting down opposite her. 'Now, as to last night – have you never heard of the pubs, alanna?'

'Ye-es, that's where they do a lot of black-market trading and so on,' Polly said. 'But I've never seen anyone doing anything other than drink and sing and lark about. Not that I go into pubs all that often,' she added. 'Because we've got the NAAFI, and the mess, and our wrennery, of course.'

'That's right. Well, if you go into a certain Dublin pub and put it about that you've trading goods, sooner or later the person wantin' those particular goods will turn up and you do a deal. That's about all,' Tad said. 'They know most of us who come across the water come over one day and go back the next, with no time to do much in the way of shopping. So they come to us, see?'

'And they bought me silk, and sugar and tea, and

sold you butter and stockings and lipstick?' Polly said incredulously. 'It can't be that simple – I bet you've never wanted lipsticks before, have you? Let alone silk stockings!'

'Well, I'm not in the habit of buyin' lipsticks,' Tad said, looking a little self-conscious. Polly realised that he might well have bought stockings for the WAAFs on his station and felt a stab of something remarkably like jealousy, which was a bit thick considering she had been telling herself ever since last night that the two of them were more or less strangers. 'But I moved about a bit, and managed to get everything on your list. All right?'

'Oh, sure an' I am grateful,' Polly said hastily. It was not fair to ask him questions, she thought guiltily, when he had done her such a favour. 'That girl Angela – I suppose she doesn't want silk stockings or lipsticks, seeing as how she's still living in Dublin?' she heard her voice say as though it had decided to ignore the advice its owner had been handing out so prodigally. She clapped a hand to her mouth but Tad, heavily engaged in his bacon sandwich, seemed to notice nothing amiss.

'Angela? I dunno. She's got another feller,' he said thickly. 'How about the bloke wit' the peculiar name? Sammy, was it?'

It was tempting to ask what was peculiar about the name Sammy, but Polly reminded herself severely that she should never have mentioned Angela and bit her tongue. 'Sunny,' she said in as offhand a voice as she could manage. 'He's on the Russian conveys, so I've not seen him for months and months, they sail from Scapa Flow, you see. But he writes regularly, like I do, so I know he's doing pretty well. He's a leading signaller now, and hoping to become a yeoman of signals before too long, and he's only young . . . about your age,' she finished.

'Oh aye? So you're still . . .?'

He didn't finish the sentence but Polly said quickly: 'Friends, d'you mean? Yes of course we are. He's a grand feller, Sunny. You'd like him.'

She half-hoped that Tad would look glum and say roundly that he would not like Sunny at all, but instead, Tad said cheerfully: 'Sure I'll like him if he's a pal of yours, Poll. And I daresay you'll like Maisie when you meet her.'

'Who's she?' Polly said bluntly. She, too, continued to eat her sandwich as though it was the most important thing in her life at this minute. 'Is there any mustard?'

Tad pushed the mustard pot across and took a long drink of coffee. Then he said: 'Maisie? Oh, she's a little WAAF working on the station. She's in the control tower, talking the kites down safely. We've been seein' quite a bit of each other lately. You'll like her.'

'So I will,' Polly said, inwardly deciding that she would heartily dislike anyone called Maisie, and wondering, just why the term 'a little WAAF' should sound so exceedingly friendly. 'If I meet her, that is. I don't get away from the old Bee all that much.'

'I'll see you get asked to our next dance,' Tad said. 'Want another coffee?'

Polly said that she would love another one, and watched his backview disappear into the scrum round the counter with an unaccountable feeling of annoyance. Why could he not have said *I'll ask you to the next dance*, instead of *I'll see you get asked to our next dance*, with its tacit inference that, since he would be taking the wretched Maisie he could not ask her, too. Not that it matters, she told herself fiercely, swinging

344

round in her seat to examine the other people in the dining area. I've got Sunny so why shouldn't he have his horrible little WAAF? She's probably got sticking out teeth, frizzy hair and a bad case of dandruff. *And* she'll be flat chested. And have spots. And not all the stockings in the world will be able to make those matchstick legs look good!

Tad, returning with two more cups of coffee, changed the subject and for the rest of the voyage they talked about the changes – all for the better – which had taken place at the flat in Gardiner's Lane and the delights of visiting Dublin, albeit briefly.

'Next time I come over I'll get in touch wit' you and we can go together again,' Tad said as they were queuing to leave the ship. 'We might have a bit of a get-together wit' some of our old pals from school. We could go round to Swift's Alley too – you had a grosh of pals there when you were a kid.'

But Polly, agreeing, thought that this was unlikely. She had done what Diane had asked of her and saw no reason for a return trip to Dublin, particularly in the company of someone who was clearly in love with a skinny, spotty WAAF named Maisie!

Chapter Thirteen

It was a brilliant summer day and for once the wind, which seemed to Tad to blow continuously from the sea which was only just out of sight from where he was working, had dropped from a gusty force six to a gentle breeze. Tad was working on a Beaufighter Mark II belonging to number 456 Squadron fitted with Merlin XX engines, but he had just about finished and now he replaced the cowling, rubbed oil marks off with the piece of soft rag which hung at his belt, and jumped down on to the grass.

Finished now, he glanced at his watch, saw that it was time for his canteen meal, and turned back towards the huts. He would clean up, go and get himself some food, and then perhaps he would get out the old motorbike and go into Holyhead; you never knew, Polly might be at a loose end and glad of his company.

Accordingly, he turned his footsteps towards the hutments clustered at the end of the runway, beginning to think about Polly and how her being so near had complicated his life. The truth was that he had not really thought of her as a girl, let alone a breathtakingly pretty one, until that trip to Ireland. She had been his little friend, the kid he had bullied, protected and teased, he had never really thought of her as a young woman. Seeing her on Francis Street had been quite a shock, but then meeting her in the full splendour of her WRNS uniform had been an even greater one. The dazzling blue of her eyes, the soft primrose curls, the rosy mouth nearly always curling into a smile, had made her very much sought after, and it riled Tad to have to take his place in the queue, so to speak.

Not that he ever let Polly know that he was one of the many admirers who would have given a great deal to be able to call her his girl. No fear! He knew his Polly too well to let her see that he was just like the others. He took advantage of their old friendship, laughed at her, carefully asked other girls to dance at the weekly hops – and kept a jealous eye on her all the time, in case she began to show real favour to anyone other than himself. But it seemed that she was 'just pals' as she put it, with half the armed forces upon the island, and that she was saving herself for that Sunny Andersen who had been such a bad influence on her as a child.

As he crossed the concrete apron in front of the mess hut he sniffed the air. 'Bangers and mash and cabbage,' he decided, not ill-pleased, for he thought the RAF food very good indeed and was always ready for his meals. And then there was a homely sort of smell of boiling cloth, which probably meant a jam duff. It might be blackberry jam, or even rhubarb and ginger, but it didn't matter much to him. When you had spent your childhood and early teenage years fighting for a bit of bread and maggie ryan to keep off the hunger pangs then jam of any description was a treat.

Tad went into the canteen and took his place in the queue at the counter behind another fitter, Phil Dunlop. Phil turned and grinned at him. 'Finished? I bet that kite's fair shinin' with every little nut and bolt looking like burnished silver! Coming into town later? I know you've got some little gal tucked away there, you dirty old Irishman! Who is she? Do you get your oats there? Is that why you aren't seein' so much of Maisie?'

Tad gave his companion a good-humoured swipe then picked up a plate from the pile and checked that his irons were in his pocket; they were. 'There's a girl I grew up wit', she's with HMS *Bee*,' he said carefully. 'I'm – I'm keepin' an eye on her, like, to see she don't get into mischief. I know her parents, and they – they expect me to see she stays on the right side of the law.'

It did not sound too convincing, even to Tad himself, but no one, not even a pal like Phil, could be told about his feelings for Polly – indeed, when she was at her most aggravating, he was none too sure of those feelings himself. All he knew, in fact, was that he could not bear the thought of any other feller with his arms round her, even if she was not precisely his girl – especially not that Sunny bloke.

'You? A guardian of decent girls? God awmighty, them parents can't know you very well, Tad! If I were a dad I'd take precious good care you din't get too close to no gal of mine, I'm tellin' you straight! Why, I'd as soon give a nice little lamb chop to old Bowser to keep safe!'

Tad grinned. Old Bowser was an enormous alsatian, one of a pair who paraded the perimeter track by night, making sure that no unauthorised person got too near the aircraft. Both dogs were friendly enough with the personnel on the station, old Bowser would probably have helped a spy to climb up into the nearest kite provided that same spy gave him a chunk of meat first.

'You shouldn't say such t'ings about the ould feller,' Tad said now, reprovingly. 'That dog had a bad puppyhood, his handler told me so. Why, he was half-starved until he was six months old, so naturally he'll do – well, anything – for a snack.'

'And you'd do anything to have your way wit' some pretty little WRN,' Phil said. 'Wouldn't we all?'

Tad said nothing but held out his plate for sausages, then moved along to the WAAF cook who was hurling spoonfuls of mashed potato on to the plates as though she had a personal grudge against it. How did Phil know I had a girl in Holyhead, Tad wondered. Then, sighing, told himself that Anglesey was a small island and Holyhead a small port. Everyone knew everyone else's business sooner or later, plainly someone had seen him with Polly. And anyway, he was glad enough to have been seen with her, because she looked so very pretty in her uniform, with her cheeky little sailor hat tipped over her eyes and her bell bottoms hugging her neat and rounded bottom. Of course she only wore her bell bottoms when she was working, but that was how he liked to think of her, tearing down the Turkey Shore Road with her hat seemingly stuck on to her curls and her slim legs going like pistons, whilst the bundles of documents she held under one arm flapped in the breeze of her going.

But anyway, even if she was working he would quite likely see her this afternoon. The girls were allowed far more latitude in the WRNS than in the WAAF, and Polly would deliver her messages, whatever they might be, and then come down to the shore. If he could find her they could have a cup of tea and a bun with him without anyone being any the wiser. She was his friend still, he knew that, but he sometimes worried a bit that it was really his motor-bike that she was interested in rather than himself.

She was desperate to become a WRN despatch rider and not just a messenger, and as soon as she had discovered that he owned a motorbike she had begun to pester him to teach her how to ride it. She was pretty good already, and liked nothing more than to persuade him to take her to some quiet country road, or to a hard, deserted beach, so that she might practise on the bike. Tad wondered sometimes just how Polly would explain her sudden ability to ride a motorbike to the Powers that Be, for she intended to apply for a despatch rider's job just as soon as she felt she was proficient. Knowing Polly, however, he thought ruefully, she would work something out in time – something which was both convincing yet not too far from the truth. In the meantime, if teaching her to ride his bike was his best way to keep close to her, then teach her he would.

'It's treacle duff for afters,' Phil said as he received a spoonful of overcooked cabbage and turned away from the counter. 'Grab the Flag, old feller, I can't face sawdust sausages without a good covering of sauce.'

'Right,' Tad said, obediently picking up the nearest sauce bottle and heading for the long table where most of the flight mechs seemed to have gathered. 'Treacle duff, eh? I thought I could smell something good!'

Polly and Diane had the afternoon off, so since it was a brilliant day, they had agreed to cycle over to Treaddur Bay for a swim. They met at Llys-y-Gwynt soon after two o'clock and set off together, Diane on a hired bicycle, down the long hill which would lead them on to London Road. They saw Tad from afar as they were skimming down the hill, with their hats on the extreme backs of their heads, though only Polly recognised him. 'It's me pal Tad,' she shouted to Diane above the breeze. 'He'll be coming over to give me a lesson on the motorbike, I daresay. Oh, damn, and I was looking forward to a swim, so I was. What'll I do, Di?'

Diane managed to shrug, not easy on a speeding bicycle. 'Tell him you can't play this afternoon,' she advised. 'After all, Poll my little parrot, you and I have planned this swim ever since the beginning of the week. You wouldn't let me down, would you?'

''Course not,' Polly said rather indignantly, the more so, perhaps, because she had definitely considered, just for a moment, begging Diane to let her off their planned expedition. She did so love the excitement of riding the motorbike and knew that Tad did not find it as easy to get time off as they did. 'Only he doesn't get as much time off as we do . . . so could he come along with us this afternoon, d'you t'ink?'

'He'll spoil it,' Diane said grimly, slowing to a halt as they reached the corner since Tad was now fast approaching along London Road. 'Besides, I don't like swimming in front of an audience. Tell him to come back another day.'

Polly giggled. Diane was a superb swimmer, very much better than her but Diane was going to be wearing her old school swimsuit which was decidedly skimpy in the bust region and, since it was made of black wool, rather baggy around the bottom. Diane had applied to her important relatives several times for a newer, roomier costume – well, roomier in certain areas, and tighter in others, Polly reminded herself – but so far they had been unable to come up with the goods. I expect all the swimwear factories are making diving suits or something, Polly told herself vaguely as Tad drew to a halt beside them and pulled off his forage cap. Still, no use being silly about it. Oh dear, thought Polly. If I tell Tad where we're going he'll come along, invited or not, and he'll see Diane's suit and won't give a thought to it, knowing Tad. Indeed, she privately thought, in some dismay, that Tad might very much enjoy the view, for the sight of Diane overflowing from her swimsuit was the sort of spectacle that most red-blooded young men would appreciate, she felt sure.

'Afternoon, girls,' Tad said politely as the girls drew their steeds to a halt beside him. 'Not going anywhere special, are you? Only I thought as it was a nice day, like, that Polly might be able to have a lesson on me old bike.'

'Oh, did you?' Diane said with more than a touch of sarcasm. 'Well, as it happens Polly and myself have a – a previous engagement. But no doubt she'd enjoy a lesson on your motorbike if you gave her some warning, and didn't just turn up as though she'd never got anything better to do.'

'Nasty, nasty,' Tad said with what seemed to be unimpaired cheerfulness, though Polly saw a slight flush steal across his cheekbones. 'I would have rung up, only she's hardly ever available during the day and I didn't know I was going to be free today until quite late on. I've been servicing kites all morning, but I got through sooner than I expected, and it's a lovely day . . .'

'I'll be free this evening,' Polly said quickly. 'In fact, by teatime, probably. Only I did promise Di . . .'

'Oh, it's just the two of you, then?' Tad said. 'Just going for a bike ride, are you? If so, why can't I tag along?'

'Because you go a good deal faster than us, and we

were planning a quiet afternoon, just the two of us,' Diane said in her crispest, most authoritarian voice. 'Honestly, airman—'

'If you tell me where you're going, I could be there ahead of you,' Tad said. He looked hard at the carriers of their bikes and clearly realised that the bundles so neatly strapped into place were towels. 'Oh, going swimming, eh? Now there's nothing I like better than seeing two beautiful girls takin' to the water . . . but I'm prepared to put up wit' watching the two of you, since it seems that's all that's on offer.'

Even Polly felt this was a bit cheeky, but rather to her surprise Diane giggled and surrendered, though not with very good grace. 'All right, all right,' she said, hitching herself on to the saddle of her borrowed bike and scooting forward a few paces.

'We're going to Treaddur Bay for a swim and I suppose I can't stop you coming along. But if you do, airman, you can bloody well swim too, then we shan't feel silly.'

Tad grinned and roared off but Polly, mounting her own bicycle, said: 'But he's not got bathing drawers wit' him, Di. He'll probably want to swim in the altogether, and I don't fancy that at all, at all.'

It was Diane's turn to grin. 'He might swim in the altogether if it was just you and himself, my dear girl, but he won't attempt to do so with me present,' she assured her friend. 'He'll probably come in in his horrible Air Force undies, whatever they may be. Why, it might be an even more interesting experience for you and I than it will be for him. Cheeky sod, making it just about impossible for us to freeze him off!'

'Oh well,' Polly said peaceably, pedalling away. 'I've always wanted the two of you to get better acquainted, so I have, and it looks as though me wish is about to be granted.'

When the two girls reached the beach it was to find Tad's motorcycle propped up against the sea wall whilst Tad himself was already in the sea and swimming strongly.

'Showing off,' Diane said icily, changing amongst the rocks on the right-hand side of the bay. 'Well, let's hope he stays well out there whilst we go in.'

Presently, respectably, if scantily clad, the two of them ran down to the waves and splashed in, shouting as the cold salt sea gradually rose to chest level. Further out, Tad did a graceful duck-dive, which caused Polly to squeak.

'Oh janey, Di, it's nekkid he is,' she gasped, turning her back on Tad in considerable confusion. 'How does he dare? Ooh, I do think he's awful!'

'I expect he's wearing his underpants,' Diane said, though without total conviction. 'Where is he now?'

'Over by the island . . . don't *look*, Diane, he'll think we're awful strange if we look.'

'Well, at least it'll stop him looking at us,' Diane owned. 'If he really is bare, that is. Oh come on, forget him and enjoy your swim.'

'Ye-es, but he hasn't got a towel,' Polly moaned presently, after doing some fancy strokes in the cool, salty water. 'If he shakes like a dog I'm goin' to die of embarrassment, so I am. I know he's me pal, but I'll never look him in the face again, I swear it.'

'It isn't his face you'll be looking at,' Diane said, giggling. 'He's a marvellous swimmer, though, isn't he? When he does the crawl he looks like a steam tug he moves so fast.'

'And splashily,' Polly said with a shiver. 'I'm going out now, Di. If he comes near us—'

'He's coming over,' Diane said. 'Not that I care.' But she began to retreat towards the beach nevertheless, whilst Tad came on faster, until he was near enough to speak to them.

'Why don't you come out a bit further?' he shouted. 'It's marvellous out here, and it's always easier to swim wit' a bit of depth under you. Well, Polly O'Brady, I never knew you were a water-funk until now!'

'I am nothin' of the sort,' Polly shouted back, stung by the remark. 'It's just . . . What are you wearin', Tad Donoghue? Because we aren't goin' to get ourselves court-martialled through bathin' wit' a bare airman!'

'Come and see,' Tad said provocatively. 'Come on, the pair of yiz, unless you're both yeller as – as flag irises!'

Diane turned her shoulder on him but Polly, enraged by such remarks, splashed back into the sea again, launched herself forward, and began to forge her way towards Tad in a rapid sidestroke. When she got near enough she trod water, staring at her old pal, whereupon he did a porpoise leap out of the water and back in again, revealing that he was clad in a pair of skimpy but respectable underpants.

'Well, I didn't think you'd be out here swimmin' in your birthday suit,' she said untruthfully. 'Only I didn't see what else you could have found to bathe in. Glory be to God, Tad, you'll be horribly wet and soggy when you have to get yourself dressed.'

'Shan't. I'm gettin' out now, and I'll lie on the rocks until I dry off,' Tad said complacently. He gave a short bark of laughter. 'Hey, didn't I have the pair of you in a state, then? Frightened to see something you

355

weren't supposed to see, and thinkin' me a shameless sort of feller!'

'So y'are,' Polly said stoutly, turning for the shore once more. 'I doubt that Diane will ever forgive you for making her feel a fool though, Tad, and I did want you to be pals.'

'Oh, pals,' Tad said, with a shrug in his voice, Polly thought crossly. 'That's what you and me are – pals. But we go back a long way, so we do. I don't make friends wit' people that easy.'

'Unless they're WAAFs,' Polly said under her breath. 'Unless they're pretty little WAAFs who t'row themselves at your head, Tad Donoghue! Why, everyone knows that WAAFs are easy, and sleep around wit' anyone. It's only the WRNS who have a bit of discretion.'

'What was that?' Tad called. There was laughter in his voice but Polly knew she could not possibly have been overheard and ignored him, continuing to swim for the shore. Presently she hauled herself out on the sand and went over to where Diane was already draped across a smooth, flat rock, her face blissfully held up to the sun and the salt water drying on her body. She opened her eyes a slit and smiled at Polly.

'If it wasn't for your precious pal we could have sunbathed naked,' she murmured, then laughed at Polly's shocked exclamation. 'Now, now, Polly, less of that middle-class morality! I know you want to learn to ride his motorbike, but don't you think it's a bit unfair to lead him on? I mean, you always say that the naval signaller is your real feller.'

'Sunny,' Polly said. She lay down on her own towel and relaxed, letting the heat begin to soak into her sea-wet limbs. 'Oh aye, he's me feller . . . but Tad and I have known each other for ever. I like him in the same sort of way I like you, Di. What's wrong wit' being friends with a feller?'

'Nothing's wrong with that, so long as he understands that you're only going to be friends and nothing more,' Diane said lazily. 'This chap seems to me to be rather more involved than you, though, Poll. Still, I daresay you know your own business best.'

'I do,' Polly said a trifle huffily, and closed her eyes firmly. As the sun began to dry her wet hair and costume, she thought about Sunny. She knew she wanted to be Sunny's girl though she hadn't seen him for ages. She only had to think of his hand caressing her neck and moving round along her jawbone to find that her stomach had begun to churn in an exciting way, whilst her knees turned to water. Resolution seemed to disappear; it no longer mattered that she was a good girl, a decent girl, intent on saving herself for marriage. Sunny's touch made her feel wicked, daring . . . and it made her want to do something more, to . . .

With dear Tad, however, it was quite different. She and Tad had been exchanging blows, wrestling each other to the ground, kissing better, for more years than she could remember. His hand on her arm, or round her waist when they danced, brought warmth and a strong feeling of safety and security. It did not thrill her one little bit. It was a shame, she supposed idly, but there it was. Sunny was wickedly exciting, poor Tad was more like a brother, and you didn't go around wanting to marry your brother. So however much she might like Tad, he was not going to be the one for her.

Satisfied with her musings – and slowly beginning to roast in the hot sunshine – Polly rolled on to her face and gave the back of her a chance to swelter. And presently, without at all meaning to do so, she fell asleep.

When she woke it was because Tad was standing over her, flicking seawater on to her extremely hot flesh and telling her that if she didn't get a move on there would be no time for a motorbike lesson before he had to return to Valley. Polly, feeling stiff and sandy and rather cross, got stumblingly to her feet and saw that Diane, looking smug, was already fully dressed, as was Tad.

'You're mean, Di,' she said accusingly, picking up her clothes and retreating to a sheltering rock. 'You could have woke me. Come to that, you could have as well, Tad,' she added in an aggrieved tone. 'Oh, I'm all burned, me legs is like lobsters and – and when I brush the sand off it hurts like hell, so it does.'

'I did try to wake you, but you swore at me and went on snoring,' Tad said unkindly. 'Look, Di, if you want to start cycling back we'll follow as soon as Polly's dressed.'

'Don't you dare go, Di,' Polly squeaked, tearing her swimming costume off with scant regard for the proprieties, though since the beach was deserted apart from themselves and she was in a private tumble of rock from whence she could see nothing but the curve of the bay she was safe enough from prying eyes. 'I won't cycle back wit' Tad on his motorbike very likely trying to hustle me to go faster than I can. Oh, and me shoulders feel like a couple o' burned steaks, so they do! You're a cruel pair, and I thought you were both me friends.'

'Sunburn is a self-inflicted wound and you could be court-martialled for it,' Tad said smugly just as Polly, fully dressed but still sandy and cross, emerged from her hiding place. 'Do you want to abandon your

bicycle and come home on me pillion, though? I'll
come back for the bike later, if you really can't use it.'

But this Polly refused to do, though she cycled
along slowly, because the friction of her shirt against
her skin was very painful. Since she was in uniform
she had not dared to leave off her underwear and
stockings, though even the thought of the long cycle
ride, clad in full uniform, dismayed her. But still, hot
and uncomfortable though she was, at least she
would arrive back in Holyhead properly dressed.
And once they got going it was a bit cooler, with the
sun sinking now towards the west and the worst of
the heat gone from the day.

'I've never envied Sunny his Arctic seas before, but
I do now,' she grumbled to Diane as they cycled
slowly along the country roads. 'Oh, I could murder
an ice cream, so I could! Come to that, I'd give a small
fortune for a nice cold bath. But when we get back to
the wrennery I suppose I'll have to let Tad give me a
lesson, after mucking up his afternoon.'

But by the time they got back to London Road,
however, Tad told them that he would have to return
to Valley. 'Sure an' you're looking mortal hot, Poll,' he
said, not unkindly. 'The best place for you is bed, once
you've had a bath to wash off the salt and the sand. I'll
see you in a day or so.'

By this time Diane had disappeared into the house
and Tad and Polly were alone in the small back yard.
Polly tried to banish her bad temper and smiled
gratefully at her companion. 'Oh, Tad, I'm sorry to be
such a grouch,' she said. 'But I hurt all over, so I do; I
don't think I could concentrate on riding your motorbike even if you didn't have to go back to the station.
I'm really sorry . . . but next time, do ring up first.'

'Sure I will,' Tad said. He glanced round quickly,

then propped his motorbike against the back wall and came over, trying to take Polly gently in his arms. 'Sleep well, alanna, and I'm sorry I codded you about being sunburnt. It's horribly painful, I know, and—'

'Don't touch me!' Polly shrieked. 'Honest to God, I'm as raw as a peeled shrimp and you go touchin' me! Gerroff, Tad Donoghue!'

Tad apologised and left and Polly stomped off indoors and presently she lay in a cool bath watching the sand float down to the bottom and feeling a good deal better and even a little ashamed of her abrupt dismissal of her old friend.

But it just went to prove, she thought drowsily, flapping her hands up and down in the water to make little waves, that she was right to wait for Sunny. And presently she got out of the water, patted herself dry and went and got into bed, where even the touch of the sheets was uncomfortable. I'll be all right once I'm asleep, she told herself, cuddling the pillow. And tomorrow I'll be right as rain, and I'll begin to have a lovely tan, just like Tad's got on him, the lucky feller. And when I see Sunny . . . Her mind drifted off into a pleasant dream in which she was back in Liverpool in peacetime, with the sun shining and Sunny holding her hand and telling her she was the only girl for him . . .

Polly slept.

It was decidedly odd getting off the number 24 tram on Stanley Road and heading for the O'Bradys' new home. Weird, really, Grace thought, that the area which she had once known so well should seem so strange to her because she herself had very likely been born on Snowdrop Street – certainly it was amongst her earliest memories. The Carberys had been at least the semblance of a family then, with a mother, a father and eight or nine children, Grace being the youngest-but-one, but by the time Grace was four or so, the family had moved away from Snowdrop Street and begun to disintegrate. Her mother was a mean, cowardly woman who would – and did – blame her children when anything went wrong so that the force of their father's wrath fell upon them rather than on herself. Stan Carbery had been a drunken brute of a docker who had become more violent and unpredictable as the years went by and the drink ate into him. They had been kicked out of the house in Snowdrop Street because they didn't pay the rent, Grace could still remember that much . . . as she could remember her father knocking her mother downstairs in a drunken fight one evening, and breaking her neck. The scuffers had come and decided to treat it as an accident, but the kids, all of them, even little Grace, had known better. They also knew that their father would keep his threat to strangle anyone who told the truth, so they had kept their mouths shut. Indeed, by the time Grace had been eight or nine she had rarely, if ever, returned to the filthy slum in a back-court where her father screamed and beat anyone who got in his way and drank not only all his own money but any that his kids might be lucky enough to make.

I wonder what would have happened to me if the Salvation Army had not taken me in and given me some pride in myself and a home at Strawberry Field? Grace wondered now as she walked, kitbag slung over one shoulder, and her greatcoat over the other, along Stanley Road. I'd never have amounted to much even if I'd lived – how could I? I was filthy, half-starved, in mortal fear of any sort of authority and constantly sleeping rough. I would certainly never have joined the WAAF, worn a smart uniform and helped to fight for my country. Indeed, she would never have gone off to America to help bring up Jamie. Yes, if it had not been for the Army and the love and schooling they had given her, her life would have been very different.

Grace reached Snowdrop Street with Thompson the tailor on one corner and the Manchester Laundry on the other and turned down it, squinting along the damp pavement, trying to remember which house the Carberys had once inhabited. Number 24? Or was it 26? She did not recall ever referring to the house by its number, she had just headed for the place which she knew was her home, though usually, in those very early days, she had been either carried or led along by Jess, her big sister, the one who had been like a mother to her until the baby, Mollie, had been born and had taken her, Grace's, place. She walked slowly along the pavement, trying to conjure up memories which were pleasant, but found herself almost totally unable to do so. It had been so long ago, and after Jess had died and Mollie had been lost, their stay here had been brief. As an older child she had once or twice been drawn back to this street, wooed by vague memories of a time when she had been Jess's little favourite and of her baby sister, but even then she had been unable to recapture those happy times, so why should she expect to remember them now?

She looked hard and curiously at the houses that she passed, though they were all very much neater and cleaner than she remembered. Their front door had had a great hole in it which someone, probably their mother, had patched rather badly with a wobbly piece of cardboard. She remembered one of her brothers coming in through that cardboard one night when someone, again almost certainly either their mother or father, had locked the door and sworn that any child not indoors by a certain time would sleep on the street. She even remembered that it had been a bitterly cold night, that there had been snow, and that the missing child had left the cardboard dangling on one side so that the draught had come sidling meanly up the filthy, bare boards of the stairwell, to rouse even the soundest sleeper with its damp and chilly breath.

But right now it was summer, though the rain was falling steadily, and Grace pushed aside her memories of this street and hurried, turning towards the house now occupied by the O'Bradys and tapped on the green-painted front door.

There was a short delay, then the door shot open and Peader stood there in carpet slippers, old grey flannels and a woollen jumper which had seen better days. But his smile could not have been more welcoming had it been his own daughter standing on the doorstep and the way in which he shouted 'It's our Grace, alanna; come and help me to get her unravelled from her luggage!' was enough to warm the cockles of a heart far less susceptible to kindness than Grace's.

'Oh, Uncle Peader, it's so good to be back,' she half-gasped, as he and Deirdre took her kitbag and somehow managed to detach her from her greatcoat and began to pull her across the narrow hallway and into the back kitchen. 'Isn't it a rotten night, though? You'd never think it was summer, it's so damp and chilly.'

'Never mind, love, I've got the kettle on and there'll be a mug of cocoa ready before you've so much as settled in your chair,' Deirdre said, pushing Grace gently into the shabby old armchair which she had last seen in the house in Titchfield Street. 'We didn't know what time you'd arrive so I've got a liver casserole cooking in the oven which must be done to a turn by now. Are you very hungry?'

'Starving, Auntie Dee,' Grace said, holding out her hands to the fire. 'Liver casserole, my favourite.' She looked about her at the solid, comfortable kitchen furnishings she had known for so long. 'Have you heard from Brogan or Sara and Jamie?'

'Brogan's been posted to a base in Suffolk, Laken-heath,' Deirdre said, bustling over to the oven.

'It feels really strange to be in Snowdrop Street again,' Grace said. 'As I walked along I tried to recog-nise our house . . . but it was so long ago . . . You knew I was born in Snowdrop Street? I think we lived here for four or five years.'

She glanced across at Deirdre. The older woman was sitting as though turned to stone, staring at her, and when Grace looked interrogatively at Peader he, too, was staring, round-eyed.

'What's the matter?' Grace said, smiling. 'Didn't you know I were born in Snowdrop Street? Not that it matters, particularly as we weren't able to pay the rent so we had to leave. I was trying to remember the neighbours, wondering whether there were any left from when we were here, but I daresay they've all either moved on or forgotten all about us. It was ages ago, after all – I was about four when Mollie was lost and Jess was killed. That was nearly twenty years ago which is a long time for memories to go back.'

'You're right there,' Deirdre said after a rather long pause, Grace thought. 'Yes, memories are short.' She got to her feet and moved over to the oven. 'I'd best dish up before we're all as hungry as Grace.'

Grace frowned across at the fire. All of a sudden the small room seemed less cheerful, less secure, as though a chilly little wind had blown under the door.

Peader cleared his throat, glanced at Grace and then at his wife, and said rather lamely, Grace thought: 'There's nothing like a liver casserole to warm you through on a chilly night.' Grace felt that the atmosphere, which had been so warm and comfortable when she first entered the house, had become strained in some way. What could she have said? So far as she could recall she had said nothing to remind them of the war. Then suddenly she remembered a topic of conversation which would please them. 'Oh, you said in your last letter that Monica had got herself a job in a factory making uniforms because she felt that she was doing nothing towards the war effort. Has she settled in well?'

'She has indeed,' Peader said heartily. 'I don't deny there's been times when we thought her rather . . . But all that's past. I don't believe she's ever looked at another feller since Martin's – Martin's ship went down, and now she's working in a factory on a big commercial sewing machine. It's not glamorous work, but useful. She's always been a keen needle-woman and seems to have taken to the work. At any rate she's a supervisor and does special jobs for them. And whilst Sara was here she used to go over to the Eventide homes to help out, and to the Strawb, as well. Oh aye, she's turned out all right has our Monica.'

Grace smiled at the 'our', because she still remembered when Monica had been very much an outsider. But how sad that a tragedy had had to happen before Monica had truly become an O'Brady. Still, that was life, she supposed.

'Come up to the table the two of you,' Deirdre said presently, carrying a steaming casserole across the kitchen and putting it down with a plonk on the scrubbed wooden table. 'Peader wouldn't eat his share earlier, so I made do wit' a sandwich. Now we're all ready for our food!'

And the three of them settled themselves round the table whilst Deirdre dished up and Grace, mouth watering, picked up her knife and fork. Home cooking, she thought ecstatically. Bliss after months of canteen food.

'It was the ideal opportunity, alanna, so why didn't you take it?' Peader whispered to Deirdre very much later that night as the two of them lay in their bed. 'You could have just said straight out that our Polly was adopted when she was a few months old, and that she was really Mollie Carbery. I meant to speak meself, but such a look you gived me – it scared the livin' daylights out o' me, I tell you straight!'

'I think Polly should be the first to know,' Deirdre insisted. 'She's our girl, we should tell her first. Grace is a dear, but we didn't bring her up, love her from the time we first laid eyes on her as we did wit' our Poll. Oh, and I'm scared that if we tell anyone we'll be in mortal trouble. I know the mammy and daddy died, but there may be relatives . . . I can't face it, so I can't.'

'Well, you're going to have to tell the pair of 'em, some time,' Peader pointed out. 'And Grace so longs for a sister! Why not tell her now, make it easy on yourself? The good Lord above knows when Polly will be on leave next, and you'll not put such news in a letter, that I *do* know, so why not grit your teeth and tell? If Sara had been here she'd have blowed the gaffe, I'm sure of it.'

'Why? Why should Sara say anything?' Deirdre asked in an aggrieved tone. 'She's me daughter-in-law, not me conscience!'

'Because didn't you hear what Grace said after supper, about Sara's gran living on Snowdrop Street too? Sara knew the Carbs, I know she did, and naturally she and Brogan both know all about Polly's being brought over to Ireland to keep her safe. Oh, Deirdre, no good ever came of deliberate deceit!'

'We've been deliberately deceiving ourselves for all of Polly's life, just about,' Deirdre pointed out. She felt tears come to her eyes and turned, burying her face in Peader's pyjama-clad shoulder. 'I don't think it's right to tell one girl and not the other, anyway. Next time they're both home on leave I swear on the Holy Book, Peader, that we'll have it all out. Will *that* satisfy you?'

'It will,' Peader said. 'Let's hope it will be sooner rather than later, then. I know Polly was only a tiny baby when she left this area, but if I'd realised we'd have been bringing her back to the very street on which she was born . . . well, I don't know but I'd have turned the house down.'

'I would have,' Deirdre said fervently. 'Still, next time they're both home on leave . . .'

She left the sentence unfinished and was soon asleep but Peader lay awake for some time, staring into the darkness. It was all very well to insist that they tell the two girls the truth and let them enjoy their relationship, but what would it do to Polly's relationship with her adoptive parents and brothers?

'Me pal Grace is home!' Polly squeaked, putting the

first page of her letter down on the table and turning shining eyes on Diane, sitting beside her and eating slightly burned porridge with as good a grace as she could manage. Polly was not a good cook and it had been her turn to make the breakfast. 'Well, she will be by now, at any rate, since Mammy wrote this . . .' she flicked the letter before her with one finger, '. . . a couple of days ago. I wonder now, could I get a forty-eight?'

''Course you could,' Diane said crisply. 'Why, if Tad was able to do the same he could take you back home on the motorbike! Go on, if she's your best friend it 'ud be nice to meet up again and you've not been home since you joined HMS *Bee*. Go and ask as soon as you get into the offices,' Diane suggested, finishing her porridge and reaching out a hand towards the teapot. 'Any more tea? Though I do think the mess should provide coffee for brekker. My mama would faint if she knew her ewe lamb was reduced to drinking tea before work in the morning.'

'Your mama must have got used to bad news about her ewe lamb by now,' Annabel Ridge remarked from her place further down the table. The three girls were having an early breakfast and none of the other WRNs had yet appeared. 'What about diving into the harbour and having to be dredged up by a whole platoon of soldiers, then? What did mama think of that?'

Diane giggled. 'Not a lot. But I didn't dive into the harbour, you utter idiot, I was coming ashore from one of the MTBs and a wave sort of jiggled it and I fell in the drink. And only two soldiers came in for me, not a platoon.'

'She's accident prone,' Polly said, finishing her toast and pushing her empty cup towards Diane, who was waving the teapot about rather uncertainly. 'Pour us another cup, me darlin', then we'd best get a move on. I want to tackle the Leading WRN before she gets all snarled up in other business.'

Chapter Fourteen

On her first day, Peader took Grace on a ramble along the Scotland Road, where Grace was duly dismayed at the empty shelves and windows filled with pictures of goods often no longer even available. They had quite a good lunch though, in a tiny workingmen's cafe filled with large and noisy dockers, and after that Peader went home and Grace went to Strawberry Field.

She caught a bus, walked up the drive, and was immediately filled with nostalgia for days past. She had been so happy here! Matron came out as she entered the familiar hall and gave her a hug, then bore her off to the staffroom where a number of Salvationists were having tea and introduced her to those few that she did not already know. Then they sat and talked and Grace told them all about being a driver, and quite a lot about Graham, who was a Salvationist as well and had introduced her to a whole host of his friends.

'You won't go far wrong with another Salvationist, chuck,' an elderly member of the staff said comfortably. She was a Mrs Farrow, a retired teacher who was 'helping out during the emergency', which seemed to mean that she was doing a very good job and would continue to do it so long as the war lasted. Which, Grace thought soberly, looks like being quite a time – it's a good job Mrs Farrow enjoys the work and loves the kids.

She refused, with real regret, an invitation to stay and share the evening meal but went through into the playroom and talked to the children for a bit. They loved meeting 'old girls' they told her and wanted to know all about the services so that they could join the right one when they were old enough.

'With luck, the only force you'll join will be the Salvation Army,' Grace told them, smiling. 'I pray the war will be over long before you're old enough to join up. But Matron tells me you've done a great deal of work in raising money for our chaps. She says you must have bought a whole Spitfire with all the old iron you collected, to say nothing of newspapers, rags and the like.'

She was back on Snowdrop Street by the time Deirdre was beginning to scrub the potatoes and prick the sausages, for it was to be bangers and mash tonight. 'Tomorrow we'll have fish and chips from the shop down the road, if they've got any, that is,' she said as Grace crossed the room towards her. 'We thought we'd have an early tea tomorrow, just a cuppa and some bread and jam, and then go to the flicks. After that we'll have the fish and chips. Would you like to do that? Only we don't want you to waste a minute of your leave, alanna.'

Grace agreed with all the plans Deirdre had made and began to lay the table for supper.

'Fish and chips and a visit to the flicks will be lovely,' she said contentedly, putting round the knives and forks. 'But the best thing of all, Auntie Dee, is being with you – being back here, in Liverpool amongst me pals. They were prime to me at the Strawb, and Uncle Peader and I had a good laugh, looking at what the shops aren't selling. But I never asked – how did your day go?'

'Grand, thanks, chuck. Oh, and I met Monica, and she's coming with us to the flicks tomorrow and having supper after that. She's looking so pale and ill, I thought it would do her good to meet someone who wasn't a hundred years old and stuck on a sewing machine.'

Peader, sitting by the fire reading the *Echo*, laughed. 'There's other girls in that factory, I'll be bound,' he said. 'Still, I know what you mean, me darlin'. Monica said right from the start that she didn't believe Martin was dead any more than our Polly did, but I sometimes wonder if it isn't a good deal worse waitin' for a feller to write, or make himself known to you, than if you accept he's dead and you won't see him again. On the other hand, whilst there's hope, there may be life as well.'

'She's right to hope, I think,' Grace said. 'With the Navy, it's awful hard to say for certain what's happened, I know that. You know Sunny and I write to each other? Well, he's on convoy duty still in his destroyer, he's on the Russian convoys now though, and in one of his letters he was telling me how his ship was dodging round the convey, keeping it safe, a bit like a sheepdog circles a flock, he says, when they suddenly realised that they were a ship short – a big merchantman had disappeared. He says it was broad daylight, with no enemy aircraft overhead for once and nothing under the surface either, so far as they could judge. Yet the ship just simply disappeared and no one saw it go. But very much later, he found that one of the men had been picked up by another member of the convoy, and was safe. Only the one – but even he couldn't say just what had happened, save that he was woken by water sloshing round his hammock and a lot of noise. He said he managed to wriggle through a hole and shot up to the surface, despite not wearing a lifebelt, and found a half-submerged life raft and clung to it.'

'Well, there you are, then,' Peader said placidly. 'There's hope for Mart yet – if he was picked up by a German ship . . .'

'That's right. Or I suppose he might have swum ashore . . . oh, I don't know, but I do believe that Monica is quite right to hope,' Grace said. 'I'll be glad to see her tomorrow, in any event. I never really got to know her before, but now, perhaps, we'll have a bit more time.'

Tad was unable to get a forty-eight, or even to find time to take Polly home on the back of his motorbike.

'The truth is, Poll, that you'll be safer on the bus and train,' he told her bluntly when she rang him that evening at the station. 'My bike's not a new machine, you know. She's totally trustworthy on a run of twenty miles or so, but it's a good deal more than that to reach Liverpool, and I'd be afraid that if she broke down and I'd not got the right spare parts with me, I might make you miss your pal Grace. If you'd given me some advance warning, it would have been different, but as things stand, you're better off by public transport.'

Polly sighed and said that she would take his advice and rang off, but she had not the slightest intention of doing anything so tame. Instead, she set off on a round of all the drivers she knew, and the next morning managed to get a lift with a driver returning to Chester after delivering supplies to the naval base.

Immensely pleased with herself, Polly proceeded to hitchhike the rest of the way and as a result arrived within a few hundred yards of her new home no later than eleven in the morning with her money still intact and feeling fresh and perky. The man who had taken her on the last stage of her journey was heading for the docks and he dropped her on Commercial Road, very near the end of Snowdrop Street, and drove off, beeping his horn cheerfully in farewell.

Polly turned into the short street, reminding herself that she had now got extra time to enjoy her forty-eight and rat-tatted cheerfully on the door. She wondered who would come in answer to her knock and hoped it would be Peader, though of course if it was Grace that would be wonderful too. It could not be her mother, who was working in the parachute factory and she was still wondering who would answer the knock when the door opened and Peader stood before her, his eyebrows gradually rising into his hair whilst a big smile spread right across his face and delight beamed out of his dark eyes. Polly bounced across the short distance that separated them and straight into his arms.

'Oh, Daddy, isn't it just great to be here? Oh, I do love you, so I do!'

'Polly! Be all that's wonderful, how've you come here? Why, me darlin' girl, you couldn't have arrived at a better moment – d'you know your pal Grace is here? She got up late this mornin', because we've planned an outing tonight, and she and meself was about to go off on the tram to the posh shops on Bold Street and round there . . . But come in, alanna, and sit yourself down. Oh, just wait till I tell young Grace who's here!'

Together, father and daughter entered the house, closing the front door firmly behind them.

*

Polly had a wonderful day. She and Grace went off by themselves in the end, Peader having admitted that he could do with a couple of hours on his allotment, and they talked non-stop, scarcely noticing the lack of goods for sale, even in the poshest of posh shops. Grace told Polly all about her work and Polly was very impressed, feeling that Grace was doing more for the war effort by rushing around in ambulances and ferrying the aircrews to and from their kites and the messes and admin buildings than she herself was doing in taking documents and messages from ship to shore and from one centre of administration to another.

'But we're all doing our bit,' Grace said comfortingly, when Polly voiced her thoughts. 'Why, without you, Poll, enemies of the state might listen in on the wireless waves or whatever they are, and hear the secrets that you carry. Anyway, didn't you say you were learning to ride a motorbike? Despatch riders are important, and they have a very interesting sort of life as well. I think I'd rather be a despatch rider than a bus and gharry and ambulance driver any day of the week! Here's Lewis's, though and they're still serving quite a decent meal, cheaply too. Shall we indulge ourselves for once?'

'But won't Daddy expect us home?' Polly asked rather anxiously. 'I know he said he'd rather dig his allotment, but I felt mean taking his morning off away from him, so I did.'

Grace, however, was reassuring. 'He was just being polite to a guest,' she assured her friend. 'Auntie Dee tried to get a day off to take me around, but the factory weren't keen, so your dad said he'd take me instead. The trouble is, most of me old pals are working so I was at a bit of a loose end. You're a sight for sore eyes, queen, and your dad's glad he can get out of a lot of window-shopping, I promise you. As for going home for a meal, he and I had planned to eat out, so I'm sure he'll expect you and I to do the same.'

So the two girls went and had lunch at Lewis's and after that they 'did' the cheaper shops in Byrom Street and the Scottie, before getting themselves a cup of tea and a bun at the nearest cafe.

They caught a tram home and told Peader all about their day and when Deirdre got back, tired after a long day at her machine but thrilled to see Polly, they had another cup of tea whilst they waited for Monica to join them. She, good girl that she was, came in just as the tea was brewing, so the five of them hurried off to the Gaiety Cinema, where the girls had a most enjoyable snuffle in the sad bits and laughed heartily over the cartoon. They walked home after the cinema and ate the fish and chips which Peader had bought from Podesta's, opposite the cinema, and then Grace and Polly walked Monica back to her tram stop before returning home and making their way, tired but happy, up to bed.

That night the two girls talked exhaustively, despite the fact, as Grace remarked, that they had been doing so all day, and did not get to sleep until the early hours, with the result that they woke late, got up leisurely and decided to spend the day calling on old friends, or at least on the homes of old friends.

Grace took Polly to the citadel, where they were clucked over and made much of by the mainly elderly people still working there, then they had the rather dispiriting business of going along familiar streets and finding that a good many of their friends had moved away after their homes had been either badly damaged or completely destroyed in the May Blitz.

Polly was sad that St Sylvester's church was still in ruins, as was the school where she and Sunny had first met, but she had seen enough of the bombing before she left to realise it was impossible to rebuild at present. There had been too much damage and building supplies of all descriptions were in short supply. Indeed, at the house in Snowdrop Street they had odd slates on the roof and the plaster on the end kitchen wall was kept in place mainly, Peader had assured them, by the thick layers of paper which he had stuck over it.

'Anyway, they're better off in Snowdrop Street,' Polly said as she and Grace made their way back towards it later that morning, for Polly's forty-eight officially came to an end at midnight and she meant to leave and start back to the island as soon as they had eaten their dinner. 'It's much nicer than Titchfield Street, don't you think, Grace? There's more room, and more neighbours too. They're nice as well. Mammy said some of them have been there years, and can remember Sara's gran – she used to live here, now isn't that a strange coincidence? Think of our Brogan coming courting all those years ago!'

'Yes, I rather like Snowdrop Street,' Grace agreed, glancing into shop windows as they made their way along Stanley Road, though the displays could not be described as tempting. 'Did your mammy not tell you that I used to live here as well, once? Oh, it was long time ago, before my older sister died, but we did live here for a few years. I was only a kid when we left though, so I couldn't tell you which house.'

'*Did* you?' Polly said. She heard the surprise in her voice and felt guilty, but she knew that the Carberys had been a poor, feckless sort of family, knew that Grace had had a hard childhood, and this did not seem to fit in with living on Snowdrop Street. 'No, Mammy never told me that – perhaps she didn't know.'

'Probably not,' Grace agreed. 'Now I can tell you're wondering what a – a family with eight or nine kids, and all of them neglected, were doing in a nice street like this. No, don't shake your head, Polly O'Brady, I don't blame you for thinking it because I thought it meself. The truth is, my father was usually in work when I was very small and though he drank like a fish and beat up anyone smaller than he was, he must have been able to manage the rent at first. Then, when it all got too much, we were chucked out, and went off to live in one of the courts off the Scottie. Still, it's true that we were here for a bit. I daresay Sara's gran knew the Carbs quite well.'

'Well, isn't life strange now?' Polly wondered as they reached the corner of Snowdrop Street. 'We'll go round the back jigger because they always hide the key under one of the slates and I know which one. Daddy may be home, of course, but once he gets gardening, you know, he forgets the time.'

They were about to turn down the jigger when a voice hailed them and, turning, Polly was astonished to see her mother hurrying along the pavement towards them and brandishing a key. 'We'll go in the front door,' she called as soon as they were near enough. 'I've got some time off work, so I have, since it's me daughter's last day. The boss said as I do so much overtime it would be all right. I'll go back to work after you're on your way,' she added a trifle apologetically. 'But there *is* a war on, as everyone keeps saying. Come along in, girls. Peader won't be long.'

The three of them hurried into the house and

Deirdre began to cut bread for sandwiches, since the main meal of the day was always eaten at night. 'It's only spam and tomato,' she said apologetically, as she worked. 'And you won't get a decent meal, Polly me darlin', until you're back in Anglesey. But I've not the time to do much cooking before you'll want to go off, and I want a word wit' you before then.'

'Oh? What've I done wrong, Mammy?' Polly enquired, immediately aware of a certain tenseness in her mother's voice, even in the way she was slicing bread and spreading margarine. 'I've only been home two minutes, for goodness' sake!'

'Oh, alanna, you've done nothing wrong,' Deirdre said. 'It's just . . . It's something we've been meaning to tell you . . . Oh, here's Peader! Let's get this dinner down us – there's cold apple pie for afters.'

Deirdre did not enjoy her meal. She and Peader chatted to the girls, joked, laughed, ate their food. Or at least, Peader ate; Deirdre crumbled her solitary sandwich and pushed a piece of apple pie round and round her plate. Not even the addition of custard, made, admittedly, with water and dried milk, could make it palatable to one who was rehearsing over and over, inside her head, what she would presently say to the two girls. She and Peader had talked it over the previous night, and had decided that it would be best, perhaps, to speak to both the girls at once.

'After all, we're goin' to tell them that they're sisters,' Peader had said reasonably. 'Why should we not tell them together, the darlin's? I know it will be good news for our Polly, but even better for Grace, situated as she is.'

But now that it had come to the point, Deirdre wondered whether they were doing the right thing.

Or rather whether she was doing the right thing, since it had been agreed between them that the news would come better from her.

So presently, with the meal finished and Polly not due to leave the house for an hour, she and both girls stayed in the kitchen to wash up and clear away and to talk whilst Peader took himself off to the front parlour with the newspaper.

Deirdre cleared her throat a couple of times, then decided she would start the washing-up and sort of – sort of throw the information over her shoulder as she worked. Accordingly, she began, though with far less ease than she had intended – or imagined – herself doing.

'I want to – to tell you a story, girls. A long time ago, when you were only three or four, Grace, and Polly here was a little baby . . .'

Peader, sitting uneasily in the parlour trying to concentrate on the paper, could only hear their voices as a sort of murmur through the wall. But he heard the shriek, closely followed by the thunder of feet on the stairs. He got slowly and awkwardly out of his chair and went into the kitchen to find Deirdre standing with her back to the sink, her hands to her face. Tears fairly spouted out between her fingers and Grace was standing beside her, patting her shoulder awkwardly and saying: 'Now come on, Auntie Dee, it were a surprise for me – well, surprise is putting it mildly, truth to tell – so what must it have been like for Polly? For me, it's really wonderful to know I've got a sister of me own, a proper blood sister. But for her . . . well, what you didn't seem to realise you were telling her was that she may have gained a sister but she's lost the parents and the brothers that she's always thought were her own. Oh, don't you *see*?'

'Where is she?' Peader said bluntly, realising that this had not gone at all as they had expected when he and Deirdre had talked over the telling of their long-held secret.

Deirdre opened her mouth to speak but was spared the necessity of answering by the thunder of feet descending the stairs and the hurling open of the kitchen door. Polly stood framed in it for a moment, looking . . . well, looking as Peader had never seen her. Her face was deathly white, her eyes scarlet-rimmed and swollen with crying. But her mouth, that gentle, generous mouth, was held so tightly that it looked lipless and the eyes, when she turned them on him, were so cold that it was like a knife through his heart.

'Polly?' he said uncertainly. 'Me darlin' child, why are you lookin' at me like that? As for poor Mammy, we t'ought you'd be pleased to know you'd a sister as well as a grosh o' brothers, we never t'ought—'

'I'm not Polly,' Polly said, her voice still tearful. 'I'm not Polly O'Brady at all, at all, Mr O'Brady, and you aren't my – my daddy, nor is *she* . . .' she pointed at Deirdre, '. . . my mammy. I'm Mollie Carbery, the little kid no one wanted once her sister was dead. And – and I'll never forgive you for lettin' me think I was one of you, wit' a proper home and a proper family of me own, when all the time I were just – just a bit of a stray kid Brogan had picked up on the railway, to oblige a dead girl.'

Peader felt tears in his own eyes and crossed the kitchen unsteadily, holding out his arms, beginning to try to explain how they had not dared to tell her at first in case the news got around and someone tried to take her from them, how they had loved her as much – more – than they would have done had Deirdre actually given birth to her. But Polly swerved round him and shot across the kitchen, hurled the back door open and ran out into the yard. Her kitbag, untidily packed, swung from one shoulder but even thus burdened, she was out of the yard, along the jigger and off up the Scotland Road, Peader guessed, before he, with his halting steps, had even reached the back door.

'Stop her, Grace! Peader, for the love of the good God, bring my little girl back to me,' Deirdre shrieked. She cast down the apron she had been wearing and ran past Peader who, following as fast as he could, was still hobbling along the jigger when his wife returned, defeat in the slump of her shoulders, the misery in her face.

'Oh, Peader, what'll she do?' she asked breathlessly, clutching his upper arms and staring earnestly into his face. 'She's in a terrible state, so she is – she'll be on a tram and halfway to Lime Street by now – I never dreamed she'd take it so badly.'

'We should have thought it out more carefully,' Peader said heavily as they returned to the kitchen, where Grace was stacking plates, cups and dishes on the dresser and looking worried half to death. 'It never occurred to me that she'd stop seeing herself as an O'Brady. I just thought she'd be mortal glad we'd stole her away, and even gladder to find she'd a sister as well as her brothers. As for what she'll do, alanna, God alone knows.'

'She'll go back to her wrennery and come to terms with it,' Grace said, heaving the big black kettle over the fire and warming the teapot. 'Give her a few days to get her sense of proportion back and she'll

382

come round. You know our Polly, she doesn't have a nasty bone in her body; she'll see that you meant everything for the best, and get in touch to tell you not to worry. But . . . well, it must be a terrible shock, to be told that you aren't who you've always thought you were.'

'We've little choice but to wait,' Deirdre said ruefully. 'I wish there was something . . . If we could go to her . . . but she'd not see us, either of us, for all our love.'

'Perhaps not. But she'll see me,' Grace said, finishing her task and turning towards the kitchen door. 'I'm going after her, Auntie Dee; I'll catch the next tram down to Lime Street, then I'll start the journey to Holyhead. And as soon as I've talked to her I'll drop you a line, or telephone your factory, Auntie. We'll get this sorted out, never fear.'

'Oh, would you? But dear Grace, this is your week's leave, it really isn't fair—'

'It's my choice,' Grace said firmly. 'What sort of enjoyment could I have, knowing Polly – my sister – is in trouble and deeply unhappy? I think I can help her; it's the least I can do.'

She left the room, closing the door quietly behind her. Deirdre walked into Peader's arms and they stood for a moment, hugging, both with tears running down their cheeks.

'It'll come right, alanna,' Peader said at length, smoothing a big, calloused hand down her face. 'You see, it'll come right. What we did for our girl we did with the best of intentions and she'll realise it, when she's calmer. And she's right, you know, we should have told her long since that she wasn't an O'Brady by birth but only by love.'

'You wanted to tell her,' Deirdre sighed. 'And I

wouldn't – I was afraid. Oh, Peader, I pray to God we get our girl back!'

Tad was in the mess, playing cards with a group of friends, when Toby Carruthers, who had gone across to answer the almost constantly ringing phone, turned towards him.

'Tad! Tad Donoghue, there's a call for you.'

'Oh?' Tad said, getting up from his chair with a sigh and laying his cards carefully down on the green baize table. He glared menacingly round at his three companions. 'Don't you go lookin' at me hand nor changin' me cards, because I've a photographic memory, so I have and I'll kill anyone who stops me winnin' this round.' Crossing the room, he thought bitterly that it was just his luck; the first time he'd had a decent hand all week and the bleedin' phone had to ring. However, he grinned at Toby and held out a hand for the receiver. 'Who is it? Not me mammy?'

'It's a female,' Toby said, putting a hand over the mouthpiece so that his words would not be heard on the other end of the line. 'I think she's crying, old feller, so you'd best go gentle. Been getting some nice little WAAF into trouble, have you?'

'Not that I can remember,' Tad said, but though he smiled he took the receiver rather hastily, almost dropping it as it changed hands. He held it to his ear. 'Hello? Tad Donoghue speaking.'

There was a pause, and then a dry sob, a gustily indrawn breath, and a voice said: 'Oh Tad, Tad! Thank the good Lord . . . Oh Tad, it's so awful, I can't be after tellin' you how awful it is . . .'

He would have known that voice anywhere, even coming distorted over the line, and ending in sobs. He said sharply: 'Polly! What in heaven's name has

384

happened to you? Where are you? I t'ought you'd be back in Holyhead by now . . . Are you back? If so, I'll come right away.'

'I'm – I'm not back,' Polly said, her voice sounding small and snuffly. She began to cry again. 'Oh, Tad, I'm in terrible trouble, so I am – can you come?'

'Where? Where are you, in God's name?' Tad shouted, terribly frightened by the fear in Polly's tone. 'Get a holt of yourself, Poll, and tell me where I can find you.'

'I d-don't know exactly,' Polly said, her voice perilously close to a wail. 'It's lost I am, Tad, and it's dark and it's pouring with rain and I just bolted into the first telephone box I saw, so I did. It's not Chester, it's further on than that . . . Oh Tad, will you come?'

'Of course I will – but, Polly me darlin', you must pull yourself together now. Have you some more pennies?'

There was a short scuffle and then Polly said in a slightly more composed tone: 'Yes, I've some more pennies.'

'Good,' Tad said. 'Now, alanna, are you in a town or in the countryside?'

'I – I'm in a sort of village, I think,' Polly said, after a moment during which she must have peered out through the glass windows of the telephone box, breathing heavily. 'But you know what it's like, Tad, they don't put big signs out no more tellin' you where you're at, in case of an invasion.'

'Right. Is there a pub near? Is it safe for you to go to the nearest pub and then ring me again? Don't worry, I won't move from the phone.'

'Ye-es, but – but suppose he's out there some-where, hidin' round a corner waitin' for me?' Polly quavered, with the fear so strong in her voice that Tad felt his own hair begin to rise on his scalp. 'Oh, Tad, I feel safe wit' you on the other end of the line . . . Can't you just come? I must be on the way back to the island, because the feller said he was goin' to catch the Irish ferry . . . Please Tad, don't make me leave the box. It's nearly dark out there and the rain is drivin' somethin' awful.'

She was desperately scared of someone . . . What on earth did she mean, *the feller said he was goin' to catch the Irish ferry*? She was supposed to have caught the bus and then the train . . . but suppose she had missed one or the other? Besides, she was on her way back now . . . If she had been coming back towards the island it might be possible to pinpoint her where-abouts if only he asked the right questions. He took a deep, steadying breath.

'Look, alanna, what time did you leave Liverpool? I take it you've been given a lift by someone? Well, how long d'you reckon you've been on the road?'

'Hours, I think,' Polly said after a rather long pause. 'Oh . . . don't go, don't go!'

The telephonist's voice cut across Polly's plea. 'Your time is up, caller. Do you wish to pay for another three minutes?'

'Yes. Yes,' Polly gabbled and Tad could hear the money rattling through the coin slot. They were not disconnected though they might easily have been; this was wartime and telephonists did not encourage long calls because there was always someone else waiting for a line. 'I'll stay right here, but Poll, you must take your courage in both hands and make your way to the nearest pub,' Tad said, putting all the command and sternness he could into his voice. 'I could spend the whole night and all day tomorrow hunting for you, else. Now, be my brave girl . . . peep out of the box, and see if you can see something which might look like a pub.'

He could imagine Polly, stuck in that little, blue-lit cube in the middle of an unknown town or village, pushing open the door, peering round it . . .

'There's buildings,' Polly said presently, her voice a little stronger. 'A shop – well, it's got a shop window, anyway, then what looks like more houses . . . Oh, I can see something with a sign, swinging in the wind. All right, Tad, I'm goin' to put the receiver down and run like hell towards the house wit' the sign. Don't go, will you?'

'Good girl,' Tad said encouragingly. 'Watch your footing, though, don't go tripping over the kerb and breaking your leg or something. And ring me back the moment you know where you are – the landlord will lend you his telephone, if you can't pay him I will, when I get there.'

'Or I could leave the phone off the hook here, run up to the pub and find out where I am, and run back,' Polly said with longing in her voice. But Tad decided that he had better veto this. After all, any half-decent man, seeing Polly's distress, would take care of her until help came.

'No,' he said authoritatively. 'Now, Poll, off you go – put the receiver down *now*!'

He heard the receiver click on to its rest and put his own instrument down, then turned and faced the mess. To his astonishment no one was taking the slightest notice of him; men went on playing cards, talking, throwing dice, writing letters. No one, he realised, could have known that he was talking to a desperately frightened girl to whom something awful but so far unexplained had happened. At the card table he had left one of the fellers called out to him, reminding him, reproachfully, that they were in the middle of a game and he had better come quickly and play his hand or he would ruin the session.

'Oh . . . one of you can play my hand,' Tad said. What cared he for cards or poker or the two bob he had hoped to gain when Polly was in trouble? 'I'm waiting for an incoming call, I don't know how long I'll be.'

In fact, he was beginning to wonder whether the call would ever come, whether he had put poor little Polly in even more jeopardy by insisting that she should find out where she was, when the telephone rang again. He had it off its rest almost before the ring had properly begun and was speaking into it.

'Polly? Is that you, alanna? Oh, thank God, I was beginnin' to think . . . but never mind that. Tell me where you are and I'll be with you just as soon as I can.'

'I'm in a pub, like you said. It's called the Bear's Paw and it's in a place called Frodsham. Oh Tad, I don't t'ink that feller was tellin' the truth when he said he was on his way to catch the ferry . . . Oh Tad, can you come?'

'Of course,' Tad said, outwardly cool but inwardly in a ferment of doubt. Frodsham? He had never heard of the place, for all he knew she could be somewhere in the wilds of Scotland! Then he remembered that she had only been travelling from Liverpool, surely she could not be that far away? Still in his calm, steadying voice he said: 'Stay where you are, alanna, and I'll be wit' you as soon as may be. But you'd best ask the landlord if you can stay with him until I arrive . . . It's nigh on eight o'clock now, it could be midnight before I reach you. But don't you worry now, I'm as good as on me way. D'you want me to have a word wit' the landlord now? Explain t'ings a bit?'

But this, Polly assured him, was not necessary. She would stay where she was, quietly in a corner, until he arrived. Closing time was ten o'clock, Tad reminded her, but Polly said, with another muffled sob, that if closing time arrived before he did, then she would be sure to find somewhere near at hand where she might wait. 'You'll be as quick as you can possibly be, I know it,' Polly assured him, sounding a little braver now, though still obviously shaken. 'Don't worry about me, Tad – just come and find me. People are awful nice, I'm sure the landlord won't turn me out into the rain – it's pourin' cats and dogs out there, so it is.'

'That's grand then, alanna,' Tad said, greatly relieved. Polly had clearly got herself in deep trouble, but she had managed to extricate herself and would surely be all right now until he arrived to bring her back to Holyhead. 'Don't you worry about anything either, alanna. Just stay put until I come.'

A couple of hours later, Tad was driving a car which did not belong to him along a road he did not know, with only the haziest idea of how to reach his destination. But he had an elderly road map spread out on the passenger seat and the words of his pal Micky echoed in his ears: 'You can't miss Frodsham – lovely little village. Head for Manchester and you'll see this damned great hill looking as though someone's took a bite out of it. The village sort of nestles under the hill, with woods above it. And the Bear's Paw is sandstone buildings on your left as you go through the village. How far? Well, I suppose it 'ud be a three-hour run normally. But in this rain . . .

Still, there shouldn't be much else on the road . . . you'll mebbe make it by midnight.'

Micky had not known, of course, that he intended to steal a car and had been imagining that Tad would be on his motorbike. Come to that, Tad had not known he intended to steal a car. Not that he had stolen it, exactly. It was more or less like borrowing it, only the owner did not know. Well, he had not been around to ask. Had he known, Squadron Leader Alan Pierce would surely have told Tad to go ahead, but Squadron Leader Pierce was not around, having gone off on a course, leaving his elderly but reliable Sunbeam Talbot to be serviced and generally fussed over by the mechanic he most trusted – Tad Donoghue. By a great piece of good fortune Tad had worked on the Sunbeam the previous day until it was in as near perfect condition as he could make it. He had even filled it with petrol so that when its owner came back he could drive it straight off. Then Tad had put it carefully away in one of the work sheds and forgotten all about it – until Polly's phone call, that was.

He had scarcely considered the motorbike as a means of rescuing Polly, however. He had known he would have to beg, borrow or steal a car or a gharry or, dammit, a perishing blood waggon, sooner than leave his Poll alone and afraid, miles from home. But no sooner had he stepped out of the mess than he had remembered the Sunbeam; remembered, too, that its owner was off in Suffolk or Norfolk somewhere . . . and had gone confidently off to the work shed.

He had not done much to prepare for the journey either, so worried was he by the state Polly had got herself into. He simply told Micky an old pal, a little WRN from his home town, was in trouble, explained her whereabouts, took Micky's advice and his map and got into the car and drove off. Now, after two hours of solitary driving through this wild night, he wished he had thought to fill a bottle with cold tea since he was parched with thirst, but it was too late for such might-have-beens. He was stuck in the car, driving steadily along black and winding roads, occasionally catching up with a military convoy.

He wished the rain would stop, though. The low grey clouds overhead and the driving rain, to say nothing of the howling wind, probably meant that there would be no activity in the air above him on such a night, but he could see very little through the slits in the car's headlights and was in constant fear of missing a turning – or finding a ditch – and so lengthening his journey still further. Once he had spotted a stream and had climbed out of the car and slaked his thirst, but that had been ages ago. Now he was thirsty again, his mouth dry as much with fear as with the long drive, and his eyes were beginning to feel tired, as though someone had thrown sand into them.

He glanced at his watch. Eleven o'clock! It could not be much further, surely? He had seen, against the cloud, the hill with the bite taken out of it, coming and going as the road wound and snaked and seemed to curve back on itself, but always there. It was appreciably closer now – surely he would arrive soon? He glanced apprehensively at the petrol gauge, but it was going to be all right. He had fine-tuned the engine and it was being gracious, sipping rather than devouring his precious juice. Of course, the slow speed at which he had been forced to drive for a good deal of his journey would have eased the petrol consumption. He grinned to himself in the dark, for it was now pitch black except for the tiny patches of light from his heads reflecting on the gleaming wet tarmac. Soon be there, he comforted himself, peering ahead. Soon be taking his Polly in his arms and hearing what had happened to her. At the thought of the fellow who had given her a lift, lied to her, deserted her, he ground his teeth with impotent fury. He hoped Polly had got his name, the number of his vehicle, anything, so that he, Tad, could find him and use his bleedin' guts for bleedin' garters just as soon as he'd settled his Polly safely back in her wrennery.

Tad slowed to negotiate a curve, glanced up at his hill and found it appreciably nearer. Grimly, he continued to drive steadily onward. At his present rate, he should be in Frodsham well before midnight.

It was not long after midnight that Tad found himself back in the car once more, but this time with Polly beside him. She sat quietly, very small and pale and huddled in one of the two rugs which Squadron Leader Pierce kept in the boot of his beloved car – a relic from pre-war outings, Tad imagined. He had found her slipping out of the pub and walking across the pavement towards him almost as he drew up. She stood in the rain for a second, glancing doubtfully at the car, and then, as he stepped out and went to meet her, she gave a strangled sob and hurled herself into his arms.

For a moment he had held her, but then she had disengaged herself briskly and returned to the pub door. She pulled it wide, called something softly – he thought it was to the effect that her pal had come – and then she closed the front door cautiously and returned to the car. Tad helped her in, noticing as he did so that she was shivering and went round to the driver's door, climbing in behind the wheel and starting the engine. After nearly four hours of difficult and tiring driving he felt strongly inclined just to sit where he was for a moment, to ask her just what had happened to her, to pull himself together, but instead, he engaged first gear, released the handbrake and turned the car in the wide road so that they were facing towards the mountains of Wales once more. It was not until they were several miles from the village that he chose a quiet stretch of grass verge and drew up on it. Then he turned to her.

'Hadn't you better drive on?' she said. 'Whose car is this, Tad?'

'I borrowed it from a – a pal,' Tad said evasively. 'Look, what wit' the rain and the wind and bein' so worried over you, Poll, I don't reckon I can drive and listen to what you're going to tell me, so why not tell me now? For a start, why didn't you catch the train?'

'Because – because it seemed silly when I could hitch,' Polly said, her voice muffled. 'And – and – I left in rather a hurry. It was all right, at first. I got a lift from the city right through the tunnel and beyond Birkenhead, but then the rain started. I walked for miles – well, it felt like miles – and then a man in a big lorry . . . Oh Tad, I don't want to talk about it! I don't want to remember!'

'Did he hurt you?' Tad said bluntly after the silence began to stretch. 'Did he get fresh wit' you, alanna?' He felt his teeth snap shut and all the muscles in his body tense at the thought of anyone offering any sort of unwanted attention to his Polly. 'Just tell me what happened, as brief as you like.'

'He *tried* to get fresh,' Polly said. 'He was hateful, Tad. Only I remembered what the Chief WRN said to us when we were doing drill, and self-defence and stuff like that. She said if a feller got fresh to kick him where he joins, so I did and he shrieked like – like the bleedin' banshee, Tad, and then he flung me out of his horrible old lorry – not that I cared, I wanted to get out – and just drove off!'

'Oh,' Tad said rather inadequately. 'But he didn't hurt you, alanna?'

'No,' Polly said firmly. 'He tried to kiss me and put his hand up my skirt so I—'

'Yes, I know, you kicked him,' Tad said hastily. 'Where were you? Still in the lorry cab? How on earth did you—'

'Yes, we were still in the lorry; he'd pulled over on to the verge, though,' Polly said. 'When he tried to kiss me I thought maybe that was all right since he'd given me a lift and promised to take me right back to the wrennery, but when his hands started moving about – *you* know how they go on, Tad – I bit him as hard as I could on his horrible chin and then I tore a great lump out of his hair and then I kicked him in the—'

'Well, you did right,' Tad said. He was beginning to feel almost sorry for Polly's assailant. Still, it would teach the feller not to give lifts to young girls in order to try his luck with them. And besides, he had abandoned Polly miles from anywhere on a filthy night in a rainstorm . . . no, he deserved all that Polly had handed out and more, Tad decided. 'But another time, alanna, don't go hitching lifts unless you're wit' a pal because . . . Oh Polly, love, what've I said?'

For Polly was crying again, the tears chasing down her pale cheeks. 'It – it's just that everything's so awful,' she said, fishing out her hanky and blowing her nose hard. 'The feller in the lorry was a bastard, all right, but it – it weren't him that got me so upset, not really. Tad, did you ever think . . . well, that I wasn't meself?'

'Sometimes, when we were kids,' Tad said rather cautiously. Sometimes, he remembered, Polly's temper had flared up at him and he had thought her a termagant and not the loving little Polly he knew so well. And he knew that Ivan had often grumbled at his sister's making him do more than his fair share of the housework. Was that what she meant, though?

'You did?' Polly brightened for a moment, but then began to cry more dolorously than ever. 'Well, I never even t'ought of it, but Tad, I'm not Polly O'Brady at all! Mammy and Daddy aren't me mammy and daddy, and the fellers aren't me brothers. And they've known all along, but never a word did they say until this afternoon . . . Oh, and they seemed to think I'd be quite *glad* to be told they just took me in out of pity, glad that I was really a child of one of the meanest, nastiest, rottenest families in the whole of Liverpool . . .'

'Liverpool?' Tad said, thoroughly startled now. He wondered if the man's attack had knocked Polly clean off her trolley, because he could still remember the baby Polly sitting on her mother's hip, patting the head of any chiseller who came within reach, always smiling, always sunny. 'But Polly me love, you were born and bred in Dublin, same as me!'

'No, I wasn't,' Polly said drearily. 'I was born in Liverpool . . . Well, I'll tell you how they telled me and then you'll know why I didn't much care, at first, if that feller upped and killed me, I was so unhappy. Why, if I'd not been crying half the time, d'you think that feller would have dared to put a hand on my – my chest, let alone up me skirt? If I'd been like I usually am he wouldn't have tried anything, I'm telling ye!'

'Yes, I can see that,' Tad said slowly. He was beginning to think back, to remember. There was Polly's story, oft-repeated, that she could remember being born, being brought out of the doctor's bag and into a firelit circle of admiring male faces. Tad, with his superior knowledge of the facts of life – he was not eldest in a family of eight for nothing – had always found this scenario difficult to credit, but now he wondered whether Polly had, in fact, been remembering her arrival in the O'Brady home in Dublin, but as a child of twelve months or so instead of a new-born babe. He also remembered neighbours whispering, a rumour in the early days that Polly had come in from the country . . . but they were such vague rumours, and of so little interest to him, that he had never really taken them seriously. Polly was an O'Brady, her entire family worshipped her, and he, Tad, had quite agreed with them that she was a darling, and worthy of the love which folk gave her so readily. But she was still sobbing, so he put a gentle arm about her shoulders and gave her a bit of a squeeze. 'All right, Polleen, suppose it's true, that you were adopted. Well, what's so wrong wit' that, then? You said *out of pity* but people don't take on an extra child in a big family out of pity. They do it out of love, alanna.'

'Th-they wanted a girl,' Polly said, her voice still heavy with tears. 'If I'd been a boy baby . . .'

'Nonsense,' Tad said confidently. 'Why, were you ever given love which belonged to Ivan, or Bev? Tell me truthfully, Poll, don't go making things up.'

There was a long pause before Polly said grudgingly: 'No-oo, Mammy always loved us all and so did the daddy. And – and they were fair as well. Even when it made me mad as fire, I knew they were being fair.'

'Well, there you are, then. Being adopted is – is a sort of compliment, I'm after thinking. Can't you see it like that?'

'They should have told me,' Polly said, after another silence had stretched until Tad had begun to wonder whether she intended to reply at all. 'Me brothers *knew*, Tad – the older ones, anyway – and they never said a word. Why, it was Brogan who brought me home, in the front of his donkey jacket, but never a word out of him to explain to me that I wasn't his little sister at all, that I wasn't even Polly!'

'But, alanna, you are Polly O'Brady by adoption,' Tad insisted, giving her another squeeze. 'So was that the reason you left home in a hurry, and hitched a lift? Because you'd flown into a temper and run out on your mammy and daddy? Alanna, they'll be worried to death, wondering where you've gone, what you've done. We can't telephone now, of course, but you must do so first thing in the morning. I suppose you didn't phone from the pub? It never occurred to me that you might have left them not knowing . . . Oh, dammit, Poll, how could you?'

'Grace is still there,' Polly said defensively after a moment. 'And don't you go tellin' me off, Tad Donoghue! And what'll I tell the WRNS? Because they've got me down as Polly O'Brady, so they have, and I'm really Mollie Carbery.'

Tad heaved a sigh. He was very tired indeed, and beginning to feel more than a little impatient with his Polly. But he tried to explain again. 'You may have been born one thing, but when the O'Bradys took you on you became something different. It – it's a bit like marriage, alanna. You knew you wouldn't always be an O'Brady, didn't you, because you knew you'd marry some day, and go and live wit' your husband? Well, you'll be married as Polly O'Brady, not as Mollie . . . what did you say the name was? And what's this Grace girl got to do with it?'

Polly took a deep breath and launched into the story, this time starting at the very beginning, with the girl Jess – her sister – carrying the baby out of their strife-torn household and down on to the railway, to keep warm and safe in one of the gang huts until morning. At first the recital was punctuated by sniffs and gulps, sometimes even by sobs, but by the time she reached the climax Polly seemed to have got a hold of herself, and the story, a rivetting one, Tad considered, was told with considerable relish. She painted the Carberys so black, indeed, that Tad felt the hair on the back of his neck stand up with horror; from what she told him, she would have been unlikely to live had she been left with the likes of them. And Polly, having got Tad up to date, turned a soulful face towards him, clearly expecting sympathy.

'Well, now I know what it's all about I can't help thinking that Brog did you just about the best service one person can do for another,' he told her. 'With your big sister gone, what sort of a chance would you have stood of being brought up properly, alanna? Indeed, from what you've said, it's Grace who has a right to feel sorry for herself. She was really left out in the cold, wasn't she? You say you're ashamed of being a Carbery, incidentally, but Grace did well for herself, didn't she? And your big sister, Jess, sounds just lovely, alanna – very like yourself, in fact. So don't condemn all the Carberys because the parents were bad, wicked people. And probably, you know, your real mammy, Mrs Carbery I mean, was a good person until her husband began beating her up and draining all the goodness out of her. Are you beginning to feel a bit better, now? Shall I get moving again?'

'I'm never going to get married,' Polly said, shrinking down in her rug once more. 'Nor I shan't have kids . . . and I do t'ink you might feel a bit sorrier for *me*, Tad, with everything I believed turned upside down.'

'It's been a dreadful shock for you, so it has,' Tad agreed diplomatically – and truthfully, now he came to think of it – pressing the starter and putting the car in gear. 'You'll come to terms with it, Poll, given time. And you must ring your mammy at work first thing tomorrow and let her know you're all right. Promise?'

'Oh, all right,' Polly said. 'And now I'm goin' to sleep so you mustn't talk to me any more, Tad Donoghue. I'm very grateful that you came for me, but I don't like you very much right now. You won't try to understand, and you say you're sorry for Grace when at least she really is who she thought she was. Goodnight.'

And with that she huddled herself right into the rug and turned away from him.

Tad could have done with the companionship of an occasional word or a look, but he drove on, realising that to Polly what had happened had been a major tragedy. She would come to her senses in the end, he knew that – his Polly had never been one to bear a grudge. And he acknowledged that finding your family were not your family, your parents not your parents, must have taken some swallowing, especially for the spoiled and adored Polly. He felt it a little unfair that he was being punished for it, for driving alone with Polly beside him and pretending to be asleep – now and then he saw her eyes glint as she glanced stealthily sideways at him – but he had enough imagination to guess pretty accurately at how she must be feeling and continued to drive in silence.

However, once they reached the island he pulled over again and turned towards her, giving her a gentle shake when she hastily closed her eyes and once more pretended slumber. 'Polly, I think you'd best wake up now. Your wrennery will be locked up for the night, and it can't be more than four o'clock now so there won't be anyone stirring for a bit. I'm out without leave too . . . but I've worked out how to get round that. What about you, alanna?'

'There's always someone up around six o'clock,' Polly said. She yawned. 'Don't worry, I'll get in wit'out any fuss. Diane will have signed in for me, I expect.'

'Right. Then I'll put the other rug round me and we can both snooze until around five.' He leaned over to the back seat and pulled the second rug across, then glanced sideways at Polly. 'Shall we both snuggle up under the two rugs, alanna? Then we can share each other's warmth and have the warmth of both rugs instead of one each.'

'I don't think we should,' Polly said, with an edge of frost in her voice. 'What would people say?'

'Not a lot,' Tad said, grinning. 'I'm not suggesting we get into the back seat, alanna! 'Tis just for warmth, you know.'

'Well, I suppose it might be all right,' Polly said, clearly not wanting to come down off her high horse but probably needing the warmth as much as he did, for Tad, by this time, was very cold indeed. His hands felt as though they might have frozen to the wheel and his feet were very little better. 'After all, you're more like a brother to me than—' Her voice wobbled and Tad heaved the rug off her and took her in his arms.

'All right, all right, darlin',' he said, his voice rough with love and compassion. 'You've had a shocking time, so you have, and here's me been trying to make you see that it wasn't so bad when it's been cruel hard on you. Now give your Tad a nice cuddle and we'll go off to sleep like a couple of babes in the wood and it'll soon be morning. Indeed, the sky's trying to lighten in the east even now.'

'Pull the rugs over us, then,' Polly said, snuggling against him. 'Oh, Tad, isn't this nice and comfy? You are kind – I wish you really *were* my brother. You'd have telled me I was adopted if you'd known, wouldn't you?'

'I don't know,' Tad said, innate honesty compelling him not to give the easy lie. 'But it's not your brother I want to be, alanna. When this lot's over I want you to change your name again, only this time to Donoghue.'

He said it with a dry mouth and thumping heart, for though he had known he loved Polly and wanted to marry her ever since they had met as two adults, he still did not really know how Polly viewed him.

Polly stirred in his arms and laughed sleepily. 'Silly! I'm going to marry Sunny Andersen, I'm sure I told you that ages and ages ago. I love you ever so much, Tad, just like I love me brothers . . . well, I mean just like I love the O'Brady boys. But it's a different sort of love, isn't it! Now let's try to go to sleep or we'll be wrecks.'

Polly slept quite quickly after that but Tad stayed awake, his heart sick and sore within him. She loved him like a brother! She was going to marry that Sunny Andersen – ridiculous name – because for him she had a 'different' kind of love! He had been a fool not to have courted her more openly, letting her believe that it was just friendship which brought him into Holyhead whenever he had a few hours free, just friendship which made him give her lessons on his motorbike, teach her how to service it, take him so for granted that she could phone him up and ask him to get her out of trouble without a second thought. She knew Tad – good old Tad – would not let her down because he was like a brother to her!

It was a long while before he slept.

Next morning, Tad was closeted with his squadron commander for a long time, rather to the surprise of his friends, for they knew that Tad had got away with his unexpected absence and also with his 'borrowing' of the car. When he came out, however, he was pale but composed, grinning cheerfully at his friends and telling them that he would surprise them all yet.

A couple of days after that, he rang Polly at her wrennery.

'Hello, Poll. Did you ring your mammy and daddy?' he enquired, for all the world as though they had parted best of friends instead of with a chill between them. 'You did? It's glad I am. Well, next time you speak to them, tell them I've been posted, will you? I'm off to foreign parts to train as a pilot, so you won't be troubled with me for a while.' And when she would have asked questions, he just said, still with unimpaired cheerfulness: 'Take care of yourself, Poll, and no more hitchhiking. Bye, love. See you – oh, some time, I guess.'

He rang off. No point in hanging around where you were not wanted, he told himself grimly. Besides, the powers-that-be had offered to train him as a pilot. It would . . . take his mind off things.

Whistling, Tad set off for his hut to get his gear packed.

Chapter Fifteen

1944

Sunny came up from the warm depths of the ship on to the icy deck and instinctively ducked his head deeper into the thick scarf wound round his neck and the lower half of his face. By God, but it was freezing out here, though that was nothing new. In the Arctic waters at the top of the world, where they took their convoy of merchantmen to the Russian ports of Murmansk and Archangel, it was always cold. Indeed, cold scarcely described it, Sunny thought morosely now. The air was so icy that it was dangerous to draw it sharply into one's lungs and even through the muffler he knew from experience that all too soon the damp of his expelled breath would form icicles on the soft white wool.

He glanced towards the rail and saw the white-tipped waves, though he had known the sea would be rough. When was it ever anything else, up here? He had been on the Russian convoys for two years – more – and had grown accustomed to the constant bucketing of the ship, the constant straining to see through the thick dark and the wicked, unrelenting cold which attacked every man as soon as he left the warmth of the mess deck below. But no one, Sunny thought now, could get used to the almost perpetual darkness up here. How did they bear it, the inhabitants of these arctic coasts, where they only saw daylight between eleven in the morning and two in the afternoon and that a pretty grey and overcast daylight at this time of the year? He and the rest of the crew, after their first few trips, had speculated on why in heaven's name did the Jerries want this God-forsaken land? Why should they fight to possess the great, sprawling mass of Russia, a land made up of empty, ice-ridden wastes and surly, ignorant peasantry? But it was all part of the war effort, to keep Russia alive and armed, so they continued to bring the convoys across some of the worst seas in the world, to suffer the perpetual dark and the endless cold, to say nothing of the dangers inherent in such seas.

However, staring out at the sea would scarcely bring them in to port any faster so Sunny made for the bridge, where the man waiting to be relieved grinned at him and then made his way as quickly as he dared across the iced-up deck and down the companionway, where he would seek his hammock and would get himself as warm as he could during his time off watch.

On the bridge, the officer of the watch acknowledged Sunny's arrival and he took his place beside him and raised the night glasses to his eyes scanning the convoy keenly for the first blue flash of a signal from another vessel. The ships showed no lights, but he could see the dim shapes of the merchantmen and could guess that the deeper darkness on the port bow was another corvette, circling their flock, as the *Snowdrop* was doing. He wondered where they were; they had rounded the North Cape a day or so earlier; going on past voyages they must be in the approaches to the harbour by now. He thought rather wistfully of his earlier days at sea, when he had sailed through warm, tropical waters and, when the ship docked at a foreign port, had taken pleasure in their surroundings, strolled around the streets, smiled at the people, admired shop windows.

Russia was different. Very different. There could be no talking to the locals because the Russian police saw to that. They were a constant presence, patrolling the dirty, wooden quaysides as though some great treasure was hidden there.

There was a slight scuffle on the bridge and moving closer to the rail he saw the ice-breaker looming up in the darkness. So the port was near! Out here, where the sea was so constantly rough, so constantly in motion, the ice did not form but as soon as the ships got into the shelter of the land – such shelter as it offered – then the sea began to freeze over. Russian ice-breakers were essential to force a way into harbour for the convoys and their escorts and now, on the port bow, Sunny saw, through his binoculars, the quick flicker of a blue light – a signal from the Russian ship. Sunny scribbled the message on his pad and read it out to the officer of the watch who told him to acknowledge it, so that the crew of that rusty, elderly vessel would know that this was the convoy for which they waited.

Very soon, Sunny was signalling the other ships to follow the icebreaker into harbour. The *Snowdrop* and her fellow guardians would not be the first into port; the merchantmen, which went right up to the quayside, were always first with the war ships following them in like sheepdogs shepherding their flock. Once the merchantmen were tied up, Sunny knew from experience that the Russian dockers would come swarming out of the collection of wooden huts which, it seemed, constituted a Russian port, and begin to unload the convoy. Meanwhile, the warships which had protected them on their long and arduous journey would not be allowed to tie up against the quays but would anchor in mid-pool. The intention,

Sunny was sure, had been to see that no British sailors went ashore, since the police must have had their hands full just watching the dockers, both men and women, working on the ships. But since the ice formed hard enough to walk on with complete safety after no more than half an hour it was possible for anyone to walk ashore.

Someone came and stood close by Sunny's elbow at the rail. It was Freddy Sales, a fellow Liverpudlian. The two men had become good friends, particularly since Sunny's mother's death the previous year when she had been killed by a stray bullet during a daylight raid on the shipping in Portsmouth harbour and though Sunny had been at sea at the time he had been given compassionate leave when the ship had docked. He had made his way to his mother's cramped little house, only to find it already occupied, since because of the bomb damage housing was at a premium in the area. Since Sunny had never spent more than a few days in the house it had never seemed like home and though he visited her grave he had left Pompey with few regrets. He and his mother had drifted apart once he had joined the Navy, and though her morals had never worried him as a youngster, he had found it more difficult to accept her way of life once he was in the Navy himself. On the couple of occasions when he had taken himself off down to Hampshire she had been 'entertaining' a friend and though she was not embarrassed to find her son on the doorstep, both Sunny and her new playmate were. He had heard nothing of his father since the start of the war, and reverted to Liverpool on his leaves, glad to return to the city where he had been born and bred. It had seemed very much easier to go back to the city where he still had many friends, including the O'Brady family, who were always warm and welcoming. They were happy to let him sleep in their spare room if he had nowhere else to go, though he usually managed to find a shipmate who was glad enough to have him to stay for the brief period of his leave. Besides, he was ruefully aware that it was far easier to make his way to Liverpool than it had been to Hampshire. At least it enabled him to get there and back in the time allotted to him.

And of course, there was the lure of seeing Polly, because she had been back in Liverpool now for eighteen months, and sometimes, when he was on leave, he managed to see a fair bit of her.

Although he acknowledged sadly to himself that his Polly had changed. She was a despatch rider now, and took her job very seriously. She whizzed all over the place on what seemed to him a very large motorbike, taking messages, instructions, secret papers quite often, she told him proudly. She was still a darling, of course, he told himself loyally now, but . . . well, different. Harder. Less – less interested in his war, being far too occupied with her own. And, he had to admit it even to himself, less interested in him. It was not as though she had another feller, not that he could discover anyway, and Polly was not the sort of girl to try to deceive anyone. No, she was honest and straightforward. It was almost – well, almost as though her interest in young men in general and himself in particular had flagged. Been beaten down by the war, perhaps, and all the various things which had happened to her. So, though he always tried to see her when he was on leave, he was uneasily aware that there was something missing; the old Polly, the light-hearted, carefree one, was gone, and that he did not really know the more serious young woman who had taken her place.

On one of his leaves about a year ago he had had a stroke of luck. Grace Carbery had also been on leave, and they had managed to meet several times. Polly, wrapped up in her work, had been happy for her friends to get to know one another better, but Sunny had been rather guiltily aware that by the end of his three days at home, the relationship between himself and the young leading airwoman was possibly a trifle warmer than the old Polly, at any rate, might have liked.

For Sunny had found that it was easy to become fond of Grace. Of course she was not like Polly had once been, not by any means so bubbly and loving, but she had, he discovered, her own charm. She was far more serious, you might even say she was a bit solemn, but she was still a very feminine young woman. Polly, he thought now, had put away her femininity for the duration. She almost always wore trousers, bell bottoms, in fact, as he did himself, and now that he thought about it, he did not think she wore lipstick, or went to dances, or if she did, she had not done so when he was in the city.

Another thing about Grace was that he and she had had their fill of the horrors of war. Grace, working on an airfield in Norfolk, was used to the tragedy of the young aircrews who were laughing and fooling around in the mess one day and missing the next. And it had changed her, made her more serious, less light-minded. Polly, though she worked hard and did a job which could be dangerous, did not have the same proximity to death which had become a way of life to himself and Grace.

Even as he thought this, Sunny felt vaguely

ashamed. He had been crazy about Polly for so long now that he took it for granted that other girls, whilst a welcome diversion, were just that. When the war was over, he was sure that Polly's conviction that she was as good as any man would change, that she would become his own his lovely, loving Polly once more. And heaven knew, by that time he would *need* the old Polly. He knew that a good deal of his own light-hearted approach to life had gone for ever. Gone with the companions who would not make it to the peace, the artificer who had been swept overboard as they passed along the Norwegian coast in a gale, with those poor devils, Martin amongst them, who had disappeared along with their ship whilst Sunny had been in hospital, suffering from the indignities of measles. He knew, now, that he had been a light-weight, someone who never thought about the morrow, who seldom worried about anything, never spared a thought for others.

It was different now. He was aware of a sombre streak in his nature, the realisation that every day might be his last. Someone had once said that the sea was a cruel mistress – well, she was that all right, but it was not simply the sea which had taken the feckless enjoyment out of his life. It was, he supposed, man's inhumanity to man, which struck home doubly hard when you considered the conditions. The icy cold which could kill you before ever you hit the sea; the sea itself, its very turbulence guaranteed to sink almost instantly any small life-raft which was cast upon its stormy bosom. Then there was the possibility of being iced to the deck, literally between one step and the next, and consequently drowned by the coming aboard of a great, heavy sea. And as well as all this, there were the U-boats, lurking beneath the surface, waiting to strike. Enemy war ships, prowling round the convoy, trying to stop the cargoes getting to their destination. And the aircraft, which came out of the blue and followed the convoy until other planes came up and the convoy could be efficiently attacked, dive-bombed, fired on, utterly destroyed.

So when he went home for his leave, it was nice to have someone who understood his sudden silence in the middle of a group of noisy drinking companions. Why he sometimes wanted to be quiet, to appreciate something other than war, violence, something other, even, than the ceaseless round of gaiety which seemed to satisfy some of the other combatants in what he was beginning to see as an increasingly terrible war.

Because of the conditions on the Russian convoys, most of the men had grown beards, and Sunny had a magnificent one. Long, blond and curly, he had grown it for a bet and now rather liked it, though it had an odd effect on girls. Some liked it, others seemed to hate it. Polly, for instance, had been instantly antagonistic, had said it was ugly, made him look old, got in the way of a kiss. Sunny had tried explaining about the cold, but Polly said flatly that she thought he had grown it more to impress than to keep warm. Grace, on the other hand, ignored it, simply, he thought now, because to her it was not important, any more than he suspected his looks were. Polly, bless her, thought that his beard detracted from his good looks, whereas he knew, or thought he knew that Grace liked him as a person and would have continued to like him had he gone bald as a coot and begun to squint. What was more they had soon discovered that they enjoyed the same sort of things – visits to the cinema, long walks on the shore, talks about what they would do when the peace came. And singing.

Sunny had not really thought very much about singing until he joined the Navy and had begun to sing with an amateur choir got up by the ratings on his first convoy to Russia. To his surprise, he had a good strong tenor voice and found it easy to keep a tune in his head. Singing relaxed him, gave him something to think about other than war. When he had gone to the Seamen's Mission for one of his leaves and had met up with Grace, staying with the O'Bradys, he had discovered that she, too, loved singing.

'I'm a member of the Salvation Army, and I sing in the choir. I was a songster – that's what they call the younger members – from the time I went to the Strawb, pretty well. Why don't you come along to a service? I'm not trying to convert you or anything like that, but you'd be welcome, and I think you'd enjoy it. Our hymns are much . . . well, much *jollier* than the hymns sung in more established churches, and somehow we seem to sing them with much more joy, and – and verve. We've a great choral tradition, us Salvationists – I often think that the roof of the citadel must be fixed down extra strongly, or we'd sing it clean off!'

He had gone along, mainly, if he were honest, to be polite because Grace was Polly's pal and was staying with the O'Bradys. But after that first visit he had known that Grace was right; the enthusiasm with which both choir and congregation sang and the simple, unassuming friendliness, was a balm to his tired, overstrained mind and body. He found that he was returning to his duty not exactly uplifted by the Army, but somehow soothed by it, by the very ordinariness of singing along with people who sang quite simply for the love of God, without giving themselves airs, or having to create an atmosphere in which, Sunny now believed, pomp and ceremony played a more important part than simple belief.

So though he had no illusions about his relationship with Grace – they were friends, nothing more – he still found sharing his leaves with her was infinitely better than being in Liverpool alone, and did his best to arrange that, when they were home, it was at around the same times. Grace, working on her airfield in Norfolk, was able, to an extent, to choose when she would take her leave, so Sunny formed the habit, as soon as he got ashore in Scapa, of ringing her and telling her when he would be having sufficient time off to get back to Liverpool. If she was able to make it at the same time that was marvellous . . . not that he ever pretended to Grace herself that they were anything other than good friends, of course. Good friends who shared an interest in music, particularly singing, though Sunny had recently bought, from a fellow rating, a somewhat battered trumpet which he was learning to play. He was being tutored by the rating, who had bought a superior instrument but was happy to show Sunny how to get the best out of his old one.

But of course, Sunny reminded himself now as the ship began to nose into the clear-water path across the harbour, Polly was still his girl. She was wrapped up in her work as a WRN despatch rider, that was why she seemed not to have the time for him that she had once had, but when the war was over . . .

There was activity now on the bridge as the first officer gave the order to let go and the chocks were knocked out, allowing the anchor chain to run out.

Above them, the sky was a cold grey and before them, the merchantmen were lining up alongside the quay. Sunny looked at the cleared path of water around them as the icebreaker, with a valedictory grunt like an old pig in a wallow, turned and made slowly for the open sea once more. He would go below now and get some rest, then when the ice had reformed and was hard enough to take a regiment of sailors, perhaps he and a pal would go ashore; there was not much to do when you got there apart from strolling along beside the ships they had accompanied to this place, and since they were, when on shore, representing His Majesty's Royal Navy they would have to wear their number ones, but it was better than spending the time below decks, or wandering round and round the corvette's tiny deckspace. Sunny wanted a long, brisk walk in this sort of weather and though they would be speedily turned back by the police if they attempted to go far from the quayside, you never knew. All Russians, his reason told him, could not be peasants bundled up in rags, too terrified of their own police guards even to exchange a smile with a visiting sailor. Somewhere, he imagined, there must be civilised men and women, some of whom might even have a few words of English. Whenever he went ashore he always took a couple of bars of the dark and bitter chocolate or even a screw of tea and sugar; one of these days he would find someone with sufficient courage to accept such gifts when offered – but so far there had been no takers. And he was sure that the people were hungry; he longed to make contact with someone, anyone, who would give him a smile, acknowledge that they were fighting the same war, facing the same enemy, damn it, *needed* each other. Why otherwise would he and his companions have

414

come halfway across the world to this bitterly cold, dark land, bringing food, clothing, implements of war or agriculture? He didn't really know what they carried save that it was desperately needed; why could the Russians not behave as allies and friends, instead of looking at English sailors as though they might eat them?

But then Russia wasn't like other countries and Uncle Joe wasn't like other leaders, either. Sighing, Sunny went across the bridge to report to the first officer that he was going below. He would check the signal log and then get some sleep and by that time the ice would have formed again and someone else, with luck, would be awake and ready for a tramp outside.

Polly was sitting astride her motorbike at the top of Everton Brow, admiring the city and the burnished gold of the Mersey as it lay in the setting sun before her, when the engine gave an apologetic cough, a couple of hiccups, and stopped.

Polly, who had been feeling fairly peaceful, immediately felt annoyance start to tighten her muscles. It was not fair! For a start, she should not have been up here at all, feeling mistress of all she surveyed, when she had been sent from HQ to Birkenhead with important messages; she should, by now, have been back at the Liver buildings, informing her superior officers that her task had been successfully accomplished. But it was such a beautiful, golden late afternoon, and suddenly the temptation to go a bit out of her way for once had come over her. What was more, there was a sweet shop on Salisbury Street which sometimes had a few off-ration goodies which the proprietor, fat little Mrs Mobbs, handed out in tiny amounts to service personnel.

Then there was the fact that her engine had done quite a bit of sly coughing when she was actually doing her duty, on a part of the road which she should have been on, and she had done nothing about it. Now that she lived at home, she had reasoned, she could wait until the weekend and then strip the machine down in the back yard. Ivan would be delighted to give a hand and she was familiar enough with her engine to be able to pick out what was wrong pretty quickly. What was more, the engine had never actually died on her before, just spluttered a bit and then recovered. Dirt in the carburettor, Polly had told herself – and had ignored it, when she could easily have taken it into the transport section and got one of the mechanics to see to it for her.

Still, she had been well taught by Tad before he had gone off to train as a pilot, and usually did all her own maintenance. And at least it had happened at the top of one of the best hills in Liverpool, she told herself, reaching into her pocket for one of the homemade toffees which Mrs Mobbs had sold her and tucking it comfortably into one cheek. She would coast down the hill, get the engine going again, and make her way back to the Liver buildings, then on to the depot where she would hand her machine over for once, and take a tram home to Snowdrop Street.

For Polly had opted to live at home over a year ago, when she had returned to Liverpool as a despatch rider. After the awful business – she admitted, now, that it had been an awful business, and all her own fault – of the row when she had discovered that she was adopted, she felt that it was the least she could do for Mammy and Daddy. She had been forced to admit, soon enough, that they had treated her as well if not better than their own natural children; that they loved her dearly, with the sort of love that can't be put on or pretended. And though she had run away from them on that first fatal night, she had gone back a few weeks later, driven there, she had told herself rather sullenly, by Saint Grace Carbery, who had come to her in Holyhead and read her lectures and told her off just as though she had been a thoughtless and selfish school child.

For Grace had indeed travelled down to Holyhead the day after Polly's horrid adventure, if you could call it that, and had tackled her head-on about her attitude to finding that she had been adopted, and further, that Grace was her sister.

'Peader and Deirdre have been kinder to me than almost anyone else, apart from Brogan and Sara, in my entire life,' Grace had said gently. 'And just think, Poll, if you'd not been adopted! Why, the sort of life I led . . . I don't think I've ever told you about it before, but . . .'

And she had proceeded to tell Polly things that had made Polly's hair stand up on her head with horror – a father who had in all probability killed his wife, a mother who was too worn down and weary to try to protect her numerous children from a violent husband, and after they had both died, her own struggle for survival. For the first time, Polly heard of Grace sleeping rough in parks and jiggers and other people's sheds. Of being attacked by a rat – Grace took Polly's hand and made her trace the faint marks of the rat's teeth, still there on one otherwise smooth young cheek – and of being constantly hungry, constantly in fear.

At the time, shocked though she had been, Polly had not intended to show it. She had turned a sulky shoulder on her new-found sister and had said: 'Sure and I'm – I'm not after sayin' that I'd have enjoyed meself in Liverpool the way I did in Dublin, am I? It's the deceit, Grace, that's what I can't take in me stride. Why in God's name didn't they *tell* me I was adopted, instead of letting me believe I was their own little daughter?'

'You know the reason, Poll; because Brogan stole you, that's why,' Grace had said with a sort of weary patience which, at the time, Polly had thought was an insult in itself. 'You were only a little kid; you might have said something to anyone, anyone at all, and they couldn't risk that, couldn't risk Brogan being took up for kidnapping. Now could they?'

And in the end, of course, Polly had had to come round, to understand why Deirdre and Peader had said nothing to her, why Grace herself had been kept in ignorance. Indeed, she was forced to admit to herself that 'Saint Grace' was a better person than she, because Grace absolutely longed to acknowledge her as her little sister, to tell people that she did have a proper relative, after all. But because of the various difficulties of the situation she had to be content with being Polly's pal, which wasn't quite the same thing at all, as Polly, in her more generous moments, acknowledged.

A few weeks after Grace's visit to Holyhead, however, Polly had felt obliged to return to Snowdrop Street and to tell her mammy and daddy that she was sorry for all she had said, that she *did* understand why everyone had behaved as they had, and to promise them that she would never think one whit the worse of them for not telling her earlier that she was adopted.

And then, when Polly had applied for the job of despatch rider attached to the Liverpool HQ of the

Navy, Deirdre had had her brainwave. 'Your daddy and meself have been thinking,' she told Polly as the two of them sat in the kitchen, knitting industriously for various members of the family who were in the Navy and needed warm clothing. 'What would you say, alanna, if we adopted Grace? Officially, I mean.'

Polly had been so astonished that for several moments she could only stare, and Deirdre, interpreting this as dislike of the idea, hastily said that it was only . . . that it seemed a sort of solution . . . that poor Grace had had a rotten deal one way and another . . .

'But she's a woman grown,' Polly had said at last, on a gasp. 'Can you do such a t'ing, Mammy? Adopt a woman grown?'

'You can; and then she can change her name by deed poll to O'Brady and the two of you will be sisters,' Deirdre said. 'Or wouldn't you like that, alanna?'

For a moment Polly had very meanly thought that indeed she would not like it. She was the only girl in the O'Brady family, the boys wouldn't want another sister thrust upon them and Polly was not too sure, in her heart of hearts, whether she truly wanted 'Saint Grace' to share her name, her brothers, her whole family. But then the more generous side of her nature came to the fore and she said: 'Well, if that's what Grace would like, it would suit me just fine, so it would. It's rare kind of you and Daddy, Mammy, when you've so many kids already.'

But as it turned out Grace, though grateful for the suggestion, had turned it down with unexpected firmness. 'It's awful kind of Auntie Dee and Uncle Peader,' she had said almost apologetically. 'But I really think it would only complicate matters.

Besides, Poll, you're going to be changing your name from O'Brady pretty soon – as soon as the war ends, in fact. Then we can be sisters without people wondering.'

'I'm not going to change me name—' Polly had begun, quite offended, before light suddenly dawned and she giggled. 'Oh! You mean *marriage*, I suppose. But you'll be changing your name as well, Grace – sooner than me, probably.'

'I might,' Grace had agreed cautiously. 'But I don't have fellers hanging on me every move like you do, Poll. Besides, isn't Sunny . . .'

'Oh yes, I reckon I'll marry him one day,' Polly had said offhandedly. 'But I dunno when – it might not be for years yet.'

But that had been some while ago, and right now, sitting astride her bike and looking down on the city as the light of the setting sun slowly deepened from gold to rose, from rose to crimson, she reminded herself that the way she was going on, she should be glad to marry Sunny just as soon as peace was declared, since she seemed to have cast off all her other boyfriends – and mostly, with no tears shed, on her side at any rate.

As for Tad . . . well, she was still cross with him, even after almost two years' absence. For as soon as he had 'phoned her at her wrennery, telling her that he was going abroad to train as a pilot, she had regretted her cruel words. Not that there was any-thing cruel in telling someone she thought of him as a brother, exactly – she had a high opinion of all her brothers, hadn't she? – but she had known she was hurting Tad even as the words passed her lips. And it wasn't true, not really, it was just that she had known him for so long that it was difficult to take him seriously as – well, as a boyfriend. So of course she hadn't tried, not really. And though he was her pal, and a better feller never breathed, he wasn't anywhere near as handsome as Sunny. Well, he wasn't handsome at all, he was downright plain was Tad. It was just that he was familiar, and very much her friend.

Which was why, she reminded herself now, that she was so bleedin' cross with him. Called himself a pal and yet had he answered her letters, which she had sent at least once a week for the first half year of his time abroad? No, he hadn't. Oh, he'd sent a couple of those miserable standard letters which meant that he had ticked boxes – I am well, the weather is fine, we have been swimming – and a couple of scruffy notes too, but they hadn't been letters. In fact, they had been downright unfriendly, as though he were telling her that if she wasn't prepared to swoon before him then he meant to forget her and the sooner the better.

This, Polly reflected now, sucking on her sweet, had been totally unacceptable. She wanted her friend Tad as a pal, not a lover. She had Sunny to take her about and impress her friends with his good looks. She wanted Tad for . . . well, for the sturdy independence and friendship which he had always shown her. The plain truth was that she missed him, infuriating though he was, but Tad's behaviour had proved that this was futile – it was all or nothing for him. So she had gradually stopped writing to him, had allowed her letters to get briefer – and colder – and had tried not to mind when still he did not bother to reply to them. And then, out of the blue, she had discovered the worst thing of all; ten months ago – ten *months* – he had returned to Britain, to fly some plane or other – she did not know whether he was still with his beloved Beaufighters – from an airfield in Lincolnshire and despite being back in Blighty he had not once so much as dropped her a line or telephoned her or – or anything. If she had not happened to meet up with an old friend of his who had told her that he was back in England, she would not even have known that much.

She had considered getting in touch, naturally, but had finally decided against it mostly because she felt that he should have been the one to get in touch with her. After all, she had written and written and he had not replied. If he was so indifferent to her then she would take the hint and leave him alone.

Nevertheless it was on her mind, and a bit like an aching tooth; she could not stop thinking about it, examining her conscience, wondering whether, since it was she who had told Tad so unequivocally that she did not intend to take him seriously as a boyfriend, it should also be she who should break the barrier of silence and contact him. But she had done so, had she not? The first three letters she had sent had been mainly apologies for her behaviour, she remembered that clearly enough. And though she had not rescinded her words – how could she, without telling downright lies, since she did not have the slightest interest in Tad as a proper boyfriend? – she had definitely said she was sorry if she had been unkind. Further than that, she told herself severely now, no girl should be expected to go. And if Tad was not interested in her then she was not interested in him either. Though she did miss him most awfully, and sometimes wished . . . wished . . .

She had mentioned the rift to Grace a month or two back and Grace had reminded her that Tad would not know that she was now working as a despatch rider in Liverpool and living at home once more in Snowdrop Street. 'How can he contact you when he's only got the Holyhead address?' she had asked in her sensible, practical way. But though Polly's heart had given a little leap at the thought that maybe Tad had been bombarding Holyhead with letters for months and months, common sense made her reluctantly discard the lovely thought. The Navy were very good at seeing you got your post – why, she had once sent Sunny a seven-page epic in a box of Mammy's homemade fudge with some ginger snaps which she had laboriously made herself, and Sunny had got both eventually, though by then the fudge had mould all over it and the biscuits were so hard that no human teeth could break them. He had described how he had battered them into fragments with a sledge hammer and then sucked the bits – she had laughed like anything over that, she remembered.

So no hope that Tad had not been able to discover her new address. If he had wanted to reach her he could have done so. The plain old truth was that he was now as indifferent to her as she was to him, and she should forget him, push him to the very back of her mind. All that was now due to him was an invitation to her wedding, when she and Sunny got spliced, she told herself vengefully. And he wouldn't come to the wedding anyway, she knew that, since he hadn't even bothered to answer her letters.

Still. Sitting there in the late sunshine, Polly told herself that however she might feel about Tad, her feelings about Sunny were at least, very definite. I'm crazy about him, she told herself now. He's the best looking, nicest, cleverest feller I've ever met, and I'm madly in love with him. Why, when he touches my hand my bones turn to jelly and my heart thumps like a drum, and when he kisses me . . . !

But this would not get the baby a new bonnet, Polly told herself, yet still she lingered. Somehow, up here on the hill with the city spread out before her, she seemed to be able to think more clearly. Being billeted at home, she acknowledged to herself, was a mistake. She missed the companionship of the other girls, the feeling that they were all in the same boat, the easy-going sharing which went on so that when kit inspections were called, each girl would help the others over some missing bit of equipment. Stockings would be passed from bed to bed, small items such as a hat or a decent pair of shoe-laces would be shot along the row of beds when the officer wasn't looking . . . All of that was impossible, of course, when you lived at home. If you lost equipment you applied for a replacement which was supplied and they could stop the cost of it from your pay if they thought you had been careless. But somehow, the fun had gone out of it. And though Mammy's meals were a good deal tastier than the food frequently served up in either the canteen or the WRNnery itself, it wasn't quite the same. Sitting down with your parents round the kitchen table at the end of an exciting day was an anti-climax for it was impossible to say much because a good deal of what she did was confidential.

But of course her rotten behaviour over her being adopted had meant that she had little choice. She could not very well live in billets in the city when she had treated her dear Mammy and Daddy so shame-fully, she had felt obliged to go home to live.

However. Polly took a deep breath and expelled it in a long sigh. She should be getting back to the transport section just as soon as she could so that her bike might be put right in time for work in the morning.

Deirdre was darning a pair of Ivan's socks which were more darn, she thought ruefully, than sock and keeping half an eye on the bake oven, where a peculiar dish of her own invention was slowly cooking on a low heat. It was a vegetable pie, made more interesting by the addition of finely minced bacon rinds with the pastry the richer for some beef dripping which the butcher on Stanley Road had slipped into her basket the last time she had been in his shop. Deirdre knew that the beef dripping was a thank you for a couple of large onions which Mr Hartley had been delighted to receive the week previously. Peader's allotment provided the family with many small treats. So now she waited for the moment when she could produce the pie from the oven, cooked to a lovely golden brown, and receive the congratulations of her family and also of Monica, who was coming to tea this evening.

Monica, Deirdre thought, finishing off a black sock with navy blue wool and telling herself that she was lucky to have found any darning wool at all, despite their initial doubts, had turned out to be a good little daughter-in-law; one of the best.

When Martin's ship had gone down she had gone into a factory which made uniforms and when this no longer satisfied her, had joined the WRNs as a writer, which was what they called the office staff. Peader and Deirdre had wanted her to live with them in the house in Snowdrop Street where there was plenty of room and where she would have been very welcome, particularly to Polly, but Monica said she would rather go the whole hog and live with her fellow

WRNs. So she had moved into the wrennery at which had once been the Royal Hotel on the Marine Terrace at Waterloo, and was a good deal happier there, Deirdre thought, than she would have been sharing a house with them and reminded of Martin at every turn.

So now, sitting in front of the fire with her darning more or less finished, Deirdre was able to contemplate the evening ahead with some satisfaction. Polly would be home very soon and then she, Deirdre, would pop into the oven the eggless, fatless sort-of sponge pudding which she had prepared, and then Polly could read her post. The back door opening brought a smile to her face.

'That's a grand smell so it is,' Peader said, taking off his earth-caked boots and knocking them on the cobbles and, stepping into the kitchen, he pulled the door to behind him. 'I hope the girls won't be long. I'm hungry enough to eat me own boots, so I am. Diggin's such hard work . . .'

The abrupt re-opening of the back door again put an end of Peader's words.

'Mammy! We're not late, are we?' It was Polly, looking flushed and pretty in her uniform, with Monica close behind her. 'Only me bleedin' bike broke down and I took it in to the MT yard, and one of the fellers said he'd fix it so that I could use it first thing tomorrow. And Monica came out of the Liver buildings as I was passing and so we came on together. What's for tea?'

'A lovely vegetable pie with beef dripping,' Deirdre said. 'And I'm just about to mash the spuds wit' a smidgin of milk; then we can eat. Oh, and there's letters for you on the mantel behind the clock.'

Afterwards, she was to wonder what had made her

say such a thing in front of Monica, for usually she tried not to remind Monica that there were no letters for her; not any more. But today, for some reason, she simply told Polly about the letters, though she added hastily: 'You may not want to read them now; wait until later when you're alone, will you?'

Polly was sensitive about letters, too, but she reached up and took the envelopes off the mantelpiece, weighed them thoughtfully in her hand and then went and sat opposite Peader by the fire, whilst Monica, having removed her jacket, put a wraparound overall over the rest of her uniform and began to mash the potatoes for Deirdre, whilst her mother-in-law made gravy with the vegetable water and some cornflour. 'I'll have a quick glance, just to make sure everything's all right,' Polly said, and slit one of the envelopes, then pulled out a number of sheets. 'Well, would you look at that! Sunny writes a grand letter so he does, but not usually a – a *book*.' She grinned at Peader, then began to read.

Later she glanced up at Monica, then away again, before shoving the letter back into its envelope as her mother told her that the meal was ready. And presently, when the first edge of their hunger was taken off, she said thoughtfully: 'Isn't it odd, now, that this letter should have arrived wit' Monica here? Because there's a bit of it which Sunny thought I ought to pass on to you, Monica. I'll read it presently, but first of all I'll tell you that Sunny wrote it on his return voyage, after he'd been in one of those Russian ports, all darkness and ice, which is where the convoys go. He said that he'd decided to go ashore – they're allowed, but they don't think the Russians like it much – and take a look around. A pal of his had meant to go with him but for some reason he wasn't able to, so Sunny went alone. He set off across the ice . . . '

Sunny, in his number ones but with his biggest muffler wound twice round his face and once round his neck and his greatcoat collar turned up, with his thickest socks – two pairs – on his booted feet and his cap pulled right down to his eyebrows, set off across the ice. He was alone, but had already decided that he would not go ashore alone. However, someone from one of the merchantmen or even from another member of the convoy guardships would surely want to get a breath of fresh air. Going ashore alone, they had been told, might well be dangerous. The Russians, or the dock police, at any rate, were a queer bunch. They would not set on a group of sailors, and indeed if they did so it would mean the end of the life-giving convoys, but no one was absolutely sure that they would not pounce on a solitary sailor, using the excuse that he was spying, and obstinately deny that they had even seen the fellow. Might, Sunny morbidly imagine, even claim that the sailor had fallen through the ice and been drowned. They could probably produce a body without too much difficulty, Sunny thought now, eyeing the straggle of dark figures unloading the nearest merchantman. He could not be sure, of course, but he certainly suspected that the men and women who acted as dockers and unloaded the stores were prisoners of some description. Certainly the way the dock police treated them meant that they were, at any rate, not held in much esteem. Life is cheap here, Sunny thought, and was grateful when he saw three muffled figures coming towards him across the quay. He hailed them.

'Hi, there. You from the SS *Rangoon Princess*? Been ashore here before?'

They had not, but wanted to see as much as they could. 'Which won't be much,' Sunny told them gloomily. 'I've been ashore several times, but there's really nothing to see. Flat, snow-covered ground, a huddle of wooden huts, and sometimes you see lorries, lining up to take the stuff away from here. As for the locals, if they *are* locals, I've never succeeded in getting so much as a word out of any of them.'

Nevertheless, the four of them walked briskly along the snow-covered quay towards the long line of muffled figures hefting the bags and boxes which were already piling up on the quay. But as he predicted, in a lowered voice, to the sailor nearest him, as soon as they got within ten feet of the working party a couple of dark-clad policemen detached themselves from the group and came towards them, making signals that they were to come no closer, whilst they spoke harshly in their own tongue.

'Right you are, mate,' Sunny said, and the four of them swung around and walked away from the working party, towards the huddle of huts.

They skirted the buildings and went on past them, into the snow-covered wilderness beyond, but after only a short way it was clear that Sunny's new companions had no urge to explore further.

'There's nothing but snow and dark,' the man nearest Sunny said disgustedly. He turned to one of the other men. 'It's a far cry from your neck of the woods, Eggy, but even if you want to see more of it, I don't reckon the rest of us do. We'll be gettin' back, see whether there's any grub going.'

'Just because my parents originally came from Italy and my brother's been troop carrying in the Med, that doesn't mean to say I want to hang about in this God-awful place,' the man called Eggy said cheerfully. He turned to Sunny. 'My brother has been taking troops across to Italy for the invasion, and bringing back wounded and so on. Lucky devil! At least he's been warm and not perpetually frozen, like our lot.'

'Italy?' Sunny said, surprised. 'Don't tell me we've taken Italy!'

The other man laughed. 'Well, not yet I don't imagine, though you must know our troops have been fighting their way up from Sicily for months and months now. And my brother . . . but look, why not come aboard the old *Princess* for a noggin and I'll tell you about it. Cooky might find us up something hot, seeing as you're one of our brave escorts.'

Sunny, agreeing, went on board the *Rangoon Princess* and was soon comfortably settled in a corner of the mess deck with a large mug of cocoa and a bacon sandwich and as soon as he could do so he asked Eggy, who proved to be a short, stocky young man with very dark hair and eyes and a swarthy skin, to tell him what had been happening to his brother.

'My brother is younger than me and so when war came he joined the Navy, whereas I was already in the merchant service,' he explained. 'Because Ben – that's my brother – speaks pretty good Italian he was given the job of talking to ex-POWS and some prisoners who were brought aboard his ship for transportation back to the UK, and he had some strange stories to tell. The partisan movement isn't highly regarded in Italy and the peasants fear them almost as much as they fear the Nazis but even so they readily give shelter to anyone they consider as oppressed as themselves. You can tell by the marvellous way they treated fellows who managed to escape from the Germans, and aircrew who weren't picked up by the jerries but managed to find friendly locals to shelter them. Of course, when they spoke Italian, as some did, it was even easier for them to stay out of jug, I imagine.'

'Yeah, speaking the language must have helped.' Sunny said, taking a large bite out of his bacon sandwich. 'And if the allies have only recently been pushing ahead, I suppose you might have been better off in a prisoner of war camp – at least they'd feed you. Or would they head for a neutral country? Switzerland, perhaps?'

'I wouldn't have tried to cross into Switzerland,' Eggy said, pulling a face. 'I wouldn't trust a Swiss further than I could throw him and that's a fact. No, if it were me I'd stay shtum in various villages and waited my chance.'

'That would be all right for you, knowing the language,' Sunny said sagely. 'It might have been a very different story if you'd been like meself, for instance. I don't speak a word of any language but English – unless you count scouse, of course.'

'Well, I dunno about that,' Eggy said. 'Ben talked about other fellers who'd been taken prisoner but escaped, or who had been sheltered by fishermen and so on, and none of them had a word of Italian to their names. Not when they first got there, though I think most of 'em picked some up. Why, he picked up one feller who had some Italian, and he told him he'd been in a remote little village in the Calabria area of the country, being hidden by a peasant family and fed on whatever they could spare – mostly goat's cheese, unleavened bread and grapes – when a cousin from another village came visiting. She was a pretty thing, and was getting married. The old woman I was staying with was a noted dressmaker, apparently, and this girl had brought her some material to make up into a wedding dress. It was pretty stuff, real

431

quality, not the sort of thing you would ever find in a remote hill village, so this young feller asked her where she got it. She beamed at him and said it had been given to her by a young sailor that her father had fished out of the water quite early on in the war. She said he was English, couldn't speak a word of Italian, and was carrying the material wrapped round his body under his clothing. It wasn't spoiled by the sea-water for it was wrapped in some sort of oiled paper, and when he moved on somewhere else, after weeks and weeks of staying with the young bride-to-be, he gave it to her. The feller told Ben it was really pretty, a sort of cream-coloured silk covered with bronze poppies.'

Sunny stared, his sandwich halfway to his mouth. 'Are – are you sure? What was the feller's name, did the girl say?'

'I dunno, I can't remember. Ben may not ever have told me his name . . .'

'No, I don't mean the story teller's name, I mean the – the chap who they fished out of the 'oggin with the silk wrapped round him,' Sunny said quickly. 'What was his name, d'you know?'

Eggy wiped his hand across his mouth and after a few moments' thought, shook his head. 'No, I doubt that Ben would have remembered it, even if the girl had mentioned it to the other feller. No, she wouldn't have used a name, them being foreign to her. And it might not have been too safe anyway, what with the jerries and everything.'

'The thing is,' Sunny said, his mouth suddenly dry. 'I've a pal called Martin O'Brady who was lost at sea when his ship went down. His wife is a dressy little thing and he got me to buy him a dress length of silk whilst I was in Gibraltar. I did as he asked and bought him a length of cream-coloured silk covered with bronze poppies. It was very unusual stuff, and . . . well, it seems strange . . . Martin's my girlfriend's brother and if it was him they fished out of the 'oggin, and he's still alive . . .'

Eggy, finishing up his own sandwich, shrugged. 'Bit of a coincidence, but things like that's always happening in wartime,' he observed. 'I can't think two sailors would have a dress length of material like that. I bet it was your pal, Sunny!'

And Sunny, grinning broadly, said that he suspicioned it was, too. But though the pair of them talked for some while after that, they could come to no firm conclusion. 'I wonder if I ought to write to Mart's wife, tell her the story?' Sunny said at last as the two of them stood once more on the windy quay, with loose snow blowing into their faces. 'I don't want to raise false hopes, but . . . well, what would you do, Eggy?'

'I'd just tell her the story and let her make what she could of it,' Eggy decided, after some thought. 'No, tell your girl, let her decide. But if it were me, I'd rather have hope than none at all, wouldn't you?'

'I think I would,' Sunny agreed after a moment. 'If only someone had mentioned a name . . .'

Eggy, shrugging, watched him climb down the rope ladder, and, as Sunny's feet met the quay, he thought of something else. 'Hang on a mo, old feller,' he shouted, cupping both hands round his mouth so that his voice carried clearly across the ice. 'One thing me brother did say – the girl said he called her "alanna", or something like that. If that's any help, of course.'

Sunny turned and grinned up at him. 'Oh, the

times I've heard Martin use that word, me ole shipmate! That decides it; I'll write to my Polly this very night.'

Polly and Monica danced around the table and hugged each other when the letter was read, and even Peader and Deirdre allowed that 'It looked as though Monica had been right all along, and Martin was still alive.' No one said that he had been alive in 1942 but might well have died in the interim, but it was probably at the back of every mind. Monica, however, pointed out that had Martin been taken prisoner they would have been informed, but that, living on the country as it appeared he was, he could scarcely have let anyone know his whereabouts.

'The allies are pushing up Italy as fast as they can go,' she said contentedly, as the family sat round the fire that evening, for although it was October it was pleasant to sit in the warm once darkness fell. 'We'll get confirmation soon enough, I'm sure. Oh, and I'm so grateful to your Sunny, Poll! Now that I know he reached land, I'm content to wait.'

Chapter Sixteen

SPRING 1945

Polly lay on a smooth, sheep-nibbled stretch of turf, with the sun hot on her closed eyelids and the sound of the sea gently lapping at the shore below the cliffs, and basked. She was on her holidays, or at least she felt as if she were, for when one is in the WRNS, and suddenly gets a whole week off, and lives at home, what is to stop one spending that week somewhere else? Peader had his allotment and his coupon-checking and points-additions and Deirdre still worked in her parachute factory on Hanover Street so if Polly had stayed at home it would have been a lonely sort of leave.

If Grace or one of Polly's pals had been able to get some leave as well it would have been a different story. But despite the fact that everyone knew the war was going to end any day now, Grace was needed on her station, and Sunny was probably still with his ship, halfway, Polly thought gloomily, between Scotland and Russia, either coming or going. At any rate, she hadn't had a letter for ages, so she had decided to spend her leave visiting old friends, visiting a place, she thought now, where she had been happier than one usually was in wartime.

Anglesey. Holyhead. In fact, in the very house where she had been billeted when she had first joined the WRNS, for Diane was still there, and most of her other friends were still in Holyhead. So Polly had rung up and asked permission to spend her leave in the tall house in London Road, and Diane had told her that she was as welcome as the day was long, and added that they would not mention her presence to anyone in authority.

'We've a spare bed or two, with people on leave, and others having left for different jobs,' she had said breezily. 'Oh, Poll, I have missed you! It'll be grand to see you again – are you coming down here to see that fellow, the one you made so unhappy? Only I've not seen him around since you left.'

'No, of course I'm not coming to see Tad,' Polly had said, annoyed. 'Why on earth should I do such a t'ing, Di? Besides, he's up north somewhere – I don't know where, we've lost touch.'

'Oh,' Diane said. She sounded a little doubtful. 'Well, you know your own business best, of course, but I always thought—'

'I don't know what you thought,' Polly had said rather reproachfully. 'But you shouldn't leap to conclusions, Di. I've told you over and over that I've got a feller, a serious one. Sunny, the chap whose on the Russian convoys. He's a signaller, and—'

'Oh, yes, I know all about your Sunny,' Diane had assured her, sounding not in the least cast down by Polly's words. 'Still, no point in talking about it now, when we're going to see each other so soon. I'll get some time off . . . Oh, Poll, I can't wait!'

So Polly had caught a train and arrived at Holyhead on the first day of her leave. She had settled into the old house as though she had never left it, and in the bright April sunshine had begun to enjoy her holiday. For the first couple of days she had revisited old haunts around the docks and the town, had gone into the clubs and messes to meet old friends and generally caught up with the local news. But even in the bustle of the naval headquarters she had the feeling that everyone was waiting. Waiting for the inevitable end of it all which could not be far off, not now.

And all the time, in the back of her mind, was a feeling of vague dissatisfaction. She had been so happy here – why could she not recapture that happiness, feel the warm glow of it in her veins? She supposed it was because she was no longer truly a part of it, as she had once been. She had no real place here, no actual purpose. And a good many of the men she had worked with had moved on, perhaps manning the invasion fleet which had left from the channel ports the previous year, perhaps taking the place of other men on the convoys or in the dock-yards, putting right the damage which had been done to such vessels. So earlier that day Polly had decided to get some food from the girls' kitchen and make herself some sandwiches. Then she could take a picnic somewhere quiet, and enjoy the wonderful sunshine.

She had borrowed a bicycle and pedalled slowly around the coast, ending up here, on the quiet, sunny cliff, sunbathing, occasionally taking a drink from the bottle of cold tea she had brought with her, and thinking.

What had gone wrong with her life of late? she wondered. She had not seen her angel for ages now, since joining the service, in fact, and had told herself rather miserably that seeing angels was presumably something which you left behind with girlhood, because now she was a woman who no longer needed an angel. But she missed that sweet-faced presence which had always made her feel safe, and loved. And now, she fell to wondering why she had ever had that guardian angel, because she had had Mammy, and

Daddy and her brothers, to say nothing of Tad ... Her thoughts broke down in confusion, until she reminded herself that she had meant she had had Tad when she had been just a kid, in Dublin, that his presence – or absence – would most certainly not have affected her need of an angel.

But Grace, who had needed an angel so desperately, her thoughts continued, had never had one. That was strange, wasn't it? She had asked Grace several times, very carefully, mind, whether Grace had ever been aware of a presence, of something glimpsed, not straightforwardly, but out of the corner of one's eye, so to speak. More an inward conviction of another's presence than a proper sighting. She had made it plain that she did not mean recently, of course, because now Grace, like herself, was a woman grown, but long ago, when Grace had wandered the streets alone, always in need, usually in fear. Grace had looked mildly surprised by the question but had said, a little regretfully, that never, during that sad time, had she ever felt any sort of strange, other-worldly presence, or not one which was well-disposed towards her at any rate. So Polly had dropped the subject, and had told herself fiercely that she should be eternally grateful for her own immense good fortune in being able to see her guardian angel now and then – as a child, of course – and not feel so deprived and cheated now that she could no longer do so.

Having settled that matter to her satisfaction, or almost so, she turned her thoughts back to her stay on the island. She had been to a dance held out at Valley, and had not enjoyed herself as much as she had hoped. She and Diane had had a lovely day out with two young naval bods. They had gone out in a dinghy and bathed from the boat, swimming in water a great deal deeper than they could have reached from the beach. It had been fun, but somehow, the faint disappointment which had seemed to come over her even as she smiled her delighted greeting to the island where she had been so happy would not be dispelled. There was something wrong, something missing . . .

Restlessly, Polly rolled from her back on to her front and studied the tiny, gold-centred daisy almost beneath her nose, with its oriole of pink tipped petals. She was being quite absurd, wholly ridiculous, and it was time she snapped out of it. She turned her thoughts to a favourite theme: her wedding. There she was, poised and lovely in a long white dress with a full skirt and narrow sleeves. She wore a white veil which billowed out beneath a wreath of lilies of the valley and her feet were clad in white, satin, high-heeled shoes. She had her hand – with the sapphire engagement and the gold wedding rings on the third finger – tucked into Sunny's uniform sleeve, and she was smiling up at him as he was smiling down at her, their eyes meeting with a look of perfect understanding and love . . . and nearby, her parents beamed, both with their eyes full of tears of love and pride as they saw their only daughter wed. And there was Diane (who often doubled in the dream as her bridesmaid, along with Grace and Monica, of course) in her uniform getting eight girls in neat WRNS navy-blue to form a triumphal arch so that she and Sunny could run the gauntlet of all the rice – no, confetti, because she would not be marrying in wartime, not now, when the whole thing was more or less over – which would be thrown between the porch of the church and the lychgate.

It was a nice dream and Polly, smiling, rolled over

439

on to her back again and then sat up and reached for her picnic. She bit into a corned-beef sandwich, liberally doused with brown sauce, and gazed blissfully up at the brilliant blue of the noonday sky. She had found a bag of dried apple rings and a few sultanas as well as the sandwich ingredients when she had poked about in the pantry and had decided the girls would not miss these odds and ends, deciding that she had done very well considering that no one, as yet, had asked her for her ration book. Indeed, apart from the vague feeling that she no longer belonged here, no holiday, she told herself, could have been nicer or more satisfying.

Sitting there, with the wind lifting her fair hair off her shoulders and the subdued sound of the waves on the rocks far below in her ears, Polly thought that the only unsatisfactory thing about her wedding dream was that she could never force herself to go any further with it. She could not imagine the going-away suit which she would wear, or the hotel, or guest-house more likely, where she and Sunny would spend their honeymoon. She could not imagine them enjoying their wedding reception, far less climbing into their marriage bed. And as for the ordinary things, her making his breakfast, him going off to work, this seemed totally beyond her. In fact, she thought now, folding her sandwich paper into a neat square and shoving it into the pocket of her uniform jacket, she could not imagine herself spending a few weeks with Sunny, let alone the rest of her life.

The thought, coming spontaneously, jolted her. She frowned down at her black lace-up shoes and then did something she had not done for years and years. She pressed the heels of both hands into her eye sockets and pushed and pushed until she could see scarlet and gold with black squiggles and strange patterns shooting across her inner vision, until she felt as though her head were a huge balloon which must burst at any minute. When she could bear it no longer she took her hands away from her face and opened her eyes. And for one startling, extraordinary minute she saw, vaguely, the faint outline of a face, and seemed to hear, equally faintly, the echo of a voice. Then both faded and she was just Polly O'Brady, sitting in the sunshine feeling remarkably foolish, and knowing, with startling clarity, the answer to the questions which had been plaguing her of late. The wonderful wedding of which she had dreamed was just that – a dream. It had no hint of reality, no possibility that it might, one day, actually happen. You've been a complete and total fool, Polly O'Brady, she told herself furiously, beginning to cram the remains of her picnic into her pockets and standing up to brush the crumbs off the front of her skirt and the creases off the back. But just because you've been a fool until now, doesn't mean you have to go on being a fool for ever. You came back here to find the happiness you thought you had lost – well, you didn't find it because it isn't here, not any more. It's – it's up in Lincolnshire somewhere, and if you don't go up and see Tad and tell him you've made the biggest mistake of your life and ask him to forgive you, take you back, then whatever happens next, it won't be marriage to Sunny because he isn't the feller for you and you aren't the girl for him.

Why, when Sunny comes back on leave are you so thrilled at the thought of just seeing him again that you can't think of anything else? When you're with him, do you hang on his every word, want to please him, put yourself out for him? No, Polly O'Brady, you do not do any of those things. You are pleased to see him all right, but you don't want to make any special arrangements and very soon after his arrival you begin to wish he wasn't quite so sure of himself, quite so handsome and self-opinionated. You find fault with him – oh, not aloud, but in your head. He doesn't come up to your imaginary expectations, so you find yourself pretending. Pretending that the two of you are perfectly matched, that you'll marry, have a family, be happy together. When all the time – all the time, Polly O'Brady – you're really trying to fit him into quite another shape. To make tall, handsome, blond-haired Sunny into . . . into . . .

She picked up her bicycle from where she had rested it against a handy gorsebush and began to coast down towards the road. It crossed her mind to wonder what Sunny would think when she told him that it had all been a mistake, that she really wasn't the girl for him. She could write to him, a sort of 'Dear John' letter, except that it wouldn't be a letter like that at all because now that she was looking honestly at her relationship with Sunny, she realised that in all probability Sunny had been aware of the problem for some time.

She reached the main road, if you could call a winding country lane a main road, and turned left along it. She would go back now and tell Diane that she wouldn't be spending any more time on the island. She could say anything, she could even tell her the truth, because she and Diane had never had any secrets from one another, and she saw no reason why she should be secretive with her friend now.

Polly gritted her teeth as she slogged up the first of the hills which lay ahead. Diane thought I'd come back to see Tad, she remembered, and though of course I hadn't, perhaps, in a way, she was right. Perhaps it was really Tad who had made Holyhead so special.

But as she rode into the outskirts of Holyhead, it did cross Polly's mind to wonder what exactly she should do next. She had three whole days of her leave left, enough to get up to Lincolnshire – and back again, she supposed vaguely – but she did not have very much money, and she realised that knowing which airfield Tad was stationed at did not mean she would be able to run him to earth easily. The chances were, she knew, that the airfield would be some considerable way from the railway station, and Tad, being a pilot now, wouldn't be available all day as he had been as a flight mech. She could go up there and find he was flying the first night she arrived, in bed all the next day, and flying the following night. I could hang around there for a week and not see him and be court-martialled from the Navy for being AWOL, she told herself, pedalling desperately. Though if Tad knew I was there, surely he would get out of bed and see me, if only for a few minutes? She would have to borrow some money from Di for the rail fare and the taxi fare out to the airfield. Now she actually began to think about it, what was more, she would need to stay somewhere overnight . . .

But she had reached the lane which led to the backs of the houses in London Road and turned down it, reminding herself rather grimly that obstacles such as she had been outlining to herself were there to be conquered. Besides, she could scarcely rush off now, without a word to her hostess; Diane would be home from work in an hour; she would have a chat with her then and between them they could work out what best to do.

'Ring him,' Diane said, when Polly had blurted out her sudden and surprising change of heart. The two of them were sitting in the kitchen, preparing high tea, for Polly had agreed to defer rushing off anywhere until the following morning at least. 'No use tearing off to Lincolnshire only to find that your chap's gone off on leave, or is having a day's sleep before a big bombing raid or something. Ring first; be sensible for once.'

'I don't know his number,' Polly wailed. 'That's to say I don't know the number of the airfield, let alone what mess he's in. They're huge places, these airfields, Grace talks about them sometimes. What I t'ink is, Di, that they wouldn't wake him up for a telephone call from someone they'd never heared of, but if I was actually there, on the spot . . .'

'Ye-es, I know what you mean. But – oh, hang it, Poll, you're old enough to realise that fellers aren't made of stone! You've not been in touch, not so much as seen each other, for nearly two years – what on earth makes you think he's not got himself another bit of skirt in that time?'

'Another . . . oh, no, Di, you don't know Tad, he's not like that, he's—'

'You got yourself a feller, and what's more, you more or less boasted about Sunny to Tad from what you told me. He might have got himself a girl in a fit of pique, almost, and then found . . . well, he might have discovered he really did like her. Didn't you tell me about some girl in Dublin . . . I can't remember her name . . .'

'It was Angela,' Polly said, giving a derisive sniff. 'Little miss Angela, all sweetness and light. Huh! She didn't wait for him for long either, did she? First it were undying love, then it got a bit cooler, and then she t'rew him over for someone who was on the spot and probably better off, too.'

Diane giggled. 'I'm sorry, Poll, but whenever you get ratty your brogue comes back hot and strong,' she said, when Polly gave her an enquiring look. 'Anyway, I'm just warning you for your own good. You've treated Tad badly, you said as much earlier, so you couldn't be too surprised, surely, if he – well, if he'd decided there was no hope and had – had moved on, could you?'

'Yes, I could,' Polly said indignantly. She could feel the warmth rising to her cheeks at the mere suggestion that Tad might have looked at another girl. After all, they had been sweethearts for *years*. If she had been foolish enough to turn away from him for a matter of months, surely that would not change Tad? 'I'm only a kid; Tad's a man grown and he made up his mind he wanted me so why should he have changed?'

'You aren't only a kid or you wouldn't have been considering marriage to Sunny,' Diane reminded her shrewdly. 'Honestly, Polly, when you want to twist things to your best advantage there's no one who does it better! Well, if you're determined to go rushing up to Lincolnshire don't blame me if you get given the cold shoulder and end up with a broken heart. In a way,' she added, frowning at her friend, 'you almost deserve it, after the way you treated poor Tad.'

'Oh, pooh,' Polly said rudely.

Polly spent the evening sorting herself out, as Diane put it. First she buttonholed a naval rating who came from up north and got him to explain to her the exact location of Tad's airfield and the railway station to which she must go in order to visit it. Then she got train times from the booking clerk at the station, and when asked, he proved enthusiastic over helping her to plan her rather complicated cross-country journey. That done, she sat down and wrote to Sunny.

'What do you want to do that for?' Diane asked curiously as Polly settled herself at the kitchen table with a piece of borrowed writing paper and her fountain pen. 'You haven't even spoken to Tad yet, you've no idea what you're going to find when you do see him. Why, he might be married with a kid for all you know.'

Polly looked up at her, puzzled. 'So? What difference would that make? I'm writing to Sunny, not Tad.'

'Oh, for heaven's sake,' Diane said, really exasperated. 'What can you tell Sunny when you don't know a bloody thing yourself, woman? Use your loaf for once, O'Brady!'

Polly laid down her pen and looked up at Diane, then took a deep breath. 'Di, don't you *see*? You pretend I'm thick, but I can't compare wit' you! I've made up me mind that Sunny and meself really aren't suited, and that it's Tad I want – Tad I always wanted, I suppose. So the right thing to do is to let Sunny know as soon as possible. And don't think I'll be breaking his heart – Sunny's I mean – because it's my belief he probably hasn't really thought much past the end of the war and getting back to – to – well, whatever he wants to do in Civvy Street. Fellers don't think about marrying and such the way women do, I don't believe, so if he's thought of marriage at all it won't be with me. Just with some girl, I suppose. So you see, regardless of what happens when I see Tad,

I've got to tell Sunny that there's nothing between us.'

'Burning your boats, you mean, I suppose,' Diane said slowly. 'It's all very grand and honourable, but what if . . . what if . . .'

'If Tad turns me down I know, now, that if I love anyone it's him and I couldn't possibly turn to Sunny,' Polly said sturdily. 'Surely you see that, Di?'

'Ye-es, only . . . look Poll, a couple of days ago – no, a *day* ago, you were saying that you and Tad were just pals and the feller you really loved was Sunny! Don't you think it's just possible that when you see Tad again – and it's been two years, love, don't forget – you might easily discover that no matter how *he* feels, you – well, you don't really want to marry him, after all?'

'Mebbe,' Polly said. She picked up her pen again and began to write. 'But even so, I know it won't be Sunny. He's awful nice, but . . . Oh, I can't explain because you aren't in love with anyone, you don't know how different someone feels when . . . well, I can't explain.'

'Then if it all goes wrong I suppose you'll end up a spinster,' Diane said. 'What a waste that would be, you conceited little baggage! Oh, go on, burn your boats, chuck out the baby with the bathwater, cut off your nose to spite your face and all the rest. Only don't come crying to me when it all goes wrong.'

'Yes, I shall, and you'll sympathise wit' me and tell me all men are bastards,' Polly said, and Diane, despite herself, gave a chortle of amusement. 'Di, you're the best friend a girl ever had, but do buzz off and let me write me letter!'

It was a long and tiring journey across country to Lincoln, the nearest railway station to Tad's airfield, and then, Polly knew, a good taxi drive. As the train neared her destination, however, she became more and more worried by what she meant to do. Simply to turn up at the airfield, she was beginning to realise, would not get her very far – would get her nowhere, in fact. It was not as if she were in the WAAF; she was in another service and could scarcely expect to be allowed simply to walk across to the mess and demand to see Sergeant Pilot Thaddeus Donoghue – if that was still his rank, of course. By now he might be a warrant officer, or a flight lieutenant . . . Oh, anything might have happened to him, including, she supposed, demotion instead of promotion. No, she could not just walk in as she had planned, she would have to telephone first.

So when she reached Lincoln she went down the road, booked herself into a guesthouse where a wiry little woman in a stained wraparound apron was charging four bob for bed and breakfast, and set off for the nearest telephone kiosk. She found one only a few streets away and went rather timidly into its noisome interior, standing and dithering for several moments, undecided what to do. Indeed, it was only when a rat-faced RAF corporal rapped on the glass with a penny and mouthed at her that she snatched up the receiver, asked for the number and pushed her pennies into the slot.

She waited, moving restlessly, shifting her weight from one foot to the other. Suddenly, she was not at all sure that she was doing the right thing. Her mouth felt dry and her heart was bumping so loudly that she felt sure she would not be able to hear the voice which spoke when someone lifted the other receiver.

The bell rang, then stopped abruptly and a voice gave the name of the station in a clear, businesslike manner. Polly's heart, which had seemed determined, two seconds earlier, to crash its way out of her chest, was suddenly suspended, along with her voice and her breathing. For vital seconds she could not say a word, then began to speak whilst, on the other end of the line, the voice repeated, with some sharpness, the information it had already given.

Oh God, it must be one-way transmission, she could hear him but he couldn't hear her! What should she do? In another moment . . .

'Press Button A, caller,' a small, impersonal voice said. 'Have you pressed Button A?'

Polly's heartbeat returned to more or less normal and her ability to breathe came back. She pushed Button A, heard her pennies rattle irrevocably into the greedy maw of the telephone box, and spoke.

'H-hello? Oh, I w-wonder if you could help me . . . I'd like to speak to Sergeant Donoghue, please.'

'You've come through to the officers' mess,' the voice said a little impatiently. 'Hold on, though . . . you don't mean Tad Donoghue, I suppose? He's Pilot Officer Donoghue.'

'Oh! Y-yes, that's him,' Polly stammered, all her normal self-confidence gone. 'Umm . . . is he there?'

'Nope. Sleeping,' the voice said laconically. 'Try tomorrow around lunchtime.'

'Oh! But I only want a word wit' him,' Polly said pleadingly. 'Won't he be around before then? Or is he flying tonight?'

It was the wrong thing to say. Walls have ears and telephones, Polly knew, were at the mercy of every interested girl on every little local exchange. So she was not unduly surprised when the voice said, suddenly suspicious: 'Who *is* that? Because if it's you, Jenny, you ought to know better than I do what's going on up here. And if it isn't—'

'I'll try tomorrer, around noon,' Polly gabbled. 'Sorry to have troubled you,' and she slammed the receiver back on its rest and almost ran out of the kiosk, completely forgetting her gas-mask case and her purse until the rat-faced corporal shouted her back.

She almost ran back to her lodgings, tired after her long journey, hungry as a wolf now that the packed lunch the girls had provided was no more than a memory, and humiliated by the embarrassing telephone call. Who was Jenny, anyway? And what was she doing ringing Tad Donoghue, who was . . . Oh dammit, he *wasn't* her feller, that was the truth, and she was behaving every bit as stupidly as Diane had said, trying to run him to earth, never considering, not really, whether he wanted to see her again.

She went in through the front door and headed for the stairs to her attic bedroom, then paused in the small, square hallway. She was terribly hungry – she wondered if Mrs Rabbit or Tebbit or whatever she called herself might be willing to provide her with a cup of tea and a sandwich? She hadn't seemed a particularly welcoming woman but surely she would not see a WRN starve before her very eyes?

Polly was standing there, considering the question, when a door in the back of the hallway opened and her landlady appeared. She stared at Polly in a manner which seemed somehow accusatory, Polly thought.

'Yes? Forgot your room key?'

'No, but I've – I've rung me pal and – and he's workin' tonight and I'm starvin', so I am,' Polly said desperately, clutching her matelot's hat in both hands and feeling like a street beggar under the woman's sharp and condemnatory eyes. 'I wondered if – if—'

450

'Chip shop two streets away, but be sure you eat 'em outside and don't trek the smell of fish in here or I'll likely be havin' complaints,' the woman said so sharply that Polly jumped. 'I lock the front door at eleven o'clock, but if you want a key . . .'

'Oh! No, it's all right, I won't be long,' Polly said, and shot out of the front door before the older woman could say another word. Horrible old hag, she was thinking. Here's me, wit' me belly flappin' against me backbone and her not willin' to give me so much as an apple to keep me alive till morning. Still, I wouldn't mind some fish and chips. What's more, it'll give me something to think about until bedtime.

She found the chip shop, which had a couple of gingham-clothed tables in the window and bought a pot of tea and a plate of fish and chips which she ate on the premises, not grudging the extra sixpence since it meant she could have as much vinegar and salt as her food required. Then she made her way back to her lodgings and went straight up to bed. And though she had expected to lie awake half the night worrying, she was so tired, and so unhappy, that she slept as soon as her head touched the pillow.

Polly spent a miserable, rainy morning waiting for the time when she could ring the airfield once again and feeling frightened, apprehensive and generally far from her usual cheerful self. But the time passed and at last, at noon, she returned to the telephone box, lifted the receiver and asked the operator for the number and this time asked for Pilot Officer Donoghue.

'I'll fetch him,' the telephone answerer said laconically, and Polly thought, a trifle dismally, that she should have left her name the day before, and asked that Tad be by the telephone at noon. It would have saved time . . . but she had a little tower of pennies standing on the side waiting to be put into the slot and anyway, it was no more than a couple of minutes later that Tad said: 'Hello? Tad Donoghue speaking.'

'Tad!' Polly said, her voice coming out high, and squeakier than usual. 'Oh, Tad, it's me, Polly.'

'Who?'

'Polly O'Brady,' Polly said, dismayed to hear a slightly apologetic note creeping into her voice. 'It's ages since we met . . . and though I wrote to you over and over, you didn't reply apart from a couple of notes. So – so I thought it might be nice to meet up again.'

'You did?' He sounded so surprised that a hot colour rose in Polly's cheeks. 'Well, it's always nice to meet old pals, but I don't get off the airfield much. Where are you, anyway?'

'Lincoln. Staying at a guesthouse in town,' Polly said. 'I – I had some leave and I thought it would be nice to – to see each other again.'

'So you said.' There was a long pause. 'But don't you think it might be better, perhaps, to let sleeping dogs lie? I don't want to upset you, but . . . Oh, how's Sunny, by the way?'

Polly felt like blurting out that she didn't know, hadn't seen Sunny for months, that it was Tad she cared about, Tad she wanted to see, but innate caution made her say airily: 'Sure and he's fine, though he's at sea a good deal. How's Jenny?'

'Jenny?'

'When I phoned last night they asked me if I was Jenny,' Polly muttered. 'So I know she's a friend of yours. How is she? Who is she, for that matter?'

'Oh, Jenny. She's fine. She's one of the WAAFs on

452

the station,' Tad said. 'So you're in Lincoln. How long for?'

'I'm going back to Liverpool tomorrow,' Polly said stiffly. 'It doesn't matter, it was just a thought since I happened to be in the neighbourhood . . . It's been – been nice hearing your voice again, Tad, but—'

'What are you doin' in the neighbourhood, anyhow?' Tad cut in. 'We don't see many WRNs in this neck of the woods!'

'Oh! I – I came . . .' Polly thought about inventing a friend, then abruptly changed her mind. She had come to see Tad, she was desperate to see him, if he was going to tell her he had met someone else, wasn't interested in her any longer, then that was sad, but she would at least know it was no good hoping. So she took a deep breath, squared her shoulders and almost shouted into the receiver. 'I came to see you, Tad, because you'd not writ, and we're old pals and I missed you. But if you're too busy to come down and meet me, that's all there is to it and I'll go back home.'

'Well, I daresay I could spare half an hour,' Tad said cautiously. 'Do you know the Albion Hotel? It's in St Mary's Street – not far from the railway station.'

'Yes, I know it,' Polly said rather gloomily. She felt she could have answered a stiff examination paper on this wretched town since her landlady had turned her out at nine o'clock and she had spent the entire morning roaming the rain-soaked streets. 'What time, Tad?'

'Well, it's noon, or just after, now. Say, one o'clock? The landlord does quite decent sandwiches – I'll buy you lunch.'

'Thanks,' Polly said. 'Oh . . . the pips! See you at one, then. In the lounge bar?'

'One o'clock,' echoed Tad and put his receiver

453

down just as the operator asked Polly to cut her connection since others were waiting.

Polly came out of the box almost at a run, hot-faced and humiliated. He had not wanted to see her again, and she had more or less forced his hand, made him do the decent thing and see her. Well, when they met she would come out with it, baldly, tell him that she realised she had made a mistake, that she did not love Sunny, and ask him to give her another chance.

Outside in the rain, she turned up her coat collar, pulled her cap down further over her eyes, and sloshed through the puddles towards the Albion. This was easily the worst thing that had ever happened to her in her entire life – she had thrown herself at Tad and he had, verbally, pushed her away. He had not wanted to meet her and she had insisted even when it was plain that Tad felt it was a mistake. I've cheapened meself, Polly thought as she slogged on. Oh, well. At least we'll get it over and then I can start trying to rebuild my life with someone else, not Tad, clearly, nor Sunny, but someone as yet unmet.

A trifle cheered by this thought, which sounded exciting, and even more cheered by the recollection that her shame and humiliation were hers alone, that no one else would know that she had chased all the way up here only to be turned down, Polly continued to slog onwards, with the rain now beginning to channel down her neck and find its chilly way to her uniform underwear. At least, she comforted herself, she was going to see Tad presently, and surely, once they set eyes on each other, they would speedily recapture their old friendship? But in her heart she was beginning to doubt it.

Tad came off the phone and stood in the mess for a

moment, gazing in front of him and trying to conquer the big grin which was beginning to spread across his countenance. Polly had rung him, admitted she had come all the way to Lincolnshire especially to see him. Surely that must mean something, indicate that her old fondness for him was still there? He crossed the room and went out of the door to get his mackintosh, for there was no point in leaving the airfield it in this downpour. He was halfway back to his hut when someone caught up with him. Jim Stratton grabbed his arm.

'Where you goin', Tad old feller? I thought you and me were going to have some grub in the mess and then going to see a flick? Who was it on the telephone, by the way? Jenny? Only I thought she was away on a course or something.'

Tad descended abruptly from the clouds. 'No, it wasn't Jenny, it was a girl I was friendly with in Dublin,' he said slowly. 'She thought she'd look me up – we were good pals once, so we were.'

'Oh? But I thought you and Jenny had a thing going.'

'I've told you often enough that me and Jenny are just friends,' Tad pointed out. 'Anyway, meeting a girl doesn't mean you're going to marry her, does it? I'm only *meeting* Polly since she's in the neighbourhood.'

'Oh aye? Isn't she the one who gave you the brushoff just before we all left for Rhodesia? Didn't she write for a bit, only you wouldn't reply, said it was best left.'

'Oh damn you, Jim,' Tad said, grinning despite himself. He and Jim had been together now for more than two years and he must have told Jim a hundred times about his Polly and how she was going to marry

455

another feller. 'Yes, that's Polly. I don't know why she's come to see me, but . . . well, I can't help hoping that she's realised that Sunny feller isn't the one for her.'

'And you are, I suppose,' Jim said, breaking into a run as Tad did so that they crashed into the hut together. 'Remember the last time she got you to go chasing off after her? Someone had got fresh with her and who did she turn to? It'll be the same this time, you mark my words. She wants something, that one, and you'll go chasing after her all over again and get asked for . . . well, whatever it is she wants. Likely she's in the club and wants advice.'

'In the . . .? Good God, Jimmy, whatever makes you think that? She said Sunny's mostly at sea, she didn't say she was in any sort of trouble, didn't even suggest that she was after help or advice. You're a bleedin' cynic, that's your trouble. Probably she simply wants to say she's sorry for the way she treated me that time. Anyway, I'm meeting her in the Albion in an hour. There's a bus which stops at the main gate in fifteen minutes, if I'm quick.'

'Shall I come in as well, then? Oh, I won't come to the Albion, I do have *some* tact, but we could meet up afterwards to see that flick,' Jim suggested as Tad dived into his room and began to sort through his possessions. 'Or are you going to spend the afternoon with her?'

'I don't know,' Tad said. He sorted out some money and shoved it into the pocket of his tunic, then grabbed his mackintosh. 'Look, I'm sorry about the flick, but I don't think it's on. I'll see you when I get back, though.' He grinned at his friend. 'Come in on the bus by all means, but you'll miss whatever delicacy the mess has to offer, and the Albion only does sandwiches.'

'I won't bother,' Jim said. He turned away. 'Have fun, Tad, and don't forget, if she's after something just you think twice before knuckling down and handing it to her on a plate. Especially if she's looking for someone to take on responsibility for a bun in the oven.'

In too much of a hurry to answer him back, Tad merely cuffed his friend across the ear as he tore past, and by a dint of running, managed to get aboard the bus, which was early. He settled himself on the back seat, shook as much rain off his coat as he could, and then concentrated on getting his fare out of an inner pocket and asking the conductor what time he expected to arrive in the city.

Having satisfied himself that he would be on time at the rendezvous, Tad then sat there and began to wonder whether Jim could possibly be right; could Polly have come to see him because she was in trouble of some kind? The more he thought about it the likelier it seemed. After all, when he had been at Valley Polly had been friendly with him because she wanted to learn how to ride his motorbike, and to service it too. And the only time she had been in trouble, the night she had been more or less kidnapped by the lecherous lorry driver, she had rung him up, with just that little catch in her voice that he so loved, begging him to rescue her.

But . . . a baby? It just was not possible that Polly could be having a baby by some bloke, or that she would dream, for one moment, of turning to him for help if the father had not wanted to marry her. But there was, he supposed wretchedly, a fair chance that she was in some other sort of scrape, that she had felt he was the only person to whom she could turn. In a way, it was nice that she still trusted him, still felt he would help her, but dammit, that wasn't the way he wanted Polly to think of him, as a mug to get her out of trouble! He wanted . . . The truth was, he did not know what he wanted. I'll just have to wait and see what happens when we meet, he told himself, hunched down in his seat staring through the smeared window at the lashing rain outside. After all, this time he was in a much stronger position than she. She had come running to him and he could either accept her or send her home with her tail between her legs, depending how he felt. And as the journey continued he found that his intentions were crystallising into a firm resolve not to be hurried or pushed into anything again, not even mere friendship. She's let you down with a big thump in the past, Donoghue, he reminded himself. This time, play it a bit more cautiously. Besides, she'll have changed, as I have. We're almost like two strangers meeting after all this time, and strangers shouldn't leap into each other's arms. I'll play it cool, and remember what Jim said. If she's in trouble then she should ask her good friend Sunny to get her out of it!

In the train going home, Polly sat back in her seat and thought of the last couple of days and, most of all, of the meeting which had taken place between Tad and herself the previous lunchtime. It had been sticky, she reminded herself, especially at first. She had been sitting in a corner of the lounge bar when he had entered the room and had sprung to her feet and gone towards him, eager for his usual beaming smile, his hug.

Instead, he had taken her hands, gazed seriously down at her for a moment, and then said: 'Well? What's gone wrong, Polly? Because I don't imagine you've come all this way just to tell me you're well and happy!'

Whether it was his words or the way he stared at her Polly could not have said, but suddenly it was just plain impossible to say: 'I came because it's you I've wanted, all along. The whole business with Sunny was a dreadful mistake, and I've never thought of you as a brother, honest to God, Tad. Will you make up, so's we can go back to being friends? Well, I hope we'll be more than friends.' Instead, she stammered that of course there was nothing wrong, that she was in her usual good health and she had come to see him because . . . because they were old pals, weren't they, and she had some leave owing, and it had seemed like a good idea at the time . . .

Here she ran out of steam and Tad, guiding her to a corner table and going over to the bar, seemed not to notice the garbled half-sentences which she had uttered. He did not ask her what she wanted to drink but came back with two halves of bitter and the good news that sandwiches were on their way. Polly, who detested bitter, sipped cautiously and tried not to pull a face, and whilst they waited for the food, Tad first of all stared into space and then, apparently deciding that this was a waste of what little time they might have together, addressed her seriously.

'Polly, it was good of you to come, I appreciate it, don't get me wrong. But you know, you've changed a great deal in the last couple of years and I guess I have too.'

Polly nodded, trying not to eye him too obviously. He was broader, more substantial altogether than the Tad she remembered, and his skin was so brown, so healthily tanned! In Dublin the pair of them might have given the outward appearance of a tan but it was usually dirt, particularly in Tad's case. This tan, however, was a real one, made by the sun which had lightened his hair from mid-brown to fudge-colour streaked with gold, and it gave him an additional confidence. So she had to admit that he had changed and supposed, with real uncertainty, that she, too, must have altered.

She had said as much in a rather small voice just as the sandwiches put in an appearance. Tad handed the plate to her, then took one himself and spoke somewhat thickly through his first mouthful. 'Look, alanna, are you in – in some sort of trouble? Because if so, I've got to know about it before I can do much to help. If I can do anything, that is.'

Polly, with a sandwich halfway to her mouth, frowned across at him. Until that moment he had seemed calm, sure of himself. Now for some reason the colour in his cheeks had darkened and he looked ill at ease, as though he thought that she must have a guilty secret which he did not much wish her to reveal. So it was rather sharply that she said: 'In trouble? Me? No, indeed, Tad, I'm fine, so I am. What about you?'

He grinned, but did not answer her last question. 'Well, all right, you're fine and just came up here to – to renew old acquaintance. Is that right?'

'Yes,' Polly said baldly. She would have left it at that, gone on to talk of other things, but suddenly a sort of wild defiance took hold of her. Why should she be ashamed to tell Tad that she was no longer going out with Sunny? Why could she not tell him that far from thinking of him as a brother . . . Hastily, before she could change her mind, she spoke. 'Tad, you once said you wanted us to be more than pals. Do – do you still feel the same?'

He looked at her then, round brown eyes rounding still further, looking first astonished and then, to her chagrin, slightly amused. 'Well, next t'ing I know you'll be proposin' marriage, Poll, and it's not Leap Year for a while yet!'

Polly felt so annoyed with him that for two pins, she told herself, she would have leaned across the table and rammed his sandwich down his self-satisfied throat. But she remembered Diane's cautions and spoke calmly, or as calmly as she could. 'I'm proposin' nothing, Tad Donoghue, I'm just asking you. Do you or do you not want to – to be a bit more than just pals?'

This time Tad neither laughed nor turned away. He gazed thoughtfully at her, clearly considering his reply, and when at last he spoke it was seriously, with no lurking smile. 'Look, Poll, you might have been right when you said – well, that I'd been like a brother to you. The truth is, I loved you when you were a little girl, a kid of three or four, but now you're a woman, and as you said earlier, we've both changed. I – I think I'd like to get to know this new Polly better, that's what I think. So how about it? I know we're a long way apart but the war's going to end soon, everyone knows it, and in the meantime we can ring each other up, write letters – well, no, all right, I'm a lousy correspondent, you've told me so – and meet up now and then. I have leaves and so do you; we could meet halfway, or if I've got a week I could come over to the 'Pool and if you've got one you could come up to Lincoln. What do you say?'

Polly stared at him, two entirely different emotions warring within her. In one way she was glad of his suggestion, because he was right, they had both changed and she felt that she needed time to get to know this sturdier, more self-confident Tad. But her other emotion was that of pique that he had almost thrown her attempt to get close to him once again back in her face. Polly had had a great many boyfriends, a great many young men had vied for her attentions. Never before, she realised, had any of them suggested that they ought to get to know one another better before going on dates and canoodling at dances. Still, she could see Tad's point. If, as seemed possible, he had only loved her with what they called puppy love, then clearly he was going to have to get to know her all over again before embarking on a more serious relationship. So finally, having thought it over for at least five minutes, she heaved a sigh and nodded. 'Right you are, Tad. But how will I know when to ring? I mean, you're flying at night and sleeping during the day . . . and I can't say ring me, because we aren't on the telephone at home – did you know I was living at home now? – and I'm hardly ever at the depot, not now I'm despatch riding.'

'You just have to phone the mess, and if I'm not there I'll leave a message that Polly O'Brady's to be told when I'm available,' Tad said, so blandly that once more, Polly's fingers itched to give him a ding round the ear. 'I could drop you a postcard when I've got leave, if I've not been able to speak to you on the telephone. Would that do?'

'I suppose so,' Polly said grudgingly, and began to concentrate on her sandwiches and beer. The beer wasn't too bad, she discovered, if you stopped breathing through your nose, swallowed hard and quickly jammed a hunk of sandwich into your mouth. She felt let down, with a sort of inner ache in the pit of her stomach, because she had had such romantic ideas of this meeting. She had been going to run into Tad's arms and their lips would have met and they would have – have melded into one person, love enveloping them in a warm glow, every eye softening with tears, mouths trembling into gentle smiles . . .

Still, there you were. It was not going to be so easy, but that didn't mean she intended to give up. She had made up her mind years and years ago that one day she would marry Tad, and though she had gone astray a bit in between, the resolve was strong in her again now. Tad was doomed, whether he knew it or not, and she, Polly, would simply have to make the best of every opportunity to see him so that he fell under her spell once more and wanted to marry her as badly as she wanted to marry him.

So the two of them drank their beer and ate their sandwiches and in between bites Tad told her a little of his life in the Air Force. His work was often highly secret, and always interesting, because his Beaufighter was what they called a pathfinder, which meant that he went ahead of the heavy bombers and their fighter escorts and saw the attackers safely to their targets. Sometimes he dropped leaflets over enemy territory, sometimes he carried a photographer, sometimes he simply went on reconnaissance flights. He talked so interestingly that Polly almost forgot to eat, but it occurred to her, uneasily, that what he did was very dangerous. Even now, with peace looming, he was in danger, she thought, whenever he flew. Of course she had known that flying was dangerous, as she had known that Sunny's voyaging through the Arctic waters on his way to and from Russia was dangerous, but she had never really thought of it quite like this. Tad's sturdy, self-reliant body could as easily spiral down to earth in a blazing plane as anyone's . . . I'm going to worry now every time I think of him night-flying, Polly thought with deep foreboding. Oh, if something were to happen to Tad I just couldn't bear it, whether he'll be my proper boyfriend or not. I wish I hadn't come, then I wouldn't have known . . . but then I wouldn't have seen him, wouldn't even have had a chance of getting close to him again, and that would have been worse, much worse. Everyone worries in wartime, she concluded, drinking the last of her horrible bitter, so why should I be any different?

When the sandwiches were eaten and Polly had told Tad a bit about her own life and work they went and saw a flick, and Tad had not even held her hand in the sad bits. He had bought her an ice cream in the interval and passed her his handkerchief when she began to snivel a bit, but that was the closest he had come to touching her. And then, when they came out of the cinema and walked back to her lodgings, she had meant to invite him in and see if he would try to kiss her, either in the privacy of her bedroom, if her landlady was not around, or on the hard little sofa in the ugly, overfurnished front room if she was. But before she could even open the front door with the key the landlady had lent her, Tad had taken her hand, squeezed it between both of his, and told her, in an infuriatingly avuncular manner, to run along in now, since he would have to belt across the city to get the bus back to camp or he would be late for his briefing and that would never do.

Polly had stood and stared after him as he had hurried away, almost unable to believe what was happening to her. This was Tad, who adored her, who had always tried to please her, who had vowed undying love at least twice when they were both stationed on Anglesey. But then the front door had opened behind her and her landlady had said: 'Are you coming in now, Miss O'Brady? I'm making meself a cup of tea, you're welcome to share the pot if you're not on your way out again,' and pride had stiffened her backbone, driven the tears out of her eyes, and got her into the kitchen to drink the proferred cup.

And now, sitting in the train chugging back to Liverpool, she wondered rather dismally where it would all end. Not, she thought glumly, with her having to fight Tad off, that at least was plain. She was going to have to woo him, by the looks of it, and she was not at all sure that she wanted to do any such thing. It was his job to woo her, not vice versa!

But oh, it had been good to see him! The way his hair fell, the deep, wicked dimple which came and went in one cheek when something truly amused him, even his habit of cracking his knuckles when he was embarrassed . . . Yes, it was worth fighting for Tad, she decided, suddenly remembering the voice on the phone asking her if she were Jenny. She had not managed to cross-question Tad about Jenny . . . but she could drop an artful little question or two into their very next telephone conversation, at least she could find out whether Jenny was competition, or merely an acquaintance.

And then there was the worry; worrying over his safety, she could see, was going to become a part of her life until this wretched, horrible war ended. She felt strongly that no one should be expected to worry over the safety and well-being of a fellow who was not even prepared to make a play for you, but there it was. When you loved someone, you worried about them whether you wanted to or not. It was even possible, she supposed, feeling a little glow of satisfaction at the thought, that Tad would worry about her now. After all, she was dashing around on a motorbike, living in a port, a prey to all sorts of dangers – oh yes, Tad ought to worry about her, all right.

Satisfied on that score, Polly leaned back in her seat and prepared to work for Tad, as well as worry over him.

Tad returned to the airfield feeling extremely pleased with himself. Dear little Polly, how cast down she had been at his apparent lack of interest, and how her eyes had sparkled as, he guessed, she decided that he *should* fall in love with her whether he wanted to or not! The truth was, he knew, that he had never stopped loving her, but he had realised long ago that Polly, little darling though she might be, did not value what came easily in the way she would value something she had had to fight for. So he had not told her he loved her and wanted her desperately, had not told her that Jenny, nice little WAAF that she was, was only a friend. In fact, he had told her he was flying tonight though he would not be doing so for another forty-eight hours. It had gone to his heart to deceive her, but if she believed she had competition for his affection, it would make her value him more.

So he felt like dancing as he made his way to the mess; he felt that his life was on course once more.

Sunny got the letter when he next came ashore, and was far less troubled by it than Polly had anticipated, in fact it relieved his mind considerably. For a start, she had said she intended to make friends with Tad again, and this, he thought approvingly, was a good thing. He had been aware for some time that Polly missed Tad and wanted to get back on good terms with him, and he had been equally aware that he was no longer the boy who had once talked of sharing his future with Polly. The war had changed them both. Indeed even the peace, when it came, was uncertain because he was going to have to make up his mind what he wanted to do after the war, and he was not at all sure that he could face up to Civvy Street. Nor, when he came to think about it, did he altogether want to do so. His skipper had suggested that Sunny might carry on with his job, for a while at any rate, and Sunny thought that it might be the best thing to do. Once peace was declared, he assumed that the need for the Russian convoys would cease, but that did not mean that ships would not be wanted.

So Sunny wrote back, saying despite her letter he hoped they could still be friends and promising to come and see her the next time he was in Liverpool.

Chapter Seventeen

From the moment that Mr Churchill announced that Tuesday, 8th May was to be 'Victory in Europe Day', and that everyone would have a day off in order to celebrate, Snowdrop Street became a place of wild excitement, with everyone planning what they should do.

Folk had known that the moment would come, of course, they just had not known exactly when, and they had been saving up goodies for weeks. Months, in some cases, Deirdre said proudly, fishing her little hoard out from the tin box under the lowest shelf in the pantry. There was to be a street party, and a bonfire, despite the fact that the government had said bonfires were forbidden. 'Who'll be on the watch if everyone's to have a holiday?' Deirdre had said when Peader had been doubtful about the bonfire. 'Besides, how else can we get rid of the beastly blackout if there's no bonfire to burn the blinds on?'

Church bells, which had been silent for the whole war, only to be sounded in case of an invasion, would ring out once more. Lights would blaze, flags would fly, folk would sing and dance and there would be a spread the like of which none of the kids in the street had ever seen.

Polly had been as wildly excited as everyone else, and had done all she could to help, both because she was looking forward to the celebrations and because of a private reason of her own. She intended, a day or so before the great event, to ring Tad at his Lincolnshire station and invite him to spend his leave – he would surely have leave? – at the house in Snowdrop Street. They would be together at last. She was in a mood of wild exhilaration, making plans for what they would do now that the end of the war had at last arrived. And in that atmosphere of gaiety and victory, surely it would be no particularly hard matter to persuade Tad to forget the bad times and remember only the good? There was the wretched Jenny, of course, but Polly always tried to put Jenny out of her mind. Tad had assured her Jenny was 'just a friend', and by and large she believed him. There was no doubt that Tad liked Jenny. He said she was great fun to be with, even-tempered and easy to please. Naturally, in view of this, Polly had sometimes suppressed a desire to say something sharp to Tad and had been as mild and biddable as possible, and she was sure it must be paying off, and that Tad would, very soon indeed, succumb to her charms and tell her that he loved the new Polly as much as the old and ask her to be his wife. Dreamily, she contemplated a future shared with Tad and looked in jewellers' windows at engagement rings.

So, as she worked, she was quietly content, quietly planning her own celebrations which would, of course, take place just as soon as Tad was hers once more. She intended to marry him in due course but occasionally common sense came to her aid and reminded her that no one, not even she and Tad, could live on fresh air. They would both have to get jobs in Civvy Street before they could possibly start planning their future together.

The bonfire which the street had planned might have been difficult some years earlier, for Snowdrop

Street was right in the city with few open spaces, but now, thanks to Jerry, there were plenty of large bombsites, already thickly overgrown with the tall pink spears of rosebay willowherb. These open spaces were just the sort of area where a nice big bonfire could blaze without danger of hurting anyone's property and all over the country, Polly imagined, they were being put to the same use. So she helped the kids from the surrounding streets, the flower streets, to collect everything burnable and piled it high, and then she went and helped Deirdre to bake a number of cakes and pies, and she and Peader borrowed every trestle table they could lay their hands on from church halls and schools, and then they sat back and waited hopefully for a fine day on which to celebrate.

At the weekend Polly put in her usual call to Tad, determined to persuade him to get leave and come to the Snowdrop Street party.

She got through easily and in her new, gentle tone, greeted Tad enthusiastically and asked him what he meant to do the following Tuesday.

'Tuesday?' Tad said, apparently less aware than Polly of the importance of the occasion. 'I dunno – why?'

'Oh, Tad,' Polly cried, softly reproachful. 'You can't have forgot – Mr Churchill's given everyone the day off to celebrate – it's VE Day!'

'Oh aye,' Tad said. 'Well now, what had I meant to do? Stay in bed late, I reckon, and—'

'Stay in bed later, wit' all the country celebrating?' Polly asked incredulously. 'You can't do that, Tad – think what you'll be missing! Why, we're having a street party, we've all give food and Mammy's made *vats* of lemonade and ginger beer, and there's to be fireworks, and flags, and games . . . We – we t'ought, all of us, that you'd come across to see us, and stay for the day and mebbe the night too. There's no one in the spare room, and I know you're bound to have leave owing, because you've not had any time off since that day in Lincoln an' even then you had to go off early, flying.'

She had tried not to sound injured, but knew that she sounded at least disappointed at his failure to leap at her idea like a trout at a fly, but she kept her tone wheedling rather than reproachful, bearing in mind that wretched, goody-goody Jenny.

'Oh, I couldn't do that,' Tad said immediately, however. He sounded quite shocked. 'I couldn't let me pals down, Poll. There's all sorts of goings-on planned in Lincoln and the NAAFI are running a big dance and a special dinner . . . No, I couldn't let me pals down.'

'But just now you couldn't even remember what Tuesday was,' Polly wailed. 'And won't your pals have just as good a time if you aren't there, then? Because you can't have done much, or you wouldn't have forgot. Oh, Tad, I've done no end, honest I have. I've beetled about getting fuel for the bonfire, and I've helped Mammy wit' the cooking and Daddy wit' fetching chairs and tables and I've even done sewin', and you know how I do hate me needle.'

Tad sighed. 'Sorry, love, it can't be done,' he said, his tone complacent. 'Well, you have fun now, and t'ink about me stuck up here doing me best to have fun as well.'

It was at this point that Polly's careful plans deserted her. 'Who with?' she demanded, her voice strident with suspicion. 'Are you goin' to watch fireworks and eat your dinner wit' that Jenny you telled me about?'

'She's bound to be there,' Tad admitted. 'After all, as I've told you a thousand times, Poll, she's me good friend so there's no reason—'

Polly cut across this thoroughly infuriating sentence. 'Tad Donoghue, if you don't want to come to our street party then I can't make you,' she shouted wildly into the receiver. 'But I'm tellin' you, when you *do* deign to come back to Liverpool, don't you bother calling in Snowdrop Street, because I shan't be after wantin' to see you! I'm going to send a telegram to Sunny this moment, asking him to come and stay and be me – me partner. Well? What do you say to that?'

'I'm sorry, Poll,' Tad said, but he didn't sound sorry, he sounded amused, which only added fuel to Polly's anger. 'But I suppose, if you feel that strongly—'

'I do,' Polly shrieked, discretion cast to the four winds and temper and disappointment bringing tears to her eyes. 'Why, if you had any feelings for me, Tad Donoghue . . .'

'You're my good pal,' Tad said soothingly. 'Calm down, Poll, and remember—'

He got no further. Well, he might have done had Polly not slammed the receiver back on its rest and stalked, trembling with rage, out of the telephone box. And presently, when she was calmer and could think straight, she realised that the careful work she had been putting into her relationship with Tad ever since the visit to Lincoln had just gone up in smoke. He would be telling himself this very minute that Polly had not changed at all, she was still the bad-tempered, spoilt child he had known in Dublin. And he would be turning to Jenny and asking her . . . asking her . . .

Tears blinding her, Polly turned round and rushed back to the telephone box. She asked the operator, in trembling tones, for the number and had a considerable wait – 'Line's busy,' said the operator impersonally – before at last she got through to the mess.

But not to Tad. 'He's not here,' the officer who answered the telephone said. 'Is that Polly? No, he's had to go out – wasn't he on the telephone to you just now? I thought he said you'd just spoken to him.'

'I – I had,' Polly said, tears running down her cheeks and tasting salt in her mouth as she opened it to speak. 'But – but I've j-just remembered something I – I forgot. I'll ring later.'

She had rung later, but somehow, Tad was never available, and it seemed pointless to write a letter. She could say she was sorry, hadn't meant a word of it, would accept him on any terms, but what was the use? If he wouldn't speak to her then he was unlikely to take much notice of a letter. So, on the eve of the day for which she had longed so passionately, Polly went to bed in a very subdued frame of mind, quite seeing that her horrid temper had ruined her whole life for her and quite at a loss, for the moment, as to how she was to mend the breach she had caused between Tad and herself.

Besides, she thought drearily, as she turned out the light and rolled up the blackout blind for the last time, by now he's probably asked that horrible Jenny to marry him, and I hope she makes him very unhappy, so I do!

Then she got into bed and after indulging in the luxury of a good cry into her pillow she settled down and, despite her conviction that she would never sleep, was soon dreaming.

On the morning of 8th May, Polly woke early to find

pale sunshine pouring in through her bedroom window. It was early, but she slid cautiously out of bed and padded over to the window, telling herself that she might as well check that it had not rained in the night because if it had, some work might be needed on the bonfire, and there might be work to do on the street itself, which must be dry and decent before they could set out the tables and chairs.

But all was well. The night, clearly, had been as fine as the day which now beamed down upon Liverpool. The sky was a deep blue, there was not a cloud in sight and the sunshine was growing brighter as the sun rose in the heavens. It's going to be a marvellous day, Polly told herself, going over to her washstand and struggling out of her nightdress. Well, it would be a marvellous day if . . . but there's no use repining. I lost my temper and now I've lost Tad, and I've just got to make the best of it. Anyway, it wasn't kind of him to refuse to speak to me when I phoned, and heaven knows I phoned often enough to show anyone I was sorry, so I was. But that's Tad for you: unforgiving. And who wants a feller like that, a feller who can't forgive a person for making one little mistake and having a bit of a shout because they were disappointed?

Unfortunately, however, Polly knew very well that the answer to this rhetorical question, which should be a firm 'No one sensible wants a feller like that,' was in fact, very different. One person wanted a feller like Tad – no, not a feller like him, she wanted Tad himself – and that of course was Polly O'Brady.

However, she could not stand around in her room feeling miserable, not with such an important day about to start. She chucked her nightdress on to her unmade bed, poured water from her jug into the pottery basin and seized the small piece of soap which was all she had left until Mammy found some more, somewhere. She washed all over, rinsed herself, dried on the small scrap of towel hanging beside the washstand and began to dress, her uniform all cleaned and pressed for this special day.

Once she was ready she headed for the stairs. Deirdre was already in the kitchen, with the kettle boiling on the hob and a panful of cold potatoes frying over the flame. Some rather suspicious-looking sausages were sharing the pan and Polly gave a sigh at the sight of them. Now bacon would have been nice but was rarely available, so it would have to be sausages and some of those delicious fried potatoes.

'Morning, Mammy,' Polly said, going over to the Welsh dresser and beginning to lay the table. 'Is Daddy about yet?'

'He's walked down to the tram to meet Monica,' Deirdre said, turning the potatoes and sucking in her breath as the fat spat. 'They'll be back in a few minutes, so we can all have breakfast together. Be a love, alanna, and slice me some bread and put it on the plates.' She glanced round the kitchen as though walls truly did have ears. 'I managed to get a few shell-eggs, so I thought we'd begin our celebration early wit' them and the sausages and spuds. After all, heaven knows when we'll have our dinner, and the party won't start until four o'clock so's everyone can be there.'

'I heard from Grace; she's coming back to the 'Pool if she can manage it, and Sunny says he might come too, because his ship's in dock for some sort of a refit,' Polly said, getting the loaf out of the crock and beginning to slice. 'Oh, it'll be a grand day, so it will, but it'll be best of all to see me pals, if we manage to meet up. Only I guess there'll be crowds everywhere, and neither Grace nor Sunny could say for certain where they'd be, or at what time.'

'Never mind; if they're home they'll make their way to Snowdrop Street sooner or later. But it's a pity Tad can't get away,' Deirdre said with a shrewd look at her daughter. Polly, noticing it, sighed inwardly. She had not said much about Tad since the fateful phone call the previous weekend, but she realised that her mammy, who knew her so well, probably guessed what had happened. 'Still, everyone will be wanting leave for today, I reckon,' Deirdre continued, moving the pan off the heat. 'Mebbe next week or the week after our Tad will turn up here, eh?'

Polly finished slicing the bread and turned to her mother with a deep sigh. She might as well spill the beans, she was no use at telling fibs, never had been. And besides, Mammy and Daddy wouldn't blame her; they would be comforting and loving. It would ease her conscience to tell Mammy the truth. 'Tad won't be coming, not today nor in a few days,' she said bluntly. 'I shouted at him when I rang to invite him here and he said he couldn't let his pals down. I – well, I lost me temper, Mammy, and told him that if he didn't come today he needn't bother to come at all. I – I said I'd write to Sunny and get him to come instead. I was horrid, so I was.'

'Lovers' tiff,' Deirdre said comfortably just as the back door opened and Peader ushered Monica inside. 'Don't you worry, alanna, these things happen no matter how we try to avoid 'em. Monica, me dear, sit you down, I'm just going to dish up.'

Sunny and Grace had met that day entirely by chance since neither could possibly have known the whereabouts of the other. Sunny's ship had come in for a refit but though he had hoped to be in Liverpool for the celebrations he knew that everything depended on the trains, on the hour that his ship's captain saw fit to dismiss him, and on luck.

In the event, luck and his skipper were definitely on his side, with the result that he was told good-humouredly the previous evening that he could make himself scarce so long as he was back at his post before the ship sailed on the Wednesday, and managed to catch the milk train next morning, arriving in Liverpool after various changes and connections, to his own delight and astonishment, before noon.

He had come into Lime Street, of course, along with a great many other men and women in uniform, and the first person he saw as he got down from his train was a neatly uniformed WAAF with light brown, shiny hair and a pale, heart-shaped face, walking along the opposite platform. As she turned towards him her face lit up in a smile of such sweetness and genuine pleasure that he felt his heart give a little leap. 'Grace! By all that's wonderful, if this isn't the strangest thing! So you *did* get leave, after all, and the first person I see when I reach Liverpool is you!'

'Hello, Sunny,' Grace said. Her smile did not falter but he saw a certain wariness come into her blue-grey eyes. 'I daresay you're off to Snowdrop Street as well?'

Sunny had been about to agree that he was indeed off to Snowdrop Street when he changed his mind. He held out a hand and took hers and watched pink roses bloom on her cheeks. 'No, why should I go to Snowdrop Street when you're here, and we can have a good time, just the two of us?' he said. 'Oh, we'll mebbe go round there later, queen, but not yet, eh? There's a lot to do and see in the city and two's easier than half-a-dozen, wouldn't you say? Besides, they've gorra street party and all sorts this afternoon. We'll spend the morning together, just catching up on what's going on, shall us?'

Grace had nodded eagerly, squeezed his hand – then sighed doubtfully. 'Well, I'd love that, Sunny, but . . . don't you think Polly will be expecting you?'

'No,' Sunny said light-heartedly. 'You know our Poll, she'll enjoy herself no matter what, and there's plenty of fellers around today. She wrote a while back, said something about someone called Tad . . . I got the feeling that he was special to her. So come on, where'll we go first? I haven't eaten since last night, how about a meal? We might find some fish and chips!'

And the two of them had set off, heading for Byrom Street where Sunny remembered a place which, in peacetime, had been famous for its excellent food.

As Sunny had said, there was plenty for two young people to do and see in a city celebrating the end of a long, hard-fought war. They ate their meal, talking eagerly about their jobs, their friends, fleshing out the letters that they had been exchanging regularly, now, for a twelve-month. And then they went out into the excited crowds to begin to celebrate.

By nightfall, Sunny and Grace had watched the firework displays, danced in the street, eaten food which had been offered to anyone in uniform at various street parties and caught up with each other's news. With some reluctance they had returned to Lime Street since both were due back in their service positions by next day, and sat on a wooden seat under the clock waiting for their trains and discussing their future. Sunny waxed eloquent on his captain's suggestion that he should stay with the service, and told Grace impressively that he could have a fine career in the Navy even in peacetime. He didn't want to be a sailor for the rest of his life, he told her, but just for a few years, until things were more settled. As he talked, Sunny caught hold of Grace's hand and thought that this was the first time he had noticed a likeness between Grace and Polly, though he knew that they were sisters. Of course Polly was a little raver for looks and Grace no more than passable, but somehow, today, he thought that had he had to choose he would have put Grace as the more striking of the two. Polly had golden curls and blue eyes and a dear little face, but Grace . . . Grace had style, he decided, and a sort of elegance which the bubbly Polly most certainly did not possess. I'm proud to be seen with her, Sunny thought, and was astonished at himself. He was a catch and he knew it, girls flocked round him, always had, and here he was with a girl he had never thought so much as pretty, admiring her style and elegance, two attributes which he had never even thought about before. But he dragged his mind away from his companion's looks and listened to her conversation, noticing also for the first time what a pretty voice she had, with almost no trace of the scouse accent which he himself had retained.

Grace, knowing nothing of his thoughts, continued to talk naturally and earnestly. She had told him several times of her life in New York with Sara, and of how she missed Jamie and her other friends, so now it seemed quite natural to tell him of her plans for the peace. 'I've had a lovely letter from Sara, telling me that I'm welcome to live in the flat again just as soon as I can get a passage,' she said. 'Poor Sara, it's been a horrid time for her, though she's known nothing of the shortages and the bombing and so on. But she doesn't think Brogan will get back as quickly as they would both like, so I suppose she'd be even more pleased to see me.'

Sunny stared at her. He could feel his mouth dropping open and, what was more, suddenly heard his own voice, with a note of almost desperate incredulity in it, say, 'Get a passage? You don't mean ... you can't mean you're thinkin' of goin' back to the States when the war ends?'

Grace, in her turn, stared. 'Well, I think so,' she said slowly. 'I don't suppose there will be much for me here, Sunny – in the way of work, I mean. What's more, though I could live at the Strawb for a bit, I suppose, I couldn't expect the O'Bradys to take me in again. They'll be having all their family home, not just Polly. No, it's better that I go back to Sara. She says the delicatessen where I used to work were delighted to hear I'd be returning there and said my job was waiting for me. So you see—'

Sunny interrupted her without apology. 'But Grace, you – you don't want to go off, half a world away from – from your pals,' he said. 'Oh, I know I said I'd stick with the Navy for a bit and so I shall, but – but sailors marry, you know, make a home ashore, raise a family. And you and me's always got on great, wouldn't you say? So why go all the way to America, when I'm on your doorstep, queen.'

There was an astounded silence. Sunny, watching Grace's face closely, saw her cheeks flush very becomingly and her eyelids droop over her eyes. Was she angry? Had she not guessed that he was fond of her? Oh, he might not have declared himself so soon, in fact he had made up his mind to tell her that they must meet more often now that peace had been declared, but at the thought of her going right away a lump of ice seemed to have frozen his stomach and a sense of panic assailed him. She was the nicest girl he knew, they had a great deal in common, he couldn't let her go without a struggle! But she was still looking down at her hands and not answering and Sunny realised that he hadn't actually said – well, what he wanted to say. So he took a deep breath and then spoke with more earnestness than he knew he possessed.

'Gracie, I want – I want you to be me girl, not just me bezzie, like you have been.'

'Oh, Sunny,' Grace said, lifting shining eyes to his face. 'It sounds – it sounds . . . But I thought you and Polly . . .'

'Polly's me pal, but only a pal,' Sunny said at once. 'A grand girl, I agree. But she's not the one for me, Grace, and she knows it. I've got me eye on quite a different sort of girl. One who won't fly up into the boughs if I say I'm staying in the Navy for a while, for instance. One who doesn't think an awful lot of herself, but who suits me just fine.'

There was a longish pause before Grace said quietly: 'Oh. I'm sorry, Sunny, I didn't realise you – you had a girl, I just hope I've not spoiled your day, taking it for granted that we'd go about together.'

'That was my idea, not yours,' Sunny said. He leaned across her and took her other hand, pulling her round until they were facing each other. 'Grace, you must know that I like you, enjoy being with you.'

'I hoped you did,' Grace said shyly, the pink colour slowly blooming in her cheeks once more. 'Only there

481

was Polly . . . and there have been heaps and heaps of other girls, you've told me so yourself.'

'Oh aye, but none of them meant anything, really, not even Poll when it came down to brass tacks,' Sunny told her. 'So if you don't mind me staying in the Navy, how about us going steady? We've done a lot of getting to know each other today and we'll need time and a lot of meetings before – well, before we think about getting engaged, but . . . well, how about it?'

'Oh, Sunny, I'd like that,' Grace said breathlessly. 'If you're sure, that is? It 'ud be better than going to the States – better than anything!'

'I'm sure,' Sunny said, and was leaning across to kiss her when, with a shriek of brakes, a train drew into the platform. Above them, the echoing voice of a railway official informed them of the train's various destinations and Sunny stood up. 'No time for anything even when there's a peace on,' he grumbled. 'I'm for this one . . . come and see me off, then I can kiss you without anyone thinking twice about it!'

The day had begun well and went on better, Polly decided as she and Monica, with Deirdre on one side of them and Peader the other, fought their way first on to a tram and then off it again, to surge amongst the cheering, stamping, flag-waving crowds and to cry a little because everyone was so happy. The crowd cheered wildly – Mr Churchill first, of course, then the King and the Queen, then the royal children. In the midst of such excitement it would have been hard to remember one's own personal troubles. Polly, determined not to think about Tad, found that for the moment at any rate she was simply responding to the happiness around her, and when someone started to play the National Anthem on an accordion she joined in with the rest, bawling out the words raucously.

'Do you realise, Mon, that some of these kids haven't ever heard the church bells ring before?' Polly shouted at one point as the bells of the nearest church began their long, loud-mouthed clamour. 'Well, I suppose they might have, but not that they can remember, I mean.'

'I know what you mean,' Monica shouted back. 'Look, fireworks!'

It was a waste, but who could resist letting off fireworks when they were so glad? Polly squeaked as the rockets whizzed past her and up into the blue, bursting in a shower of almost invisible sparks, so strong was the sunshine. And presently she began to pick out the faces of people she knew – old friends from school, mostly in uniform, neighbours, shop-keepers, even. It's an odd thing, so it is, Polly found herself ruminating, but to Liverpool people the city's like a honeypot to bees – they have to come back. They can go to the ends of the earth, I do believe, but at the end of the day they'll come back to Liverpool. Why, neither Sunny nor Grace had any thought about spending VE Day where they were stationed; they both wanted to come home, to come back here, and so they have, no doubt. If they aren't here yet, they soon will be, I'm sure of that. Oh, I do hope they come round to Snowdrop Street, otherwise . . . well, it will be a quiet sort of day for me.

It was a day to remember, the sort of day, Polly reflected, which would still be in people's memories in fifty or so years' time. People who scarcely knew one another hugged and danced together, boys climbed on to the statues in St George's Plain and hung flags from the ears of a great bronze horse, girls put wreaths of spring flowers on the statue of Queen Victoria and decorated the huge stone lions crouched on their plinths in the same way. And as darkness fell everyone watched the uprush of rockets, the whirl of Catherine wheels, the flaring brilliance of Roman candles.

The street party in the late afternoon had been a great success, with the children so excited at first that they could scarcely eat, and then so drunk with the wonder of it that they could scarcely stop and crammed their mouths with sausage rolls, sand-wiches and little cakes until their parents declared they were quite ashamed – though they, too, had been busy reducing the feast to a memory.

Yet two things stood out in Polly's mind as the family made their way slowly homewards. One had occurred halfway through the afternoon, when she and Monica had gone off for half an hour to join in the dancing taking place in a nearby gardens, and she had seen, through the crowd, a young man she was almost certain was Sunny. Well, she told herself reasonably, how could she mistake that bright blond hair and the height of him?

She had caught Monica's arm, shouting that she had seen Sunny, that he was probably searching for her . . . and then, even as she fought her way towards him, she had seen him sling an arm around the shoulders of his companion and lean down, to lightly kiss the side of her face. The girl had looked up and in that instant, Polly had recognised her and stopped pushing her way through the good-humoured crowd.

It was Grace! Grace Carbery who was Polly's sister and whom Polly had always considered to be good but plain. But now, in that fleeting moment, Polly saw that Grace was not plain at all, she was very pretty, with silky brown hair and a straight little nose. And when Grace looked up at Sunny – for it was definitely he – Polly also saw, with a cold little shock, that Grace's eyes were brimming with affection for the young man whom she, Polly, had once thought of as her own property. Oh, she did not want him, not if she could have her dear old Tad, but nevertheless . . .

It had shaken her considerably, however. She stood where she was for a moment and saw the couple swallowed up in the crowd, and then turned and made her way back to Monica. 'Did you find Sunny?' Monica asked, pushing her hair behind her ears and smiling at Polly. 'Only the crowd's so thick—'

'No,' Polly said shortly. 'Never mind. Come on, let's go back to Snowdrop Street.' And they had done so, with Polly trying very hard not to keep searching the surrounding faces for Tad, because though she knew he was not coming, she could not help hoping that he might still turn up.

The second thing that she would remember, she thought now, plodding tiredly along beside Monica through the dark and emptying streets, was Monica herself. At one point, when the fireworks were at their most dazzling, Polly had looked at her sister-in-law and she had seen that Monica's face was streaked with tears.

It had brought it home to her, then, that on this wonderful day which she was enjoying so much, there were people shut up in their homes with hearts which must be breaking when they thought of their own young people, their husbands, children, lovers, who would not be coming home now that the peace had come. There were girls like Monica who were brave and loving, who told themselves every morning, every night, that they were waiting for news, that their husbands, lovers, brothers were safe. But in their hearts there had to be a little seed of doubt, a suspicion that what they were rejoicing in was premature, that for them there might be no cause to rejoice.

As the glare from the rockets died down Monica turned away for a moment, and when she turned back Polly saw that she had rubbed her face dry, that her eyes seemed to be no brighter than other eyes in that great throng. 'What a day!' Monica said, taking Polly's arm. 'We shan't forget today in a hurry, our Poll!'

And Polly, giving her a hug, talking brightly, though with a little catch in her voice, thought that Monica was braver and more loving than anyone she knew. She wouldn't want to spoil anyone's fun by showing a long face on this day so she was putting all her courage and strength into an enormous pretence – Oh God, let Martin be safe, Polly prayed. I'll buy the biggest candle in the city and light it for Martin tomorrow so I will. And I'll have a word with God about Monica, too, while I'm about it. Because it had been two years since the last sighting of Martin, if it had been Martin, and in that time the allied forces had over-run Italy, releasing prisoners and searching out the men who had gone on the run. Even to Polly's desperately optimistic hopes it seemed strange indeed that Martin had not got in touch with them. If he was alive that was. Peader, with his eyes full of sympathy, had tried to tell her not to expect miracles.

'Hope is good, but I can't help thinkin' if our Mart had been alive that someone would've been in touch,' he had said. 'Just you pray, alanna, same as your mammy and I do.'

But right now Polly turned to Monica with her brightest smile. 'I'll walk up to the Pier Head with you because you'll be wanting a number 17 and then I'll have to come back here to catch my own tram,' she said. 'It's been such a grand evening that making it last a little longer suits me just fine.'

When the two girls reached the Pier Head, however, there were still a great many people about and the queue stretched a considerable distance. 'But it doesn't really matter,' Polly said as they joined the end of the queue, 'because we'll be able to lie in for a bit tomorrow morning. Oh, but you've got to walk from Seaforth to Waterloo if you catch this tram . . . Is there anything that would take you all the way, alanna?'

Monica, however, assured Polly that she did not mind the walk and since there were several WRNs in the queue ahead of them she would have company all the way home. The wrennery, which had once been the Royal Hotel on the corner of Marine Terrace, was an enormous building and housed a great number of girls, so some at least of the WRNs in the queue would be making their way back to it. Indeed, Monica spotted several friends ahead of them and assured Polly that the walk, in such company, would be more enjoyable than a taxi ride – and far less expensive.

'Not that we'd gerra taxi at this time of night,' she added comfortably. 'Don't you worry, Polly, your mam said I could stay over if I wanted, but I decided to go back. Me and me mates will have a good jangle before settling down to sleep, and – and it takes me mind off things.'

And presently, two trams, both 17s, drew up at the stop and Monica crammed on to the second one, Polly stepping back but waiting to wave as the tram drew away.

'It's been a grand day,' Monica shouted over her shoulder as she was pushed and shoved further down the tram. 'Tell Mam and Dad I'll come over later in the week. Night, Poll!'

'It was much more fun 'cos we were together, Monica,' Polly called back, and then turned away and with one last wave started to make her way towards Lime Street and her tram home. Polly was luckier than Monica, boarding a 24 no more than two minutes after arriving there and when they reached her stop she got thankfully down off the step into the comfortable warmth and brightness of Stanley Road. What a good thing the blackout's done with at last, she told herself, for with most of the shop windows brightly lit she could see her way perfectly. Only fancy, she said to herself as she turned away from the tram stop, this time last month the sight of one of those lights would have brought a warden's wrath down on the head of whoever had neglected to draw curtains or blinds. Oh, isn't peace a wonderful thing now?

Smiling to herself, Polly turned her steps towards Snowdrop Street and her own bed. She was very tired indeed, and now that she and Monica had parted and the excitement was over she could no longer deny a sort of inner flatness, as though the day had sucked all the life and enthusiasm out of her, leaving her little more than an empty husk.

It's that old Tad, I did think he might have turned up despite what he said, Polly told herself as she plodded along the pavement, but though she was no longer buoyed up by the mad excitement of the day she soon began to enjoy the walk. Lights streaming out of so many windows despite the lateness of the hour were still a novelty, a bonfire on a bomb-site glowed red and the trams, bicycles and occasional cars making their way along the street were comforting to one used to the pitch darkness of a blacked-out city.

And presently, Polly reached Snowdrop Street and turned down it, realising that her legs were extremely tired, that she would not be at all sorry to climb the stairs and get into her bed, even though her day had not been quite what she had planned. Her house was in darkness, however, which meant that if she went by the front door she would have to wake someone up, so she retraced her steps and went down the jigger, finding her way easily despite the fact that it was a good deal darker here than in the main street. She opened the gate into their own yard, headed for the back door and the key always kept hung up on a nail behind the bird-box fixed to the wall – and gave a startled squeak. A man detached himself from the shadows where he had apparently been waiting and came towards her.

'Polly?'

Polly's hand flew to her heart. It was Tad, after all – Tad, who had said he couldn't get here, wouldn't get here! He was right here in front of her, a grin on his brown face, teeth gleaming white, hands going out to her . . .

She had meant to say that he had frightened her, she had even meant to reproach him a little before admitting that she was glad to see him, but somehow nothing happened quite as she had intended. Instead, she heard herself give a muffled sob as she crossed the distance between them in one jump and threw herself into his arms. Those arms closed round her, infinitely

489

warm and comforting, and Tad's voice said in her ear: 'You're not cryin', are you, Poll? And I t'ought you'd be pleased to see me, so I did!'

'Oh, I – I am pleased, I am, I am,' Polly snuffled against his tunic. 'Oh, Tad, I was horrid to you, wasn't I? And I do love you most awfully much, so I do, and I t'ought you didn't like me one bit and I couldn't blame you because I'd been horrid, not a bit nice, and I was jealous of that Jenny girl, and I wanted to punish you . . . Only Tad, I love you more than anyone else in the world, and I want to be with you even if you know I'm not a nice girl at all. So there!'

'That's good to hear,' Tad said, a hand smoothing the curls away from Polly's hot forehead and then caressing her cheek, wiping away the wet of her tears. 'But we need to talk, Poll. Where can we go?'

'Indoors,' Polly said at once. She reached up and plucked the key from its hidden hook. 'In the kitchen; there's no one still up, Mammy and Daddy will have been in bed hours since.'

As she spoke she was unlocking the back door and ushering Tad into the kitchen, still warm from the day of sunshine as well as from the fire smouldering away in the stove. Now, she took off her coat and hung it on the back of the door, motioning Tad to do likewise. Beaming with a pleasure which she was quite unable to conceal she lit the lamp with a taper from the fire and then turned to her companion. 'We can talk very well in here,' she said, pulling one of the chairs nearer to the fire. 'I'll put the kettle on – how long were you standing in our back yard waiting for me to get home, dearest Tad? And when did you leave Lincoln? Oh, and why did you come, when you said you wouldn't? Couldn't, I mean,' she amended hastily as Tad opened his mouth to speak. 'I know it wasn't your

490

fault really, I know you were only being fair to your pals, but . . . well, here you are, so . . .'

'Here I am,' Tad agreed. He had taken off his own coat and hung it next to Polly's and now, as she bustled about getting out tea, milk and cups, he sat himself down in the chair she had indicated. 'Well, the truth is, Poll, that I didn't altogether trust your sudden desire for me companionship. After all, alanna, you'd spent months keeping me at arm's length, you'd told me over and over how fond you were of Sunny What's-his-name, you'd assured me that you thought of me as a brother . . .'

'I didn't mean it,' Polly muttered, turning back towards him. 'I – I was all mixed up that night, you know, Tad. I know I was thinking backwards – all wrong, I mean – but it's a strange t'ing to discover that you're not your own mammy's and daddy's girl, after all. I reckon I didn't know what I was saying, not really. Oh, and I know I probably said the same thing again in me letters, but I was still all muddled up in me mind, you see,' she added hastily. 'For ages and ages I just told meself that I wanted you as a friend. Then I realised that I couldn't bear a – a future which didn't have you in it.'

'That's grand to hear, so it is,' Tad said, but Polly thought he still didn't sound as though he completely believed what she was saying. 'The trouble is, Poll, it took me a long while to get you out of me system, like, and I don't fancy having to do it again if your mind does one of its quick-change tricks. You see, I don't know *why* you've suddenly decided that – well, that I'm the feller for you and not Sunny What's-his-name.'

Polly began to pour the tea. The trouble was, she reminded herself, that her own realisation that Tad

491

was the only person she could ever love had come, not as a result of any one thing, but more as a gentle flow of gradually increasing conviction. In fact, now that she thought about it seriously, it had been her awareness that Sunny was not the man of her dreams which had made her realise it was Tad who mattered to her. But how to explain to him so that he would understand, see that this time there would be no changing of her mind, no going back. She was the old, loving Polly who had known from the time she had been just a child that Tad was her other half, her mate. This, she realised, was an important moment in her life and this time there must be no mistakes, no wrong words or misunderstandings. This time she must make Tad see that she was in deadly earnest.

So she carried the tea over to the fire and sat down in the chair opposite him. 'It happened because I wanted to go back to Holyhead, where I'd been so happy, and have a leave there,' she said, speaking slowly, her eyes on his face. 'I needed some time alone, I think, Tad. Time to consider just what I did want in my life. So anyway, I went back, and some-how, Holyhead wasn't as special as I'd expected it to be. It was almost as if there was something missing. Anyway, I went off by meself to the clifftops above the sea with sandwiches and that, and I lay on the turf and thought. I thought about Sunny, and being married, and then I *knew* that marrying Sunny would be the greatest mistake of me life. He's a grand feller, he's handsome and tall and girls like him, but . . . I realised when I had a chance to think properly, on that quiet clifftop, that I didn't love him. Not even a tiny bit and – and the feller I wanted to be beside me for ever wasn't tall or golden-haired or any of that rubbish, it was – well, it was you, Tad.'

'Right. And this was how long ago?' Tad asked rather dryly. 'A year? Nine months?'

'Well, no, it wasn't as long as that—' Polly began, to be swiftly interrupted.

'You mean it was just weeks ago? Oh, Poll, who's to say you won't change your mind again in another few weeks? After all, you've not seen Sunny once since your trip to Anglesey, have you? You might set eyes on him—'

'I have seen him, so,' Polly said vehemently, standing her mug down on the floor beside her and getting to her feet. 'I saw him this very afternoon, and did I get one single feeling that he was me feller? No, I did not! He was with Grace, what's more, but if he and she were to get together – which I know very well they won't – Oh, Tad, I want you!' The last words came out almost as a wail and with them, Polly cast herself at Tad's knees, clasping them tightly and then burying her head in his lap. 'Don't – don't you want me even a little bit?' she said on a snuffle.

There was a moment's silence and then Tad leaned down and heaved her on to his lap. With both arms tightly round her and his mouth against her hair he said: 'Polly me darlin' girl, you don't know how much I want you! You're all I've ever wanted, that's God's truth, and when you decided you didn't want me – well, I was cut to the heart, so I was, and for a bit life just didn't seem worth living. Only I made meself think sensibly and I got over it, more or less. That's why I don't want to go through all that pain again.'

'Oh, Tad,' Polly muttered. 'Oh, Tad, it wasn't the real me, it was just plain stupidity, and – and being a bit bedazzled by Sunny's looks. But all that's over and done, I swear it on a stack of Bibles, I'll never look at

493

another feller so long as we both live.' She looked up at him, seeing him through a dazzle of tears. 'Won't you give me a chance to prove I mean it, though, darlin' Tad? Because if you won't – or can't, even – then I don't know what I'll do.'

'Well, we'll give it a go, then,' Tad said, suddenly cheerful. 'Ooh, you're a cuddly armful, so you are! But we can't sit here like this all night. I've only got a forty-eight, so I'll have to be off back to Lincoln at the crack of dawn, which means trying to grab some sleep tonight. I'd best see if I can find a lodging house still open.'

'You'll do no such thing,' Polly said softly but with determination. 'Mammy and Daddy would be shocked at me if I let you go off when we've an inch of space to spare. And – and tomorrer, I'm coming wit' you back to Lincoln so's we can talk some more, because there's things we need to say, Tad.'

'But not tomorrer,' Tad said with emphasis. 'I don't want to see you court-martialled, alanna. We'll do everything the proper way, for once. I'll go back to Lincoln and get meself some leave and you'll go back to being a despatch rider until you're demobbed. Agreed?'

And Polly, opening her mouth to say hotly that she would do no such thing, that she did not care if she were court-martialled so long as she was with Tad, heard her own voice saying meekly: 'Sure an' if that's what you think is best, darlin' Tad,' and knew that she had grown up at last.

It was comfortable in the O'Bradys front parlour, with a couple of blankets and a pillow and the comfortable couch all to himself, but even so Tad found it hard to go to sleep. For one thing, he was uneasily conscious that it was past midnight which meant that he could only sleep for about five hours at the most. His squadron leader had given him a forty-eight as a special favour, it really would be a shabby thing if he was late back, so he must be at the station early because he had no idea what time the first train heading for Lincoln left, but no matter how unearthly an hour it should prove he really meant to be aboard.

For another thing, though, he was as pleased and excited as he had ever been, and pleasurable excitement is no aid in getting to sleep. He knew, now, that he had been right to call Polly's bluff when she had simply turned up unannounced in Lincolnshire to tell him she was fond of him and wanted to resume their old relationship. He had not told her so this evening, but in fact he had decided not even to try to get back to Liverpool for the celebrations, only once the great day dawned he had found it quite impossible not to try to get to Polly just as soon as he could. Having told his squadron leader that he would be staying on the station he had had to explain that things had altered and leapt aboard the first transport heading into the city. He had gone at once to the station and from then on had cursed every slow train, every missed connection, as he worked his way steadily cross-country towards his girl. But he had made it at last, only to realise that the house in Snowdrop Street was deserted. He had imagined Polly in Sunny's arms, being comforted because he, Tad, had been so cruel to her, and had ground his teeth with rage at his own foolishness. Why hadn't he admitted that he loved her, wanted only her? Why had he played out the charade that he was too hurt to risk being hurt again? But now he was glad, because his little darling really was his little darling now. He had no more doubts, only a wonderful, warm glow of certainty. Polly was his and he was Polly's, and now they could stop wasting time and start to plan their lives together.

So after he and Polly had kissed goodnight she had gone upstairs to fetch blankets from the spare room, and had come down again with a pile of bedding and the information that Mammy had still been awake, and had said to say sorry she wasn't coming down herself to welcome him but it was awful late, and would he make himself at home, please, and not to leave in the morning before Polly had got up and made him breakfast and a packed lunch for the train.

Tad had felt good after that. He was no longer an interloper in the O'Brady house but an invited guest, and since Polly had promised to set her alarm for five o'clock so that she might come down and wake him and see to his breakfast he should have had no qualms about going to sleep and fitting himself for another day of travel on the morrow.

The trouble was, he could not sleep, and it soon occurred to him that Polly, too, would be wide awake and this re-activated his worry about her finally dozing off and sleeping through the alarm clock's bell, and very soon he was sitting up on the couch, with the pillow across his shoulders, determined not to risk so much as half an hour of slumber.

When, after about an hour of this, the parlour door creaked open and a small figure wrapped in a pink eiderdown and with an alarm clock in one hand and a very guilty expression crept into the room, he was so pleased that he nearly cried out. In fact, he remembered in time that there were two O'Brady parents upstairs and merely whispered: 'Poll! I can't sleep, I was scared of not waking in time for the early train, but I see you guessed how it would be and brought me the clock – thanks, alanna. But you need your rest, you've had a long day, same as I have, so you go up again now, and go to sleep and don't bother about waking up for me. I can get meself a bit of bread and scrape and a cuppa and then be on my way. Off wit' you, Polly me darlin'.'

Polly, however, came over to the couch and sat down beside him, standing the alarm clock on the small occasional table in front of it. She smiled at him but shook her head in a very determined fashion. 'No, Tad, I'll not be going back upstairs to lie awake and worry that you'll miss the bleedin' train,' she told him in a very composed tone. 'Besides, there's a lot we've not had time to talk about, I want to ask you . . . oh, about lots of things. And since we can neither of us sleep – I'm still all lit up and excited inside about us, and about not being at war, and remembering the fireworks and the bonfires – we might as well be awake together, don't you think?'

'So I do,' Tad said, giving in happily and putting an arm around her slender shoulders. 'Lean on me, Poll, and let's talk!'

'Where will we start, though?' Polly said, settling herself comfortably in the hollow of Tad's shoulder. 'I feel as if I've lived *years* that you don't know about, Tad. Are you goin' to tell me what you did after I'd said – the things that I said? Only I don't think I want to know.'

Tad laughed. 'No, I don't suppose you do, and it wouldn't make very interestin' listening,' he agreed. 'So let's start with you, Poll. You don't mind about being adopted now, do you, Poll? And you don't mind that Grace is your sister?'

'No, I don't mind, exactly,' Polly said in rather a subdued voice. 'Because I know that Mammy and Daddy love me ever so much and did everything they

497

could to make me happy. But I do wonder about my angel, Tad. Do you remember her? I told you about her when I was only a kid, and you thought I was going soft in the head I daresay, but – but I really did see her, Tad, often and often. In fact, it's only this past year or so that I've not seen her.'

'I believe you saw your angel,' Tad said. 'I'm not saying I understand it, Poll, but I do think you saw . . . well, something, at any rate.'

'Someone, not something,' Polly put in. 'But what I don't understand, Tad, is why the angel came to me? Why didn't she go to Grace, who needed an angel so very badly? She was the one who was left alone, not me.'

'Oh, Poll, you will keep looking at things from your own point of view and never from anyone else's,' Tad said, sighing and kissing the top of Polly's curly golden head. 'Can't you see, even now? Your mammy told you that she thought your angel was really your big sister Jess, didn't she?'

'Sure she did, and I suppose she might have been right,' Polly said rather grudgingly. Tad, grinning, thought that if you'd imagined a guardian angel with great white wings and a good deal of influence with the Lord it was rather a comedown to admit that the angel was just a skinny, dirty little slum child who had been killed by a train whilst searching for shelter in the shunting yards. Still, Polly was clearly coming round to the idea. 'But if it's true that my angel was really Jess, then why didn't she take care of Grace? Grace was her sister too, remember.'

'That's what I'm trying to tell you, alanna,' Tad said gently. 'Sure an' you will look at things from your own point of view all the time – amn't I telling you so, time and again? Look at it from Jess's angle, won't you! She was in charge of a young baby, the baby she had looked after almost from birth. And because she was cold and worried and in a hurry she went and got herself killed by a train, leaving that little baby to fend for itself. Don't you see now, alanna?'

'But I was all right; Brogan took care of me, carried me over the sea to Mammy and Daddy, and after that I didn't really need anyone – except for you, Tad,' Polly said quickly. 'So that dog won't run, me fine friend!'

'But Jess wasn't appearing to you because you needed her, Poll. She was doing it because she needed *you*,' Tad explained as patiently as he could. He had found it hard to understand himself, at first, but now that he had come to terms with Polly and her angel it seemed impossible that Polly should still not see. 'I guess that she loved you with a deep, possessive love – and why should she not? She'd made a pretty good job of bringing you up from what Brogan told your mammy, and she *needed* to see you, to watch over you, to make sure you were all right.'

There was a long pause whilst Polly clearly gave this new idea all her attention. Then she heaved a great, deep sigh. 'I do see, now,' she said at last. 'Then – then I won't ever see my angel again, will I? Because I'm really grown up now – and I've got you, Tad. For ever and ever.'

'That's right, Poll,' Tad said gently. 'You've got me now, for ever and ever.' And he put both arms around her and drew her close. 'Do you know, I've never kissed you, Poll? And if we're giving it a go, then I think . . .'

Polly put her face up to his and their lips met and clung.

*

At five o'clock the alarm went off and by six Tad was kissing her goodbye and setting off for the station. Polly would have liked to have gone with him, but Tad said she should go up to her room and get a bit of sleep before her work started later. Polly agreed, therefore, to telephone his airfield that evening to make sure he had got back safely, waved him off and then went meekly back into the house. Light was beginning to filter through the curtains as she climbed the stairs to her room, filled with a happiness yet with a thread of sadness running through it because she was going to have to say goodbye to her angel, and, she knew, to her carefree girlhood.

I've grown up at last, so I have, she thought to herself, sleepily climbing the stairs. I thought I was a woman ages ago, but now I know it took almost losing Tad and then finding him again and sharing a real, proper love to grow me up. And as she reached the head of the stairs she looked back . . . and thought she saw, standing on the half-landing, a barefoot girl in a long, draggly shawl who looked up at her fleetingly for a moment and gave her the most beautiful smile before she was gone, and only the shadow of the bannisters remained, and dust motes swirling in a pale sunshine's ray.

Polly stopped still for a moment. 'Goodbye, Jess,' she said in a voice no louder than a whisper. 'I'm proud to have known you, and in a way I'll miss you . . . but I'll have Tad now, so long as we both shall live, and that's enough for anyone.'

For a moment she waited. For a sign? For one more glimpse of that sweet, fragile presence? But she knew suddenly, with a deep inner certainty, that she would never see her angel again. Not, at any rate, in this world.

As she let herself into her bedroom she realised that there would be no more blackout, no more dark, dangerous streets, and very soon no more despatch riding, no more exciting uniform. No more war.

Polly crossed the room and threw the blanket she had wrapped herself in back on to the bed, then climbed between the sheets. What a day – well, what a night, come to that! She and Tad had talked and talked, and worked out how their life would go on for the next few months and she hadn't thought once about a white wedding or a wonderful honeymoon somewhere exciting, she had simply thought how marvellous it would be not to have to say goodnight to Tad and go their separate ways. I'm lucky, so I am, she thought, snuggling down. Peace is beginning and Tad and I will tackle whatever it may bring together. Come to that, everyone is having to tackle it now. Sunny will leave the Navy and Grace the WAAF and the boys will come home and . . . For a moment she thought about that odd sighting across the crowd, of Grace and Sunny in each other's arms. Had she really seen them? If so, what did it mean? But her own happiness was so enormous that she could not speculate for too long on anyone's else's future. Tomorrow, she thought drowsily. Tomorrow I'll get down to wondering what Sunny and Grace were doing together, tomorrow I'll think about Martin and the others and pray they all get home safe, tomorrow . . .

And Polly was asleep.

A Long and Lonely Road

Katie Flynn

Rose McAllister is waiting for her husband, Steve, to come home. He is a seaman, often drunk and violent, but Rose does her best to cope and sees that her daughters, Daisy, 8, and Petal, 4, suffer as little as possible. Steve however, realises that war is coming and tries to reform, but on his last night home he pawns the girls' new dolls to go on a drinking binge.

When war is declared Rose has a good job but agrees the children must be evacuated. Daisy and Petal are happy at first, but circumstances change and they are put in the care of a woman who hates all scousers and taunts them with the destruction of their city. They run away, arriving home on the worst night of the May Blitz. Rose is attending the birth of her friend's baby and goes back go Bernard Terrace to find her home has received a direct hit, and is told that the children were seen entering the house the previous evening. Devastated, she decides to join the WAAF, encouraged by an RAF pilot, Luke, whom she has befriended . . .

arrow books